A NOVEL BY JUDITH KRANTZ

WARNER BOOKS

A Warner Communications Company

For Steve
With all my love
Always

*I*n Beverly Hills only the infirm and the senile do not drive their own cars. The local police are accustomed to odd combinations of vehicle and driver: the stately, nearsighted retired banker making an illegal left-hand turn in his Dino Ferrari, the teen-ager speeding to a tennis lesson in a fifty-five-thousand-dollar Rolls-Royce Corniche, the matronly civic leader blithely parking her bright red Jaguar at a bus stop.

Billy Ikehorn Orsini—whose faults did not normally include a tendency to erratic driving—brought her vintage Bentley to a stop with an impatient screech in front of Scruples, the world's most lavish specialty store, a virtual club for the floating principality of the very, very rich and the truly famous. She was thirty-five, sole mistress of a fortune estimated at between two hundred and two hundred fifty million dollars by the list makers of the *Wall Street Journal*. Almost half of her wealth was tidily invested in tax-free municipal bonds, a simplification little appreciated by the IRS.

Hurried though she was, Billy lingered in front of Scruples, casting a piercingly proprietary eye over her property on the northeast corner of Rodeo Drive and Dayton Way, where, four years ago, Van Cleef & Arpels had stood, a white plaster, gilt, and wrought-iron landmark, which looked as if it had been clipped off the Carlton Hotel in Cannes and shipped intact to California.

Billy's tawny wool cape was lined in golden sable against the chill of the late afternoon of February 1978. She pulled it around her as she looked quickly up and down the sumptuous heart of Rodeo Drive, where the two facing rows of immodestly opulent boutiques outglittered each other to create the most staggering display of luxury in the Western world. The broad boulevard was made gay by pointed fiscus trees, vivid green all year round, with low, wooded mountains visible in the near distance, like the background of a Leonardo da Vinci.

A few passersby acknowledged their recognition of her by that tiny sideways flick of an eye with which the true New Yorker, or the Beverly Hills regular, reluctantly validates the same celebrity who would draw a crowd in some other city.

Since her twenty-first birthday Billy had been photographed many hundreds of times, but newspaper pictures had never quite caught her challenging reality. Her long, dark hair, the deep brown of the best mink, so brown that it looked like black licked by moonlight, was thrust behind her ears, in which she always wore her signature jewels, the great eleven-karat diamonds known as the Kimberley Twins, which had been her wedding present from her first husband, Ellis Ikehorn.

Billy was five feet ten inches tall before she put on her shoes and her beauty was almost virile. As she crossed to the entrance, she took a deep breath of anticipation. The Balinese doorman, graceful in his black Scruples tunic and tightly wrapped pants, bowed low as he opened the heroically scaled double doors. Inside those doors lay another country, created to beguile and dazzle and tempt. But today she was in too much of a rush to scrutinize any of the details of what her Boston background, for she had been born Wilhelmina Hunnenwell Winthrop of the undiluted Massachusetts Bay Colony strain, caused her to refer to as a "business" rather than as a fantasy she had brought to life by pouring out close to eleven million dollars. She strode rapidly, with her characteristic pace, that of a huntress, in the direction of the elevator, determined not to catch the eye of any of the customers with whom she might have to stop and chat. As she walked, she threw open her cape and exposed her long, powerful throat. She was that most disturbing and rare of combinations, a female of rampant sexual vitality combined with an ultimate and totally authoritative sense of personal style. To any observant male, her smoky eyes, which had irises striped with faint horizontal lines of tortoise and dark brown, and her full mouth, ripe rose under a thin coat of colorless lip gloss, sent one message, while her long, slender body, severely clad in dark green kidskin trousers and a heavy cream silk tunic, cut wide and casually roped in at the waist, sent another message, a contradiction of the first. Billy knew that any emphasis on ass and tits played bloody hell with elegance. The absolute chic of her clothes was at war with her innate sensuality. She put people off-balance, almost certainly on purpose, because she wore her offhand yet splendid garments as if she was equally prepared to tear them off and tumble into bed, or to stand in front of a photographer and pose for *Women's Wear Daily*.

Billy arrived at the elevator without having to do more than nod toward a half dozen women with a brisk friendliness, which simultaneously indicated that she was pleased to see them there getting rid of a tiny part of their unmitigated wealth but couldn't possibly stop. She went straight to the top floor, where her destination was the private office shared by her two chief employees, Spider Elliott, who managed Scruples, and Valentine O'Neill, head buyer and custom designer. She gave a brief knock, which was not a question but an announcement, and entered an empty room, all the more deserted for the incongruity of the scarred English mahogany partners' desk, which Spider had fallen in love with in an antique shop on Melrose Avenue and insisted on transporting to Scruples. It stood like an island of rugged reality in the center of the room, which had been decorated by Edward Taylor in future-wordly tones of melting taupe, fawn, biscuit, and greige.

"Damn, where have they got to?" Billy muttered under her breath, flinging open the door into their secretary's room. Mrs. Evans jumped nervously at her unexpected appearance and stopped typing immediately.

"Where are they?" Billy asked.

"Oh dear, Mrs. Ikehorn—I mean, Mrs. Orsini—" The secretary stopped in confusion.

"It's all right, everybody does it," Billy reassured her quickly and automatically.

She had been married to Vito Orsini—that most independent of independent film producers—for only a year and a half, and people who had read of her over the years as Billy Ikehorn made the same mistake with her name without even realizing that they were doing it.

"Mr. Elliott is with Maggie MacGregor," Mrs. Evans informed her. "In fact, he just got started with her and he said he'd be at least an hour, and Valentine is working in her studio with Mrs. Woodstock—they've been there since right after lunch."

Billy tightened her lips in annoyance. They couldn't be disturbed, not even by her. Just when she wanted them, Spider was closeted with perhaps the most important woman in television and Val was busy designing a complete wardrobe for the wife of the new ambassador to France. Balls! Billy had painted herself into a corner in establishing the fact that she was above acting like a Queen Bee in such matters as appointments and fittings at Scruples. Let Dina Merrill act, Gloria Vanderbilt paint, Lee Radziwill decorate her friends' homes, and Charlotte Ford, followed by a whole pack of socialites, "design" collections of clothes, she, Billy Ikehorn Orsini, ran a flourishing retail business, the most successful luxury shop in the world, a brilliant combination of boutique, gift shop, the world's best ready-to-wear and haute couture. The fact that Scruples represented the smallest part of her fortune didn't make it any less important to her, because, of all the sources of her income, Scruples was the only one she had been personally responsible for establishing. It was at once her passion and her plaything, a cherished secret come to life, tailored on a human scale that she could see, smell, touch, possess, change and make perfect and ever more perfect.

"Look, I need them *soon*. Please let them know I'm here the minute they're through. I'll be somewhere in the store." She stalked out and went into her own office before the flustered Mrs. Evans could offer the little speech of good luck that she had been nervously preparing for weeks. Tomorrow was the day on which the nominations for the Academy Awards were to be announced, and Vito

Orsini's film *Mirrors* had a possibility of being nominated as one of the five Best Films of 1977. Mrs. Evans didn't know much about the film business, but she knew that Mrs. Ikehorn—Mrs. Orsini—was very tense about the nominations from the gossip she had picked up around the store. Perhaps, she thought, considering how abrupt her employer had been—perhaps, it was just as well that she hadn't said anything. The protocol of such occasions escaped her.

Maggie MacGregor felt both depleted and electrified by the adrenaline of acquisition. She had just spent at least seven thousand dollars for clothes to wear on camera during the next two months and ordered an entire wardrobe for the Cannes Film Festival, which she would be covering in May. The festival wardrobe had cost an additional twelve thousand dollars for clothes that would be made by Halston and Adolfo in New York in special colors and fabrics just for her and delivered in time for her trip, or she'd have someone's head on a platter. Naturally, it was stipulated in her contract that the ganefs at the network paid. No way she'd spend her own money like that.

If anyone had ever tried to convince her, ten years ago, when she was a short, jouncingly plump teenager named Shirley Silverstein, daughter of the owner of the biggest hardware store in tiny Fort John, Rhode Island, that spending nineteen thousand dollars on clothes was hard work, she would have—laughed? No, Maggie reflected, even back then she was ambitious enough to have been able to imagine such a situation and smart enough to understand that it involved a lot of psychic strain to say nothing of what it did to her feet. She just wouldn't have thought of it in any relation to herself. Even now it hadn't become routine, although, at twenty-six, she was a television superpower, as tough as—many thought tougher than—Mike Wallace, and a hell of a lot less obvious about it; even prettier than Dan Rather, and blessed with an inborn talent for interviewing as strong in its own way as the talent that makes Beverly Sills sing. She had her own network show in the choicest cut of prime time. For a half hour every weekend more than a good third of the television sets in the United States were tuned in to Maggie as she reported, with the help of a faithful crew who had virtually grown minicams out of their shoulders, the inside news of show business, particularly the film industry; tightly researched, completely authoritative stories, which had nothing in common with the tiny turds of coy gossip that were served up only three years ago to an incurably curious public.

Right now she was just an exhausted female whose Betty Boop-round black eyes had seen so many dresses in the last three hours that they were all jumbled around in her sassy head. But the network insisted that if she reported on show business she had to look as if she belonged in that glamorous world. As she waited for Spider Elliott to come in and tell her which of the outfits she had chosen were absolutely right for her, she looked disarmingly disheveled, her bangs and black hair separating into a dozen cowlicks. She didn't bother to look in the mirror. Maggie knew that no matter how much money she spent, the only time she looked put together was during the half hour after the studio makeup man and hairdresser had finished with her just before she went on camera.

Spider knocked and Maggie merely answered, "Help!" He came in and shut the door behind him and leaned against the wall of the dressing room, looking at her both quizzically and tenderly.

"Hey, Spidy, did you study leaning from old Fred Astaire movies? Just like you practiced walking and sitting down? Where's your top hat?" Maggie asked.

"Don't try to change the subject. I know you. You probably bought stuff you can't wear and you're trying to put me on the defensive."

"You," she said, enunciating clearly, "are a putz, a schmekel, a schmuck, a schlong, and a shvantz. And a WASP putz, at that."

"Her ladyship." Spider kissed her hand. "You're a class act, kid. I may be just an ex-UCLA beach bum, but I know when I'm being called a prick. So, you have a guilty conscience and I haven't even seen the clothes? One thing I'll never understand about women, Maggie—why, when you call a man a prick, is it considered an insult? 'Eunuch,' now that would really hurt."

Maggie made a throaty sound of resignation. She knew

already that she'd gone a bit overboard on those evening dresses for Cannes. Spider, that cock-sucker, could read minds, female minds, no question about it. Where did such a gorgeous stud get his gift for women? As Maggie well knew, it was rare in a red-blooded American heterosexual, that quick, instinctive intuition that no system of psychology could explain. And as horny as a whole herd of young goats too.

Spider pressed a button and Maggie's saleswoman, placid, well-bred Rosel Korman, popped her head in the door.

"Rosel, would you please get Maggie's new things for us?" Spider asked, with a smile. Spider and Maggie were the best of friends, but she felt a quiver of apprehension as Rosel disappeared. He was such a fucking dictator. On the other hand, he was always right. She knew already that he wouldn't let her keep that batwing Bill Blass she loved so much. But no matter what he did to frustrate her, there was a bond between them based on the sweetness of non-possession. They cherished not having had each other because it created a current of continual warmth, which, they both knew, was more important to them than sex. Sex they could, and did, get everywhere. Warmth was rare.

Spider Elliott, at thirty-two, was, in Maggie's opinion, one of the most attractive men in the world, and she was in the business of observing the mechanics of what makes men and women attractive. Her shrewd, measuring eyes were trained to miss nothing of the workings of seduction; if a performer is not also a seducer of some sort or another, he or she will never become a star. Certain obvious things were in Spider's favor, she thought. The All-American Golden Boy with a great body never goes out of style. And he had the hair, the naturally blond hair that had turned a darker, richer, more streaky gold as he grew up. And he had the eyes, Viking eyes, as blue as if they reflected nothing but the sea. They squinched almost closed when he smiled, as he had at Rosel, and the semisunburst of lines at the corner of each eye deepened, making him look merry and wise, as if he'd been somewhere very far away and had many a good tale to tell. He even had that nose, broken in some long-forgotten high-school football game, and a tiny chip in one front tooth, which lent an agreeable toughness to his face. But basically, Maggie decided, it was Spider's very special knack for moving through a woman's mind, trading easily in her idiom, speaking directly to her, cutting across the barriers of masculinity and femininity without any of the warping caused by fag bullshit that did the trick. He had a passionate absorption with the sensuous secrets of raw femaleness, which drew him naturally into the center stage of the erotic-narcissistic atmosphere that reigned at Scruples, as essential a masculine counterpoint as a pasha in his harem. And no matter how cunt-happy he was, he was never unprofessional. If the men of Bevely Hills, La Jolla, or Santa Barbara had guessed of Spider's underground reputation as a dedicated, world-class cocksman, spread through impeccably firsthand reports, they might not have paid their women's staggering Scruples' bills with such good-humored resignation.

Now Rosel reappeared, followed by her assistant wheeling a heavy rolling cart with a rack. A white linen slip-cover concealed the contents. Billy Orsini had devised this system as one way of maintaining the customer's privacy at Scruples, a privacy almost nonexistent in most of the other expensive shops of Beverly Hills. Rosel left them as soon as she had unveiled the clothes. Spider always worked with the customers alone, their interchange undiluted by the saleswomen, who had a habit of falling in love with the dress that would have looked well on them rather than on the woman who would wear it. Together he and Maggie went through her choices. Some of them Spider passed on without comment, some he eliminated, some he asked Maggie to try on before he made his decision, which she did behind the four-panel screen in one corner of the large room. When they had got through the lot, Spider picked up the phone and asked the chef to send up a big pot of Earl Grey tea, a bottle of V.S.O.P., and a tray of fresh caviar and smoked-salmon sandwiches.

"We'll have your blood-sugar level back to normal in no time," he reassured the exhausted girl. As they shared the strong tea, laced well with brandy, they both relaxed with the sense of a difficult job accomplished.

"You realize, Maggie," Spider said lazily, "that you still haven't picked out the most important dress of all."

17

"Huh?" She was groggy with relief and fatigue and her back hurt.

"What are you going to wear for the Academy Awards, little one?"

"Who knows? Something. Haven't I bought enough, you momser?"

"Not yet. Are you trying to ruin my reputation? That monster rally is beamed by satellite all over the world—audience of one hundred fifty million. That's *three hundred million eyes* looking at you. You'd better wear something pretty special."

"Oh, shit, Spider, you're giving me the chills."

"You've never been head honcho on an Award show before. We'd better get Valentine to design something really special for you."

"Valentine?" Maggie's eyes were uncertain. She had never bought custom-made clothes because her schedule was too tight to allow for many fittings.

"Yep. And don't worry, you'll find the time. Don't you want to astonish the whole fucking world?"

"Spider," she said gratefully, "if I kissed your feet, you wouldn't think I was coming on to you, would you?"

"You don't have the strength," he answered. "Just stay put and answer a few questions. What are Vito's chances for the nomination? Just between us."

"Only fair, good, or excellent, depending. There are seven other pictures out there that made a good number of the ten-best lists and have lots of backing behind them. Obviously, I want him to get one . . . but I wouldn't bet my next paycheck on it."

"How can you know as little as I do?" Spider complained.

"That's show business. Is Billy showing any signs of wear and tear? She's really addicted to that divine wop she married."

"Wear and tear? Obsession is more like it. But then she never has gone in for mild emotions, not since I've known her. If there were a few more weeks to wait, she'd wake up one morning, look in the mirror, and see Lady Macbeth. Hell, I like Vito and he's a very talented guy, but sometimes I wish she'd married someone who did something less dangerous, like sky diving or Grand Prix racing."

"That bad, huh?"

"Worse."

While Maggie and Spider were talking, Billy was restlessly studying some of the stock of the gift section of
Scruples, prowling around in a thief's paradise of Chinese
export armorial cachepots, Victorian silver cookie jars,
eighteenth-century beaded evening bags, French shoe
buckles of rose-cut diamonds, Battersea candlesticks, and
Georgian snuffboxes, the corner she called "the pillaging
of Peking." Simultaneously she kept a discreet eye on the
backgammon tables in the pub where six men were having
a friendly game while they waited for their women to finish
shopping, a game at which probably not less than three
thousand dollars would change hands. Scruples had developed into the most popular unorganized yet exclusive
men's club in town. Billy managed, at the same time, to
notice the two women from Texas who had each just
bought four identical vicuña lap robes lined in chinchilla,
mink, nutria, and, for a giggle, mole dyed in beige, brown,
and white stripes. Sisters? Best friends? She had never been
able to understand women who shopped together and
bought the same things. An abomination. Her irritation
at the two women was, Billy realized, merely a reflection of
her growing annoyance that Valentine wasn't finished yet.
Damn and blast her client, Muffie Woodstock, that leathery
creature. And Spider, why the hell wasn't he around?

Abruptly disgusted with the people around her, she
walked to one of the four sets of double doors on the north
and south sides of the main salon of Scruples and looked
out at the formal gardens that surrounded the store like an
oasis. Dwarf privet and gray santolina were set in intricate
patterns in front of the tall boxwood hedges that shielded
Scruples on three sides. Two dozen varieties of geraniums,
in antique terra-cotta urns, were already in full bloom,
brought in from Billy's own greenhouses. She could smell
the fruitwood-and-eucalyptus fire that snapped behind an
ornate brass fire screen in the Edwardian winter garden at
the far end of the salon and hear the murmur of voices as
a few late shoppers drank tea and champagne. But none of
these familiar sights and sounds could quiet her nervous
agitation.

Valentine O'Neill, in her design studio, had been enjoying herself thoroughly all afternoon. Mrs. Ames Woodstock presented the kind of challenge she enjoyed, a woman who was terrified by beautiful clothes yet was going to be forced by circumstances—and Valentine—to wear them and wear them with panache. Nor did Valentine underestimate the princely amount that Mrs. Woodstock's millionaire husband, wise in the diplomacy of international oil and just appointed ambassador to France, was willing to pay for the privilege of having an entire wardrobe made to order at Scruples. No Frenchwoman would.

Although Valentine hadn't lived in Paris for five years and was half Irish on her father's side, now, at twenty-six, she remained as unmistakably French as the Eiffel Tower. The final, secret detail of what made her so French, in defiance of her wild Irish coloring, might have been in the whimsical tilt of her lips or in her slender, deliciously pointed nose with its three freckles or in the speculative glint in her eyes, light green as young leaves. She had mermaid eyes in a small, white face, an alive, alive face, which never fell into dullness or fixed itself in a pout. She was as alert as a vixen, as humorous as the song by Maurice Chevalier after which her homesick war-bride mother had named her. There was, under Valentine's ever-changing expressions, a bedrock of sturdy reasonableness, a base of stubborn French logic, which was all too often combined with her quick Celtic temper. Even her cap of short, red curls, Mrs. Woodstock thought apprehensively, as Valentine draped another length of silk over her shoulder, was the most assertive, even aggressive, hair she had ever seen.

Muffie Woodstock had the bewildered expression of a woman who has always lived in pants, peacefully breeding her dogs and riding her horses, and now finds herself being shown a sketch of the dress she will be wearing to a gala reception at the residence of the president of France.

"But, Valentine, it's rather, well, I don't know—" she said helplessly. Washington had advised her that she'd need at least half a dozen suits suitable for ladies' luncheons, a number of "small-dinner" dresses, and a minimum of a dozen full evening dresses and coats for the diplomatic round.

"But, Mrs. Woodstock, *I do*," said Valentine, who had spent most of her childhood tucked away in the corner of a great atelier in the couture house of Pierre Balmain in Paris, watching ball gowns being made while she did her homework. She was totally confident and she was determined to make this nice woman confident too.

"You do not like the idea of a gala, then, Mrs. Woodstock?"

"Good heavens, I loathe it, my dear."

"But Mrs. Woodstock, you carry yourself very well."

"I do?"

"And you have the very best, truly the best kind of a body for clothes. I am not flattering you. If there were defects we would work together to hide them. But you are very tall, very thin, and you walk so well. I know exactly the kind of evening clothes you think are 'proper'—simple, unpretentious, quiet, just like everyone else's, with perhaps a small jewel at the neck—am I right? Ah, I thought so— and they are indeed proper at your chalet in Sun Valley, at your ranch in Colorado, at your estate in Santa Barbara. But at the Élysée Palace! At the Paris Opéra! At the big embassy parties! No, never, you would feel silly, improper, out of place. Only if you dress like all the other women there will you be able to feel that comfortable, inconspicuous way you like to feel. It's interesting, is it not? Only by being very, very chic will you not look wrong, different, foreign."

"I suppose you're right," Muffie Woodstock said reluctantly, but convinced by Valentine's last three terrifying words.

"Good! Then it's settled. I'll be ready for the first fitting in two weeks. And when you come, could you please get your jewels out of the vault and bring them with you? I need to see what you possess."

"How did you know I kept them in a vault?"

"You are just not the kind of woman who would wear them more than twice a year—a shame, because I'm sure they're magnificent."

Muffie Woodstock looked embarrassed. Evidently Valentine was some sort of a witch. She'd better go and buy some new shoes before she set foot in here again; Valentine would undoubtedly notice that her evening slippers had seen better days. Oh goodness gracious, why did her husband want to be an ambassador anyway?

"Cheer up," said Valentine. "Think of the wonderful riding you will have in the country there."

Muffie Woodstock brightened. One thing she really spent money on was riding boots. But . . . could she ride in jeans and an old sweater?

"Valentine, while we're at it, let's make some riding clothes too."

"Oh no!" Valentine responded, scandalized. "For that you must go straight to Hermès, when you get to Paris. I can make you anything but that—it simply would not be correct."

As she ushered her client to the door of her studio, Valentine felt doubly delighted. Her own designs would now once again be seen in competition with the best that European couture had to offer. And Mrs. Woodstock, who had no idea of her own assets, would soon learn about them as she wore the dashingly dramatic, yet seriously elegant, clothes Valentine had planned for her. "Inconspicuous" indeed! With her height and her walk she'd equal any duchess. She'd be the talk of Paris—they'd stand on chairs to see her. And she'd learn to love it! Or perhaps not. That, unfortunately, Valentine, conjurer though she was, could not control.

In addition to this, Valentine had once again proved to herself that she possessed the essence of conducting a commercial transaction, a talent every true Frenchwoman appreciates. Making and selling clothes was an important and significant business as far as she was concerned, even when it was conducted in this absurdly extravagant, eccentric, and lavish playland called Scruples. Once again she had proven that even in Beverly Hills, which, next to Palm Springs, is the headquarters of the worst-dressed rich women in the United States, she could provide haute couture, for those who cared about it, for whatever reason.

Still wearing the crisp, anonymous white smock she always worked in, Valentine left her studio and went into her office, carrying the estimates for Mrs. Woodstock's new wardrobe. Spider was there with his feet up on the worn oxblood leather of the desk they shared.

"Oh, Elliott, I didn't expect to see you here," she exclaimed, suddenly uneasy. Since Christmas, only six weeks ago, since that absurd fight they had had, which had been over in a flash yet was still lingering on in the air, they had both avoided the conversations they used to have every morning before the opening of the store, sitting opposite each other at the big desk.

"Just dropped in to tell you I've promised Maggie you'd make her a dress for the Oscars," he said distantly.

"My God," she exclaimed. "I'd forgotten the Oscars!" She dropped into her chair. "Mrs. Woodstock put it all out of my head—perhaps I'm finally going mad?" To every important figure in the retail business in Beverly Hills, the Oscars are regarded as manna from heaven, a cause for celebration equal to New Year's Eve. It is not who wins an Oscar that matters, but who wears what.

"Perhaps," Spider said in a neutral tone, which she ignored, still thinking about her lapse of memory.

"For three whole hours I didn't realize it exists, this Oscar business," Valentine said in wonder. "Yet tomorrow, at last, we'll hear who was nominated and there'll be so many customers coming in to buy—finally they'll know whether they go to the Awards and pray or whether they just sit at home and watch. Just think of it, for the next six weeks we will have the most awful tension, and then, for a handful of people, a few hours of happy relief. Is it not marvelous theater, keeping a whole huge industry in suspense, making the whole country argue and even care a little about the fate of a few actors, a few pictures?"

"How condescending you sound."

"Not at all. It's merely admiration, Elliott. Just put your mind on all the lovely money this comedy spreads around! The studios spend fortunes in public relations and advertising, movie ticket sales will benefit by many millions . . . but what do I really care about that? After all, it's only the dresses for the big night that are our concern."

"I suppose so," Spider answered, still without inflection. His tone of voice instantly infuriated her.

"Oh, it's all very well for you, this Oscar business. You run the whole store, I grant you that, Elliott, but as far as clothes go, it's only ready-to-wear that has to concern you, just a question of which Chloé or Holly Harp your little women will decide to buy. But up here we have the real problems. You don't have to worry about whether La Divina Streisand has gained another fifteen pounds on her already not petite derriere, which the dress, of course, must hide—and yet be skintight." She jumped up from her chair and walked over to him, her green eyes locked in battle with his blue gaze. "You, Elliott, don't have to worry if Raquel Welch has decided to look like a nun this year, but a nun who shows her titties, or whether Cher is convinced that she still won't be noticed in the crowd unless she's done up like a Zulu princess on her wedding day. And it's not just the presenters I have to think about. What about the nominees? And the producers' wives and the actors' mistresses?" And, she thought wrathfully, but did not say, he also didn't have to be constantly on the alert to fend off questions about his sexual activities. Valentine always knew, from the different shadings and tonalities of their casual inquiries to her whether Spider had not yet made love to a particular customer, whether they were in the middle of an affair, or whether the affair was over. She was adept at acting as if she knew nothing and cared less—as was the case—but she was totally sick and fed up with being subtly catechized either by Spider's conquests or their inquisitive friends.

"Look, Val," Spider said in a tone of indifferent coolness, which only made her angrier, "you know the Oscar gowns aren't what keeps Scruples profitable. We get every rich woman who sets her foot west of the Hudson. So if those touchy entertainment types are such a pain in the ass, why don't you turn them back to Bob Mackie and Ray Aghayan and Halston and all the other boys who used to do them before you came along and latched on to some of them?"

"Are you completely crazy—" she blurted before she caught the mockery in his eyes. Once it would have been indulgent laughter, today it was hurtful. And yet he knew, as well as she did, just how important it was to her to have captured so many of the stars of Hollywood. For all her Gallic grumbling, she wouldn't give up a square inch of her territory, particularly when it was so recently won. Valentine was perfectly well aware that although she was now the new necromantic name on the Beverly Hills-Bel Air circuit, it would still be a while before she became a firm fixture in the larger fashion establishment. And Spider knew it too. What the hell was wrong with him? He could certainly remember, just as well as she did, the rancidness of failure they had shared less than two years ago in New York, the dingy color of defeat. Even now they were employees, irreplaceable perhaps, but Scruples belonged to Billy Ikehorn Orsini, from the many million dollars' worth of land on which it was built to the latest dress shipment from Seventh Avenue waiting to be picked up at the airport.

At that moment Billy walked into the office and caught them there, glaring at each other. She cast a malevolent glance at the two of them and spoke in a voice that was low, yet so pitched that it had the power to make them both forget their anger with each other.

"Mrs. Evans was under the impression that the two of you were working and couldn't be disturbed. Have either of you any idea of how long I've been waiting for you?"

Spider rose from his chair and turned his smile on her, a smile of thorough sensuality, innocent of any trace of guilefulness or mordant wit, a smile that held a straightforward expectation of pleasure. Usually it worked.

"Don't bother with that fucking wholesome smile, Spider," Billy snapped.

"Billy, I finished with Maggie only five minutes ago. She's still in her fitting room getting herself together. Nobody expected you here today."

"I have just seen Mrs. Woodstock out," Valentine announced with dignity, "and I should like you to see just how profitably I have spent my afternoon." She held out her estimates. Billy ignored them.

"Look! Goddamn it to hell, I bought a big hunk of the highest priced land in the country and built the world's most expensive store on it and hired you two—out of the depths of unemployment, I might add—to run it and make your bloody fortunes and all I expect, just once, is that I shouldn't have to mooch around like some kind of time-killing idiot of a customer when I *need* you!"

"Neither one of us is a mind reader, Billy," Valentine said calmly, her temper in control because of the very strangeness of the way Billy was talking. She had never seen her employer so senselessly outraged.

"You don't have to be a mind reader to know that I would need you this afternoon!"

"I thought you'd be at home with Vito," Spider said.

"At home—" Billy was incredulous. "Anyone with half a head should have known I'd be here to order a dress for the Awards. By tomorrow *everyone* will be here—do you think I want to be bothered with that mob?"

"But, Billy, until tomorrow—" Valentine began, her hair almost frothing as she shook her head in bewilderment.

"Billy," Spider said gently, "what's the rush? You have at least a hundred evening dresses hanging in your closet. Until the nominations are announced you won't know if—" He broke off as she took three quick menacing steps toward him.

"Won't know if *what?*"

"Well, realistically—"

"Realistically WHAT?"

Now, angry himself, he answered bluntly. "If *Mirrors* will get a nomination. You certainly won't need a new dress unless it does." There was a long pause.

Suddenly Billy laughed and shook her head at both of them, as if they were silly children, foolish but forgivable. "So *that's* it, is it? It's lucky you're not in the movie business, Spider, you'd never make it. And you, Valentine. Just what the devil do you think Vito and I have been up to all year? Practicing to be gracious losers? Get off your asses, you two. Now *what* am I going to wear to the fucking Oscars?"

U ntil Ellis Ikehorn died, at seventy-one, Billy Ikehorn had not realized the extraordinary difference between being the wife of an enormously rich man and being an enormously rich young woman without a husband. For the last five years of their twelve-year marriage Ellis had been in a wheelchair, partly paralyzed and unable to speak as the result of a stroke. Although, from the day Billy had married him, she had thrown in her lot with the rich and powerful of this world, she had never really established a position in that stronghold from which to organize her widowhood. During the years of her husband's last illness, she had lived, in many ways, as a recluse in their Bel Air fortress, enduring, as far as her peers knew, the restricted life of the wife of a serious invalid.

Now, suddenly, she was thirty-two, without responsibilities to a family, and the mistress of an income that was virtually unlimited. Billy realized with amazement that it scared the shit out of her, all this endless money. Yet was that not what she had craved during the long years of her childhood as a poor relation? But now her fortune was so great that it was deeply disquieting. The potentials of vast sums of money seemed to flatten out, to shadow, to turn into prospects and perspectives so blurred at the edges that they led nowhere.

On that last morning when one of Ellis's three male nurses had come to tell Billy that he had had a final stroke in his sleep, she felt relief mingled with sadness for that part of the past that had been so good. But she had grieved over the past for five years; she had had too long to prepare herself for his death to feel a fierce personal loss. Yet, even less than half alive, Ellis had protected her. During his lifetime she had never bothered to think about money. A corps of lawyers and accountants handled all that. Of course she was aware that after their marriage he had given her ten million dollars' worth of tax-free municipal bonds, on which he had paid the gift tax, and that he had repeated the same practice on each of her seven birthdays until his first stroke in 1970. Even before she became his sole heir, inheriting all of his stock in Ikehorn Enterprises, her own fortune had swelled to eighty million dollars from which she derived an income of four million tax-free dollars a year. Now a platoon of IRS auditors spent weeks working on the Ikehorn-estate tax return, but do what they would, Billy was still left with roughly one hundred twenty million additional dollars. This new money confused and frightened her. In theory she understood that she could go anywhere, do anything. It was only by reflecting that she certainly could not pay for a moon shot that Billy was able to bring herself back to a sense of reality. Her magnifiying mirror reassured her as she looked into it to put on her mascara. All the familiar tasks remained. Bathing, brushing her teeth, weighing herself as she had done every morning and every evening since she was eighteen, dressing—it all restored the grain and texture of life. She would make one move at a time she told her image in the mirror, which showed none of the panic she felt. To a stranger who might have seen her for the first time at that moment, and assessed her height, her proud walk, her strong throat, her imperious head, she would have looked as autocratic and as strong as a young Amazon queen.

The immediate need was to decide about the funeral. Billy almost welcomed it because it gave her such a precise and limited set of decisions to make.

Ellis Ikehorn had never been a religious man, nor was he sentimental except on matters that touched on Billy. His will contained no instructions about a funeral, and he had certainly never expressed any preference about the matter of his burial. That form of anticipatory intimation of mortality held as little appeal to him as it did to most men, rich or poor.

Cremation, obviously, thought Billy. Yes, cremation followed by a memorial service in the Episcopal Church in Beverly Hills. Whatever his religion might have been, and he had always refused to discuss it, she had been brought up as a Boston Episcopalian and that would have to serve. Fortunately, there were enough local employees of his corporation and men he had done business with in the past to fill the church. If Billy had had to depend on her own personal friends to make up a respectable crowd, she could, she estimated, hold the service in the back room at La Scala's and still have space left over for a large choir and a three-piece combo.

She telephoned her lawyer, Josh Hillman, to ask him to make the necessary arrangements, and then directed her attention toward the next thing, a dress suitable for the funeral. Mourning. But she had lived in California too long, even for a woman who had spent years on the Best-Dressed List. There was nothing in her wardrobe, enormous as it was, that resembled a short, thin black dress appropriate for daytime wear in September 1975 with temperatures in the nineties accentuated by hot, dry Santa Ana winds. If only Scruples were finished she could go there, she thought longingly, but it was still under construction.

As she picked out several black silk linens from Galanos at Amelia Gray's, her gaze again went to the mirror. She was plagued by so much *unused* loveliness. Billy was not modest about her beauty. She had been desperately unattractive throughout her first eighteen years, and now that she was beautiful she gloried in it. She never wore a bra. Her breasts were high and almost lush. Any hint of support, which always provided uplift, would have made her too bosomy for chic. She thanked heaven that her ass was flat for a wide handspan below her waist, not becoming full until safely past the point where it would have destroyed the line of her clothes. Naked, she was unexpectedly rich in flesh. Flesh, Billy thought, with a dry, brittle heaviness of frustration, that had not felt the touch of a man's hand in many, many months. Since Christmas, when Ellis's decline had become more terrible day by day, she had, whether out of pity or a sense of taboo, deliberately deprived herself of the secret sexual life she had established almost four years before.

As she put her own clothes back on and waited for the new dresses to be packed, she turned her thoughts away from herself and attacked the next problem: the question of the ashes. She knew only that she had to do something with them. Ellis, when she had first met him, would probably have wanted to be dusted lightly into the speaking end of as many telephones as possible, she thought with a small smile of memory. He had been not quite sixty then, a vigorous emperor in the world of international wealth, who had made his first million of what he called "keeping money" a good thirty years before. Perhaps he would have preferred to have his ashes rubbed, a pinch at a time, into the linings of the briefcases of his battalion of executives. He had always enjoyed keeping them off-balance. The saleslady looked at her oddly, and Billy suddenly realized that she had made a small sound of mirth. She mustn't start that. It would be all over town by lunchtime that Billy Ikehorn was laughing on the morning her husband died. But hadn't there been something, besides their life together, that Ellis had been sentimental about before he got sick? He used to say that a glass of good wine and the new issues of *Fortune* and *Forbes* magazine was his favorite way to spend a quiet evening—of course—the vineyard, Silverado. Perhaps she was in more of a state than she realized, after all. Normally she would have thought of it immediately.

They couldn't use the Learjet. Hank Sanders, the head pilot, explained it to her. For the purpose she had described to him they needed a plane that could fly slowly, with a window open. The young pilot had been on the Ikehorn payroll for a little more than five years. It was he who had flown them all out from New York City to California after Ellis's first stroke, he who had occupied the left-hand seat on the many trips the sick old man and his remote young wife had made to their vineyard in St. Helena or to Palm Springs or to San Diego. Occasionally Hank had left the controls to the copilot and walked back to the main cabin to report on weather conditions to Mr.

Ikehorn, sitting by the window in his wheelchair; a formality, since he either paid no attention to them or seemed not to. But Mrs. Ikehorn had always thanked him gravely, pausing in whatever book or magazine she was reading to ask him a few questions about how he liked his new life in California, to tell him how many days they would be in the Napa Valley, even to suggest that he try a bottle from a particular vintage while he was there. He admired her dignity enormously and felt flattered when she looked him in the eye during their brief exchanges. He also thought she was a flaming, fabulous piece of ass, but he tried not to dwell on that.

But now, with Mrs. Ikehorn sitting inches away from him in the rented Beechcraft Bonanza as they took off from Van Nuys Airport four days after the cremation, he sat rather nervously at the controls. His uneasiness did not stem from any unfamiliarity with a small plane. Actually, Hank Sanders owned a secondhand Beech Sierra for weekend trips to Tahoe and Reno. There was nothing, he had discovered, like flying a girl away for a weekend to insure as much pussy as you could eat. No, it was sitting next to Mrs. Ikehorn, so serious, so preoccupied, and so unreasonably sexy—too close for comfort considering the circumstances. He carefully avoided looking at her. If only she had some relatives there with her, sisters or something.

He had filed a round-trip flight plan for St. Helena, some six hundred and fifty air miles in all, a trip that the Bonanza could make in no more than four and a half hours, maybe less, depending on the winds. As they approached Napa, Billy finally broke her silence.

"Hank, we're not going to land there on the strip. I want you to follow Route 29 straight up, losing altitude all the way until you get to St. Helena. Then bank to the right. Please enter slow flight by the time you've reached our boundaries at Silverado. Then level off as low as you possibly can—five hundred feet is legal, right?—and then circle the vineyards."

The Napa Valley is not wide, but it is exceedingly lovely, especially as the September sunlight showered down on the densely planted, miraculous acres of valley floor and the steep wooded hills that shelter it on all sides.

The finest wines in the United States, considered by many experts to rival and often surpass the greatest wines of France, come from these mere twenty-three thousand acres, where wineries jostle each other almost as closely as they do on the hillsides of Bordeaux, although they are each many times as large as the French holdings.

In 1945, Ellis Ikehorn, who detested the French on principle, which principles he did not choose to divulge, bought the old Hersent and de Moustiers property near St. Helena. That fine winery had fallen on ruinous days and had been badly neglected as Prohibition and the Depression and World War II dealt successive blows to American wine making. Its three thousand acres included a vast, elaborately shingled, twin-turreted, stone manor house, unmistakably Victorian in style, which Ikehorn restored to glory and renamed Château Silverado after the old road, once a coaching trail, which followed the length of the valley. From Germany he lured Hans Weber, the celebrated cellar master, and gave him free rein. The purchase of the winery and the interest Ellis Ikehorn took in consuming the great Pinot Chardonnay and the equally splendid Cabernet Sauvignon, which were eventually produced, some seven years and nine million dollars later, was the closest he ever came to having a hobby.

As they circled the vineyards, speckled with workers in the last days before the harvest, Billy opened the window on her right. In her hand she held a massive Georgian presentation box of solid gold, about six inches square, bearing the London hallmark for 1816-1817 and the maker's mark, that of the great craftsman Benjamin Smith. Inside the box were engraved these words:

Presented to Arthur Wellesley,
Duke of Wellington
On the occasion of the first anniversary of
The Battle of Waterloo
By the Respectful Company of Merchants
and Bankers
Of the City of London
"The Iron Duke will dwell eternally
in our hearts."

Billy carefully put her right hand through the small window, tensing her wrist against the rush of air. As the Bonanza circled low over the Silverado vines at eighty-five miles an hour, Billy barely released the catch on the lid of the box and, little by little, allowed Ellis Ikehorn's ashes to drift down on the rows of heavy bunches of grapes hidden beneath the deep green leaves. Her task completed, she returned the empty box to her handbag. "They say this will be a vintage year," she murmured to the speechless pilot.

During the flight back, Billy sat wrapped in a strange, quivering silence, which seemed in Hank Sander's tense imaginings to expect something of him. However, they landed at Van Nuys uneventfully, and as he pushed the Bonanza back on its blocks on the tarmac and went inside the Beech Aero Club to return the keys to the plane, he felt that the strangeness of the episode must have been due solely to the reason for the trip. But when he came out to the parking lot, he found Billy waiting for him, sitting in the driver's seat of the enormous, dark green Bentley Ellis had favored and which she had never sold.

"I thought we'd take a little drive, Hank. It's still early." Her dark eyebrows were raised in amusement as she looked into his confused face. This was an invitation for which he was totally unprepared.

"A drive! Why? I mean, yeah, sure, Mrs. Ikehorn, whatever you say," he answered, struggling between politeness and embarrassment. Billy laughed at him gently, thinking how like a strong, young farm boy he looked with his fresh, blunt, freckled features, his straw-blond hair, and his absolute lack of interest, as far as she had been able to tell over the years, in anything besides airplanes.

"Then get in. You don't mind if I drive, do you? I'm the wizard of the right-hand drive. Isn't it fun in this old thing? I feel as if we're about ten feet off the road." She was as natural and gay as someone going off to the beach.

Billy drove expertly, seeming to know where she was going, gaily humming a bit to herself, while Hank Sanders tried to relax, as if going for an outing with Mrs. Ikehorn was something he did frequently. He was desperately uncomfortable, so preoccupied with the etiquette of the situation that he hardly noticed as Billy left the freeway,

34

took Lankershim for a few miles, and then turned off the broad street into a narrow road. She made an abrupt right turn and pulled into the driveway of a small motel. She stopped the Bentley in one of the carports, which were built next to each room.

"I'll be right back, Hank—it's time for a drink I think, so don't go away." She disappeared into the motel's office for a minute and came back, casually flourishing a key and holding a plastic container full of ice cubes. Still humming, she handed him the ice, opened the trunk of the car, and took out a large leather case. She opened the door of the motel and laughingly waved him in.

Hank Sanders looked around the room with apprehension mixed with wonder, while Billy busily opened the portable bar case, made to order in London ten years before for race meetings and country-house shooting parties, a relic of an era in her life that seemed as archaic as the silver-topped decanters she set in a row on the carpet for lack of a table. The floor of the air-conditioned room was covered from one wall to another in thick, soft raspberry carpet, which also covered three of its walls all the way up to the ceiling, which, like the fourth wall, was entirely mirrored. Hank nervously walked about, noting that there were no windows in the room, no chairs, nothing but a small chest in one corner. Light came from three poles, which reached from floor to ceiling, to which were attached small spotlights fitted with pink bulbs, which could be pointed in any direction. A large, low bed took up almost half the space. It was covered in rosy-pink satin sheets and piled with pillows. He was pointlessly investigating the spotless bathroom when Billy called to him.

"Hank, what are you drinking?"

He walked back into the bedroom. "Mrs. Ikehorn, are you all right?"

"Perfectly. Please don't worry. Now, what can I offer you?"

"Scotch, please, on the rocks."

Billy was sitting on the floor, leaning against the bed. She handed him a glass as naturally as if they were at a cocktail party. He sat down on the carpet—it was either that or the bed he thought wildly—and took a long pull on his drink, which she had poured into a sterling-silver cup.

In her white, handkerchief-linen blouse and her French-blue cotton wraparound skirt, with her long, brown legs sprawled on the carpet, she looked as if she were at a picnic. Billy drank too, playfully clinking her cup against his.

"To the Essex Motel, garden spot of the San Fernando Valley—and to Ellis Ikehorn, who would approve," she toasted.

"What!" he said, deeply shocked.

"Hank, you don't have to understand it, just believe me." She moved closer to him, and with the same casual, yet precise, gesture she might have used to shake hands, she deliberately reached out and laid her elegant hand directly over the tight V of his jeans. Her fingers expertly searched out the outline of his penis.

"Jesus!" In an electric reaction, he tried to sit up straight but only succeeded in spilling his drink.

"I think you'd enjoy this more if you just sat still," Billy murmured, as she unzipped his jeans. His cock was completely limp with shock, curled on a broad mat of blond hair. Billy took a long breath of delight. She loved it like this, all soft and small. This way she could get every bit of it into her mouth with ease and hold it there, not even tonguing it yet, just feeling it grow and grow in the wet warmth, experiencing her power without moving a muscle. Even the hair on those pouchy globes squeezed together between his legs was straw-colored. Gently she nuzzled them, inhaling deeply the secret smell. Until a woman has smelled a man precisely there, she thought, driftingly, she can't know him. She heard the pilot moan protestingly above her questing head but paid no attention. He was recovering from his surprise, his cock beginning to twitch and grow. She cupped his balls with her free hand, her middle finger stealthily sliding and pressing upward along the taut skin of his scrotum. Now her lips and tongue were working together around the almost erect penis, which, though fairly short, was thick, as sturdily built as the rest of him. He lay back against the edge of the bed, abandoning himself entirely to the novelty of the passive role, feeling his cock jerking and leaping with a pulsating movement as more and more blood filled it. As he grew thick and then thicker still, she shifted her mouth slightly and and worked only on the swelling tip, treating it with a strong, unfaltering suction while the fingers of both her hands now slid up and down his wet, straining shaft. With a groan, unwilling to come too soon, he raised her dark head up from his lap and buried his face in her hair, kissing her beautiful neck, thinking that she was only a girl, only a girl. He lifted her onto the bed and flung his jeans to the carpet. Soon he had unbuttoned her blouse—her bare breasts were bigger than he had ever imagined them, the nipples dark and silky.

"Can you imagine how wet I've been for the last hour?" she muttered against his mouth. "No, I don't think you can—you'll have to see for yourself—I'll just have to show you." Billy undid her skirt in one movement; under it she was naked. She sat up and pushed him down on the bed, holding his shoulders on the sheet with the heels of her hands. She threw one knee over him and moved higher, straddling him, so that her cunt was directly over his mouth. His tongue reached out to capture it, but she kept undulating back and forth above him so that he was only able to lap at her from second to second. Finally, maddened, unable to stand her teasing, he clutched her ass and pulled her down, firmly planting his mouth between the tumid, plump lips, sucking and licking and pulling and tugging blindly. She tensed, her back arched, and with a muffled scream she came, almost immediately. His cock was so hard he was afraid he might spurt into the air. Frantically he took her by the waist, pulled her down on top of it and plunged up into her savagely while she still shuddered with her own spasms.

The hours that followed never happened again, but Hank Sanders would have remembered them for the rest of his life even without the Georgian presentation box, once the property of the Duke of Wellington, which Billy gave him late that night as she said good-bye to him back at the mansion on the hill in Bel Air.

As she walked up the wide staircase, the house seemed empty even though it was full of a dozen sleeping servants. Ellis was really and truly gone now, she thought, remembering the lusty man she had married twelve years before. When she had told Hank Sanders that Ellis would have approved of them that night, he hadn't understood, but she had been speaking the truth. If it had been she who had died, an old woman, and Ellis who had survived, a young man, he would probably have fucked the first woman he could lay hands on, in private celebration of the past, a past in which they had loved each other so thoroughly. It might not be everybody's idea of a sentimental way to salute a memory, but it suited both of them perfectly. His ashes clinging to the ripe grapes, the smell of cock in her hair, the welcome soreness she felt between her legs—Ellis would have not only approved, he would have applauded.

When Wilhelmina Hunnenwell Winthrop was born—in Boston, twenty-one years before she became Billy Ikehorn —people who cared about genealogy, and Boston is to family trees what Périgord is to truffle lovers and Monte Carlo is to yacht owners, considered her a very lucky little girl indeed. Her vast cousinage included the indispensable number of Lowells, Cabots, and Warrens, a good handful of Saltonstalls, Peabodys, and Forbeses, as well as a splash of imperial Adams blood mixed in every other generation or so. Her paternal line began with a Richard Warren, who was on the Mayflower in 1620—one could hardly hope for more than this—and on her mother's side there was not only impeccable Boston blood but she could also trace her descent straight back to the patroons of the Hudson River Valley, as well as to some of the many Randolphs of Virginia.

The fortunes of old Boston families, by and large, were founded on clipper ships, countinghouses, and the West India trade. These fortunes, conserved and husbanded by the prudent overseers of the clans, now form a network of interlocking trusts, which virtually insure that every proper Bostonian infant will never need to worry about money and, indeed, will grow up wondering why money problems loom so large in the concerns of most people. As long as the family trusts are quietly but mightily prospering and producing, many Bostonians are simply *beyond* money, just as a person in perfect health is beyond thinking about breathing in and breathing out. Fortunately, Old Boston has developed, in each generation, men with exceptional talents as money managers, men who watch over the investments of their relatives as brilliantly as they care for the investments of the large institutions they have under their charge. These men enable the rest of Boston to consider talk of money vulgar.

However, even the very best of Boston families have branches that, as they may choose to put it, "do not enjoy the same means" as the rest of the family.

Billy Ikehorn's father, Josiah Prescott Winthrop, and her mother, Matilda Randolph Minot, were both the last of their respective subsidiary side branches of these great dynastic tribes. His family's money had been all but wiped out in the financial disaster that befell Lee, Higginson & Co., the great brokerage firm, which lost twenty-five million dollars of its clients' money when Ivar Kreuger, the "Match King," went bankrupt and committed suicide. Matilda's family hadn't had money since the Civil War, although it was rich in history. Whatever was left of the ravished family trusts that Josiah brought to their marriage had been reduced to an income of little more than one thousand dollars a year. No fresh money had been introduced into either withering family in the past five generations. Again, not typical of the sensible Bostonian practice of restoring a faltering family fortune by marriage into a neighboring clan with nicely healthy trusts, the past generations of Winthrops had stubbornly married demure, sensitive daughters of educators and men of the cloth, both honorable Boston professions but not financially rewarding. The last decent sum of the family money was used to send Josiah Winthrop through Harvard Medical School.

However, he was a dedicated student who had graduated high in his class and served with distinction as an intern and resident at the renowned Peter Bent Brigham Hospital. His specialty was gynecology and he could look forward to an excellent practice even if he only treated friends of his own female relations, who numbered in the hundreds.

Late—much too late—in his last year of residency, Josiah Winthrop discovered that he wasn't interested in private practice. He fell in love, passionately and permanently, with pure research the minute he began to look into the new field of antibiotics. Going into research is the only way a doctor can positively insure himself against ever making a decent living. On the day on which he should have gone into practice for himself, Josiah Winthrop joined the staff of the private Rexford Institute as a junior research fellow at a salary of three thousand two hundred dollars a year. Even this small sum was about seven hundred dollars more than he would have made at a federally funded research establishment.

Matilda, high-minded from the day she left the high chair, was too involved in the last months of her pregnancy to worry about the future. Together, she thought they could certainly manage on four thousand two hundred dollars a year and she had the greatest confidence in her Joe, tall, skinny, long-boned, his dark eyes filled with the quintessence of Yankee strength of mind. His single-mindedness and determination to follow his star struck her as the very model of a man destined for greatness. Matilda herself, a slender, dreamy, dark-haired beauty, seemed to have stepped from the pages of Hawthorne. There was little in her of the high-living Dutch and the hot-blooded Virginia gentry who decorated some of the branches of her family tree.

When their daughter was born they named her Wilhelmina, after a beloved aunt of Matilda's, a middle-aged scholar who had never married. However, they both conceded that Wilhelmina was a burdensome name for a baby and they called their tiny daughter Honey, an acceptable diminutive of her formidable middle name, Hunnenwell.

A year and a half after Honey was born, Matilda Winthrop was run over and killed as she crossed Commonwealth Avenue against the lights, in a fit of absent-mindedness resulting from a suspicion that she was pregnant again.

For a short while, Josiah, stricken and disbelieving, hired a nurse for litle Honey, but he soon realized that he couldn't afford such a luxury. The idea of remarriage was unthinkable, so he did the only possible thing left to do and resigned from his beloved Institute, where he had already achieved an enviable reputation. He took a despised but better paid job as a staff doctor, specializing in everything from measles to minor surgery, at a small and under-manned hospital in the undistinguished town of Framingham, about forty-five minutes' drive from Boston. This job had several advantages. It enabled him to rent a small house on the outskirts of town, where he established

Honey with Hannah, a good-hearted, simple woman who worked as both nursemaid and a cook-housekeeper; it was near a good public school system, and it left him enough free time to continue his researches in the small lab he constructed in the basement. Josiah Winthrop did not even consider going back to gynecology because he realized that he would never have time to himself in that branch of medicine.

Honey was a dear child. Far too chubby, of course, and much too shy went the verdict of the countless aunts who drove out to Framingham with her cousins, unto the fourth degree, to visit the little girl or to fetch her and take her home with them for days at a time. But who could blame her for anything, that unfortunately motherless creature whose father—although one had to admit that he was a dedicated man—was almost always at the hospital or doing whatever he did in that basement. Honey had no one but Hannah to bring her up, after all. Hannah managed marvelously, but there were—well—limits—to her education. The aunts decided that next year, when she would be three, Honey really must start at Miss Martingale's nursery school in Back Bay with Cousin Liza and Cousin Ames and Cousin Pierce, where she could get the right background for her future appreciation of music and art and become acquainted with the children who would form, in the natural course of events, her network of lifelong friends.

"Out of the question" was her father's answer. "Honey lives a good, healthy country life here and there are dozens of perfectly nice children around for her to play with. Hannah's a good woman, decent and kind, and you aren't going to persuade me that a three-year-old who gets plenty of fresh air and has normal intelligence needs to be 'introduced' to finger painting and, God save us all, organized block building. No, I simply won't do it and that's that." None of the aunts could change his mind. He had always been the most stubborn of a stubborn family.

And so Honey, at the age of three, began to become an outcast from the tribe. The visits from even the best meaning of the aunts slowed to a trickle, since their children were busy with nursery-school obligations on weekdays and they wanted to play with new friends on weekends. To say nothing of birthday parties! It was more sensible to wait until the holidays when dear Josiah could bring Honey to them for the day. It was a pity that he would never stay overnight, but he insisted on getting back to his work every evening.

Honey didn't really seem to miss the diminishing connection to her horde of stolid cousins and managerial aunts. She played quite contentedly with the children who lived in the modest houses on her street and attended a local kindergarten when the time came. Nor did she feel lonely with Hannah, who baked her cookies and pies and cakes every day. Josiah almost always came home to eat dinner with her before he disappeared downstairs to his work. This was the pattern of her life, and with nothing to compare it to, she accepted it.

After two years at a local kindergarten Honey entered the Ralph Waldo Emerson Elementary School in Framingham. There, from the early days of first grade, she became very gradually aware that she was somehow different from her schoolmates. They all had mothers and brothers and sisters instead of just Hannah, who was not a relative, and a father whom she saw only during a hasty dinner. They had a kind of daily family life, made of jokes, and fights and the intertwining of emotions, which fascinated and puzzled her. On the other hand, they did not have cousins who lived on enormous estates in Wellesley or Chestnut Hill or in glorious town houses in Louisburg Square or in Bulfinch mansions on Mt. Vernon Street. They did not have aunts who belonged to the Sewing Circles and went to Mrs. Welch's Waltz Evenings—even if now they rarely came to Framingham. Nor did her schoolmates have uncles who had all gone to Harvard, who all either played squash or sailed large boats, who belonged to the Somerset Club or the Union Club, the Myopia Hunt and the Athenaeum. They were not taken by one aunt or another to the Boston Symphony on occasional Friday afternoons.

Honey fell into the habit of boasting about her relatives and cousins and their houses in order to make her lack of a mother and siblings and an ordinary homelife seem unimportant. Gradually her classmates stopped liking Honey, but this didn't affect her boasting because she never understood precisely *what* it was that they resented. Soon they stopped playing with her after school or inviting her to their houses or including her in their parties. She began to compare them more and more unfavorably with her Brahmin cousins. Although her cousins didn't seem to particularly dislike her, neither did they like her. Slowly, inevitably, helplessly, and without understanding why, she became a very lonely child. Hannah baked more and more, but even apple pie with vanilla ice cream was little help.

There was no one to talk to about it. Honey never considered telling her father how she felt. They didn't talk about *feelings;* they never had and they never would. She knew, without knowing that she knew, that he would disapprove if he found out that she was unhappy. Her father often told her that she was a "good" child, too heavy of course, but she'd soon grow out of it. A good child cannot, dare not, allow it to be known that she is not liked or approved of outside of the home circle. Not being popular, to a child, seems to be a final judgment that has been made against her for reasons she does not understand but everyone else does. A child accepts this severely damaging judgment and is ashamed for herself. The humiliation of unpopularity is so great that it must be hidden from anyone who still loves that child and approves of her. That love is too precious to risk with the truth.

When the time came that the aunts insisted that Honey be sent to dancing school, even stubborn Josiah Winthrop had to agree. He was too much of a bred-in-the-bone Bostonian not to accept unquestioningly the sacred ritual of Mr. Lancing de Phister's Dancing Class. Naturally, without need of explanation, it was simply part of Honey's heritage, just as was her future membership in the Colonial Dames. Without even thinking it over, he knew that if Matilda had lived, she would have been one of that elect band of well-groomed mothers who escorted their small daughters to the ballroom of the Vincent Club every other Saturday afternoon from October until late May.

Children started at Mr. de Phister's when they were a minimum of nine years old, not a day before. From the ages of nine till eleven they were considered beginners; from twelve to fourteen they were intermediates; and when the students of fifteen to seventeen had mostly gone off to boarding school, the classes were held on holiday evenings and became, in effect, predebutante dances.

Much later in her life Honey was to discover that almost every woman who had ever been to dancing school had retained horrified memories of gloves lost at the last minute, of petticoats that fell down in the middle of a waltz, and of sweaty boys who stepped on their toes on purpose. But she was secretly convinced that they enjoyed trotting out these nostalgic minor traumas as evidence that they had come from the kind of families who sent their children to dancing school. She never told anyone about Mr. de Phister's. The lessons she learned there had little to do with dancing.

Instead of an appropriate nine, she had been almost ten years old that first year of classes because of her inconvenient November birthday. A ten-year-old who stood five feet six inches tall and weighed one hundred and forty-five pounds. A ten-year-old in a dress bought in the teen department of the Wellesley branch of Filene's because nothing in the children's department fit her. A terrible dress, that Hannah had helped her pick out, a genuinely hideous bright blue taffeta dress.

Various aunts kissed her as she came into the lobby of the Vincent Club, an embarrassed Hannah at her side, and then gave each other appalled glances. "Blast that thick-headed Joe anyway," one muttered to another with fury, quite forgetting to wave good-bye to her own dainty daughter, neatly turned out in a dusty-rose velvet with an Irish lace collar. Honey's scattered cousins gave her small waves of greeting as she shyly sidled into the crowded room.

Much of Mr. de Phister's success depended on the fact that he charged the parents of boys half of what he charged the parents of girls so that every class had a guaranteed surplus of males. His first rule was that every boy must try to find a partner. No boy could sit out a dance until every little girl was dancing. There was, however, no way to prevent the boys from scrambling in a shoving group to ask certain precocious girls to dance, those who had, at nine, already discovered the power of certain looks, certain smiles, the note of a private voice telling a private joke. Nor was there any way to prevent one girl from being the last girl to be asked to dance by an obviously miserable, foot-dragging boy. (Every psychoanalyst in Boston eventually became familiar with the name of Mr. de Phister's classes.)

Dancing practice alternated with six periods of instruction given by Mr. de Phister and his wife before the break for refreshment in the middle of the two-hour lesson. Six times Honey was the last girl to be asked to dance. When the nightmare came to a temporary halt, she went to the laden table at the side of the room and stood by herself, gorging frantically on small, rich cakes and cookies and many cups of sweet fruit punch. She stood alone in a corner and gobbled as quickly as possible. When Mrs. de Phister signaled the beginning of the second half of the lesson, Honey stayed in her corner, forcing the last cookies into her mouth and gulping down a tenth cup of the grape punch. Mr. de Phister spotted her quickly. This had happened before.

"Honey Winthrop," he said loudly, "please be kind enough to join the other girls. We're about to start."

Honey threw up violently in a horrible purple gush. All the cookies and all the punch disgustingly splashed across the table of refreshments and the white linen cloth, even splattering the polished dance floor. Mrs. de Phister led her quickly into the ladies' room and left her, after a few minutes of attention, to recover there on a chair. Later, when the class was over, Honey heard some girls approaching her hiding place and ran to conceal herself in a stall.

"Who in earth is that—yech—*fat*, awful, funny-looking girl in that *icky* blue dress—imagine woopsing like that! Do you really know her? Someone told me she's your cousin," a strange voice asked. Then Honey heard her first cousin Sarah answer with obvious reluctance.

"Oh, that's just Honey Winthrop. She's only—some sort of a distant cousin, a very distant one, she doesn't even live in Boston. Promise you won't tell anyone, but she's a *poor relation*."

"Why, Sarah May Alcott, my mother told me no lady ever uses that expression!" The strange voice was sincerely scandalized.

"I know," Sarah giggled, unrepentant, "but she *is*. I

heard our Fräulein telling Diana's Mam'selle just last week in the park. Just a poor relation, that's exactly what she said."

The rest of the memory was lost, although Honey knew that she must have been returned to Hannah eventually and that the aunts must have held a family conference because from that time on one or another of them always took her shopping for her dancing-school dresses at a discreet shop on Newbury Street that specialized in clothes for the "early bloomer."

From time to time Honey went into Cambridge to visit her great-aunt Wilhelmina. This professorial maiden lady was her favorite relative because she never asked about school or dancing class or little friends but talked about France and books and served a sumptuous array of cakes and sandwiches at teatime in her tiny, neat apartment. Honey suspected that Aunt Wilhelmina was a poor relation too.

From 1952, when she was ten, until 1954, Honey endured and endured and grew taller and steadily fatter. Two years of Mr. de Phister's, two years of Ralph Waldo Emerson, where she lost the few friends she had left when the other girls began to give pajama parties and talk about boys and experiment in secret with makeup and bras. Two years of celebrating Thanksgiving and Christmas and spending an odd week in Maine or Cape Cod with the aunts and the cousins, the unbearable words "poor relation" never out of her mind. She had been unhappy before but friendly. Now those two words made her awkward, sullen, and uncomfortably hangdog. She could have formed friendships with various cousins if she had felt at ease with them, for they were by no means unkind or unapproachable. After all, she was a Winthrop. But her memory of that afternoon at dancing school convinced her that behind each smiling face was scorn, that behind each remark was hidden condescension, that they would all disavow her if they could. Her remoteness provoked even the best of them to indifference, and their indifference validated her convictions.

Honey began to hate her bossy aunts and her many cousins who all acted as if they never thought about money. She knew better. She knew it was the only thing that really mattered. She began to hate her father for not making more money, for working at a dull job so that he could save long hours for the research that must be far more important to him than she was. She began to hate Hannah who loved her but couldn't help her. She began to hate everything but the thought of having money, lots of money. And food.

Josiah Winthrop talked to Honey severely about her eating habits. He gave her a number of stern, informative lectures on her fat cells and her body chemistry and balanced nutrition. He told her it was merely a matter of proper diet, that no one in her family was born to be fat, and he instructed Hannah to stop baking. Then he went off to the hospital or his lab and both Hannah and Honey ignored him. She was almost twelve and weighed one hundred and sixty-five pounds.

During the summer before Honey's twelfth birthday, Aunt Cornelia, Josiah Winthrop's favorite of all his family, came out to Framingham to see him on a Sunday afternoon.

"Joe, you really must do something about Honey."

"Cornie, I assure you that I've talked to her about her weight on many occasions, and she has no opportunity to eat fattening foods in this house. She must get them from her friends. Anyway, my parents were both big boned, as you probably remember, and she'll slim down as soon as she reaches puberty. In two years—perhaps three—she'll be right down to her proper weight. There has *never* been a fat Winthrop! Of course she has the Winthrop height—but there's nothing wrong with that."

"Joe! For a brilliant man you can be unbelievably stupid. I'm not talking about Honey's weight, although, heaven knows, something has to be done, and, what's more, she's small boned, not big boned, as you'd notice if you ever looked with half an eye. I'm talking about the way she's growing up. She simply isn't part of *anything*. You're so wrapped up in your blasted work that you don't realize just how unhappy that child is. Don't you see that she doesn't have friends to get fattening food from? She doesn't even know the people she would just naturally know—she's hardly a part of the family. And, heaven knows, Mr. de Phister's has been a tragedy. Joe, you know perfectly well what I mean, so don't try that bland look on me. Or if you don't know, the more shame on you. Her own kind of people, to be blunt, our *sort* of people, since you force me to be crude, are going to exclude Honey if you don't do something."

"Aren't you being a little snobbish, Cornie? Honey *is* a Winthrop, even if we happen to live on the wrong side of the tracks." He was on the defensive, a self-willed, arrogant, selfish man who loathed being called to account and could spin out his excuses endlessly.

"I really don't care what you choose to call it, Joe. I only know that Honey is growing up as an outsider in a group where we have precious little time for outsiders. I wouldn't want to live anywhere in the world but Boston, but I know our faults. They don't matter when you belong, but Honey is beginning *not to belong,* Joe, and that is both cruel and unnecessary."

Josiah Winthrop's expression changed. He had always belonged, so completely, so unquestioningly, that wherever he lived, however little money he had, whatever he did, he knew he belonged with the kind of conviction that needs no reassurance. He would be a Boston Winthrop if he became a leper, a murderer, even a maniac. It was unthinkable that a child of his might not belong, unthinkable and impossible. His thoroughgoing self-centeredness had been penetrated by Cornelia's cannily chosen words.

"What are you suggesting that I do, Cornie?" he asked, hastily, hoping that it would be something that wouldn't take any of his time. He was making great progress down in his little lab, but he needed all of his time, every minute.

"Merely that you let me take over in certain areas, Joe. I have tried before, as you may remember, but you always rebuffed me. Now it's almost too late. George and I would consider it a pleasure if you would allow us to send Honey away to the Emery Academy. Our Liza is going there this year—I've always felt that twelve-year-old girls—impossible creatures—are better off at boarding school than they are at home—and there will be any number of nice Boston girls there. After all, it was your mother's school and your grandmother's school—I don't have to tell you that lifelong friendships are formed in boarding school, do I? If Honey goes into junior high here in Framingham, she'll never make those friendships. It's really her last chance, Joe. I detest sounding dramatic, but I think you really owe it to Honey, and to poor, dear Matilda, to accept." Cornelia never minded pulling out all the stops when it was absolutely necessary, although she knew it was a fearfully un-Boston thing to do.

It was charity, there was nothing else you could call it, Josiah Winthrop thought, but he certainly couldn't afford the fees that the Emery Academy asked. He had prided himself all his life on the fact that no one had ever dared to offer him charity; he had chosen not to go into private practice and was prepared to pay the price, but Cornelia had frightened him badly.

"Well—thank you, Cornelia. I accept with gratitude. I've been reluctant—well, that's not relevant—I'm sure we both know what I'm trying to say. Please tell George how I feel. I'll tell Honey the news tonight, at dinner. I know she'll be delighted too. What about the application forms and all that sort of thing?"

"I'll take care of them. There's room for her, of course —I've already checked. And, Joe, tell Honey to take the noon train to Boston next Saturday. I'll meet her at Back Bay Station and we'll go and order her uniforms. It really couldn't be simpler, my dear; I have to do it all for Liza anyway."

Cornelia was gracious in her victory. She could hardly wait for her weekly lunch with her sisters at the Chilton Club. In one sweeping triumph she had vanquished that troublesome bear Joe Winthrop, displayed considerable generosity, not that they couldn't afford it—but nevertheless—and quieted her conscience, which had disturbed her recently whenever she saw poor Honey being left out of swimming races and pony-jumping contests on her Chestnut Hill estate.

That fall, equipped with everything her cousin Liza had, Honey left for Emery where she was to spend the next six years—lonely, hideously lonely, outrageously lonely years, more of an outsider than she had ever been before.

Of all the various kinds of snobbishness that make youth such hell for so many, an utterly cruel snobbishness never again equaled among adults, there is perhaps no stricter hierarchy than that which reigns at a really exclusive girls' boarding school. It makes the permutations of privilege in the court of Louis XIV look democratic. In each class there is a ruling clique, then a second-best clique, a third-best, a fourth-best, and even a fifth-best. And then there are the freaks. Honey, of course, was a freak from the day she arrived. There is no law that says a member of a clique can't be fat, no law that says she can't be poor (although few poor girls are found in such schools), but there is a law that says each class must have its freaks and that a freak is distinguished on the first day of school and stays a freak until she graduates.

There were certain compensations. Honey worked hard at her studies, since she had no offers to waste time at gossip or bridge. She discovered several teachers who appreciated her good mind, and she got excellent marks in French, which was taught strictly as a language to be read and written. Even at Emery the teachers soon gave up at attempts at French conversation. Honey made a few tentative friendships with some of the other freaks, but these relationships were always overshadowed by the knowledge that if they hadn't been freaks they wouldn't have been caught dead talking to each other. Her closest human contact was with Gertrude, one of the cooks at the school, a fat, young woman who nursed a deep resentment against all the slim girls she was employed to feed. Here was a girl almost as large as Gertude herself. She understood completely that Honey couldn't subsist on the plain fare of the school. Every night Gertrude, with both malice and sympathy, left a large covered tray of leftovers hidden in the dining-room pantry, supplemented by the baked goods bought in the local village with the money the Winthrop girl gave her, money that Aunt Cornelia had given Honey for her extras.

By senior year Honey had reached her full height of five feet ten inches and weighed two hundred and eighteen pounds. She would have weighed more, but Emery prided itself in its healthy, low-starch, high-protein diet. She had been accepted at both Wellesley and Smith. Aunt Cornelia planned to send her niece through college in the same first-cabin manner in which she had sent her through boarding school. But Honey had another plan, conceived in grief and rage. On her last visit to her great-aunt Wilhelmina, who was being taken care of by the family in a nursing home, the ancient lady had given her a certified check for ten thousand dollars.

"It's my savings," she said. "Don't let them know you've got it or George will take it away to manage for you and you won't even see the interest on it. Use it while you're young, do something foolish. I've never done anything foolish in my life and oh, Honey, how I regret it now! Don't wait until it's too late—promise me you'll spend it on yourself."

A week later, Honey confronted Aunt Cornelia. Quaveringly, she announced, "I don't want to go to college. I can't stand the idea of another four years in a girls' school. I have ten thousand dollars of my own and I intend to—I intend to go to Paris and live there as long as I can."

"How—where on earth did you get ten thousand dollars?"

"Great-Aunt Wilhelmina gave the money to me. You don't even know where I've deposited it. I'm not letting anyone, not even Uncle George, invest it for me." The fat girl quivered with unexpected defiance now that she had finally begun to speak. "If I want to, I can run away and be in Paris before you know I've gone—and you won't be able to find me."

"Absolutely impossible. Out of the question, my dear child. You'll adore Wellesley. I loved every minute of my four years—" Cornelia had begun to look at Honey closely for the first time in this incredible conversation. What she saw was not reassuring. The girl obviously meant every word she was saying. In fact, if you wanted to be fanciful, you might almost say it was a question of do or die. And old Wilhelmina had certainly been most unorthodox. Giving cash to a child! Unheard of—she must be senile. Still, perhaps something could be rescued from this contretemps. Honey could hardly be *made* to attend college. Cornelia had long wondered what the girl would do with herself after college. Graduate school most likely and perhaps a teaching career. After all, she had been at the top of her class in French. It did seem a pity, Matilda's daughter becoming another spinster schoolteacher.

"Honey, come here and sit down. Now—I promise to consider your plan, but on two conditions. First, we must find a good French household for you to live in where you will be looked after properly. I can't have you living in a hotel or one of those sinister student hostels. Second, you may stay only one year—one year is quite sufficient for Paris—and when you come home you must promise to go to Katie Gibbs and take their one-year program. If you do that you'll be assured an excellent job as an executive secretary, since you'll obviously have to begin thinking about earning a living."

Honey was silent for a few minutes, considering. Once she actually got to Paris it wouldn't be easy to force her to come home again. And her money would go farther if she lived as a paying guest with some family. She had heard, at Emery, that French families really didn't bother about what their paying guests were doing just as long as they paid their pension on time. And she'd get out of Katie Gibbs somehow. Who could possibly face life as a secretary? Or go to that stuffy, strict school?

"It's a deal!" She gave her aunt a rare smile. The child really did have an enchanting smile, even with her fat cheeks and triple chin, Cornelia realized vaguely. But one saw it so seldom.

That night Cornelia wrote to Lady Molly Berkeley, a Lowell by birth, and one of Boston's chief conduits to "people one knows" in Europe.

Dear Cousin Molly,

I have some rather exciting news. Honey Winthrop, Joe's girl, is planning to spend the next year in Paris perfecting her accent before going on to Katie Gibbs. She is a good child with a kind heart—although not much of a heartbreaker, I'm afraid. I wonder if, among your many French friends, you might happen to know of a really nice family in which Honey could live as a paying guest. She is not comfortably off, unfortunately, so she will have to earn her living eventually, but she does have a small sum that should be more than adequate to see her through the next few years, with proper management. I do hope to hear from you,

*dear Molly, before we arrive. We'll be at Claridge's,
as usual, in June and we're both looking forward to
seeing you then.*

Love,
Nelie

Lady Molly Emlen Lowell Lloyd Berkeley, who was
then a lively seventy-seven, loved nothing more than
making such arrangements. She wrote back within three
weeks.

Nelie my dear,

*I was delighted to receive your letter and I do have
promising news for you! I've poked about and discovered that Lilianne de Vertdulac has room for Honey.
You must remember her husband, Comte Henri—such
a nice man. He was killed during the war, alas, and the
family's business was ruined. Lilianne only takes one
girl a year and we are most fortunate because she is
thoroughly appropriate in all ways, a rather remarkable
and very charming woman. She has two daughters,
younger than Honey, but they will certainly provide
lots of youthful company for her.*

*The pension, with all meals of course, will be
seventy-five American dollars a week, which I do
think is a jolly fair price considering what food is these
days on the Continent. I'll confirm the arrangements as
soon as I hear from you. My love to George—*

Fondly,
Molly

The true French aristocracy, not those with new titles
conferred by Napoleon but the ancient royalist aristocracy,
which traces its ancestors back to the Crusades and beyond, is twice as interested in money as the average
Frenchman. This is to say that the old French aristocracy
is perhaps four times as interested in money as the average
human being. To them, all money is new money unless it
is their own family money or becomes their money. If

one of their sons marries the daughter of a wealthy wine merchant whose great-grandparents were peasants, instant transubstantiation takes place and her dowry immediately glows with all the grace of an inheritance from Madame de Sévigné herself.

The French aristocracy has taken a lively interest in the good people of Boston ever since the days of the French Revolution when a Bostonian, Colonel Thomas Handasyd Perkins—whose daughter had married a Cabot—personally rescued the son of the Marquis de Lafayette and brought the boy to safety in the New World. Of course, it had to be recognized that the Bostonians were all merchants or sailors to begin with, generally of untitled English stock if you insisted on tracing the line back before Plymouth Rock—and many did so insist—yet one had to admire their ability to establish and enlarge their fortunes, while with each generation, they became more and more distinguished. Indeed, a good number of their daughters had become so distinguished over the course of history that they now wore some of the most glorious titles in France. And these Bostonians, although they rarely possessed those venerable family acres adorned by a château, which alone could really satisfy the French deification of real estate, nevertheless did own a gratifying number of mills and plants and banks and brokerage firms. Also they had *ton*. They were never vulgar. They lived with their fortunes in a quiet way, which was compatible to the many great French families who had had, perforce, to renounce the outrageous, indeed fatal, ostentation and grandeur of their ancestors after the Revolution.

It has always been understood that a young male French aristocrat, without a family fortune, must marry money. It is a sacred obligation to his parents, to himself, and to the future of his family. And it is the only way to hold on to the land. A French aristocrat, female, without money, who does not obtain it through marriage, has an equal obligation to maintain certain forms, certain ways of dealing with the world, until she literally starves to death, although it is hoped that it will not come to that.

La Comtesse Lilianne de Vertdulac had lost everything in World War II except her sense of form, her courage, her style, and her kindness. Her style was a mixture of innate taste stripped down to its simplest expression and a personal evasiveness, a quality of holding herself back, eluding intimacy, which gave her that fascination that forthcoming people never inspire. Even her basic kindness had been all but extinguished by the yearly succession of paying guests, young and usually American, who provided the bulk of her livelihood. She was more than pleased to be able to shelter, for the next year, Miss Honey Winthrop, about whom Lady Molly had written so warmly. The girl obviously had only the very best connections, indeed she seemed to be related to most of Old Boston quite the way in which Lilianne was related to most of the Faubourg St.-Germain.

The tiny, blond Frenchwoman of forty-four lived in an apartment on Boulevard Lannes, facing the Bois de Boulogne. Through complications in the rent freeze of the war years, which still had not been untangled, she and her two teen-aged daughters were able to afford to live in this exceedingly fashionable part of Paris, although she had not been able to spend any money on her apartment since 1939. It was rather grand, if very shabby, with high ceilings flooded by sunlight. The apartment was pervaded by a kind of intensely feminine coziness that is found only in homes where no man lives or is catered to.

Madame La Comtesse herself came to the door when Honey arrived. Normally her cook, Louise, who lived in a room in the attic of the house, answered the bell when they expected guests, and Lilianne remained curled in the deep, worn cushions of the couch in the salon until the guests were shown in, rising only for an older woman, but today she wanted to show marked hospitality.

Her smile of welcome remained fixed, but her eyes widened in shocked astonishment and quick disgust as she shook hands with Honey. Never, no never, had she seen such an immense girl. She was a baby hippopotamus—it was incredible, a disgrace. How could this have happened? And what would she do with her? Where would she hide her? As she led Honey into the salon where tea was waiting, she tried to comprehend this unexpected horror. Although Lilianne had never expected to spend her life taking in paying guests, she nevertheless prided herself on the fact that any girl who spent a year in her home left it improved in two ways: first with a command of French as good as the girl's brain and her application would allow and, even more important, with a sense of style, absorbed from the very air of Paris, which she never would have acquired if she had not had this opportunity. *But with this girl?*

As they sat down in front of the tea tray she spoke with perfect calm in spite of her emotions.

"Welcome to my home, Honey. I shall call you Honey, no? and you may just call me Madame."

"Please, Madame, would you call me by my real name?" Honey had rehearsed this speech over and over in the plane from New York to Paris. "Honey is just an old, childish nickname and I've outgrown it. My real first name is Wilhelmina, but I would like to be called Billy."

"Why not?" It was certainly more appropriate, she thought, for such fat rendered the girl almost sexless. "Then, Billy, this is the last time we shall speak to each other in English. After I've shown you your room and you have put away your clothes, it will be almost time for dinner. We dine early in this house—at seven-thirty—because my daughters have a great deal of homework every day. Now, from dinner on we will speak French to you all the time. Louise, the cook, knows no English at all. It will be difficult, I know, but it is the only possible way for you to learn." Lilianne always made this condition plain to each of her new girls. "You may feel very foolish and embarrassed at first, but unless we do this you will never learn to speak French as it should be spoken. We will not be laughing at you, but we will correct you constantly—so do not become angry when that happens. If we allow you to continue to make the same mistake, we will not be doing our duty." Lilianne realized that her remarks had almost no hope of penetrating Billy's mind. In spite of her best efforts, her paying guests spent their days and often their nights with the American students who flooded Paris, and never gave themselves a chance to truly sink into the language. Apparently they had all "studied French" in school. In her opinion every one of them had been abominably taught and they usually remained content to stumble along in ignorance.

Billy's eyes were shining. Instead of the trapped look

that usually came over the faces of pensionnaires when she made this announcement, this disaster of a girl looked eager. Well, Lilianne mentally shrugged her shoulders, perhaps she would turn out to be somewhat serious. It was certainly the most one could hope for, considering. In any case she would not be like the girl from Texas who treated the apartment like a hotel and asked for fresh sheets three times a week, or the girl from New York who complained about there being no shower because she wanted to wash her hair every day, or the girl from New Orleans who got pregnant and had to be sent home, or the girl from London who brought four trunks, demanded dozens of extra hangers, and actually had the idea that she could share Lilianne's closet.

The domestic arrangements practiced at the home of the Comtesse de Vertdulac were simple. Louise did all the housework, all the cooking, all the laundry, and all the shopping. She worked an eighteen-hour day and was perfectly content. She had been with her Comtesse all her working life, and neither she nor Lilianne thought there was anything unusual in this arrangement that was so mutually agreeable.

Every morning, long before breakfast, Louise went to the shops on the Rue de la Pompe and purchased the food for the day. She bought exactly what was necessary and not one item more. The kitchen did not contain a refrigerator. Anything, such as milk or cheese, that had to be kept cool was put into the *garde-manger,* a ventilated box built into the kitchen window, which would then be locked.

Louise was a skilled manager, particularly adept at finding bargains in the market, a well-known figure to the shopkeepers who had long ago stopped trying to sell her anything but the best quality at the lowest possible price. Even so, food accounted for at least 35 percent of the family's budget. Lilianne de Vertdulac knew, every day, exactly how much money Louise had spent because she doled it out from her purse the night before and took back all the change when Louise returned. It was not a lack of trust in her servant that accounted for these measures but the simple fact that the money she received from the pension she charged her paying guest was the money on which her entire household lived. The rent she received from her small country house, in Deauville, paid only for her clothes and the girls' school, but food and rent and all other necessities came from taking in a pensionnaire.

Billy put away her modest supply of clothes, mostly skirts and blouses in dark colors, and stood at the balcony of her room, inhaling with almost beatific rapture the smell of Paris of which she had read meaningless descriptions so many times. Now she understood why authors who should have known better had been tempted to do the undoable, to convey a smell through words. From her narrow balcony she could actually see the chestnut trees and the long grass of the Bois. The room itself was simply decorated, with a high, lumpy bed covered in a worn spread of faded yellow damask and boasting a fat bolster covered in the same material. Down the hall was a toilet, in a tiny tiled room of its own, with a pull chain and thin, slick, pale brown toilet paper. In her own room she had a sink with a little mirror above it. When she wanted a bath, she had been told that she must inform the Comtesse who would then make her own bathroom available.

Excitement had made her almost forget food, but when the rap on her door came to announce dinner she realized she was as hungry as she'd ever been in her life. She entered the salon, one end of which was given over to a small, oval dining table, and sniffed expectantly. Unlike dining rooms in Boston and at Emery, there was no smell of cooking in the air.

The Comtesse's two daughters were waiting to be presented to Billy. Each of them shook hands and said a few words in French, with grave courtesy. Billy had never seen girls quite like them. Although Danielle, the younger, was sixteen and Solange, the elder, was seventeen, they both looked as young as American girls of fourteen. They had almost identical, pale, pointed, stern little faces with severely perfect features, long, straight blond hair parted in the middle, and pale gray eyes. They were dressed alike in their convent uniforms—pleated dark blue skirts and pale blue blouses; they wore no makeup at all and they gave off an aura of untouched dignity, like protected

58

English schoolchildren. There seemed to be nothing French about them.

A creaking, rumbling noise growing closer announced that Louise was wheeling in an ancient double-decker wooden cart from the kitchen, which was located at the far end of the L-shaped apartment. Billy was seated next to the Comtesse, who carefully ladled out a thin, delicious vegetable soup, first to herself, then to Billy and then to each girl. After the soup there were soft-boiled eggs in the shell, one apiece, followed by a large green salad with one thin slice of cold ham for each of them. After each course either Solange or Danielle would clear the plates and stack them neatly on the cart. A basket of bread stood on the table, but Billy realized that no one was eating it yet and she didn't want to be the first to start. In any case, she discovered to her incredulous terror that she wasn't sure of the right way to say "Pass the bread, please" in French. Was it *"Voulez-vous me passer le pain?"* or was it *"Passez le pain, s'il vous plaît?"* It seemed absolutely important not to say it unless she said it correctly. The French language that Billy had read and written so confidently at Emery didn't seem to have the slightest connection with the sounds she heard swirling and dipping and bubbling and hissing around the table as the girls talked to their mother. One word in a hundred sounded vaguely familiar, but soon any comprehension she had disappeared in her growing panic, her realization that somehow, somewhere, she had made an incredible mistake. If this was French, she did not speak it. Not at all.

After the salad plates were cleared, fresh plates were put on the table and Madame placed a small platter in front of her own place. On it was displayed a small cheese sitting on a mat of woven straw and surrounded charmingly with fresh leaves. The Comtesse judiciously cut herself a slice and passed the platter to Billy. Billy cut herself a slice exactly as large as Madame's, too intimidated to take more. The bread was finally passed and a round crock of butter, a very small crock, although a pretty design was stamped into the butter. The cheese was not passed a second time. Dessert was a bowl of four navel oranges, which the girls and Madame all peeled adroitly with their knives in a way Billy had never seen before but imitated as well as she could. A carafe of wine stood near the center of the table, but only Madame helped herself to a glass. The girls drank water and so did Billy, who had never been offered wine at a meal.

After dinner Danielle and Solange whisked away the cart, and Louise brought in a tray holding two demitasse cups and a pot of café-filtre. She put it on the coffee table in front of the couch in the salon, and the Comtesse waved her hand to Billy in indication that she was to join her there, while the girls left to do more homework. So far Billy had not uttered more than four words. When a question was put to her by either of the girls she just smiled broadly— and, she felt, stupidly—shook her head and said, miming a combination of sadness and confusion, *"Je ne comprends pas."* Neither of them showed the faintest surprise. They had lived with a parade of voiceless, speechless strangers all their lives and they only bothered to speak to them to show a polite interest. If Billy had answered them they would have been amazed.

After an abashedly silent five minutes of drinking strong black coffee sweetened with a big, brownish lump of blessed sugar, Billy ventured a timid *"Bonsoir"* and retreated to her room. She was ferociously hungry. That one lump of sugar had started a craving for sweets that she assuaged only slightly with the last two chocolate bars in her handbag. However, she remembered, before she reached utter despair, that the French eat their main meal at lunch, not dinner, so tonight's meal was just the equivalent of lunch. But still, why were there no second helpings, why were the portions so incredibly tiny—*one* boiled egg, *one* slice of ham, for God's sake!—and why did everyone take such a small piece of cheese? Meditating on this, thinking of bowls and bowls of Cream of Wheat with butter, sugar, and raisins in it, she finally fell asleep.

Had she but known it, the dinner she had just eaten was to live in her memory as one of the largest evening meals she would consume under the roof of Lilianne de Vertdulac. The vegetable soup and the slice of ham had been special festive touches to welcome the new guest.

Billy soon discovered the normal way in which the Comtesse, her daughters, and Billy herself were to eat. Breakfast consisted of two *tartines,* slices of toasted French bread cut on the bias and covered with a thin scraping of butter and jam, accompanied by a large bowl, like a deep soup bowl without a handle, filled half with hot coffee, half with hot milk. For lunch there was always a plate of soup made of a puree of the vegetables left over from the day before with a few spoonfuls of milk added just before it was served, followed by one fair-sized slice, sometimes two, of roast veal, lamb, or beef, all lean, tasty, and inexpensive cuts Billy had never seen before. The meat was accompanied by a small handful of perfect shoestring potatoes and a sprig of parsley. Next came a separate, generous plate of hot vegetables, marvelously fresh, served steamed, with a faint gloss of butter sometimes visible. Then the small cheese, each of which was expected to last for two days, a large lettuce salad, and a bowl of fruit. Dinner normally consisted of an egg, in one form or another, cheese, salad, and fruit. Billy was getting about eleven hundred calories a day, most of them from lean protein and fresh fruit and vegetables.

After two days of these beautifully cooked, elegantly presented, and hopelessly unfulfilling meals, Billy began to seriously consider how she was going to survive. She made a terrifying nightmare foray into the kitchen, tiptoeing past the bedrooms like a thief, to discover that the *garde-manger* was unlocked because it was empty. Until Louise went shopping the next morning there was literally not a single crust of bread in the house. She thought about making friends with Louise, but since she couldn't speak French that was impossible. She thought about going to a café or a restaurant to buy herself a decent meal, but the quarter of Paris in which she lived was entirely residential. In any case, Billy knew perfectly well that she didn't have the nerve to sit down alone in a café and order in French. How could she? She considered going to the Rue de la Pompe to buy food to eat in her room. She could just point at what she wanted and pay the price marked on it. But she was afraid that someone would catch her at it and ask questions. That was unthinkably embarrassing. She even plotted to buy food and eat it on the street, but that, too, was mysteriously out of the question. She had never seen French people eating on the street in her luxurious neighborhood, bordered by Avenue Foch and Avenue Henri

Martin, the two finest avenues of private dwellings in Paris, although sometimes she saw a schoolchild hurrying home, furtively biting the end off a *baguette* of bread.

Billy's attempts to solve her food needs were complicated by the intuitions she had developed during her eighteen years of life, intuitions about having and not having.

Without possessing the slightest notion of cash value, she nevertheless knew to a fairly exact degree the amount of money a person had *relative* to the amount of money other people in their circle had. She was able to judge which of her cousins were richer, which less rich, which richest; which of the girls at Emery were really rich, which were merely quite rich, and which were barely rich. All of her life had been spent dealing with the problems of *entitlement*. She, Billy, was not an entitled person and never had been. Some people were entitled, without question, to everything they chose to want. Still others were partially entitled—thus far and no farther. She had absorbed this into her value system. Billy had pondered for many years over why some were entitled and others were not and had never reached a satisfactory answer. It was revoltingly unfair. But it was.

Therefore she felt, in all its strength, the taboo on the subject of food that existed in the home of Lilianne de Vertdulac. The amount of available food—it was communicated to Billy from some source she recognized and immediately acknowledged—was as much food as Madame could *afford* to serve. It was as much food as there was or was going to be. It was also perfectly understood, without words, that it would have been most grossly and crassly impolite to indicate that this amount of food left Billy empty and aching with hunger pains. The only time she felt able to ask for a second helping of meat was when the Comtesse's carefully carved portion, which indicated to the others how much they could take, was less than one-fourth of the food on the platter. At these times, the left-over meat would be evenly distributed among the three girls.

Billy cried herself to sleep every night. Her days were agony. And she lost close to a pound a day. She was living on at least three thousand calories a day *less* than she had absorbed since her childhood days. If she had been at Maine Chance or the Golden Door, they couldn't have kept her there at gunpoint, but her increasing interest in the mysteriously charming Comtesse and with the French language kept her in thrall. In any case, she had nowhere else to go.

After the first month Billy started to dream in French. She began to catch the meanings of stray phrases in the conversations around her. Timidly she began to point at things and ask how to say their names in French. She tried to answer questions at the table and committed the corrections of her French to her excellent memory. Since she had no experience in French conversation she had no wrong accent to unlearn. Her spoken French was atrocious, barely literate, but her accent and her intonations were those of Lilianne de Vertdulac.

One evening, during the fifth week of Billy's stay, Danielle and Solange had their first argument about her. They had become so indifferent to their mother's paying guests that they rarely mentioned them to each other.

"It's curious," Danielle said, in her clear, pure voice, "we've had lots of thin girls before who got fat, drinking up all the wine and going out to restaurants every night with their boyfriends, but we've never had a fat girl before."

"One is enough," snapped Solange.

"Don't be horrid. Perhaps it isn't her fault, perhaps it's a question of glands," suggested the softer Danielle.

"Perhaps it's a question of greedy Americans who eat everything in sight."

"Solange, I believe she is getting thinner. Truly."

"That would be difficult. Haven't you noticed that she always takes three *tartines* for breakfast—she'd take four if possible—and I'm sure that she steals sugar. When I took the coffee tray back to the kitchen last night the sugar bowl was almost empty and Maman always drinks her coffee black."

"Even so, notice that her skirt is too big all over. And her blouse as well."

"They never fit to begin with."

"Idiot! I tell you she is getting thinner. Just look at her for yourself."

63

"Ah, no thank you! Go back to work, little imbecile, you are keeping me from my Racine."

During the occupation of France and the hard years that followed the end of the war, Lilianne had developed a habit of seeing things that distressed her and immediately blocking them from her mind. She had not looked directly at her new pensionnaire since that first day, from which she retained an impression of an immense grotesquerie, truly out of bounds: lots of dark hair untidily flopping around a puffy face, eager dark eyes, impossible clothes, surprisingly excellent shoes, and a good wristwatch. Although she did her duty as a temporary guide to Paris, taking Billy to all the obligatory historical sites, she showed her about in a perfunctory way without watching for Billy's reactions. She had no intention of making a habit of these outings. Her other paying guests had soon learned to fend for themselves, and she always waited eagerly for the inevitable day when they would not come back to Boulevard Lannes for meals because they had more amusing things to do. But this Boston hippo, Lilianne reflected, seemed to have attached herself to the household, borrowing her copy of *Le Figaro* every morning after she had finished with it, reading Colette in her room all afternoon, hanging around in the salon before lunch and dinner, never missing afternoon tea, taking occasional walks in the Bois but not venturing far enough from the neighborhood to miss a single meal. And now Danielle had some notion that this Billy was losing weight.

That evening Lilianne took her second good look at Billy. She believed her eyes. A Frenchwoman always believes her eyes, whether it is a fresh pullet she is inspecting or the new collection at Yves Saint Laurent. Lilianne saw a grossly overweight girl, much too heavy, heaven knows too tall, but a girl with some small possibilities. The other girl, the one who had arrived from Lady Molly, had had no possibilities. None.

A Frenchwoman likes possibilities almost more than perfection. They give her a chance to arrange things, and arrangements, of all sorts, are a Gallic passion.

Arranger, s'arranger, verbs used in France to include the successful disposition of anything from a complicated legal problem to a worn-out love affair, from the resolution of a change in government to the choice of the right button. *"Ça va s'arranger," "Je vais m'arranger," "L'affaire est arrangée," "On s'arrangera"*—the key phrases of France, the promise kept, the assurances given, the obligations met. No people on earth, except, perhaps, the Japanese, arrange matters as well. Difficult circumstances are merely a question of more complicated arrangements.

Lilianne decided that the matter of Billy Winthrop must be properly arranged. It looked to her as if the girl had lost as much as twenty pounds, perhaps more, although on one so fat it was hard to know for certain. If she could do that in five weeks, in two or three more months she might, just, be made presentable, and if she were presentable, who knew what might then arrange itself? Meanwhile there was the question of her clothes. She could *not* wear that brown cotton skirt, which, Lilianne now noticed, was held together by a large safety pin clumsily attached inside the waistband. Also that blouse! A horror. Typically Boston, without doubt.

"I find this a very chic combination, don't you?" Lilianne asked Billy. They were at a shop on the Avenue Victor Hugo where elegant women of the Sixteenth Arrondissement did much of their moderate priced ready-to-wear shopping. Billy was bewildered. She did not know what was chic. Chic was not a word that she had ever supposed could be used in relationship to anything she could wear. Serviceable and appropriate were words she understood. How could she estimate if something were chic?

"Yes, Madame, very chic," she answered, because she could tell from her expression that she had made the decision already. Billy, from as far back as she could remember, avoided looking at herself in a dressing-room mirror. She was an expert at just standing there in a cross-eyed dream, docile and unresisting, while the saleslady and one of her aunts picked out her clothes. She had no opinions. There was no reason to care.

Her tone of voice, attempting enthusiasm but not attaining it, made Lilianne notice, for the first time, how young Billy was. She was a child really, only one year older than

Solange who was still a schoolgirl. Her Pygmalion impulses, disappointed by self-assured paying guests who had rejected her hints or advice, had never entirely withered. She felt an impulse of her old kindness.

"Just look, Billy, how well this gray-flannel skirt hangs. It is truly very cleverly cut; it makes you look so much thinner that I can hardly believe it. Turn around and look at yourself and you will understand. The disposition of the pleats here—they take kilos off! And these dark red sweaters are really an excellent color for you. Just see how they warm your skin—"

Billy turned unwillingly. This was the humiliation she feared the most, the confrontation with her image that she had managed to escape at all times, cleverly spotting potential reflections in shopwindows blocks away. But she realized that Madame was not going to be content until she seemed to really interest herself in the skirt and the sweaters. The Comtesse could not be easily satisfied, like an aunt. In fact, Billy had never heard her speak in such an intent tone of voice, as if affairs of state were being settled there in the shop.

Quickly she ventured a glance into the triple mirror and turned away again. Puzzled, she dared another look. She stared at her mirror image face on. Then she looked at herself from one side, turned awkwardly and looked at the other side. Finally she arranged the panels of the mirror so that she could see herself in a back view. Tears flooded her eyes, blurring the miraculous vision. She looked OK. Really OK. It was the only time in her life that she had thought so. She reached for the fragile Comtesse and embraced her for the first time, rupturing forever the formality between them.

"Vive La France!" Billy sputtered, laughing and crying at the same time. Lilianne de Vertdulac could not imagine why, but she was weeping too.

The birth of an obsession can be a beautiful thing—especially when it involves first love and hope. Billy had not loved herself for many years, and for as many years, hope had been slowly extinguished in her. Paris was her last act of hope and now, seeing herself in the mirror of the shop on the Avenue Victor Hugo, she felt her first glimmer of self-love.

As if she had been using them all of her life, Billy began to exercise her father's Winthrop characteristics: total dedication to a cause, stern self-discipline, the willingness to struggle toward achievement at all costs, the determination to move relentlessly toward an ideal of perfection. All of these obsessive-compulsive qualities are as necessary in becoming a great medical researcher as they are in the successful transformation from a fat girl to a thin one.

Billy had always been intelligent, but she had fled any impulse toward introspection. She ate to avoid thinking about herself and why she was not loved. Now, with great shyness at first, and then with more and more freedom, she became her own love object. Soon she loved herself enough to welcome hunger and discover that, for her, it was a necessary feeling. Within weeks she developed an obsessive terror of ever leaving the table feeling comfortably full, a feeling that would last all her life.

On the return from that first shopping expedition, Lilianne had presented Billy to her daughters with triumph, as if she were giving them a gigantic, unexpected Christmas present. Danielle danced around her in a jig of glee, filled with self-congratulations, and even cool, caustic Solange had to admit that their paying guest was slightly less embarrassing to have around at one hundred and eighty pounds than at two hundred and eighteen. Lilianne found a bathroom scale in a closet and installed it in her bathroom. There, each week, the four women held a weighing-in. Billy was modestly wrapped in a toweling peignoir, which they determined in advance weighed a kilo in itself. Living on their normal diet, Billy maintained a steady loss of just over five and a half pounds a week, for which she was rewarded, each Sunday, by an extra piece of lean roast chicken without its skin. As she approached one hundred thirty-five pounds, the weight loss tapered off until it stabilized at one hundred and twenty-seven pounds on a five-foot ten-inch frame.

As her fat melted, Billy discovered her bones. They were small bones, like those of her mother's family, and long bones, like those of her father's family. "Small, long bones—long, small bones," she murmured to herself like a mantra, over and over for hours—"small, long bones." Soon she discovered that she didn't have any muscles, except in her legs, thanks to years of compulsory field hockey and bike riding up the steep hills of Emery. She joined a daily afternoon modern dance class in the Rue de Lille, several miles from home, and she never missed a class.

Many rituals, all connected with her body, took her over. She must walk at least one way to class, or if she missed a day, both back and forth on the next day. She must never take the third *tartine* at breakfast. She drank her coffee black. She must brush her hair exactly two hundred strokes every day. The new underwear she had bought must be washed every night before she went to sleep no matter how tired she was. Billy wrote down the contents of each meal in a secret notebook and estimated how many ounces of food she had consumed each day. She embraced the religion of thinness as if she had had a spiritual conversion. If a hair shirt had been necessary, Billy would have worn it joyfully.

Her new gray skirt had to be taken in and taken in again by Lilianne's little dressmaker. Soon Billy's dark red sweaters hung on her, but she was determined not to buy others until she had finished losing weight. She threw out all her old clothes except for her winter coat, made of dark brown nutria, which Aunt Cornelia had given her as an eighteenth birthday present. While she was still shrinking, Billy and the Comtesse made an expedition to Hermès, where Billy bought a wide belt to hold in the coat and a narrow one to rope in the sweaters. In addition, she bought her first Hermès scarf. Lilianne had taught her that with a well-cut skirt, a good pair of shoes, a decent sweater, and that one indispensable Hermès scarf, any Frenchwoman may consider herself as well dressed as the Queen of England, the Queen of Belgium, or La Comtesse de Paris, the wife of the pretender to the French throne, because it is thus that those royal ladies have always dressed in their private lives.

Billy had a secret. She was beginning to understand almost everything that was said at the table. She did not speak often to the others, for there was all the difference in the world between understanding and actually venturing out into the dangerous high seas of conversation. But every day she was sure, inside, that she was making progress. It filled her with a tremulous, quaking feeling of frightened expectation, which she tried to push away. The rules of grammar and lists of vocabulary words that had once been memorized and consigned to exam notebooks started to spring back into her mind. Now they lived, they jumped, they sang, and even verb endings took on an air of absolute rightness, necessity. It all seemed, suddenly, to make perfect sense. Billy felt that French was her miser's treasure, the secret hoard that would unlock the entrance to a kingdom. But she wasn't ready to test herself yet in front of a group.

Danielle was the first to notice.

"Maman?"

"Yes, chérie?"

"I think Billy has the ear."

"Truly?"

"Yes, I'm certain. We were alone the other day for just a few minutes and I complimented her on her loss of weight and then she answered me and we had a little talk. She has the ear. Her grammar and her vocabulary are not good yet, she does not understand the subjunctive at all, but the ear is there."

Lilianne felt a spurt of triumph. The ear was everything. A person can live in France for twenty years and speak impeccably correct textbook French, but without an ear for the language, it will never be accepted as French by the French themselves. The French, unlike Americans, do not think it is charming in the slightest to hear someone speaking their beloved language with a delightfully foreign accent. Unless that person is obviously noble and English, in which case it is understandable, even forgivable, if not agreeable. If Billy truly had the ear, and Danielle could not possibly be wrong about a thing as important as that, it was because she, Lilianne, had insisted that no one speak English to her. Her own daughters, who were sent to live in the homes of English friends every summer, spoke perfect upper-class English. As everyone knew, a second language was the foundation of any good education. But Billy had never guessed that she could communicate with them in her own language and be understood. That would have ruined everything. Indeed, things did seem to have an air of arranging themselves.

Toward the end of December, the Comtesse received a gift of four fine, plump rabbits from her nephew, Comte Edouard de la Côte de Grace, who had bagged them in the fields of his Ile-de-France hunting lodge, about forty miles outside of Paris. Louise, who had been famous for her traditional regional cooking in the lavish days before the war, made an especially important trip to the shops one morning and came home with all the ingredients for both a classic *ragoût de lapin* and her specialty, an open-faced apple tart glazed in syrup. The Comtesse invited her distinguished aunt and uncle, the Marquis and the Marquise du Tour la Forêt as well as another middle-aged and amiable couple, the Baron and the Baronne Mallarmé du Novembre, whom Billy had met before at one of the Comtesse's small, infrequent dinner parties, which had been made possible by the gift of game from one or another of her hunting friends.

Lilianne de Vertdulac was motivated no less by hospitality, for she cherished her circle of old friends, as by the desire to show off her achievement. Billy, she judged, would reflect credit on her. True, the girl still had no chic. If all it took was one Hermès scarf, the whole world might be chic. But she had attained something far more important in the Comtesse's mind. She had *quality*. Her skin was absolutely clear, her teeth, thanks to Aunt Cornelia's insistence on an orthodontist, were perfect, her long, dark hair, pulled back in a simple ponytail, was thick and well cared for, and her skirt and sweater were of good enough material to suffice, just. Her manner was modest, her posture, since she had been taking dance class, was excellent, and she looked exactly like what she was, *une jeune fille américaine de très bonne famille*. The Comtesse knew her friends well. They judged by the highest and the oldest of patrician standards; they could not be fooled by an imitation, even the cleverest. She would never have invited them to dine, in intimacy, with the girl from Texas or the girl from New York, but the girl from Boston was another matter. She could pass inspection. Her muteness in company would pass for reserve, and, most important of all, she was no longer fat, a thing unheard of in people of quality unless they were very old or very royal.

Sometimes of late, Bill had shown signs of what the Comtesse believed to be true beauty, but she told herself severely that it was too soon to calculate if they were a promise of things to come or simply wishful thinking on her part. It was enough that Billy stay thin, Lilianne cautioned herself.

The Marquis du Tour la Forêt, who admired the courage of his niece in her limited financial circumstances, brought an offering of three bottles of champagne to accompany the dinner, and he gallantly insisted that Billy drink a glass as each bottle was opened, absolutely refusing to pay attention to her protests that she was not used to drinking wine at all. The table was expanded to accommodate the four guests, and while Danielle and Solange served the apple tarts, the Baronne Mallarmé du Novembre tried to engage Lilianne's shy, young paying guest in conversation by asking her if the old rhyme about Boston was true: If the Lowells still spoke only to the Cabots and the Cabots spoke only to God?

This is not a question that may be lightly put to a Winthrop. Not even in jest. Billy found herself, before she had time to smile yes or smile no or smile in any of the many ways she had developed for answering questions without speaking, launched into complicated and detailed explanations of the relative merits of the Gardners, the Perkinses, the Saltonstalls, the Hallowells, the Hunnenwells, the Minots, the Welds, and the Winthrops, in relation to the Lowells and the Cabots. She touched lightly on the family trees of the Wolcotts, the Birds, the Lymans, and the Codmans before her impassioned, champagned-gilded genealogical flight ended as something in Madame's incredulous expression caught her attention and made her realize that she was speaking—was it too much?—was it too loudly?—no—*in French!*

The barrier was down, never to rise again. One such breakthrough experience in a language is enough. It opened all the doors of Billy's mind, destroyed all her hesitations, vanquished her timidity.

Speaking French, Billy found herself another person than she had ever been. In French she had never been a freak at school, never been a poor relation, never been the last and the least of her cousins. Never, it seemed, been fat. Or lonely or unloved. She found that the lessons she had learned by rote, and just as quickly forgotten, came flooding back into her mind, filled with such obvious and logical reality that she gasped in distress at the ignorance of their meaning in which she had memorized them only a year or so before. She talked and talked and talked. To bus conductors, to Louise, to Danielle and Solange, to children in the park, to all the girls in her dance class, to ticket sellers in the Métro, and most particularly to Lilianne.

Every day she stretched herself in French as she stretched her body in dance class. She greedily accumulated the minutiae of French life. It was perfectly correct to address a duchess simply as "Madame" after you had met her, but you must take care to address the concierge by her full name, "Madame Blanc," each and every time you saw her; you could not live happily in France unless you knew how to build an efficient fire because the law required the landlord to heat the building only when the pipes were about to freeze; an unmarried girl must never expect her hand to be kissed, but if it is, she must never indicate that she has noticed the impropriety; at a buffet dinner the women of the household fill the gentlemen's plates before they take any food of their own—at least *chez* Madame; and, astonishingly, the Comtesse considered herself a good Catholic, although she went to Mass only at Easter. Also, to send a flower arrangement is insulting because it indicates that you do not trust the recipient to be able to arrange cut flowers, but it is not as bad as writing a personal letter on a typewriter.

Now she bought new clothes, with what the Comtesse thought was typical Boston caution. A few sweaters and skirts, several silk blouses, a tailored wool coat, and one simple black dress, which she wore with the exceedingly good pearls Aunt Cornelia had given her for graduation from Emery. Each purchase was made at the shop on the Avenue Victor Hugo with the advice of Lilianne, who initiated Billy once and forever into the small company of women who totally understand the vast gulf between clothes that fit and clothes that do not fit. Slowly she explored the mysteries and significance of cut and quality. Together they went to the collections at Dior, where the directrice, husky voiced, lanky Suzanne Luling, who was a friend of Lilianne's, gave them excellent second-row seats only five weeks after the collection had opened, as soon as the serious buyers had come and given their orders, so that there was room for mere observers. They went to other collections, chez Saint Laurent and Lanvin and Nina Ricci and Balmain and Givenchy and Chanel, the seats less good, sometimes quite bad, for impecunious comtesses are not treated with much respect in the great couture houses; however, the whispered commentary that Lilianne poured into Billy's ear was just as canny and sharp-eyed as if they had been looking with every intention of buying.

"That number would never be for you, it is too sophisticated for anyone under thirty; that dress is too extreme— it will be *démodé* by next spring; now, that one will be good for three years; that suit is made of too heavy a tweed —it will bag; that coat makes one awkward; that color would make one look faded; that dress is perfection. If you were to buy only one number, that would be it." Privately she wondered why Billy did not permit herself at least one Chanel suit. Even the fabled Bostonian practice of living on the income of the income of one's income could surely, in Billy's case, accommodate itself to such a small indiscretion during a year in Paris. It was a shame she did not profit by the occasion. However, the expenditure of money was not a subject that Lilianne felt she had the right to discuss with her paying guests, even so dear a one as this.

The woman of infinite sophistication and the nineteen-year-old girl often strolled together along the Rue du Faubourg-St.-Honoré, analyzing and judging each object in each shopwindow as if it were one vast art gallery and they were the most discriminating of collectors. Billy absorbed Lilianne's standards of quality. Since the Comtesse had no means to satisfy her tastes, she could afford to approve of only the very, very best and then, only after the most judicious comparisons.

It had never been a part of the Comtesse's reception of paying guests to introduce them to suitable young men. In the first place she did not know a great many young Frenchmen and in the second place it would have added an unnecessary complication to her life. As it was, soon there would be her daughters to launch in worldly life, a prospect she dreaded, since she was not of the match-making disposition and they would be girls with nothing to offer but themselves and their ancient blood.

However, a temptation entered her mind as she thoughtfully surveyed the young woman who now occupied such a special place under her roof; a tall, slim girl of unmistakable distinction, yes, a girl of beauty, a girl who spoke French no American could be ashamed of, a girl who was connected with all the great fortunes of Boston, a girl who had come to her recommended by the venerable and enormously wealthy Lady Molly Berkeley.

If Boston, Lilianne told herself, had sent her a baby hippo who couldn't even ask the time in French, why should she return this girl, whom she had transformed, to what must obviously be an uncongenial and sad environment? Billy, unlike other girls she had sheltered, had never shown the first signs of homesickness. If those rich merchants of Boston didn't know how to bring out the best in their own daughters, they deserved to lose them.

Why not, after all, keep Billy in France? Why not introduce her to several of her nephews and perhaps one or two of their friends? All of them had one thing in common: Their families had been impoverished by the war to varying degrees and these young sprigs of the old aristocracy had been reduced to working for their living just like everyone else. World War II had finished, for much of Old France, a decline that even the guillotine had been too selective to accomplish.

In any case, Lilianne assured herself, whether anything came of it or not, it was surely not normal for Billy to still live like a schoolgirl months after her nineteenth birthday, with no company but that of other women, dance students, and old family friends. (The Comtesse had, naturally, a private life of her own—she was still a young woman, *voyons*—but that was a very discreet one indeed and no paying guest, no matter how close she became, was ever to be included in it.)

74

Yet when she suggested to Billy that it might amuse her to meet a few young men, Billy's response was violent.

"No, Madame! I beg of you! I'm so happy the way I am, my life is perfect just exactly as it is. There is nothing more embarrassing than a blind date—or whatever you call it in French. I know you're being kind, but, truly, I'm not interested at all. The family is more than enough for me. Don't ever talk about it again, *please*."

Nothing she could have said would have consolidated Lilianne's nebulous plans more firmly. This would not do at all. What was the purpose of a transformation if there was no one to admire it? What if Cinderella had not gone to the ball? She had been right in thinking the situation was not normal. How could Billy be truly the credit to her that she deserved after all her efforts if the girl was without a single male admirer? She had not, after all, been preparing her for the religious life. Obviously, this Boston virgin must be outwitted. One must arrange it—it was no more than one's duty.

Comte Edouard de la Côte de Grace was Lilianne's preferred nephew. Unlike the physically undistinguished heritors of many great names, he carried about him a genuine hint of nobility, an air of another time. He looked truly like one of the last of the grand seigneurs, although Lilianne had to smile at some of his pretentions. Edouard had great height, a superbly aquiline nose, thin, arrogant lips, and an expression both stern and, when he chose, humorous. At twenty-six he still lived at home with his parents since his salary at L'Air Liquide wasn't enough to enable him to maintain his own place in the style he would have accepted. However, his future in the giant corporation was assured in the long run through family pull, since he had, on his mother's side, as one said in slang, *du piston*.

One afternoon Billy returned from her dance class almost too late for tea. She had chosen to stand outside on the platform of the No. 52 bus during the half-hour trip, in spite of the bitter cold of early February, because it was such a clear and brilliant evening that she didn't want to miss a minute of Paris. Her cheeks flamed and her lips stung. Her hair was loose around her flushed face, blown about by the wind, and she dashed into the apartment on Boulevard Lannes with her long, eager stride, holding herself tall, laughing with anticipation of a cup of hot tea. In front of the blazing fire, feet planted wide apart, stood Edouard de la Côte de Grace, clad in full morning dress, tailcoat and striped trousers, warming his backside with all the assurance of the Sun King.

"This is my nephew, Comte Edouard de la Côte de Grace, Billy," Lilianne said casually. "Edouard, this is Mademoiselle Billy Winthrop, who lives with us. Billy, you must forgive the figure Edouard sets—he doesn't always dress this way at this hour. However, today he is going to be initiated into the Jockey Club and he has come to show himself off to his old aunt before he goes to drink an entire bottle of champagne, all by himself, mind you, so that then he will officially be a member of the Club. What folly! It was thoughtful of you, Edouard, to drop in to see me before this curious ceremony, rather than afterward."

And so it began. Utterly beguiled, drenched in the glamour of Edouard, in love for the first time in her life, Billy surged into romance with reckless abandon, an impulsiveness that disturbed Lilianne de Vertdulac in spite of her smugness at the success of her plot.

All of Billy's occupations became new ways of becoming worthy of Edouard, her mind and her emotions focused entirely on him. She could not believe her luck when he took her out shooting rabbits on the weekends or invited her home to dinner with his parents. Once he even invited her to have a drink in the bar of the sacrosanct Jockey Club, the most exclusive men's club in the world.

For Edouard's part, he was well pleased. This little American of Lilianne's was far more attractive than he had expected, considering the fairly decent quality of her birth. It had been his rueful experience that the other girls of great fortune he had met were not girls he found physically possible, or he would have married one several years ago. Billy would be quite suitable in the role of Comtesse de la Côte de Grace, provided that the arrangements were correct, of course. He found her both suitably innocent and properly in awe of him. With

the right coiffure, the right clothes, and the right ma-
quillage, she would become a striking woman of the world.
When his father and his uncle died, and she became
Madame La Marquise de la Côte de Grace, she would
be ready for the dignity of the name. He thought of
his hunting lodge, so badly in need of repairs—to be
reduced to hunting on foot!—he considered the family
château in the Auvergne, waiting to be restored to its
former beauty. It was clearly time to settle down.

Part of the bargain Billy had struck with Aunt Cornelia was that she would write weekly from Paris. She
had deliberately been very vague about her weight, in-
tending to surprise and stun all Boston when she returned.
She rarely mentioned Edouard, except in passing, but
by spring, Cornelia sensed that something was going on
between Billy and this young count, although what it
could possibly be she found difficult to imagine. One
day in May two letters crossed each other.

Dear Cousin Molly,

*Thanks to your great kindness in finding
our Honey a place with Madame de Vertdulac,
who has been quite wonderful to her,
she's been having a marvelous year! From what she
writes, I believe that her French has improved
immeasurably—I am so glad! She has even taken up
dance class, which can only do her good! Recently
she had mentioned one name rather frequently—
that of a Comte Edouard de Côte de Grace, who seems
to be squiring her about Paris. Do you happen
to know anything about him or his family? I must
confess that I'm as surprised as I am delighted that she
should have found a young man, since the dear girl
was not a great success in Boston in that particular
way. I have always hoped she might be a late
bloomer—unlike you, dear Molly! I would
appreciate any news you may have for me.*

With much love,
Nelie

77

Nelie my dear,

I have just received a most puzzling letter from Lilianne de Vertdulac. Apparently your young niece is having a serious romance with Comte Edouard de la Côte de Grace, whose family I know fairly well, although not intimately, and Lilianne believes it might turn into an engagement at any moment! All well and good, he comes from the very top drawer, as my maid would say, but, my dear, he is no more well off than she is, except for his job. Great expectations but nothing for years, as I understand it. The extraordinary thing is that Lilianne is apparently unaware of Honey's exact circumstances as she spoke of a marriage settlement. She actually seemed to think that Honey's father would have lawyers!!! who would want to meet with Edouard's father's lawyers, should it come to that.

Reading between the lines I got the strong impression that she believes Honey to be an heiress merely because she is a Winthrop. How frightfully French of her. There are so many Winthrops. But then, how was she to know that? Edouard's family is very proud and very grand, even for the English. They seem to take themselves very seriously, and I'm quite sure, in fact certain, that Edouard must marry an heiress. There could be no question of his marrying for love alone unless he were prepared to badly disappoint his entire family—he is the only son, you know. What am I to tell Lilianne? I'm quite distraught over this matter. Has Honey, perhaps, a trust fund that she will come into in the future? You spoke of a small inheritance, as I remember, but was there anything else—or could there be? I'm still American enough to disapprove of the dowry system on principle, but when in France—In any case, do write me immediately and tell me exactly how things stand.

> *With love to you—as ever—*
> *and to dear George too—*
> *Molly*

Cornelia hadn't been so disturbed since her daughter refused to go to the Christmas Cotillion or to join the Vincent Club. Not even when her nephew Pickles failed to make A.D. at Harvard. In fact, this was actually worse than the time her son Henry seemed to be falling in love with a Jewish girl from Radcliffe—even if both of her greatgrandfathers *had* foughtt in the Civil War! She cared more for Honey, she discovered, than she had realized.

Three weeks before Lilianne received Lady Molly's enlightening answer to her letter, Edouard had made the decision to assure himself of his prize American virgin. Had Billy been French, he might well have waited until after the wedding, but since she was American, and not Catholic, he felt that the event might be conducted with a bit more promptness. However, the occasion of Billy's initiation into lovemaking was a ceremony both solemn and painful. It took place on his bed in his rather bare bedroom in the tumbledown hunting lodge, with its empty stables and uncared-for garden. Billy would always remember that the ceiling of the room was draped with dusty cloth striped in dark blue and red, like one of Napoleon's battlefield tents, that the furniture was heavy Empire and unpolished, and that her pain was as extraordinary as it was unexpected. Her main memory, however, was of her amazement that a stiff penis pointed upward, rather than straight out, horizontally, as she had always imagined it would. Edouard assured her that it would be better for her the next time, but, he told her, even for a virgin she was the tightest woman he had ever had. She felt supremely proud of that for some reason she never understood.

They returned to the lodge each Saturday and Sunday for three weeks and it did get easier, if not better, although Billy had no standards of comparison by which to judge sexual pleasure any more than she could have once judged chic. Edouard was the first man she had ever kissed on the lips. All she really cared about was pleasing him as she became more and more obsessed by the mere fact of actually being in love. She was awkwardly ardent and utterly credulous under his kisses, warmed by his body into an innocently burgeoning belief in the future possibilities of passion. She emerged from her trance of wonder from time to time to say to herself, with trembling pride, mingled with only a faint whisper of caution, "Comtesse Edouard de la Côte de Grace—Billy de la Côte de Grace—oh, wait till they hear this back in Boston!" And then she went out and spent more and more of her Katie Gibbs tuition money on beautiful clothes for Edouard to see her in.

When Lilianne received Lady Molly's no-nonsense letter she locked herself up in her room and wept, as much for herself as for Billy. From her own experience in such matters she could not but believe that Billy would recover in time, but she, Lilianne, would never pardon herself. The mistake had been normal, in her estimation; in fact, the true facts made her feel like the victim of a deception, however unplanned. Also, she told herself, the wish to arrange matters for Billy was, in itself, perfectly reasonable. But the result was cruelty and she was guilty.

That same day the Comtesse went to talk to Edouard in his parents' drawing room. She told him that Billy could not expect a dowry. Her father was a greatly respected man, a medical man, a savant, but poor. She was absolutely a Winthrop, but there was no money on her side of the family. But whatever small hope she sheltered that he might still marry Billy died as soon as she spoke.

Edouard de la Côte de Grace was exceedingly angry. She should have known, he raged at her. How could a woman of her good sense, her experience, have let him believe that Billy possessed a fortune? What had given her that assurance? What had happened to her judgment, her prudence, her interest in the future of their family. As his aunt, how could she have led him to make such an error? Yes, of course, he agreed that Billy was uncontestably delightful, much more than she knew, and absolutely suitable, perfect in fact, except that the entire affair was, without need of further discussion, impossible. Utterly impossible—what to do? Who was to tell her? He, Edouard, as a gentleman, had never been involved in such a distressing affair. His honor—

"No! Edouard, it is your duty, please do not play at the

great seigneur with me any longer. I have had enough of your reproaches! You will tell her and you will tell her the truth or else she will think it is herself that you do not wish to marry, rather than the circumstances that make it impossible. Perhaps—perhaps she has lived in France long enough to understand."

Years later, when Billy could think about Edouard with only disdain for him and a touch of pitying contempt for her young naïveté—or had it been stupidity?—she was grateful for his bluntness—at least it was based on brute necessity—and for her poverty. Had she possessed any respectable sum of money of her own she would have become another of the dozens of dull, young comtesses of the rigid Faubourg St.-Germain, bound for life by the kind of stuffy conformity that her husband would have demanded of her. A French version of Boston—only the food and the clothes were better. She had been too close then to the agony of her school years to have ever dared to rebel. Certainly she would have become a Catholic in order to please her in-laws, and by now she would be totally the captive of a bloodless tradition that would hold her with the inescapable and still strong fingers of a dying class that can survive only by clutching new flesh. She would have smothered before she had found her chance to live. From future lovers she would learn that Edouard was as unimaginative and pompous in bed as he was in life.

But all that knowledge, the perspective from which she could make these judgments, was still years away. She decided to leave Paris before her time was up and to come home on a boat, to give herself an empty space in which to cross from one world to another.

So there was to be no happily ever after, Billy thought, as she paced the decks at night. Somehow it didn't surprise her. If she had been a typical young girl, accustomed all her life to being petted, admired, and loved, Edouard's actions might have shattered her. But she had had so much confirmation about the possibility, indeed the probability, or rejection, that unknowingly she had become toughened to it. She was able, only days after it happened, to accept the experience as another example of what could happen to someone who didn't have money, rather than seeing it as a totally personal affair. There was even something gratifying, no matter how painful, in finding out that she was right about life.

She was thin and she was beautiful, Billy told herself fiercely. Those were the important things. The necessary things. The rest she would have to get for herself. She had no intention of dying for love of a man, like one of the nineteenth-century women in the books she had read. She was no Emma Bovary, no Anna Karenina, no Camille— no spineless, adoring, passive creature who would let a man take away her reason for living by taking away his love.

The next time she loved, she promised herself, it would be on her terms.

*T*he inspired heterosexual, the devout lover of women, the man whose life is a celebration of the fact that there are females in the world, arouses very little psychological interest. Volumes have been devoted to homosexuality and to the Don Juan complex, but the man who deeply, hungrily, passionately and persistently enjoys women in all their characteristics, not merely sexually, is as rare as he is little acknowledged.

A look at Spider Elliott's life history might—or might not—give a psychologist some inkling of a working hypothesis.

Harry Elliott, Spider's father, was a Regular Navy officer who spent twice as much time at sea as on land, by choice Spider always suspected, since he and his wife, Helen Helstrom Elliott, a nice Westridge graduate from Pasadena, fought with a military unruliness whenever he had shore duty. These battles had few satisfactory results except the peace treaties that produced Spider, the oldest child and only son, born in 1946, and three sets of twin daughters.

Holly and Heather, the oldest girls, were two years younger than Spider. The next pair, Pansy and Petunia, was born at another two-year interval. The last two, appearing punctually on a now familiar schedule, were called June and January. Spider barely winced, even as a teenager. He loved his mother too much to try and curb her raging whimsy, and in any case, it was all done before he was old enough to offer suggestions.

All six sisters in the Elliott household revolved around Spider like doting little sunflowers. From the days of their earliest memories there had always been a wonderful big boy who belonged to them, a strong, blond boy who taught them all kinds of magic things and had time to read Spider Man comics out loud to them before they were old enough to read themselves, and told them how beautiful they were, and was their prized and adored hero, to be freely shared by all, for he had plenty of love to go around.

As far as Helen Helstrom Elliott was concerned, her son, Peter, unfortunately called Spider by his sisters, was the light of her life. Peter could not put a foot wrong, in his mother's eyes, although she sometimes found herself ridiculously irritated by his devotion to her daughters. Peter, she noted with satisfaction, had inherited his looks from her side of the family. Perhaps his height came from his father, but the bright blond hair and sailor-blue eyes were pure Swedish Viking. All of her family on both sides had been Scandinavian—blond until they were old enough to turn gray. The fact that there hadn't been any real Vikings around since the tenth century—and never any in California—was a mere detail to this romantic woman.

Spider had that most unliterary of American experiences, a very happy childhood. Commander Elliott, a ruefully cheerful man, whose chief distinction was that he had graduated from the Naval Academy a year before Jimmy Carter, turned to Spider for masculine companionship when he had shore duty. He taught his son sailing and skiing, helped him with his homework, and from the time the boy was three, took him away for backpacking, trout fishing, tent pitching, heartily male weekends, as often as possible. He loved his wife well enough, but if they kept on fighting, he was afraid they might end up with yet another set of female twins.

The Elliotts lived in a comfortable house in Pasadena. Spider's mother had family money in a genteel, just-enough-to-make-all-the-difference kind of way, and Spider's school days were spent there, in that self-satisfied suburb of Los Angeles that looks like the best part of Westchester. He grew up in the 1950s, a comfortable conformist decade in which to be young and southern Californian, and he entered UCLA in 1964. For the next four years, while his peers were protesting and rioting at Berkeley and Columbia, an occasional pot party was an antiestablishment a gathering as he attended.

There were really only two things about Spider that made him distinctly and permanently different from that prince of the world, the healthy, upper-middle-class American male. First, he *adored* women. He had a passion for everything and anything that was part of the female element in the world. And second, he had great visual taste. His graphic sense was inborn and unself-conscious. It demonstrated itself, for the one or two people who noticed it, in the way he arranged the huge corkboard in his room, on which he pinned up a constantly changing gallery of photographs from newspapers and magazines, and in the way he used his bookshelves to display "found objects" long before the concept of found objects had been heard of: a row of empty Dundee Orange Marmalade jars, discarded street signs, and a pair of child's ice skates, forming a group that pleased the eye in a way that could not be explained. He even wore his jeans and t-shirts with a subtle difference from the way every other boy wore identical jeans and t-shirts.

When he was thirteen his maternal grandparents gave him his first camera, a small Kodak. Although Commander Elliott had made sporadic attempts to photograph his family, he never had been able to get all the girls together in one picture without the use of threats, and invariably one of them made a face and spoiled the photo. What they wouldn't do for their father, however, they clamored to do for Spider, vying with each other in this new game, dressing up in Mrs. Elliott's old garden hats and high-heeled shoes, hanging from tree branches, posing in a ring around the statue of a Grecian nymph at the bottom of the spacious garden, a frieze of femininity in bud.

By the time Spider was sixteen he had bought a secondhand Leica in a pawnshop. It had a broken shutter, so he got it cheaply, and after he had it cleaned, polished, the lens replaced, and the shutter fixed, it was a fine camera. Spider paid for all this by working summers in a shop where he developed passport photos overnight. His camera was his hobby; his sisters were not so much his inspiration now as his work load, for, suddenly, they "needed" pictures of themselves with their best friends and, in the case of Holly and Heather, to give to boys. Spider turned his bathroom into a darkroom, buying a used enlarger and trays from his summer employer, and taught himself the finer points of developing and printing by trial and error. Often, inspired by photographs in *Life,* he would go out and take rolls of pictures of trees, mountains, and industrial buildings or drive into downtown Los Angeles to try to capture the feeling of the streets. But, invariably, he found himself happiest when working with his sisters, who were now growing more beautiful and more self-conscious in front of the camera. He learned how to make them relax and cooperate. For graduation from high school he received a new Nikon from the same proud grandparents who had given him his Kodak, and now, at UCLA, his opportunities for photographing women became unlimited.

Spider joined the Photography Club, but his real interest was in capturing images of California girls doing all the gorgeous things California girls are famous for doing so well. By the time Spider graduated with a major in political science, he knew that he had picked the wrong field of study. His hobby had gradually turned into something he intended to do professionally. He was determined to become a fashion photographer and for that he had to work in New York City, which is to fashion photography what Amsterdam is to diamond merchants.

This was a sensible aim for a man who loves women, a man with an exceedingly keen graphic sense and his own Nikon, but about as easy an ambition to fulfill for a boy just out of college as that of getting a job as a cub reporter in the city room of the *Washington Post.*

However, Spider Elliott arrived in New York in the fall of 1969, armed with the savings he had accumulated from twenty-three years of birthday checks, Christmas checks, and summer jobs, some two thousand seven hundred dollars in all, and immediately looked for a cheap place to live. He quickly found a loft in the grimy lower Thirties, near the wholesale fur district of Eighth Avenue. It was one enormous, long, skinny room, which seemed to sag in the middle, but it had a view of the Hudson River—

and the ceiling was eighteen feet high and had seven skylights. It contained a miserable bath, which could also serve as a darkroom in a pinch, a kitchen table, and a sink. A previous tenant had installed an old stove and an older refrigerator. Spider bought a minimum of furniture, built a platform topped by foam rubber to sleep on, and invested in a few pillows, sheets, two pots, and a frying pan. Then he painted the old floors a golden sand color, the walls four slightly different shades of sky blue and the ceiling off-white. He installed three ten-foot-tall Kentia palms he got wholesale at Kind's, lit them from underneath with uplighters, and soon, at night, lying on his raft of a mattress, looking up at the clouds of the city through the seven skylights, the shadows of the palm fronds making a tropical play on the walls, a little Nat King Cole or Ella Fitzgerald playing on his old turntable, he felt as loose and free and happy as a beach boy.

The building in which Spider's loft was located was a musty, old business structure, not legally meant for people to live in. It had an ancient elevator with doors like folding iron gates, and the lower floors were occupied by a jumble of dusty mail-order firms, semibankrupt button manufacturers, seedy jobbers of yard goods, and two firms of accountants whose offices had attained positively Dickensian squalor. On the top floor, where Spider lived, there were several other tenants who kept mysteriously odd hours and seldom crossed his path in the hallway.

After two and a half months of unsuccessful job hunting, talent, persistence, patience, and luck eventually paid off, as they do with dependable infrequency, and Spider landed a job as darkroom assistant in Mel Sakowitz's studio. Sakowitz, a third- or possibly a fourth-rate photographer, did a lot of hack catalog work and occasional shots for the "About Town" shopping pages of minor magazines.

One Saturday morning in the late autumn of 1972, Spider, like Robinson Crusoe finding a footprint in the sand, discovered his new top-floor neighbor in person. He was coming back from the Italian markets on Ninth Avenue with a bagful of groceries, taking the shallow old stairs at a deliberate run and wondering, as usual, if life without tennis was going to incapacitate him. As he reached the top of the third flight, sprinting at full speed, he rounded the corner of the landing and stopped with a skid. Only his excellent reflexes kept him from knocking down a woman who was struggling along and swearing angrily to herself in French, heavily burdened with a bundle of clean laundry, two full shopping bags, a bunch of yellow mums wrapped in newspaper, and two bottles of wine, one tucked tightly under each arm.

"Hey! I'm sorry! I didn't think there'd be anyone on these stairs—here—let me help." She was standing with her back to Spider, unable to turn around as the bottles slowly slipped out from under her arms.

"Idiot! Get the bottle! It's going to fall."

"Which one?"

"Both!"

"Got 'em."

"About time! 'Which one?' Couldn't you see they were both slipping? 'Which one?' indeed!"

"Well, it's not terribly smart to carry wine under your arms like that," Spider said mildly. "A bag would make more sense."

"How could I carry another bag? My fingers are about to fall off as it is. That monster landlord—on Saturday no lights in the hall, no elevator service—it is truly disgusting, atrocious." She turned to face him and in the dim skylighted stairwell he saw that she was young, in spite of her perfectly vile temper.

"I'll follow you upstairs and help you with all that," he offered politely. She nodded agreement, dropped everything in his arms except the flowers and the wine, and silently sped up the three flights, to the top floor, without a backward glance. She stopped at her door, about twenty feet away from Spider's own, and took a key out of her bag.

"So I've finally met a neighbor in the flesh," Spider said, smiling at her back in a friendly way.

"So it would seem." She didn't turn, smile back, nor did she open her door.

"Shall I bring all this in for you?" Spider nodded down at the load of bags and bundles he was carrying.

"Just put them on the floor. I shall attend it later." The woman put her key in the keyhole, opened her door, slipped in, turned quickly, and shut the door in Spider's face. In contrast to the dark hallway, the sunlight was pouring into her room, and he had a brief flash of curls like crazy red lace, a delectably tilted nose, and green eyes, as surprising as a flashflood.

He stood there for a moment, dumbfounded by her abruptness, staring at the blank door, the image of her face still imprinted on his mind. Then he turned and ran back downstairs, conscious of experiencing a strange feeling, one he couldn't quite identify. It was like the disorientation, the short, empty pause, that follows in a busy restaurant immediately after a waiter has dropped an entire tray of glasses and silver. All conversation stops for less than a second, then, recognizing what has happened, the diners resume their conversation in mid-sentence. Only today, for Spider, the pause was a longer one. Unlike a dropped tray, what had just happened to him had happened for the first time. For the first twenty-two years of his life in California and during the almost three and a half years he had worked in New York, no female had ever treated him with such a total lack of interest. He had met women who actively didn't like him, for one reason or another, but if they didn't fall into that category, they responded to him with some degree of warmth—and frequently, heat. A woman who simply didn't notice him at all—Spider shrugged his shoulders, decided it was her problem, and went on up to Madison Avenue for his weekly tour of the art galleries.

He returned late in the afternoon. There, on his doorstep, was the paper bag of his own groceries, which he had completely forgotten about. Next to it sat a bottle of wine and a folded sheet of paper on which were scrawled the words "Have a drink on me." Not even a name, he noted, amused. He walked down the hall, holding the bottle, and knocked on her door. When she opened it, he stood outside, making no move to enter.

"My mother made me promise never to accept drinks from strangers," he said solemnly.

She gave him her hand to shake. "I forgot to present myself when we met before. I'm Valentine O'Neill. Please—come in and let me offer my excuses. I'm afraid that I was a bitch—was I not?"

90

"I'd say that was a fair description—a little on the kind side maybe."

"A bad-tempered bitch who lacked gratitude?"

"That about covers it." Spider's gaze wandered around her room, noting its half shadows lit by lamps with rosy shades. She had a fat, red-velvet sofa with old ball-fringe trimming, several armchairs in pink-and-white toile de Jouy with flounced skirts, a flowered carpet, and fringed red draperies, and in the background Spider could hear Piaf singing something familiar about the unfailingly poetic misery of love. Every little table in the room seemed to be covered: framed photographs, ferns, flowers, paper-covered books, records, and magazines. It was a small room with only two skylights, and something about it was powerfully evocative, familiar to Spider, although he knew he had never seen such an interior anywhere before.

"I like your room," he said.

"It is only my old furniture," she said, vanishing behind a screen also covered with the faded toile. "I'm afraid there is too much for this room, but I have to keep the other one free for my work." She emerged, carrying a tray on which was an open bottle of chilled white wine, two glasses, a loaf of French bread, a crock of pâté, and half of a ripe Camembert on a pottery plate. She set the tray on the floor in front of the sofa. "Shall we drink to something? Or perhaps first you will tell me your name?"

Spider sprang to his feet. "I'm sorry—I'm Spider Elliott." Absurdly, they shook hands again. He took his second quick look at her. All he noticed in detail was that her hair, two crucial shades deeper than carrot, covered her head in a heap of bumptious, undisciplined curls that fell over a small, fine, white face. Everything fell into place—the room, the tray of food, her voice, the Piaf record.

"Say, I just realized—you're French—this room—it's like being in Paris. I've never even been in Paris but I'm sure—"

She interrupted. "I happen to be an American—born in New York at that."

"How can you look at me with that French face and that little touch of accent, plus the way you get your words just kind of wrong, and tell me you're an American?"

Valentine deliberately ignored his question. Aggressively she asked, "What kind of a crazy name is Spider?"

"It's my nickname, after Spider Man." She looked unenlightened. "Now, just wait a minute, you *don't* know—and you say you're American! That's a dead giveaway."

"I refuse to have a neighbor called Spider," she said crossly. "I am allergic to them—I break out in spots just at the thought. Such a name. Truly it is too much! I shall call you 'Elliott.' "

"Swell. Whatever," he grinned. What was with this cute nut? The most harmless question seemed to get her up in arms. No way was she American, and he didn't believe she was allergic to spiders either.

Responding to his easy acceptance, Valentine finally deigned to satisfy his curiosity. "I was born in New York, but when I was a child I went to live in Paris and until only last month I lived there. Now, shall we drink?"

"What to?"

"To my getting a job," Valentine answered promptly. "I need one."

"To your getting a job and to my getting a better job."

As they touched glasses Valentine thought how American he looked, so undamaged, so careless, so—pleased to be alive. He was the first young American male she had ever spoken to socially in her life. She felt off-balance, almost like a teen-ager. He was excessively informal, disconcertingly open, so that she hardly knew how to talk to him except defensively. Valentine was not used to being flustered.

"What do you do?" she asked, remembering from some article in *Elle* that all Americans ask each other this question immediately after they are introduced.

"I'm a fashion photographer—at the moment only an assistant to a photographer. What about you?"

"Come, I will show you." She led him into the second room, smaller than the first. Next to the window stood a chair and a table with a sewing machine on it. Bolts of fabric were piled neatly on one long table. A dressmaker's dummy draped in a fluid fall of material stood in the center of the room and a few sketches were pinned up on the wall. Otherwise it was bare.

"You're a dressmaker? I don't believe it."

"I'm a designer. It doesn't hurt to know how to sew—or did you not know that?"

"I never thought about it," Spider answered. "Did you design what you're wearing?" She had on a bloused, open-necked, cozy slide of a long dress in a heavy, apricot wool, and although it wasn't, in any particular detail, astonishing or striking, somehow Valentine projected an air of rare luxury, a note of casual yet quite specific originality that he wouldn't have expected in a fellow attic mouse.

"Designed and made, every stitch—but come on back to the other room. The cheese is just ripe enough. We must eat it before it runs right off the plate."

As she gave him a crust of bread spread with Camembert, Valentine also gave Spider the most appetizing but unprovocative smile Spider could remember receiving from a woman. He realized that she was not flirting with him, not even a little bit. How could she be half French? Or even half Irish? Or even female, for that matter?

Spider Elliott had lost his virginity in his senior year in high school to a horny, big-breasted girl's basketball coach who admired his dunk shots only less than the fit of his gym shorts, which one of his sisters had shrunk three sizes in a loving attempt to make them whiter than white. For the rest of his life Spider got a hard-on whenever he smelled a locker room, a condition that made it embarrassing for him to work out in a gym. He took up tennis and running.

UCLA had been as ripe with nookie as with smoggy sunshine, but Spider soon discovered that fashion photographers' studios are the heartland of verbal sex. Although a great many of the photographers are homosexual, to work effectively, they must create an aura of sensuality. A model is encouraged in her work by the lavish application of a stream of instruction, almost in the way a nervous small-plane pilot can be "talked down" to a landing by an air-traffic controller. The words of instruction, which are always flattering even when they are said through clenched teeth, are almost always hyped up by subliminally erotic music playing in the background. The field of sexual force built up in a fashion photographer's studio is sometimes sincere, but far more often the fact creeps through that it is basically a synthetic, a fake, with a nervous, brittle undertone that carries a touch of the hidden hostility of the photographer for the model who falls short of perfection.

When Spider was hired by Mel Sakowitz, he arrived on the fashion scene with something of the impact made on the decadent European courts hundreds of years ago when sea captains arrived to display their "noble savages." Spider in his working clothes, old white denims and a UCLA t-shirt, was tangible evidence that men, real, pagan, lusty, loving men, existed, even inside the hothouse of fashion.

In a matter of weeks, models who didn't know Printol from bubble bath began to show an unusual interest in negatives and enlargers, making it necessary to visit Sakowitz's darkroom and clutch Spider's muscular California forearm. "From tennis? How freaky!" Soon Spider found that the smell of a darkroom was beginning to give him a hard-on too. However, he could and did do something about it. He even smuggled in a bunch of pillows for his girls' comfort, because he couldn't stand the thought of their delicate little ass bones getting bruised on the floor. Most of Spider's models insisted on cunnilingus because it didn't mess their clothes or their hair. All they had to take off was their panty hose. They weren't all that keen on fellatio because it always messed their make-up one way or another and they really had to watch out for their fingernails, but Spider was a strict tit-for-tat guy, as they soon learned. At any rate, there were no complaints, and the people at the model agencies found that it was easier and easier to get girls to accept jobs at Sakowitz's, normally a booking of last resort.

Spider warned each girl what to expect before he made a move.

"I'm only promising a short story, babe. There's a beginning and a middle with me, but absolutely no end. I'm not interested in commitment, enduring relationships, and unique interpersonal bullshit. And I don't make promises, not even about tomorrow night."

"Spider, sweetheart, what if I told you that there's got to be a first time for everything?"

"You'd only be saying something I've heard many times before. The one thing I'll never understand about women is why they refuse to believe you when you tell them honestly that there is absolutely no future in something. And yet, how can you possibly say anything more clearly than that?"

"Hope springs eternal and all that jazz. Why don't you just shut up, Spider, and fuck me—nice and slow. I'll take my chances."

By the time he met Valentine, Spider had advanced from the darkroom through two increasingly good jobs as assistant to established photographers. He had become something of an institution in the fashion world in three years. The thing was that he dearly liked all his girls in his honest, sensual, big-hearted way, and they knew it. They had been fucked by too many men who talked about love and didn't truly *like* women. When a girl made love with Spider it was as if she had been given a marvelous surprise birthday party—she felt so *good* about herself for a long time afterward. Just like a real girl.

Spider had discovered, sometime during his first months in New York, that most models don't think of themselves as "real girls." Almost none of them had had a date for their high-school senior prom. Until the boys began to sprout in the late teens, the girls had always been the tallest, skinniest, most awkward people in their classes, the butt of a million jokes, their mothers' disappointments, no matter how well hidden. By the time they learned what to do with their faces and discovered that their extra-long waists and lack of breasts and hips made them perfect living clothes hangers, their self-images were firmly established at close to zero. Of course, some of them had had the luck to be conventionally pretty enough throughout their early lives so that they were able to compete in things like the Miss Teen-age America Contest, but the top models, the most interesting-looking ones, still thought that a real girl was no more than five feet five, took a 36C-cup bra, knew how to talk to boys from the day she was born, and had never hit a ball with a bat.

While they were growing up, almost any one of them

would have given anything to be cuddly. Spider made them feel cuddly, kissable, cosseted, hugable, teasable, pinchable, altogether adorable. He liked them all—the lanky ones from Texas who still had retainers on their teeth, which they religiously whipped on between jobs; the tough ones who loved to talk dirty even though it shocked no one but themselves; the ones who constantly lost their contact lenses in thick carpets; the sad ones of twenty-four who looked upon their twenty-fifth birthday as the end of the world; the lonely ones who had been discovered in Europe long before they were really old enough to leave their homes; he even liked the ones who didn't eat all day, ruining their nerves, and then expected him to buy them the leanest steaks for dinner. Quality protein for starving women was Spider's biggest expense.

The makeshift days of erotic confusion on the floor of Sakowitz's darkroom were now forgotten as Spider discovered that what he really liked best was fucking in bed, in a girl's bed, in a girl's bedroom, smelling of girl smell. Although he was making good progress professionally, he still missed the atmosphere of a female's dwelling, and the closest he could get was sniffing around a model's apartment, picking up on all the evocative details. With bliss, he inhaled the smell of talcum and hair spray and Carmen Rollers getting hot. He particularly enjoyed messy girls who left things all over the place, underwear on the floor, wet towels slung over the tub, shoes forgotten where he'd fall over them, old favorite bathrobes, wastebaskets overflowing with Kleenex, sink tops littered with half-used lipsticks and eye-shadow brushes—all those girl-child artifacts gave Spider deep pleasure. His sisters, he thought longingly, were such a glorious bunch of little slobs. How he enjoyed their appetites, whether it was for each other's newest clothes or three helpings of chocolate ice cream. To Spider, appetite was a sure sign of the female principle.

The only place Spider never considered using for sex was his own apartment. He would have brought a girl there if he had been in love with one. But Spider knew he had never been in love. His bittersweet, sensitive heart was stubbornly his own. He had turned into an intelligent, feeling man and he understood perfectly that he loved women generically, as a group, a species. His very avail-ability was a sign of some deep inaccessibility to a special one among them. Someday, he hoped, he would fall in love with one woman, but that day had not yet come.

Meanwhile he had his popsies and he had his friend, Valentine, whose cozy, crazy stage set of a Paris attic had become a special refuge for him, the place he wanted to be when he felt especially fine or, as occasionally happened, flat and grumpy. Valentine's own blend of food, sympathy, and plain talk always set him right.

One evening, several months, many bottles of wine, many of Valentine's savory stews, many long conversations, after they met, Spider burst into her room without knocking.

"Val, where the fuck are you?" he shouted and then stopped in confusion as he saw her almost hidden in one of her flounced armchairs. She was holding the burning end of a Gauloise Bleu cigarette a foot away from her nose, and with her eyes closed, she was sniffing the smoke with relish.

"So that's what you do! I wondered why it always smelled of French cigarettes in here and yet you don't smoke yourself—you burn it like incense. Aw, sweet baby." He hugged her. She blinked at him, startled out of her dream and embarrassed at being caught in her sentimental secret.

"Oh, they don't smell like Paris really, nothing does, but it is as close as I can get. And why, Elliott, don't you knock before you come in?"

"Too excited. Listen, I've got something for you that tastes like Paris—*Bollinger Brut.*" He produced the bottle of champagne from behind his back.

"But that's so very expensive—Elliott, has something good happened?"

"Bet your ass. Next week I start as chief assistant to Hank Levy. He's light-years ahead of the guys I've been working for. Sakowitz, Miller, Browne—none of them have done as much high-fashion work as Levy. His studio is busy as hell—lots of commercial work. He's not in demand as much as he used to be for editorial but still he's in the big leagues—not the biggest league, he never was there, but it's a giant step for me. I heard Joe Verona —his assistant—was going back to Rome this morning from some gal and I went over to see Levy as soon as I could get out of the studio. Luckily it was a slow day—anyway, I start next week." Elated, he dropped down on the rug at her feet.

"Oh, Elliott, I'm so happy! That's the most marvelous, marvelous news. I have a good feeling about it and you know my feelings are never wrong." Although she was an utterly practical woman in many things, Valentine had great faith in her occasional "feelings"—Spider teasingly said it was her wild Celtic blood trying to drown out the voices of French realism. Looking at Spider clutching his bottle of champagne, Valentine congratulated herself that he was not her type. He was a lecher and a womanizer and a heartbreaker, and any woman who felt sentimental about him was doomed to misery. She was happy to have him for her friend, but it would never go farther than that—she was basically much too sensible to think of such a promiscuous man as anything but her good neighbor. Thank God she was French and knew how to protect herself from this kind of man.

"You look hungry, Elliott. It so happens that I made a *blanquette de veau,* which is too much for one person. And it goes with champagne."

Hank Levy was almost a nice guy, kind of. He had a lot of your basic Brooklyn charm—an aging Huck Finn, a tall, skinny version of Norman Mailer, with more freckles and fewer furrows, and a receding hairline instead of a noble brow. He dressed in standard Hollywood-director drag: French jeans, work shirts carefully unbuttoned almost to the waist, under which hung only one gold chain, but that was a very heavy one from Bulgari. His particular trademark was a Professor Henry Higgins cardigan made of four-ply cashmere, which cost him fifty-five English pounds at Harrods. He had a dozen of them in different colors and liked to tie them around his waist or throw them over his shoulders, sleeves dropping straight down à la Balanchine. If he had known when he hired Spider that in winter Spider wore irresistibly authentic, aphrodisiacally mangy sweat shirts and crew sweaters from his father's Annapolis collection, he might not have wanted to have that kind of competition around the studio—too much the real thing for comfort.

The twin burdens of bisexuality and Jewish guilt weighed heavily on Hank. He considered that he'd been had. Shit, one day he was giving some pussy a try-on-for-size with a cute, little, blond fashion coordinator who was game for anything, and in what seemed to be only forty-eight hours later he found out that she was not only pregnant, indisputably by him, but also a Nice Jewish Girl who had several dozen relatives in Brooklyn, some of whom belonged to his mother's branch of Hadassah.

So Hank ended up married and a father before he found out for certain if all-gay might have been more fun, not that he ever stopped trying to make sure.

However, it was far from a total loss. Chicky was a lot smarter than he was. She was also more aggressive and more ambitious. She wore sable hats before anyone had ever seen one except in the movie version of *Anna Karenina*. She wore the no-lipstick look before it was invented, or perhaps she invented it; she wore the first pants suit and the first miniskirt and the first midi and made *Women's Wear Daily* at least five times a year. She shaped up Hank's act, giving shrewd and cunning little dinner parties to which she managed to entice enough impossibly rude celebrities to make everyone else who was invited feel that they had had a brush with the glittering world of high fashion. Still, it kept the jobs rolling in to Levy's huge studio, where the obligatory newest records played all day on the obligatory fabulous sound system, and the obligatory butcher-block table was always loaded with the obligatory feast of French cheeses, Italian and German sausages, dark, twisted breads from Bloomingdale's gourmet department, and kosher dill pickles. All in all, a swell arrangement, and Spider learned a great deal during the year he was Levy's assistant.

A photographer's assistant spends nine tenths of his time handing his boss a camera that he has just loaded with fresh film, pulling down rolls of paper for backgrounds, checking the light meter, moving tripods from one place to another, fiddling with temperamental strobe lights, and shifting props. The other tenth of his time is devoted to changing the tapes on the sound system. However, Hank Levy was lazy and he was heavily involved in the social rumble, so he let Spider actually *take* a lot of pictures. Meaning that now Spider finally got to do all the things that had made him want to become a fashion photographer in the first place, like posing the models and deciding on angles and inventing his own lighting and focusing the camera and pushing the buttons and making the camera go click. It was even better than it looks in those movies about fashion photographers because Spider turned out to be a genius in talking to the models.

However, Hank Levy wasn't so simpleminded or preoccupied that he ever let Spider take any of the pictures on magazine assignments. If anyone was going to go down to the Virgin Islands and shoot three models in next year's monokinis, getting it off on the beach with a steel band, it was Hank. Not that he got a great many jobs like that. He had almost been a star photographer at one time in his career, but lately he was being asked to shoot Kimberly Knits on the Staten Island Ferry or White Stag separates at the West Side Tennis Club. Still, it was for *Vogue* and that was where you got your name underneath the photo. The money was lousy but the prestige was essential. Hank only let Spider loose on the small ads for watches and shoes and creams to bleach body hair, and not too many of those either—only when the smaller ad agencies were involved and he was sure that they didn't plan to send their own art department people to observe the proceedings. Spider worked strictly on the low end of Hank's business, the end that paid almost all of the rent.

The ad that launched Spider was for a new type of fingernail hardener, put out by a shoe-string company. The model, who was suppose to embody the essence of the romantic South, was young, inexperienced, and stiff in her hoopskirts and laced waist. Spider inspected the awkward-looking girl with frank appreciation.

"Perfect! Honey, you're perfect! We finally booked someone who looks the part. I'm on to you, kid—you're just that sort of proud little tease who used to drive

100

the boys to drink in old Virginia. Too bad you weren't born in time to play Scarlett O'Hara in the movie. My Lord, if this isn't one irresistible girl—a little more to the right, sweet—I'll bet there isn't a man you meet who wouldn't like to nibble his way up under that hoopskirt—now try to look remote, baby, remember you're the plantation belle they went to war for. Great! It's going great—bend a bit to the left, no that's your right, lover—Christ, it's fun to work with a fresh face. Oh, you are a clever little darling—this is better than a time machine—you can call me Ashley or Rhett, whichever you choose, because when a girl is as beautiful as you are, she always gets her pick. Come on, Scarlett honey bun, let's try it sitting in that garden swing—lovely!"

And the now giggling girl, who had lived all her life in New Jersey, believed every word he said because she had only to notice the hard-on Spider got when he was shooting—and it was impossible to miss—to know that she really *was* divine. And that knowledge *made* her divine to the ninth power faster than Spider could say "Lick your lips, doll baby, and give me that smile again."

The difference between the way a model looked when a fag photographer flung out a perfunctory "Fabulous, absolutely fabulous, darling!" and the way she looked when Spider was standing there clicking away with the bulk of his massive prick clearly outlined inside of his tight, white denims—and she felt her pussy begin to twitch, my God, actually get wet under that crazy hoopskirt—was the difference between a good fashion shot and a great fashion shot.

Harriet Toppingham, the fashion editor who discovered Spider, was at the top of her field. However, all fashion editors, no matter how important, do not just breathe the electric, perfumed air of high fashion and gossip over expensive lunches. They work like dogs. One of her jobs was to scrutinize the ads in all magazines, not just purely fashion magazines, because ads are the life-blood of the magazine business. The cost of the paper and printing and distribution of each individual copy of a magazine is usually more than its newsstand or subscription price. Without advertising revenue there would be no magazine, no reason for a fashion editor's job to exist.

There are only a handful of top magazine fashion editors in the United States. Each of the straight fashion magazines has an editor in chief, who is usually assisted by two or three subordinate fashion editors. There are always special editors for shoes, lingerie, accessories, and fabrics, each of whom has an assistant, since companies in these businesses advertise widely and have to be given particular attention and hand holding. On a general women's magazine, like *Good Housekeeping,* the fashion department may have a staff of one fashion editor, her assistant, a shoe editor, and an accessory editor, but they fill only six editorial pages or less each month. At *Vogue* there are something like twenty-one editors of varying degrees of importance, including those stationed in Paris, Rome, and Madrid who are socialites first, editors second.

Only the very top fashion editors on any magazine make impressive salaries. The others are paid no more than a good secretary, but they willingly slave for the status, the excitement, and the prestige of the job. These lesser editors must be not only talented but ambitious. It helps if they come from backgrounds where a working-woman doesn't need her own money to keep her in Laszlo soap and an occasional leg waxing.

When a fashion editor, like Harriet Toppingham, is at the top, or close to it, she is courted by those seeking favors as Madame de Pompadour was when she enjoyed the ear and favor of Louis XV. Her lunches are bought for her in that handful of acceptable French restaurants by dress manufacturers and designers and public-relations people; her clothes are, if not free, at something considerably less than cost; and at Christmas she has to hire a car and driver to clear her office of gifts twice a day. Naturally, she travels free. A discreet inclusion of even part of the logo of an airline or the image of a corner of a hotel swimming pool in a fashion photograph, with several words of acknowledgment in the body of the copy, takes care of the transportation and lodging for the editor, photographer, models, and assistants.

Harriet Toppingham had arrived at the top of the business on merit, not because she could pay her own way, although her private income from a father who had manufactured hundreds of thousands of bathtubs was considerable. She was a woman of such hard, sharp style that she seemed to have a cutting edge. Her feeling of authority was so genuine that it inspired equally genuine fear in her entire staff, and her creative imagination had as few limits as Fellini's. Her innovations were first hated and then imitated and eventually became classics. When she first noticed Spider's work she was in her early forties and many people called her ugly. She had never become what the French call a *jolie laide* because she saw no reason to make the attempt to exaggerate any good points she might have had. She preferred to be that other thing the French know how to admire, a sacred monster. She took what she had and presented it uncompromisingly, full front—plain, thin, brown hair pulled back severely, a large, masculine nose jutting forward, thin lips covered with bright red lipstick, and plain brown eyes, small and shallow, set like a mud turtle's, taking in every detail and discarding all but the most delicate, the most intricate, the most important and recherché. She was of better than medium height, built like a stick, and she always wore splendidly and shriekingly chic clothes, since nothing she put on could do anything to overpower looks she didn't possess. She made no concessions to what was currently fashionable. If this was the season for the "American sportswear look" or the "return to softness" or "dressing with clear color," you could count on Harriet to wear a look that couldn't be pinned down to a year or even a decade, a look that would make any other woman, no matter how perfectly turned out, feel like just another sheep in a pack. She had never been married and she lived alone in a large apartment on Madison Avenue, which she filled with her collections, treasures from her countless trips to Europe and the Orient, most of them too odd and too unharmonious, often too grotesque, to fit in anywhere as well as they did in her crowded, brown interiors.

At least once a year or so Harriet Toppingham liked

to "make" an unknown photographer so that she could drop, at least for a while, one of her regulars. What was the point in having power unless people knew you wouldn't hesitate to use it? Once she had established a new photographer, he, or she, was indebted for life, and even after her favor had passed elsewhere, they retained the cachet she had bestowed on them. She thought of the photographers she had unearthed as her creatures, as much her property as the objects in her collections. As head fashion editor of *Fashion and Interiors,* she could bypass her enemy, the art director, and interview photographers themselves (for she refused to deal with photographers' agents) in her own office, known in the trade as the Brown Hole of Calcutta.

When she saw the ad for the nail-hardening product, tucked away in the back of *Redbook,* she checked with the agency to find out who had taken the picture. "They say Hank Levy," she told her secretary, "but I find that impossible to believe. He hasn't done anything that original since the late sixties. Get Eileen or one of the other agencies on the phone and find out who posed for the shot. Then get the gal to call me here."

Two days later she summoned Spider to an audience. He brought his portfolio, a big black-leather folder, accordion pleated and tied together with a strip of heavy black braid. It contained the best prints of the best pictures he had ever taken, a few of them results of his work for Levy, but most of them had been taken for his own pleasure on weekends. Spider kept his loaded Nikon F-2 near him at all times, for his passion was to capture women in moments when they weren't posing, in passages of brief, intimate communication with themselves. He celebrated the female when she was feeling most her own woman, whether she was cooking eggs or daydreaming into a glass of wine or tiredly undressing or waking up yawning or brushing her teeth.

Casually, Harriet Toppingham leafed through the prints, easily hiding her disbelief as she recognized girls with five-hundred-dollar-an hour faces wearing old bathrobes or casually draped in a towel.

"Hmmmm—interesting, quite nice. Tell me, Mr. Elliot, who is your favorite artist, Avedon or Penn?"

Spider grinned at her. "Degas, when he's not doing ballet girls."

"My, my. Still, better Degas than Renoir—so predictably pink and white. Tell me—I hear you're a famous stud. Is that rumor or fact?" Harriet liked to attack as unexpectedly as possible.

"Fact." Spider gave her a friendly look. She reminded him of his fifth-grade math teacher.

"Then why haven't you ever worked for *Playboy* or *Penthouse?*" Harriet was not ready to abandon the field.

"A girl twining a string of fake pearls through her pubic hair or all dolled up in a Frederick's of Hollywood garter belt and playing with herself while she looks in a mirror usually seems a bit lonesome. Masturbation isn't a great big turn-on in my life," Spider answered politely. "Then, when they shoot two girls together it gets so artsy-craftsy soft focus that it doesn't look like sex. In fact, it depresses me—and it seems like such a waste—"

"Yes. Perhaps. Hmmm." She lit a cigarette and smoked as if she were alone, occasionally glancing at the prints she had littered all over her desk in an indifferent manner. Abruptly she spoke.

"Can you do some lingerie pages for us for the April issue? We need them by next week at the latest."

"Miss Toppingham, I'd give everything but my left nut to work for you, but I have a full-time job with Hank Levy—"

"Drop Levy," she commanded. "You surely don't intend to work for him forever, do you? Open your own studio. Start small. I'll give you enough work to keep you going until the April issue comes out. If you can do the job I hope for, you won't have trouble paying the rent."

Harriet favored Spider with the nearest she ever came to an encouraging look. This moment, this tangible use of power, this ability to alter people's lives in the way she chose was the most important of the things she lived for. She felt heated, potent, supreme. The pictures she had just asked Spider to take had already been scheduled for Joko by the art director. Joko had become a bit boring lately—tame and lacking in fantasy. He needed a kick in the ass. The art director always needed a kick in the ass. Besides, this Spider Elliott had taken the sexiest pictures of women she'd ever seen. Those girls who were paid to look so otherworldly beautiful in cosmetic ads looked more enticing than she'd ever dreamed they could be, and somehow more approachable, more real.

Lately, she realized, there had been a problem with lingerie photographs at *Fashion and Interiors*. The pages had become so sleek that they were creating a backlash. Some of their biggest advertisers, men with important girdle and bra accounts, were calling to say that while they appreciated the editorial credits, their clients were getting flack because the showroom models on Seventh Avenue didn't look one tenth as good as the girls in *Fashion* did. This, in turn, made the department-store buyers worried that ordinary women would expect to look like the photographs and then, when they actually saw themselves in the merchandise, blame the garments rather than their own bodies. The photos, quite simply, were a con. When advertisers were unhappy with editorial pages something was wrong and when something was wrong, Harriet Toppingham always played her hunches. Today she had a strong hunch that Spider Elliott could be important to her.

Spider found a studio in an old building off Second Avenue that hadn't yet been turned into a restaurant or a singles bar. It was too rundown to tempt any but the most desperate tenant. The landlord hadn't repaired anything for twenty years, waiting for the day when Warner Le Roy would pop out of a cloud of wonder dust and offer him a fortune for the premises. However, there was water for the darkroom, and on the top floor, where Spider rented two big rooms, the ceilings were high. His own apartment would have made a better studio, but he knew it was too inconveniently located.

For this first assignment, Spider decided not to use the usual lingerie models, girls whose bodies are so perfect that no sane person would believe that even once, in all their eighteen years, they would have dreamed of wearing a panty girdle or a bra. And he didn't use the usual poses:

dance students caught all unaware practicing stretching positions in their undies; or languid beach shots in which the sand-strewn model seems to have mistaken her underwear for her bikini; or storytelling voyeur shots in which a man's hand, dangling a diamond bracelet, or a man's foot, in a polished evening shoe, somehow wanders into a corner of the picture.

Instead he hired models in their mid-thirties, still beautiful but with faces and bodies that were at an undeniable remove from youth. He built a set designed exactly like a fitting room in a department store. Piles of discarded lingerie cascaded over a single chair and were draped all over the little shelf so unhelpfully provided in these cells. Models glared at themselves suspiciously in three-way mirrors; sat on the edge of the only chair, dressed only in a half slip, and lit badly needed cigarettes; struggled angrily out of tight girdles; searched in bulging tote bags for a lipstick that might improve matters; did, in fact, in Spider's photos, all the things every woman does when she has to go out and buy new underwear. The pictures were funny and loving and even though the models undoubtedly needed all the help they got from the lingerie they were wearing, they still looked like fine bodied, luscious women with a lot of mileage left on them.

Men who saw that issue of *Fashion and Interiors* felt as if they were getting a good look at something they normally were never allowed to see, glimpses of feminine mysteries much more private than an open centerfold had to offer. Women compared themselves to the models, as they always do, no matter how miserable it makes them, and did not find the results as upsetting as usual. In fact, those bras looked as if they might really hold up a pair of normal boobs—how strange. And how reassuring.

The art director of *Fashion* had threatened to resign when he first saw the contact sheets, screaming in some low Hungarian dialect—normally he screamed in French. Harriet actually laughed out loud when she heard him.

By the time the April issue was on the newsstands, Spider had completed three other assignments for *Fashion:* perfume pages so outrageously sentimental, so romantically Victorian that a movie critic would have awarded them three handkerchiefs; a series of shoe shots that foot fetishists kept as collector's items; and a totally lovable layout on children's nightgowns and pajamas, which persuaded more than one woman to stop taking the pill and see what happened. However, for the last four months he had been utterly dependent on Harriet Toppingham, who doled out these assignments like a stingy hostess who has been forced to serve fresh caviar. In any case, the small sums that a photographer is paid for fashion editorial work, as compared with the large amounts he is paid for advertising shots, is barely enough to keep him in film, shaving cream, and cornflakes. Spider was reduced to letting his girls of the moment pay for his dinners even though their business managers disapproved.

The appearance of the lingerie pictures still did not bring him any commercial work. Although the department stores that carried the merchandise were delighted with the results, advertising agency art directors, much as they respected Harriet, thought that perhaps she had finally gone too far. However, the perfume pictures were something they could understand, and within months, by the end of 1975, Spider felt safe in considering himself a moderate success with all sorts of good things in prospect. At almost thirty, he was finally a New York fashion photographer with his own studio, his own Hasselblad, his own strobe lights. It had taken almost six years since graduation.

Melanie Adams walked into Spider's studio one day in the early May of 1976. She had arrived in New York precisely three days before from Louisville, Kentucky, and with the maddening innocence of ignorance had simply marched up to the Ford Agency's waiting room to wait. Both Eileen and Jerry Ford, who know more about photographic models than anyone alive, happened to be out of town for the day, but for a girl who looked like Melanie Adams, there really was no better place to wait. The Fords hadn't trained their staff to overlook miracles. In fact, their entire operation is based on the premise that the miracle of true beauty exists. Of course, they know that almost all beauty has to be mined and polished like a diamond; they invented the process by which prospective models are put on diets, taken to the best hairdressers, made-up by experts, taught to sit and stand and move, and then sent to see as many photographers as possible, hoping that some of them will spot a girl's potential.

As soon as one of Eileen's assistants laid eyes on Melanie she decided to bypass all that preparation and find out immediately how this stupendously beautiful girl photographed. She phoned Spider and asked him to take some test shots, since Melanie's own pictures were hopeless. She'd never done any professional modeling before and all she had were some out-of-date family-album snapshots and her high-school yearbook photograph.

Melanie stood just inside the open door of Spider's studio until he noticed her. "Hi," she said shyly, pushing back the heavy curtain of her hair with one hand. "The Ford people told me to come over for tests—"

Spider thought his heart might truly stop. He just stood there, looking at her. It was as if every other girl in his life had been part of a montage of pictures flashing under the opening titles of a movie. Now the camera had finally focused on the star, and the film was about to start. Had started.

"Right. They called me. I've been expecting you." He spoke automatically, out of sheer habit. "Let's get started. First I want some shots in natural light—just throw your coat on the chair and go and stand over by that window and look out." Jesus, he thought, there have to be thirty different shades of color in her hair, everything from curry to maple sugar—there aren't even names for some of them. "Now, move a little closer to the window and lean on the sill with your right elbow, profile toward me. Chin up. Little smile. A little more. Now, turn toward me, lower your hand. Good. Chin down. Relax." He was aware that fortunately there was no possible way to get a bad angle on this girl. The way his hand was trembling he'd be lucky if the pictures were in focus. "OK. Come over here now and sit on that chair where the lights are set up. Just look around the studio as much as you want and don't pay any attention to the camera."

As she turned her head this way and that, Spider, considering her, was almost idiotically stunned at the violence of his emotions. He was bedazzled. His brain struggled vainly to make any logic out of his feelings. He considered himself the last man in the world to be affected by mere beauty in a girl. He *expected* beauty and looked past it for the person. But now he felt as if he could spend the rest of his life trying to understand what made this face so significant. Why were her eyes placed in her flesh so that they seemed to have meaning beyond meaning? Why did the molding of these particular lips make him ache to trace them with his finger, as if a touch would explain their mystery? Her smile was wanton, delicately wanton, yet full of hidden withdrawal. Something in the way her bones lay under her skin told him he would never possess her. She was so perfectly *there,* yet her reality eluded him in some maddening, incomprehensible way.

"I've got everything I need," he told her as he turned off the lights. "Here—come and sit here." He guided her to a couch and sat down next to her. "Listen, how old are you? Do you love your parents? Do they understand you? Was anyone ever mean to you? What are your favorite things to eat? Who was the first boy you ever kissed? Did you love him? Do you dream a lot—?"

"Now, just stop!" Her voice was offhandedly southern, with just exactly enough sweetness, the warm ice of the archetypical belle. "Nobody at Ford's warned me that you were mad! What on earth are you asking me all that for?"

"Look, I'm—I think I'm in love with you. No, *please* don't smile like that. Oh God! Words! I'm not playing games. It's something I have to tell you right now at the beginning because I want you to start thinking about it—don't look so suspicious. I've never told a woman I loved her before, not until you walked in here. Please! I don't blame you for looking that way but try to believe me." Spider took her hand and placed it on his chest. His heart was beating as violently as if he'd run a mile for his life. She lifted her eyebrows in acknowledgment, finally looking directly at him. Her irises were the clear, warm color of a glass of rich, sweet sherry held up to the light, and her look seemed to be seeking some ultimate truth with a yearning yet gentle anguish.

"Tell me what you're thinking right this minute," Spider implored.

"I hate it when people ask me that," Melanie answered gently.

"So do I. I've never done it before. Just promise me you won't get married to somebody right away, give me a chance."

"I never make promises," Melanie laughed. She had learned not to box herself in years ago. It always saved a great deal of trouble, sooner or later. "Anyway, how can you say things like that? You don't know me at all." She wasn't really caught up in this game, but she was enjoying it, as she had enjoyed the dozens of declarations that had been made to her since she was eleven. Her earliest memories were of being told how beautiful she was. Something in her never believed the words, never felt satisfied. It wasn't modesty; it was a craving for more proof than anyone had ever yet given her. Her mind worked constantly at trying to understand for herself *exactly* what other people saw when they looked at her. She could never grasp it whole and living. Her deepest fantasy was to step outside of her skin and look at herself and find out just what people were talking about. She spent her life experimenting with people to see how she could make them react, as if, in their response, she could discover herself. "I never make promises," she repeated, since he didn't seem to have heard her, "and I don't answer questions."

Her poise was almost Victorian, straight-backed and attentive, like a good, demure little girl. Yet the faint, unmistakable invitation of her smile was set in a timeless quietude, as if she were certain of triumph. She started to stand up.

"No! Wait! Where are you going?" Spider asked frantically.

"I'm starving and it's lunchtime."

Spider felt enormous relief. Food was familiar ground. If she could get hungry, she had to be human.

"I've got a whole refrigerator full of food. Just wait one minute and I'll make you the best liverwurst and Swiss on rye you ever had in your life." As he made the sandwiches, Spider thought that if he could just lock the door and throw away the key and keep her there, it would be the most splendid thing the world had to offer. He wanted to find out everything about this girl from the day she was born. A hundred questions tumbled about in his mind and were rejected. If she would only tell him everything, he thought, he might eventually make some sense out of the way he was feeling.

Spider had never been introspective. He grew up just living his highly enjoyable stretch of life without self-analysis. He didn't realize that basically he was a man who kept himself hidden from himself, partly through liking so many other people and being so warmly available to them. He fell in love the way someone might fall through a gaping hole in a floor that had been solid the day before. He was as unprepared for passion as a schoolboy.

They ate without banter. Everything Spider wanted to say seemed, even before he said it, to go against her rules. She was not at all bothered by the silence between them. Melanie had always been quiet, serenely, evasively so. Her absorption in herself was such that she had little curiosity to discover things about other people. They always ended up telling her more than she was interested in, in any case. But she gazed at Spider intently, trying to catch a glimpse of herself in his eyes. The image would be distorted, but it might tell her something she needed to know. Sometimes, alone, she could get a feeling of being a certain person, of possessing a certain face, of having a certain clearly outlined image, but it was always the image of some actress she had seen in a movie. She would smile like that woman and feel that other face fall like a mask over her own. For that moment she would sense what it was to be in the real world, and then the moment would pass, and she would be left with her endless quest.

The light in the studio changed as the afternoon sun left the room. Spider looked at his watch.

"Christ! In five minutes three tiny tots and their mommies are going to be here—I'm shooting party dresses—and nothing's set up." He jumped up and headed for the other end of the studio as Melanie put on her coat. He stopped short and spun around, disbelieving.

"Hey, what did you say your name was?"

Two weeks later, in front of a long mirror in Scavullo's

dressing room, one of Spider's former girls said to another, "Have you heard the news?"

"What do you mean, *the* news? There's plenty of it around."

"Our divine mutual Spidy has been caught at last—he's going down for the third time."

"What are you talking about?"

"Love, that poor darling fool is in love with the new Garbo. You know who I mean—Eileen's latest, El Mysteriosa Magnolia Blossom."

"Who told you? I just don't believe it."

"He told me—otherwise I wouldn't believe it either. But Spider can't shut up about her. You'd think he invented love. The way he carries on it's Cole Porter time in Dixie. I find it absolutely stomach turning, particularly when you remember how he never—wouldn't ever—"

"I know exactly what you mean."

"I had a feeling you would."

"Oh—the little southern cunt!"

"I'll drink to that."

When Billy Winthrop returned to Boston three months before her year in Paris was supposed to be up, she told her Aunt Cornelia that she had been homesick. She said she had felt a sudden desire to spend the summer with the family in Chestnut Hill before she had to leave for New York to begin studying at Katie Gibbs. Convincingly, Cornelia accepted this lie, the enormity of which might well have been overlooked by most Bostonians, whose love of their city and its surrounding countryside makes the charms of even Paris pale. However, Cornelia knew better. The last letter from Lady Molly had told her the whole story of the despicable way in which that Côte de Grace boy had dropped her niece flat. Her good maternal heart ached to tell Honey—Billy—how unhappy she was for her, but the girl's absolute dignity prohibited any intimate conversation.

And the way she looked! All of Boston—the part that counted—buzzed with it. Brahmin mamas, looking at their own uninspiring daughters, almost forgave Billy her long, sleek body, her mass of black hair, her magnificent way of walking, her perfect skin, but did so slowly, feature by feature, and, even then, only because she was, after all, a Winthrop. After thinking of her as that pathetic, fat, hopeless Honey for so long, it was wrenching for even the most-good-natured woman to have to accept the fact that Honey had returned from France a raving beauty. If she had been born a beauty—but now, this transformation was almost unfair. One had to do entirely too much mental readjustment. It was as if a perfect stranger had come to town, a dashing, lovely stranger who didn't look like anyone they were used to and didn't somehow dress like a Boston girl was supposed to, but who calmly proceeded to greet them all with the unawed familiarity of a member of the family. As indeed she was. Most unsettling.

The girls of Billy's own age found the change even more irritating. Duckling into swan was all very well and good for the Brothers Grimm, but in Boston it was downright theatrical, you could call it—well, frankly—showy. Even a tiny bit—vulgar?

Cornelia waded into the fray. "Amanda, shame on your daughter, Pee-Wee, for her sour grapes. I happened to hear what she was saying about my Billy at Myopia yesterday. So it is 'absurd' to change your first name at her age, is it? You might do well to remember that she was named after your own second cousin, Wilhelmina. She did not 'change' her name—she merely resumed it. And so Billy 'doesn't know how to dress to watch polo.' If Pee-Wee ever took her riding britches off we might find out if she knows how to dress for anything else. And does she intend to be called Pee-Wee until she's a grandmother? If I were you, Amanda, I'd write to Lilianne de Vertdulac and find out if she has room for your daughter next year. It wouldn't do that girl any harm to find out that there is a life outside a stable."

With Billy, Cornelia was very direct and very kind.

"Billy, I have the feeling that your year in Paris may have cost you more than you expected."

"I'm afraid so, Aunt Cornelia. I got carried away—"

"Nonsense. Any girl who looks as glorious as you do deserves to make the most of Paris. I don't blame you for a second for buying those clothes. You wear them well and, after all, it was your own money. I would have insisted on sending you off with a nice check for a new wardrobe, myself, but when you were so plump it didn't seem worthwhile."

"Plump. How dear you are, Aunt Cornelia. I was a disgustingly gross cow. Admit it."

"Now, let's not quibble over words. You were another girl altogether. The problem isn't that—it's the future. Wouldn't you like to stay in Boston and go on to Wellesley after all?" Cornelia asked hopefully. This new Billy could marry anyone she liked. No need for her to go to Katie Gibbs to study to become a dreary secretary.

"Good God, no! In the fall I'll be twenty, much too old to start school all over again."

Cornelia sighed. "I hadn't even thought about that aspect of it. But there is still no need to leave home surely? You know how your uncle and I love to have you here with us."

"I do, and I'm deeply touched, Aunt Cornelia. But I have to get away from Boston, at least for a while. I've known everybody here all of my life and I don't have one close friend, only you and Uncle George. Father's buried in his research—he took one look at me, said 'I always knew you had the Minot bones' and went back to work. Oh, damn, it's hard to explain, but as soon as I came back I began to feel like a freak again, not the way I used to be, but still out of place. The French would say I'm not at home in my skin here. I want to go somewhere where no one comes up to me and says 'My God, what's happened to you? How much weight did you lose? I can't believe it. Fat Honey Winthrop!'"

Cornelia made an understanding face. She'd heard the very same words.

"Aunt Cornelia, don't you remember how you made me promise to go to Katie Gibbs when I got back from Paris?"

"But dear, I wouldn't hold you to that now. I mean, you have so many more choices—so many nice boys calling you—"

"So many nice *kids*. I feel as if I'm ten years older than they are. I can't just sit around, doing the proper charity work, living on you and Uncle George, and waiting to find someone to marry me who isn't totally juvenile. Yet I'm good for nothing else *but* that, if you stop to think about it."

"Well, my dear, that's all most of us ever did."

"Oh, you know what I mean."

"As a matter of fact, I do. I think you're quite right, and much as I hate to see you leave, somehow I don't quite see you at a Sewing Circle." Cornelia felt a pang of loss, but she had never balked at accepting the self-evident. "So. Katie Gibbs it is!" She turned to the familiar consolation of organizing someone else's life with her usual brisk efficiency. After all, the Katharine Gibbs School, which had been founded in 1911, was the only secretarial school in America that the families of young women of good social position found entirely acceptable. Hats and gloves were still mandatory for students, other "nice" girls went there, and its social credentials were equaled only by its reputation as a school that turned out first-class secretaries.

Within a week Cornelia had unearthed a suitable roommate for Billy. One of her old friends, from her own college days, had a daughter who was working in New York City and living at a most proper address. There was an extra bedroom in her apartment, which her mother was anxious to rent. Cornelia also went ahead and paid a year's fees in advance at the school, working on the correct assumption that after her Paris purchases Billy would be short of money for both tuition and expenses. Under the guise of "taking advantage" of the August fur sales, she whisked Billy to Roberts-Neustadter on Newbury Street and presented her with an advance twentieth-birthday present: a slim-fitted coat of velvety black seal, belted at the back, flaring in the skirt and trimmed with a notched collar and cuffs of dark mink. "Keep the old one for rainy days," she advised, waving away Billy's hugs of appreciation. Cornelia's generosity was boundless. It was having it acknowledged that she couldn't bear.

Billy sat in her parlor-car seat, traveling from Back Bay Station to Grand Central Station, on a hot, sticky day during the first week of September 1962. Her stomach gave a sickening downward jerk every time she thought about the coming meeting with her future roommate, Jessica Thorpe. What a haughty name that seemed, so starchy, so dry and complete in itself. Even worse, she was twenty-three, a summa cum laude graduate of Vassar, and she had a job working for *McCall's* in the editorial department. What a frightening paragon she must be, Billy thought. Even her background was impeccable. Her parents were both descended from the oldest families in Providence, Rhode Island. Not like being from Boston,

Aunt Cornelia pointed out, but happily not as—ordinary—as being from New York. And her apartment was located on 82nd Street, between Park and Madison. These details alone convinced Billy that this inevitable, inescapable roommate was going to be sophisticated, full of herself, and a competent career girl in total charge of her life. Perhaps, oh horror, an intellectual.

Meanwhile, Jessica Thorpe was having a most unpleasant morning. It had started when Natalie Jenkins, the articles editor, had ripped to shreds Jessica's last rewrite of the Sinatra profile. The article, originally tossed off by a well-known raconteur, had been turned over to Jessica to be "cleaned up," and she had worked on it for weeks, trying to give its confused anecdotes and scrambled syntax the smooth touch suitable for a women's magazine. Mrs. Jenkins, famous as the first woman in publishing to survive a daily four-martini lunch, had hated her first attempt, disliked her second attempt, and this very day she had taken the third attempt and done the rewrite herself in three quarters of an hour, eviscerating the guts of the piece and demolishing all the parts that meant anything. Now it was just another bit of Pablum, old-fashioned sob-sister stuff, but Mrs. Jenkins, sitting in triumph at her typewriter, was finally satisfied. She had proven, once again, that no one could really do any job around the office without her help.

And if this wasn't dismal enough, the Girl From Boston was arriving today. Wilhelmina Hunnenwell Winthrop. The very thought made Jessica's clouds of Pre-Raphaelite baby hair droop. Jessica was much given to drooping regardless of circumstances. Her skirts always drooped because her hips were too slender to hold them up properly, and it never occurred to her to have the hems altered. Her blouses drooped because she forgot to tuck them in. Her body drooped because she was only five feet two inches tall and she never remembered to stand up straight. But even when her spirits drooped, as well as everything else, she was irresistible. Men, seeing the drooping of Jessica, found the idea of an upright woman downright masculine. She had a tiny little nose and a tiny little chin and enormous, sad, lavender eyes and a lovely wide brow. When her adorable little mouth drooped, men were overwhelmed by an urge to kiss her. When it didn't droop, they felt precisely the same way.

Men were Jessica's favorite thing. She thought that she had managed to hide this dangerous propensity from her mother, but obviously she hadn't succeeded or otherwise her mother would not have forcibly insisted that she had to have a roommate or else move to the Barbizon Hotel for Women, that Devil's Island of Chastity. Chastity was Jessica's least favorite thing.

The Girl From Boston was certainly her mother's spy, Jessica reflected, as she drooped ravishingly homeward, ruining the evening of at least a dozen men on the Madison Avenue bus by not even looking at them. In normal spirits, Jessica looked directly at every man she saw for a fraction of a second, rating him on a scale of one to ten, the only criterion being "How good would he be in bed?" A man had to be actively unattractive to get less than a four because Jessica was very nearsighted and hated to wear her glasses in public. The number of sixes and sevens reached into the dozens in the course of Jessica's average week. She could never be positive about them because her eyes were so poor, but she gave generous marks, to be fair.

Billy had trouble getting a cab during the rush hour, and it was after six-thirty when she arrived, frozen with nerves, at Jessica's apartment. The doorman rang up from the lobby to announce her just as Jessica had finished hiding five unmatched men's sock's, a Brooks Brothers belt, and, in a last-minute flurry, her douche bag. Would a girl use a douche bag if she was a virgin? Jessica was too terrified to think that one out. She stood at the open door of her apartment and watched a pile of impressively good luggage being wheeled toward her on a dolly. Behind the luggage was the second doorman and behind him strode, to Jessica's nearsighted eyes, an Amazon. She exchanged flustered greetings with the tall blurred figure while the doorman disposed of the luggage, waiting unhappily for the moment when they would be alone together. The Amazon stood, silent and uncertain and voiceless, in the center of the living room. Although Billy had finally found herself relatively at ease, as long as she was speaking French, even when she was meeting strangers, the prospect of living in close association with a superior girl of her own background, a girl who was three years older than she was, brought back every one of the dozen of insecurities she had been tattooed with during her first eighteen years. And the sight of tiny Jessica, so slight, almost frail, had the strange effect of making Billy feel enormous again, just as if she were still fat.

The doorman left and Jessica remembered her manners. "Ah—why don't we just sit down?" she fluttered timidly. "You must be absolutely exhausted—it's so hot out there." She waved hesitantly toward a chair and the tall figure sat down with a gasp of relief and fatigue. Jessica groped for some common ground, something to make the stranger speak. "I know," she ventured, "why don't we have a drink—I'm so nervous—" At these kind words the Amazon burst into tears. So, companionably, did Jessica. Bursting into tears was another of her favorite things, really more useful, she found, for difficult moments than anything else.

Within five minutes Jessica had put on her glasses and inspected Billy thoroughly. All her life she had wanted to look like Billy and she told her so. Billy answered that she had always dreamed of looking like Jessica. Both of them were telling the exact truth and they both realized it. Within two hours Billy had told her all about Edouard, and Jessica had told Billy all about the three number nines with whom she was currently having affairs. From there their friendship progressed in geometric proportions. Neither of them could imagine how there would ever be enough time to tell each other as much as they had to tell. Before they finally retired to their respective bedrooms— at 4:00 A.M.—after ceremoniously retrieving Jessica's douche bag from its hiding place, they had, with great gravity, made a pact never to tell anyone in Providence or New York or Boston anything more about the other than her name, followed by the sacred formula "a very nice girl." They kept that pact all their lives.

As Billy stepped off the elevator into the entrance of the Katharine Gibbs School, the first thing that met her eyes was the gaze of the late Mrs. Gibbs, preserved with all its stern, implacable presence in the portrait that hung over the receptionist's desk. She did not look mean, thought Billy, only as if she knew all about you and had not decided whether to actively disapprove—yet. Out of the corner of her eye she was aware that someone was stationed by the elevator door checking out each girl for gloves, hat, dress, and makeup, of which there must not be much. That, at least, was not a problem for a girl who remembered only too well the folkways of Boston.

Gregg, on the other hand, was. Billy cursed Gregg and Pitman, whoever they were. Why had people been so cruel as to invent shorthand, she wondered, as the infernal, eternal hourly buzzers went off and she moved hurriedly, but with the required precision, from the steno room to the typing room and then back to the steno room again. Many of her classmates had some knowledge of typing before they entered Katie Gibbs, but even those who thought they had a leg up on the system were swiftly disillusioned about their skills. Being "Gibbs Material" meant that you were expected to reach certain degrees of proficiency that struck Billy as outrageous. Were they seriously expecting her to be able to take one hundred words a minute in shorthand and type faultlessly at a minimum of sixty words a minute by the time she had completed her course? They were indeed.

Within a week Billy decided it was a waste of time to revile Gregg and Pitman. Like the laws of gravity, they were not about to go away. It was the same as losing weight. She had suffered, almost more than she could remember, but it had been worth it in the end. Everyone at school had her own talisman story of a Gibbs graduate who had started as secretary to an important senator or well-known businessman and then gone on to more important jobs. Billy could feel her strong obsessive drives finally coming to her aid, helping her to bite into the work with the confidence that she would master it, make it her own.

Jessica, on the other hand, was worried about Billy's lack of what she euphemistically termed "beaus."

"But, Jessie, I don't know a soul in New York and I came here to work. You know how I feel about becoming independent and making some money of my own."

"How many men did you look at today, Billy?" Jessica asked, brushing aside her friend's ambitions.

"How do I know? Maybe ten or fifteen—something like that."

"What numbers were they?"

"Well really! I wasn't playing the game; that's your department."

"I thought so. If you don't look and give them numbers how are you ever going to have any basis for knowing when you meet an eight or even a nine?"

"What difference does it make?"

"Billy, I've been thinking about you. You're a cliché, like a rider who falls off a horse and doesn't get right back on. You're plain afraid of men because of what happened, aren't you?" Jessica murmured all this in her tiny voice, but Billy knew her well enough to realize that under that adorable whimper there lurked a ferocious intelligence that it was useless to contradict. Jessica saw through walls and around corners.

"You're probably right," she admitted wearily. "But even if I wanted to meet a man, look at the realities. I simply can't pick up some number nine on the street, now can I? No, Jessie, don't give me that eye—even you wouldn't do that. I think. Now, the alternative is to scribble a note to Aunt Cornelia and let her loose among her New York friends. She'd dig up some 'nice boy' here who is connected by a wire through his belly button to Boston. Whatever happened between us would be all over the Vincent Club in a week. You don't know how they gossip! I simply will not let anyone there know what I'm doing with my life. I'm going to graduate from Gibbs, get a terrific job, and work my way up until I'm a big success, and I'm never going back to Boston again!"

"Well, who ever said anything about getting involved with someone from your own circle, silly?" Jessica said with indignation. "I'd never, ever, do it myself. All my lovely nines haven't the faintest idea who my family is. They don't even care where I come from. I wouldn't dream of having a thing with someone who might know the man I'll eventually marry, whoever that lucky fool may be. The trick is to go outside."

"Outside?"

"Dummy." Jessica moaned, smiling at Billy's skimpy grasp of life's possibilities. "Outside of your own world. You have no idea of how limited that tiny little world is. Just because they all know one another, just because the people your aunts know in Boston, Providence, Baltimore, and Philadelphia are all connected to the people you might meet through them in New York, doesn't mean that when you get just one step—one tiny step—away from the connections you can't drop out of sight completely."

"I just don't see how," Billy complained. Jessica was maddeningly elliptical sometimes.

"Jews." Jessica gave Billy the smile of the smartest cat on the block, the cat who has just cornered the market on whipped cream and sardines. "Jews are perfect. They don't want to have things with nice Jewish girls either, because they're all connected just the way we are, and they don't want anything to get out about it any more than we do. So all my nines are Jewish."

"What if you met a Jewish ten?"

"I'd run like a thief, I hope. But stop trying to change the subject. Now, how many Jewish men do you know?"

Billy looked blank. "Well, you must know some," said Jessica.

"I don't think so, except maybe that nice shoe salesman at Jordan Marsh." Billy looked puzzled.

"Hopeless. I thought so. And they're the best too," Jessica muttered to herself, her lavender eyes bemused, unfocused, her summa cum laude brain picking and choosing and sorting possibilities.

"The 'best'?" Billy asked. She had never heard that Jews were the best, except maybe for violin playing and chess and of course there was Albert Einstein and, well, you really couldn't count Jesus. He had converted.

"For fucking, of course," Jessica answered absentmindedly.

Billy took to fucking Jews with an enthusiasm even Jessica couldn't have matched. Jews were like Paris, she thought. A new world, a free world, a foreign world that was all the more exciting for being forbidden. In this unknown, secret world she had no secrets to keep. A Winthrop? From Boston? Perhaps historically interesting but essentially unimportant. If they had gone to Harvard it would be highly unlikely that they would know any of Billy's cousins because they would not have been asked to join any club more select than the Hasty Pudding. But just to be on the safe side, Billy never saw a Harvard graduate more than once and never let him kiss her. Even if he was a nine. There were so many nines it seemed. It was one big, wonderful world of Jewish nines if you knew where to look, and soon Billy became an expert. NBC, CBS, ABC, Doyle-Dane-Bernbach, Grey Advertising, *Newsweek,* Viking Press, *The New York Times,* WNEW, Doubleday, the executive training programs at Saks and Macy's—the list was rich, endless.

Billy became clever at avoiding German Jews, particularly those whose families had been in the United States for many generations. They had a disconcerting way of producing mothers who had been born Episcopalians, from families who might well know the Winthrop clan. Billy warned Jessica to stick to Russian Jews, if possible second- or third-generation Americans only. Anyway, they were more fun.

It was from Jews that Billy learned that she had never suspected the depths of her own sensuality. Gradually she learned to sink down into it and let herself go with the current. As she allowed herself to feed her appetites, her appetites grew. She became avid, avid for the feeling of absolute power she got when she felt the jutting stiffness of an engorged prick through an expensive pair of trousers, and she knew that in one swift movement she could uncover it, hold it, smooth and quivering and hot in her hand. She became avid for the electric moment when a man's slowly exploring hand finally settled on her clitoris and found it already plump and wet, offering itself to his repeated, burning, stroking. She became avid for the rapturous time of expectation, which she drew out until it almost became pain, before a new lover parted the lips of her cunt with his cock and she finally knew what he felt like when he was all the way up inside her.

She became so sexually charged that sometimes, between classes at Katie Gibbs, she had to duck into the ladies' room, lock herself in a stall, thrust a finger up between her thighs, and, rubbing hastily, have a quick, silent, necessary orgasm. Her Gregg improved steadily.

Billy had seven proposals of marriage from nines she didn't love, and, reluctantly, she had to replace them. It would not have been playing the game fairly to keep them on the string after honorable intentions had been declared. Jessica had twelve proposals in the same period of time, but they decided that it amounted to an even number, because only men over six feet tall proposed to Billy, while tiny Jessica had a much wider field to appeal to.

All in all, she and Jessica decided, as they reached the end of the spring and Billy approached her graduation from the one-year course at Katie Gibbs, it had been a very good year. A vintage year. It was the spring of 1963, Jack Kennedy was President of the United States, and Billy, about to go for job interviews, took herself to the custom-order millinery salon at Bergdorf Goodman's, at Aunt Cornelia's behest, in order to have Halston, then Jackie Kennedy's favorite hat designer, make her one perfect pillbox. "I want to look intelligent, efficient, capable, and chic—but not too chic," she instructed him firmly.

The year at Katie Gibbs, with its punishing discipline and high standards, combined with the revelation of the possibilities of her body and its infinite uses, had given a final polish to the transformation that had started in Paris. Although Billy was five months short of her twenty-first birthday, she looked and sounded a superbly balanced twenty-five. Perhaps it was her height; perhaps her way of standing, poised as a ballerina waiting for her cue in the wings; perhaps her unconsciously patrician Boston accent, smoothed down but not entirely hidden by a combination of Emery Academy, Paris, and New York; perhaps it was the way she wore her clothes, so that she stood out from any crowd as instantly as a flamingo would among a flock of New York pigeons. Altogether a formidable girl.

"Linda Force? You mean you're going to work for a woman?" Jessica cried incredulously. "After all I've told you about Natalie Jenkins, how could you?"

"First of all, there's the money. It's top dollar. They're offering one hundred fifty dollars a week, which is twenty-five more than anybody else. Secondly, it's a giant corpora-

127

tion with lots of room to move around in—up, up, and away! And my boss is very close to the powers that be. She's the executive assistant to the mysterious Ikehorn himself. Anyway, when she interviewed me, I liked her and she liked me. I could tell—sometimes you have to go on your instincts."

"Well, don't say I didn't warn you," Jessica said, drooping lugubriously.

During the first few weeks of Billy's new job, the vast office next to Mrs. Force's was empty. The Ikehorn Enterprises New York headquarters occupied three floors of the Pan Am Building and from the president's office, thirty-nine floors above the street, all of Park Avenue unrolled into the dim distance of Harlem. Ellis Ikehorn was on a world tour of his various subsidiaries. His corporation, which Billy was only beginning to understand, reached into a circle of overlapping areas: land, industry, lumber, insurance, transportation, magazines, and building and loan companies. Linda Force talked to him several times every day by phone, sometimes for as long as an hour, and dictated a great quantity of letters to Billy after each conversation. Nevertheless, there was a feeling of a summertime lull in the offices in spite of the hundreds of employees moving busily about their tasks.

Billy was delighted when Mrs. Force asked her if she'd like to join her for lunch on a day when she didn't have to eat at her desk while she patiently waited for one of the daily transatlantic phone calls. She was curious about her superior, a rounded, graying woman in her early fifties, who displayed no quirks of personality or dress but whose calm strength was obvious the minute you met her. Mrs. Force was commanding, in a beautifully unassertive way, Billy had observed. She had the vast, complicated business of Ikehorn Enterprises at her fingertips; she was on good-natured first-name terms with the presidents of all the Ikehorn companies; her word, in the absence of Ellis Ikehorn himself, was as final as his own, and as unquestioned. Here, certainly, was a woman at the top of the ladder.

"I'm a Katie Gibbs girl myself," Linda Force told her after they ordered, smiling in memory. "Hell, wasn't it?"

"Sheer hell," Billy sighed, delighted to find her theories

of how to succeed in business validated. "But worth it, wouldn't you say?"

"Definitely. Of course one can't give them all the credit. There is just so much they can do."

"Yes," Billy breathed fervently.

Mrs. Force went on, musing. "When I think that all through college I couldn't take shorthand—a crime, really."

"What was your major in college?" Billy ventured.

"Prelaw at Barnard, with a heavy emphasis on business law, and I squeezed in some office management courses at CCNY during the summers," Mrs. Force answered, sipping her ice tea. "Then I had a year at Columbia Law School before the money ran out. I'd been studying accounting during the summers, fortunately, so I was able to become a CPA without wasting too much time. As a matter of fact, it was during that last year that I went to Katie Gibbs, as a backup position." She started on her chicken salad with gusto.

Billy was speechless. She had flunked algebra and geometry at Emery and was rocky on long division. Law —accounting—office management!

"Oh, it sounds a bit complicated now, but when you have to make a living—" Mrs. Force continued, looking encouragingly at Billy. "Why, twenty-five years ago I started just where you are today, as secretary to Mr. Ikehorn's secretary."

"But you're his executive assistant!" Billy protested.

"Oh, that—that's my title for—inspirational purposes I suppose. But in actual fact I'm just his secretary. Of course, I'm a super executive secretary, I don't deny that. And it's a marvelous job, but there is just no room in a business like this for a woman to go farther. After all, when you really think about it, what could I be? Plant manager? Board member? Chief counsel? I don't have the proper training and I don't have the ambition, frankly. Of course, without my law and accounting background I couldn't have come this far."

"Aren't you being very modest?" Billy said, without much hope.

"Nonsense, my dear, just realistic," Mrs. Force answered briskly. "By the way, Mr. Ikehorn's coming back on Monday and I'm putting on two other girls to help me besides you. When he's here the amount of work triples. You may not see much of him, but you'll know he's here."

"I'm sure I will," Billy said in a flat voice. So she was one of three secretaries to the secretary of the boss, and *trapped*. It would be fatal to her employment record if she didn't stick it out in her first job for at least one year, especially in such a prestigious company. Billy Winthrop, New York career girl, she thought ruefully. Well, at least it paid a living.

When Ellis Ikehorn entered his domain on Monday morning it was, Billy observed, something like Napoleon making a triumphant return from a successful campaign. The population of the office did all but stand up and give three cheers; he was followed by a procession of field marshals carrying heavy briefcases filled, unquestionably, with booty, and the big corner office immediately took on the qualities of a command post. Billy imagined, dourly that she could almost hear the sound of trumpets.

She was briefly introduced to Ellis Ikehorn by Mrs. Force as he left the building for lunch, and as she rose to greet him, she had the impression of meeting a westerner, not a New Yorker, a tall, deeply tanned man with thick, white hair worn in a crew cut, who looked a little like an American Indian because of his hooded eyes, his hawk nose, and the deep lines that ran to his wide, taut mouth.

Later that day, between letters, Ellis Ikehorn casually asked Mrs. Force, "Who's the new girl?"

"Wilhelmina Hunnenwell Winthrop. Katie Gibbs."

"Winthrop? What kind of Winthrop?"

"The Boston, Plymouth Rock, Massachusetts Bay Colony kind. Her father is Dr. Josiah Winthrop."

"Jesus. What's a girl like that doing in your typing pool, Lindy? Her father's one of the top men in antibiotic research in the country. Don't we fund the research he does? I'm sure we do."

"Among many others, yes. His daughter's here for the reason the rest of us are. She has to earn a living. No family money she told me, and you ought to know that even if her father has a research chair he can't make more than twenty, maybe twenty-two thousand a year.

That money you give goes for equipment and lab costs, not salaries."

Ikehorn looked at her quizzically. She was earning thirty-five thousand a year with some stock options and worth every penny of it. Leave it to Lindy to know everyone's salary.

"Did you make my appointment with the doctor?"

"Tomorrow morning at seven-thirty. He wasn't too happy about the hour."

"Tough."

"Ellis, you're a fucking medical miracle," said Dr. Dan Dorman, the most eminent specialist in internal medicine east of Hong Kong.

"How so?"

"It's not often I get the chance to see a man close to sixty with the body of a forty-year-old and the brain of a two-year-old child."

"How so?"

"We've checked everything twice since you were in the other day. We did every lab test and X ray known to science, plus a few I invented as I went along. I gave you a going over that wouldn't have missed an enlarged pore. There is no reason whatsoever for you to feel lousy."

"Yup. But I do."

"I believe you. You haven't had a checkup in five years in spite of my requests. If you didn't feel lousy you wouldn't be here."

"So what's wrong? Think I'm senile?"

"I said the mind of a two-year-old because you treat yourself with a monumental lack of niceness—the 'terrible twos' they call them."

"Do they now?"

"At two a child has tantrums when he can't get what he wants; he's physically active every hour of the day, messing in everything he sees; he sleeps only when he falls down with exhaustion; he eats only when he's starving, and he drives everyone around him crazy."

"Anything else?"

"For several months of his life he doesn't have much fun because he's so busy butting his head against obstacles.

Fortunately for the human race, sometime around two and a half he starts to get more sense."

"Cut the preliminary crap, Dan. Spit it out."

"Ellis, you have to stop treating yourself this way. You're OK physically but mentally you're working on a heart attack."

"You mean cut down on work?"

"That's too obvious, Ellis. Don't play doctor with me. I caught your act years ago. How long since you've had a good time?"

"I always have a good time."

"Which is why you feel lousy, I guess. What about fun?"

"Fun? *Kids* have fun, Dan. Don't be an idiot. What are you going to tell me? Golf? Shit! Art collecting? Shit! Backgammon? Double shit! Politics, flying my own plane, deep-sea fishing, raising purebred horses, bird watching, becoming a patron of the ballet? Come off it, Doctor. I'm not too old to do anything the fuck I want to, but culture and sport aren't among my aspirations."

"How about pussy?"

"You shock me, Dan."

"Like hell I do. There are only two things you've ever enjoyed Ellis since I've had the honor of being your doctor: business and pussy. How much time do you give to pussy these days, Ellis?"

"Enough."

"How much exactly?"

"You sound exactly like a pimp. Since Doris died—I guess two, maybe three times a week when it's around. Less if it's not easily available. Maybe once a week, maybe not at all for a week or so—or two—when I'm really getting things done. I'd like to see how much time you'd have for pussy during an eighteen-hour day, Dan."

"You just proved me right. Ellis, you'd better start acting sensible. Get yourself a regular woman who doesn't give you heartburn. Begin to treat yourself like a human being. Be good to yourself for once in your life. You've got all the money in the world, but you don't have all the time in the world. It's a waste of breath to tell you to take it easy, but I can say *indulge yourself*."

"Indulge myself?"

"Look, Ellis, how the fuck do I know what you want? Maybe you'd like to buy the Taj Mahal and walk around polishing the marble. Maybe you want to get dead as fast as you can. So go around the world a dozen times and forget what a pair of boobs feels like. Who knows what you really want to do with the last part of your life? But whatever it is, you'd better start thinking about it."

"You've made your point, Dan. I'll give it some thought. The body of a forty-year-old man, you said?"

"That's just a medical opinion."

"Which is what I came to you for. Not the other stuff, you closet shrink. In just about six years I'll be eligible for Medicare and I'll get rid of you then. You talk too much." Both men got up and walked to the door of the doctor's consulting room, their arms affectionately over each other's shoulders. Dan Dorman was one of the few men in the world Ellis trusted completely.

Billy and Jessica had established a ritual: One night a week they had dinner together, come what may. Otherwise, they risked missing each other entirely for weeks at a time because of their complicated social lives.

"What's Ikehorn like, Billy?"

"I've only seen him for a few minutes at a time really—it's hard to be sure, but I think, I'm almost certain, that he used to be a ten."

"Used to be?"

"Jessie, the man's almost sixty. I mean, after all."

"Hmmmmm. Jewish, isn't he?"

"The *Wall Street Journal* thinks so. *Fortune* doesn't. The *Journal* also thinks he's worth about two hundred million dollars and *Fortune* thinks it's more like one hundred fifty million. Nobody really knows. He hasn't given an interview in twenty years, and he keeps six people busy full time in our P.R. department keeping his name out of the media, refusing requests to speak, that sort of thing."

"But what do you think?"

"He's a little like a non-Jewish Robert Oppenheimer."

"Ah-ha!"

"Or else like a Jewish Nelson Rockefeller, only taller."

"Gracious!"

"Maybe a non-Jewish Lew Wasserman."

"Goodness!"

"On the other hand—"

"Don't stop!"

"Quite a lot—don't laugh, Jessie!—like a Jewish Gary Cooper." Jessica stared at her, goggle-eyed. That was the best combination she could imagine if she lived to be a hundred.

"All in all, he's rather devastating. God, Jessie, you're hyperventilating! Pull yourself together, girl."

"Tell me everything you know. Where's he from? How did he get started? Tell!"

"I've been doing a little quiet research. All anyone knows is that he started in an old factory in Nebraska with a sick company. Where it came from or what he was doing in Nebraska is a mystery. He made the sick company well and bought another sick company. When that company got well he bought another—not as sick a one that time. Finally, it got to the point where the canning company bought the bottling company, which bought the trucking company, which bought the insurance company, and the insurance company bought the magazine company because it owned the lumber company that provided the paper for the printing presses, which he also bought. Or maybe it was vice versa. That's just the beginning. You know."

"I didn't really, but I do now. Thanks awfully."

"Well you *did* ask!"

Ellis Ikehorn, to his amusement, found himself actually considering Dan Dorman's advice. Every once in a while, in the middle of a conference or a phone call, one phrase of the many the doctor had used kept coming back to him, "the last part of your life." It wasn't one of the lines that Dan had laid special emphasis on, yet, more than anything else he had said, it illuminated reality. Ikehorn had never been interested in birthdays, but, at almost sixty, he reflected, they seem to start to mount up, whether they interest you or not. In principle he had nothing against the idea of indulging himself. He just didn't know where to start. His wife, Doris, dead ten years before, had learned to indulge herself as soon as he started making

134

real money, if you could call keeping forty rare Persian cats in fabulous luxury self-indulgence. Personally, Ikehorn had found it both messy and pathetic, a poor substitute for the children they didn't have. But she was happy and busy all day with their snit-fits and ailments and eventual lyings-in, which she insisted on managing herself, attended by two vets, "just in case." Ellis resolved to keep an eye out for opportunities to indulge himself. It was like finding a new company to buy: First you had to know what you were looking for and eventually it was bound to turn up.

In the middle of one night Billy was suddenly awakened by a bundle of Jessica landing on her bed, shaking her out of her sleep.

"Billy, Billy darling—it's happened. I've found a ten and he's the most heavenly man in the world and we're going to get married!"

"Who is he? When did you meet him? Oh, stop crying, Jessie, stop it right away and tell me everything."

"But you know all about it, Billy. It's David of course. Who else could possibly be so wonderful?"

"Jessie, David is Jewish."

"Well, of course he's Jewish—I don't sleep with any other men."

"But you said—"

"I was an idiot. I thought I could keep it all under control. Ha! But I didn't know David then. Oh, I'm so terribly happy, Billy, I just don't believe it."

"And how about Mumsie. How's she going to like it?"

"She won't feel nearly as bad about it as his mother will. Didn't I ever tell you that David's father is the senior partner of the second-biggest investment banking firm in New York? I didn't always pay attention to your advice about staying away from German Jews, thank heavens. My mother will bear up very well indeed and my father will be the most indecently relieved man in Rhode Island. After all, I'm twenty-four, Billy, and Pa has been harboring this idea that I've been leading a life of sin."

"He must have a dirty mind. A nice girl like you!" As Jessica shook her head happily over her suspicious parent,

Billy remembered something. "But how will you bring up your children? Jewish or Episcopalian?"

"That's the one thing I can't figure out. See, they'll know *everybody*, so how will they be able to get away with anything? Well, let them figure it out—by the time they're old enough there'll probably be another way."

"Oh, Jessie, what will I do without you?"

Ellis Ikehorn was waiting impatiently for Linda Force. She hadn't appeared for work that morning and they were late in leaving for Barbados where he was going to meet the heads of two of his Brazilian lumber companies. Damn it, it was after nine, and he had three phone calls stacked up already.

Billy knocked timidly on the door of his office. She had never been inside since his return. When he gave dictation, he gave it directly to Mrs. Force, who passed it on to the three girls in the office next to her own.

"Excuse me, Mr. Ikehorn, Mrs. Force just called in on my line because yours were all tied up. She says she thinks she's got the flu. She woke up this morning and feels too sick to even get out of bed. She said not to worry, her maid was there to take care of her, and she was terribly sorry to let you down."

"Jesus, I'll get Dorman to go over right away. The day Lindy can't get out of bed! She probably has double pneumonia. OK, get your hat and coat while I call Dorman. Don't forget your notebook. Do you have to call anyone to let them know you're leaving for Barbados?"

"What, go with you? Like this?"

"Naturally. You can buy what you need when we get to Barbados." The tall, tan man with the white crew cut turned impatiently to the telephone. "Oh, collar one of the other girls on your way out. She's got to stay at Lindy's desk and take messages. I'll call in as soon as we arrive. Come on, we're late."

"Yes, Mr. Ikehorn."

As they sped out to the airport where the Ikehorn Enterprises Learjet was waiting, Billy sat nervously next to her employer as he steadily dictated letter after letter. A warm spot was quickly developing in her heart for the late Katharine Gibbs.

Billy had never been south of Philadelphia before. When she stepped out of the air-conditioned plane into the humid, voluptuous, spicy air of Barbados she entered a new dimension of the senses. The touch of the stealthy wind was insinuating; the unfamiliar ripe smell of the earth was sweetly stimulating and taunting, giving Billy a sense of breathing things she understood at once but could never fully know. She was disoriented by the island itself, the swift drive on the wrong side of narrow, winding roads, bordered by pastel shantytowns and deep-green scrub, ending in the pillared, arched elegance of the old bricks of Shady Lane. Her suite opened directly onto the wide, tree-shaded beach. It seemed to her that she could see 180 degrees of horizon, with piles of yellow and violet clouds riding far away just above the lowering sun.

Mr. Ikehorn had told her that she had just enough time to buy everything she needed for a two-day stay from the arcades of shops in the hotel and, sticky in her wool suit, she hastily chose several simple silk shifts, sandals, underwear, a bikini, a nightgown, a bathrobe, and toilet articles from the drugstore. She charged them all to her room and hurried back in time to see the sun set in a frightening burst of beauty before night fell abruptly and millions of native insects instantly set up a nerve-racking combination of a chirp and a screech. She was relieved to find a message from Mr. Ikehorn under her door, which instructed her to order dinner from room service and go to bed early. They would start the meeting right after breakfast the next day. She was to be ready promptly at seven.

For the next two days, while Ikehorn and his two South American division heads met and talked for hours on end, she and a Brazilian secretary took rapid notes, put through phone calls, and, while the men had lunch together, managed to steal a few hasty swims in the warm, seductive water in which stinging corals lurked under the clean sand. Nina, the girl from Brazil, spoke excellent English, and she and Billy ate their meals together at a small table placed a good distance from the three men. They all dined on the great curve of outdoor terrace overlooking the sea, lit only by hundreds of candles. The hotel was more than half empty and would remain so until the Christmas season when it would be packed with families who had made their reservations at least a year in advance.

On the third morning the South Americans flew off at dawn, back to Buenos Aires, and Ikehorn alerted Billy to be ready to leave by noon. When the chief pilot called toward midmorning to inform them that the weather had changed and that hurricane warnings had been posted, they hardly needed telling. A sheet of rain, with no space visible between the drops, was already falling between their windows and the beach. The branches of the stunted trees that bore small poisonous fruit were dragging in the sand.

"You might as well take a break, Wilhelmina," Ellis Ikehorn finally said. "This is only going to let up when it lets up. It's the hurricane season all over the Caribbean this time of year—that's why the hotel's so empty. I thought we'd get off in time, but it's too late now."

"Actually, Mr. Ikehorn, it's Billy—what people call me, I mean. Nobody calls me Wilhelmina. That's just my name, but I don't use it. I didn't think I should mention it while Mr. Valdez and Mr. de Heiro were here."

"You should have thought of that sooner. You're Wilhelmina as far as I'm concerned. Or do you hate it?"

"No sir, not at all. It just sounds odd."

"Yup. Well, tell you what, call me Ellis. That's an odd name too."

Billy was silent. There had been no rules at Katie Gibbs about this. What would Jessie do? What would Madame de Vertdulac do? What would Aunt Cornelia do? Jessie, she thought, in the blink of an eye, would probably go so droopy that shed'd melt, the Cometsse would favor him with her most enigmatic smile, and Aunt Cornelia would call him Ellis, without further ado. Billy found herself combining all three reactions.

"Eliis, why can't we walk in the rain? Would it be dangerous or something?"

"Don't know. Let's go see. Got a raincoat? No, of course you don't. Never mind, put on your bathing suit."

Billy's idea of a walk in the rain was based on a drizzle on the Boston Common. This was like standing under a warm waterfall. They had to hold their heads down to avoid choking on the falling water, and they both ran,

138

instinctively, toward the ocean and plunged in, as if the sea would protect them from the rain. Three waiters, caught by the rain, huddled under the beach bar and snickered at the crazy tourists splashing around in the shallow water for a few blinding minutes before they gave up, raced back over the sticky sand, and disappeared into their respective rooms.

When they met for lunch Billy blurted, "My God, Ellis, I'm sorry. What a dumb idea! I almost drowned and your raincoat was soaked through."

"I haven't had so much fun in—too long a time. And you ruined your hair."

Billy's thick, long hair, which had been carefully bouffant and sprayed with lacquer in the early Jackie Kennedy style was now towel-dried and fell heavily to her shoulders. She wore a hot-pink shift and her skin was lightly tanned from her lunchtime swims. Never in her entire life had she been so beautiful and she knew it.

Ellis Ikehorn felt keenly the weight of the ironic distance he maintained between himself and other people. It seemed to be dissolving or fading away into the air of the air-conditioned indoor dining room where the hurricane still seemed to quiver. Dan, he reflected wryly, had told him to indulge himself, but even that pussy-fixated man wouldn't mean with a girl in her twenties, a Boston Winthrop, Dr. Josiah Winthrop's daughter.

As they chatted casually and pleasantly through a leisurely lunch, both Billy and Ellis Ikehorn drifted in and out of five distant states of mind, neither aware of the other's thoughts. On one level they were taking the basic inventory of any new acquaintance, asking and answering carefully superficial questions about each other's lives. On another level, as all people do without thinking about it, they were taking note of the other's physicality: details of skin texture, muscle tone, directness of gaze, movements of the lips over teeth, luster of hair, mannerisms, gestures, everything the greedy, constantly judging eye can register. On a third level they were each thinking of getting the other into bed. Not if. Just how and when. On a fourth level they were each thinking of all the excellent and compelling reasons why they would not, should not, must not seriously contemplate such a thing. And on the fifth level, the rock bottom, they were both filled with the clear and thrilling knowledge that no matter how many reasons there were against the idea, it was simply going to happen. Something had been set in motion as they ran together through that warm, heavy rain, a sensual connection had been born that years of knowing each other might never have brought about. They had skipped every one of the normal preliminaries, and as they ate their civilized lunch, the great man unbending to put his young secretary at her ease, the secretary displaying becoming poise and breeding, combined with the proper respect for the great man, they were both as much in rut as any male and female could be.

That condition, no matter how it is covered over by convention and prohibition, has rarely, if ever, failed to become evident. Words are not necessary. Humans still retain enough of their animal perceptions to feel when they want and are wanted.

After lunch Ikehorn suggested that Billy should get some rest while he made preliminary evaluations of his Brazilian meetings. The phone service was out and he had no more letters for her. Actually he was fighting for time. He needed to put some distance between himself and this woman. He was a man whose acquisitive instincts had formed his life from his earliest memories. His success was based as much on following his drive to acquire as on his business genius. He had honed down to the last percentage point a philosophy that dealt with just how much he really wanted anything in this world. To Ellis Ikehorn, certain things weren't worth more than a 58 percent investment of time plus a 45 percent investment of energy. Others were worth a 70 percent investment of time but only a 20 percent investment of energy. When he went after a new business it had to be one that, putting aside all purely financial considerations, caused him to be willing to give it 80 percent of both his available time and energy. Otherwise, he had proven to himself, the move was bound to be a wrong one, no matter how promising it appeared.

Wilhelmina Winthrop? He didn't know whether to feel like an old fool or a young fool, but he wanted her 100 percent. He couldn't remember when he'd last thought something was worth 100 percent. Certainly nothing after the first five, maybe ten million. He paced the sitting room of his suite, damning Dan Dorman, damning Lindy Force, damning the hurricane, happier than he'd been in dozens of years and without any idea of what to do next.

Billy sat in front of her dressing table brushing her hair. She had decided that she was going to have Ellis Ikehorn. Calculation did not enter into her decision; it came directly from her heart and her cunt. She wanted him, and no matter how almost unthinkable it was, she was going to get him and get him now, before anything happened to change the opportunity the weather had given her. The pupils of her eyes narrowed in concentration, her lips, without lipstick as always, were a deeper rose than usual and she bit them to keep them from trembling. Moving precisely, as if in a preordained pattern, she put on her transparent, white lawn bathrobe over her completely naked body and strode boldly, a huntress with bare feet, across the empty corridor to the door of his suite.

Before he opened to her knock he knew who it was. She stood silent, unsmiling, very tall. He drew her into the room, locked the door behind them, and took her in his arms without a word. They stood together for a time, not kissing, just pressing tightly against the firm length of the other's body like two people who meet after an absence too long to be interrupted by mere words. Then she led him by the hand into his bedroom in which the curtains had been drawn against the storm. Two bedside lamps were already glowing. Suddenly, they fell on the bed, ripping off the few clothes they wore, consumed with a lust that knew no barriers, no hesitancies, no pride, no age, no limits. Time out of mind.

The hurricane lasted two more days. From her room Billy fetched her handbag, her hairbrush, and her toothbrush. From time to time they got out of bed, ordered from room service, and peered out at the wind- and rain-battered beach, both dreading the moment when it would stop. As long as the cocoon of the hurricane enclosed them, there was no other world. They thought that they had pushed all memory of it out of their minds, but, always, it was there. Not once in the endless, intense flow of conversation did they refer to the future. On the third morning Billy awoke knowing that the sun must be shining outside. They could hear dozens of men raking the beach, several carpenters already at work, dogs barking as they chased each other in the sand.

Ellis signaled Billy not to pull open the curtains and picked up the phone to tell the operator not to put through any calls.

"How long can we play hurricane, my darling?" she asked wistfully.

"That's exactly what I've been meditating on since five this morning. I woke up then and saw that the rain had stopped. We're going to talk about it."

"Before breakfast?"

"Before anything or anyone from the outside world comes into this room. The minute that happens we'll stop thinking straight. The only thing that matters is what you and I decide. Now, *today,* we can make our own choice."

"Is that really possible?"

"It's one of the things that money can buy. I've never fully understood that before. We have the freedom to choose."

"What *do* you choose?" She hugged her knees with her elbows, intensely curious. Even in the midst of a business meeting she had never seen him so concentrated, so powerful.

"You. I choose you."

"But you have me, don't you know that yet? The sun won't change it. I don't melt."

"I'm not talking about an affair, Wilhelmina. I want to marry you. I want you for the rest of my life."

She nodded, stunned, incapable of speech, her whole being instantly assenting to an idea that had not consciously entered her mind until that second. Although they had spent the last two days in the perfect equality of nakedness and passion, in the back of her mind she had always discounted a future. Too much separated them, too many years, too much money. She had accepted the inequality of their positions because she had grown up trained to live with inequality. She had not dared to hope beyond the present because she had learned that hope was dangerous. She had given herself freely, without expectations, because she had wanted this man. Now she loved him.

"What does that mean? Yes or no?" Her nod could have meant either, he thought, as unhinged as a boy.

"Yes, yes, yes, yes yes!" She launched herself at him and pulled him down on the bed, pounding him with her fists to emphasize her point.

"Oh, my darling! My darling, darling! We're not leaving this island until we're married. I'm afraid you might change your mind. We'll keep it as secret as possible. We can stay here for our honeymoon—or forever if you like. I'll just have to make one call to poor Lindy. She'll know what to do."

"Do you mean I can't have a church wedding in a long, white dress with eight cousins for bridesmaids and Lindy to give you away?" she teased him. "It would be one of the events of the year in Boston—Aunt Cornelia would see to that."

"Boston! When this gets out it'll be in every paper in the country. 'Elderly Millionaire Marries Child Bride'—we'll have to be prepared for that. How old are you anyway, darling, twenty-six, seven?"

"What day is this?"

"November second. Why?"

"I'm twenty-one, as of yesterday," she said proudly.

"Oh Jesus," he groaned, burying his head in his hands. After a minute he began to laugh, unable to stop, gasping "Happy Birthday" at intervals, which only set him off once more. Finally Billy had to join in the laughter herself. He was such a sight, doubled up like that. She just didn't understand what was so terribly funny.

During the next seven years no public-relations department in the world could have kept Billy and Ellis Ikehorn from being in the public eye. To the millions of people who read about them and saw the frequent newspaper and magazine pictures of the magnificently dressed, aristocratic, young beauty and the lean, tall, white-haired man with the hawk nose, the Ikehorns seemed to be the essence of what being in the great world of wealth and power is all about. The thirty-eight-year difference in their ages and Billy's patrician, historic Boston back-

143

ground added a degree of rampant, romantic titillation that was missing in more evenly matched society couples.

Speculation never ceased on the question of whether Billy had married Ellis for his money. Obviously, knowing the circles they lived in, both of them realized that this deliciously vile question simply had to be somewhere in the minds of everyone they met and that most people would assume money had been the motivating force. But only two or three people knew how much Billy loved Ellis, how totally she depended on him.

But would she have married him if he had been poor? This was basically a meaningless speculation. Ellis was the man he was *because* he was immensely rich. Or perhaps he was immensely rich because he was the man he was. Without money he would have been someone else entirely. It was as futile an exercise as asking if Robert Redford would still be Robert Redford if he were ugly, or Woody Allen the same Woody Allen if he lacked a sense of humor.

Six months after their marriage in Barbados the Ikehorns went to Europe on what was the beginning of their many travels. Their first stop was Paris, to which Billy wanted to return in triumph, and triumph she did. A four-room suite at the Ritz, facing on the noble symmetry of the Place Vendôme, became their base for a month. Their rooms had great high ceilings, walls tinted in the most delicate "château" tones of blue and gray and green, superbly intricate moldings picked out in gold leaf, and the most comfortable beds on the Continent. Even Ellis Ikehorn, for all his anti-French bias, had to admit that it wasn't a bad place to stay.

Lilianne de Vertdulac had seen Billy off on the boat train back to the United States just about two years before. Now she gasped in surprise as she saw the changes that so little time had made in the girl. It was something, she thought, like seeing pictures of the young Farah Diba, that lovely, almost lanky, shy and unassuming student, soon after she had been transformed into the absolute and unquestioned consort of the emperor of Iran. The same face, the same body but an altogether different air, something touchingly new in the way she moved and looked at those about her, something unexpectedly splendid, tentatively imperial, yet wholly natural.

Now Billy, too, saw a side of the Comtesse emerge that was a complete novelty in her experience of that lady. Lilianne flirted with Ellis as if they were both no more than twenty-three, found nothing more endearing than his uneasy attempts to speak a few words of French, called him frequently and under almost any circumstances "my poor darling," and freely exhibited her command of Oxford-accented English. She accepted Billy as an adult woman, called her Wilhelmina the way Ellis did, and insisted on being called by her own first name, which Billy found, at first, strangely difficult to do.

Ellis escorted the two women to all the couture collections. They asked the concierge at the Ritz to arrange, by phone, for their invitation cards to each showing, as is the custom when tourists visit Paris, but their place in the showrooms was not a detail the concierge could guarantee. The same haughty directrices who had, only a few years earlier, granted the Comtesse seats during the fifth or sixth week of showings, and not necessarily good seats at that, took one look at Ellis, a great tanned chieftain in a Savile Row suit, barely bothered to register Billy and Lilianne with peripheral vision, and instantly led the three of them to the best seats in the house. A couture directrice can spot a rich and generous man almost before he comes through the door; some say she must be able to smell him at a hundred paces—blindfolded—in order to really merit her job.

They went first to Chanel, whose two-thousand-dollar suits were being worn like uniforms by every chic woman in Paris. It was a period during which women, lunching together at the Relais Plaza of the Plaza Athenée Hôtel, the most elegant "snack bar" in Paris, invariably devoted the first hour of their meal to deciding which of the other women in the room were wearing *"une vraie"* and which were wearing *"une fausse"* Chanel. Clever copyists were able to reproduce everything, even to the gold chain that weighed down the bottom of the jacket lining and made it hang perfectly, but something always gave *une fausse* away: a slightly less than authentic button, fringe on the pockets that was two millimeters too long or one millimeter too short, the right fabric in the wrong color.

At Chanel, Billy ordered six suits, still in part guided by Lilianne's advice. Ellis, to Billy's surprise, seemed to be making notes on the tiny pads they had been handed when they entered, using his old Parker fountain pen rather than the dinky little gold pencils that were passed to the others. As the three of them walked up the Rue Cambon, back to the Ritz for tea, he said, "Lilianne, your first fitting is ten days from today."

"My poor darling, you are quite mad," she answered.

"Nope. I ordered three suits for you, numbers five, fifteen, and twenty-five. You didn't expect me to sit through all that without having a little fun, did you?"

"It is totally out of the question," said Lilianne, deeply shocked. "I could not possibly let you. Never. Absolutely never. You are too kind, Ellis, but no, simply no."

Ellis smiled indulgently at the stunned Frenchwoman. "You have no choice. The directrice gave me her solemn assurances that she was going to be personally responsible for making sure that work will have been started on them this very minute."

"Impossible! I wasn't measured and they would never do anything without measurements."

"This is an exception. The directrice promised me that she could make an excellent guess. She's almost exactly your size. No, they're under orders to go ahead, no matter what. If you won't wear them, I'll have to give them to the directrice."

"This is ridiculous," Lilianne said, protesting wildly. "I told you at lunch that I've disliked that woman for years. Ellis, I accuse you of using blackmail."

"Yup. You can call it whatever you like, poor darling."

"Oh. Oh!" For once in her life the Comtesse couldn't find the right words, and the right words to a Frenchwoman come with the milk of maman. Ellis had picked exactly the suits she would have chosen for herself. She would do anything short of murder to own either number five, fifteen, or twenty-five. But all three!

"Look at it this way, Lilianne, either you do it my way or you're in big trouble with me. You don't want that, do you? I'm forcing you, poor darling, in my brutal American way, and you can't help yourself." Ellis tried to look as menacing as possible but only succeeded in looking delighted.

"Well, of course," the Comtesse said, more mildly, "I am totally helpless, after all, am I not? When you are fond of a crazy man, you cannot risk offending him."

"Good, that's settled," said Ellis.

"Ah, but wait. Tomorrow we go to Dior and there you must promise not to play those tricks on me."

"I won't order anything else without letting them take your measurements first," Ellis assured her. "But those suits at Chanel were all for the daytime, weren't they, Wilhelmina, my sweetheart?"

Billy smiled assent with tears of pride in her eyes. To be able to give to someone who had given her so much was a joy she had never known existed.

"So, Lilianne, you still have to get some things for evening, right Wilhelmina? Only makes sense."

"No, I will not go with you under those conditions."

"Oh, Lilianne, please," Billy pleaded. "Ellis is having such a good time. And I wouldn't enjoy it if you weren't there. I need your advice. You simply must come—please?"

"Well," the Comtesse relented, filled with bliss, "in that case I will accompany you, but Ellis may choose only one, only one number for me."

"Three," countered Ellis. "It's my lucky number."

"Two, and that is final."

"You've got a deal." Ellis stopped in the middle of the dazzling, long corridor lined with showcases displaying the best Paris has to offer that connects the back of the Ritz to the front. "Let's just shake on that, poor darling."

The press soon became particularly fascinated by Billy's wardrobe. The average rich woman doesn't come into her own, in fashion, until she has been married a number of years, if, indeed, she ever finds the style that suits her. But Billy had had that intensive apprenticeship with Lilianne de Vertdulac to educate her to the limitless potential of elegance, and now, with Ellis behind her, insisting that she dress as superbly as she had ever dreamed of, as much to delight him as herself, she became one of the fashion world's chief customers.

Billy could carry any dress ever made. The carte blanche she received at the age of twenty-one might have made a laughingstock of a woman with less taste and less height, but Billy never overdressed. Lilianne's strict sense of perfection as well as her own innate eye kept her from excess. Nevertheless, when grandeur was called for, she went full out. At a state dinner at the White House she was the most resplendent figure there, only twenty-two years old, wearing pale lilac satin from Dior and emeralds that had once belonged to Empress Josephine. At twenty-three, when she and Ellis were photographed on horseback on their thirty-thousand-acre ranch in Brazil, Billy wore plain jodhpurs, boots, and an open-necked cotton shirt, but at the presentation of a new Yves Saint Laurent collection two weeks later, she wore the landmark suit from his previous collection, while Ellis, who was becoming an old Paris hand, whispered to her the numbers of the dresses he thought she should order in a way that made people with serious fashion backgrounds remember the black-tie spring collection at Jacques Fath in 1949, sixteen years earlier. At that presentation the late Aly Khan, sitting beside a young, glorious Rita Hayworth, had decreed, "The white for your rubies, the black for your diamonds, the pale green for your emeralds."

Billy, too, had a treasure of princely jewels, but her favorites always remained the peerless Kimberley Twins, the perfectly matched eleven-karat diamond earrings that Harry Winston had said were, among the finest gemstones he had ever sold. Heedless of convention, she wore them morning, noon, and night, and they never looked inappropriate. In her twenty-third year Billy spent more than three hundred thousand dollars on clothes, not counting furs and jewelry. A substantial part of the money was spent in New York because Billy, a perfect size eight in American designer clothes, wanted to avoid too many of the time-consuming fittings in Paris that kept her away from Ellis and their enjoyment of the city. That was the year she first appeared on the Best-Dressed List.

Soon after their return to New York the Ikehorns rented and redecorated an entire floor high in the tower of the

Sherry-Netherland Hotel on Fifth Avenue, which became their main address. From their windows they had a 360-degree view of the city: All of Central Park spilled like a green river at their feet. Ellis Ikehorn still dominated the vast holdings of which he held a voting majority of the stock, and they were often in Manhattan. Since Ikehorn Enterprises was a publicly-owned company, his board of directors and executive officers had been consistently and brilliantly chosen by him to carry on after his death. All of them owned enough stock to guarantee their loyalty. Now, increasingly, he found that he was able to spend his time with Billy in far-off places. When Billy was twenty-four they bought a villa at Cap-Ferrat with legendary gardens and grassy terraces that descended toward the Mediterranean like a vast Matisse; they maintained a permanent suite of six rooms at Claridge's for their frequent trips to London, where Billy collected Georgian and Queen Anne silver whenever Ellis had to spend part of the day in business meetings. They bought a hideaway house on a hidden cove in Barbados, to which they often flew for a weekend; they traveled widely in the Orient; but of all their homes, they both preferred the Victorian manor house in Napa Valley, where they could watch the grapes for their Château Silverado wines being tended in a countryside as pastoral, as comforting to the spirit as that of Provence.

Whenever Billy and Ellis were in New York, Aunt Cornelia, who had been widowed shortly after Billy's marriage, came to spend a week or two with them. A deep friendship had sprung up between Cornelia and Ellis, and he was almost as bereft as Billy when Cornelia died suddenly some three years after their marriage. Cornelia, to whom bad health was something one simply didn't do, had a first and fatal heart attack, dying, as she would have wanted to, without fuss, in a brisk and well-organized fashion, without even waking the servants. Billy had resisted going back to Boston during her marriage because the city held such painful memories for her, but now, of course, she and Ellis traveled there for Cornelia's funeral.

They stayed at the venerable Ritz-Carlton, a dowdy relation of the parade of other Ritzes they knew so well, the Lisbon Ritz, the Madrid Ritz, and, still best of all, the

Paris Ritz. Nevertheless, the hotel beat with the heart of a Ritz in spite of its muted Boston flavor.

Before setting off for the church in Chestnut Hill where the services were to take place and where Cornelia was to be buried next to Uncle George, Billy looked one last time at herself in the mirror. She was wearing a sober Givenchy dress and coat in black wool with a black hat that she had telephoned Adolfo to send over to her as soon as she heard the news of Cornelia's death from her cousin Liza. Ellis watched as she removed the diamonds from her ears and slipped them into her handbag.

"No earrings, Wilhelmina?" he asked.

"It's Boston, Ellis. I just think they look wrong."

"Cornelia always said you were the only woman she'd ever known who could look natural wearing them in the bathtub. Seems a shame."

"I'd forgotten, darling, so she did. And why am I worrying about Boston anyway? Poor Aunt Cornelia. She spent so many years trying to make this ugly duckling into a swan—you're right, I should do her proud. She'd like that." Billy put the earrings back on, and as they flashed the winter sunlight back into the mirror in a most unfuneral splash of brilliance, she said softly, "Supremely vulgar for church, especially in the country. I wonder if anyone will have the gall to tell me that?"

If anyone even thought it at the Bostonian version of a wake that followed the burial, in the drawing room of a great house in Wellesley Farms, which belonged to one of Aunt Cornelia's sisters, it was never mentioned aloud. As always, after a funeral, everyone drinks either a lot or at least a little more than usual, and the subdued exchange of greetings of the first half hour was soon followed by a surprisingly hearty hubbub of talk. Soon Billy realized that she and Ellis were the center of a group of her relations who seemed sincerely and openly delighted to renew old acquaintance with her, some of them even claiming a closeness that had never existed. She had been braced for remarks like, "Just what kind of name *is* Ikehorn, Billy? I've never heard anything like it before. Where on earth was he born, my dear? What did you say his mother's maiden name was?" But these remarks never came.

"I don't quite understand, Ellis," she said when they

finally returned to the hotel. "Somehow I imagined they'd all be just polite to me but standoffish toward you. But there were the uncles treating you as if you'd been born here, and my aunts and cousins were all over me. Even my father, who hasn't spoken to anyone but a microbe for years, was talking to you with what I can only call animation. I've certainly never seen him like that in my life. If they weren't Boston and I didn't know them too well, I'd think they were impressed by your money."

No, thought Ellis to himself, they aren't impressed by money unless it's money that has been given in the name of Ellis and Wilhelmina Winthrop Ikehorn to their hospitals and research centers and universities and museums. He was deeply glad that he had quietly contributed so much money to Boston's varied philanthropic institutions since he had married Billy, in the certain expectation that someday she would return to that city.

His protectiveness of his wife was complete and extended to every detail of their life together. As the years went by she lived entirely within this magic circle, forgetting more and more of even the most minor problems of ordinary life, becoming so accustomed to having her every desire fulfilled that she grew gently yet totally autocratic without either of them realizing it. With a limousine and chauffeur at her disposal twenty-four hours a day, it quickly became unimaginable that she had ever owned an umbrella. Wet feet became as remote a possibility as bed linens that weren't changed every day. A room that wasn't filled with fresh flowers was as foreign to Billy as the idea of running her own tub. When the Ikehorns traveled to any of their homes, they took their chef, Billy's personal maid, and their housekeeper to supplement the permanent staff already in residence. The chef, who knew their tastes in food perfectly, presented the menus for each day for Billy's approval, and her maid was also a trained masseuse and hairdresser. She grew spoiled in a way only a few hundred women in the world could begin to understand. This particular kind of spoiling, no matter how graciously accepted, has a subtle way of changing a woman's character, giving her a thirst for control that becomes as natural as a thirst for water.

No one who read about the Ikehorns in the newspapers

or the magazines, which carried so many stories about their life, understood that while Billy and Ellis *seemed* to be part of the world of society and privilege, they nevertheless always held themselves just to one side of it, never truly joining in. They were encapsulated in a world of their own, which made close relationships with other people not just unnecessary but impossible. They never identified themselves, as a couple, with any particular crowd or set or clique or pack or group. Jessica Thorpe Strauss and her husband were their only close friends, no matter how much they entertained or were entertained. When they had to spend time with Ellis's business associates and their wives, Billy felt abruptly out of synchronization with the world. Why was she sitting at a table with men in their sixties and their grandmotherly wives while around them dined tables of young people, people her own age? Mustn't she look like someone's daughter or granddaughter, brought along because she didn't have a date for the evening? Yet, as soon as she and Ellis were alone, they seemed to be the same ageless age, two loners who traveled together as a tight team. When Billy was twenty-seven, it was with a particular pang of fear that she realized, on Ellis's birthday, that he was now eligible for Medicare.

In the world of that band of New Yorkers or Parisians or Londoners who are photographed at the Prix Diane, at Marbella, at Ascot, or at Broadway opening-night parties, Billy felt much more at home. There were many young women of her age sprinkled in among the middle-aged women of the world. At a certain level of society, heiresses are treated with the same attention as women of accomplishment, just as a Princess Caroline of Monaco or a Princess Yasmin Khan took their places while still in their teens at great events. There, in this press of fame and luxury, Billy Ikehorn and Ellis Ikehorn were a fascinating and enigmatic couple because they never allowed themselves to be labeled and classified and, in a certain sense, owned by those who choreograph that particular social whirl. They were amused and diverted by the passing spectacle, but neither of them took it seriously. It was as if they had made an unspoken pact, on the day they decided to get married, that none of the conventions of ambition and social position were going to reach them.

In December 1970, when he was sixty-six and Billy was just barely twenty-eight, Ellis Ikehorn had his first stroke, a minor one. For ten days he seemed to be making a rapid recovery, but a second, far more serious stroke removed those hopes forever.

"His brain is active, just exactly how active we can't tell," Dan Dorman told Billy. "It's his left lobe that has been affected. That's most unfortunate because the speech center is located in the left lobe of the brain. He's lost his ability to speak as well as the use of his entire right side." He looked at her sitting rigidly in front of him, her powerful throat bare and white, and he felt as if he were running a knife across that taut skin. He knew he had to tell her just how bad it might get, now, while she was still in shock.

"He'll be able to communicate with you with his left hand, Billy, but I can't predict how much effort he will be able to expend. Right now I'm keeping him in bed, but in a few weeks, if nothing else happens, he'll be able to sit in a wheelchair in relative comfort. I've ordered three male nurses, around the clock. They'll be necessary as far in the future as he lives. We've already started physical therapy to keep the muscles of Ellis's left side functioning."

Billy gave him a mute nod, her hands bending and unbending a paper clip she couldn't seem to put down. "Billy, one of my chief worries is that Ellis will become terribly restless, claustrophobic, if you stay here in New York. Once he's able to get about in a wheelchair you should live in a place where he can sit outside, be moved around, feel in touch with nature, see things grow."

Billy thought of the old men she had passed on the streets of New York being wheeled to Central Park by an attendant, their frail knees covered by a thick blanket, dressed in expensive topcoats, muffled in cashmere, eyes blank.

"Where should we go?" she asked softly.

"San Diego probably has the best climate of any city in the United States," Dan answered, "but you might get bored to death there. You can't fall into the trap of thinking that you're going to sit by Ellis's side every minute of every day for the rest of his life. He would hate that far more than you would. Are you listening to me, Billy? It would be the height of cruelty, and he wouldn't be able to tell you how he felt."

Billy nodded. She had heard what he said and she knew he was right, but it didn't seem important. "I understand, Dan."

"I think you'd better move to Los Angeles. You'll know lots of people there. But you'll have to live above the smog belt. Ellis can't take smog in his condition because only one lung is really working. Find a house high up in Bel Air and I'll be out at least once a month. The medical men there are superb. I'll refer you to the best. Of course I'll make the trip out with you to get him settled."

Dr. Dorman couldn't bear to look at Billy, sitting as straight and still as a queen, as lost as a child. It would have been far better for both of them if Ellis had died. He had been afraid of something like this since the day he learned of their marriage. He assumed that Ellis must have had his fears too. It would explain the scale on which they lived, one that Dan Dorman knew had never been the style of his old friend, and the uncharacteristic way Ellis had thrown himself into a world he had ignored in the past, as if he were living to give Billy a splendid time while he could.

"Are you sure that we can't live at the house at Silverado, Dan? Ellis would like that so much more than a strange place."

"No, I don't advise it. Go there for the vintage, by all means, but you should be near a major medical center as much of the time as possible."

"I'll send Lindy out to buy a house tomorrow. She could probably get it ready for us as soon as Ellis can be moved."

"I think you can plan on packing up by mid-January," Dorman said, rising to leave. As Billy went with him to the door she could hear the pain in his voice, which he tried to keep so matter-of-fact. He had really known Ellis as well as anyone in the world except herself. Yet, in his professional capacity he was supposed to remain unemotional, dealing only with the facts, a support, not a griever. She felt she had to offer him some comfort, although the situation held none at all. She put her hands on his shoulders after he put on his coat and looked down at him with a faint smile, the first smile since Ellis had had his second stroke.

"Know what I'm going to do tomorrow, Dan? I'm going out to buy some new clothes. I've got absolutely nothing to wear for California."

Among her collection of sentimental souvenirs Valentine loved one best. It was not even a family photograph, merely a yellowing newspaper picture, one of hundreds that had been taken on August 24, 1944, the day on which the Allied Armies liberated Paris. It showed grinning, waving American soldiers triumphantly driving up the Champs-Elysées in their tanks. Almost delirious Frenchwomen had hoisted themselves aboard the war machines bringing bouquets of flowers and indiscriminate kisses for the jubilant, long-awaited victors. One of those soldiers, not in the particular picture she cherished, but somewhere in that glorious, legendary parade, was her father, Kevin O'Neill, and one of those rejoicing, tearful women was her mother, Hélène Maillot. Somehow in the wild carnival of that day they had managed to stay together long enough for the redheaded tank commander to write down the name and address of the little midinette with big green eyes. His tank corps was stationed outside of Vincennes, and before it was ordered back to the United States, at the end of the war in Europe, he had taken a French bride.

Kevin O'Neill sent for Hélène as soon as he could, and they lived in a walk-up apartment on Third Avenue in New York City where the witty, tempestuous Irishman, brought up in a Boston orphanage, was fast learning all the skills of a master printer. Until Valentine was born in 1951 her mother worked for Hattic Carnegie. Although she was much younger than many of the other highly skilled dressmakers in that illustrious couture house, her Paris-trained workmanship was impeccable. Within three years she had become a fitter, specializing in the fabrics that are most difficult to handle, chiffon, crepe de Chine, and silk velvet.

After Valentine was born, Hélène O'Neill left her job and settled happily into domesticity, vastly indulging her other great talent, cooking. To Valentine, even before the little girl was old enough to understand a word of any language, she always spoke French. When Kevin was home they all talked English, and what a jolly, disputatious, loving noise they made, thought Valentine. She didn't have too many specific memories of those early years, but she still felt, and would feel throughout her life, the warmth and gaiety and optimism in which the small family was enclosed, as if they lived on a tiny, safe island of grace and happiness. The music of those days included the songs of France: Charles Trénet, Jean Sablon, Maurice Chevalier, Jacqueline François, Yves Montand, Edith Piaf. The only way in which her mother betrayed her occasional moments of homesickness was in these records and in the words of the song she so often sang, which began, *"J'ai deux amours, mon pays et Paris . . ."*

In 1957, when Valentine was six, the summer before she was to start first grade, Kevin O'Neill died, in a matter of days, of viral pneumonia. Within a week his widow decided to return to live in Paris. Hélène O'Neill had to earn a living, and Valentine needed a family to love, now that they were only two. All the big Maillot family lived on the outskirts of Versailles but if Hélène and Valentine stayed in New York they would be alone.

Jobs above the rank of simple seamstress in the haute couture are either almost impossible to find or instantly available because of a fluke. In the Paris of the late fifties the women who worked in the great design houses were almost as devoted to their jobs as if they had taken vows. The head fitters, in particular, who had the responsibility of an entire atelier, composed of from thirty to fifty workers, lived for the glory of their firm. It sometimes seemed that they had no life outside the feverish, controlled hysteria of their particular *maison de couture,* and often they grew old in its service, where their abilities were appreciated and their idiosyncrasies became the stuff of tradition.

In the early fall of 1957, at the worst possible time of the year, just after the presentation of the fall collection, the incredible happened: A chief fitter and a pillar of dependability at the house of Pierre Balmain eloped. Her persistent suitor, a lusty, middle-aged restaurant owner of Marseilles, had told her that after four years of spring collections and fall collections being used as an excuse for delaying their marriage, it was now or never. The fitter, who was almost forty, looked at herself in the mirror and knew that he was right. Intelligently, she decamped without telling anyone in advance. The next day, when the extent of her crime was discovered, the wrath of the entire house of Balmain almost set number 44 Rue François Premier on fire.

On the afternoon of that same day Hélène O'Neill applied for a job at Balmain's. Normally she would not have stood a chance of starting as anything more important than a first or second "hand," the level of a highly skilled seamstress, but Balmain, facing a deluge of orders for the most remunerative season of the year, had no choice but to hire her immediately as a fitter. By the evening of the first day, the stocky *Savoyard* knew how fortunate he had been. Hélène's slender hands handled chiffon with the authority and patience that the fabric demands. The test of battle came when she had had to fit a dress on Madame Marlene Dietrich, Dietrich who knows as much about how a dress should be made as anyone in the world and is twice as difficult and demanding than it seems anyone in the world could possibly be. Everyone at Balmain's breathed a collective sigh of disbelief mixed with relief when the fitting went off without a word. When Dietrich said nothing, it meant that the work was perfect. Madame O'Neill's reputation as a wonder worker was made—her place secure.

A fitter's hours are long. In a house like Balmain, which dresses not only rich women of the world but also busy actresses, there are many fitting appointments scheduled for early morning and late afternoon. If just one client arrives late, and there is always at least one such tardy lady every day, the tight work schedule becomes a nerve-racking race against the clock. A fitter is on her feet or on her knees all day, except during lunch, and by the time evening comes she is often close to physical and nervous collapse. Before a collection, she will often work until four or five in the morning, fitting the new models on girls who often faint with fatigue. In the fifties and sixties what the French couture was really all about was not the endless succession of "new" looks that the fashion press wrote about so breathlessly but the *fit* of the dress or suit or coat. Without good fitters, any dress house, designer's inspiration or no, would have been bankrupt within a year. (These days, with only three thousand women in the world regularly buying all their clothes from the Paris couture, the dress houses remain open in order to sell their ready-to-wear and their perfumes; haute couture is merely a loss leader, a loss leader which, nevertheless, makes the world brighter.)

Shortly after beginning to work at Balmain, Hélène O'Neill realized that she couldn't possibly live in the heart of her family at Versailles. If she added the burden of the journey back and forth each day, on that crowded little train, she could never maintain the stamina necessary for her difficult work. She found a tiny apartment for herself and Valentine in an old building in the network of streets within walking distance of Balmain and arranged for her daughter to begin school nearby. On Sundays and holidays the two of them visited one or another of Hélène's brothers or sisters who lived as close to each other as possible and vied with each other in spoiling their widowed sister and fatherless niece.

Most French schoolchildren go home for lunch. Valentine's home became the house of Balmain. By the age of six and a half she was accustomed to walking inconspicuously through the employee's entrance and being greeted with a grave handshake from the guard. Gliding silently upstairs through the corridors deserted by the lunchtime exodus, she found her mother sitting expectantly in the corner of her atelier, one of the eleven at Balmain. There was always something hot, nourishing, and delicious in Hélène's covered basket for them to share. Many of the other workers also brought their lunches from home, and soon Valentine found herself adopted by forty women, many of whom were not on speaking terms with each other from one year to the next, but all of whom had a soft word for Madame Hélène's well-behaved, little half-orphaned daughter.

After school, Valentine refused to go home to an empty apartment. Instead, she took her heavy book bag and crept back into her own corner of the atelier, sometimes doing her homework with quick concentration and sometimes intently observing the busy, self-important comings and going of the room. She took great care to never get in anyone's way, and within a few months she was such a familiar figure, there in her corner, that the robust, often irreverent working-women spoke as freely to each other as if she hadn't been there at all. She heard wonderful tales of the clashes of temperament that took place in the fitting rooms, of the good and bad points of customers named Bardot and Loren and the Duchess of Windsor, of the fights to near death between one *première vendeuse* and another over the location of seats for the collections or the possession of a new customer, and of the antics and scenes of jealousy in the *cabine* where the mannequins dressed—gorgeous, dramatic girls with theatrically heavy eye make-up and names like Bronwen and Lina and Marìe Thérèse. But, for the most part, when Valentine had time to spare from her homework, she was fascinated not by gossip but by the work she saw going on so steadily: the way in which a dress, which she saw start out as several unpromising pieces of stiff white muslin cut into a pattern, would, over a number of weeks and at least one hundred fifty hours of hand labor and three or more fittings, be worked, stitch by stitch, into a chiffon ball gown destined for a Duchesse de La Rochefoucauld and priced, even in those days, at something between two and three thousand dollars.

It went without saying that the echelon of command at *chez* Balmain did not know that a child was being all but brought up in one of their workrooms. Pierre Balmain, for all his kindness, and Madame Ginette Spanier, the all powerful directrice, who ran the house from her desk at the top of the main stairs, would have taken a decidedly dim view of such a lapse. Several times, on the rare occasions when Madame Spanier, raven-haired, explosive, superbly exuberant, and quite irrepressible, burst into the atelier to successfully mediate an impending revolution, Valentine had always hidden behind a rack of finished ball gowns, which was placed just next to her little stool for exactly that purpose.

When Hélène's last fitting was finally over and her customer had departed into the Paris night in her waiting limousine—for, in those days, twenty to thirty thousand women flocked to Paris each season to outfit themselves completely in great custom clothes—the mother and daughter would walk home to their simple supper. After they had finished, Valentine always had more homework, but an evening rarely passed without her asking her mother about the happenings at Balmain. The details of workmanship fascinated her. She wanted to know the rationale behind each seam and buttonhole. Why did Monsieur Balmain always use an odd number of buttons, never an even number? Why did Madame Dietrich send one skirt lining back six times to have the seams changed? Wasn't it just a lining, after all, not the dress? Why were all the ateliers for tailoring completely separated from those for dressmaking? Why was one atelier in charge of the jacket and skirt of a suit, while another worked on the blouse and the scarf that belonged to that suit, since they were destined to be worn together? What was the vast, apparently unbridgeable difference between being able to cut wool and cut silk? Why did men fitters always work on anything that was tailored, and women fitters work the softer designs?

Most of her questions Hélène found easy to resolve, but the one question that interested Valentine the most was one she could not answer. "How does Monsieur Balmain get his ideas?" Finally she told the persistent child, "If I knew that, my little one, I would be Monsieur Balmain—or perhaps Mademoiselle Chanel or Madame Grès." And they would both giggle at the idea.

Valentine never stopped wondering. One day when she was thirteen she began drawing her own ideas for dresses and found the answer. The ideas just came—that was all. You imagined them and they came and you tried to draw them and if they didn't look right you tried to think why and then draw them over again, and again, and again.

But that wasn't enough, of course. You had to know if

the sketches you drew would work on a human body. She, Valentine, could sew beautifully. She had been learning from her mother for eight years. But just knowing how to sew could lead, at best, only to a job like her mother's, which seemed to get more exhausting every year. Or perhaps to becoming a little neighborhood "couturière" who stole ideas from the great collections and reproduced them as best she could for her middle-class clients. Even then Valentine knew that such a future wasn't good enough.

Valentine had never been just another French schoolgirl. When she arrived in Paris at the age of six she was a boisterous, red-haired American kid ready to fit easily into first grade—in New York. Overnight she had had to turn into a French schoolchild, one of the legion of overburdened, well-behaved, pale, little creatures whose youthful lives are expected to be devoted to learning. Even the smallest French village schoolhouse gives its children an education that puts any American public school to shame. She made the transition well, and by the time Valentine was ten she was studying Latin as well as making her first acquaintance with Molière and Corneille, perfecting her exquisite penmanship, and spending long hours with the terrible labyrinth of French grammar, which can be learned only by years of endless repetition and analysis.

She had become an arresting-looking young girl. Her features, pointed, delicate, and full of quick intelligence, were classically Gallic. Yet her coloring, the furiously red hair, the brilliant, naughty, light green eyes, the three freckles on her nose, the splendidly white skin, all were classically Celtic. Even in the uniform of the French public-school girl—a drab pinafore, always just a little too short, worn over a long- or short-sleeved blouse, according to the season—she managed to stand out from the crowd of others. Perhaps it was the particular way she had of tying back, with bright plaid ribbons, her thick braids from which curls nevertheless escaped. Perhaps it was her vitality, which couldn't be contained within the strictly required limits of schoolgirl docility. Valentine was always a creature of extremes. She led her class in English and drawing. She was last in math, and as for deportment, it was best not spoken of.

By the time she was a teen-ager, Valentine was the only

girl in school who collected Beach Boys records; all the others adored Johnny Halliday. With a sense of dedication she went to American movies every Saturday afternoon, preferring to go alone so that no one could distract her. Although she thought in French, she never allowed her English to be forgotten or even grow rusty, as usually happens with so many languages spoken fluently in childhood. She always remembered that she was half American, but she never talked about it, even with her mother. Her dual citizenship was like a magic talisman to Valentine. Too precious—and too remote—to be exposed.

As Valentine approached the age of sixteen she decided that there was no point in continuing her education. After sixteen she could legally leave school and take a job. What good was there in being able to repeat by heart vast amounts of the literature and poetry of France, to say nothing of more mathematics, for someone who was destined to become a designer? For she was going to be a designer, although she was the only one who knew it.

Even if there had been a Parsons School of Design or a Fashion Institute of Technology in Paris, as there are in the United States, at that time Valentine would not have had the money to pay for years of schooling. The only route for her was to become an apprentice. An apprentice is not supposed to be creative. Even the great fitters and cutters of the couture are not supposed to be creative— creativity is left to the master couturier, each one of whom has learned his métier working for other couture houses, often beginning as a sketch artist. Even Chanel lacked technical knowledge when she started, set up in a hat shop by her lover of the period. It is rare when a designer can actually cut and sew, as can Monsieur Balmain and Madame Grès.

But very few great designers, if any, started in as lowly a position as did Valentine. In 1967 she became a midinette, one of the slaves of the couture. Her mother's position was responsible for her getting the job, but from then on she was on her own. A midinette can ruin a yard of brocade worth two hundred dollars and that is the last of her. A midinette can take too long to finish basting hemlines and that is the last of her. Every dress in the collection is priced to include the cost of every last stitch, every last hook and eye, every inch of trim, each button, right down to the number of pieces of tissue needed to pack it in the big, white Balmain box. One careless midinette can cost the house its profit on a dress or suit.

For five years, from 1967 to 1972, Valentine progressed steadily, from midinette to second hand to first hand, making, in only a few years, a leap that usually takes twenty years if it is ever made at all. She had started far ahead of the others in technical skill, thanks to the intensive training her mother had given her on the sewing machine at home, and now she absorbed the side of the business that took place outside the atelier. After the first two years she was often needed in the fitting rooms, where princesses and movie stars and the wives of the richest men in South America stood in their lingerie for hours, sometimes with sweat pouring down their faces in the perfumed, airless atmosphere, sometimes in tears of rage and disappointment at the way their new clothes looked on them. Valentine learned to anticipate within seconds the moment at which a woman would try to blame the house of Balmain for the fact that she could not wear a garment with the same allure as could a mannequin who was four inches taller and weighed sixty pounds less than she. She also absorbed the techniques used to deal with this frequent occurrence, techniques developed over lifetimes of selling by the hardened, canny, cynical chief vendeuses. From the women who were fitted, often in pain from the discomfort of standing absolutely still for hours at a time in their beautiful, handmade, high-heeled shoes, she learned the power of vanity and the stubbornness of the determination to possess exactly the right dress, no matter what agony was involved. She learned more about women, especially rich women, than any girl her age should know.

Now Valentine was able to attend the rehearsals of the new collections, held for the staff only, where she could see the dresses she had worked on herself, and hundreds of other designs she had never seen before, pass by on the quick-stepping, nerve-sick mannequins. Now she could watch as Balmain and his assistants conferred over what pieces of jewelry, what gloves, which hat, and what fur scarf was needed to complete each ensemble to perfection. Valentine had been born with taste. Now, daily, it grew in the Balmain forcing garden. She found that she became able to divine accurately, from seeing the rehearsal of a collection, which dresses and suits would sell the most and which original designs would never be bought, not even when they ended up on the sale rack after that particular collection was completed. These dresses are picked over by women who wait like vultures for this occasion, buying dresses that have been worn every day for four or five months by the mannequins, all of whom sweat like race-horses crossing the finish line as they calculate whether or not they have intrigued a customer into ordering the dress they are showing, thereby earning themselves a tiny commission.

Valentine herself would never have deigned to buy something *en solde,* even if she could have afforded it. She made all her own clothes and very artful they were. It would not do for her to appear at work in anything but the traditional black skirt and sweater and white blouse, yet even these somber garments, designed to indicate the vast social gulf that separates the workers in the couture from the customers, looked special on Valentine, but not special enough for anyone to take much notice. She had cut her impossibly curly hair as short as possible and left the plaid ribbons in a drawer, so that now she looked almost like a sober, industrious working girl—if you happened never to glance above her neck or look her in the eye, and customers of the house, totally intent on their own reflections, rarely did.

In spite of her quick temper, it never caused Valentine any irritation that she was obliged to disguise herself like this. Even Madame Spanier herself, who was dressed entirely by Balmain, always wore a severe suit, either black or gray flannel, set off by her inevitable triple strands of pearls. The awed gossips of the atelier reported, however, that she possessed the most magnificent clothes for evening, which she wore when she and her husband went to every important first night in Paris with their closest friends, such stars as Noel Coward, Laurence Olivier, Danny Kaye, and the terrifying Madame Dietrich herself.

But on Sundays and holidays Valentine could dress as she pleased, in her own designs. From the age of fourteen she was her own mannequin, with her mother helping her with the fitting. After a day of pinning and repinning the clothes of perfect strangers, Hélène O'Neill gladly spent hours working on the creations of her extraordinary daughter. She did not, of course, tell Valentine that she was extraordinary. That was a mother's private opinion, perhaps prejudiced, for she did not want to be vainglorious, but this slim, quick, alert girl, with her father's sudden, unaccountable Irish moods and her mother's skillful hands and logical approach to life, was certainly not ordinary—Hélène O'Neill was positive of that, no matter if she were her own daughter.

Valentine was aware, from the day she started to design, that even if she could somehow bring her creations to the notice of Monsieur Balmain himself, it would have been a worthless exercise. Whatever he might have thought of her talent, her style did not fit into the prevailing tone of the house, which was rich clothes for rich women. Valentine did not design for multimillionaire wives in their early-to-late middle age who spent their time at charity balls or having lunch at the Ritz. She did not have the stately Begum Aga Khan or the altogether too stiffly dignified Princess Grace in mind when she sketched a dress. In her imagination she was designing for another kind of client entirely. But who, besides herself? She knew, as surely as she knew anything, that her clients existed. But where? And how would she find them? Never mind, she told herself with the vast optimism that lived side by side with her vast impatience, it would all come together—it was bound to. And she ran gaily across the Rue François Premier to La Belle Féfé, the red-awninged café that was almost an annex of the house of Balmain, to fetch a pot of strong tea for a buxom English countess who had just announced that she was about to faint dead away and the dress for her daughter's wedding not half fitted yet.

Hélène O'Neill kept getting thinner and thinner. Her hands worked fabric just as deftly as ever, but as she had to pin and re-pin more and more times before she was satisfied, the clients became restless. She had taught Valentine to cook as well as she did herself. Now, frequently she couldn't finish the dinner Valentine had made for her.

Sometimes, although not often, she uttered a little moan of pain when she thought she was alone. By the time Valentine persuaded her to see a doctor—"What do *they* know," she would say, sniffing in disdain—she had only a few months to live. Dead at forty-eight, of a swift spreading cancer, Hélène O'Neill was mourned by the entire staff of Balmain, all of whom came to her funeral in the old Versailles cemetery.

A week later Valentine went to the American Embassy on the Place de la Concorde with her birth certificate, which her mother had always carefully kept with her marriage documents and her husband's army papers. She had not discussed her decision to apply for an American passport with anyone, neither with her mother's sensible, unimaginative family nor with anyone at *chez* Balmain. Now, finding herself alone, she was operating on pure instinct, allowing the surge of direction-finding impulses that had always whispered to her in the past, to guide her wholly, completely.

She was not quite twenty-two, but she had five years of experience at Balmain's, she had been a first hand for a year, and she knew, without thinking about it twice, that she would be a first hand for another five years at least and then, certainly, a fitter if she stayed in Paris. And there her promotions would have to stop. Unless, of course, she got married and retired from the couture. But the idea of turning into a housewife more interested in the price of a kilo of beef than in the doings of the great world to which she had been insidiously exposed in the rarefied atmosphere of Paris couture—oh, no! She had always been bored by her nice, middle-class girl cousins, who admired her Sunday clothes so extravagantly but otherwise found little in common to talk to her about. Anyhow, the last time she had been in love was at the age of sixteen with the young Versailles curé who assisted at Sunday Mass, and even that deliciously impossible passion had lasted only six months. No—no—Paris was over for her, Valentine thought, weeping for her mother. She would pack up everything in the apartment and send it to New York. After she had given her month's notice and removed her own and her mother's life savings from the Crédit Lyonnais, she would follow her furniture and seek her fortune —in the United States. Was that not, after all, a very traditional thing to do?

New York City had changed during those fifteen years she had been away, and decidedly for the worse, Valentine thought, as she walked in discomfort on the streets bordering Third Avenue on which she had played as a child. Now she was barely able to push through the crowds of Saturday's Generation happily waiting in line to get into a movie theater, as if the act, or was it perhaps the art, of waiting in line was the main event, rather than the film. She had spent a week searching the dimly remembered streets for a cheap apartment, but Bloomingdale's, that fabulous flower of American culture, and the multiplying profusion of art movie houses had made the neighborhood so trendy that the rents were absurdly high.

Valentine had a nice sum of money from her savings and inheritance as a cushion to sustain her while she looked for work as a designer. If worst came to worst, she knew that with her technical skills she would be hired in a millisecond anywhere on Seventh Avenue, but she had no intention of sewing for a living ever again. That was not why she had left all the family she had in the world, her blood relatives and, far harder to leave, her loving Balmain collection of surrogate mothers and aunts, who made her last month there nothing but a succession of tearful scenes, which slowed up any number of fittings, much to the consternation of Monsieur Balmain himself. Things had reached such a pass—not just one but two Baronesses de Rothschild had actually been kept waiting—that the head of Valentine's atelier had tried to enlist the efforts of Madame Spanier herself to persuade Valentine not to leave France. But Madame la Directrice, that quintessence of the French businesswoman when matters of commerce were concerned, owned a thoroughly bold and British heart. She had been born and brought up in England, although her mother was of French birth, and this quintessential Parisian was 85 percent English by inclination, with the other 15 percent of her heart belonging to New York. When she took a good, long look at Valentine's lovely, vivid face and learned that she spoke perfect English, her own adventurous blood leaped in excitement at the challenge and the opportunity she saw for her. She couldn't think of anything more absolutely divine, more absolutely exciting, more absolutely thrilling than for Valentine to become a great, *great* success in New York, she informed the dumbfounded girl. She must not even dream of wasting her life in a workroom—hadn't she, Jenny Spanier, started by selling gifts in the basement of Fortnum and Mason's in London and quickly become the special saleslady to the Prince of Wales when he came in for his Christmas presents? Of course Valentine must go! And when she came back, she would come as a client—and they would make her a special price!

Remembering her inspiring interview with Madame Spanier, Valentine took fresh courage and decided to follow up a tip she had had from the room clerk at the inexpensive hotel at which she was staying while she looked for an apartment. There were old office buildings all over town, he had told her—not advertised though, it wasn't strictly legal or something—in which lofts were to be had. The floors were now too ancient to hold up heavy machinery, but the lofts could be made livable if she wasn't too choosy.

Valentine turned down four different lofts, each one more dilapidated and dubious than the other. The fifth loft she saw was on the top floor of a building in the Thirties. The janitor told her that three other lofts on the floor were inhabited, one by a couple who had night jobs, one by a quiet old man who had been writing a book for the last ten years, and one by a photographer. The two rooms she inspected did not seem to have holes in the floor, and something about it, perhaps the windows looking toward the Hudson, perhaps the two skylights, reminded her of Paris. Valentine rented it immediately. Was she always going to be nostalgic, she wondered. In Paris she had spent all her pocket money on American records and American movies. Now, in New York, she was attracted by a place that had a suggestion of Paris in its shape and light. Within two weeks she had all her furniture out of storage and arranged much as it had been in Paris. Her room lacked only a full larder to make her feel really at home, she decided, and she set out on a shopping binge that ended with the rescue of her two bottles of wine by Spider.

This Elliott, she reflected after he had left, his appetite having fully justified the supply of pâté and cheese she had bought, was easy to talk to, once she got over the shyness of entertaining a man, an American man at that, alone in her apartment for the first time in her life. Her French cousins had been introducing her to prospective boyfriends from the time she was sixteen, but none of them had even remotely resembled her vague idea of a man. She had turned up her freckled nose at even those good catches whose secure office jobs at Renault or any of the other factories that ringed Paris had allowed them to purchase their own little Simcas. Either they sounded like silly schoolboys to Valentine, who had always been too wise for her age, or else they seemed like premature grandfathers, so stuffy and boring and predictable that she could imagine them presiding over a table full of descendants before they even took a wife. Valentine didn't realize it, but her idea of what a man should be had been formed by the years of American films she had seen on Saturdays. She had gone to watch *Butch Cassidy and the Sundance Kid* no less than nine times, *Bullitt* six times, *Bonnie and Clyde* eight times. Her ideal man was an amorphous mixture of Redford, Beatty, Newman, and McQueen. Small wonder she hadn't found him in a middle-class Frenchman.

Compared with almost any American girl of her age, Valentine was sexually very unsophisticated. At twenty-one and seven-eighths, she was still a virgin. Her evenings had been filled with homework until she was sixteen. From sixteen on she had worked at the luxury equivalent of ditchdigging nine hours every day and spent her evenings with her mother, designing and sewing clothes. Her rare free times, spent alone at the cinema and with her family on Sundays at Versailles, did not lead to sexual adventure. Who could fail not to be a virgin under those circumstances, she asked herself indignantly. She had reluctantly allowed herself to be kissed by some, but only a few, of those uninteresting young men she had been introduced to. Her nature was straightforward and abrupt, and she'd never had the need nor, she thought, the inclination to learn how to flirt. She was not one of the women to whom it comes naturally. The only time Valentine had burned with passion, it had been for a priest who wasn't even the one who had heard her confession—that, at least, would have been an experience she thought ruefully. And everyone had the idea that French girls were so sexy, so racy, so "oo-la-la," as if they hadn't changed from the stereotypes of Mademoiselle from Armentières in World War I. " 'Hinky dinky parlez-vous' indeed!" she said haughtily to herself and turned to her treasured pile of the last three weeks' issues of *Women's Wear Daily*.

Valentine, who gravitated toward extremes, who combined, with occasionally dizzying results, Gallic logic with Celtic fancy, had, as it frequently happens, failed to understand herself. Her lack of sexual experience had nothing to do with her capacity for sensuality. That capacity had always been there, held in close restraint by the enormous demands made on her concentration and energy by the life she had led in Paris. However, her sensuality had found an outlet she wasn't aware of, in the one area of her daily life that was hers alone, her fashion designs. They had a quality that is usually expressed only by a woman herself—a quality called, in French, *du chien*. When a woman has du chien she has something that is not chic nor elegance nor even glamour, yet falls somewhere in the same category of descriptive terms. *Chic* is in the way a woman wears her clothes, not the clothes themselves. *Elegance* is in the line and quality of the clothes and the line of the body under them and in the wearer's personal intensity about the importance of perfect details. *Glamour*, a word that is so impossible to pin down that it doesn't exist in any language except English, is a combination of sophistication, mystery, magic, and movies. *Chien* is spicy, tart, amusing, pungent, tempting, and puts the male world on notice that this is no ordinary woman. Chic and elegance have nothing to do with sexiness, glamour has much to do with sexiness, chien has everything to do with sexiness. Catherine Deneuve has glamour, but Cher has chien. Jacqueline Bisset and Jacqueline Onassis both have glamour, but Susan Blakely, Brenda Vaccaro, Sara Miles, and Barbra Streisand all have chien. So did Becky Sharp and Scarlett O'Hara and so did Valentine O'Neill, both in her person and in her work. Chien is often only recognized by the effect it has on others, and Valentine's ignorance of her own quality was normal, considering how surrounded she had always been by females at school and at work. Chien is one of the aspects of a woman that must be reflected by men. Other women do not give her credit for it since it stirs no particular response in them.

Valentine had started buying *Women's Wear Daily* from the first day of her arrival in the United States. This newspaper of the fashion industry is completely indispensable to anyone connected in any creative or executive capacity with the enormously important business of selling things to wear. If you are a manufacturer of buttons in Indiana or a maker of tennis shoes in Japan or a fabric designer in Milan or a department-store buyer in Wisconsin or are in any significant way connected to the fourth largest industry in the United States, you are a fool if you do not read *Women's Wear Daily*. It is the most important daily trade newspaper in the world. In addition it has excellent critics of all the arts, fascinating Washington coverage, important inside glimpses of the film and theatrical world, and consistently revealing columnists. And, finally, it deals with design, with designers, and with the people who wear the prettiest clothes and go to the very best parties all over the world. A society woman who had to choose between *Women's Wear* and all the fashion magazines and society columnists put together would always pick the newspaper.

Valentine had been able to form an excellent idea of where to go to look for a job by simply absorbing information through *Women's Wear*, and on the Monday following her unexpected picnic with Spider, she set out, carefully dressed in her most successful and original dress and coat, perfectly accessorized, with her portfolio of sketches under her arm. She knew exactly what she wanted to be—a designer's assistant.

Any designer of the slightest importance must have an assistant to translate sketches into hard reality, to act as a go-between between the designer and the workroom, to provide a backboard on which to bounce off new ideas, sometimes to provide the ideas themselves. When Anne Klein died, her assistant, Donna Karan, until then unknown, became an overnight heroine as she produced a perfect "Anne Klein" collection. Now she has her own assistants and the business is bigger than ever.

From *Women's Wear* Valentine had compiled a long list of designers whose work she admired and she had located them through the phone book. The design center of the United States is located in just a few tall office buildings on Seventh Avenue. Just reading the list of tenants in the lobbies took Valentine's breath away, whatever breath she had left after pushing her way through the crowds on the street, the crowds in the lobbies, all of which were minor league compared with the crowds in the elevators. The heart of Seventh Avenue is a claustrophobe's nightmare, as busy as all the alleys of Hong Kong crammed together into several nondescript buildings entirely without charm.

Every wholesale showroom has a hard-eye receptionist who looks at a top editor from *Harper's Bazaar* with precisely the same suspicion with which she regards a Hasidic rabbi collecting for his temple. Valentine, however, had a knack for dealing with suspicious women: Any vendeuse in the French couture can double as a prison matron when dealing with those beneath her. Only sheer affrontery, Valentine knew, stood a chance.

"I am Valentine O'Neill," she announced precisely, with that air of quiet, taken-for-granted arrogance and the same slight, condescending smile she had observed on so many truly secure clients as they announced themselves at Balmain's. Valentine exaggerated her French accent. "I should like to see Monsieur Bill Blass."

"What about?"

"Please tell Monsieur Blass that Valentine O'Neill, the assistant of Monsieur Pierre Balmain, would like to see him."

"What about?"

"Business. I have just arrived from Paris and I don't have time to waste, so could you kindly ring Monsieur Blass for me."

Sometimes it didn't work; sometimes Valentine was told to come back later, but almost always there was enough authority in her manner and enough devastating luxury in her clothes, enough easy confidence in her posture, to get her into the office of the designer or, more frequently, that of his assistant. Her story of being a former Balmain assistant was not closely questioned. She looked the part so perfectly, in spite of her youth, that she usually got a chance to show her portfolio. Seventh Avenue designers don't like to overlook any possibilities of new blood. Once they were all hopeful beginners with portfolios themselves, and they know that in any portfolio there is always the chance of finding something good.

But 1972 was a very bad year to be looking for a job on Seventh Avenue with a portfolio full of original designs that leaped totally out of the ordinary. The garment industry had just emerged from the bloodbath of the midcalf length, and department store sales had never been worse as American women refused to buy new clothes, defiantly clinging to their old pants for a few more years. No one really knew what direction to go in, but anything that looked new and fresh had to be wrong.

"Elliott, I've been turned down cold by twenty-nine designers in three weeks. If you tell me not to get discouraged I'll throw this dead chicken at you."

Spider had fallen into the habit of going with Valentine on her Saturday marketing expeditions to the Italian street markets on Ninth Avenue. His excuse was that she couldn't possibly carry all the heaps of provisions she bought, but he also took a deep interest in seeing what she was planning to cook so that he would know what to look forward to. The model he was currently having an affair with kept only skin freshener in her refrigerator. On the nights when he didn't take his girl out to dinner, he clomped up the stairs to his apartment as noisily as possible. Valentine, who complained that it was not amusing to cook for one person, would wait until she heard his record of Ella and Louis singing "A Foggy Day in London Town" before she slipped a little scrap of paper under his door. *"Pot-au-feu"* it would say or *"Choucroute Alsacienne."* Elliott was the only person she knew in New York and she saw no reason to eat alone. It was only reasonable.

"It's not a question of getting discouraged," he answered her. "I think that you're simply going about things the wrong way. You want them to hire you on the basis of designs that scare them shitless. I think your stuff is incredibly exciting, but I'm not making clothes for a living and I don't have to worry about what women in Oshkosh are going to want to wear. You're ahead of your time and in the wrong country and you're too pigheaded to admit it. You can't ram your ideas down anyone's throat, I don't care how brilliant they are."

"So, what do you suggest I do?" She glared at him wrathfully, her eyes gripping his face. "If *I* don't get a job soon, *you* may starve to death."

"Low blow! You French bitch! How many times have I begged and begged you to let me pay for these things?" He hugged her, refusing to respond to her anger.

"Today, Elliott, you pay. For everything. And I have a long list."

"Giving in at last? Good. And since you're in a reasonable mood, how about another tiny concession?"

"Tell me what it is first—I don't trust you, Elliott."

"Make some new sketches. A whole new fucking portfolio. Throw out all your ideas of how women *should* dress in the best of all worlds and just walk around this city for a few days and look at what women are actually wearing, not the terribly rich women, not the poor women, but the in-between women, over eighteen and under sixty."

Valentine dropped three tomatoes back in a bin, bruising them unmercifully, and looked at him in horror.

"You mean *copy!* You mean base my designs on what women have on their backs already? What a disgusting, vulgar idea—it's vile, Elliott, I tell you, it's—"

"You really are such a dummy. How did you ever grow up?" Spider enjoyed indignant females. At least one of his sisters had always been indignant about something. "Now, listen. Just shut your mouth and listen. You go see what women are already wearing and then you make designs that are *better,* but not so *different* that they will have to rethink their whole approach to clothes. People really hate to change—I mean they loathe it!—but the whole fucking fashion industry is based on making 'em change, because if they don't change, they don't need new clothes. That's why you have to do it gently, so that they don't have to worry about whether something new is too oddball or too freaky or what would they wear it to—or with—or will it make them look too unlike from everyone else. Creep up on 'em—nobody loves a prophet."

Valentine was sullenly silent. She was torn between her entire conception of fashion as an individual expression of her creative spirit and her immediate understanding of the rightness of what that bastard Elliott was saying. She knew, from the reactions of all the designers she had seen, that she wouldn't get a job from the sketches she had shown. Even the kindest and most honestly impressed and encouraging of them had told her that her ideas were too different, too impractical. But how she hated to give in! How she hated to tailor her beliefs to mundane reality! For five minutes she concentrated on finding the perfect head of lettuce, while she raged within. Spider, reading her emotions on her face, felt sympathy, but determined not to give an inch.

"Bourgeois, conservative shit!" she flung at him. He laughed. That meant he'd convinced her. "What makes you think you know so damn much about women, Elliott? Look at you! You dress like a bum and you presume to tell me what goes on in a woman's mind, you slob in tennis shoes!" His confidence infuriated her, particularly since she knew he was right and she had been unforgivably blind not to figure it out all by herself.

"Modesty forbids—" Spider started to answer. She picked up a large bunch of grapes and advanced on him menacingly. He dropped the shopping bag he was carrying and picked her up, holding her easily off the street until their eyes were on a level.

"I know you want to express your gratitude, but I can't take those grapes, Valentine. Think of Cesar Chavez. But you may kiss me, if you like." He held her astonished gaze, thinking that her eyes had the color of fresh growing things.

"If you don't put me down, Elliott, I'll kick you in the balls!"

"Frenchwomen lack a sense of poetry," he said, still holding her close. He wondered if he should kiss her or not. He certainly felt terribly much like doing it, and normally Spider never wondered about such things. Any woman he felt like kissing, he kissed. But Valentine was such a prickly pear, such a funny, proud thing, and she was feeling humiliated now, he could tell. A kiss might seem condescending. He lowered her gently to the pavement, removing the grapes from her grasp. Besides, he informed himself, she was his neighbor and his friend, and he wanted to keep that relationship. He didn't want to fuck Valentine, because if he fucked her, sooner or later the romance was bound to end. Even if they stayed friendly later, as almost always happened with his girls, it wouldn't be the same kind of friendship as it was now.

"I forgive you," he told her, "for your lack of poetry, not to speak of your lack of romance, but only because you're such a good cook. What's for dinner?"

"I see through you, Elliott. A man like you can't even be insulted because all you think of is your stomach. Just for that, for dinner we have cold jellied calf's head." She started into the Italian butcher shop where skinned rabbits and veal heads hung hideously in the window.

"Aw, Valentine. Come on, that's not nice."

"You'll love it. It's time you got over some of your narrow-minded provincial American ways. You need to enlarge your horizon, Elliott."

"Valentine." He grasped her hand and stopped her dead. "I don't stand still for blackmail. What's for dinner?"

Startled, she stopped short and looked intensely at the littered pavement—orange peel, crushed red peppers, scraps of newspaper, bread crusts. What a typical American he was. No gastronomic imagination, taste buds half alive. Still—she felt a curiously warm swell of gratitude toward the big barbarian.

"I'm sorry if I have offended you, Elliott. I didn't realize you were so hungry. If *tête de veau* is too unfamiliar to you, we will have a simple *côte de porc* in the style of Normandy, cooked with Calvados and a heavy cream sauce, garnished with shallots and apples—it won't be too exotic for your taste, will it?" She knew this was his favorite of all her dishes.

"I accept your apology," Spider said with dignity. And gave her a tiny little goose, just enough to let her know who was who and what was what.

For the next two weeks Valentine haunted the city from downtown in Greenwich Village north to the Guggenheim Museum. She roamed the department stores, the better markets, the lobbies of large office buildings, and, of course, the streets, particularly Madison Avenue, Fifth Avenue, Third Avenue, and 57th and 79th streets on the East Side. On five evenings Spider took her on a round of middle-priced but popular places to eat and drink. She didn't bring her sketch pad, only her eyes and her memory. She wanted to immerse herself in a flood of pure impressions. Then she retired to her apartment for a week, alone with a terrible head cold, aching feet, and a mind reeling with ideas. After a week of almost constant work, Valentine emerged with a full portfolio. Spider flipped through the pages eagerly.

"Holy Mary Mother of God!"

"I didn't know you were Catholic."

"I'm not—just bowled over. It's an expression I save for really big events, like when the Rams win in overtime."

"Huh?"

"Never mind—I'll explain someday when I have six or seven hours with nothing else to do. Now you just get out and hustle lady—your work is so good I don't even know how to tell you."

The next day Valentine donned her persona of Monsieur Balmain's former assistant and got in to see the assistants of several designers she hadn't approached before. The first two assistants begged her to leave her porfolio so that they could look it over and perhaps, who knows, find a place for her. But she was wiser than that. At Balmain there existed a long list of people, including some American designers, who were never allowed in the door because their photographic memories could register an entire line in the course of a collection and reproduce it in detail before the first customer's order had been filled in Paris. In any case, these assistants she talked to, Valentine suspected, might steal her ideas and never even mention her to their bosses.

The third firm she tried was a very new one called simply Wilton Associates. The designer was out of town, but the receptionist, miraculously, was young and new at her job. She invited Valentine to wait and see Mr. Wilton himself. "He's not the designer, dearie, but he does all the hiring and firing—he's the man to see, whatever it's about."

Alan Wilton was an impressive man. He was as well tailored as Cary Grant and quite untraceable in his looks. Anywhere in the Mediterranean Basin he would look like a rich, well-traveled native. In Greece he would be taken for a minor shipowner, in Italy for a prosperous Florentine, in Israel for a Jew but never a sabra. However, in England he would instantly be seen to be some sort of foreigner. In New York he looked like the spirit of the city incarnate. He had dark brown eyes, as impenetrable as a wildcat's, olive skin, and beautifully tended, straight, black hair. He seemed to be about thirty-five, although he was actually eight years older, and his manners were superb. His deep voice gave no hint of his birthplace or his background.

As he sucked thoughtfully on a pipe he looked through Valentine's sketches with care, occasionally nodding his head.

"Why did you leave Balmain, Miss O'Neill?" He was the first person who had bothered to ask her that question. Valentine felt herself turning white, as she always did, when other people would have blushed.

"There was no future there."

"I see. And how old are you?"

"Twenty-six," she lied.

"Twenty-six and already Balmain's assistant. Hmm. I could call that a very promising situation at your age." She realized from the way he bit on his full lower lip that he had seen through her from the beginning.

"The question is, Mr. Wilton, not why I left Balmain but whether you like my designs." Valentine summoned all her Irish spunk and her most exaggerated French accent.

"They're sensational. Perfect for today's crazy market. Exactly what I need to start women buying again. The problem is that I already have a designer and he has an assistant with whom he has worked for years."

"That's—unfortunate."

"But not for you. Sergio's assistant will have to go. I don't run this business to make people happy, Miss O'Neill. I'm not just the moneyman—I make all the decisions around here. When can you start?"

"Tomorrow?"

"No—not a good idea. I'll have a bit of shuffling around to do first. Why don't we say next Monday morning? By the way, can you sew?"

"Naturally."

"Cut?"

"Of course."

"Make samples?"

"Obviously."

"Fit?"

"Certainly."

"Make patterns?"

"That's basic."

"Supervise a workroom?"

"If I had to."

"If you can do all these things you could make a great deal more than the hundred fifty a week I intend to pay you."

"I'm perfectly aware of that, Mr. Wilton. But I am not a sample hand or a patternmaker. I am a designer."

"I understand." He gazed directly at her, his thick eyebrows raised in quizzical, knowing amusement. Her technical experience was too thorough to have allowed her time to assist Balmain, whose assistants were, in any case, always men, not young girls.

Valentine gathered up her portfolio as quickly as she could without losing her dignity.

"I'll be here on Monday," she said, walking out of Wilton's large office with the businesslike air of someone quite accustomed to being hired. While she waited for the elevator, shaking with thanksgiving, she prayed that Mr. Wilton wouldn't come out of his office after her and ask her any more questions.

Nothing in Valentine's experience could have prepared her for Sergio, the designer for Wilton Associates. Her knowledge of the homosexual world as a whole had been largely confined to the last weeks she had spent making the rounds of wholesale firms. All she really knew about gay designers was that they were good at giving her the brush-off. At Balmain's the prevailing atmosphere was one of intense, simmering femininity. The middle-aged male cutters and fitters had as much sexual definition, one way or another, as tame gray tabbies. Her own family life included no contact with the homosexual side of Paris, although she knew it existed, of course.

When she met Sergio on Monday morning as she reported for work, she found not just another queen but rather a very royal, very grand, very petulant princess. He was young, with a beautifully molded chin and neck. His lips were pouting and provocative, and he had a classically voluptuous face and fairly long, glossy brown hair. He dressed in the height of Italian fashion, his pure silk body shirt unbuttoned to the navel, showing a great deal of his smooth tan chest, and his slim waist clasped by a heavy solid-gold link belt. His trousers might not have seemed too tight in a Spanish bullring, but on Seventh Avenue they made a definite statement.

Sergio, at that moment, was a very, very angry princess who had come back dreadfully bombed out from a much too brief vacation to find that his dependable workhorse of an assistant had been replaced by some little tricky numero Alan had put over on him in his absence. You could trust nobody in this business! A French twat. How was that for sneaky?

"Stop whimpering, Sergio. The girl has talent and you need her. If you're planning on stamping your teeny-weeny feet and having hysterics, do it someplace else." Alan Wilton looked at Sergio with scarcely concealed contempt.

"You'll regret this, Alan."

"Don't you dare threaten me, you little cunt. You know who's boss around here, don't you? Don't you? So, get those tight, little, fancy pair of buns of yours into the studio and start working. And if you're planning to pull any of your Miss Bitch ratshit with Valentine—I really and truly would *not*, if I were you."

Sergio left, slightly mollified by Alan's words. In some situations he had a weakness for—being told what to do. Alan could be such a tough son of a bitch. He'd be damned if he was going to work right away, not now, with his cock suddenly so stiff that he had to get off or come in his pants. Sergio took the fire stairs up two flights to a public men's room, which was known all over Seventh Avenue, along with several others. He looked quickly in both directions, made sure that no one he knew was in the corridor, and slipped inside. A dozen men were there, a few in low conversation, others roaming around nervously, some just standing and smoking, their eyes flicking from side to side. Sergio recognized an important menswear buyer, a Puerto Rican stock boy, the vice-president of a major department store, a blond male model, and a young wrapper for a dress manufacturer. He didn't greet any of them nor did they greet him. Sergio's heart beat hard as he fumbled in his pocket as if for a cigarette, making sure that the outline of his stiff prick was emphasized by his manipulation of the thin, tight fabric. One of the men, a stranger as conservatively dressed as a banker, came over to him immediately with an outheld lighter.

"How do you like it?" he asked Sergio.

"Up the ass."

"You've picked an awkward place for that."

"Yeah—you can't have everything—so, you want to suck?"

"How could you tell?" The stranger's lips were open with lust.

"ESP. Go in that cubicle, the third from the end—it's the right height."

The stranger obeyed immediately, locking himself in. Sergio sauntered over to the cubicle, the door of which was neatly punctured by a hole about four inches in diameter, padded comfortably by a rim of foam rubber. All the doors in the room had similar arrangements, the "glory holes" varying only in their height from the ground. Sergio stood as close to the door as possible, his back to the room full of men, and unzipped his fly, sticking his hard penis through the hole until his balls pressed closely against the door. The man inside, who had dropped to his knees, took Sergio's cock in his mouth with a muffled moan of ecstasy. His own half-stiff penis was already out of his tweed trousers, and while he grasped Sergio with one hand and sucked passionately, he used the other hand to rub himself with a hard, merciless stroke. Sergio stood perfectly still, his hands at his side, his eyes closed, lost in the delicious tugging, licking, pulling sensations he felt on the other side of the door. He knew dimly that he was going to disappoint the guy inside. He was so ready, that tongue-lashing of Alan's, that he came in less th[?] minute in a series of wildly relieving jerks. The stranger in the cubicle had barely started to really work on Sergio's prick when his mouth was filled with sperm. He gulped it frantically, trying to hold the pumping cock in his mouth as long as possible. But, once finished, Sergio unceremoniously removed himself from the glory hole, zipped up, and was out the door in a practiced movement. The stranger, cursing under his breath, carefully eased his distended, purple, and aching penis back into his pants and left the cubicle. He was going to try his luck again—he couldn't settle for a nothing quickie like that, not after coming in all the way from Darien for it.

Valentine would have liked to stay out of Sergio's way. He wasn't nasty to her in any straightforward manner to which she could, at least, have reacted, but his unfeigned air of absolute disdain seemed to fill and solidify the space around them. However, their work kept them together constantly, often bending over the same piece of fabric or paper, constantly needing to consult on this matter or that. He had taste, she granted, particularly in the firm's specialty, women's sports separates made in fine wools and cashmeres, leather, linen, and pure silk. Although Wilton Associates was only six months old, it was solidly capitalized by Alan Wilton, who had formerly been a partner in an enormous dress business. Valentine gradually learned, through office gossip, that Wilton had sold out his former partnership when he and his wife, the daughter of the bigger firm's founder, had been divorced. No one seemed to know any details about his past since they were all, like Valentine, fairly recent employees. Sergio was the exception. He had worked for Wilton at his former business and had gone with him when he left it.

Sergio was engrossed in the preparation of Wilton Associates' summer line, but not so involved with his own designs that he didn't find time to incorporate large numbers of Valentine's ideas in his own sketches. Often he resketched her drawings without bothering to make any changes in them at all.

One afternoon, about two months after Valentine had

been hired, Alan Wilton asked her to come to his office.

"You haven't asked, Valentine, but I want you to know that I think you've added something very important to the look of our line."

"Oh, thank you! Has Sergio—"

"Sergio's not famous for sharing credit—he's said nothing. I just happen to have a very good memory." The wildcat eyes looked steadily into hers. "Will you have dinner with me this Friday? I'd like that very much—or do you have to be somewhere for the weekend?"

Valentine felt a shock run right up into her hair. Until this minute Alan Wilton had treated her with pleasant formality on the frequent occasions when he came into the studio. She found him intimidating, although she would never admit it to anyone, not even to Elliott.

"No! That is—I'm not going anywhere for the weekend —I'd love to have dinner." She was thoroughly confused.

"Perfect. I'll pick you up at your place then?" Valentine had a vision of this exquisitely dressed man climbing six flights up to her loft in the light of the forty-watt bulb that lit her staircase.

"That might not be a good idea." Idiot, she told herself, that doesn't make sense. "I mean—the traffic—Friday night. Why don't I just meet you somewhere?" What traffic she asked herself, mortified. On Friday night all the traffic was leaving the city.

"Whatever you say. Come for a drink at my place first and we'll go on to Lutèce. You can tell me how it compares to La Tour d'Argent." He looked at the white work smock she was wearing. "It'll give you a chance to wear one of your Balmain dresses. And we can chat about dear, old Pierre. I haven't had dinner with him in at least three years."

"I think Sergio needs me," she answered hastily.

"Well, there's certainly no doubt about that. Shall we say eight o'clock? I live in the East Sixties, here's my address. It's an old town house. Just ring the bell on the outside and I'll let you in. It's the first door straight ahead."

"Yes. Well—until Friday then—" She left his office precipitously, realizing too late that she would probably see Wilton a dozen times before Friday in the course of her work.

Valentine arrived at Alan Wilton's door wearing a short, soft, black chiffon dress with an open matching jacket, trimmed in black satin ribbons, of her own design and workmanship, which Balmain would have been proud to acknowledge. She expected to find his home decorated in the spirit of his office, which incorporated all the executive clichés of gray-flannel walls, a black-and-white geometric David Hicks carpet, and furniture of polished steel and glass, an office as severely masculine and strictly organized as the man himself.

But when Wilton answered her ring he led her into a duplex that combined fantasy and fine art in bewildering profusion. A collection of rare Art Deco furniture was placed on brilliant Persian carpets; eighteenth-century Chinese chairs stood on either side of a splendid naked Greek torso of Alexander the Great; sinuous Cambodian dragons guarded an upright Ptolemaic sarcophagus. The colors were all rich and dark—wines, bronzes, lacquered shiny black, and terra-cotta. Mirrors were everywhere, competing for space with books, antique Chinese wall hangings, framed photographs, and small Cubist paintings, two Braques, one Picasso, several Légers. Leather and velvet sofas were partly covered with fur throws and unexpected pillows in silver and gold lamé. On every table stood an amazing clutter of vases and small sculptures, Lalique and Gallé glass, Chinese ceramics, Assyrian stone figures, flexible metal fish. It was an apartment at once so personal that Valentine imagined that if she had the time to absorb and analyze it, she would know the man who had created it, yet it was so full of surprising contrasts and ambiguous juxtapositions that it might as well have been designed as camouflage.

Valentine was speechless. This was such a complete work of art that she really felt nothing yet but astonishment. Wilton waited, drinking in with pleasure this reaction on the part of his guest.

"I see," she finally said, "that you do not believe that 'less is more.'"

He gave her the first entirely open smile she had seen on his face. "I've always thought old Corbusier was unnecessarily dogmatic about that," he answered, and began to show her around the two floors and the small formal garden with unabashed pride in his treasures. From the minute he had answered the door, Valentine had ceased to feel frightened by him. He seemed a different man entirely in his own home. He hadn't mentioned "dear, old Pierre" once, and she felt, somehow, that he didn't intend to tease her ever again.

Valentine had been taken aback when Wilton had mentioned dining at Lutèce. Even after a mere three or four months in New York she knew its reputation as the most expensive restaurant in town, supreme in its standards of haute cuisine. She expected the kind of grandeur she had read about in French magazines when they described the glories of Maxim's or Lasserre. Instead, she found it was a narrow, friendly brownstone, with a tiny bar. They climbed up a steep, open, circular iron staircase into a small cream-and-pink room, lit entirely by candles, overlooking a garden filled with roses and other tables. There was not a single note of ostentation, yet the room breathed depths of luxury and comfort because of the use of the finest materials: heavy, pink linen tablecloths and napkins, fresh roses in bud vases, fine crystal, and solid-silver flatware. Even the waiters, in their long, white aprons, were protective and approving, instead of exuding the stiff pomposity that Valentine had dreaded in anticipation. As they drank Lillet on the rocks in delicate, round goblets with long, thin stems, Valentine inspected the menu, which, to her surprise, had no prices on it. Later she discovered that only the host's menu had the prices listed, a delicate way of making the guest unself-conscious about the cost of his choice. Let the host wince—or, if he had to wince, let him stay away.

Although some of Valentine's strange sense of shyness had been dissipated in Wilton's apartment, where his objects provided a safe topic of conversation, after the business of ordering was over she suddenly wondered what on earth they were going to talk about during dinner. As if he sensed her new attack of uneasiness, Wilton began to tell her about the history of the restaurant. He had been coming there since it opened.

"I hoped it was going to be a success from the first day," he said, "but I was absolutely sure of it on the day I heard the owner, André Surmain, refuse to serve a regular customer iced tea with his dinner, although the man swore that if he didn't get his iced tea he would never set foot in the place again."

"I don't understand," Valentine said, confused.

"I knew that the place hadn't begun to break even yet, but there was André, so determined to maintain the standards of French cooking that he preferred to lose a good customer than do what he considered an abomination, a desecration of great food. With nerve like that—he had to be a little crazy—how could he fail? And the man never did come back either."

Valentine felt a return of her natural self-confidence. She wouldn't let anyone drink iced tea here either, certainly not with the roast duckling garnished with poached white peaches she was eating.

Alan Wilton felt something stir inside that had been dormant for many years. It was an enchanting child, indeed. He had suspected it would be. So young, so innocent, in spite of its airs, so amazingly unspoiled in spite of its beauty. How restful, how touching, to show it a bit of the world. And how well it knew how to accentuate its type—slender as a young boy, tiny breasts, a curly, short cap of absurdly red hair above the simplicity of the black chiffon—how very well done.

During the next five weeks Valentine had dinner with Alan Wilton some fourteen times. He introduced her to the authentic, noisy bistro atmosphere of Le Veau d'Or; the subdued, badly lit reverse chic of Pearl's, where the thrill came not so much from the Chinese food, which no one ever admitted was only fair, but from the feeling of being a member of a privileged elite who had made it their own; and to the very special charm of Patsy's, an unpretentious but expensive West Side Italian restaurant where entrenched Democratic Party politicians, and men whose methods of business did not encourage investigation, dined on some of the best Italian food outside of Milan. Mainly they ate at Lutèce, sometimes downstairs in the less formal, slightly larger dining room, sometimes outside in the garden, protected by awnings and tall lamps, which radiated heat on chilly nights, sometimes in the room in which they had first sat. Slowly Valentine came to know Wilton a little better. He was a man who had the trick of offering tiny bits of information about himself at odd moments and at the same time managed to convey, wordlessly, the fact that probing questions were not just unwelcome but out of the question. He had two sons, both young teenagers; he had been divorced for five years after a marriage of twelve years; his wife had remarried and was living happily in Locust Valley.

He never discussed business with Valentine. In fact, his chief interest seemed to be in Valentine herself, in her past life, which she gradually described to him in full detail. It was a relief to her to be able to stop misrepresenting herself. Now that she was really a designer's assistant she could admit the truth about her years at Balmain. Yet somehow she didn't feel free to be as easy and open with him as she was with Elliott. Although she could now relax with Wilton, his perfect manners constrained her own impetuous frankness.

She puzzled endlessly about her relationship to him. Everyone in the office knew they were seeing each other, since he had his secretary make all his restaurant reservations. Valentine managed to evade the questions her friend the receptionist and some of the more important women in the workrooms slyly tried to put to her. She thought she understood Sergio's attitude completely. The more often she saw Alan, the more frigidly vicious Sergio became. Only natural, considering that she was a potential competitor for his own job with the unfair advantage of being involved in a man-woman relationship with the boss.

But was she? That was the stone at the heart of the question. They had established a pattern in their evenings. She met Alan at his home for a drink, they went out to eat, they had a brandy or two in a bar after strolling a while, and then he took her home in a taxi, insisting on seeing her all the way up to her door. He invariably kissed her goodnight on both cheeks, in the French manner, but he never came in, although, after the first three evenings, Valentine always invited him to do so.

Wilton had subtle charm and formidable glamour. Valentine had never been courted by a man she took seriously, and she was beginning to fall more and more under his spell. He was the first man of the world she had ever known, but she had no basis of comparison to use as a yardstick to judge his impeccable behavior. After fourteen dinners she certainly expected something more than the kind of kiss one French general gives to another on dress parade! More and more frequently she found herself staring at his full mouth, imagining what it would feel like to her lips, until, with a start of realization, she dropped her eyes. Sometimes she noted a strange flash of what looked like pain in his expression, and she would hurry to distract him with an anecdote on the mad pace at Balmain's because she feared, for no reason she knew, whatever it was that he might have been about to say. Yet, what *was* he waiting for? Was there something she was supposed to do? Some sign, some word? Did he think he was too old for her? Was she perhaps not his type? No, that, she concluded, was just not possible. No man would spend hundreds and hundreds of dollars to feed a woman who wasn't his type, common sense told her that and common sense never failed. Perhaps because she didn't know the right way to flirt, perhaps he was frightfully shy deep down inside, perhaps he had been so hurt by women that he didn't want to get involved, perhaps—

Valentine was disgusted with herself. All these fake wonders and doubts when what she really wanted to know was when she was going to bed with Alan Wilton? Her twenty-second birthday had passed and she was still so intact a virgin that if she had still been a practicing Catholic she could have gone to confession without a blush. Why, even that dolt of an Elliott had never made a move—

Bitterly, she remembered a recent conversation she had had with a runaway model who had come to Wilton's to have some of the new collection fitted on her for a fashion show. She was a flip creature with a Cockney whine as aggressive as her pelvic bones.

"Do you mean that Spider the Cocksman is your neighbor? What perfectly fabulous luck!"

"I beg your pardon?"

"You know, that's considered vulgar in England but terribly grand in New York. I wonder why?"

"What on earth are you talking about?"

"That expression you just used, 'I beg your pardon.'"

"Spare me a wandering mind," Valentine snapped, "what did you mean exactly about Elliott?"

"He's a bloody famous stud—you do understand 'stud,' Valentine? Not to put too fine a point on it, he fucks early and often. Ever at the ready is our Spider—and he specializes in the most ravishing creatures. I've never had a good whack at the man myself, worse luck, but I hear he's fantastically good."

"Salope. Conasse!"

"What did you call me?"

"A gossip," said Valentine, who had used two words that, roughly translated, mean, respectively, "pig of a slut" and "dirty cunt."

"Well, gossip is the soul of this business, I always say. So—I take it you haven't had a tumble with the old darling. Not to mind, dearie, he probably thinks of you as a sister. I hear he adores his sisters—ouch! That hurt!"

"Sorry," said Valentine, removing the pin.

So where did that leave her? A sister to Elliott—not that she'd have him anyway, she thought savagely, the promiscuous, disgusting pig—and a question mark to Alan Wilton. There must be something wrong with her.

A week later when Alan Wilton suggested that Valentine return to his place for a drink after dinner, she felt a sharp snap of relief. She'd seen enough movies to know that it was the classic seduction ploy. Now that he'd finally made his move, she was enchanted with herself for having waited without betraying her impatience.

When they had left his apartment earlier in the evening, he had turned off almost all the lights, and now he made no move to light them again. With endearing nervousness he poured them each a large brandy, and silently, trembling slightly, he guided Valentine's elbow with his warm hand, leading her to his bedroom. He disappeared into his bathroom and Valentine gulped the brandy quickly, kicked off her shoes, and went to stand by the window, looking out at the dark garden. Her mind refused to work. She just stared outside as if she might see something vitally important if she kept on looking long enough. Suddenly

192

she realized that Alan was standing closely behind her, entirely naked, kissing the back of her neck, unbuttoning the tiny buttons that ran down the back of her dress. "Lovely, lovely," he murmured, slipping off her dress, undoing her bra, pushing down her half-slip. She tried to turn to face him, but he held her firmly with her back to him as he slid off her wisp of underpants. His fingers slowly traced the line of her backbone and her rib cage, his hands came around to clasp her breasts briefly and then returned to their delicate, deliberate celebration of her back, gradually reaching her small, firm bottom. There he lingered a long while, cupping her buttocks in his hands with hot, eager fingers, squeezing them together and then, alternately, flirting with the line that separated one from another until gradually he had worked a finger in between them for an inch or two. Valentine felt his penis rise and grow stiff against her back, but still he had said only "lovely," repeated over and over.

Now he knelt on the floor and gently widened her stance so that her legs were parted. She felt his hot tongue tracing her ass and the sensation was so maddeningly good that she pushed back against him and found herself rotating her pelvis without conscious design. Just as she felt that she couldn't stand still one minute longer without turning around, he lifted her in his arms and carried her over to the open bed. There was no light except a small bedside spot, which he turned off before he laid her down on the sheets and finally kissed her repeatedly on the open, waiting mouth.

As Valentine felt herself getting wetter she tried to clasp him close to her, exploring with her hands the well-muscled, hairy body she couldn't see. She didn't dare to touch his penis. She had never felt one in her life and she realized that she didn't know what to do—how to touch it. But his kisses were so hard, so devouring that she let herself stop worrying about whether she was responding properly. Suddenly, unmistakably, she felt him trying to turn her over on her stomach. She felt a clutch of dismay —she wanted more kisses on the mouth, her nipples ached for his lips, but she turned over obediently. He began kissing her softly down the back, but very soon he was licking and sucking her bottom, almost bruising her with the ferocity of his demanding lips, bared teeth, and strong hands, kneading her ass in an eruption of passion. She was disoriented in the dark; she wasn't sure exactly where on the bed he was, but now she realized that he was kneeling over her, his legs were holding her thighs wide apart and his hands were clasping the cheeks of her rump so that she was spread wide open. She felt the firm head of his cock thrust into the entrance of her vagina. It went in easily for an instant and then stopped as she gave a gasp of pain. He pushed again, and again she gasped. He pulled out and turned her over abruptly.

"You're not a virgin?" he whispered, horrified.

"Yes, of course." Her virginity was so much on her mind that it had never occurred to Valentine that he wouldn't know.

"Oh, shit—no!"

"Please, please, Alan—keep on—go on—don't worry if it hurts a little—I want it," she said urgently, as she tried to find his cock in the dark with her hands to show him that she meant her words. She heard him grinding his teeth, and suddenly, as she lay sprawled on her back in a jumble of sexual quickening, pain, and the beginnings of a huge embarrassment, she felt him shoving roughly into her with two of his fingers, like a battering ram. She bit her lip but forced herself not to cry out. When Wilton had assured himself that the passage was open all the way he turned her over on her stomach again and, with a cock that felt less firm than it had a few minutes earlier, slid into her. As he rooted and grunted inside, Valentine felt him growing stiffer, bigger, until, much too soon, with a cry of triumph that sounded like agony, he came.

Afterward they lay silently, Valentine filled with unspoken words. She was totally confused, almost in tears. Was this how it was? Why had he not been more tender? How could he not know that she was aroused and unsatisfied? But in a minute he put his arms around her and pulled her over so that they were lying face to face.

"Darling Valentine—I know it wasn't good, but I couldn't believe—I was so surprised—forgive me—let me —" and with his fingers he played so expertly with her clitoris that she too finally came in a burst of pleasure that made her forget her questions. Of course, she thought hazily, when she came back to her sense of logic, he didn't expect a virgin—that explained everything.

The next few weeks were among the most puzzling of Valentine's life. She and Alan Wilton had dinner every second or third night and, invariably, afterward they went back to his house and made love. Since that first time he had been much more determined to arouse her before he entered her, driving her to a pitch of sexual rapture with his lips and his fingers, but he insisted on doing everything silently and in the dark, which she found terribly frustrating. She wanted to see his naked body and she wanted him to see her. With innocent vanity Valentine knew that her very white, perfect skin and her fragile body with the dainty, uptilted breasts and the lusciously tight, firm bottom would please any man. But even worse was his evident reluctance to enter her from the front as she had always imagined a man would do. Now when he pushed his prick into her as she lay on the big bed, he raised her ass in the air with several pillows so that he could use his expert fingers to caress her clitoris in the front while he fucked her from behind, but rarely did he want to try the ordinary position that she longed for. He explained that she wouldn't feel as much that way, that it was manual stimulation that brought her to orgasm, not mere penetration, which wouldn't, in any case, stimulate her clitoris directly. But something in her demanded face-to-face confrontation, which seemed, in a symbolic way, to be a meeting of equals in the game of love.

And love it must be, she told herself, as she found herself unable to think about anything besides her rapidly growing feelings for Alan Wilton. She was not just in love; she was obsessed by him because he continued to mystify her. He treated her as one would a beloved, he showed her extraordinary consideration and admiration, he shouted her name out loud now when he came, but she didn't feel that anything between them was—settled? No, that wasn't the right word. It was some sort of deep understanding that was lacking—a *compréhension*. With all the dining and talking, all the lovemaking, she still waited to divine the true man she knew she had not yet seen in him.

As the new line of clothes neared completion, Valentine was forced to work late several nights during the last two weeks. Normally Wilton left the office at six, leaving Valentine, Sergio, and their technical helpers to continue without him when his own day was finished. One Monday, rather late, as Valentine passed his office door on her way home, she saw, with surprise, that it was slightly open and that voices, Alan's and Sergio's, were coming from it. She started to hurry by when she heard her own name. Was Sergio complaining about her, she wondered, stopping to listen. She would put nothing past him.

". . . your dirty piece of French gash."

"Sergio, I forbid you to talk like that!"

"You make me puke! You *forbid* me! Mr. Straight forbids me! If there is anything as pathetic as a fag trying to convince himself that he can make it with a woman—"

"Listen, Sergio, just because—"

"Because what? Because you can get it up for her? Sure you can—that's no surprise. You got it up for Cindy for almost ten years, didn't you? You got it up often enough to have two kids, didn't you? But why did Cindy divorce you, Alan, you sickening hypocrite? Wasn't it because you couldn't get it up for her any more after you found out what you really wanted? Do you think that just because you do it to me instead of my doing it to you that you are any less of a fag?"

"Sergio, shut up! I admit all that shit, but it's in the past—ancient history. Valentine is different, fresh, young—"

"Christ! Will you listen to the world's biggest lying cock-sucker. Until she came along you couldn't get enough of me, could you? And just where were you last night? I seem to remember you sticking that big thing of yours up my ass until I thought I'd burst—and afterward, who was that sucking me off and moaning and groaning—Santa Claus? It was you, you shithead—and you loved every second of it!"

"It was a lapse. It's not going to happen again—that's over."

"Over! Sure it's over. Just look at me, Alan, look at my prick. Don't you want to put it in your mouth? Nice and juicy? Look at my ass, Alan—I'm going to bend over this chair and spread it apart, nice and open, just the way you like it. Can you tell me you aren't hard already? Can you?

"You're dying for it—it's the only thing you really want—stop kidding yourself. I'm going to lock this door and you are going to give it to me in the ass right here on the floor—every way, Alan, every way you want. Oh, the *things* you're going to do to me. Aren't you, Alan? *Aren't you?*"

Valentine only heard him gasping "Yes, yes!" in a voice of abject, joyful surrender before she was able to break out of her trance and flee down the hall.

Once she reached home Valentine stopped functioning. She was incapable of doing more for herself than brushing her teeth and washing her face. She spent two days and two nights huddled in bed, under her blankets and quilt, wearing the heaviest bathrobe she had, but she was unable to feel a moment's warmth. She drank only a few glasses of water and ate nothing. Time had stopped. She felt as if there were two enormous knots linked together inside of her, one in her head, one in her heart. If she dared to think, one of the knots would come undone. She was unable to imagine what would happen to her then. She was paralyzed with fear.

On the morning of the third day Spider began to worry seriously. He had vaguely noticed that there were no signs of life coming from her loft, but he hadn't seen her regularly since she started going out with Wilton. Still, he should have seen some light, at least, since she couldn't be away for the weekend in the middle of the week. True, he'd been working late for Hank Levy for the last two days, but quite suddenly he knew that something was wrong.

He went to Valentine's door and knocked for a long time. There was no answer, but he had the strong impression that Val, or someone, was inside. Months ago they had exchanged keys to their apartments. In case of an emergency, he told her, feeling street smart, it's always a good idea to have a neighbor who can get into your place. Certainly none of the other characters on the floor were trustworthy—in fact, who knew if they were even there? He fetched his key, knocked again, and when there was still no answer, he entered. At first he thought the room was empty. Puzzled, he looked around carefully. Nothing. No noise except the hum of the refrigerator. Then he realized that the long, almost imperceptible lump under the quilt was a body. He tiptoed over in terror, knowing that he had to investigate. With infinite care he peeled back the quilt and uncovered the back of Valentine's head, her face, pressed sideways against the mattress, allowed just enough room for her to breathe.

"Valentine?" He went around the bed and bent close to listen to her breathing. He inspected her face carefully. She was not asleep, he was almost certain, but she wouldn't or couldn't open her eyes. "Valentine, are you sick? Can you hear me? Valentine, baby, darling try to talk to me!" She lay unmoving, unresponsive, but by now Spider was convinced that she heard him. "Valentine—it's going to be all right. I'll just call Saint Vincent's and have them send over an ambulance—whatever it is that's wrong, you'll be taken good care of soon—don't worry—I'm phoning right away." As he backed away from the bed toward the phone, she opened her eyes.

"Not sick. Go away—" she rasped.

"Not sick! Jesus—if you could see yourself—Valentine, I'm getting you to a doctor right away."

"Please—please, leave me alone. I swear I'm not sick."

"Then what are you? Come *on,* baby."

"I don't know," she muttered and then fell into a heaving contortion of tears, the first she had shed. For more than an hour Spider sat on the bed and held her tightly in his arms, unable to do or say anything more to comfort her. She wept with extraordinary violence, keening and howling, but not one intelligible word came from her. He was totally bewildered, but he held on to his little, wet, shaking bundle and waited tenderly, patiently, thinking from time to time of his sisters. How many little girls, miserable, heartbroken little girls, he wondered, had he ministered to?

When her sobs seemed to be descending to the level at which she might be able to hear him, Spider risked a few tentative questions. Was it bad news from Paris? Had she lost her job? Was there anything he could do?

She raised her eyes, swollen almost closed, and spoke to him with an intensity he had never heard in her before.

"No questions. It's over. It didn't happen. Never, never."

"But Valentine—darling—you can't just shut things up—"

"Elliot—*not another word!*" He was transfixed. Something fearsome and dreadful in her voice made him understand that if he asked one more question he'd never see her again.

"Know what you need, baby?" Spider said. "I'm going to make you some Campbell's cream-of-tomato soup with buttered Ritz Crackers." Spider's mother believed that this combination was too much of a treat to be given to anyone but a very sick child, and every one of her seven offspring considered it the ultimate remedy.

For the next week Valentine lived on cream-of-tomato soup, cornflakes and milk, and the only other thing Spider knew how to prepare, melted-cheese sandwiches. She allowed him to persuade her out of bed, into the shower, and back to her favorite chair, but she refused to dress. Every morning he brought her hot tea and cornflakes. She sat in the chair all day staring into space, tortured by agonizing spasms of loss, tearing grief at the way she had been used, and hideous, filthy humiliation, because her emotional gift to Alan Wilton had been turned into splattered mockery by blows of reality, the reality of memory. Spider hurried home after work every evening, made the soup and a cheese sandwich, and sat with Valentine until midnight, putting on records from time to time but mainly just keeping her silent company.

Spider was not just alarmed by this collapse in Valentine, he was also intensely curious. He knew it wasn't medical help that she needed. Since she was so adamantly silent and so passionately secretive, he didn't know how to go about getting psychiatric help for her. So he just did the only thing he could think of; he combed *Women's Wear* looking for a clue since it was obvious that she wasn't working for Wilton any more. He found nothing for six days. The reports had started to appear on the spring American Designers' Collections. Twice a year, during several jam-packed weeks, the new collections are shown to buyers and the press, staggered in such a way that everyone has a chance to get to most of them. Every day during Market Week *Women's Wear* devoted a double-spread, sometimes two, to sketches and photographs of the best of the new lines. On the sixth day they covered Wilton Associates' collection with a fire storm of extravagant praise. A double-spread was allocated to the collection, including four detailed sketches. Three of them Spider recognized immediately as being straight from Valentine's portfolio, although her name was not once mentioned. It seemed impossible that this could be the explanation for her breakdown—after all, he knew that other assistant designers had had the same experience—but it was all he had to go on. Spider made several phone calls.

That night, as he and Valentine sat together, Spider said softly, "You have an appointment with John Prince tomorrow at three."

"Oh, sure—" She wasn't even curious. She had hardly listened.

"I called him up today and told him."

"What are you talking about?" Prince, like Bill Blass or Halston, was one of those giant designers whose name is so valuable that they are able to license the use of it for everything from perfume to luggage, racking up, in certain cases, as much as one hundred million dollars annually in retail sales, not counting the money they make on their clothes.

"I called Prince and told him how much of the Wilton collection is yours, and he checked with Wilton, who confirmed it, and he wants to interview you for the job as his chief assistant at twenty thousand dollars a year, starting right away. He expects you in his office tomorrow."

"Are you completely crazy!" It was the first time he had seen any animation on her face since he had found her.

"Wanna bet? I told him I was your agent—that means you owe me a commission, I'm not sure how much yet. But don't think I won't collect."

Nothing rings as true as the truth. That Spider was not making this up was instantly plain to Valentine, even as she pretended not to believe it, reluctant to struggle out of her limbo of mourning and depression.

"But my hair!" she cried, abruptly snapped back to basics.

"You might consider washing it," Spider said judiciously. "Maybe even use a little makeup. You could take off your bathrobe now. It's not as if you didn't have a thing or two to wear."

"Oh, Elliot, why did you do this for me?" she asked, almost beginning to cry again.

"I got sick of making melted-cheese sandwiches," he laughed. "And if I see one more tear out of you I'm never going to make you any more tomato soup again either."

"Please God," she breathed, "no more tomato soup, whatever you do," and ran into the bathroom to start washing her hair.

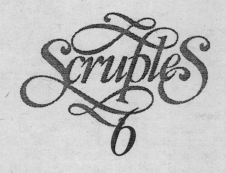

*T*he mansion in Bel Air that Lindy selected for the stricken Ellis Ikehorn had originally been built in the late 1920s for an oil baron who had fallen under the spell of the Alhambra in Granada. A Spanish-Moorish castle, as authentic as many millions could make it, it stood on a hilltop more than two thousand feet above the Los Angeles basin, surrounded by fifteen acres of formal gardens in which the play of multitudes of fountains was always the focal point. Thousands of cypresses and olive trees, planted in avenues, led from the mansion in every direction, always downward, since it stood on the highest point of the hilltop, glimpsed here and there from other points of the Bel Air peaks, never fully revealed, tantalizingly romantic in its foreignness, always admitted to be the most remote aerie of all in this remote enclave of millionaires' estates. Only people who had a map ever found their way to the gatehouse through the bewildering maze of overgrown, twisting, dangerous roads that led there; even if a stray tourist was to attempt to get closer to the dwelling, he would see only the gatehouse and the massive double gates, the only break in the tall walls that surrounded the entire property. The oil baron must have had enemies, Billy reflected, when she realized how completely the house was cut off from intruders.

But in spite of the inconveniences imposed by its location, the mansion, which was often and justifiably called the citadel, the fortress, or the castle, had one overriding advantage: a climate of its own. It was spring there all year round except during the rare rainy days in winter. During most of the winter, however, the many balconies, terraces, and courtyards were so sheltered that Ellis could sit outside in the warmth of the sun a large part of the day. In the summer, when the hot Santa Ana winds blew, the cloistered interior patios, planted with hundreds of tree roses and pungent herbs, were cool and sheltered and filled with the sound of falling water. When there was smog, it could be seen only as a yellow-brown layer of air below them, and fogs from the Pacific never rose as high as their hilltop. And the gloomy month of June, when the sun seems to shine only an hour a day on the streets of Beverly Hills, was bright and filled with the smell of spring high on the hill.

Only after Billy realized how many people would have to be housed in the mansion did she fully appreciate how well Lindy had chosen. The entire staff had to live in, except for the five gardeners, and the servants' wing contained more than enough room for them, fifteen in all—chef, butler, kitchen helpers, a hand laundress, maids, and a housekeeper, who had a suite of her own. There were five cars permanently at the disposal of the servants for use during their time off. No one who lived at the mansion could be without transportation, for it was a good four miles from the East and West gates of Bel Air on Sunset Boulevard and the nearest bus stop. The three male nurses lived in the guest wing. Each of them worked one eight-hour shift a day, so that Ellis was never unattended, and they too had to be provided with room and board so that their rotating schedules meshed perfectly. They also were provided with cars so that they would not become restless with their isolation from the attractions of Westwood and the Strip. Twenty people ate three meals a day at the lonely citadel on the hilltop.

Mrs. Post, the housekeeper, was busy almost all morning arranging for deliveries from Jurgensen's, from Schwab's, from the United Laundry, which handled all the towels, sheets, and nurses' uniforms, from the dry cleaners, and from Pioneer Hardware, which held Beverly Hills in a tight monopolistic grip.

Lindy had accomplished miracles in preparing the

huge mansion to receive them. A new kitchen had been installed; the old swimming pool, at the bottom of an avenue of tall, dark cypresses, had been fitted with a new filtering and heating system; and the pool house had been redecorated. Much of the vast house was closed off, but the main living quarters had been totally redone in a cheerful, luxurious way, so that a bright, Spanish quality now banished the musty, gloomy Moorish feeling it had had before. None of it was Billy's own taste, but she didn't have the heart to care. The gardens were halfway to restoration, and work was proceeding on the servant and guest wings. The old garages, fortunately, had room for a dozen cars.

When Lindy had made the house habitable, Billy and Ellis and Dan Dorman flew out in the company jet, which had been refitted to accommodate an invalid. The cabin was converted into two large rooms, one a pleasant bedroom containing a hospital bed for Ellis and a couch for Billy, the other a living room in which there was very little furniture besides easy chairs and side tables so that Ellis's wheelchair could be easily moved around. The three nurses had their own lounge up front near the crew.

The problems involved in hiring the male nurses, converting the jet, giving her approval to Lindy's choice for the new house, closing up the apartment in New York, and selling the houses in the south of France and in Barbados had all occupied Billy's mind and given her a minimum of time to think about the new realities of her life. In the absolute shelter of Ellis's love—Ellis, who had been lover, husband, brother, father, and grandfather to her, all the protective males she had lacked during her life—Billy had bloomed and yet not grown in any essential sense. She had glowed for seven years as the twenty-one-year-old girl-woman he had married, not becoming more mature, as she would certainly have had to do had she married a young husband. It was Ellis who had become younger during their marriage, Billy who remained the same.

Now, in her castle on the hill, three thousand miles away from her New York acquaintances, her New York activities, alone in a house filled with servants, nurses, and one paralyzed old man, she felt panic begin. Nothing had prepared her in any way for this responsibility. Everything frightened her, there was no comfort anywhere, no safe place, nothing to hang on to. Lost. Lost—and now, twenty miles away, even the sun was setting over the Pacific. "Stop it Billy!" she scolded herself in Aunt Cornelia's abrupt manner. Aunt Cornelia, she decided, was to be the example she would follow until she could find her own way. Briskly she turned on all the lamps in her bedroom and sitting room and drew the curtains on the darkness. What did Aunt Cornelia do every day of her life? Billy sat down at her desk, took out a pad and pencil, and began to make a list. One, find a bookstore, *tomorrow*. Two, learn to drive. Three, arrange tennis lessons. Four—she couldn't think of a four. It should be a list of people to call, but there was no one here she felt close enough to telephone. But she felt slightly less panic already. How Billy wished that Aunt Cornelia were still alive—she'd call Jessie in New York—maybe she could be persuaded to leave her five children and come out for a visit—

Within a month Billy had found a workable formula for her life. The first priority in each day was the time she spent with Ellis, four or five hours, either reading aloud or to herself, watching television, or just sitting quietly with him, holding his good hand, in one or another of their many gardens. She was with him for two hours every morning, from three to five in the afternoon, and an hour after dinner before he slept. She talked to him as much as she could, but he responded less and less. It had turned out to be easier for him to spell out words with little alphabet blocks fitted with tiny bits of magnet, which he arranged on a metal blackboard, than to learn to write with his left hand. Increasingly, even this cost him a great effort. Dan Dorman had explained to Billy, during one of his monthly visits, that a number of tiny strokes were bound to be taking place imperceptibly in Ellis's brain as time passed, so that the brain damage was slowly increasing. The stricken man's general health continued to be excellent, his body fairly strong. In the circumstances, Dorman thought to himself but did not tell Billy, Ellis might easily live another six or seven years, possibly more.

Billy had followed Dorman's advice not to spend all her time with her husband. Every day she took a tennis lesson at the Los Angeles Country Club, and three times a week she exercised at Ron Fletcher's studio in Beverly Hills. She made a number of casual women friends at both places, and she was careful to make several lunch dates each week with one or another of them. These lunches represented 99 percent of her social life.

Ellis refused to have her present while he was being fed and he slept a long time after lunch, so during those midday hours she felt free of the obligation to be at the mansion. Without the support system of a nearby family or a network of old friends, without the free time necessary to undertake a serious commitment to charity work or even some sort of part-time volunteer job, Billy realized that she had three chief resources in her life: books, exercise, and buying clothes.

There was something which almost relieved her constant tension in prowling daily through the boutiques and department stores of Beverly Hills, buying, always buying—what did it matter if she needed the clothes or not? She had hundreds of elegant robes to wear at dinner; dozens of pairs of beautifully tailored pants; forty tennis dresses; silk shirts by the hundreds; drawers and drawers full of handmade lingerie from Juel Park, where a pair of panties could cost two hundred dollars; closets full of two-thousand-dollar dresses from Miss Stella's Custom Department at I. Magnin to wear to the few dinner parties to which she was invited; three dozen bathing suits, which she kept in the elaborate pool house where she changed for her daily swim. Three empty bedrooms in the mansion had been turned into closets for her new clothes.

Billy knew perfectly well, as she walked into the General Store or Dorso's or Saks, that she was falling into the classic occupation of rich, idle women: buying supremely unnecessary clothes to feed, but never fill, the emptiness within. "It's that or get fat again," she told herself, as she walked up Rodeo or down Camden, feeling a sexual buzz as she searched the windows for new merchandise. The thrill was in the trying on, in the buying.

The moment after she had acquired something new it became meaningless to her; therefore, each time she went out looking for something to purchase it was the same need that drove her. But she couldn't buy just anything. It had to be worth buying. Billy's Paris-born discrimination about quality and fit had become even more important to her as she noticed the casual way other women in Beverly Hills dressed. If she ever allowed herself to go around wearing jeans and t-shirts, what reason would she have to go shopping? Day by day she became an increasingly difficult and autocratic customer. A missing button or a badly finished seam became personal insults. The flesh around her full mouth would tighten in a fury when she found any defects.

Women's Wear occasionally did roundup features on how California women dressed, and Billy's picture was always included as an outstanding example of West Coast chic. Keeping her body clothed to perfection, staying on the Best-Dressed List, the exercise classes,which kept her muscles firm, strong, and supple, the frequent visits to the hairdresser, the manicures, the pedicures—all these became obsessions that almost managed to cover over her desperate, growing craving for sex.

Until the day of his first stroke Ellis had been able to provide Billy with enough sexual pleasure to keep her satisfied if not satiated. Now, for well over a year, she had had no sex at all, except for occasional masturbation. And even that lesser relief was tainted by a feeling of deeply etched guilt left over from a childhood in which she had believed, as long as she could remember, that masturbation was a sin. A sin against what or whom had never been made clear, but Billy couldn't get over feeling depressed and sad afterward whenever she now resorted to masturbation to try to lower the gnawing degree of sexual need with which she lived all of the time.

She spent long hours thinking about the problem of achieving some sort of normal sex life. She tried, as always, to think with Aunt Cornelia's head but abandoned the attempt as quickly as if she had unwittingly picked up a piece of shit on the street. Aunt Cornelia would have repressed such thoughts if they had, indeed, ever dared to creep into her mind. She tried to think with Jessica's head. Jessie, she knew, would not have wasted time with such consideration—she would have gone out and gotten herself fucked, good and proper, months ago. But she wasn't Jessie. She was still married to a man she deeply loved, even if now he was less than half alive, and she couldn't, she wouldn't belie that love with a meaningless affair with one of the pros at the club or one of her friends' husbands.

As far as she could tell, there were no other possibilities. Billy accepted only a few of the invitations that came to her, going only to the homes of women who were not, she felt, using her as an attraction, almost as a sideshow, to satisfy the curiosity of the other guests. Even then, when she was introduced to strangers, she found them treating her as if she were a new widow to whom condolences, embarrassingly, could not be offered. They—indeed, all the world—had seen newspaper photographs of Billy walking next to Ellis in his wheelchair, crossing the landing strip to the jet as they left New York for California, and it seemed to her that everyone who heard her name immediately thought of that dying man in the fortress as they shook hands. At those stupendously wealthy Beverly Hills-Bel Air-Holmby Hills dinners to which Billy was invited as an "extra woman," the "extra man" invited to sit next to her at dinner was either a homosexual or a professional leech who dined out every night by mere virtue of being unmarried and mildly presentable. The rare, newly divorced man always brought his own dinner partner, usually a woman twenty years his junior. And, in any case, she realized, she had become too famous a face, too much an object of gossip, to carry on an anonymous affair even if a man had been available.

More important to Billy than all these deterrents was the absolute need she felt to defend herself from the speculation that would follow any relationship she might have with a man. She was Mrs. Ellis Ikehorn and that fact alone made her invulnerable, no matter how bereft she understood herself to be. Should she become simply Billy Ikehorn, sleeping with this one or that one, all her security, her proud place in the world, the regal girl-queen role she had played so eagerly during her marriage, would disintegrate in a flood of sneering, knowing, leering malice.

She could actually *feel* the gossips lurking out there—waiting for her to do the wrong thing.

Billy's only regular masculine company were the three men, all registered nurses, who tended Ellis. Often she would invite the two of them who were not on duty to eat dinner with her, and she enjoyed their gentle, amusing company. All three were homosexuals, who often cruised the gay bars of Los Angeles and the San Fernando Valley.

Once they had realized how much Billy needed their companionship, they lost their reserve with her and made her laugh, dubbing the guest wing "Boys Town," telling stories of their adventures, always, however, leaving a wide margin of discretion. The fifteen hundred dollars a month and keep, plus use of a car, which they each earned for their work, was good money indeed, and they did nothing to jeopardize it by overfamiliarity.

Billy didn't realize just how dependent she had become on the trio until two of them announced that they had to leave. Jim, who was from Miami, had to return home for family reasons. Harry, a wisecracking westerner, had become his lover during the last months and freely admitted to Billy that he had become too involved with Jim to let him go alone.

"We're both real sorry, Mrs. Ikehorn," he said reassuringly, "but there's an excellent nurses' registry in L.A. You won't have any trouble replacing us—the woods are full of ex-medics from Vietnam who finished their nursing training after they got back. See, most of them were drafted out of high school and now it's good living for them. No sweat."

"Oh, Harry, that's not the point—you've been with us right from the beginning. Mr. Ikehorn will miss you too."

"Ma'am, it would have happened sooner or later anyway—we sort of drift from job to job—you tend to go stale after awhile. No offense meant—it's the best job I've ever had."

Billy understood Harry perfectly. If she could have drifted on, who knows? But the bogus castle was her prison, and she was stuck fast in it for an unlimited period of time. She was determined to be very certain that the two new nurses she hired were pleasant people, since they would become such a large part of her world.

Billy had a month before Jim and Harry left in which to interview applicants for the jobs. She saw fifteen men before she found two who were suitable by virtue of both the excellence of their training and the ease of their personalities. The first of them, John Francis Cassidy, known as Jake, had a droll and artful street-urchin look to him and typically Black Irish coloring with thick, white skin and unabashed blue eyes. The second nurse, Ashby Smith, was Georgia born and bred. He wore his red-brown hair rather long, and in his soft voice there was a feeling of fastidiousness mixed with pride, which went agreeably with his slender height and graceful, long hands. They had both been medics in the war, and Billy had the suspicion, if not the certainty, that neither of them was homosexual.

Months passed, an unusually hot spring settled over southern California, and Billy found herself sinking deeper into depression. Every day she had to force herself to get dressed and drive to her tennis lesson or to her exercise class because if she stayed home she found it impossible to sleep at night. When it became too hot to run around chasing tennis balls in the sun, she took to swimming laps in the big pool, trying to exhaust her body, but even when she swam so much that her muscles quivered with the strain, she almost always had to take a sleeping pill, often two of them, before she managed to sleep. She found that liquor helped the process, although she knew it was dangerous. She never permitted herself more than a small wineglass of warm vodka. The lack of ice made it taste like medicine, and she tossed it off in one gulp, the unpleasantness of the taste taking away the tinge of impermissible pleasure that followed.

Billy found herself spending more and more time in the pool house. There, the decorator Lindy had chosen had exercised all the abandon he had not been permitted to put into the big house. It was a large pavilion with a big central room, intended for entertaining, with two wings of dressing rooms and showers for men and women. Looking around at the lavish, voluptuously appointed pavilion, Billy wondered dispiritedly if the decorator had assumed that she would be having many pool parties.

There were three puffy divans, ten feet square, covered in thick, red terry cloth and the floor was tiled in a Moroccan design of various shades of purple, pink, and white. Big, soft terry cushions in many shades of purple were piled everywhere. The domed ceiling had been painted in stylized arabesques, and beaded curtains made a slippery whispering sound when anyone passed through them. In one corner there was a bar, which had gradually become covered with the books Billy always carried with her. The pool house had become her favorite place to read because it was so removed, so private and secluded; there, for hours at a time, she could forget the house on the hill and all its occupants. No one, not even the gardeners, was allowed to work near the pool house after midmorning.

One evening of that sultry spring Billy found herself having dinner alone with Jake Cassidy. Morris, the one male nurse left over from the old days, was on duty, and Ash had taken himself off in his car. Billy had no appetite, but she forced herself to take tiny bites of her avocado and crab-meat salad. Every time she put her fork to her plate she caught sight of the black hairs on the white skin below Jake's cuff. She was almost hypnotized by the movement of his strong wrists. She felt a hungry heaviness, a grindingly good ache, begin between her legs. She let her lids fall over her dark eyes so that he couldn't see them, couldn't guess that she was imagining the thickness, the wiriness of his pubic hair, wondering how far up his belly it reached.

"Jake," Billy said casually, "why is it that you never use the pool?"

"Don't want to disturb your privacy, Mrs. Ikehorn."

"That's thoughtful of you, but it's a shame to let it go to waste. Come on down tomorrow afternoon and have a swim—it won't bother me."

"Hey, thanks! I'll take you up on that if it's my afternoon off duty."

Billy smiled. It would most certainly be his afternoon off. She'd make sure of that right after dinner.

Billy lay full length on one of the red divans, covered only by a large turkish towel, a big soft pillow under her head. The pool house was dim; only an orange glow from the sun outside penetrated, with occasional flicks of light reflected from the surface of the pool. Her eyes were almost closed in the soft light and she sighed deeply in almost unendurable impatience. Finally she heard the whisper of the beaded curtains as Jake Cassidy entered, wearing only a pair of thin, nylon racing trunks. He stopped dead when he saw her, stretched out there, her long, black hair loose and wild in a way he'd never seen it before, her long, tan legs spread carelessly on the red terry cloth.

"It's almost too hot to swim, isn't it?" Billy murmured.

"Well—I'll just have a quick dip—"

"No. No you won't. Not yet. Come over here, Jake."

He moved hesitantly toward her and stood close to the divan.

"Sit down, Jake. Right here—there's plenty of room." The young man perched gingerly on the edge she had indicated. Billy reached out, took his hand, and drew it toward her.

"Just move a little toward me, Jake, you're not close enough."

This time he obeyed quickly, with the final dawning of understanding. Billy took his large hand and guided it under the towel that covered her. He held his breath as he felt her pressing it down her body until it reached her cunt. Her clitoris, already engorged, pouted out from her pubic hair. She took his middle finger and placed it on the hot, wet flesh and slowly slid it back and forth over the precise spot from which her burning body radiated. He immediately took up the rhythm as she pulled off the towel and let him see her, magnificent in her nakedness. Jake bent to suck fiercely on her dark nipples. Billy's whole body arched upward in longing as she responded to that authoritative finger, that hard man's hand, that hot man's mouth. Oh, the difference when it was the flesh of another that touched her. After a minute she looked down the length of his body as he still savaged her breasts. Pushing out, above the drawstring that held his trunks low on his hips was the distended tip of his imprisoned cock. She pulled the drawstring open, on an indrawn breath, and looked, dry mouthed, at his large penis, rock hard and rosy against the whiteness of his belly and the dark thicket of his hair.

"Put it in me," Billy commanded.

"Wait—I want to—"

"Now!"

Jake straddled her and kneeled on the divan. She took his thrusting stiff prick in her hands and eased it, inch by inch, prolonging the delight until he growled in frustration. Finally, when he filled her entirely, Billy could feel him about to plunge wildly inside her.

"Hold it, Jake," she whispered into his lips, "got something good to teach you—you'll like it—" She put her hands on his hips and pushed him backward until his cock was almost entirely withdrawn from her, then she slowly released her forearms so that he reentered her vagina. She could hear his teeth grinding with barely restrained lust, but she paid no attention. Several more times she repeated the maneuver, and the last time she pushed him so far that his cock came out of her entirely. She took it in her hands and leisurely drew the whole length of the underside of his prick across her clitoris and up toward her navel, then drew it back just to the entrance of her cunt. He caught on quickly and rubbed it up and down, again, and again, over her belly, never losing contact with her tumescent clitoris, which Billy now visualized as a dark red, ripe fruit.

"Look at it, look at it," he muttered. Billy couldn't take her eyes off the glistening, superb penis on which the veins stood out in bold relief. The head of the cock had grown twice as big while he was inside her, and now she moaned with an excruciating need to have him back inside.

"No, you don't," he whispered. "Not so fast—you wanted it like this—you're going to get it all right, get it good and hard—you'll get all of it—don't worry—look at it—look—that's what you're going to get—as much as you can take—now!" And he drew back and rammed his prick all the way up, brutally, wonderfully, just as she came in violent, mindless, racking shudders.

They lay on the divan for long minutes, speechlessly waiting for his cock, which was still half hard inside of her, to subside. Billy felt the warm trickle of sperm between her legs and couldn't imagine how she had gone so long without it, without the quivering, sticky, sweaty reality.

That night Billy dined in her sitting room, telling the butler just to put everything on the coffee table.

"Just leave it, John, I'll help myself," she said. "I'm a little tired. Please see that I'm not disturbed."

She didn't touch her food. She was in the grip of a snarl of conflicting emotions: deep worry and a return of tearing lust. While part of her mind was concentrated on the memory of the afternoon, even while her cunt twitched involuntarily with the thought of it, even as she lightly, unconsciousy fingered her tangle of pubic hair under her light robe, she mulled anxiously over the repercussions of the incident. Would he tell the others? Boast of it? Would he try to blackmail her? What if this ever became public knowledge? What did he think of her? Not, she reflected, shaking her elegant head for a second at her vestigial puritanism, that it mattered. But what did she know about Jake? How far could she trust him? Billy had the answers to none of these questions and there was no one she could ask. The only thing she was sure of was that she had to have Jake Cassidy again. In her. Deep inside. Soon. Her fists clenched. She licked her lips and paced back and forth. She wanted him *now*. Her sexual appetites, starved for more than a year and a half, gripped her more violently than they ever had before in her life, even during the times in New York, even during any of the days of her marriage.

Billy abandoned almost all her excursions into Beverly Hills except for the hairdresser and refused all lunch dates. She was afraid to rearrange the nurses' schedule so that Jake would have every afternoon off, for fear of alerting the others. But two days out of three she went to the pool house after lunch and waited, lying naked, thighs opened shamelessly wide, until he came.

After that first afternoon he had treated her in public exactly as he always had. There was not a flicker of an eye or a secret glance to indicate that he even remembered what had happened between them. He was as respectful and punctilious as ever. All her sharp perceptions told her that no one suspected anything. Nor would they, as long as she didn't betray herself. And even in the pool house, vibrating like a steel rod inside of her, working his cock in and out of her cunt, he called her by no name and discreetly left her afterward so that there was no need to speak, to use words to talk about what they had been doing, even to get to know each other in this new relationship. How strange, she thought, that she could taste her own juices in his mouth and yet this most intimate communication was nonverbal. It was as if they shared a place that existed only under certain circumstances, at a certain time, a space in which their own everyday personalities dropped away entirely.

Billy's eroticism became more and more focused on the secrecy and the illicitness of the pool house. Nothing that happened there *counted* in the real world, yet nothing in the real world mattered compared to the pool house. In the pool house, where she had absolute disposal of the powerful and marvelously willing body of Jake Cassidy, their fucking became more and more experimental and animal. She was not Billy Ikehorn, the sad, rich wife of a dying man; she was somebody—somebody she didn't give a name to—but somebody who hadn't existed before. She almost felt as if she could sense this new person being born, separating itself from her, a new person without guilt or standards of behavior, to whom everything was permitted—as long as it was secret. Utterly secret.

In the beginning of her afternoons with Jake Cassidy Billy wondered at what seemed the abnormal way he had of keeping the time they spent together in a separate compartment from all the other times they were in contact during the day. Then she realized that she too wanted it that way, not just because it was safer but because she *did not want to know* Jake any better than she did. He was likable and efficient in his professional capacity; at the pool house he was a man with an ardent mouth and a stiff prick, but beyond this, she did not care to probe. She didn't want to know about his family, about his childhood, about his feelings, about his likes or dislikes or any of the other idiosyncrasies that make a person individual and meaningful. It was not that she was deliberately shutting him out of her heart; it was rather that he failed, in some fundamental way, to appeal to that heart, an intransigent heart that steadily refused to confuse lust with sentiment. Billy remembered too well what love had been like. Jake Cassidy had nothing to do with love. But she could live without love, if she had to. She had no choice.

Dan Dorman looked at Billy shrewdly. Since his last visit she was getting some, somewhere, he'd bet his life on it. She had that luminous look he hadn't seen since before Ellis got sick. Good for her. It was about time.

"You're looking well, Billy. I'd take up tennis myself if I didn't think I'd drop dead first time on the court at my age."

"Swimming, Dan, not tennis. I swim about a mile a day now—wonderful exercise. But why don't you? You could start just doing a few laps a day."

"In New York? Maybe deep knee bends. Now, about your plan to take Ellis to Palm Springs again, this winter —well, I'm not sure it's really necessary. It just isn't going to make that much difference to him this year, unless you enjoy it there, yourself, of course."

"Good God no. It's geriatric paradise, Dan. Even the young people look old and dried out. And our house there isn't nearly as comfortable for us as this one—I'd like to sell it."

"What about the jet—going to keep it?"

"Definitely. I'm sure that Ellis still enjoys going to Silverado and it's worth keeping the plane even if we only use it twice a year—with the nurses and everything, we're like a safari when we set off. Anyway, the cellar master at Silverado would kill me if we didn't show up for the vintage this year. Do you have any idea of how many vines we had to uproot to build the landing strip? But Dan, why did you say it wouldn't make any difference to Ellis about Palm Springs this winter?"

"He's much more withdrawn, Billy. You probably don't notice it as much as I do because you're with him every day, but he's losing interest in life month by month, going away more and more each time I see him. When it rains here this winter he'll be just as happy indoors, watching the fire or television, if it still interests him. He won't miss a few days of sunshine."

"I have noticed it, Dan—his—enormous—remoteness. I was afraid it might be something I wasn't doing right."

"Don't ever, ever think that Billy. He's getting the best possible care. You can't compensate for what happens inside a person's brain when a tiny blood vessel pops. You can only do so much. What are you now, Billy, almost thirty? It's not much of a life for you."

"Oh, I manage, Dan, I manage."

As Billy's afternoons in the pool house continued, she felt herself changing even further. She had never guessed how aggressive she could become with a man. Except for the two times in her life when she had taken the initiative —once when she crossed the hotel corridor in Barbados to go to Ellis and the first time with Jake—she had always assumed that it was the man who reached out for the woman, who indicated his desire, who aroused the passive yet alluring female. Now she was tasting the thrill of a fresh and almost excruciating pleasure in becoming the one who sought, who demanded, who explored, who drained. When Jake arrived at the pool house she was always there, hungry for him. In early autumn when he started to arrive first a half hour and then an hour late, she found the waiting, the uncertainty, more viciously painful than if she had known he couldn't come at all. He always had a plausible excuse, but she didn't believe them. She began to suspect that he enjoyed the power of knowing that she was already there, aroused almost to the point of violence, a voluntary prisoner focused totally on the animal release only he could give her. She had taken him. Now he was trying to turn the tables. She became sure of it the afternoon he didn't come at all, explaining later that he'd just fallen asleep in the sun. Raging with hidden anger, horrified and humiliated but in the grip of her need, her obsession, unable to do anything else, Billy raised his salary by a thousand dollars a month.

Her lust for Jake's body chewed at her constantly. In the mornings as she saw him passing in the hallways, she followed him with lidded eyes, visualizing the details of their next meeting. When she dined with the nurses, if he was among them, she could barely swallow as she looked at his hands and thought of what they could do to her. One Monday morning after he had had the weekend off, she came upon him passing the door of her room and gripped his wrist. She pulled him into the room, locked the door behind them, unzipped his pants, searched frantically for his cock, and made him hard with her hand. Then she rubbed herself against him until she came, still wearing her nightgown, the two of them leaning and panting against the wall like a pair of teenagers. Another day, when he had been on duty during the afternoon, she waylaid him after dinner and led him to a guest bathroom on the first floor of the mansion. She ripped off her panty hose and panties, sat on the lid of the toilet, forced him down on his knees, and pushed his head between her spread legs, thrusting her aching, wet cunt at his lips. He brought her to a quick, sharp orgasm with his tongue, but somehow it wasn't enough of what she wanted. She made him stand up in front of her, and still sitting, she took his penis in her mouth and sucked him off, the world reduced to that jut of flesh that she attacked so thirstily, with such craving. When he had slipped out of the door she sat in the locked bathroom for almost an hour, disconcerted and still unfulfilled. Billy knew that she was getting out of control. Either the incident in her bedroom or their joint disappearance of tonight could have been observed by any one of the servants who came and went about the house.

Within a day in early November the weather changed. The long, hot spring, summer, and fall were unmistakably over. An unusually rainy winter had come to southern California, a winter that might seem merely like a disappointingly wet fall anywhere else, but here, with the temperature in the fifties, long afternoons in the unheated pool house, far down an avenue of dripping trees, were self-evidently impossible. Billy became aware that until true spring came, perhaps until April, almost six months away, she would have to find an alternative location for her secret life.

She spent a long, thoughtful afternoon prowling about the great citadel on the hill, wandering speculatively through the many empty rooms Lindy hadn't bothered to

220

have redecorated because they served no function. Some of the rooms could be observed from other parts of the house, some were located too close to corridors often used by the servants, still others displeased her because from their windows she could see the wing that contained her own suite of rooms and Ellis's rooms, a part of the house that instantly made her aware of its true function as a private hospital. But finally, at the top of a long unused turret staircase, she came upon an octagonal room that might have been built simply for the quaint aspect it had from outside the castle, since it seemed to have never been used. She leaned out of one of the narrow windows and felt her hair caught by the newly brisk wind. The rain clouds that pressed down on Bel Air looked as if they could almost touch this high room and she remembered Rapunzel, the princess held prisoner in a tower. This particular Rapunzel, she mused, was about to acquire a hobby. Should it be sketching, watercolors, or oils? Or perhaps pastels? It scarcely mattered. The important thing about her art was that it required long hours alone in her studio, hours during which no one would question the fact that she was incommunicado. Everyone respected an artist's need for privacy and who, she wondered, was there left in the world to ask to see her work?

Within several days Billy's new studio was furnished. First she made a whirlwind stop at Gucci's, where she had recently spotted a thick silver-fox throw lined in silk and at least twelve feet square. Then she descended on the May Company, where a bewildered salesman, used to customers who measured, hesitated, compared, and consulted, barely managed to keep his sales slips filled in, as, in half an hour, Billy bought a floor sample couch from Milan's most experimental designer, which the buyer had been worried about because it was too dominating and too expensive to fit into any normal room; an ancient, fine Oriental rug, which was, in the salesman's opinion, too rare to be used as anything but a wall hanging; and several wildly extravagant lamps, which he knew, but didn't tell her, could give only dim light.

Billy's next stop was at Sam Flax, an art supply store, where her salesman enjoyed the odd experience of selling almost two thousand dollars' worth of painting necessities to a lady who seemed more interested in the sable brushes than in anything else she bought. He would have been even more intrigued if he had seen Billy struggle the next day to set up her new, unfamiliar easel. That finally accomplished, she fished out one of the dozens of canvases, positioned it carefully, and drew a jagged streak of red across it with a stick of pastel. Then she carefully lettered, on a page from one of the sketchbooks, "Studio. Work going on. Do not disturb under any circumstances." She tacked the page to the outside of the door, which could be locked from the inside, and, satisfied, she then removed all the sable brushes to her dressing room where they would come in handy for her eyebrows.

During the time it took to set up her studio Billy noticed that, in spite of the change in the weather, Jake maintained his attitude of imperturbability and public reserve. His black-fringed choirboy eyes met hers as frankly as ever, without a flicker of question, although he must have realized that it had been more than a week since they had touched each other. He did not even pay her the homage of a glimpse of impatience. Billy had first planned to surprise him with her studio, but now some instinct prompted her to keep it secret from him.

When it was all finished, she joined Jake and Ash for dinner one night dressed in a long, silver-lamé robe bordered in black mink, her hair combed loosely back, and heavy ropes of cabochon emeralds, baroque pearls, and rubies twisted around her strong throat. She studied Jake dispassionately across the table as he favored her with one of his cocky, impersonal smiles. Suddenly she saw him as not only unnecessary but dangerous. She had never forgiven him for the times he had kept her waiting, nor would she, as long as she lived.

Her lawyer, Josh Hillman, could handle the matter of Jake tomorrow, she decided. No, she'd have to attend to it herself. Josh would never understand the large bonus, the most inappropriately large bonus, that Jake would receive on his rapid departure. That and a few carefully chosen words should settle it. Perhaps Jake wouldn't fully understand, but somehow Billy knew that he wouldn't be too surprised. He must at least have wondered if he had gone too far. He'd been playing a game that was over his head.

Billy looked down the table at Ash, Ash with his gentle southern voice and his fine, long fingers, Ash who trembled when, without thinking, she stood too close to him, Ash who followed her with longing eyes when he believed she wasn't paying attention—slim, gallant Ashby. What would he look like naked?

"Ash," she asked, "are you interested in art?"

"Yes, Mrs. Ikehorn, I always have been."

Billy smiled faintly, her eyes looking right into his. "I'm not surprised. Somehow I imagined you would be."

Twiggy, Veruschka, Penelope Tree, Lauren Hutton, Marisa Berenson, Jean Shrimpton, Susan Blakely, Margaux Hemingway—Harriet Toppingham had spotted them all as they first appeared on the scene. Sometimes she was too late, and the new girls were already so identified with another magazine that she either would not or could not use them. The competition among fashion editors to find The Next New Beauty before another magazine does is enormous. They rely largely on tips from spies inside the model agencies and from their favored photographers. Naturally Spider brought the test shots he had taken of Melanie to Harriet as soon as he finished developing and enlarging them.

Her dull brown eyes narrowed secretively as she looked at the enlargements. She felt a lunge of acquisitiveness catch her in the gut. When she saw something or someone she wanted, it started all her juices flowing. This was where her emotions lived, in getting hold of the illusive, in laying hands on the rare and special.

"Well. Hmm. Yes, indeed."

"Is that all you're going to say, Harriet?" Spider demanded, almost angrily.

"She's quite killingly beautiful, Spider. Is that what you want to hear? Ruthlessly, killingly beautiful."

"My God, you make her sound like something out of *Bonnie and Clyde.*"

"Not at all, Spider. Merely that this is not a face we're

going to forget. A little scary, don't you think? No? Well, you're young."

"Harriet, that's nuts. You've never been scared by anyone in your life. Admit it."

"I admit nothing." She blew in his face, enjoying the prolongation of the inevitable. Of course she had to have the girl. A great model has to be unique. One merely beautiful girl looks like another, but this was an entirely different face. It held something joltingly special she couldn't put a name to. Finally she continued, "I'll book her solid for the next two weeks and shoot the most important part of the fall designer collection on her. The cover too." Her voice was carefully flat, without inflection or exhilaration, but she could feel her heart swelling with excitement. Power glowed like a hot stone in her stomach.

"I'll clear my decks," Spider said with joy. "There's nothing I can't get finished before then."

"Oh? Really?" She sounded mildly surprised, with a hint of embarrassment.

"Harriet! Harriet! I found her! You *are* going to give me the job?" Spider hadn't imagined that she would use Melanie and not use him.

Harriet's bright red lips curved in a thin red smile, barely permitting herself amusement. She waited, thoughtfully, putting out her cigarette meticulously in a heavy jade ashtray before she spoke.

"You're good Spider, I don't deny that. But very new, very untested. What have you done for us so far? Bras? Shoes? Kids' pajamas? Remember, the September issue is the most important one of the year for us. I simply can't afford to make a mistake." She took another cigarette from a bronze Empire-style box and lit it carefully, with the air of someone who has successfully closed the subject.

Spider bit down on his rage and forced himself to speak calmly.

"You wouldn't be taking a chance, Harriet. I'm aware that just because I brought Melanie to you first, instead of taking her pictures to *Vogue* or *Bazaar,* doesn't mean you have to give me the assignment. You want to use Melanie? She's all yours. But I don't think there's anyone she'll work with as well as she'll work with me. She's green, she's never modeled before. You didn't know that, did you? It didn't show in these pictures, and I took them in her street clothes, without special makeup or hairstyling. Trust me, Harriet. I'm ready for this. More than ready."

Harriet stared vaguely up at the ceiling and tapped her nails reflectively on her desk. She leafed through the pictures again, leisurely, feeling simmering flutters of pleasure fill her as she kept him waiting. Spider's work had already caused more talk than that of any other new photographer in years. If she let him slip through her fingers, he would be snapped up in a second. And he could do the job—she had known that from the beginning. However, she hated to be pushed into anything—still—on occasion—

"Well, I'll just have to think about—no—perhaps— after all, Spider, on second thought, I'll take the chance. I'll let you have a shot at it."

Never before in his life had Spider known what it was to be in someone's power. The relief of her words had not reached him yet. He stood shaking with fury and an astonished awareness of injustice at the pleasure he perceived in her baiting of him. Harriet watched him carefully. Had he finally been made afraid? Fear was out of Spider's normal emotional range—she had sensed that from the beginning and prized it in him—it made him more interesting to work on.

"Thank you." Spider gave her a glance that was too complicated for her to read immediately for all her cunning: a look of scorn, hurt, surprise, and disgust mixed with gratitude and the beginning of a private excitement. But no fear. She saw that at once. He gathered up the pictures and walked quietly out of her office. Harriet smoked meditatively. That boy still had a lot to learn.

While the September issue was being photographed, Spider's studio was jammed with people, each of them tensely looking for a way to make some impact on the main event. Harriet and her two assistants hovered; the accessory editor and shoe editor and their assistants, all four of them as heavily loaded with bags and boxes as little Italian market donkeys, came and went; Spider's own assistant, a bright kid from Yale, whom he had just hired, was never far from his side. A changing stream of people arrived from the various designers carrying precious original models over their arms. They waited around nervously, looking anxiously at their watches, for the pictures to be taken so that they could rush the garments back to the showrooms, while Harriet's assistants nagged at them to stay out of the way or ineffectively tried to convince them to go away and come back at the end of the day. Men from David Webb and Cartier brought cases of borrowed jewels and watched carefully until they could take them back again, while the assistant shoe editor's apprentice, a young beglamoured du Pont debutante, fresh from Vassar, was reduced to bringing everybody coffee and sandwiches and taking away half-empty cups and paper plates. In the dressing room a star hairdresser and his crew worked in coordination with a makeup expert and her helper, not just on Melanie but on the succession of male models who were booked to pose with her. The art director of *Fashion and Interiors* kept coming in, watching for a while, grunting to himself and leaving, only to return in an hour.

Spider worked in an electric trance. As far as he was concerned there was no one in the studio except Melanie and the cameras and the shadow of his assistant.

Melanie was as collected as he was concentrated. While she was being dressed and undressed and lipsticked and combed and told how to hold her head or move or smile, the tight bud of some gigantic question seemed about to unfold its petals in her depths, some perception seemed to stir, a perception that was in itself another question, not an answer. She found the long hours of posing surprisingly easy, in spite of her inexperience. It seemed a very natural, a very right thing to be doing. The more they asked of her, the more she gave, happier than she'd ever been.

At the end of each day Harriet and the art director, in a temporary truce, huddled together over the tiny 35-mm slides, projecting them on a white wall. Their lack of discussion indicated more clearly than any words could have that they both knew it was going well. They didn't want to give each other the satisfaction of showing approval, and with nothing to complain about, they had no reason to talk. They could tell, from years of experience, that a number of the slides would become some of the most ravishingly pure fashion photographs that they had ever published. Classics. The poetic, impenetrable beauty of the model lent each dress a dimension it had never had, except perhaps in the designer's first inspiration.

During the late spring and short summer that followed, Melanie's career was in a state of suspended animation. Until the September issue of the magazine appeared, in late August, Harriet had advised her not to do any commercial work, so that when she burst upon the fashion scene, she would be a completely new face. She kept Melanie busy doing editorial pages for *Fashion's* future issues throughout the summer months in such a way that Melanie was never available to any other magazine, all of whom shoot on roughly the same day. It is normal for a fashion editor to use one favorite model consistently, issue after issue. It keeps the model out of the hands of other editors, and it develops a certain look for the magazine.

Melanie accepted all of Harriet's guidance unquestioningly and avoided the Ford Agency's offices, dealing with them by telephone. Some instinct told her that Harriet, more surely than anyone she had ever met, might hold the answer to her still formless question, might tell her what it was that she wanted to know. She was fascinated by Spider's pictures of her. She spent hours studying them, with strained curiosity. Sometimes, when she was alone, she held up life-size enlargements of her face next to her own face and looked in the mirror for long minutes. The pictures told her some things she had not yet known about what she looked like to other people, but they still didn't satisfy that parched hunger in her that cried out for an absolute answer. Spider's photographs, which showed her what she looked like to him, showed her at the same time a mystery that only deepened her own perplexity. Perhaps if she could be photographed by another photographer, she thought, but Harriet was playing her cards very close to her chest and didn't want Melanie to work with anyone but Spider until September.

"Darling, Melanie darling, you've never talked about yourself." They were sitting at the kitchen table in Spider's loft, eating hero sandwiches.

"Spider, you're terribly nice to me, but you're the most inquisitive person I've ever met. I've told you everything there is to tell. What more do you want?"

"Jesus, all you've given me is bare bones—it sounds like the beginning of a fairy tale. Handsome, rich father, beautiful social mother, no sisters or brothers, parents still madly in love, envied by all Louisville. As for you, a perfect childhood and a year and a half at Sophie Newcombe before you talked your doting dad into letting you come to New York to try your luck. End of story. How can you say that's all there is to know?"

"What's wrong with having had a perfect childhood?"

"Nothing. I just don't understand the human connections there. Everyone is beautiful and loving and it's all so goddamned nice. I can't taste it, it doesn't have texture, it's too bright and light to be true."

"Well—it was. Honestly, Spider, I don't know what you expect from me. It seems to me that you had a pretty good time as a kid too—so what's the difference? You make it sound as if I'm hiding something. Would a blow-by-blow description of my first high-school dance make you happy? It was a genuine Gothic horror story." Melanie wasn't impatient. She was used to people who wanted to dig and dig at her. She had told him the truth as she knew it. Her private fantasy, about getting out from behind her eyes, wasn't something she had really put into words and certainly it wasn't something she'd tell anyone about.

Spider looked at her in indignant rapture. She didn't even seem to have any idea how mad she was driving him. He didn't think she was a tease; he didn't feel that she was holding out on him deliberately; but he knew that there had to be more, something that would make him feel she had given him something special of herself, something that responded to his love. She was so damn ungettable—at that it was almost like being in love with the world's most beautiful deaf-mute. And yet, the hellish thing was that the less she gave, the more he wanted it, the more she deflected his questions with bland disclaimers, the more he was convinced that she was refusing him something— some key detail—that he absolutely had to know.

Before he fell in love Spider had been lazily and good-naturedly willing to listen to his woman-of-the-moment's endless discussions of her psyche, her inner consciousness, her traumas of childhood, her parents' lack of understanding, even her astrological forecasts. He was amused and often charmed by the way the women he had known probed and poked around in themselves, dredging up bits and pieces for him to see. He had given no more of himself to them than he had promised, but now, when he wanted to understand someone's soul and to give her the most intimate access to himself, she was afflicted with a kind of softly unyielding dreaminess. He was filled with a desire to envelop her, to engulf and enfold her, to hear about her most private wishes and hopes and fears, her wildest ambitions, her most petty and ignoble feelings, her saddest days, her silliest faults. Everything.

Even while they made love he didn't feel she was totally there for him. They had made love for the first time on the day after the pictures for the September issue were completed. Melanie hadn't been a virgin, but she might just as well have been for all the difficulty Spider had had in coaxing her into bed. Finally, perhaps because it was easier to say yes than to keep saying no, she allowed him—quite crazy with love and desire—to take her to his apartment. He had been careful and patient and artful, curbing his lust, totally intent on her pleasure rather than on his. Spider was used to women who wanted him, who were as excited as he was, who met him halfway, who flung themselves into bed greedy for his body. Melanie made love with an unrelenting fragility. She responded to kisses and touching like a child being petted. She prolonged these gentle preliminary caresses, keeping him at her lips and her nipples, until he began to think that she wouldn't let him go any farther. Finally, wistfully, almost disappointedly, she allowed him to enter her. Then she urged him on with what he thought was passion, realizing too late that she wanted him to satisfy himself as quickly as possible.

"But, my darling you didn't come, please let me—there are so many things I can—"

"Spider, no, it's perfect like this. I'm happy, I don't need to come, I almost never do, just hug me and kiss me and pet me some more—pretend I'm your little baby—that's what I like best." But even in those long, soft, sweet moments he sensed a turning inward in her, a withholding of communion, a direction of her attention somewhere away from the two of them, lying so closely intertwined that it seemed impossible that they weren't together. And yet they were not.

After that first time he used every art he knew to bring her to an orgasm, as if that might be the key that would unlock the door between them. Sometimes she achieved a fleeting little spasm, but he never knew that it came from her one recurring sexual fantasy. In her mind she was being made love to by an anonymous lover, lying on a low bed surrounded by a ring of men who were watching her avidly, men with unzipped pants, whose cocks got harder and bigger as they watched her lover work on her, men who concentrated completely on her reactions as she was being fondled. These men whose cocks were now so huge that they were hurting, almost bursting, were making a movie of what they were watching. If she concentrated hard enough on their excitement and their frustration, she was able to come.

Naturally, there had been much speculation in the fashion world about what Harriet Toppingham did for sex. Many people assumed that she might be a Lesbian, but they never turned up any evidence of it, so gradually they added up her uncompromising ugliness, her solitary life, and her immense prestige, and the general impression grew that she was a sort of neuter, interested only in her work.

However, the evidence seekers had all looked in the wrong places, the obvious places, searching for a liaison between Harriet and some young beauty.

They had no means of knowing that Harriet was a member of the most hidden of all major sexual subgroups, an international network of middle-aged and powerful Lesbians, women who range from the late thirties to the early sixties, women in high positions of authority or fame, all of whom know each other or know of each other, whether they live in New York, London, Paris, or Los Angeles. These women include legendary actresses, famous literary agents, brilliant industrial and interior designers, successful theatrical producers, top advertising executives, and creative artists in many fields. They form a loosely connected but supportive group, which has none of the visibility of the highly placed male homosexuals in these same occupations. Many of them have been solidly married for many years, some of them are devoted mothers and grand-mothers. Unless you have seen such a woman without her mask you might easily know her for twenty years and not have the faintest suspicion of her strongest sexual orientation.

As a matter of basic self-protection these women keep their Lesbian lives and their working lives severely separated. Their sexual partners are most often women like themselves, at the same degree of power. Sometimes they may be anonymous, absolutely unimportant young girls, picked up in Lesbian bars, but such cruising is always dangerous. For such women of status, the flauntingly open, gay-is-chic, all-the-fun-people-play-together style of life of the fashionable male homosexual is an impossibility that might cost them the respect they inspire and the power they wield. They operate with the same tacit protection that used to be given to a President with a mistress or a congressman with a drinking problem. Of course, some people know about them, certain important and knowledgeable people, but it is considered to be no business of the public's. Lesbianism, in high or low places, still carries with it a much greater stigma than male homosexuality, and the vast majority of successful Lesbians are firmly determined to remain hidden.

Harriet had made it a rule, when she started in fashion as an assistant shoe editor, never to have anything to do with a model, even if the model was herself a Lesbian on the make. In her twenties her sexual experiences were all with women in their thirties and forties, and gradually, as she grew older, she was accepted into the worldwide network. When Harriet first saw Melanie's pictures she was involved with an important Madison Avenue copy chief, some two years older than she was. Their affair was an old one, comfortable, unexciting, yet it served a purpose. Those people who assume that "neuter" men and women live without sex are almost always wrong.

Now, after years of iron self-control, Harriet found Melanie's magically remote eyes and Melanie's delicate body moving relentlessly through her dreams, waking and sleeping. In the past she had been briefly in love with certain models, but she had never made the slightest gesture toward them, never looked to see if there was any signal she could read. The risk was too great. It was unthinkable that one of the girls whom she could lift to fortune by raising a finger and saying "I'll use that one" might come to possess the knowledge that would enable her to penetrate Harriet's secret. She watched the relationship between Spider and the girl and observed, almost as soon as it happened, the moment when he became her lover. She was used to being a spectator of heterosexual romance; she had cultivated a leaden indifference toward it, but this time she felt pain. The pain was unmistakably jealousy, and Harriet, a woman as proud as she was hard, did not know which was worse, the jealousy or the knowledge that she was weak enough to feel it. All that spring and summer she watched them—Spider, brilliant with happiness, Melanie, seeming to save for him those prim, cool, exquisite smiles that held a half-given invitation.

On the first night of every Fourth of July weekend, Jacob Lace, the publisher of *Fashion and Interiors* and the six other sister magazines that made up a publishing empire, gave a party. It was more than a command performance; in the world of fashion an invitation to that party was the confirmation of a patent of nobility. Harriet always attended, abandoning for the occasion her normal policy of staying clear of business socializing. This year Spider had been invited, because of his steady work for *Fashion,* and, of course, he brought Melanie.

Lace lived in Fairfield County on twenty-five acres of green fields and woods, not far from the Fairfield Hunt Club. His house had been built in the 1730s and lovingly restored and expanded over the years. On the night of the party, many thousands of tiny, white lights flickered in all the great old trees and turned every copse into a set from *A Midsummer Night's Dream.* People flew in for this party from Dallas and Houston and Chicago and Bel Air and Hawaii. Hostesses on Fire Island and the Hamptons and Martha's Vineyard, cursing the publisher, planned their own Fourth of July parties so as not to conflict with his and be left without their key guests, the ones for whom the others came. There were no photographers present taking pictures for the society pages, no society editors taking notes. This was a strictly private party for the elite and potential elite of the worlds of fashion, the theater, the dance, advertising, merchandising, publishing, and designing.

Jacob Lace's clever wife had long ago solved the problem of what to feed hundreds of guests by sticking to what she called "traditional American food"—hamburgers, hot dogs, pizza, and all thirty-one flavors of Baskin-Robbins. This bicentennial year it was more appropriate than ever. In keeping with her all-American tradition, she had four heavily stocked bars, built inside red, white, and blue striped tents on the lawn and near the pool.

Harriet Toppingham loved to drink. She never drank during business hours, but every night, as soon as she reached the haven of her apartment, she immediately poured herself a double bourbon on the rocks and then another and perhaps another before she sat down to her late dinner, served by her silent cook. She didn't like wine, and she never drank anything at lunch or after dinner because it might impair her efficiency at work, but those predinner drinks were a necessary habit of twenty years' standing. She was afraid to drink with people who were not part of her inner circle because she knew that some sort of change came over her when she drank. When she was alone, or with her own kind of women, it didn't matter—no one had ever seemed to notice—but she felt that it was wiser to take no chances.

She came to Lace's party by herself, in a chauffeured limousine. Like most New Yorkers, Harriet didn't own a car. Normally, she would have invited any one of a number of willing male escorts, men she met through her work, but this year there didn't seem to be anyone she wanted to single out for the honor of coming with her. Harriet, who knew almost everyone at the party, was greeted as a peer by a very few, as a star by everyone else. She moved from group to group with the glitter of a matador, encased in a vintage, shocking-pink-and-black satin Schiaparelli, thickly encrusted with gold braid, a dress that belonged only in a museum or on Harriet Toppingham. She was strolling about, holding a glass of tonic water, when she caught a glimpse of Spider and Melanie, walking alone, holding hands, and gazing around them with fascination. They had met very few of the other guests, and it wasn't the sort of party at which anyone made introductions—people were on their own. Spider, with his golden tan and his golden hair, was as splendid as a decathlon winner at his moment of triumph. Both he and Melanie wore white, and people turned to look after them when they had passed.

As soon as they saw her, the two of them hurried to greet Harriet; Melanie's pleasure was frank at seeing a familiar face in this crowd of impressive strangers. The three of them chatted for a few minutes in a way that seemed oddly self-conscious in this nonworkday setting. Then Spider, restless, insisted on taking Melanie off to see the stables, which were Lace's hobby. As she watched them go, Harriet asked the nearest waiter for a double bourbon on the rocks. An hour later, when the currents and eddies of the huge party brought the three of them together again, near the pool pavilion, Harriet had had two more double bourbons and one ice-cream cone.

"Spider, leave Melanie with me for a while." She was commanding, not suggesting. "I'm going to introduce her to some people I think she should know and they'll never get to talk to her with you leaning all over her like that. Go and talk to some of your discards, Spider. God knows, there are enough of them here to fill a brothel."

Melanie looked beseechingly at him.

"My feet are hurting, Spider, and I do believe I've had too much champagne. I'd better stay put with Harriet. But you go on and have fun—I'll feel better soon."

Spider turned on his heel and walked away.

"Do you think he's angry?" Harriet asked. The two women moved inside the pool pavilion and sat down in a corner on a wicker couch with sailcloth cushions. Melanie kicked off her shoes and sighed in relief.

"Honestly, Harriet, I couldn't care less. He doesn't own me, even though I know he'd like to. He's a darling, really, and I am grateful, but there are limits—limits—*limits*."

"I thought you and Spider were head over heels?" Harriet had never asked Melanie such a personal question before. She expected the girl to answer in her usual impersonal way.

"Whatever in the world gave you that idea?" Melanie was shocked out of her passivity. "I've never been head over heels—hate that expression anyway—I don't think

I'll ever be, I don't even *want* to be. Why, if I gave part of myself away to everybody who wanted a piece there wouldn't be anything left of me by now. I just can't say 'yes, I love you too' just because someone else feels that way."

"Still, you are living together—that's supposed to mean something more than just gratitude, even these days." Harriet knew she should stop herself from probing like this; she was getting too inquisitive, but she couldn't resist going just a little farther.

"We are *not!* I've never spent a whole night at Spider's place and I won't let him touch me in my own apartment. I feel very strongly about that, Harriet—I insist on my privacy! Goodness, it's awful—dreadful—to think that you thought we were living together—that's such a tacky thing to do. Maybe everyone does it in New York, but it's not my style. I'm so ashamed—if you thought so, everyone else must think so too." Melanie had tears of indignation in her eyes. She had pushed herself away from the cushions as she spoke and now she was bending emphatically toward the older woman. Harriet was dimly aware of danger, great danger, but she didn't hold herself back. She put her arms around the girl, pulled her forward, and held her close. She brushed her lips lightly over Melanie's hair, so carefully that Melanie didn't feel the caress.

"I didn't really believe it. I never believed it. No one believes it. It's all right, all right, baby, all right." For a long moment they remained there—Melanie grateful and comforted, completely unalarmed. Then Harriet knew that she had to push her away before she kissed the girl's glowing flesh. As she lifted her head from Melanie's hair she saw Spider hurriedly turn away from the doorway, the beginnings of comprehension openly written on his face.

The following morning was a Saturday, the first day of a three-day weekend for most businesses. Harriet Toppingham let herself into the deserted offices of *Fashion* with her own key and walked quickly through the empty corridors until she came to her office. There she scooped up the September issue of the magazine, one of the three copies that had just come back from the printer's in rough form for editorial correction, and searched her files for all the pictures of Melanie that had been taken for future issues. She invaded the art director's office and found some layouts that featured Melanie for the October and November issues and added them to her loot. Then she hurried home and made a person-to-person call to Wells Cope in Beverly Hills.

Wells Cope was considered the luckiest producer in the film industry. He had been chief of all production for a major studio until six months ago. During his three-year tenure, the studio had had five major box-office hits as well as the average inevitable number of failures and break-evens. However, the grosses from the successful pictures, which all happened to be special projects and pets of Cope's, had boosted the studio's earnings and the price of its stock high above that of the competition. Cope decided that if he was ever going to make any money for himself, this was the time to leave, since the history of the survival of a studio production head is somewhat less reassuring than that of a Mafia hit man.

With a combat-trained, elite shock squad of lawyers and accountants, he worked out a deal that would make him an independent producer, with the ability to call on the studio for financing for his own projects, yet able to keep a much greater profit participation than his salary and pieces of the net had given him in the past. A sweetheart deal, people said enviously. He was, quite possibly, the most envied man in an industry that drinks envy for breakfast and dreams envy at night.

There is a great deal of cross-pollination between the movie and fashion worlds. Models act, actresses model, movies promote new trends in design, fashion magazines give editorial attention to moviemakers. And the top people in both worlds often work together in ways that concern only themselves.

"Wells, it's Harriet. What are you doing with yourself on this glorious weekend?"

"Frankly, my dear, I'm in hiding. Nobody knows I'm in town. I couldn't take the idea of going out to Malibu for one more beach and fireworks party—too many ex-wives floating around there. Right now I'm still in bed with twenty-five scripts, none of which I'm panting to read, and some disgustingly soggy French toast. These lousy long weekends are un-American—fuck leisure."

"I agree entirely—it's obscene. Listen, there's something I wanted to see you about. Business. I was thinking of flying out this afternoon and going back Monday. Would you be free for a while?"

"Not just free—rhapsodic! Thank God there's someone in the world who's minding the store this weekend. We'll have an orgy. I'll call Bob at The Wine Merchant to send over some big pots of fresh beluga and tell my chef to do his pompano in a paper bag. I remember that's your favorite. Harriet, you're a blessing."

Wells Cope, wearing a Dorso sweater, pale beige twill trousers, and black velvet evening pumps embroidered in gold, sat with Harriet on the deep, gray velvet couch in his vast living room. Pictures of Melanie were spread all over the Lucite coffee table and some of them lay on the twelve-thousand-dollar Edward Fields rug. Air conditioning kept the room at a cool 70 degrees, a wood fire blazed in the grate, and the butler had left a decanter of cognac on a side table and gone to bed. Although it was early July, it could have been any season in the year in any place in the world where there exists a climate of total luxury.

Cope looked at Harriet shrewdly through his blue-tinted glasses.

"She's unreal. Fucking unreal. Glamour seeping out of every pore. I didn't know they still grew girls like that. She's like one of the great stars of the thirties when they were young. But I still don't quite get it, Harriet. This issue won't be out for another six weeks. You don't have to worry about losing her to us until then. Why are you showing me these pictures now? You could tie her up for the next six months if you wanted to—or rather, if Eileen Ford let you."

"Because I know perfectly well that everyone will be after her and, inevitably, someone will get her. I'm resigned to losing her for the magazine sooner or later, but I want to be the one to decide to whom. She has a lot of faith in my advice, and I believe you'd be the best for her. Or, we can put it this way, Wells. I want to do someone a favor rather than look like a loser."

"And I'll owe you?"

"You'll owe me," she agreed. "I probably won't ever collect, but it's nice to know it's there. You'll honor the obligation and most wouldn't—and we go back a long way."

"So we do." He was wondering what the old dyke had been up to. She was acting like a fucking stage mother. This wasn't Harriet's style at all. But so what, if he got the girl.

"I suppose it's absurd to ask if she can act?"

"That's for me to know and for you to find out," Harriet answered. When she got what she was after, she was capable of a little show of schoolmarmish high spirits.

"I intend to. Next week. Could you possibly call her for me and arrange to get her on a plane as soon as possible?"

"No, Wells, you'll have to handle that end. Tell her anything you want to but don't mention my name. I'll give you her home phone number—say you got it over the grapevine—you'll think of something. I don't want *anyone* to know I've shown you these pictures. I'll take the credit when the moment comes. That is a *must*, Wells. I've never been more serious. It wouldn't help me at the magazine if they knew."

"Harriet, I understand perfectly. I give you my absolute assurance." He didn't understand at all, but he knew he would eventually. In any case, Wells Cope hadn't built his Hollywood career on betraying trusts. Secrecy was one of his major talents.

Harriet flew back to New York on Tuesday. Wells had persuaded her to stay over the extra day to keep him company in his hide-out vacation. His was one of the only houses in the world where a person could grow sick of pâté de foie gras, beluga *malossol, canard à l'orange,* great wines, and private screenings of unreleased movies in just three days. Harriet felt pleasantly cosseted and anxious to get back to work.

On Wednesday morning Harriet made eight phone calls, two of them to women she considered the most important fashion editors in town, besides herself, and the other six to the art directors of huge advertising agencies. She set up lunch dates with them for what was left of that week and all of the following week.

Long before the final lunch Spider was dead professionally.

"But, Harriet, everyone's heard he's your new fair-haired boy."

"No one will *ever* know what I went through with him, Dennis. Talent isn't enough to excuse everything. He's simply incapable of being on time—it must be some sort of compulsion. He always kept us waiting around the studio for a minimum of two hours before he finally deigned to show up! More than half the time the models had to leave for other bookings before he got there. And then the retakes! There weren't more than a handful of shots we didn't have to retake once, sometimes twice. In fact, although I hate to give that bastard credit, if our art director hadn't been there to hold his hand every step of the way, we wouldn't have been able to use him at all."

"Christ, why did you put up with it?"

"Because if you can possibly hang in there, he *is* good. But now I'm cutting my losses. You can imagine what it cost. I'm so far over budget for every issue I used him for that Lace is frankly ready to kill. He's usually understanding about these things, but this time it's way out of bounds. Spider Elliott just has a Stanley Kubrick complex. If I wasn't such an old hand, I'd probably be out on my ass."

"Retakes, huh?"

"That wasn't all. I put up with his screwing the models in the dressing room, but now I find that his latest work is simply unusable. Just plain *bad*. We'll have to re-shoot all of November with another photographer. It's all my fault when you get right down to it. When will I learn not to give inexperienced kids a chance? But enough of my horror stories, Dennis. I'm sorry I had to cry on your shoulder, but this has been one of the worst experiments I've made in years. Let's forget it—tell me about what's going on over at your shop. How's your new account coming along? I think the ads are smashing—who are you using?"

"Really, Spider, I just don't understand what you're getting so upset about." Melanie's ice-sweet voice didn't betray any anger, just a sort of plaintive wonder. "I still

242

don't know exactly how Wells Cope heard about me, but I checked it out with his office on the coast and there's no doubt that it's perfectly legitimate. He just wants me to come out and be tested. They said I'd only be gone about two weeks—that's not forever—and anyway, it sounds sort of thrilling. You're acting like he might be a white slaver when you know perfectly well he's one of the top producers in Hollywood." Melanie was speaking from Spider's huge canvas chair, designed for lolling rather than sitting, but she retained her upright, demure poise. "Oh, Spider, I know it's a million to one nothing will come of it, but all my expenses will be paid and I'll get to see California, so how can you be so negative?"

"But what if you don't come back from the Casbah? Haven't you heard tales of people who went to Hollywood for only two weeks and were never seen having lunch in Gino's again?"

"Silly." His fear and his need had showed plainly through his attempt at a joke. Nothing could have made Melanie more certain that she was right to leave. First, Spider had started making really ridiculous insinuations about Harriet, who had only been trying to comfort her—such insanely sinister hints—she was glad she'd refused to even listen—and now he was actually trying to prevent her from having a screen test. In the beginning, when they were shooting the September issue, she had thought that Spider was the most exciting and unpredictable man she'd ever met—so sure of his talent, able to help her be something she hadn't known she could be, but lately he was getting just like all the others, wanting too much, wanting more than she ever intended to give. Because she'd let him make love to her, she'd let herself get into this position where he thought he had rights. Rights!

Spider suddenly scooped her up out of the chair and gently laid her on his bed. "My love, my little love, let me be your slave—only what you want, darling, only what you want." He was actually shaking in the shamelessness of his passion. Melanie, taken by surprise, realized that it wouldn't be easy to slip away from Spider when he was this wild. He knew she was taking the first plane tomorrow morning. It seemed simpler to let him have his way.

She lay back, offering herself docilely, while he undressed

her and then hastily stripped himself naked, his graceful athlete's body a shadowy bulk against the faint light of the room. She wouldn't do a thing, she thought, not a single thing, just lie there and let him have his fun.

Spider bent tenderly over her, all his weight on his knees and his elbows, staring at her composed wide-eyed face. His heavy cock was already so hard that it was horizontal, almost flat up against his belly as he knelt. She didn't look at it. Slowly, never touching her except with his lips, he kissed her marvelous mouth, outlining her lips with the tip of his tongue as carefully as if he were creating them. When she didn't open her lips to him, he thought that she was asking him, without words, to suck her nipples. He settled back on his heels, leaned forward, and cupped a small breast softly in each hand. He paid homage to each breast in turn, rimming the nipple with his tongue until it stood up, then sucking it with his mouth for long intent minutes—the silence unbroken except for his suckling sounds. Once he whispered, "Good? Is it good?" and she breathed quietly, "Hmm." After a long while Spider gently pushed Melanie's breasts together with both his hands so that the nipples were only inches apart. Holding them firmly, he darted his tongue from one to the other, now sucking, now nuzzling, now nipping her delicately with his teeth, now opening his mouth as wide as possible to take in as much of her breast as he could, the suction coming from his cheeks and throat as well as from his lips. Her breasts were wet and pink and suddenly they seemed bigger, fuller, than he'd ever felt them before. Spider hadn't felt the touch of her hands anywhere on his body; her arms were still lying at her sides. Playing virgin, he thought tenderly. But she must be ready. He slid down the bed to enter her.

"No," she hissed. "You said you'd be my slave. You may not put it in me—I forbid you. Absolutely. You may not!"

"Then you know what a good slave would have to do, don't you," he said deeply in his throat, on fire at the prohibition. "That thing you've never let me do to you—that's what you have a slave for."

"I don't know what you mean," she said tonelessly, giving him tacit permission.

He cupped his hands under her buttocks. She hastily

244

laced her hands together over her pubic hair but made no protest. After searching with his tongue, Spider found a tiny space between her fingers and pushed his strong, impatient tongue through it until he reached the silky hair and the warm skin. Still she said nothing. Victoriously, he spread her knees apart, firmly grasped her wrists and pinned her hands at her sides. He slid down further on the big bed and lay flat on his pulsating penis, his head held just above her pussy. The feathers of fine hair barely covered her deliciously white and childish-looking outer lips. He covered her pubic hair with long lappings of his tongue, so that the hair grew wet. Then, using only the tip of his tongue, he traced and retraced the indentation deep between the outer lips and the pinker inner lips, folded secretly inside. Finally his tongue found the furrow between those soft inner lips and pushed upward into her vagina. He curled and pointed his long tongue so that it was as firm as possible and plunged it in deeply.

"No! Stop. Remember your promise—no farther," she panted, beginning to wriggle away from him in earnest. Still holding her down with his hands he pulled his tongue back and sought the nub of her clitoris with his lips. It was tiny, almost hidden, but he sucked persistently on it once he had found it, stopping only to slowly rub his tongue back and forth across it several times before he resumed sucking. As he sucked he found that rhythmically, unconsciously, he was rubbing his hugely engorged penis on the sheets that covered the bed. Suddenly the silent girl started to make lunging movements toward his mouth as if she wanted him to take her whole pussy in his mouth at once. She pushed it in his face with total abandon, grunting, "Don't put your cock in—whatever you do—keep your promise, slave." As he sucked and licked frantically, increasing the pace, he heard her moaning and muted ferocity, as if she could hardly keep from screaming out loud. He forgot his own self so completely that it seemed as if all the world contained was this wide-open cunt, which he was not allowed to enter, only to pleasure. Suddenly she went very still, all her muscles rigid. Finally she was shaken by contractions and she shouted. As he felt this climax, Spider's cock had been excited beyond endurance from the friction of the sheets as he worked on her. He felt himself shooting sperm convulsively, over the bed, unable to hold back another second.

They fell apart, exhausted, as their orgasms subsided. After a minute Spider, still lying face down on the bed, felt her stir. "Don't move—I'm just going to the bathroom." She slipped away as he lay there, too happy and too drained to look after her. She's finally made it, he thought, finally, finally. So that's what she'd wanted all along. What a shy, repressed silly darling, afraid to do the thing that delighted her beyond all else—next time I'll know what she really wants—and I'll give it to her, and give it— His thoughts trailed off into a short sleep.

When he woke up she was gone.

"Val, darling Val, tell me the truth. Do you think I'm being paranoid?"

Valentine looked carefully at Spider. He was huddled, as if he were cold, in her biggest chair, yet his hair was streaked with nervous sweat, his skin gray and tight-looking around his mouth and eyes. Why, she wondered, did she feel as if her heart might crack for him? He was her best friend, nothing more. Of course, friendship was an important thing, more important really than love, for it lasted, while love— just look where love had brought him. She could have warned him about Melanie, but it had been none of her business.

"You are a bigger fool than I thought the first time I met you, Elliott," she said softly.

"Huh?"

"Of course you're not paranoid. One night you see Harriet Toppingham trying to make love to your little friend. Seven days later your little friend is in California and your new agent has called to tell you that all your bookings for this week have been canceled, not just for *Fashion* but for three different advertising agencies. And now he tells you that you have no bookings at all for next week and he can't even get in anywhere to show your stuff. You'd have to be mad if you didn't put two and two together."

"But it's so fucking unbelievable. Why would anyone do something like this? What did Harriet think I was going to do? Tell people—broadcast it maybe? Blackmail her or challenge her to a duel at dawn? She has no reason to destroy me!"

"Elliott, sometimes you are naive. You have told me a great deal about this Harriet Toppingham and her ways, and I can tell you, from being brought up in a world full of women most of my life, that she is evil. Can't you feel it? Can't you put yourself in her place and imagine how a woman like that must have felt about you when you didn't bow down and kiss her ass like everyone else does?". Valentine's bright, untidy head bobbed angrily to emphasize her words. "I have known many women who live for power and I know what wicked things they are capable of when they are threatened. You thought that because she was female she must have liked you? Elliott, I know you are considered delectable—but not to her."

"Is that what you think it's all about? Her being a dyke?"

"Not at all. It would have probably happened sooner or later even if there had been no Melanie. You didn't give her what she wants from a man, every man she does business with."

"I just don't see what you mean, Val. I always respected her—everyone does—and I did my best for her and she knew it."

"But did you fear her?"

"Of course not."

"*Alors*—" She said the one word with the dismissive, trailing-off sound the French make when they have scored an incontestable point, one that requires no further proof.

"There's something else, something very odd about the way Melanie sounds on the phone," he finally mumbled, breaking the silence that had fallen over them. He was ashamed and humbled in his pain. "She doesn't really say how things are going, just that she's working hard, but she sounds a lot farther away than three thousand miles. I wonder if that old bitch told her some filthy lies—" He stopped, arrested by a fleeting expression of pity and disbelief on Valentine's stubbornly logical little face. "You don't think that's why, do you? You think it's something different. What? Tell me what!" He could not forget that last evening with Melanie, when he was convinced that he had finally found the secret that would make her surrender wholly to him, yet, when he spoke to her on the phone, she had seemed as noncommittal, as distantly poised as ever.

"Elliott, it is none of my business, what goes on between

247

you and Melanie. Perhaps she is being overwhelmed by it all. Why don't we open some wine and I'll heat up a little—"

"Jesus, Val! You remind me of the story about the mother whose son came crawling into the house bleeding from five gunshot wounds. 'Eat first, talk later,' she told him. Now stop trying to feed me and tell me exactly what you think about Melanie. I always know when you're lying, so don't pull anything cute. And it is your business. You're my only friend."

"And what are friends for?" Valentine said mockingly, stalling for time, trying to think of the right words to say.

"Tell me," he pleaded. "What do you think is happening —just give me your best guess—I won't hold it against you —but someone has to talk to me."

"Elliott, I don't think it has anything to do with you. I think that Melanie wants something you can't give her. I thought so from the first day I met her. She's not a happy girl—even you didn't make her happy. No, don't interrupt. You would have made her happy if anybody could have, but it's not a man she wants. Not a woman either. Not another person—something else."

"You just plain don't like her very much," said Spider, holding back a feeling of resentment.

"Perhaps it is merely as Colette says, 'Extreme beauty arouses no sympathy.'"

"Colette!"

Valentine continued, ignoring him, "Maybe it's as simple as your typical American fantasy—to be a movie star. Why did she leave so quickly? She had to cancel a week's bookings? Why should you think that Melanie wouldn't have exactly the same ambitions as ten million other American girls? She's beautiful enough—"

"Enough!" he said savagely.

"More, far more than enough. It is strange, is it not, how an accident of a millimeter here, a millimeter there, makes one face so important. Think about it, Elliott. She has two eyes, a nose, a mouth, just like everyone else. It's all in tiny degrees of placement, such a small area of magic to make such a big difference. For me, Elliott, I must tell you it is a hard thing to understand—why these things, these millimeters, are so crucial to you, you of all men. How sublime it must be for her not to need charm. Did she make you laugh? Did she love you as much as you loved her? Did she protect you and warm you and keep you from suffering?" Valentine turned her eyes away from him, unable to face the empty answer in his face but not wanting to stop saying what she had thought for so long. "I saw how fascinating her mystery was to you. For my part, I think that the mystery is always greatest where there is the most—emptiness. A person full of life is never mysterious, on the contrary. If Garbo had had something to say for herself, she'd just be another woman now."

"Christ! The fucking, objective, know-it-all French. How can you dissect emotions like that? You've never been in love—that's obvious!"

"Perhaps—perhaps not. I'm not at all sure. Now, damn it, we eat. You can starve for love's sake if you like but I bloody well won't." Valentine poured them both some wine and watched him as sternly as a mother hawk as he drank it. In her heart grew the most profound wish, a prayer, very unselfish, for that spoiled little nothingness of a Melanie to become the world's biggest movie star.

Melanie had been staying in Wells Cope's guest house. For ten days she had worked all day long with David Walker, a great drama coach. Cope's butler drove her to Walker's house in the Hollywood Hills each morning and came back for her at four. It all felt, she thought, so right, so weirdly right. Perhaps she was crazy, but she had an idea that maybe she could act a little. David didn't exactly overload her with encouragement, but, on the other hand, he hadn't been as critical as she had expected. And the day before yesterday, before the test, he'd given her a fatherly kiss for luck—she didn't think he did that for everyone.

At night she dined with Wells, always at his house—a dream of flowers, paintings, crystal, silver, music. She had never met a man like him. Witty, incurious, restrained, aloof, clever, wordlessly understanding, wanting nothing from her, yet taking enough obvious pleasure in her company so that she didn't feel unappreciated. She wished in a way that he hadn't seen the test today—that this could just go on forever, this protected, soothing world where nothing was asked of her except that she learn to pretend to be someone else—

it felt so good. She floated in being someone else. She hadn't felt the old need to *see* herself when she was acting a part.

In the distance she saw the gates open and Wells's Mercedes being driven through. But he didn't, as usual, go into the house. He crossed the garden, skirted the pool, walked over the lawn, and came to where she was sitting with a drink in her hand and a book in her lap. He took the book and the drink and put them on a table. Then he grasped both her hands and pulled her to her feet. She didn't have to ask—the sight of his face was enough. But she did anyway, for sheer delight.

"I can act?"

"Of course." He was triumphant, transfigured.

"What now?" An unexpected joy, awaited yet unpredictable, unfolded suddenly, as at the end of a long labor in childbirth.

"Now I shall *invent* you. Isn't that what you've been waiting for?"

"All my life. All my life!"

That night Wells Cope took Melanie to Ma Maison for dinner and introduced her to everyone he knew. He gave no explanation of who she was, but Melanie was conscious that half the people in the restaurant were glancing at their table whenever they thought they wouldn't be noticed. She could feel the heat of their greedy, questioning looks on her even when she couldn't see their eyes. It felt terribly good.

After dinner Wells Cope made love to her for the first time. It was perfect, she thought later, like a slow waltz. He must have spent an hour just looking at her naked body, turning it this way and that, touching and exploring it all over with his undemanding fingers, like a blind man, lost in a dream that wanted no participation from her beyond her precious, empty self. Finally, when he possessed her, it was just an extension of the dream—deliberate, languid, and full of the grace of the flesh, with none of the sweaty, hot, urgent intensity that she feared. Best of all, he didn't want to know if she had come. Why did men always ask that? It was no one's damn business but her own. She had not, but she felt supremely good all over, like a cat whose fur has been smoothed in the right direction for hours. And when she finally got up, he seemed to know, without asking, that she never spent an entire night in bed with a man. He had let her go back to the guest house peacefully, with only a look from his visionary eyes, which made promises she was certain he would keep.

July 25, 1976

Spider,

    Please don't telephone me again. I won't answer the phone if you do. It just disturbs me and I don't want to be disturbed. I don't know why, but I've never been any good at saying things out loud and making people believe me, but maybe I can convince you in writing. I don't love you and I will not marry you. I'm not coming back to New York—I'm staying here, and as soon as Wells finds the right property, I'll be making a movie.

    Why can't you understand when something is over? Couldn't you guess from the way I sounded every time you called? I realize now that you've been trying to tie me up in ropes. You've wanted every bit and crumb and last drop of me, like a cannibal. I could hardly breathe when you were around the last few weeks—you stifled me. You might as well realize that you don't have any choice in this. I've gone away from you for good. Can I be any more convincing than that?

    I can act, Spider. This movie business isn't a "crazy idea" as you said on the phone. I think I first knew I could act that last night at your house when you insisted on making love to me even though I didn't want to. I convinced you that it was good for me that time, didn't I? But I felt nothing. *Nothing, I swear it.*

Melanie

John Prince, the designer for whom Valentine was working when Spider received his letter from Melanie, was one of the kings of Seventh Avenue. He liked to tell interviewers that the people who surrounded him in his various enterprises were special. "They are the Vivid People," he said boastfully. "Every once in a great while," he expounded, "you meet someone extraordinary and something immediately happens between the two of you—that's how I know who My People are—it's purely an instinctive thing."

In point of fact, his troupe of assistants, like Valentine,

was chosen entirely for their talent, hard work, and crafts-manship. Prince never merely licensed his name to a manu-facturer and took the money. If a line of sheets and towels bore the legend "By John Prince" it meant that he had personally approved of the designs created in His image by one of His People. The same held true for His bathing suits, shoes, raincoats, costume jewelry, scarves, sunglasses, wigs, belts, furs, lounge wear, and perfume. Prince was far too protective of his reputation as a designer to choose anyone to work for him on mere instinct. However, in order to pro-duce Vivid People he had often been known to take over a new employee and transform that person into someone ex-citing enough to be worthy of the Prince label.

He had all but hired Valentine sight unseen when he saw the rare new talent in her designs for the Wilton collection, which Spider Elliott had brought to his attention. When she arrived in his office he was content to see that, for once, he had found someone vivid enough for two. She marched in with her crop of curls smoldering brightly above her astonish-ingly pale green eyes and white face. Although Valentine always used three coats of black mascara on her lashes, which served to emphasize the Rue du Faubourg-St. Honoré quali-ty of her looks, today she had applied green eyeshadow as well, to draw attention away from her body. Since finding out about Alan Wilton she had lost fifteen pounds she badly needed, and dressing at the last minute, she had to fling a bulky rust-and-orange plaid poncho over the brown jump-suit that now hung on her body.

"Well, pet, I feel as if I could warm my hands on you," he said with a flattering smile, as he rose from his chair to shake her hand. Prince led Valentine to a tufted leather Chesterfield, which faced his desk. His office looked like the smoking room in a distinguished London club, all dark woods, fine bindings, gleaming leather, polished brass, and dignity. Prince was a high-school dropout from Des Moines who had reincarnated himself as an English squire. It was not good taste but linguistic inability that stopped him from assuming a British accent. An agreeably bulky man with graying hair and a pleasantly lined face, Prince looked, simultaneously, like a high-ranking, semiretired British general in mufti and a fabulously successful racetrack tout.

He created this impression by artfully combining various pieces from his own line of men's clothes and never wearing anything that was not either tweed, checked, or plaid—unless it was herringbone. If his pants were in a brown-and-white tweed, his vest would be in a green-and-brown Glen plaid, his jacket in a very hairy, large houndstooth check, and his tie a Paisley that matched the lining of the jacket collar. He had always hankered to carry a shooting stick but compromised on an umbrella. One of his employees was fond of saying that Prince had to be immortal because he didn't own anything plain enough to wear to his own funeral. Prince secretly saw himself as a great landed gentleman, the Earl of Northumberland perhaps, who supported a band of traveling players. None of these harmless fancies kept him from being the richest designer in the United States.

"When I spoke to your agent yesterday," he said to Valentine, "I told him that I needed you to work directly with me on my women's ready-to-wear. Now, I don't want to pry ino your reasons for leaving Wilton Associates, but the one thing we have to understand, up front, is that your name cannot be used in connection with my line. You see, my dear, you'll be my associate until you go on to someplace where they'll give you billing—as you undoubtedly will in time—but, in the meanwhile, there won't be any personal credit for anyone but me."

When Valentine merely nodded in quick and understanding agreement, he thought to himself that his hunch had probably been right—she'd had trouble with that notoriously nasty, high-busted queen, Sergio. Her agent, Elliott, whoever he was, had hinted that it was a question of credit, but somehow he hadn't thought that was the whole story. And Alan Wilton had been very quick to praise her to the skies. Ah well, the intrigues of other shops rarely interested him—God knows, he had enough to handle under his own roof. Right now he was involved in creating a line of men's grooming products, and after six months the chemists still hadn't come up with a scent he thought was sufficiently masculine. His criterion was "Would the Duke of Edinburgh wear it?" and somehow, the answer was no. Press on, old chap, he encouraged himself, press on. The Empire wasn't built in a day.

Of all the male dress designers visible today in the world of American fashion, some 95 percent, if not more, are homosexual.

They have a variety of ways of being gay. John Prince was individual in his solid British gentry style, noticeably masculine and tempered with good midwestern roots. Others were austere functional-gay, given to wearing dark glasses at all times and dressed in a careful, unvarying uniform of a dark turtleneck and dark trousers, as if they had come out of the future by first-class spaceship. They lived in steel, plastic, and glass apartments, so spare and fined down that people felt tense just looking at photographs of their living rooms in which no trace of comfort was permitted. Then there is the sweet flock of Gatsby-gays, young beauties who dress in perfectly cut navy blazers and white pants, innocent, Ivy League open-necked pale blue shirts and Shetland crew sweaters, impeccably ready for a yacht to sail in and anchor at their feet. There is also a block of elder statesman-gays who have been secure for long enough to affect jeans and beards and amulets and strange-looking jackets without buttons. All of these designers are in enormous demand as guests and escorts by many of the most powerful—but single—women in the country. Without her priceless list of gay reliables, few society hostesses could put together a party.

There is also a tiny but influential married-gay set, whose wives are invariably as decorative as they are clever. They make a religion out of the art of living well, possessing marvelously beautiful apartments and country homes in which they give inventive dinner parties on small round tables, which are little museums of rare porcelain and cutlery. This is the group without which no major society party or important press junket is complete.

Advancement in the world of fashion design is dictated by this gay mafia. It is, for all the superficial differences of life-style in its members, a club in which no straight man is likely to make any progress. Women, yes: A number of important women designers, such as Holly Harp, Mary McFadden, Pauline Trigère, and Bonnie Cashin, as well as a number of good female designers in California, have been allowed entry, but they are a decided minority.

A durable working alliance exists between the gay

designers and the generally heterosexual businessmen who either own or run the financial side of the garment business. These men, generally Jewish and, for the most part, strong family men with firm ties to the New York Jewish community, are active in charities of all kinds. They provide the ballast that keeps the world of Seventh Avenue on a firm course. Outside of the business day little or no mingling between the two groups occurs, barring a department store publicity party or some sort of fashion establishment event, such as the Coty Awards.

The gay designers are leaders in almost everything that exists of the glamour of New York City. If a new restaurant opens, they find it first; a new artist, a new ballet, a new place to dance, a new hair stylist, can be made or broken by their favor. They are, in effect, Stars, with all the special privileges and perks of Stars. Each one of them attracts to himself a court, an entourage, that revolves around him, glorying in the air he projects of being superior to the dull norm of humanity. He invests himself and his followers with the conviction of being wittier, more daring, more artistic, more experimental, more sophisticated, more wicked, more knowledgeable, and, particularly, of *having more fun* than others.

No one did this better than John Prince.

His Vivid People were, in all the most important ways, his real family. He followed his impulses toward the openhanded largesse of one born to be a patron and never felt contented unless he was surrounded by those of his chief associates he secretly thought of as his "retinue," as well as a collection of others.

After the business day, Prince held court in his town house in the East Seventies. It had originally been two large town houses built side by side. When he bought them, he had the wall separating them torn down. The twin houses were then unified by a new Palladian facade, made of blocks of honey-beige marble with a noble center entrance. Inside the house a manorial staircase, with wide landings, ran up four flights through the old center of the two houses, the interiors of which had been completely gutted. Prince had depleted the rarest stocks of Stair and Co. and Ginsberg and Levy, two of the finest antique dealers in the world, before he realized that he—even he—was in need of a decorator. Within a year "Sister" Parish—Mrs. Henry Parish II, society's favorite decorator, famous for her seductive bedrooms and voluptuous sense of color, as well as for redecorating the Oval Room of the White House and for decorating President Kennedy's private quarters—had given him an unquestionably ducal setting. Quite properly he had forced himself to draw the line at even hinting to Mrs. Parish that he would like to have a family crest embroidered in gold thread on the hangings of his wide Chippendale four-poster—somehow he guessed that the firm-minded grandmother from Maine would not approve. Nor had he dared to mention the minstrel gallery he longed for, but otherwise he was vastly satisfied with his stately home.

Prince even had a majordomo: his lover of many years, Jimbo Lombardi, a cocky, tough cherub of a man, no more than five feet four inches tall but a born brawler, who had been one of the most decorated noncoms in Korea. When he wasn't efficiently killing the enemy, Jimbo was a gifted but essentially lazy painter, who was well content to spend his afternoons languorously occupying the beautifully equipped studio Prince had built for him under the eaves. In the morning, long after Prince had left their bed for his office, Jimbo finally descended to the lower regions of the house where he, the master chef, Luigi, and the two robust pantry maids, Renata and Luchiana, swapped tall and naughty tales in the kitchen Italian of Jimbo's boyhood in far-off, exotic Bridgeport, Connecticut. Jimbo was in charge of menus, inviting guests, and planning all the details of the week's parties.

If Prince had been born to be a host, Jimbo had been born to be master of the revels. He had a genius for bringing animation and good humor to every gathering and a superb eye for plucking potentially Vivid People from someone else's party and incorporating them into Prince's band of loyalists.

Jimbo took to Vallentine as soon as he met her. He had the security of being an indispensable, totally beloved mate in Prince's life, so he could afford to give vent to his friendly feelings. He had become a little bored lately by Prince's regulars: a skinny, black male model who was six feet seven inches tall and the wildest disco dancer in New York; a female jewelry designer who came from one of the aristocratic families of Brazil and simultaneously sported a crew cut and three heavily jeweled crosses; a Puerto Rican lad who painted gloriously on silk; a twitchy Hollywood superstar who flew religiously to New York when she was between pictures to order a completely new Prince wardrobe and bask in his genial warmth; a newly married young couple from two of Philadelphia's oldest families who brought Prince unwanted presents of hashish and then consumed most of it themselves; a legendary Russian ballet dancer who had defected so long ago that the IRS considered him one of their favorite Americans. Not that they weren't still all Vivid —it was just time for new blood.

Jimbo sensed that Valentine didn't want anything from Prince. She had an alluring self-sufficiency drawn around her like a lovely but durable carapace, and she was obviously not overanxious to become one of Prince's band of brothers. Nothing could have intrigued Jimbo more, accustomed as he was to people who felt that entrance into Prince's circle would grant them a cachet that nothing else could. Prince not only entertained his group at home but often took them out on the town, half filling a restaurant with them, buying two rows of seats for the hottest show on Broadway, leading them en masse, like part of a very elegant circus parade, into a charity exhibition or party given by a thrilled hostess. A Prince entrance was often photographed by *Women's Wear Daily* for their "Eye" section, the powerful gossip department that is usually read first by everyone but the most crotchety of zipper manufacturers.

Jimbo had always been the kind of homosexual who really likes women and, for that matter, so was Prince. But Jimbo knew how to create instant intimacy; in all but sexual matters he was wildly seductive with females. Valentine, with her cracklingly assertive hair and spunky ways, was a challenge to him.

She went to work for Prince in early 1973 and by the end of that year Valentine, coaxed and wooed by charming little Jimbo, felt comfortably at home in Prince's crowd. She never did anything to qualify herself as a Vivid Person —since she was born one—but the refreshing difference about Valentine was that she didn't try. Nothing works so well in a competitive social situation, such as the one in which Prince's People were caught, as a genuine lack of effort. When they perceived that Valentine just didn't care; that she could accept an invitation and enjoy it or fail to get an invitation and not have it matter one way or another to her; that she was secure enough, for whatever reason, not to be anxious to stamp herself with the stigmata of status or to step up the social ladder, she became the one ball of catnip in a room full of kittens.

Valentine's experience with Alan Wilton had, after she recovered from the worst of the emotional damage, inoculated her for a long time against romantic adventures. This deep coolness came across not as an antisocial attitude but as a self-confident, serene refusal to involve herself in high-flown personal expectations. Although the sexual ambiguity of Prince's People allowed Valentine to avoid relationships that might lead to another love affair, her sexual proclivities were one of the favorite topics of discussion among them. Was she a Lesbian? Did she have a lover somewhere who was married? Was she a fag hag, condemned to feel emotion only for men who didn't want women? It never occurred to anyone that Valentine's heart, like that of the Snow Queen in the old fairy tale, was pierced by a sliver of ice that prevented her from loving. To Prince and Jimbo, she seemed perfectly happy with her place as a design associate and her membership in the encircling world of his entourage.

From 1973 to 1976 Prince and Valentine worked side by side. Although his licensing activities brought in the really big money, their value was directly dependent on the continued success of his ready-to-wear line, which had made him famous in the first place. If Prince ever started to slip, and several bad collections in succession can almost put any American designer out of business, both with buyers and editors, the licenses might possibly not be renewed when the time came. Prince often brooded angrily over the case of the late Christian Dior, who had been dead well over a dozen years when the brand of panty hose that bears his name was invented. And that was only one example. How did the beastly French do it—so typical of the wogs.

Valentine learned how to work with Prince as if she were his second head. She mastered the conceptual fundamentals that made his expensive clothes different from any other designer's expensive clothes, and only an informed person could have told which of the two of them had worked on any part of any one sketch or chosen one fabric over another.

But Valentine was far from satisfied. She was content with her job as a job: Prince now paid her forty-five thousand dollars a year and she had her own assistants, but she was only a shadow figure and she felt it keenly. She was, if one insisted, doing something "creative," but creative in the image of Prince: She was nothing but a disciple, gifted but absolutely limited in what she would accomplish. Prince's rich clients were not innovative women: They wanted a Prince look they could count on as being immediately recognized by their peers as a Prince look. Valentine's work gave her less personal satisfaction than that of a professional art forger, since she couldn't even feel that she was putting something over on a gullible public.

Valentine had never stopped her own designing. Uninfluenced by what everyone was wearing on the streets of New York, uninfluenced by Prince's strong talent, she continued to fill page after page with sketches of her own ideas. Her only audience was Spider, her only model herself. Only rarely now did she have the time to actually make up one of her own designs, particularly since Prince demanded that she dress exclusively in his clothes, which he made for her for nothing. He dressed, as a matter of course, the permanent female members of his Vivid People, and Valentine was indispensable to him, since she lent the garments, destined for wealthy, still young, conservative, society matrons, her own brand of *chien* with which none of them would ever be blessed. However, every season Valentine doggedly made at least four garments of her own and added them to the others in her closet. She refused to give up that private side of her talent.

Several times a year Prince was forced to venture out of New York to show his new line at important charity fashion shows in major cities across the country. He even did the much loathed but highly profitable "trunk shows," for which Prince himself, along with a key salesperson and two house models, would accompany the sample collection to a major department store and for three hectic days, backed by heavy local newspaper advertising and store promotion, take orders for future delivery from the women who came in feverish flocks to squeeze into the samples. Oscar de la Renta, Bill

Blass, Adolfo, Kasper, Geoffrey Beene, in fact most important designers, recognize that there is nothing like a trunk show for stimulating interest in the rich women who rarely get to New York to shop. It is not just a way of making and keeping influential customers, it is also an important opportunity to see what women, uninfluenced by super-cautious store buyers, are anxious to choose when they have an entire line to pick from.

In the summer of 1976 Prince planned a longer trip than usual. He decided to combine a fashion show benefit for Chicago's Gastrointestinal Research Foundation with a trunk show at the local branch of Saks, going on to Detroit and Milwaukee for two more trunk shows, since he would be in the Midwest in any case. He also decided to fit in a secret trip home to Des Moines, where his widowed mother was a local celebrity for having produced him, although her friends, as working class as she was, knew of him only through the publicity clippings she pressed on them.

Valentine was tempted beyond the power to resist. With Prince away from the office for a full week and a half, she realized that she could sneak her own latest creations into her private office without anyone knowing that they were there. Then she would ask one of the house models to put them on for her. At last she could see what they looked like when they were worn by someone else. There was something ultimately frustrating in making clothes that you saw only on yourself in a mirror. Lately she had been troubled by the growing idea that her work was becoming too inbred, too personal. Perhaps her things wouldn't work on a girl with different coloring and a different way of holding herself.

Lately, she hadn't even had Spider to show them off to, Valentine mused. She had seen almost nothing of him since he had met Melanie Adams. Even now, with Melanie off in Hollywood, Spider was keeping largely to himself. The dinners she cooked went unshared, the comradeship she almost took for granted had disappeared. She didn't admit it, but she felt cast adrift. Never would she have believed that her love-'em-and-leave-'em, freewheeling Elliott could fall so insanely in love as he had with that disgustingly beautiful bitch. He was absolutely possessed, the damn fool, and she, Valentine, thought that it was too bad Spider wasn't Catholic. She would gladly have arranged for his exorcism.

Clearly he had the devil under the skin, as her mother used to say. No good could come of it; the girl didn't love anyone but herself as any idiot could see, but what man would listen to reason when he was in love? Or what woman either, Valentine added, grimly remembering. Hastily she turned to packing her most recently finished clothes in opaque plastic bags. She would get to the office early today, before anyone was around, and hang them in her private closet. There was no risk. Beth, the black model, was a good friend and renowned for her ability to withstand the temptation to gossip.

A half hour before lunchtime Valentine asked Beth if she could spare her some time later in the afternoon to try on a few things for her.

"Why not do it now, Val? I've got my yogurt right here and I wasn't planning to go for lunch anyway. If we wait till later there may be buyers dropping in and they'll need me in the showroom."

"Oh, would you really, Beth? That's wonderful! But listen, this sounds silly, but could we do it in my office? I'd prefer that no one sees them—they're just a couple of things I ran up myself for kicks, nothing important, but, well, you know how Mr. Prince is—"

"Enough said." The black girl was only an inch taller than Valentine and just as slim. In every other way they were as unalike physically as two women could be, and Valentine was dancing with anticipation of how her clothes would look on Beth.

An hour later both women were happily collapsed on Valentine's couch, each wearing one of Valentine's dresses, all the other garments heaped on the chairs, falling just as they had been left when Beth had taken them off.

"I haven't had so much fun since I gave up playing with dolls," Beth exploded. "I didn't know I was sooooo gorgeous! Baby, you're just nuts to worry that they might look good only on you. I like you in that number just fine, but I like me a lot better!"

"Beth, you are divine, divine, divine!" Valentine was almost drunk with relief and the excitement of seeing Beth, who ordinarily showed clothes with a bored hauteur, kicking up her heels and almost prancing as she tried on each new garment, entranced by their flair and fantasy and originality.

Suddenly they both jumped, in guilt, as someone knocked urgently on the locked door of Valentine's office.

"Who is it?" Valentine called, rolling her eyes at Beth.

"It's Sally," answered the receptionist. "Val, there's an emergency, come on out. Fast!"

"What's going on—is Mr. Prince back?" Valentine asked, not unlocking the door.

"I wish he were! Mrs. Ikehorn is here! Mrs. Ellis Ikehorn —and she won't talk to anyone but you or Mr. Prince. She's mad as hell—didn't know he was out of town. Come on— what are you waiting for? She's in the showroom, but she'll be in your office in a minute if you don't hurry."

Beth had already stripped and put on the gray satin wraps models wore between changes. She and Valentine exchanged appalled glances. They both knew, as did everyone on Seventh Avenue, that Billy Ikehorn, whom *Women's Wear Daily* had lately dubbed "The Golden Witch of the West," was John Prince's most cherished and adored private customer. Now that she had built Scruples, the dream store in Beverly Hills that everyone in the fashion business was gossiping about, she had become even more important to Prince since she was buying for the store as well as for herself.

"Beth, go tell the other girls to get into their first numbers and fast! Then go and tell Mrs. Ikehorn that I'm coming— no, never mind, that will take too much time—just go change and get out there in the showroom," Valentine said in a quick undertone, running her fingers through her hair and putting on her shoes in one swift movement. Beth vanished and Valentine headed toward the showroom at a fast trot.

Billy Ikehorn was standing in front of one of the showroom mirrors, every patrician bone in her body registering annoyance.

"Really, Valentine—what on earth is John doing in Middle America for heaven's sake?" she burst out, not even bothering to conceal her anger. "I made a special trip down to this God-forsaken neighborhood in this ghastly heat— and I find he's off on one of those silly charity shows instead of tending to business." She glared at Valentine, but even her furious expression did little to mar her regal, dark beauty.

"He will be absolutely desolated when he hears that he missed you, Mrs. Ikehorn," Valentine said, turning on a little French accent as she unconsciously did in moments of stress. "In fact, if he hears that we didn't give you the most satisfactory private show you've ever seen, I fear for our lives."

"I don't have much time," Billy answered, in her most curt manner, without a smile, not willing to be mollified. Finally she settled down in one of the booths, behind a small Lucite desk, where buyers sat and wrote their orders.

Valentine snapped her fingers and the house models, five in all, paraded in front of the two women, managing to change so quickly that there was no break between the presentation of the various items of the large collection. However, as smoothly as the showing went, Valentine noticed, with sinking heart, that Mrs. Ikehorn said nothing and wrote as little on the pad in front of her. Her posture was immobile and unbending, exuding irritation. It was not possible that she didn't see anything she wanted; the collection was an excellent one. Was she keeping the numbers in her head, Valentine wondered, in a panic.

When the last model had passed there was a small pause. Billy Ikehorn drew a deep breath and said in tones of withering assurance, "Dull, dull, *dull*." Valentine gasped. "I said 'dull' and I meant it. It's Prince, but it isn't new; it's so fucking dependable that it makes me want to scream. I know it will sell, Valentine, I'm not saying it won't, but it just doesn't make me want to buy. I can't get excited about one single thing. Not one piece—it's a bomb."

This was a catastrophe. Valentine knew that if John Prince had been there he would have cajoled and jollied Mrs. Ikehorn out of her bad mood long ago and had her writing numbers like a machine. She jumped up and faced the formidable woman who was sitting in judgment with total conviction that her word was law.

"Mrs. Ikehorn, you have to realize that your own taste is developed way beyond that of the average customer." Valentine knew that she shouldn't be this bold, but she had to do something to save the situation. "After all, now with your new store you are buying for other women, who will almost certainly not be able to wear what you wear or even understand it—" Valentine's voice trailed off as she noticed a spark of interest come into Billy's eyes.

"What about that dress you have on?" she demanded. With amazement, Valentine realized she was still wearing one of her own designs. She had run out of her office so quickly that she had forgotten to change into her Prince.

"Dress?" she said.

"Valentine, I know you can't be stupid, but it's getting hard to believe. You are wearing a dress. I like that dress. I want that dress. Sell me *that dress!* Is that plain enough for you?"

"I can't." Billy Ikehorn looked as stunned as if someone had deliberately thrown a large glass of red wine in her face. Valentine would have laughed if she hadn't been so terrified.

"Can't? Whose dress is it? Or is that a secret? I want to know!"

"It's my dress."

"Obviously. Who designed it? Don't tell me Prince because I can damn well tell he didn't. So—this *is* interesting! When the boss is out of town you won't even wear his clothes. Are they too fuddy-duddy for you, Valentine? Is that it?" There was menace in her tone and Valentine quickly decided that it was better to admit the dress was her own design than to let Mrs. Ikehorn think she was wearing something from the competition.

"Sometimes—almost never—I make a little something for myself, just so that I don't forget how to sew. That's all it is, Mrs. Ikehorn—just an inexpensive little thing I ran up at home. That's why I can't sell it to you. This is the only one."

" 'Inexpensive!' This is Norell quality wool jersey at a hundred dollars a yard and you know it better than I do. Stand up and turn around," Billy commanded. As Valentine reluctantly rotated, the stock boy entered the showroom wheeling a rack on which hung all her other designs.

"Say, Miss O'Neill, the receptionist told me to get all of these things of yours out of the office. Where do you want 'em?" he called.

"Over here and right away," Billy Ikehorn ordered.

"Bon Dieu d'un bon Dieu!" Valentine heard herself groaning.

"Parfaitment!" Billy replied, smiling wickedly. It was her first smile of the day.

If Valentine had entertained the most unrealistic prayer that John Prince would not find out what had happened while he was away, the hope was demolished by the look on his face when he called her into his office two minutes after his return. He was almost unrecognizable in his fury. She would never have believed that the generous man she had worked for for three years was capable of such uncontrolled rage. He could hardly articulate for anger, screeching words at her in a voice she didn't know.

"Conniving little cunt—ungrateful little bitch—filthy, underhanded, deceitful, always knew you couldn't be trusted —a knife in my back," he ranted, brandishing a piece of paper at her.

"It wasn't my fault—she insisted—" Valentine started to say.

"Don't try to lie to me, you thieving slut! Read this!" And he almost rubbed the paper in her face. It was a letter from Billy Ikehorn, scribbled in her large, elegant handwriting on her personal notepaper.

John my pet,
  Such a pity you weren't there when I came. I was sorry to miss you, but perhaps it was all for the best, since, I'm embarrassed to say, there just didn't seem to be anything in the collection I felt I simply had to have. I'm sure that won't happen again—just one of those things. I did adore seeing all of Valentine's own designs—so charming and fresh and new—and I'm desperate to hear that she can't sell them to me. Won't you let her, for pity's sake? I never realized how brilliant that girl is. You should be very proud of her, instead of hiding her talent.
  Will you be at Mary Lasker's party for Dr. Salk? I'm thinking of flying back for it. If you're going, perhaps we might join forces? Did miss you, sweet—

                                                          Billy

"You don't understand how it happened—it wasn't the way you think—I didn't want to show her—" Valentine stopped, aware that he wasn't paying any attention to her.

"You're through!" Prince spat at her. "Through here, through on Seventh Avenue when they hear what you've done to me—I never want to see you again. When I think that I took you in and taught you everything you know—I've never been so betrayed, so shit on—"

"*Assez!*" Valentine's lusty temper finally snapped.

"What did you say, you guttersnipe, you—"

"I said 'enough!' I would not stay here for anything. You will find out that you're wrong, but nobody may talk to me like that—never! I do not stand for it!" Valentine ran to her office, picked up her handbag, and left the office without speaking to anyone she passed on the way. She found a cab and gave him her address. Only then did she begin to shake. She didn't cry—just shook and shook. It was all so fucking silly, all so fucking sad.

"Aren't we the fun couple?" Spider said brightly.

"Who do you think you are, Elliott, Woody Allen?" Valentine answered.

"No moxie, that's your trouble—why do foreigners never have a sense of comedic irony?" he complained.

"If you sounded any more jolly, I'd take you out and shoot you." Valentine tried to joke, but she was more concerned about the way Spider was lacerating himself than about her own jobless situation. Her crazy Elliott, so resilient, so skillful, so valiant, was like a fearless bullfighter who had just been badly gored for the first time. Even demolished as he was, he still wanted to sound hard-boiled.

"Do you know you've got great tits?"

"Elliott!"

"Just trying to change the subject—cheer you up. And they are—small but great, perky, pointy, piquant—lots of nice words that start with a 'p.' "

"Piss off!"

"Aw, come off it, Valentine. How about some tender, loving care?"

"Red or white?"

"Whichever is open." He leaned back in her big chair and drank a glassful of wine in one long gulp. He had started on vodka at home—quite a lot of vodka—but then he remembered, thank God, that Valentine was in her room —he'd hate to get drunk by himself. He had burned

Melanie's letter, but every word of it crawled through his mind like endless subtitles to a very bad German horror movie. And this had been going on for three days and nights. Valentine, even Valentine, especially Valentine, must never know what had happened.

"More wine?" she said.

"Since you insist. Hey, I delivered a job today." Valentine raised her eyebrows in surprise. "Would I kid you? My first job in almost three weeks. Girl drifted in, couple, three days ago, and wanted me to take test shots for modeling. Gorgeous but hopeless, a *numero uno* hooker if ever I saw one; no way she could work except for *Hustler*. But I shot three rolls anyway. The sexiest pictures I've done in my life. Why the fuck not? She came back to pick them up today and *plotzed* for joy all over the studio. It was Make-a-Hooker-Happy Day. I wouldn't let her pay—at least I can still give it away. Why don't I open another bottle?" he said, opening it as he spoke.

"Elliott. Some food?"

"You have a fetish about nourishment, my tootsie. Let's talk about you. I don't like the way you're behaving."

"What!" She sat up, feisty.

"Yeah—you should be out looking for a job instead of just sitting here drinking all that wine. Bad for the liver. Prince isn't the only game in town. I'm not going to play agent this time—you don't need one."

"Stuff that."

"Stuff 'em all—stuff 'em all, the long and the short and the tall," Spider sang to himself.

"I have no intention of ever working on Seventh Avenue again. Enough is enough! It's finished—you couldn't drag me there."

"Can't say as I blame you. But what'll you do?"

"Take in washing. Look, I've saved my money. It's nothing I have to decide today."

"Wish I could say the same." Spider looked dismal. If some jobs didn't come in his agent had warned him that he couldn't afford to keep the studio—in fact, his agent was about to jump ship; he could see all the signs. Oh, what the fuck! "I wanna propose a toast—to the two most talented people in New York who are not yet on Welfare." Spider drained another glass of wine and poured out some more, slopping it on the floor. "Sorry 'bout that—I'll just drink from bottle—easier that way." He weaved over to the bed and flopped down, taking a long pull on the bottle.

The phone rang. Valentine was startled. She'd only been out of work a week. She wondered who would be calling her here so late in the afternoon of a working day.

"Yes?"

"Valentine, it's Billy Ikehorn. I'm in California. I don't know what to say—I simply could *not* be more upset. I just heard what happened last week from one of my sales staff who's an old buddy of Jimbo's. It's incredibly unfair and it's all my fault. Entirely."

"You don't say?"

"Of course you think I'm a bitch and I certainly was a prize that day. But nothing is going right out here. Scruples is the most beautiful store in the world and I've got nothing to sell, no one to organize it. I was in that rotten, stinking mood because the whole thing is falling apart—you can't imagine how awful it is."

"Dear me."

"I don't blame you for being bitter, Valentine, but you've got to believe that when I wrote that letter I thought it might do you some good."

"Wrong."

"I know that now. Prince and I have made up. You'll be hearing from him—that's what I wanted to tell you—he just doesn't know how to approach you after—"

"I won't talk to him."

"It was that bad?"

"Worse."

"Your mind is made up?"

"Absolutely."

"I was hoping you'd say that! Valentine, come out here and work for me. You can write your own ticket. I'm desperate for a designer—without couture we're just another expensive store. And you'll go to Paris for the collections. Of course, I'd want you to be my buyer too. You can go to New York as often as you want to. I've decided that I'm just not about to spend my entire life in those elevators on Seventh Avenue—too grim."

"You don't want much, do you? A designer, a buyer—how about a lady's maid?"

"At least listen to my offer, Valentine. Eighty thousand dollars a year and five percent of the profits."

Valentine, stunned, didn't answer. Then her wild Irish spirit took over. "A hundred thousand. Who knows if there will be any profits?"

"Well, in that case it would be straight salary, no profit participation," Billy answered.

"No way, Mrs. Ikehorn. Why not be optimistic? Maybe there will be profits. The five percent stands."

"But that's a fortune!"

"Take it or leave it. Either you need me or you don't."

"Oh, all right—it's a deal."

"And, of course, my partner gets seventy-five thousand and two and a half percent."

"Your partner?"

"Peter Elliott. The best salesman in the world, lots of retailing experience. He will be able to reorganize Scruples to your complete satisfaction, I have not the slightest doubt."

"Since when do you have a partner, Valentine?"

"Since when have we exchanged confidences, Mrs. Ikehorn?"

"But I've never even heard of him."

"Since when are you a retailer? Excuse me, but it is necessary to face facts."

Billy was momentarily silenced by Valentine's effrontery. Still, anyone who thought she could afford to speak to her that way must know what she was doing.

"All of this goes very much against my grain, Valentine, but I'm simply too busy to quibble. I'll hire the two of you, and believe me, I expect you to produce. There won't be any contracts."

"We must have one-year contracts, Mrs. Ikehorn. After that—I'm not worried."

Billy didn't hesitate. Scruples was losing money at an almost incredible rate. Not that it made the slightest difference to her; she could afford it indefinitely, but the figures would look so embarrassing when they were published in *Women's Wear*. It was worse than embarrassing—it was a waking, unending nightmare. People would laugh at her and the one thing in the world she must never be, never again as long as she lived, was a figure of fun. She had to turn the operation of Scruples into a success. Scruples must be *faultless*.

"When can the two of you get here?" she asked. Valentine calculated rapidly. Today was Wednesday. If they started getting ready now and took the plane Sunday—

"Next Monday. Will you please make hotel reservations for us? At your expense, of course. But just until we find places to live."

"I'll get rooms for you at the Beverly Wilshire. It's just down the street from Scruples."

"Indeed? That will be convenient for a twelve-hour day," Valentine said.

"Eighteen hours," Billy laughed, having gotten her way.

"Until Monday then, Mrs. Ikehorn."

"Good-bye, Valentine. I feel so much better about your losing your job now. All it's cost me is a couple hundred thousand dollars."

"Not quite all that much. But don't forget the seven and a half percent."

"Prince will shit a brick," Billy said with a giggle.

"He'll probably enjoy it," Valentine answered, and hung up.

She had been so engrossed in the conversation that she hadn't paid any attention to Spider. Now she was afraid to face him. His silence was accusing. How had she dared to make such decisions for him? Why didn't he say anything? Valentine glanced carefully through her lashes to where he lay on her bed. He was sound asleep. Obviously, he had been throughout the conversation. One thing was incontestable. He did not snore.

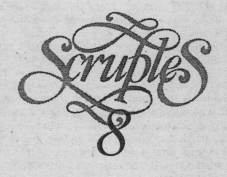

Spider Elliott was as little prepared to like or even approve of Billy Ikehorn as she was of him. He had burned with anger at every detail of the high-handed and arrogant way she had treated Valentine, carelessly causing her to lose her job with Prince. The fact that Valentine had managed to con the woman into giving him a job as, God help us all, a retailer, made him suppose that she must be fundamentally stupid, a woman with such a need to grasp whatever she wanted that it destroyed her good sense.

Billy, on the other hand, had checked with those of her women friends who read *Women's Wear* as carefully as she did and none of them had ever heard of a well-known figure in retailing named Peter Elliott. And if *WWD* didn't mention him, he couldn't exist. Valentine had pulled a fast one; the guy, whoever he was, must be her lover, and Billy had no intention of letting him get away with it. She'd wait just long enough for him to make a fool of himself and then confront him. A "contract" indeed. If Valentine wanted him as some sort of half-assed assistant, she could have him, but not for the salary she had promised. Not for a tenth of it. One of the most annoying things about having money was the way people never stopped trying to separate you from it.

Since Ellis had died, a year ago, Billy had evolved in several ways. When she found herself a widow and one of the world's great heiresses, her first move had been to sell the prison citadel high in Bel Air and buy an estate in

Holmby Hills, a comfortable four-minute drive from the shopping area of Beverly Hills. If she had planned during the five years in Bel Air what she would do when she was free to live however she liked, she would never have assumed that she would remain in California—but now it seemed like the only thing to do. Scruples was here, her exercise class was here, the women she lunched with were here. While Ellis was well, California was merely the place they went when he wanted to visit the winery at St. Helena; when he was sick it was where they had to live because of the suitable climate. Imperceptively, it had become the only logical place left in the world for her to call home.

As Billy, punctual to the minute, stood waiting for Spider and Valentine at the entrance of Scruples, her dashing, virile beauty had never been so potent. She was the kind of woman who only reaches her peak in her thirties, and the constant, illicit lubrication of secret sexual stimulation and satisfaction from the parade of ex-medics had given her face, particularly her voracious mouth, a voluptuous ripeness and readiness that made a complex and subtle contrast to her studied perfection of dress.

"Trouble," thought Spider, the minute he caught sight of her.

Billy, spotting him with Valentine at the same instant, found that she still thought with her cunt, a habit she had believed was confined to the hidden side of her life. It did not belong in her normal, daily existence and she would not permit it there—the risk was too great, too much was at stake. Her reputation, her special status, which was demonstrated by the respectful way in which the media treated her, all came from a position that put her above the crowd; her necessary safety lay in never showing a chink in her armor. These considerations had become more necessary to her every year that passed. The sight of Spider was like a punch in the gut: The impact of sheer masculinity carried without swagger or shyness, that happily sensuous aura— her practiced eye measured the insistence of his physicality and her practiced brain clamped down immediately. This was one man she could never allow herself. Too close to home. Enough of that, Billy told herself, as she advanced to greet Valentine, putting both hands on her shoulders in a gesture that was not quite a hug, yet more friendly than a handshake.

"Welcome to California," Billy said wholeheartedly. She was delighted to see Valentine. She needed her.

"Thank you, Mrs. Ikehorn," Valentine answered tensely. "This is Peter Elliott, my partner."

"I'm called Spider," he said, and bent to kiss Billy's hand with that grace he was unaware of, that early Fred Astaire grace that is either born in the bones and the muscles or will never exist, since no training can develop it. Valentine had never seen him make this gesture to any other woman but herself.

"And I'm Billy—you too, Valentine. Everyone who moves to the Coast has a whole new set of manners to learn. Well, this is Scruples. What do you think of it?" She gestured proudly toward the exquisite building that put all its splendid neighbors to shame. Spider walked to one end of the building, turned and walked the full length of the frontage, and then returned to them. "Bad windows," he said flatly.

"Bad! This building has already won three important architectural prizes and it's been finished less than a year. Everyone in the art world knows about it. And you criticize the windows!" Billy was instantly outraged. "Just how would you redesign perfection?"

"I wouldn't touch them. Only a vandal would. But the merchandise is overwhelmed by them. This is a store, after all. It's just a small problem, Billy, once you spot what's wrong. I'll find a way to get around it. No sweat. Why don't we go inside?"

Spider put one hand lightly in the small of each woman's back and gently propelled them toward the double doors, nodding a greeting at the unknown doorman, grinning to himself. The windows really were a disaster. Thank God for small favors. A few more would be welcome.

Billy could hardly wait till they received the full impact of the interior of Scruples. It was her pride and joy. She had had it modeled exactly, meticulously, and at great expense after the inside of the House of Dior in Paris.

Spider stood stock-still inside the front doors of Scruples and looked around, sniffing the air like a hound dog. "Miss Dior," he commented noncommittally about the perfume that pervaded the air.

"That's not your department," Billy snapped, still smarting from his remark about the windows. "This place is perfect, just as it is. We're going back to the stock rooms to look over the merchandise. I want to know exactly what you think and what your plans are for a new buying policy and—"

"Billy, excuse me, but I don't think so," Spider interrupted. "We'll get to the stock in good time, I promise you. Retailing isn't just stock. Retailing is romance. Retailing is mystery." Especially, he thought, to me. "I assume that your stock changes from month to month, so let's take a look at the romance first. Ladies?" He led the way, not bothering to see if they were following, into the great room. Spider explored the interior of Scruples from top to bottom, including the underground parking garage, without making any comment except a vague rumble in his throat, which expressed nothing at all but sounded thoughtfully judgmental, at least to his ears. Valentine's bewilderment, scarcely contained, was so strong he could almost taste it, but he paid no attention. Billy pressed her lips together repeatedly in vexation, but she was so confident that her store was impeccably elegant in its appointments and so vastly superior to all others in the size and luxury of its fitting rooms that she wasn't sorry to give them the full treatment.

Toward the end of the tour, Spider looked at his watch and suggested that they have lunch together and hear his comments on Scruples before they attacked the stock. Billy agreed, only because she was hungry.

"Where is the nearest place to eat?" he asked.

"We could go to the Brown Derby across Rodeo, but since it changed hands over a year ago, I haven't liked it. There's no reasonably decent place closer than La Bella Fontana in your hotel—we'll go there." The three of them made the two perilous crossings, rushing across Rodeo at its widest point, hopping over traffic islands, dodging cars making legal right-hand turns on the red light, and then dashing across Wilshire Boulevard, hurrying so that the light wouldn't change before they reached safety. Finally they found themselves in a peaceful, curtained booth in La Bella Fontana, with its walls covered in red velvet, a fountain trickling in the center of the room, flowers everywhere, and, surrounding them, the atmosphere, artfully contrived, of an old-fashioned hideaway in Vienna or Budapest.

"This is charming, Billy," Valentine said, looking around her, happy just to be sitting down.

"And *that's* the second thing that's wrong," said Spider.

"What do you mean?" Billy asked querulously. Her feet hurt.

"Let's suppose you were a woman who was buying lots of clothes for a trip to New York or London or a wedding or winter in Palm Springs or the Cannes Film Festival, something so important that you needed hours to pick and choose, not to mention alterations."

"That's not exactly a novel thing to suppose. Scruples customers do that all the time," Billy responded tightly.

"Suppose this customer had arrived at Scruples at eleven in the morning and suppose she had spent two hours looking and trying on things and hadn't finished yet?"

"Well?"

"Would she be hungry? Would her feet hurt? Billy, I see you've taken off your shoes."

"What has that to do with retailing, Spider?" In one minute she'd tell him about her investigation of his non-existent credentials.

"Your shoes? Nothing. Your customer's shoes? Everything. Your customer's empty stomach? Even more. It is the *key.*"

"You'll have to be a little more explicit. We don't sell shoes. We're not running a restaurant—we're running, or trying to run, a store."

"Not until you start running a restaurant." Spider smiled at her benevolently. "What happens when your hungry customer's feet begin to hurt? Her blood sugar goes down. If she continues to try on clothes she gets irritable and difficult, and she decides that nothing she sees suits her. If she stops to get dressed to go somewhere for lunch, the chances are that she'd have to be absolutely desperate to find a particular dress on that particular day in your particular store for her to come back to Scruples after lunch. If you lose her at lunchtime, she'll try another store later. So, first we're going to build a kitchen by shutting off part of the garage, which is much bigger than you need. Then we hire a couple of cooks, maybe only one at first, and some waiters and offer

276

our customers lunch on the house. Nothing too fancy, Billy, just salads or open-faced sandwiches. I noticed that there's a chaise longue in each fitting room. Our customers can sit there and eat while they get a foot massage. A good one can rejuvenate the whole body." He quirked one eyebrow at Billy. "You probably know the best masseuses in town? I doubt you'll need more than three of them in the beginning. Then, after lunch, we'll sell those ladies the whole fucking store." He signaled the captain to bring the menus.

For a minute Billy was mesmerized. She could see it, just as Spider described it. But then she returned to herself. "Excellent idea. It solves exactly one small and nonessential problem—how to keep your customers from leaving at lunchtime. But, at the moment, I haven't got that many customers to leave. Business is getting slower day by day. I haven't got the right stock to show them, and no obvious gimmick like a new kitchen is going to make a difference. Are you sure you were never in the catering business, Spider?"

Spider turned to her with his most wicked grin, his cowboy-look, thought Valentine furiously, the one where she expected to see him kick a piece of shit and say, "Ah, shucks, Ma'am, it weren't nothin'."

"That's for openers, Billy. I haven't even gotten down to the God-awful, tight-assed way the store is decorated yet—and that's a good half of your problem." Billy stared at him in utter shock, too disbelieving to be angry yet. Spider thought then that she was going to be a pushover. "But we'll talk about that after we've signed the contracts. 'No point in giving it away,' a gal I once knew used to say. Come on, ladies, let's eat."

The law firm of Strassberger, Lipkin, and Hillman took up two entire floors of one of the newly built towers of Century City, the twin glass monsters that make Beverly Hills residents shake their heads and think about earthquakes and doomsday whenever they drive past them on Santa Monica Boulevard. The firm, which enjoyed the quiet prestige of being one of the most powerful Jewish law firms in Los Angeles (where, as in many big cities, law firms like country clubs are either predominately Jewish or Gentile), had been decorated by someone who wanted, above all, to assure the firm's clients that even if an earthquake should happen to hit while they were trapped high on the twentieth or twenty-first floor, they would perish in style, even splendor.

Valentine and Spider stepped out of the elevator into a wilderness of walnut and rosewood, of thick new rugs and thin old ones, of fresh flowers, of genuine antiques and a genuine smile on the receptionist's face. The possession of a truly welcoming and charming receptionist is an infallible mark of any topflight business in Los Angeles. They had an appointment to sign their contracts with Billy Ikehorn's personal lawyer, Joshua Isaiah Hillman.

Although the legal work of Ikehorn Enterprises was still carried on in New York, since Ellis's death, Billy relied more heavily than before on her lawyer Josh Hillman. Much of his work now involved double-checking on the work done by the New York attorneys. Before Ellis died, she had just signed any necessary papers without worrying about them. In spite of the fact that Ellis could not advise her, she still felt as if she were under his protection. This essentially unreal state of affairs lasted until she became majority stockholder on inheriting Ellis's shares in the business. Now Billy felt she should at least be thoroughly briefed before she signed her name to anything. Soon Josh Hillman found that more than half of his time was spent on Mrs. Ikehorn's business; he employed several top attorneys within his firm just to oversee her affairs and report to him. Her legal fees became proportionately immense. No one suffered from this arrangement; even Billy's New York lawyers approved, because Josh Hillman was an exceedingly brilliant lawyer. His advice was faultless. He protected Billy's interests without trying to second-guess their own, far more informed, decisions.

At almost forty-two, Josh Hillman was exactly where an ex-child prodigy should be: at the top of his profession and possessed of an unlimited future.

He had grown up on Fairfax Avenue, the heart of the Jewish ghetto of Los Angeles, an only child, the son of the rabbi of a small, shabby synagogue. By the age of two-and-a-half, he could read; by fourteen-and-a-half he had been granted a full scholarship at Harvard; at eighteen-and-a-half he had been graduated summa cum laude, and at twenty-one-and-a-half he had been graduated from Harvard Law School as an editor of the *Harvard Law Review,* an editorship that is no more eagerly sought or won than that of *The New York Times.*

At this point, tradition dictated that he should go to work as a clerk for a Justice of the United States Supreme Court and start dreaming about that day in the future when, after perhaps forty years of consistently more brilliant legal work, he would take his mentor's place.

But Josh Hillman didn't like the odds: There was never more than one Jewish Justice on the Court at any one time and Supreme Court Justices seem to live forever, longer than anyone except the widows of rich men.

He had more than a passing interest in making money, after living on scholarships for the last seven years. Only twice in that time had Josh Hillman been able to return home on holidays to see his parents, who still lived on Fairfax Avenue. He had earned enough money during the summers to clothe himself, get his hair cut, and buy those two round-trip plane tickets. He had missed most of the social life of a Harvard undergraduate because he couldn't afford it, and if there was fun to be had during law school, he didn't know about it. He joined Strassberger & Lipkin in 1957 and now, twenty years later, although he was the junior partner in terms of age, he was the senior partner in terms of real power.

He was a serious man who thought romance was something invented in the Middle Ages to keep ladies at court occupied at home during the Crusades. He enjoyed sex, but he saw no reason to make a big deal out of it. He felt smugly superior to other men of his age who ran around getting divorced because their wives bored them in bed and then proceeded to make horses' asses of themselves with young girls. The whole business was overrated. His wife bored him too, almost from the beginning, but was that a reason to play around? Not for a serious man it wasn't.

Josh Hillman had married seriously and intelligently. Joanne Wirthman was Hollywood royalty—the genuine article. Her grandfather had founded one of the great movie studios. Her father was one of the great movie producers.

Behind her were two generations of private screening rooms. Not her mother, but her grandmother, had had the first all-Porthault bathroom in Bel Air.

Joanne Wirthman had never even heard of belly lox until she met Josh Hillman, but she soon discovered that it was tastier than Scotch salmon, just as he was more impressive, more of a *mensch*, than the rich boys she had grown up with. To their amazement, they discovered that both their grandfathers had been born in Vilna. Not that the genealogical fact —which, who knew, might make them distant cousins?— was necessary to quell any objections on the part of the Wirthman family to Joanne's marrying a poor boy from Fairfax Avenue. They were only too happy to see their hefty, placid, well-organized daughter carrying off a *Harvard Law Review* editor who also happened to be tall and handsome, in a somewhat not-fully-finished-growing way; and with a shining future like his, he was obviously not interested in her money alone.

Actually, it wasn't just Joanne's money he was interested in. To be fair, Josh told himself, he liked her well enough, and the year that he had allotted himself to marry and settle down was almost over. He was serious when it came to sticking to schedule. He was very serious about just about everything.

Joanne proved to be disappointing in bed but great at pregnancy, producing two sons and a daughter. She was superb at winning women's tennis tournaments at the Hillcrest Country Club and positively triumphant at raising money for the Music Center, the Childrens Hospital, Cedars-Sinai, the Arts Council, and the Los Angeles County Museum of Art. By thirty-five, she was a leader among that very tightly knit group of women in Los Angeles who are indispensable to both Jewish and Gentile charitable endeavors, thus socially bridging the gap between old California society and the wave of Jewish businessmen looking for sunshine, that the invention of the movie camera had brought to the land where money was supposed to come from land grants, lumber, railroads, and oil, not the sound stage.

Over the years that separated him from the rather untidy, overgrown student he had been, Josh Hillman had grown into a lithe, trim man with the look of power about him. His dark gray eyes slanted slightly upward at their outer corners, giving him a permanently quizzical look, which did nothing to detract from his reputation for cleverness. His smile was rare but full of sardonic humor. He had high Slavic cheekbones and a straight, broad nose, about which both his grandmothers argued, each delightedly accusing the other's mother of having been raped by Cossacks. Dozens of them. He wore his graying dark hair short and dressed in ultra-conservative custom-made suits with matching vests from Eric Ross and Carroll and Company, made from the finest British cloth in subdued colors and cut. He had his shirts made for him at Turnbull and Asser whenever he was in London. His ties were remarkable only for their price. None of this was vanity, merely a feeling of how it was necessary for a lawyer to look.

Until he saw Valentine, Josh Hillman had considered himself satisfactorily married. His mother, a lady of the old school, had repeatedly and solemnly warned him that there is a yellow-haired, blue-eyed shiksa lying in wait for every good Jewish boy, and if he listens to her siren's call, he will be lost and disgraced. However, Josh had never been attracted to the classic Anglo-Saxon type; he thought blandly beautiful girls were boringly alike; he considered *Portnoy's Complaint* an example of sick, fetishistic thinking, attaching as it did sexual attraction to snub noses and blond hair. But, alas, his mother had been limited in her imaginative forebodings. She could not have conceived of the spark struck in her serious son by the lure of a flaming French-Irish damsel with pale green mermaid eyes and a witty, delicate look, which made Joshua, that least romantic man, leap instinctively to his feet as Valentine entered his office. Spider seemed only a tall blur behind her as she advanced toward him with her positive step. Josh Hillman felt something that he found impossible to name, except he knew that he'd never felt it before.

Valentine noticed the tall lawyer's slight confusion as they shook hands and attributed it to some change of heart on Billy's part after Spider's outrageous behavior of the morning. Instinctively she intensified her slight French accent, further nibbling away at Josh Hillman's composure and making him endure impossibly distracting subliminal flashes of Paris in the spring.

While the three of them waited for the secretary to bring in the contracts, Hillman's mind raced.

When Billy had first told him about the contracts she had agreed to with Valentine over the phone, he had been horrified. He had considered his client too sensible to give away a percentage of her profits in Scruples as well as these enormous salaries to some young designer she had only met a few times and to a man about whom she knew nothing. He had advised her to add a cancellation clause to the contracts, which would allow her to terminate their employment as well as their profit sharing within a period of three weeks' notice. He patiently explained that it didn't matter that Scruples was leaking money like a burst dam or that there were no profits to protect. It was the principle of the thing. She had to have control over these people. Billy had seen his point at once. Now he wished he hadn't been quite so clever. The idea that Miss O'Neill might find herself fired at the whim of his most dominating, most spoiled, most demanding client was not a pleasant thing, but at this point it was too late to change.

While Spider and Valentine read the contracts, Hillman studied her from behind a tent he made of his hands. By resting his thumbs on his cheeks and his index fingers just above his eyebrows, he was able to hide a large part of his face while maintaining a contemplative look, a trick he employed often. He watched the play of expression on Valentine's small face with fascination, so bemused that he paid no attention when Spider stopped reading and said, "There's something wrong here."

But when Valentine popped out of her chair with a loud cry of *"Merde,"* he came out of his dream with an undignified jolt.

"What is this merde—this shit?" she demanded, smacking the contracts on the desk, gone so pale with rage that if it hadn't been for her hair she would have looked like a photo in black and white. "This clause that we may be fired on three weeks' notice! That was not in the conversation I had with Mrs. Ikehorn. How dare she? What kind of woman does a thing like that? It is dishonest, dishonorable, vile, disgusting! I did not expect it of her, but I should have known! We will *never* sign these contracts, Mr. Hillman. Call her up and tell her that immediately! And tell her what I think of her. Come on, Elliott—we're leaving!"

"It wasn't her idea," Josh Hillman said urgently. "I suggested it—just ordinary lawyers' prudence. Don't blame Mrs. Ikehorn. She had nothing to do with it."

"Ordinary lawyers' prudence!" Valentine's wrath was enough to make him blink in amazement. "I spit on lawyers' prudence! Then it is *you* who should be ashamed of yourself. It was contemptible!"

"I am," he answered. "Please, believe me!" His chagrin and dismay were written large on his face. He hadn't looked so helpless or so appalled since the day of his Bar Mitzvah speech, when all knowledge of Hebrew deserted him for one long unforgettable moment, a memory that still made him shudder. Valentine just glared at him balefully, all of her tempestuous nature seething in her eyes.

"Val, baby, shut up a fucking minute, will you," Spider ordered pleasantly. "Now, Mr. Hillman, if it was your prudent idea to put the clause in, is it now your prudent idea to take the clause out? Sir?"

"I'll have to talk to Mrs. Ikehorn," the lawyer admitted reluctantly.

"We'll wait outside while you reach her," Spider said, pointing at the telephone with a stern finger. "Maybe you could prevail on your secretary to bring us some coffee." He took Valentine's arm in a bruising grasp and led her, willy-nilly, to the door before she could turn the offer down again.

Josh Hillman silently punished the leg of his desk with his shoe for a minute before he leafed through his private phone book, found a number, and made a call on his private line. He talked rapidly and intently for a short while and then buzzed his secretary to bring Valentine and Spider back in.

"All settled," he announced, with a relieved smile. "I'll have those changes made in the contracts in five minutes. One year, guaranteed, no strings."

"Hah!" Valentine sounded scornful and suspicious. When the papers were brought back she read every word with a look of historic French skepticism. Once Spider was satisfied that there were no more trick clauses, they finally signed.

As soon as the two of them left, Josh Hillman told his

secretary to hold all his calls. He would need at least a half hour, maybe more, judging from past experience, before he could track down Billy Ikehorn and inform her that in spite of everything he had tried to do or say, in spite of his best efforts, those two had not been willing to sign the contracts until he took out the offending clause. He estimated that it might take another ten minutes alone to persuade her that the cancellation clause actually had never been absolutely necessary, but he knew he could do it. He could persuade anyone to do just about anything. Or, so he had thought until this afternoon. "Merde," he said to himself, smiling at the memory, as he told his secretary to start calling around and find Billy Ikehorn, on the double.

When Valentine arrived back in her room early that evening, on the coffee table stood a low basket woven in Ireland. Seeming to grow from the green moss that filled the basket were seven tall stems of white butterfly orchids, some fully opened, some just in bud. They were all of springtime in one swoop of heartbreaking grace. On the card next to them was written, "With my most humble apologies for the contretemps of this afternoon. I hope I may be allowed to invite you for dinner after an appropriate period of penance. Josh Hillman."

Valentine forgave him immediately but would have forgiven him twice over if she had known the trouble he had had in spelling "contretemps" to the salesperson at David Jones, the best florist in Los Angeles. The order had been given over the phone earlier that day while she and Spider had been sipping coffee in his secretary's outer office right after they had discovered the three weeks' notice clause in the contracts.

That same night, at three o'clock in the morning, Spider, still awake, heard a faint tap on his hotel door. He opened it to find a woebegone Valentine, huddled in her deep blue robe. He bundled her into the room, deposited her in a chair, anxious and surprised. "What's wrong, Val—my God, don't you feel well?" She looked like a terrified child; great green eyes, without their usual frame of heavy black mascara, swam in unshed tears, even her farouche curls seemed to have lost some of their fight.

"Oh, Elliott, I'm scared shitless!"

"*You*, darling? How do you think I feel?"

"The way you acted today, I thought—you were so nervy, so sure of yourself, so impudent to Billy."

"And what about you, almost walking out of that lawyer's office, going up in smoke like that. I've never seen you so angry, not even at me."

"I still don't know what happened—when I get mad I don't think. But, Elliott, I've been lying in bed thinking now, and I just realized that we're a couple of complete fakers, both of us. I've never bought for a store in my life, but I know enough from working with buyers to realize that they have years and years of training behind them. And you, you don't know one single thing about retailing. Nothing! I was just so mad when Billy telephoned that I asked for the moon because I didn't have anything to lose and now that I've got the moon I'm petrified that I'll lose it. Elliott, what are we *doing* here?"

He shook her gently and put his hand on her neck so that she had to look him in the eye. "My silly Valentine. You've got the three-in-the-morning blues. Didn't anyone ever tell you never to think about anything serious at three in the morning?" Her eyes refused to be comforted by his words. He grew solemn. "Now look here, Valentine, if I didn't think that together we have the taste and the imagination to make this thing work—so what if we never actually sold clothes? Fashion *is* our business, remember. You design clothes to make women look better than they really do; I take pictures to make them look beautiful. We're both illusionists—the best! All we need is the time to get the lay of the land and we can turn Scruples around. I know it."

"If it were only that simple." She still looked bereft. "There are so many things I'm unfamiliar with here in this California. I'm out of my element—it's frightening. And the way you talk to Mrs. Ikehorn, Elliott, it frightens me. Have you any idea how she is treated on Seventh Avenue—like a goddess—and not just there, everywhere. Today, yes, she took it from you, but tomorow she could turn on you. She can be ruthless. Don't forget what happened to me when she wanted to see my dresses and I didn't want to show them."

"Did you ever hear that good old American expression 'pussy whipped,' Valentine?"

"Never, but it is self-explanatory, is it not?" Valentine smiled for the first time that day.

"Try to understand, Val darling. Some men are pussy whipped from the day they are born, some have it happen to them later in life, some never. I was born king of the castle; I never knew what it was like to have a woman try to pussy whip me until I met Harriet Toppingham. And when I didn't let her have her fun, she ruined me." He didn't mention Melanie Adams, Valentine thought. "Billy Ikehorn has the qualities to become a topnotch pussy whipper, if she isn't one already. I won't and I can't let her. It isn't a question of just pride or saying 'you can't get away with this'—the whole thing goes so deep with me that it doesn't stop. There's no job, no contract, no success that would mean anything to me if it involved a pussy-whipping boss."

"I understand you, Elliott. But does that mean that you will have to always be antagonists with her, always insulting what she's done and getting her furious?"

"No. You're right. I laid it on a bit strong for the first day."

"Or even the second or third day? Elliott, she is so *rich!*"

"If you start thinking about her money, baby, you're lost. You're not dealing with another human being then. You won't be able to talk straight to her because you're not dealing with reality. So she *is* very, very rich and she's built herself a store that may never creep out of the red, no matter how hard we work, and she tells herself she's creative and queens it queenily over Camelot like Marie Antoinette playing at milkmaid. But Golda Meir or Barbara Jordan or Queen Elizabeth or Madame Curie she ain't. If you start adding up her income your imagination will get paralyzed. It's like trying to imagine how far it is to the nearest star or how small the planet Earth is in relation to the Milky Way. Billy Ikehorn is a *female person*. She shits, she fucks, she pees, she farts, she eats, she cries, she has emotions, she gets anxious, she worries about getting older, she's a woman, Valentine, and if I ever forget that I won't be able to deal with her. Nor will you."

"Oh, Elliott, she isn't Jeanne d'Arc either, and she isn't Madame Chanel or Gerry Stutz; she isn't even Sonia Rykiel and oh, I'm an idiot!" The waif Valentine had vanished. Her eyes had turned incandescent. She slipped out of her chair and had the door half open in one swift moment. "Thank you, Elliott, for keeping your head. Now we'd better get some sleep. Tomorrow is going to be a big day for fakers."

"Not even a goodnight kiss, partner?" Valentine eyed him with an immediate return of the suspicion she had felt toward this disgustingly promiscuous friend. Since Melanie Adams, she knew he had not been with a woman. Graciously she extended her hand, at arm's length, so that he could kiss it, then fled down the corridor, whispering, as French mothers do to their children as they put them to bed, *Dors bien, et fais des bons rêves.*

Billy Ikehorn had gone to sleep relatively early, a mistake, she realized, when she found herself awake at five in the morning. She woke up with a start, filled by a nasty, heart-thumping feeling that something was very wrong, and as soon as she had a chance to snuggle into a more comfortable position in bed, she realized what it was, what it had been every day for almost a year. Scruples. If she could wish it away, vaporized in a cloud of dust, she would—in an instant.

Billy had been seized by the idea for Scruples during the almost endless last year of Ellis's dying, some two years ago. By that time she had smoothly established her secret sex life in her studio. After the brief period of her interest in Ash had run its course, she had changed all three male nurses who attended Ellis, and as carefully as if she had been Catherine the Great choosing soldiers for her notorious personal guard, she had hired new nurses, feeling an almost incredulous elation at the knowledge that she was free to evaluate any number of men until she found the ones she wanted. Sometimes one of her choices failed to please her, sometimes the same young man would hold her sexually captive for months, but eventually she found that she grew weary of even the best of them. The remedy in either case was always the same—a day's notice and a huge bonus. For a while the ritual of choice, the power of control, the consciousness of domination, were enough, but soon habit had bled out the illicit overtones, the forbidden coloration of her octagonal studio in which one canvas still stood in its place and the cases of art supplies remained unpacked. For a long while she had centered her thoughts, day as well as night, around the clandestine atmosphere of that locked room, but gradually it had become less and less compelling. Eventually it was only as necessary to her as a call girl is necessary to a man with no other sexual outlet. The obsession that led her from one fresh, unknown male body to another, aggressively making them her possessions for as long as she wanted them, had burnt itself out in the last year of Ellis's life. Whatever fulfillment she had sought in that studio, whatever answers to her lonely spirit she had once thought she might find there, she now knew did not exist.

Meanwhile, Ellis had almost entirely withdrawn from contact with her and from his nurses. He no longer seemed to really recognize her when she came to sit by him, or perhaps he did and didn't care. When she held his hand and looked at his sunken face, the face of a man who had once commanded an empire, Billy's heart hurt so terribly that sometimes she had to hurry away. Often, after one of these moments, she reflected that at least it proved she still had a heart.

She had enormous amounts of time on her hands during the day. Billy had never been the kind of woman who finds herself comfortable on charity committees. Perhaps it was a result of her virtually friendless childhood, but when she found herself surrounded by large numbers of women of her own age she retreated into a stiffness and shyness that was taken for haughtiness and snobbishness. She knew it and couldn't seem to help it. It was easier to let the Ikehorn Foundation give away her millions than to force herself to plan a fund-raising event.

Nor could she fill her time with tennis. She had an instinctive dislike of becoming one of the tennis-beset women she saw all around Beverly Hills. She went back to her regular exercise sessions at Ron Fletcher's, where no one gave a damn who the sweating, swearing women in the leotards were: Billy Ikehorn, Ali MacGraw, Katherine Ross—it made no difference when it came to those great levelers like the saw stretch or the pendulum series, which reduced them all to mere muscle and willpower.

Billy telephoned her few casual women friends, many of whom she hadn't spoken to in well over a year, and made lunch dates with them, explaining her virtual disappearance with a single reference to Ellis and the need to stay close to home. She realized that she had lost her fine edge of chic. Two years ago she had been dropped from the Best-Dressed List. She hadn't bought anything new since her affair with Jake. Suddenly her passion for clothes revived. She had to have them now to provide some sort of emotional juice, to make her feel, outwardly at least, as desirable and romantic as she had been when Ellis was still himself and she was a queen of *Women's Wear*. Nothing, absolutely nothing she owned looked right any more. They seemed to have been bought by a different person in a different life.

Billy embarked on a piratical raid of the Beverly Hills boutiques and department stores. Although her reasons for buying had changed, her critical eye and unconcealed distaste with anything less than the best had grown. Very little satisfied her, yet she was chained to California, unable to leave for a long shopping trip to New York or Paris.

One day, as she was walking on Rodeo and observing the amount of new building going on in that lovely, long avenue of luxury stores, each corner of which she knew by heart and no corner of which could seem to give her what she wanted, the idea of building Scruples seized her.

For two days she haunted that corner of Rodeo and Dayton, measuring the amount of footage she wanted, eyeing the Van Cleef & Arpels building and the building next to it, which housed Battaglia and Frances Klein's, an antique jewelry store, with such scorn that it should have reduced them to rubble on the spot. She also needed to build over the parking lot next to Battaglia—all in all, 160 feet of Rodeo Drive, 145 feet deep. Her heart pounded with yearning, a craving she hadn't known in years. Scruples would fill the empty spaces of her life. She *wanted* it. She would have it.

Josh Hillman's objections and doubts were brushed away. At three mililon dollars, Billy insisted, that half block was a bargain. She paid for everything from the fortune Ellis had given her over the years. This wasn't an Ikehorn Enterprises business; this was Billy Winthrop's business. She would show Beverly Hills how a fine store should be run. Scruples would be the talk of the fashion world, an outpost of the elegance and grace and refinement that, until now, had existed only in Paris.

Throughout the year it took to build Scruples, she plunged wholeheartedly into her new obsession. She tried to hire I. M. Pei as her architect, but he was occupied with a seventy-million-dollar addition to the Rockefeller Foundation; she had to be satisfied with his most brilliant associate, who gave her a building that was destined to become a landmark. Billy haunted the site, harassed the workmen, maddened the contractor, and almost drove the architect into leaving the project. Her life was filled with expectations and impatience, but at least she knew that the fulfillment of her dreams was only a question of time.

When Ellis died, in the fall of 1975 just before Scruples opened, Billy realized that she had long ago finished mourning for him. The first two years of his illness had been one long, terrible work of true mourning. She would always love the Ellis Ikehorn she had married in 1963, but, she admitted to herself, the paralyzed, expressionless, old man who had died had not been Ellis, and there was no use being hypocritical about it. But still, she would call the store Scruples, a tribute, a salute to Aunt Cornelia, to all of proper Boston, to Katie Gibbs, to the pathetic Wilhelmina Hunnenwell Winthrop who had left for Paris and come back transfigured, to all the scruples she no longer felt. She knew that, in the whole world, only Jessica perhaps would see the joke, but it was enough. It was a gesture for herself, a counterbalance to the tower room in the Bel Air citadel. Something in Billy was deeply pleased with the name.

Lying there in bed she thought miserably of how well it had all started. It seemed, at first, as if every rich woman from San Diego to San Francisco wanted to see the new store. They came and bought and bought and for a few heady months Billy felt that Scruples was a success. *Women's Wear Daily* kept a close watch on this new venture. Billy Ikehorn was one of their special people, and society women who went into commerce were always news. The newspaper devoted a double-spread to photographs of Billy in front of Scruples and a retrospective collection of pictures of her life with Ellis. Later, when then store opened, they gave it another double-spread for itself—twice as much space, gloated Billy, as they had allocated C. Z. Guest and her patented jumpsuit, her book on gardening, and her scented insect repellant. Such ladies were just piddling around, Billy thought smugly, compared to such a venture as Scruples. She was especially pleased with her inspired idea of making the interior of Scruples an exact duplicate of Dior.

How well she remembered the emotion she felt when she and the Comtesse had ventured through those famous doors on the Avenue Montaigne fifteen years ago, waiting in thrilled awe as seats were found for them in the main salon, sitting breathless with the beauty of it all, as the collection, otherworldly, the stuff of dreams, passed by. Afterward, she and Lilianne de Vertdulac had explored the boutique on the street floor with hopeless desire, each knowing, but not admitting, that she couldn't afford even one of these ravishing follies and frills. Now she would have it all. A Dior in Beverly Hills.

Of course, Billy really didn't expect Scruples to make a profit. She had been too thoroughly warned by Josh Hillman that the money she had poured out without stint on the land, the building, and the interior decoration was money gone forever. There was no possible way, he said, in which the profit on expensive clothes could recoup the original cost of Scruples, even though such clothes retail for 100 percent more to the customer than they cost the store to buy.

"Josh," she had chided him, "I'm not doing this to make money. You know I can't spend my income. Why even with everything I give to charity, even with those millions every year, it just keeps on increasing. I'm *indulging* myself and I won't let anyone tell me I can't afford to. Of course I can and you know it. This is between me and me!"

If only, Billy reflected bitterly, it had remained between her and her. If only *Women's Wear* hadn't kept such an interested eye on her, she wouldn't be so frantic now. It was one thing to see the disappearance of money that she would never use if she lived to be ten thousand but quite another to have that fact published loud and clear in the one newspaper in the world whose opinion she cared deeply about. Lately there had been a few references to "Billy's Folly," signed by that pseudonymous "Louise J. Esterhazy," undoubtedly the editorial voice of *WWD,* and she could feel the winds of the future. When the next set of half-yearly figures became known, she would be the laughing stock of the whole retail world. She had little hope that she could suppress the figures. Although only her own accountants would be aware of the losses, since Billy owned the store entirely, there were leaks and spies everywhere. And even if there were not, you only had to go into Scruples to see that there was very little selling being done. It was, Billy thought, like having the world's most beautiful corpse lying on your doorstep with no way to remove it and knowing that soon the whole neighborhood would wake up and come to investigate that strange and horrible stink.

Why the fuck was she so impulsive? She could scream with rage, she could pinch herself black and blue, at the memory of that phone call with Valentine. She had wanted that girl so badly, she had been so convinced at the time that a talent like Valentine's running a custom-order couture department was what Scruples needed that she had bribed her insanely to come to California. Of course, custom work couldn't make the difference! Even St. Laurent and Dior and Givenchy, in fact every couture house in Paris, complained that they lost money on their couture business, but it kept their names alive and those names sold perfume and ready-to-wear all over the world. The French couture was dead, financially. It existed only to maintain the aura and ambience of Paris before World War II: to inspire department-store buyers and dress manufacturers from all over the world to trek to Paris twice a year; to allow the woman who bought an Yves St. Laurent ready-to-wear dress for three hundred dollars in one of his many boutiques to feel that some of that Paris magic was rubbing off on her. And Billy had known it all along. There was no one to blame but herself. And now she had hired two complete amateurs to do a job only professionals could successfully undertake.

And yet. And yet. Perhaps, Billy thought, perhaps being impulsive wasn't always such a bad thing. Looking back, it was impulse that had led her to Paris in the first place, impulse that had told her to cross the corridor in Barbados and go into Ellis Ikehorn's arms. Of course, it was impulse, too, that had let her imagine herself as a French countess merely because she had lost her virginity to a fortune-hunting count and impulse that had made her believe that one year of Katie Gibbs had given her the training to make a success in business. In the darkness of her bedroom, Billy shook her head ruefully as she realized how many times in her life she had

292

expected miracles to happen because she *wanted* them to. Like Scruples. But, after all, she had come back from Paris thin and she had married Ellis and been happy for seven perfect years. Without her bad habit of impulse, what would she be now? A grotesquely fat Boston schoolteacher, no doubt, eating her way through a death in life, still the eternal outsider, the freak, trapped within the closed circle of Boston aristocracy to which she, so inappropriately, "belonged."

And with the help of impulse? She was divinely thin, fabulously rich, and enormously chic. The classic merry widow. If only she felt merry. It was all the fault of Scruples. It was a total disaster and the sooner she faced it the better. She had been impulsive once too often.

The next morning, as soon as she woke from the brief sleep that had come over her as dawn was breaking, Billy Ikehorn telephoned Josh Hillman at his home, a bad habit that she had caught from Ellis Ikehorn in the days of his glory and power.

"Josh, how committed am I to those two, Elliott and Valentine?"

"Well, they have contracts, of course, but they could always be bought out for less than it would take to pay them for the entire year, if that's what you have in mind. It's unlikely that they'd sue. They probably don't have the resources to pay a top attorney and, to my mind, unlikely that a good man would take their case on a contingency basis. Why?" His question had an uncharacteristic note of uneasiness.

"I'm just considering my options." Billy didn't want to admit outright that she was planning on getting rid of Spider and Valentine. In the subtle seesaw of unexpressed second-guessing that takes place between lawyer and client she didn't want to lose this round too ignominiously. When she had awakened actually flirting with the idea of selling Scruples, she had realized that she had been right about one thing, at least. The land was already worth more than she had paid for it, and perhaps a Neiman-Marcus or a Bendel might want to buy the building. Even if no one wanted it except as a great bargain, at least she would be free of the suffocating embarrassment of running a moribund store.

Better for her to seem to have merely lost interest in Scruples than to cling to it while her peers laughed and sneered at her pretensions and secretly rejoiced to see her humbled. She felt depression creeping over her. She had put so much into her hopes for Scruples. It was still her baby. But she couldn't take public humiliation. Of all the things that could happen to her, that was the one she was most afraid of. She had escaped the misery of her first eighteen years only physically. The scars they left would always remain. They had deformed her, and whatever else had happened to her later had not permitted her to forget the past.

A few hours later, while she was dressing, Spider telephoned.

"Billy, I've been up half the night thinking about how to turn Scruples around, make it a smash. Can we talk today?"

"I'm just not in the mood. Frankly, the subject is beginning to bore me. Yesterday you were tap-dancing all over the ceiling with a restaurant here and a massage parlor there. I'm just not up to any of your tricky schemes today, Spider."

"I promise serious business only. Listen, I've latched on to a car. It's a gorgeous day—let's drive up to Santa Barbara and have lunch at the Biltmore. We could talk there. I haven't been up the coast in ten years. Don't you feel like getting away for a few hours?"

Oddly enough, she did. She felt as if she'd been trapped for an eternity between the city of Beverly Hills and the low Santa Monica Mountains, which rose behind West Los Angeles and separated it from the San Fernando Valley. It had been forever since she'd gone anywhere out of town for lunch except for predictable Sunday brunches at the Malibu Colony.

"Aw, *come on,* Billy! You'll have fun, scout's honor."

"Oh—all right. Pick me up in one hour."

Billy hung up reflectively. If it had been years since she had driven ninety miles for lunch, it had been much longer since anyone had asked her to go anywhere in quite that tone of voice, as if she were no more, no less than a slightly reluctant girl.

Billy remembered perfectly well how people talk to people who aren't rich. For the past thirteen years, since she had married Ellis Ikehorn, people had talked differently to her, using that special intonation reserved for the very rich. She had often meditated on the great American game of trying to find out why, *exactly why,* the rich are different. Fitzgerald and O'Hara and dozens of lesser writers had been passionately absorbed by the rich, as if money were the most fascinating thing a person could possess—not beauty, not talent, not even power, but money. Billy thought privately that the rich are different only because people treat them as if they were. Sometimes she wondered why people bothered. It was not as if knowing someone rich rubbed off on them, put more money in their own bank accounts. Yet, there it was, that slight self-consciousness, the faint over-consideration, that eagerness to charm, the instinctive putting-the-best-foot-forward that she heard all day.

Perhaps she never would have realized that people don't talk to the rich the way they talk to others if the change in her own fortunes hadn't been so abrupt. If she had been born rich, she suspected, she wouldn't have had enough experience to be impressed by Spider's informal manner. Aside from certain, very few, women who had the power and position in Los Angeles to ignore her fortune, no one else spoke to her as Spider just had.

As only he could, Spider had promoted a classic Mercedes convertible, and an unspoken cease-fire seemed to have gone into effect between them from the minute Spider asked if she wanted the top up or down.

"Oh, down, please," said Billy, thinking that, for all her thirty-three years, she'd never ridden in a convertible with the top down, something every American woman is supposed to have spent her youth doing. Or was that another, past generation? In any case, she'd missed it.

Once past Calabasas, the freeway was almost deserted and the valley stretched out around them in a series of brown, sun-dried, rolling hills dotted with live oaks, a landscape almost as simple as a child's painting. And soon, past Oxnard, they could see the Pacific on their left with nothing between them and Japan except an occasional oil rig. Spider drove like an angry flamenco dancer, cursing the speed limit as if somebody had taken away his high-heeled boots.

"Last time I was on this road you could go an easy hundred—we used to make Santa Barbara in less than an hour."

"What was the rush?"

"Oh, just the fun of it. And sometimes, after a late party, I had to get a girl home before her parents sent out a statewide alarm."

"A real California kid, weren't you?"

"The genuine article—one step away from a surfer. If you're going to have a misspent youth, have it right here." He laughed his joyous, lazy laugh at a million memories.

Billy observed the perfect conversational opportunity to lead Spider into revealing what, just exactly, he had been doing since those days, but she felt too good to bother at the moment. The wind in her hair, the sun on her face, the open car—it was like being the girl in an old Coca-Cola ad; she could sense her clenched anxiety diminishing as every mile put her farther away from Rodeo Drive.

She had never been to Santa Barbara. When Ellis was alive, the only trips they took were by jet. Nor had she ever been tempted by the few invitations she had received to come to parties in Montecito, a community just outside Santa Barbara where the very rich live on a closely guarded few square miles famous not only for their natural beauty but also for their laws prohibiting the sale of liquor and their fabulous private wine cellars. Although the Biltmore hadn't sounded too inviting, she was stunned as they drove around a curve and the grand, rambling old hotel was revealed on its high bluff overlooking the sea, romantic and beautifully maintained, a mirage out of a gracious, dignified past. Blue mountains stretched up the coast in the background, while nearby, surf pounded the cliffs.

"This is the way the French Riviera could have looked fifty years ago!" she exclaimed.

"I've never been there," Spider said.

"My husband and I used to go. Oh, but this—it's perfect. I didn't know there were places like this so close to the city."

"There aren't. This is the first one. Then you keep going up the coast and it just gets better and better. Shall we eat outside or inside?" Spider was dazzling, Billy thought, as they stood in front of the entrance to the hotel—his smile, that seemed to expect, happily, only good things. A damn knockout if she'd ever seen one. Such an obvious combination: golden hair and blue, blue, blue eyes. Why did it always work?

"Outside, of course." He wanted something, but she knew what it was, so she was prepared. He might be a knockout, but she was no pushover. And she still intended to cut her losses.

When Josh Hillman sent Valentine the basket of butterfly orchids, he committed, perhaps, the first absolutely unnecessary act of his life. When he called to ask her to dinner the next day he committed the second one.

He knew exactly where he wanted to take Valentine, to his special place, the 94th Aero Squadron out at Van Nuys Airport. He had never taken anyone there before. Five years earlier, Josh had taken up flying. He'd never been interested in sports, but he'd always yearned to fly. As soon as he felt he could reasonably spare one afternoon a week away from the office and one afternoon a weekend away from home, he started flying lessons, much to his wife's disgust. Joanne flew only Pan Am, and then only after two Miltowns and three Martinis in the airport bar. As soon as he had earned his private pilot's license, Josh bought a Beechcraft Sierra and began to steal more and more time on the weekends to indulge in the intoxication of flight. Joanne never cared; she always had a full schedule of tennis and backgammon tournaments. Nor did she mind the many nights he worked late at the office; she had literally hundreds of phone calls to make each week to keep track of the multitude of women she herded into working their asses off for culture and better hospitals. Often, after Josh landed, he went to the 94th Aero Squadron for a drink before driving home.

It was an authentic oddity, a restaurant constructed exactly like an old French farmhouse built of weathered bricks and crumbling plaster, which, one was asked to believe, had been commandeered by a British flying unit during World War I. It had hundreds of sandbags piled high around its ground floor, with early sten guns concealed behind them, a farm wagon full of hay by the front door, Muzak that played "It's a Long, Long Way to Tipperary" and "Pack Up Your Troubles in Your Old Kit-Bag," signs directing guests to the "Briefing Room," and faded photographs of brave, dead pilots on the walls. An old biplane was parked between this apparition from another world and the real end of the parallel runways of the Van Nuys Airport, where some seventeen hundred private planes landed or took off every day of the year. Josh enjoyed the nostalgia and sweet melancholy of the place, which somehow managed not to feel fake no matter how much it had to be. But Joanne would have scorned it as a "theme" restaurant, and wondered why, if they were forced to eat in the Valley, they hadn't gone to LaSerre.

Valentine was totally charmed by the Aero Squadron. It was so exactly what she had hoped to find in California, a glorious hoax. In fact, she found herself beginning to be charmed by Josh Hillman. Except for Spider, she had spent the last few years with men who weren't men, or men who might be men but whose main interest in life was buying and selling women's clothes. Enough! She was ready for a serious man, but not a solemn one, a man of substance, but not a stuffy man—in short, a real man! And Josh Hillman, having broken the habit of twenty years of dutiful marriage in inviting Valentine to dinner, felt a sense of freedom and unlimited choice in the air. Suddenly there were 360 degrees of space around him instead of a long, straight road. For a minute he remembered his grandfather's favorite proverb: "If a good Jew finally decides to eat pork, then he should enjoy it so much that the fat runs down his chin." Was Valentine O'Neill as tasty as a pork roast? Josh Hillman certainly intended to find out.

Their table was at the window, and as darkness fell and the lights of the descending planes floated past, the aircraft, behind soundproof glass, looked like wondrous fish with luminous eyes.

"Valentine—how did you get that name?" he asked. She was curious to note that he pronounced it in the French manner, Val-en-teen, strange for an American.

"My mother was a Chevalier fan—I was named after a song."

"Ah, *that* Valentine."

"You know her? It's impossible!"

He hummed the first bars of the melody and, almost too shyly to be heard, said the lyrics: " *'Elle avait de tout petits petons, Valentine, Valentine, Elle avait de tout petits têtons, Que je tâtais à tâtons, Ton ton tontaine!'* "

298

"But *how* do you know?"

"My roommate at law school used to play the record endlessly."

"Ah, but do you know what the words mean."

"Something like—she had tiny little feet and tiny little breasts."

"Not precisely—*tétons*—that's slang, it means 'tits.' And the rest?"

"I'm not sure—"

"Tiny little tits, which I *tâtais,* felt—*à tâtons*—gropingly."

"I can't imagine Chevalier ever having to grope."

"Nor can I. But do you know all the rest?"

" '*Elle avait un tout petit menton,*' " he answered, "a tiny little chin—and *'elle etait frisée comme un mouton!'*— she was curly like a lamb. Like you."

"Extraordinary—and the rest? No? Ah ha! You missed the best part—she did not have a good character! No indeed—and also she did not have a great intelligence and she was jealous and bossy—*autoritaire.* And then one day, you see, years later, Chevalier meets her on the street and she has big feet, a double chin, and a triple *poitrine!*"

"Valentine! You're breaking my heart. I was happier not knowing."

They both rocked with laughter, the aphrodisiac laughter that comes when two people have decided to run away together from their real lives, even if only for an evening, that special, tingling laughter of complicity that is the first sign that they are finding each other altogether more entrancing than they had expected.

"So you, Joshua, are the hero of the Bible, who brought down the walls of Jericho, and I am merely Valentine, the first mistress of Chevalier, the eighteen-year-old girl he met in the Rue Justine. Not an even match."

"No? Do you have a more impressive middle name?"

"But it is a dreadful secret."

"Tell me."

"Marie-Ange." Wickedly, she tried to look humble. "Mary-Angel."

"How modest, such an unpretentious little name. Your mother must have felt she shouldn't take chances."

"But you are right. We are prudent, we French."

"And you are crazy, Miss O'Neill—you Irish."

"And you Jews—you are not prudent? And you are not a little crazy?"

"Every last one. Haven't you ever heard the theory that the Irish are really the lost tribe of Israel?"

"It would not surprise me. But I wouldn't walk into an Irish bar on Third Avenue and give them the good news," she responded, with a snap of mischief in her voice.

"You're a real New Yorker, aren't you?"

"Not a real anything, I fear. A woman without a country, not a real Parisian, not a real New Yorker, and now—California. How ludicrous. Does anyone ever become a real Californian?"

"You already are. Almost all real Californians are from somewhere else. There are a handful who came here, oh, possibly as long ago as two hundred years. Before that there were only Indians and Franciscan Fathers—so we are a state of immigrants in a country of immigrants."

"But you feel at home here?"

"I'll take you to Fairfax Avenue someday soon. You'll see why." Josh had a moment to feel astonishment at his invitation. He had never taken Joanne to Fairfax Avenue. They had driven past on the way to the Farmers Market, but they never stopped. She hated it. Why did he want to show Valentine, whose elegance seemed to float on the very air of Paris, the lively, noisy, crowded, and most unstylish ghetto of his childhood?

Spider and Billy ate lunch outside, under the spread of awnings of the Santa Barbara Biltmore, a glass screen framed by flowers and palm trees sheltering them from the brisk breeze that blew inland off the Pacific. Billy waited calmly, knowing that Spider had to make the opening move. Meanwhile, she drank Dry Sack sherry on the rocks, ate a club sandwich with extra mayonnaise to make it a double sin (for which she would later penalize herself with abstinence), and felt deliciously in command of the situation.

Soon his experienced eye told Spider that this lady was as relaxed as she was ever going to get while she was upright. Carelessly he said, "Nice here, isn't it?" She merely smiled agreement, guarding her words. "I've been on the East Coast so long," he continued, "that I didn't really remember what California was like. And Beverly Hills! Christ, I fully expect it to vanish one night like Brigadoon and not be seen again for a hundred years, don't you?"

"Probably," Billy answered incautiously.

"I had a feeling you'd understand, Billy. When we hit town yesterday Val and I realized that we'd walked into a whole new ball game." By now Billy was reassembling her forces, but Spider pressed on. "If you took Scruples and set it down in Paris or New York or Milan or Tokyo, you'd have the eighth wonder of the world—women would be lining up around the block to get in—it's so perfect, what a class act! But Billy, Billy, in Beverly Hills! Home of the most casually dressed rich women in the universe! I'm so used to New York that I had to keep reminding myself yesterday that most of the women we saw on the street in pants and t-shirts could afford to buy anything they wanted, couldn't they?" Since Billy had so often had the same thoughts herself, her eyes signaled faint agreement in spite of herself. Before she could interrupt him, Spider fixed her with his most persuasive gaze and continued. "I'm sure that if you give Val and me a week or two, at the most, to get acclimated, to wander around town and look at what women actually do buy when they're shopping for expensive clothes, to see what they wear out at night, to case The Bistro and Perino's and Chasen's and all the new places —could you make a list of them, incidentally—it would help a lot—if we had the time to get a fresh feeling of the place, we can make Scruples the most successful store in town. It figures that no matter how those women look on the street, there wouldn't be a Saks' and a Bonwit's and a Magnin's and all those dozens of expensive boutiques squeezed together in one small place unless many women are spending huge amounts of money. There's no reason on earth why Scruples shouldn't be where they spend it, Billy, but you can see for yourself, we need a little time."

"A little time?" Billy tried to make the words as sarcastic as possible, but simple logic told her that she couldn't deny him a week or two without looking stupid, irrational, like a simpleminded, rich bitch who changed her mind from day to day—a dilettante.

"Exactly. As much time as you'd give a new hairdresser.

The first time he works on you, you don't really expect a good job, now do you? You'd let him do it again a week later, maybe even a third time. By then he'd know how your hair grows, how it takes a curl, where your cowlicks are, how much body your hair has, whether he has to tease it or whether he can blow dry it. Then if he did a poor job, you'd get another hairdresser."

"I most certainly would," Billy snapped.

"Of course you would." Spider looked at her approvingly. His years of listening to garrulous models was paying off. "Val will be working on the stock side of things—I'll be working on the concept."

" 'Concept'? Wait a minute, Spider. On the phone Valentine told me that you were the best salesman in the world and that you could completely reorganize the store. What's 'concept' got to do with it?"

"I *am* the best salesman in the world, but first I have to know something about who my customers are and how they live, exactly what the target area is, and what will make them want to buy at Scruples. The 'concept' is what will make them buy. Don't you see, Billy, *buying clothes should be as satisfactory as a good fuck?* There are many kinds of good fucks—I just need to know which one will work best in Beverly Hills."

Billy was shocked to realize that she was nodding her head in agreement. She'd never heard a statement that she could understand so viscerally. She had not forgotten the days when her sex life existed only in the moment of purchase.

"All right, Spider. You've made your point. Clearly. When can I expect your 'concept' to be unleashed on a waiting world?"

"In no longer than two weeks. Now, if you've finished your lunch, we'd better get started back or we'll be caught in the rush-hour traffic. Ready, Billy?"

On the way back to Holmby Hills Billy found plenty of time to reflect that whatever Spider Elliott was or was not in reality, he certainly couldn't be called a poor salesman. Still, all she had granted them was two weeks. If he didn't come up with something solid, he and Val would be out, with no further dithering. It was a firm promise she made to herself.

After dinner Josh Hillman had a problem that he had never before faced in his life, an absurdly old-fashioned kind of problem but a real one. He and Valentine were two people who were intimate only by virtue of the restaurant roof over their heads. They didn't know each other well enough to go to a private place without discussion. He needed a Lovers' Lane, for God's sake. In the old days, before he had married Joanne, he remembered that Mulholland Drive had had a reputation as the only place to park and neck, but now, as far as he could guess, dozens of new houses had been built on that tradition-hallowed land. But, damn it, if he didn't get a chance to at least kiss Valentine O'Neill tonight—he was too square for this, he told himself, which reminded him of what his sons called him. Then inspiration finally came, the Pickwick Drive-In in Burbank, of course, one of the kids' favorite haunts. Josh hadn't been to a drive-in since high school.

"Valentine, since you really want to feel like a native, I'm going to show you one of our great California traditions," he announced while he was paying the check.

"Could we go to a Hollywood movie premiere?" Her vixen face was filled with a question, a question that seemed to hang in the air, a question that had nothing to do with Hollywood premieres.

"Not tonight. Anyway, they're really kind of old hat. They don't really have them very often any more, not the way they used to. I was thinking of showing you a drive-in movie."

"What's playing?"

"That's part of the point—it doesn't matter. Come on!"

They drove to the drive-in in a fizzing silence. Once outside the restaurant they had both been filled with a sense of the immediate future that was too exciting to make other conversation possible, but in itself absolutely impossible to discuss. Josh bought the tickets as if he'd been going to drive-ins regularly, for years, and solemnly instructed Valentine in the functions of the speaker. She had just time to see four cars on the screen all meet in a head-on collision before he slid over from behind the driver's seat and took her into his arms. For long, long stunned minutes that was all. As Josh wrapped Valentine tightly in his arms, she burrowed deep into them. They didn't speak. They just held each other, listening to the soft sounds of breathing and heartbeats, made inexpressibly happy by the warmth, the closeness, the simple humanity of just holding fast to each other. The unquestioned silence of their embrace was more moving than hundreds of words. It was a moment in time that stood apart from thought or arrangements or declarations or anything artful or formal, the kind of rare moment that makes perfect sense without making any sense at all, the kind of moment that creates a knowledge of mutual need and surrender that is as frightening as it is necessary and right. But after a long while, each of them, as if moved by the same tide, searched for the other's lips, saying only the other's name, kissing. Kissing Valentine was like plunging his face in a bunch of fresh spring flowers after a long, parched winter. There were endless discoveries to be made from her lips, but first he licked the three freckles on her nose, something he had wanted to do all during dinner, and she nipped him back like a puppy. She gave him butterfly kisses on his cheeks with her spiky black eyelashes and he tasted her neck with his tongue.

The titles of the second feature were flashing on the screen before they drew apart. When two people are grown up, kissing cannot go on forever. When two people are as complex and self-defined as Valentine and Josh, kissing cannot lead to anything else without some words being spoken. But what words? They were suddenly as shy as schoolchildren, both of them overtaken by belated surprise. How had they arrived at this moment after only a few hours together? Selfconsciousness came flooding back.

"What happens next?" Josh asked slowly. "Valentine darling, do you know?"

"No," she answered, "I know as little—much less—than you."

"Then we'll both learn together," he said, as cautiously as someone finding his way in the dark.

"Perhaps," she answered, drawing back slightly.

"Perhaps! Why do you say that?"

"I am only being prudent—for me—for you."

"To hell with prudence. We can both be prudent all the rest of our lives. But this time, Valentine, lovely, beautiful Valentine, oh, just once, let's be crazy, just this once in our lives!"

He kissed her again and again, like a boy, planting impetuous, fervent, random kisses on her eyes, her ears, her chin, her hair. He felt all the starved spontaneity of his studious youth crying out to be expressed in romantic words, but all he could manage to say was, "Be crazy with me, Valentine."

"Perhaps." Something in Valentine, something very strong, would not allow her to be swept away. After giving in completely to the first, unimaginable, mindless comfort of feeling his arms around her, she had retreated, retrenched, gone back a step to her sturdy inner self. Her sense of reality had returned, and with it disquiet, disbelief that she was here, kissing this man, a man she had met only yesterday, a married man with children. Madame Hélène O'Neill's clever, skeptical, logical daughter could not agree to be crazy. At least not yet, and most certainly not in a drive-in. One shall see, she said to herself, using a time-honored French formula for any sort of style of indecision, from downright refusal to near acceptance. Aloud, she said only, "Perhaps."

With regrets, Spider returned the Mercedes to the dealer in used classic cars opposite the Beverly Wilshire Hotel—unfortunately it wasn't exactly the car he was looking for, but he'd be back—and went to scare up Valentine to tell her the story of his day with Billy. When he couldn't find her, he ordered dinner from room service and lay on his bed to think. His superbly sensitive antennae for the hidden thoughts of women had never told him anything as strongly as that the next two weeks were crucial. He suspected that he and Valentine might have been taking a plane back to New York tomorrow if he hadn't sweet-talked Billy today. That lady was quirky, skittish, and just one baby step away from washing her hands of the whole venture. She was so used to having things go her own way that she'd almost lost all consideration for others, if she'd ever had it; she was spoiled rotten, trigger-happy, and yet there was something that was still vulnerable in her. Spider estimated that, all in all, he could manage her, given the right amount of inspiration.

She was not another Harriet Toppingham, as he had wondered the night before; she did not want to see fear in a man; on the contrary, she wanted to see courage, she responded to boldness, she could be fair. She was fundamentally decent, he had to admit.

But first, Spider warned himself, before he went in for missionary work on Billy Ikehorn, he had to learn two things, and learn them within two weeks. He needed to absorb the climate of retailing as it currently existed in Beverly Hills in successful stores. Second, he had to find out about the way California women spent their money on clothes, the *how* of it. Obviously, they didn't base their wardrobes on the sorts of things he was used to noticing in New York: wonderful urban coats, good-looking suits, polished street and office dressing. Spider almost fell asleep, thinking of how different the women looked on the corner of 57th Street and Fifth than they did on the corner of Wilshire and Rodeo, when two words sprang into his mind and shocked him awake, cursing himself for being so slow to remember and blessing himself for being lucky. *Native son.*

Jesus Christ Almighty, it was the fucking treasure of Sierra Madre! He'd been out of touch so long—three or four years since he'd been back for Christmas, and the last six months he had barely let his family know he was alive—but my God, how could a man, even bleeding from every pore because of Melanie Adams and punch-drunk from changing his life's work in less than a week, to say nothing of the craziness of yesterday and the business of the contracts and today's drive with Billy Ikehorn, lady razor blade—how could a man forget that he was *back home!*

Pasadena, or rather San Marino, the quiet, wealthy part of Pasadena, had been his home until he was eighteen and UCLA in Westwood had been his Eden for the rest of his life in California, but even if Beverly Hills was relatively unexplored territory for Spider Elliott, it was still a part of the world where he had his roots, his friends, and hallelujah—his family. *Six sisters!*

A man with six sisters, Spider realized with glee, was a rich man—unless he was Greek and had a duty to marry them off. He began to jot down notes on the pad on his bedside table. Five of the girls had married—three very well—he remembered, and unless the bottom had fallen out of oil and lumber and insurance, they must be socially secure young matrons by now. Holly and Heather were twenty-eight, and Holly had married an oil heir and lived in super-conservative, old-money Hancock Park. Pansy had married the only son of a man who owned half the redwood trees in northern California, but her husband owned and operated an insurance company from a home base in San Francisco. Even one of the kids, little June, had done awfully well for herself; only twenty-four, she was the richest of them all; her new husband's fast-food franchises had given her a spread in Palm Springs, a beach house in La Jolla, and a vast house and stables in Palos Verdes. Not that the other girls had done badly—Heather and January were also married, not rich-rich, just nicely well-off; and Petunia, Spider guessed, liked screwing around too much to settle down. For his purposes, Spider needed to know about the social life of both the well-off and the rich-rich. Thoughts of the rich-rich reminded him of Herbie. He'd forgotten Herbie! His best friend at UCLA. Movie money, piles of it, and Herbie had gone into the family business.

Christ, Spider finally understood that while he was living in a loft in New York probably 90 percent of the golden lads and lasses he had known in his school days had become respectful and affluent citizens. He'd been tempted, for a moment, earlier that day, to ask Billy to give a party for him and Valentine so that they could see how women dressed out here at night, but on second thought he hadn't wanted to ask her help; he'd wanted to do it on his own. Damn good thing he'd waited until his brains unscrambled. At the bottom of his list of names, Spider wrote in letters one inch high: EVERYBODY— WELCOME HOME PARTY NEEDED WITHIN LESS THAN TWO WEEKS—DRESSED UP! and with the other hand he dialed an old familiar number, the only one he'd ever bothered to memorize.

"MOM! Hi, Mom—I'm home!"

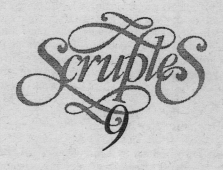

*I*n the two weeks that followed his call home, Spider needed all his resilience, all his trained eye for detail, all his leaping sense of taste, all his imagination and sense of what works visually and what doesn't quite make it. Fortunately, it was late August, the busy time, when Beverly Hills stores begin receiving their fall merchandise. Also it was still sale time for summer things all over town.

Separately, both he and Valentine worked the streets foot by foot. North of Wilshire, they covered Rodeo, Camden, and Bedford drives up and down both sides of the streets. Then they investigated every shop on Dayton Way and Brighton Way and on "little" Santa Monica, crisscrossing them from east to west. They left little but the pavement unturned on Wilshire Boulevard, from Robinson's on the west boundary, delving through Saks, Magnin's, Elizabeth Arden's, Delman's, and finally, on the east corner of the shopping part of the street, Bonwit Teller's. It all formed a dense, vaguely triangular grid, which in New York City would have been stretched out into blocks and blocks of Fifth and Madison avenues but in Beverly Hills was so compressed that any boutique, any store, was easily reached by foot. An average, medium-sized boutique on Rodeo paid a yearly rent of ninety-six thousand dollars so that the unsuccessful quickly closed.

Sometimes Spider, who did everything but lick the paint off the walls in his efforts to fix the qualities of a store in his mind, would bump into Valentine, busily

310

going through the sale racks to see what they hadn't sold last season, driving salesgirls to murder in their hearts as she carefully inspected every piece of new merchandise, filing it away in the sketchbook of her mind but never being "carried away" enough to buy, as she apologetically explained. Spider, obviously a potential customer in his beautifully cut, new clothes, hastily bought before he left New York, often pretended to be buying a present for his mother or one of his sisters as he loitered and eavesdropped and fell into conversation with unsuspecting store owners and customers and sales personnel. Together and separately, they covered all the smaller boutiques and such major shops at Dorso's, Giorgio's, Amelia Gray's, Jax, Matthews, the Right Bank Clothing Company, Kamali, Alan Austin, Dinallo, Ted Lapidus, Mr. Guy's, Theodore's, Courrèges, Polo, Charles Gallay, Gunn-Trigère, Hermès, Edwards-Lowell, and Gucci.

During those two weeks eight parties were given for Spider, hastily arranged but large and festive.

Although the Elliott girls as children had always felt that there was such an abundance of Spider's love that they did not need to compete for it, now, as adults, they found themselves rivaling each other in entertaining the legendary brother their friends had heard so much about but rarely seen. Since not one of them could bring herself to even begin to believe that Valentine was merely Spider's business partner—who was he kidding, with that sexy French look, that sparkly way she had, and those eyes—they were all exceedingly, excessively polite to her. Valentine's often reflected, when she had time to think at all, that while it had not been too difficult to be friendly with Elliott's women, good God, the ladies of his family could think of only one thing. Nevertheless, it was well worth being treated with the utmost charm of course, as if she had come to steal away each sister's particular treasure, since these parties, more than any other single element in the two exhausting weeks, gave Valentine a chance to see how affluent women dressed at night from San Francisco to San Diego. Josh telephoned her every day, but she had, truly, no time for him until this marathon was over. Valentine missed him, but she couldn't afford to indulge in any emotional feelings at this crucial, crazy time.

During the two weeks she had allotted to Valentine and Spider, Billy made several infuriating visits to Scruples, where racks and racks of clothes were on sale, a sight that disgusted her to the marrow of her bones, much as she knew it was necessary. Only her need to keep up a good face kept her from hiding all the sale clothes and shipping them away to the Salvation Army, for she could imagine just how fast the story of such a caper would spread. She could scarcely contain her desire to have the final conference with those two imposters and get the whole abortion over with.

When the day came, Billy sat behind her desk as if it were a stone wall, eyeing Valentine and Spider with the air of an indifferent, paid executioner. By now she had almost convinced herself that everything that wasn't working at Scruples was their fault.

Spider lounged against the wall, splendidly nonchalant in a lightweight Glen plaid, one of the several extremely good suits he had bought at Dunhill Tailors in New York. Billy was grimly pleased to see that, in spite of his casual pose, he looked serious and concerned. Valentine perched on a chair, obviously waiting for him to speak first. Billy thought that the girl looked exhausted, almost punch-drunk.

"Let's have it, Spider," Billy said, in a flat, bored voice. Everything about her breathed lack of interest, even her posture.

"I've got good news."

"Surprise me."

"You have only one rival to surpass to become the number-one store in Beverly Hills and you have only one way to do it."

"That's just insane. Try to make sense, Spider. I thought we'd agreed that fancy footwork was out."

"Your rival is Scruples." He held up a hand to forestall her interruption, locking eyes with her so that she subsided, only her dark eyebrows quirked in angry suspicion. "I could put it more plainly. Your rival is your *own dream* of Scruples, of the store you wanted it to be, the store you were convinced southern California was waiting for. *You were wrong, Billy*. By about six thousand miles. I understand your dream; it was the inevitable outcome of your personal taste, but it was as futile as expecting to build the Petit Trianon on the site of the Hollywood Wax Museum. Some things just don't transplant. You can sell Coca-Cola in Africa and there may be as many Mercedes in downtown Abu Dhabi as there are in Beverly Hills, but there is only one possible Dior and it is located on the Avenue Montaigne and that is where it should stay. *Give up your fantasy of Dior, Billy, or buy a ticket to Paris*. The light is different there, the weather is different, the civilization is different, the customers and their needs are different, the entire approach to buying a dress is absolutely, completely different. You, of all people, know what a serious business it is there to choose a garment—it's a monumental decision."

Billy was so taken aback, more by *how* he was talking to her than by *what* he was saying, that she didn't even try to answer him.

"Look at the facts. In Beverly Hills you have a shopping area that equals in sheer luxury and choice, the best of New York. It's not as big, but neither is the population. Now, obviously, this area wouldn't be here, and growing every day, if the customers weren't here to support it. But Scruples isn't getting them. Why? Because it *doesn't work*."

"Doesn't work?" Billy glared. "It's more elegant and comfortable than any store in the world, including Paris! I made sure of that."

"It doesn't work as ENTERTAINMENT!" Both Valentine and Billy just stared at Spider as he went on. "Shopping has become a form of entertainment, Billy, whether you like it or not. A visit to Scruples is *just not fun* and your potential customers demand fun from the stores they visit. You can even go all the way and call it the Disneyland concept of retailing."

"Disneyland!" Billy said it in a low, horrified, repelled voice.

"Yes, Disneyland—shopping as a trip, shopping as a giggle. The same money changes hands, no mistake about that, but if your customer, your local customer or your customer from Santa Barbara or a tourist from another country, has a choice between Scruples and Giorgio's, your neighbor across the street, which will she pick? You walk into Scruples and you see a vast, ornate space decorated in twenty-five shades of supremely subtle gray, with little gilt chairs here and there and a terrifying herd of chic, elderly, haughty saleswomen who all act as if they would far rather speak French than English—or you go into Giorgio's and you see a crowded, merry mob of people drinking at the bar, playing pool, salesladies who wear nutty hats and look at you as if they've been hoping you'd come in for a good gossip, all of them ready to make you feel expansive and cosseted."

"Giorgio's happens to stand for everything that Scruples is NOT," Billy said in a glacial voice.

"And Giorgio's is the number-one retail specialty store in the country, including New York City."

"What? I don't believe it!"

"Would you believe one thousand dollars of business per square foot per year? They have four thousand feet of selling space, which means four million dollars a year just on clothes and accessories. And we're talking about what is just a big boutique. In comparison, our local Saks, which has one hundred fifty thousand square feet, only did twenty million dollars in 1975, so you can see how well Giorgio's is using its space. There are dozens of women who spend at least fifty thousand dollars every year with Giorgio's, customers from every wealthy city in the world. There are even women who come in every day to see what's new—it's one way for them to keep busy. And they buy—how they buy!"

"How do you know you're right about this, Spider?" Billy was somehow managing to sound indifferent.

"I—ah, more or less, fell into conversation with the owner, Fred Hayman, and he told me. Later I confirmed the figures with *Women's Wear*. But don't think it's just happening at Giorgio's, Billy. All the stores in town that are *fun* to shop in do wonderfully, Dorso's most particularly. Just going in there makes you feel good, whether you buy or not; it's half like going to a good party, half like going to a friendly museum—a sensuous experience either way. Billy, Billy, people want to be *loved* when they buy their clothes! *Especially rich people.*"

"Really, Spider," Billy shrugged.

"And they don't want to be *judged* by salesladies," Spider continued.

"I was playing pool at Giorgio's the other day, and I saw two gals come in together, one in tennis shorts, the other in dirty jeans, a t-shirt without a bra, and scuffed sandals. By the time they'd left, and I was able to watch every move they made because the few fitting rooms they have are so small and inconvenient that you have to come outside to see yourself properly in the mirror, each of those two ragamuffins had bought three dresses, a Chloé, a Thea Porter, and a Zandra Rhodes—not one of them much less than two thousand dollars. I asked one of the gals if she shopped at Scruples—as a matter of fact we even played a little pool—and she said that she'd come in right after it opened but—and, Billy, I'm quoting her exactly—'It's too much trouble to get all dressed up to go shopping in a stiff, stuffy place with all those snobbish salesladies.' "

"Was she the one in tennis shorts or dirty jeans?" Billy asked contemptuously.

"No matter. The point is that I'm so convinced that unless you will accept the Disneyland concept of making retailing fun, there isn't any point in my staying here. You can have my resignation if you want it." Billy looked at him testily. He wasn't using that astonishing smile for a change. He was really in dead earnest. She had had enough experience with men to know a ploy when she heard one. This creature meant every word he was saying.

"Christ, I'm beginning to think I should have bought Giorgio's instead of building Scruples!" she said with a bitter laugh and sudden tears in her eyes.

"Wrong! Scruples can be ten times the store Giorgio's is because you have three things they don't have: *space—Valentine—and me.*" Spider had already smelled a change in her. Billy had abandoned something with her last remark and stepped an inch away from a fiercely defended position.

"And what do you plan—to put in a pool table and ask my salespeople to dress funky?"

"Nothing that simple, or that copycat. Complete redecoration, including your immaculate fitting rooms.

315

They have to be made sexy, individual, and amusing. It may mean another seven or eight hundred thousand dollars spent on top of the millions you've sunk in here already—but it will be enough to turn the store around. Example: When you walk in the front door of Scruples *after* we redecorate, you'll find yourself in the most extraordinary, charming country store in the world: bulging, chockablock full of everything necessary and unnecessary from antique buttons to lilies growing in pots, penny candy in Waterford glass jars, antique toys, the most expensive pruning shears in the world, handmade writing paper, pillows made from grandmothers' quilts, tortoiseshell boxes and bird whistles to—you name it. And the country store is so much fun that it puts you in a good mood, whether you buy or not. The way I've planned it, they'll buy there on the way out, impulsive gifts, but it's planned to be the entrance to the Fun Fair.

"The Fair, Billy—that's the main part of the ground floor. For the men, we'll have a pub. And while they're waiting for the women to shop, and so they don't feel silly, as if they'll trapped in some embarrassingly feminine place, we'll give them all kinds of those new pinball machines, the electronic ones, and at least four backgammon tables and, of course, a men's department, accessories only, but the finest in the world. Maybe a couple of Ping-Pong tables—I'm not sure about that yet. Now, the rest of the room, except the back end, is going to be accessory heaven for women—just heaps and heaps of gorgeous goodies, only the best, the most expensive, the latest, the newest, most exclusive beautiful things—you know what I mean—but all done with such a sense of abundance, of accessibility, of touchability that they won't be able to resist. The Arabian Nights. The Sultan's Treasures. That's why they shop, Billy—not because, God knows, they *need* another bag or scarf but because it just feels so damn good. They *want to be tempted*—they can afford it. And in the back, an Edwardian winter garden, cozy, intimate, old-fashioned, just the place to revive yourself with tea and crumpets or a chocolate soda or a glass of champagne. And, of course, all the showcases and display pieces will be easily movable—even the walls in between the country store and the winter garden can be sliding walls—so that when you give the parties there'll be lots of room for the orchestra and for the dancers—" He paused for breath.

"Dancers?" said Billy in a strange tone of voice.

"Well sure—we'll have to close to redecorate, so we'll reopen with a gala ball. After that, you'll give dancing parties twice a month—I included the cost of turning the first floor into a ballroom in the decorating plans—because, except for charity parties and a very few private parties, women don't have enough chance to get dressed up here. They all want to, as what woman doesn't, but hostesses have gotten into the habit of giving rather informal private parties, unless it's a big occasion. So if you were to give dancing parties, by invitation only, twice a month, women will simply have to have more pretty clothes, won't they? And then, maybe once a month, on boring old Sunday nights when there's nothing else to do in this town, we'll have a gambling party here. The prize could be a Scruples dress, but it would be real gambling. The money would go to charity, of course, but it's cheaper than going to Vegas and a billion times more classy, and they'd have to dress for that and—"

"The clothes, Spider, where do we put all the clothes while they're dancing?" Now there was only one note in Billy's voice: curiosity.

"Oh, we never keep the clothes down here. I thought I'd mentioned that. The clothes are the serious fun of Scruples. We sell upstairs. That way our customers can have real privacy between them and the mirror. Christ, even in the Saks Park Avenue Room they only have curtains, which don't even close properly—anybody can see a woman in her underwear just by passing through, no matter how expensive her dress may be—I don't understand why they put up with it. No, at Scruples when you come to buy, you go upstairs and get the full treatment, the fitting room, the luxury, the free lunch, the foot massage, remember? Even if you just come to look, you'll be treated like a princess. The kind of 'just lookers' we'll get will all become customers someday."

"Spider, that's all very—interesting. But how will our customers know what we have in stock upstairs? All you've talked about are accessories and gifts on the first floor. I don't understand how you could overlook that," Billy drawled.

"I was just getting to that part, Billy. On the first floor, where shoppers are going to congregate in any case, we have a large, permanent staff of models, maybe a dozen, maybe more. They'll change into new outfits every few minutes and walk through the floor showing the stock. I detest mannequins, they're a turn-off, but models make women want to touch the fabric and ask questions and see themselves in the dress—models do everything that a hanger can't do. Now, for the windows, did I say that they'll be crammed, packed, full of beautiful things, like Christmas morning, all year round? Changed every three days, we'll draw crowds—look, I'll draw it for—"

"Please, don't bother, Spider." Billy interrupted again. "Would I be wrong in saying that you want to turn Scruples into a kind of penny arcade with pinball machines and penny candy and free lunch and sexy fitting rooms and a hoard of models parading around and foot massage and gambling and dancing parties, or am I exaggerating?" She bit off each word as if she were reading from a laundry list.

"Basically, yes." There was much more, but he'd stand on that, Spider decided. If she couldn't see—

"I LOVE IT!" Billy leaped up from behind her desk as if she'd been detonated and kissed a dazzled Valentine who had yet to open her mouth. "Valentine! Darling! *I LOVE IT!*"

"As they say," said Spider, "everyone has two businesses: his own and show business." He left his wall to give Billy the kiss he decided she wanted to give him but was too embarrassed to offer. He thought he was beginning to understand her. A bitch, but not totally stupid.

The next morning Scruples closed for redecoration. Billy spent the day on the telephone locating the world-famous decorator Billy Baldwin, who was to take over the individual redecoration of each of the twenty-four fitting rooms. He had never done this sort of job before, but she had developed a good working relationship with him when he had redone the apartment in the Sherry-Netherland, the house in Barbados, and the villa in the south of

France that she and Ellis had owned. They understood one another, and for Billy Ikehorn, Billy Baldwin would turn his attention to fitting rooms. She left the first floor to Ken Adam, the brilliant theatrical designer, since essentially it was going to be a dramatic tour de force, like a stage set.

Billy was not just a good loser, she was a totally committed one. Now that she had accepted Spider's basic concept, she threw herself into making sure that it was done as magnificently as possible. Having given in on the idea of building a restaurant in Scruples, she stole away one of the best chefs from Scandia and gave him carte blanche in the workings of the kitchen. Spider, who had envisioned a simple tray of sandwiches, listened bemused as she and the chef conferred on how much smoked salmon should be ordered from Scotland, how much caviar from Iran, how many endives from Belgium, how much crab meat from Maryland, how many freshly baked croissants from Paris. The simple tray became a specially designed Lucite folding tray table, the china was the viciously expensive Blind Earl pattern, the crystal was Steuben, the heavy silver from Tiffany's, and the tray mats and napkins classic Provençal cotton prints from Pierre Deux on Rodeo because Billy thought that everyone was bored with Porthault.

Spider decided to write Billy Baldwin a memo because he wasn't sure that his employer had really understood what he meant by making the fitting rooms more sexy.

Dear Mr. Baldwin,
Our customers come here in part because they have an itch to spend money, in part because they need a new dress, often, largely because they would like a little romance in their lives without actually deceiving their husbands. They are sophisticated, spoiled, self-indulgent, self-involved, much traveled, and utterly youth-conscious, no matter what their age. To a woman they want to be STROKED, psychically. To be brutal, you may think of them as gratification junkies.

Please unleash all your fantasies. You have not one client here but hundreds. Each individual fitting room will have its particular admirers, whether you choose to do it as a villa in Portofino or as a Moroccan seraglio or even as a Queen Anne boudoir in Kent. Our only specific requirements are a large armoire or built-in closet in which accessories can be kept, lots and lots of mirrors, and a comfortable piece of furniture on which each customer can lie down at full length. Finally, at the risk of sounding lewd, could I suggest that the mood, the ambience of each room be that in which a bidet, in a corner behind a screen, would seem possible and appropriate? I don't mean that we install a real bidet, just the atmosphere that suggests the possible need for such a convenience.

With admiration and respect,

Spider Elliott

It was Billy who had inspired him to add the request for an armoire. She knew that women tended to wear their most comfortable old shoes when they went shopping and to leave their best jewelry at home. She couldn't bear the idea of losing the sale of a Galanos chiffon because of the lack of a pair of evening shoes and the ropes of pearls that should complement the dress and clinch the sale. She intended to stock the armoires with heaps of the newest shoes and scarves and costume jewelry of every description, not for sale, just to accessorize the outfits.

Perhaps Billy's greatest personal contribution to the new Scruples was in her body-snatching capacity. She was well known to every saleswoman in town from her many years as a compulsive shopper, and once convinced that a knowledge of French mattered not a whit compared to charm and warmth, she proved an adroit kidnapper: first Rosel Korman, formerly of the Saks Park Avenue Room, dignified, calm, and lovable; then Bohemian, behatted Marguerite from Giorgio's; wise, ponytailed Sue from Alan Austin, both Elizabeth and Mirelle, two tiny, young Frenchwomen from Dinallo, friendly, blond Christine and relaxed, redheaded Ellen, both from the General Store, Holly, tactful and enthusiastic, from Charles Galley, as well as another dozen of the top salespeople in town. She also hired the best alteration experts, headed by Henriette Schor from Saks. Her only recruiting failure had been lovely Kendall, who wouldn't leave Dorso's for any inducement, but, as even Billy had to admit in frustration, Dorso's was a special sort of place. Billy also established a delivery service in a town where multimillionaire customers have to do their own pickups in every boutique.

While the store was closed, Valentine and Billy went over the stock. From the day she had conceived of Scruples Billy had been her own buyer. Her chief complaint about the other stores in Beverly Hills was that she could never find what she wanted in them. She had been convinced that if she could go to New York and see all the wholesale lines, she herself could choose far more exciting merchandise.

But Billy didn't know the first thing about buying. It was as total and disastrous a mistake as attempting to duplicate Dior. Valentine wasn't a professional buyer either, but at least she had worked closely with buyers on Seventh Avenue for four years and before that she had drunk in the buyer's point of view at Balmain's as it was reflected in the rehearsals of the new collections and in the hot arguments over whether this or that dress would "please." Gently she unfolded to Billy the basic fact that it is not the buyer's personal taste that must dominate but an understanding of the needs and the taste levels of her customers.

The art of buying for a store is intricate, and even for carefully trained, highly experienced veterans with many years of success behind them, each new season is fraught with pitfalls. There are the obvious pitfalls such as errors in judgment and wrong decisions about the acceptance of customers toward the new clothes being shown. Then there are the traps that cannot be anticipated: late deliveries, wrong fabrics, the permutations of Seventh Avenue politics, broken promises, bad weather, and the ups and downs of the stock market.

Billy felt her humiliation about the lack of sales at Scruples grow lighter—it could have happened to anyone. As Valentine sensed that Billy had become less touchy on the subject of stock, she ventured to suggest to her that perhaps much of what she had ordered in the past had been simply too—intellectual—for most women. Yes, Valentine said, a totally chic woman, as tall as

Billy Ikehorn, could wear all that she had bought for Scruples, but where were the clothes for the women less dedicated to strict chic, where were the pretty clothes in good taste, the sexy clothes, the feminine clothes, the touch-me clothes, the frankly glamorous clothes? In short, the clothes that would sell. Where were the "little numbers" that fulfilled many different needs without being so ruthlessly memorable that they could not be worn frequently? And did Billy not feel that while women were in Scruples buying from designer collections, they should be able to pick up sports clothes, separates, resort clothes, casual clothes? Less expensive, of course, but, on the other hand, why should another store get even those dollars? Of course they would never compromise on quality, but they must extend their horizons.

"You're leading me somewhere in a very crafty way, Valentine," Billy observed.

"But sensibly," Valentine countered.

"And, I trust, with good judgment?"

"Yes."

"Which means?" asked Billy, trying to see one step ahead of this demoniac creature she had hired.

"Before we can reopen we must have completely new stock. I must go to New York, of course, and also to Paris, London, Rome, and Milan for designer ready-to-wear. There is still time to get fall-winter deliveries before it's too late. For sportswear, you must hire another buyer—perhaps two—but we must have the best. Our customers are lazy and they don't like to have to park here for one kind of dress, then drive around and repark somewhere else to find pants and sweaters and blouses."

"Now that I know the extent of the job and the dangers if you guess wrong—" Billy said thoughtfully.

"Yes?"

"Do you think—after all, you have never bought for a store before, Valentine—do you think we should hire someone with lots of background to go to New York and Europe?"

"It is as you prefer. When you hired me you wanted me to be your buyer. But I am content to remain your custom-order designer—on the same terms of course. Or you can try me. At worst, we lose one season."

Billy pretended to be considering the alternatives. There weren't any at this late date, and she knew it, and Valentine knew she knew it. There simply wasn't a minute left in which to look for another buyer. Valentine should have left on her buying trip a week ago.

"My Aunt Cornelia used to say 'In for a penny, in for a pound,' or perhaps it was 'If a thing is worth doing, it is worth doing right.'"

"A most sensible woman," said Valentine in a neutral tone.

"Yes. Indeed. When can you leave?"

Experienced travelers often debate which is the more devilishly inconvenient airport, Chicago's O'Hare International or London's Heathrow. Valentine, who had never been to Chicago and certainly never intended to go, was passionately in favor of declaring Heathrow an outpost of hell by the time she had trudged three quarters of a mile through bare, glass-windowed corridors with damp English night visible outside, carrying her heavy hand luggage and weighed down by her bulky knit coat, only to find that she now had to negotiate what looked like at least another mile of moving pavement. The flat metal grid quivered unnervingly as she gingerly stepped on it, but it was better than walking. By the time she had gone through British passport control and approached customs she was almost whimpering with fatigue. Her whirlwind buying trip had been draining, both mentally and physically. She passionately wanted Scruples to be a success, but no matter how cleverly Elliott packaged it, there would be no real future if the stock didn't measure up to the demands of the very special customers she had observed so carefully in Beverly Hills and at the parties given for Elliott.

But as she was waved quickly through customs her only thought had nothing to do with Scruples. She wanted to find the man from the Savoy. Billy's last instructions had been clear.

"Look for the man in the gray uniform with a cap that says 'The Savoy' on his hatband. He's stationed there to watch out for people booked into the Savoy chain. I've arranged for you to stay at the Berkeley. It's the best now, or so I've heard, and they'll take good care of you."

Valentine spotted a tall, kindly looking man in a smartly tailored gray uniform and walked up to him with relief.

"I'm Miss O'Neill. I have a reservation at the Berkeley. Could you get me a taxi, please, and do something—anything at all, about my baggage?"

He looked at her in a perfect combination of respect and admiration, as if he had known her for years and had spent his entire life at the airport just hoping that she would arrive someday.

"Ah, Madame! Yes indeed, Madame! A pleasure, I assure you. I hope you had a satisfactory flight from Paris. I believe there is a car and driver waiting for you. Porter. *Porter*. Just follow me, Madame, never mind the porter, he'll be along in a minute." He took Valentine's hand baggage and coat and walked briskly off as she trailed numbly behind. A car and driver, now that was thoughtful of Billy—she certainly could have used one in Paris, Valentine thought, as the man from the Savoy handed her into a surprisingly huge gray Daimler with a uniformed chauffeur sitting up front behind a glass panel.

"I know what you're thinking," said Josh Hillman from the back seat. Valentine stared at him incredulously. "You're wondering how much to tip the man from the Savoy and how much to tip the porter. Don't bother, I've taken care of them."

"What are you doing here?"

"This is a snatch—you're completely in my power."

"Oh Josh!" She went limp with laughter. "You make the most terrible Bogart."

"Wait till you hear my Chevalier again. Valentine—Valentine—I missed you so much—I had to come—I thought I'd go nuts when you left so quickly. I've never had to fly six thousand miles before to get a second date, but just seeing that little, woeful face of yours—it's worth every mile."

"But I don't understand. How did you get away? Where does your wife think you are?" Valentine managed to ask these questions even though he was kissing her so persistently and so adroitly that ten miles of London suburb went by before she uttered the last query.

"London, on business. Shut up, darling. Stop asking

questions. Don't be so obsessed with detail, just accept that I'm here."

Valentine relaxed. He was right. She didn't have the strength to make sense out of anything right now. "Wake me up when we get to Buckingham Palace," she whispered and immediately fell asleep in Josh's arms.

Half an hour later he kissed her awake as the car approached Buckingham Gate. As they drove slowly down the Mall with St. James's Park and its great trees, noble and mysterious in the dark, on one side and the glory of Carlton House Terrace on the other, she kept whisking around to look at the illuminated palace behind her. The bulk of the Admiralty Arch loomed ahead of them. It is perhaps the most thrilling promenade in the world to those who love London.

Valentine, who had never been to London before, was dithering with rapture. As they reached the hotel, she gazed in wonder at the huge entrance foyer with its flag-poles flying banners from all four walls, like the dining hall of a regiment. Inside, a Telex machine was humming in a corner, and the marble floor was crisscrossed by a dozen discreetly scurrying, uniformed men, each with a clearly defined part, although she could not guess what, in the smooth functioning of the hotel. She and Josh followed a tailcoated, young, pink-cheeked desk clerk through many corridors before they came to their suite. As soon as the clerk left, Valentine ran to the windows, parted the curtains, and gazed out breathlessly.

"Oh, Josh—come quickly, look, there's moonlight on the river and if I lean out I can see the—I think—yes—the Houses of Parliament—and across—what's that big building all lit up—and look, just under us, a garden and a monument—what is it all, quick, explain it to me. Billy never said the Berkeley had a view like this."

"Perhaps that's because the Berkeley isn't on the Thames, Valentine darling."

"Where are we?"

"Precisely? We are above the Victoria Embankment Gardens. That is Cleopatra's Needle you see down there, across is the Royal Festival Hall, and, to be even more exact, you are in the Maria Callas suite of the Savoy Hotel." Valentine slowly sank down on one of the velvet couches in the grandly paneled, beautifully appointed, Chippendale sitting room and gazed into the blazing fire. It was so deliciously like an old-fashioned risqué novel: innocent girl in distress met at destination by darkly handsome semistranger, carried off to unknown hotel in unknown city, surrounded by sinister luxury.

"Are your purposes dishonorable?" she asked, giving him a sideways glance that betrayed very little.

"Christ, I hope so!" he groaned. For an enormously important lawyer to get himself unsprung from the legitimate crises and clutches of both Strassberger and Lipkin plus a wife and three children in order to run off to London in pursuit of a hauntingly perverse will-o'-the-wisp girl—"dishonorable" was hardly the right word, but it conveyed the message.

"In that case," Valentine said, at her most haughty, "I shall first require a hot bath, cold vodka, soup, and, and —I must unpack." Josh pressed three buttons arranged on a little metal rectangle on a side table. Within minutes three people stood in the doorway: a valet, a maid, and a waiter.

"Please run Madame's bath and turn down the beds," he told the maid; "I'd like a bottle of Polish vodka, two bottles of Evian, a bucket of ice, hot cream of watercress soup, and a tray of chicken sandwiches," he instructed the waiter; and to the valet he said, "Madame's luggage is in the bedroom. Would you please unpack it and take away the garments that need pressing. I'd like them back by tomorrow morning." All three matter-of-factly disappeared about their tasks.

"It isn't the most fashionable hotel anymore; they're all in W.1," Josh explained to a wide-eyed Valentine, "but you can't beat it for service." They were both thoughtfully silent until the maid and valet left.

"There is just one thing I should warn you about."

"One thing?"

"Don't, for heaven's sake, drown in the bathtub. It's very deep and about three feet longer than you are."

"Perhaps I need a lifeguard."

"Perhaps—but not for your first bath, darling—we'd both drown. And your hot soup is coming."

"The waiter—he would be shocked?"

"A *Savoy* waiter, never!"

Valentine disappeared into the bathroom with a captivating backward look, an entirely imprudent spark in her green eyes, a half smile as provoking as an unopened present beautifully wrapped. It took Josh, who hadn't been seduced in twenty years, a good four seconds before he started to struggle out of his jacket.

Neither the maid, the valet, nor the waiter, as they discussed it later, were at all surprised. In the Maria Callas suite—the Diva's favorite when she had been in London—such behavior was the rule rather than the exception. "Perhaps it's something in the air," the valet suggested. "Wouldn't be surprised," sniffed the maid. The waiter, as always, had the last word. "I told my wife, it's that Cleopatra's Needle, I told her. A notorious woman she was, that one."

They had five days, five days in which discretion was never calculated—five impervious, inviolate days in which the only things that existed were the excellent satisfactions of the flesh and the thrill of being marvelously unwise, even as they knew that the time for accounts would be in the future, but so far in the future that it didn't matter, almost didn't exist.

Valentine dispatched her business with Zandra Rhodes, Bill Gibb, Jean Muir, and Thea Porter with speed and certainty. Josh made a few phone calls and sent a number of Telex messages, but otherwise they were enclosed in the approving luxury of the Savoy, venturing out to explore London and dine at Tramp's and Drone's and Tiberio and the White Elephant Club and the dining room of the Connaught only for the pleasure it gave them to be in public and yet alone together.

There is a period, early in every romance, when lovers must show each other off, admiring each other and themselves reflected in the other. Even the noblest of backgrounds is merely a stage setting. Did doomed Lady Jane Grey really accept the crown of England more than four hundred years before in this long, dim, lavender-and-gold gallery of Syon House? How the other tourists must be admiring Valentine, Josh thought, as they wandered through, listening to the guide tell that melancholy tale.

It was too soon for them to question the texture of their

love. Valentine was too enthralled with his adoration of her body, with her own physicality, truly alive for the first time. She had never been allowed an experience so purely animal as waking up in a bed that smelled of their earlier passion, to feel Josh quicken as he reached out for her again, the pungent odors of their bodies blending so that she didn't know if she smelled of him or he smelled of her. She tried to fix in her memory the scent of Josh and the bed in the Savoy. She knew that the image of the man and the pink-and-cream bedroom, vaguely Art Deco, with a large, curving bay of windows over the Thames, would always be there, perhaps blurred or faulty, yet irradicable, but that exact smell—she inhaled, already nostalgic. It was the first time in Valentine's life that she had been granted the luxuriant repletion of the senses, those long hours of twilight when merely being alive is entire unto itself, when there is enough—enough of everything, and the joy of the body makes the entire world seem good.

Josh was too filled with astonishing freedom, the bursting of the dam of duty and direction that had held him on one firm path from the day he learned to read, to ask himself where this was going, what future it could have. For the two of them, that certain moment, which in any potentially permanent love affair decides its outcome, was held in temporary suspension, intercepted by their tacit acceptance of the foolishness of trying to ponder the future.

"I don't think I could stand making love with a man who didn't have a hairy chest," said Valentine, her nose pressed to his skin, sniffing like an ardent gourmet at the roots of the dark body hair, mixed with a few strands of gray, that covered his chest. "Could you?" And that, for five days, was perhaps the most serious question she asked.

Valentine boarded the polar flight one day ahead of Josh. His wife and, unfailingly, some of his children always met him at the airport after any business trip, a fact that caused Los Angeles to become a reality again. Even then, in the departure lounge, she did not speak of the next week or the next month. What, after all, was there for her to say? Only as the future unfolded itself would she see the shape of it. The Irish strain of fatalism that had always existed in her impetuous nature seemed to have taken her in hand. Nothing could have made Josh Hillman fall more deeply in love with her than this refusal to plan, to scheme, to make arrangements—this acquiescence to the evanescent. It drove him quite mad that she wasn't trying to pin him down, to make sure of him, to demand something, anything. What was this? Two ships that pass in the night? Bullshit! He'd get this woman, no matter what. He saw her through the final gate, noted the loving farewell in her eyes as well as the nonchalance of her light, quick step, and almost ran to his waiting car. "The British Museum," he told the driver. Only those monumental stone hallways, crammed with the heavy plunder of centuries, were suitably gloomy to witness the barbarian sense of abandonment he felt.

> Billy Ikehorn
> requests the honor of your company
> at a Celebration
> at Scruples
> on the first Saturday of November 1976
> 9:00 P.M.
> DANCING
> BLACK TIE

Almost before the invitations went out, *Women's Wear* predicted that it would be the most famous party since Truman Capote let people know who Kay Graham was. When Billy had wondered whom to invite, Spider had answered, "Everybody."

"But I don't know 'everybody,' Spider. What are you talking about?"

Spider had noticed, as they worked together bringing the new Scruples back to life, that Billy was curiously out of touch with the social scene in which he imagined she would have been involved. To him, her personal life, with its lack of family ties and intimate friends, seemed strangely empty and deprived. He had no way of knowing that she had been essentially alone for much of her life. The accidents of life had created an isolated woman. Her youth had stolen from her, perhaps forever, the ability to make friends easily. The years of being a freak had left her with scars that no amount of outward physical change could ever erase. She had left family behind when she quit Boston. When she left New York, after Ellis's stroke, she hadn't replaced her acquaintances there, who had never, in any event, except for Jessica, been true friends. In Los Angeles, where she might have made an entirely new start, her years of near-isolation—and preoccupation—in the citadel in Bel Air had kept her from forming close connections with other women.

Although millions of magazine and newspaper readers knew that "Billy" meant Billy Ikehorn, just as they knew the last names of "Liza" or "Jackie," she, Billy, had never accepted the reality of her media celebrity status. She didn't *feel* known. Ellis had taught her to distrust the pettiness of what is usually termed "Society" in New York, and she had been happy to stay just outside of it. When she moved to California she never made, in any substantial, meaningful way, the first move to swim freely in Los Angeles society. In addition, although Billy did not subscribe to the ultimate viewpoint of Boston society that no other "Society" exists worthy of the name, her Boston mannerisms and her residue of a Boston accent had never really disappeared, and they accentuated the impression she gave of being, in some final way, an outsider.

"Even if you don't know everybody, they all know you," Spider insisted.

"Well, what does that matter. I can't invite perfect strangers—can I?"

"You damn well better," Spider answered. "We've just spent about a million dollars, lady, and it would be a shame to let only the neighbors in on it."

"Look, Spider, since you're such an expert, you make out the list." Billy fled, feeling for an embarrassing minute out of command. Spider tended recently to have that effect on her. He was such a wiseass, she reflected, annoyed at her own lack of social sophistication.

Spider had a field day. He started his list with the important local residents, then the barons and baronesses of the entire West Coast from the Mexican to the Canadian borders. Customers first, after all. Then he added selected notables from New York, Chicago, Detroit, Dallas, and Palm Beach. Hollywood—The New and The

Old. The Fashion Establishment, of course. Washington? Why not the best? Well, maybe not President Carter, but certainly Vice-President Mondale, and it wouldn't be a party without Tip O'Neill. Then he added what he could still only call the International Jet Set, but carefully culled, that fucked-up bunch. Was anybody left out? Jesus! *The press!* Spider hit himself on the forehead for his stupidity. That was what it was all about. He'd been jerking off over celebrities and politicians and overlooking their creators. So—the press; not just the fashion and society press but the right people from *People* and *New York Magazine* and *New West* and *Los Angeles* and the newsmagazines and Condé Nast and Hearst and network big shots. *Rolling Stone?* Maybe not. Would Walter Cronkite come? And Norman Mailer? How about Woodward and Bernstein? Hell, Scruples could easily hold six or seven hundred people when all the sliding walls were opened and all the display cases whisked away, just as Ken Adam had planned. That gave him room to invite at least four hundred couples since, Spider assured himself, many of the people he was inviting probably wouldn't travel all the way from wherever they lived to attend a ball. He invited several dozens more, not forgetting his family or Josh Hillman and his wife. Maybe he was getting carried away, he reasoned, looking at the pages in front of him. He crossed out some names from Florida and Texas—how often did they get to California anyway? Then he went over all his lists, crossing off any names that were faintly dubious, either as potential customers or in their celebrity value. He ended up with three hundred and fifty couples and the party of the decade. Perhaps The Last Great Party. Certainly the most expensive party, the most photographed party, the most electric and talked-about party of the 1970s.

Without thinking it through, Billy had chosen well to give her ball on the first Saturday of November 1976, right after the presidential elections. Those whose candidate hadn't won wanted to forget, while those who were glad about the outcome of the election wanted to celebrate. Above all, everyone wanted to think about something besides politics, the British pound, and pollution.

The last flower arrangers and lighting men left just as

the caterers arrived to set up the bars and the buffets. On the first floor, which had been cleared for dancing, there were several large bars. Spider's tour de force was putting a buffet, a bar, and a dozen chairs in each one of the twenty-four large fitting rooms. No one who came that night could miss a tour of the second floor of Scruples, which Billy Baldwin, working as fast as he had in his illustrious life, had transformed into a fascinatingly amusing and erotic pastiche of delectable rooms, each one of which provided his less inventive colleagues inspiration for years to come. Downstairs the dancing never stopped; Peter Duchin's three best bands alternated so that there was never a moment without music. The Edwardian winter garden's doors were thrown open so that people could stroll in the formal garden behind Scruples. There was even a full moon. Some magic lay over that warm night; women looked more beautiful in Ken Adam's lighting than they had ever looked at any age in their lives; men felt more romantic and yet more powerful, perhaps just because they had been invited to the most glamorous and star-filled of all gala balls, perhaps because all of Scruples blended to touch somewhere, everyone's most luxurious fantasy. Even the constant popping of flashbulbs added a note of delight. You have to be one of a half-dozen genuinely misanthropic celebrities to truly dislike having your picture taken.

Scruples reopened for business on Monday. By midmorning they knew that they had triumphed. Valentine's merchandise, ordered so late in August, had arrived in time and combined with the best of Billy's earlier fall buys performed that immensely lucrative maneuver called, in fashion shorthand, "walking out of the store." Spider had to call a secretarial service by 10:30 A.M. to order six temporary clerks just to handle the opening of new charge accounts. The chef, accustomed to the mountains of food served at Scandia, had prepared wisely, but even he was amazed to find his giant refrigerators almost empty by the end of the day. His four waiters, three kitchen assistants, and two wine stewards were trembling with exhaustion. The salespeople were trembling with exalted disbelief; none of them had ever before sold so much in one day.

The weary Oriental masseuses almost, but did not, quit en masse.

After the doors had closed for the day, Billy, Spider, and Valentine met in Billy's office. Spider lay full length on the floor and Valentine, who had pitched in as a sales-woman all day long, stretched out on Billy's priceless Louis XV sofa and kicked off her shoes.

"Can it last?" asked Billy very softly.

"Fucking right it can," said Spider.

"Christmas shopping is just around the corner," mused Valentine.

"WE MADE IT!" Billy yelled.

"Fucking right we did," answered Spider.

"YOU ARE BOTH WONDERFUL!" exalted Billy.

"Fucking right, we are," said Spider.

"Thirty-eight women asked me to design originals for them—I need an assistant, workrooms, workwomen, fabrics—everything—" uttered Valentine.

"Whatever you need, you get, tomorrow," Billy assured her.

"Fucking right she does," Spider said.

"And I have to leave on another buying trip. Even so, I'm already a few weeks late for the French and Italian spring-summer ready-to-wear," said Valentine wearily.

"Spider, tell me finally, were you ever in retailing before?" Billy asked.

"Why, of course, Billy—whoever made you think I wasn't?" Spider laughed.

"He is now," Valentine murmured.

"FUCKING RIGHT HE IS!" Billy yelled in jubilation.

All of that week, all of that month, business at Scruples exceeded their most extravagant hopes. Even when the novelty value and the curiosity factor of the store had worn off to some extent, customers settled down into a pattern of buying that didn't falter.

The country store, designed primarily for its whimsy and sense of gaiety, became the ultimate place to buy gifts and things-you-didn't-know-you-needed, so success-ful that for the following Christmas Scruples issued a coveted mail-order catalog.

The trellised winter garden—with its cozy discreet corners, its plumply tufted love seats, antique wicker armchairs, and round tables covered in sublimely out-of-date mauve and pink hydrangea chintz; its baskets of begonias and cyclamens and orchids, its huge potted ferns, and its dim, insinuating light—became the local community's favorite place for the exchange of idle gossip and vital information, which, in many cases, were one and the same.

The main salon, Spider's Fun Fair—with the men's department, the Ali Baba's cave of women's accessories, the pub, the backgammon tables and the pinball machines—became that substitute for Bloomingdale's that people always complain is missing in Beverly Hills, a playground for grown-ups, a place to be seen, to bump into people, to be both stimulated and soothed by abundance piled on abundance.

Valentine's couture designs soon took up so much of her time and energy that Billy hired two highly experienced buyers to leave her free to do the work that added so much to the prestige of Scruples, but she still remained head buyer for the store. Two additional buyers, one for accessories and one for gifts, toured almost constantly, their shipments arriving from all corners of the world.

And Spider? Spider supervised the whole thing, from the parking garage to the smallest stock boy, from the windows to the kitchen. But his most important function was that of arbiter of elegance, one he had cut out for himself during the first week Scruples was in operation. No woman left Scruples until Spider had approved of what she had bought. He was always in at the kill. His taste was literally flawless and his specialty was twofold: to convince a wavering woman that she did indeed look beautiful in a particular garment, or to talk her out of something she adored but which didn't suit her. He operated independently of concern about any individual sale. He would far rather see a customer leave without having made a single purchase than have her go home and decide, regretfully, that she'd made a mistake. If Spider detected that slight hanging back that a woman feels when she is compromising on something she isn't truly enthusiastic about, he used all his wiles to dissuade her. He was only really happy with a sale in which a customer displayed her conviction by trying to sell *him*. And, with deliberation, he invariably managed to make each customer decide against at least one thing she loved so that when she got home, any pangs of guilt she might feel over having spent so much money would be annulled by her feeling of virtue in not having bought that one thing she had *really* wanted. To pass Spider's inspection, you had to pick clothes that were utterly right for you and you had to be hot for them, dizzy with a desire that can't be forced any more than a faked orgasm can be enjoyed. In the final analysis, it was Spider, with his firm control over what was sold and to whom, rather than any other feature of Scruples, that made it, within a year, the most successful luxury specialty store per square foot of selling space in Beverly Hills, in the United States—in the world.

*M*aggie MacGregor was responsible for Spider's first assuming his role of arbiter of taste at Scruples, although he never told her and she never suspected it. Maggie prepared her weekly television show with the help of a staff of trained journalists, who did a great deal of the preliminary investigatory work. She enlisted as well the aid of countless contacts planted in strategic places with access to the secrets of agents' offices and studios' inner circles. However, on camera, she carried her show alone, without a co-host. Outspoken, sassy, often tilting, but never falling, over the edge into vulgarity, Maggie was alone on the television screen whenever the camera was not trained on the face of the celebrity she was interviewing. Shrewd Maggie knew that only split-second cuts away from the performer were tolerable to a public fanatically curious to see if their eyes could tell them why this one or that one had become a star. That was part of the essential itching appeal of her show, the chance to get a long, close look at every pore, every eye blink, every facial line of a screen personality who was not, for the moment, saying words from a script, a temporary exile from the pedestal, who was at the mercy of Maggie's questions. The fact that this glimpse told you nothing, absolutely nothing, to explain the whys and wherefores of the mysteries of who reaches stardom and who does not, did not matter as long as the audience thought they were getting a peek at something with a grain of reality in its core, something that would allow them to feel that they "knew" the star as a human being.

Maggie MacGregor had arrived at Scruples early on the Monday morning after the reopening gala in her pale blue Mercedes 450 SLC, reluctantly leaving it for James, the head parking attendant, whom Billy had hired away from Saks, to deal with. Her most intense emotional relationship at the moment, she reflected, wryly, was with that Nazi car. And, at that, in a town where the Mercedes repair department closed down tight every day for an hour's lunch break, just as unconcerned about their customers' convenience as Gucci, which did the same thing. She pacified her conscience by reminding herself that the Mercedes was manufactured in West Germany, a country that paid substantial reparations to Israel, but still—enough of that, she told herself, she was thinking like Shirley Silverstein again!

Shirley Silverstein had joined, informally, the vast clan MacGregor right after high school, just as soon as she knew that she was smart enough and tough enough and hardworking enough to go all the way. All the way where? Obviously to Beverly Hills, Maggie thought, the promised land, where Moses could and certainly should have led his people if, dummy, he hadn't turned right instead of left after crossing the Red Sea. When Maggie changed Shirley's name she also altered Shirley's nose and left behind Shirley's extra thirty pounds and Shirley's anonymous future, but she had never tried to put a veneer of Anglo-Saxon gentility over her salty Jewish tongue. Just as her mother had never wearied of saying in pride and mock dismay "The tongue on that one!" Maggie had always believed that her tongue was her only hope at fortune. If you could think smart enough, talk smart, loud, and bright enough, and sustain conviction, with a little bit of luck, you could own the American public. Maggie's first-class brain, not her tongue, got her the scholarships to Barnard and to the Columbia School of Journalism. However, Maggie's mother, whose truly inspired abilities to nag and harass had driven her unwilling daughter through three summer-school stenography courses, was able to say, with justification, that she had gotten Maggie the first job of her brilliant career.

Newly hatched journalism-school graduates emerge, like an annual plague of monster mosquitoes, to torment the personnel departments of New York's national magazines. Maggie managed to get past the personnel department at *Cosmopolitan* by applying for a job as a secretary, not as an editorial assistant, which is what she actually intended to be. The articles editor, Roberta Ashley, looked at the tiny, twenty-two-year-old girl, with a round, guileless baby face, surrounded by dark hair that threatened to hide her bright brown eyes, and asked, with her famous, forthright charm, "Do you take speed-writing or only fast longhand?"

"Pitman. One hundred words a minute. As fast as you can talk, not to worry," Maggie cockily assured the editor, who, since she was a very wise woman, immediately began to worry about just how long this windfall would last.

It went on for one-and-a-half beautifully efficient years, while Maggie sucked in all she could learn about magazines from observing and remembering everything that was discussed in the constant stream of memos and meetings between her own boss and Helen Gurley Brown, the editor of *Cosmopolitan*.

One winter morning in 1973 Maggie overheard the news that Candy Bergen had had dinner the night before with Helen Brown and her producer-husband, David Brown, during an unheralded, one-day stopover between London and Los Angeles.

Five minutes later, from a place where she couldn't be overheard, Maggie phoned the star at her hotel.

"This is Maggie MacGregor of *Cosmo*, Miss Bergen. Helen just asked me to call you. We know it's the last minute and Helen's in an editorial meeting, or she would have called you herself, but the thing is—we were wondering if we could do a quick interview before you left? I know you don't have much time—no time at all?—but listen, I could pick you up with a limo and take you to the airport and just tape some stuff on the way out. You know, life, love, lipstick, that sort of thing. Hmm? Wonderful! Helen'll be delighted! I'll call up from the lobby in half an hour."

The plane was four hours late in leaving, the divine Candice was in a mood to spill her guts, and Maggie had an interview so remarkable that it almost reconciled Bobbie Ashley to the loss of a great secretary. It was one of the very few celebrity interviews ever published that posed the obligatory question "What Is Candy Bergen Really Like?" and then proceeded to answer it until the reader felt she not only knew Candy, but that she really *cared* about her.

Once a month, for nearly the next two years, Maggie's spectacularly revealing interviews with film stars blazed on the pages of *Cosmo*. It became as much the stigma of arrival at stardom for an actor or actress to be shown by Maggie with his or her soul hanging out as for a political figure to be vivisected alive by Oriana Fallaci. "I don't *yentz* them," Maggie explained, Coca-Cola-colored eyes all innocence, "they just yentz themselves and I try not to run out of tape."

During her journalism years Maggie dressed in casual skirts and shirts, the perfect costume for a reporter who wants to make herself unthreatening and inconspicuous, while her subjects forget the purpose of her being there long enough to be lulled into saying the things their public-relations people have begged them never to mention.

Her real taste in clothes didn't surface until she broke into television and signed the network contract that included all her wardrobe expenses. The sponsor, eyeing Maggie's inoffensive, nondescript separates, let it be clearly understood that she would be expected to dress the part of a serious intimate of the film world. Network executives had already learned that the television audience won't begin to credit the intelligence and capacity of a mere local newswoman unless she is well turned out and perfectly groomed. Still less would they believe in a Maggie who didn't reflect the lingering glamour of Hollywood, a pervasive, intrinsic glamour that has never really been dissipated in spite of the attrition of years.

Given carte blanche and told never to wear the

same thing on the air twice, Maggie was able to give free rein to her passion for elaborate, ultra-high-style fashion. Unfortunately, physically, she had the same body structure as the female members of the House of Windsor. Like Queen Elizabeth and Princess Margaret, the ex-Shirley Silverstein was short, short-waisted, large-breasted, and had to fight fat every day of her life. But the royal ladies had designers whose lives were dedicated to concealing these defects with perfectly cut and fitted clothes. They also had kilos of jewels to lead the eye away from the shape of the body. Yet they were *still* badly dressed. Maggie, unprotected by skillful designers, was at the mercy of her own freedom to choose. Oh, how she chose! There were never enough sequins or beads or ruffles or feathers to satisfy her. Only if she could have worn the superb extravaganzas hung on Cher would Maggie have felt clothed in a manner that would fulfill her dreams. But even in her least lucid moments, Maggie knew that was impossible. Still, she tried her best.

That first morning at Scruples she bought enough new clothes to carry her through the next six weeks of television. Rosel Korman, who was to become her permanent salesperson, bumped into Spider, who was busy giving instructions to the window dresser he had imported from Bloomingdale's. Elated with the amount of her sale, she gave him the news.

"Has anything been fitted yet?" he asked.

"No, she's taking them with her."

"What dressing room is she in?"

"Number seven."

"Rosel, bring back everything to the room, please, everything she picked. Don't wrap anything, OK?" The saleswoman's look of astonishment was wasted on Spider's back.

Spider knocked on the door of Maggie's room. "Are you decent?"

"For the moment, yes."

"I'm Spider Elliot, Miss MacGregor, director of Scruples."

"Hail and farewell, Spider," Maggie said, surveying him with keen interest. Physical appeal in the male had long ago ceased to automatically impress her, but she was always enough of a woman to hear an inaudible fanfare as this tall, marvelously made man smiled at her from the doorway.

"I adore this place," she added, "but I've got to get to work, and as fast as I can."

"Then we'll do this as quickly as possible," answered Spider, as the heavily burdened saleswoman and a stock girl, both carrying Maggie's eight thousand dollars' worth of garments, came in through the open door.

"Do what? And why aren't my things packed up already? All you have to do is put them on hangers in plastic bags, damn it!"

"I have a policy that none of our customers should be sold anything that doesn't do justice to her—it's part of the Scruples approach." Spider was winging it. He had been visited by a flash of inspiration as soon as he heard the name Maggie MacGregor, whom he had long considered to be the worst-dressed woman in public life. He still wasn't sure where this was going to take him, but he knew he was on the track of something. The chaise and the chairs in the room were rapidly being covered with a crazy quilt of brilliant fabrics and glitter as Rosel and her helper spread out Maggie's clothes. It was the season immediately after Yves Saint Laurent had unleashed his rich Russian fantasies, and everything Maggie had bought reflected Seventh Avenue's adaptations of the look. She had picked the most richly encrusted, elaborately detailed examples she could find. Catherine the Great would have felt at home in her new clothes. So would Mae West. The room now looked like an explosion in the costume department of the Metropolitan Museum of Art.

"Since when has the age of Big Brother come to retailing?" Maggie said furiously. "Nobody tells me what I can or can't buy." She was as taken aback as she was angry. Like many powerful people who have come to their power recently, she was fiercely protective of her rights and privileges. Anything that seemed to return her to any past dependency on the rest of the world was a threat. Spider ignored her words and circled around her, eyeing her like an object he might photograph.

There wasn't more than a little over five feet of her, he thought, and probably one hundred and fifteen pounds, at least fifteen of which was bosom. Angles—none. Volume—in abundance. His eyes narrowed, his nostrils quivered like a hound dog's on the scent, he seemed to be talking to himself, but Maggie heard every word.

"Yeah—yeah—it's all there. Tall she's not, doesn't have to be, no bones showing, that's all right too if—tits, yeah, *great,* shoulders terrific—cute neck, too short but cute—soft—sexy—eyes gorgeous, skin gorgeous, waist-line—never mind—we can fake it—hips—hips—not as difficult as the boobs—it's quality raw material, just needs—needs—"

"Needs *what,* for God's sake?"

"Needs bringing out, needs a new way to be displayed," he said, still to himself. He turned swiftly to the sales-woman, "Rosel, bring us everything you have in an elegant eight that's slender, simple, and soft." As she scurried off, Spider turned back to Maggie, who was hesitating between fury and fascination. Like most people, she was willing to stand still for any amount of verbal dissection as long as she was the focus of attention. Spider finally stopped his detailed inspection of her body and looked her directly in the eyes, a look that combined intimacy and intensity without a hint of flirtation or sell.

"It boils down to a question of self-image, Maggie. You dress wrong because in your mind's eye you see yourself incorrectly."

"Wrong? Incorrectly?"

"Look, I'll lay it out for you. It's a question of per-spective." Spider took Maggie by the shoulders and turned her around so that the two of them were reflected together in the large triple mirror.

"Now look very carefully, as if you were looking at a big picture. With someone next to you in the mirror you can get an idea of how you *really* look compared with other people. When any of us look in the mirror alone, we all tend to concentrate on the parts, not the whole. Now, pay attention, Maggie. What's the first thing you see?" She was silent, unable to answer. "Small, right?" Spider responded to his own question. "Super feminine right down to the bone. Rounded, rounded, petite, female. That's what we've got to play with. Everybody should be so lucky. But you have never accepted the reality of what you actually look like. The clothes you buy would take a Margaux Hemingway to wear properly. Now watch, I'll show you what I mean."

Spider took a sumptuous gypsy dress in a gold lamé from a chair and held it up in front of her. "See, you've just drowned, disappeared." Rosel had just come back with a heap of dresses piled over her arm. Spider grabbed a Holly Harp crepe from among them and draped it so that the unadorned, supple, flowing red fabric fell from Maggie's shoulders. "All right! Now you're back in the picture. Now we see the essence of you, pretty Maggie MacGregor, small, soft, pretty, female Maggie—a real live girl. We're free to focus on your eyes and your skin, not the dress."

"But that gypsy look is the new thing!" Maggie complained. "Crepe has been around for years—don't you read *Vogue?*" she said plaintively.

"You must never try to follow fashion, Maggie," Spider said severely. "You simply don't have the height —you're seven inches short of it—and you don't have the right kind of body. It's a swell body for a lot of things—but it can't carry important clothes. You have one best look and I'll help you to find it. Then it's up to you to be consistent, to stick with it. Fashion exists *only* to be adapted to you. The Maggie-ness of Maggie is what you should be looking for every time you buy something. Ask yourself, 'Am I still there or have I vanished?' Think thin, think soft, think simple, think easy, with the emphasis on your eyes and your skin. That way you won't ever get lost."

Maggie felt like weeping. Not because she was disappointed about the gaudy heap of costume party clothes, which she now understood were all out of the question, but because Spider was taking such a serious interest in her *self,* in the Maggie who was a woman, not just a television star, the Maggie who had always been smart enough to have a suspicion, a disturbingly insecure inkling that maybe she didn't know fuck-all about clothes, the Maggie whom everyone flattered and to whom no one told the straight truth about the way she looked.

"Do you have any idea how much I resent finding out that I'm wrong?" she asked Spider, in tacit surrender. He didn't let his exultance show. This was the first time he had ever verbalized his hazy ideas about fashion.

As a photographer, Spider had always worked with fashion editors who picked their models carefully so that the dress and the girl were equally enhanced. Valentine had spoiled him for the taste of ordinary women by the wit and authority with which she wore clothes. Suddenly he realized that very few women he had ever seen in normal life really dressed to make the most of whatever aspect of their physical selves was especially attractive. Very probably, he thought, they didn't even know what it was. Back in the days—only weeks ago—when models used to tell Spider their troubles, he had often been amused and puzzled that the very thing he found beautiful in a girl—her wide, big-toothed smile, for example—was often the thing she most deplored, the thing she envied other women for not having. Was there ever a woman who could say "I want to look exactly, precisely like me, no one else?" He doubted it. Maggie never knew that she was the very first Galatea to Spider Elliott's Pygmalion, the first in a line of hundreds.

Maggie didn't learn the term "star fucker" at the Columbia School of Journalism. During her first year at *Cosmopolitan,* while she was still Bobbie Ashley's secretary, she heard it only on one or two occasions. Although *Cosmo* is dedicated, among other things, to the celebration of more and better sexuality, its editors, given their clue by Helen Gurley Brown, retain an almost dainty purity of phrase. As Mrs. Brown once put it, "You can say anything you want to so long as you say it like a lady."

Star fucker. It means so many things. It can mean the taxi driver who keeps a mental list of every hapless celebrity who ever hailed his cab or the hairdresser who gives a perfunctory comb-out to his regular customer while telling her of the marvels he performed yesterday for a television-game-show regular. It reaches from the office of the powerful multimillionaire whose walls are covered with photographs of himself standing next to a series of politicians, to the exercise teacher who lingers on the tense upper-back muscles of a minor movie actress while dozens of angry civilian women wait impatiently for his attention.

Star fucking is something millions of Americans do, in a minor key, every time they buy a movie magazine or an issue of *People*, every time they listen to Miss Rona or watch Dinah or Merv, every time they read a syndicated gossip column or society column. It is, generally speaking, a harmless way of sprinkling yourself with a glint of stardust, of gratifying, for a second, the need to feel in the know.

But, to Maggie MacGregor, after eight months of writing her celebrity interviews for *Cosmo*, star fucker meant fucking stars, in the most direct possible way: sexual intercourse with famous actors.

It started mildly enough. Her third assignment, the first one in which a man was the subject, called for her to spend several days following Pershing Andrews around New York. He was a young movie name who had recently broken into major success through one of those twelve-hour prime-time television dramatizations of popular novels. Since Maggie had interviewed only women before, she had no way of knowing that talking to male celebrities would touch on a deep vein of shyness that she had had no suspicion she possessed. Suddenly, in spite of the armor provided by her notebook and her pile of sharpened pencils and her tape recorder, in spite of the protected position conferred by her magazine connection, she began to wonder if she was looking as well as she possibly could during the interview. She had to constantly fight the fear that her questions might be considered a sexual come-on. Although Pershing Andrews seemed to be at ease with her, the interview felt—and sounded—like a strangely awkward blind date. She was getting only routine answers to her questions without the well of female-to-female understanding to fall back on. Maggie suddenly understood that there is a very difficult line to draw between being a journalist out to get a good piece and being a woman; asking a man she has just met aggressive, decidedly overintimate questions, the kind of questions she had to ask to get the answers that made good copy. It didn't help at all that she was only twenty-three, with a tiny, lush body, droll, round, dark eyes, and smooth, rosy skin. To get the kind of story she wanted, to feel free enough of her body to wade into her subject's psyche with both feet, Maggie thought she should look like Lauren Bacall, not as she used to be, but as she is now. Or, better still, Lillian Hellman.

Even before the Pershing Andrews interview Maggie had smelled out the essential fact that stars basically hate, fear, and despise the press to the precise degree that they know they need the press. And the press is both star-struck and simultaneously half-disparaging, half-contemptuous. While members of the press are free to vent their ambiguous feelings in their writing, the stars must conceal their feelings behind a mask. With male journalists the mask is that of good-fellowship; with female journalists it often takes the form of seductiveness; verbal seductiveness always and actual seduction far more often than the public imagines.

Pershing Andrews was followed everywhere not by just Maggie but also by a public-relations man who had been assigned to him during his entire visit to New York. This is standard procedure for all but the most established, most stubborn stars: Talent agencies are determined to protect their investments by gluing a sheep-dog chaperon to every piece of talent they possess for fear of what the talent might say or do if left alone. The presence of a cautious press agent virtually guarantees a hopelessly dull interview, but better dull than controversial or foolish, the talent agency feels. They so distrust the actors and actresses they represent that they are literally terrified of what a smart reporter might find out if left alone with them. The talent agency people are usually right.

After Maggie had spent the first two days of her time with Andrews and his press agent, receiving only stiff, dull answers to her leading questions, she began to devise a plan to create enough collusion between them so that she might persuade Andrews to sneak away from his keeper. At Sardi's, while the press agent took a quick leak, Maggie struck.

"Look, Pershing, I've got nothing here." She waved her notebook at him in an accusing way. "I looked over my notes before lunch and you're coming over like pasta without salt. Yech! I just don't think Helen is going to be interested in this unless I can manage to interject a little insight into the piece. I know that good stuff is there—you could make a terrific article—but having that creep attached to you like a second head is drying me up, and you too. Did you ever hear of three people waltzing together?" She made a funny face at him, a what-the-hell-you've-tried-but-you-can't-win-'em-all kind of face, which indicated clearly that if *Cosmo* couldn't run a piece on Pershing Andrews they could immediately replace it with one on Warren Beatty or Ryan O'Neal.

"Shit! Is it really that bad?"

"Afraid so. But, after all, what can you do? He's got his job to do like everyone else. That's the system." Maggie shrugged so expressively that Andrews literally saw his name being penciled out of the coveted December issue.

"The fuck it is. I can't get rid of him till after dinner, but then he has to go home to Larchmont. We can get together afterward, can't we?"

Maggie considered the idea exactly long enough to be convincing. "Why not? I'll just break my date—it's no big deal—so, where and when?"

"My hotel at eleven—he'll be gone by then."

She was at her most dry and professional when she said "Right." But her mind was speeding ahead. Maggie had had a number of more or less unimportant love affairs, but she'd never been alone with a young movie star in his hotel room. She reminded herself sternly, comfortingly, that this was business. Yet the combination of Pershing Andrews, who was, after all, exceptionally good-looking and had been recognized everywhere they went for the last two days by hundreds of thrilled women, who was, after all, a MOVIE STAR, for Christ's sake, and the idea of being alone with him in his hotel room at night seemed to give the interview the character of a rendezvous. She had a momentary feeling that she was doing something incredibly glamorous and slightly sleazy.

"We could have a late supper," he added. "I got a

great suite with a view of the Park." A suite. Good. That word changed things. There was nothing suggestive about supper in a suite, nothing taken for granted in that invitation.

And she did get a great interview, that night and the following one, good enough to make her piece, "The Life and Hard Times of a Hot Property," a minor classic of its kind. She also got thoroughly and inevitably fucked just as she had planned to be. Consciously? Unconsciously? What difference did it make? And she found out something about herself, after the same pattern of seduction had been repeated with every male heterosexual movie personality she interviewed. She was a belt notcher. What became important to her was not whether the sex had been good, bad, or indifferent, but the fact that she, Maggie MacGregor, had had sex with famous men, men whose names were household words. Fame turned her on. She was three quarters of the way to an orgasm with a famous man as soon as they were alone together. He didn't have to do much to make her come. All that had to happen was for her to see that famous face over her, or under her, or alongside her, *that famous face fucking her,* Maggie MacGregor, who wasn't famous, and sex took on another dimension altogether, the eroticism of the situation was totally contained in the fact of the man's celebrity, which during the period of fucking she shared.

Maggie learned to take it for granted that once the days of the interview were over there would be no more sexual contact. At first she thought there might be a carry-over into real life, but she found out that unless she was actively working on an article about him, an actor was not about to have an affair with just another magazine writer. As far as they were concerned, once the interview was over she fell into the category of super-groupie, cute but not to be taken seriously.

Each month brought a new assignment, a new notch for her belt, a new name for her private collection. Although she was a small-town Jewish girl, who had once had small-town Jewish values, Maggie's sexual adventures with stars never seemed to her to violate anything she had learned at home. They had nothing to do with love or commitment or caring. It was one of the perquisites of her growing talent. Still, something about it bothered her, although not enough to make her give it up. It was nothing moralistic or petty; it had nothing to do with feeling, inside, that she was acting in a cheap or easy way—oh, those fatal words from high school, which she had put behind her—but, undeniably, there was something.

It wasn't until Maggie interviewed Vito Orsini that she learned what it was.

Vito Orsini was Maggie's first movie producer. Her ideas about producers were vague and reflected the common wisdom. There hadn't been any great producers since Thalberg, or was it Louis B. Mayer or Selznick? In any case, everyone knew that the day of the producer was long dead, that the people who called themselves producers were probably agents putting together a package of star, writer, and director and selling it to a studio, or else a producer was somebody on a studio payroll who was used chiefly as liaison between the studio heads and the director, a glorified gofer. The director and screenwriter reigned supreme—to them belonged the credit. Those anonymous middle-aged men, usually at least two of them, who came up to the podium on Oscar night to receive the Best Picture Award—were they the producers or people from the studio or what? Not that it was important. Producers were businessmen—not stars. Well, of course Bob Evans was a star producer. But he was special—he used to be in movies.

The common wisdom, or rather common ignorance, which Maggie accepted so easily, was, as it frequently is, right to a degree.

In the case of Vito Orsini it was utterly wrong. He belonged to the small group of producers who are the magic glue that holds every facet of a finished picture together. There are a small number of such men, alive and flourishing, in Hollywood, England, France, and Italy, and probably there always will be. There is no substitute for the kind of man who makes a picture happen from the moment of germination to the time the lines start forming at the box office.

Vito Orsini was a passionate producer. His properties often sprang from one of his own ideas, sometimes from a book he had read or a script that had been sent to him. Once he had settled on a project, his first task was to raise the money needed to finance the picture. When this basic element of the production was nailed down, he was free to divert much of his attention to the screenplay, conferring with the writer or writers on every revision, playing a major hand in shaping it in its final form. Often he had personally taken the risk of advancing money to the writers for a treatment or an option even before finding financing for the picture. Vito Orsini himself hired the director, chose the actors with the director's help, found the right key technical people, selected possible locations for filming. He was fully in control of every aspect of his film until it reached its start date. By this point he had given at least one year of his creative life to the project. Unlike some massively successful producers, such as Joe Levine, who have managed to put their names as producer on hundreds of films, Vito did not delegate responsibility. He never abandoned to highly paid employees his right to imprint each film with his personal taste. His interest was in the film, not in the deal. Stanley Kubrick has produced eleven films in the course of twenty-two years. Carlo Ponti has produced more than three hundred films in fewer than forty years. There are producers—and producers.

From his first success in 1960, when he was twenty-five, until the day in 1977 when he married Billy Ikehorn, Vito Orsini had produced some twenty-three pictures. He did this by sometimes working on as many as three pictures at a time, one in its preproduction stages, one actually in photography, and one in postproduction.

Although Vito Orsini worked in Europe so frequently that many people assumed he was Italian, he was actually born in the United States, the son of a Florentine jeweler, Benvenuto Bologna, who had immigrated to the United States long before his son's birth. Quickly understanding the disadvantage of being named after a luncheon meat, Benvenuto took the noble name of Orsini, as many another Italian has done with as little justification. He made a handsome fortune in the wholesale silverware business and brought up his family in the prosperous corner of the Bronx called Riverdale, where his neighbor was Maestro

Toscanini. In 1950, when Vito was at the impressionable age of fifteen, he saw his first Italian film, *Bitter Rice,* produced by Dino De Laurentiis. From then on he bathed himself in the thrilling, ground-breaking excitement of postwar Italian movies and took for his three heroes De Laurentiis, Fellini, and Carlo Ponti. He went to the University of California to major in film, and after graduation, while other film majors were busy getting jobs in the mailrooms at Universal or Columbia, Vito took off for Rome. There he worked as a propman, extra, stunt man, writer, assistant director, and unit production manager before producing the first of his own films at the age of twenty-five. Vito's success was due to the fact that his passion for film making was equaled by his intelligence, gilded by his nimbleness, and propelled by his raw talent and energy. His first film was one of the genre that later became known as Spaghetti Westerns. It made money and so did his next three highly commercial, totally unpretentious works. Finally, in 1965, just as he reached thirty, he had enough of a track record to enable him to raise the financing to make the kind of pictures he really wanted to make. He hadn't looked back since.

As each one of his twenty-three pictures reached its start date, Vito was forced, reluctantly, to loosen the tight reins he held over the production in order to allow the director freedom. Once the camera starts to roll, the film essentially belongs to the director. He tried, but rarely succeeded, to force himself to restrict his visits to the set to two each day, one in the morning and one in the afternoon, feeling like a mother who isn't permitted to be present during the upbringing of her own baby. On the set he could be found hovering a tactful twenty feet behind the director, slightly to one side, observing everything the director was seeing by narrowing his focus, yet far enough away to watch the functioning of the crew, to observe the attitude of the cast members who were not in the particular shot, to keep his eye on the supporting actors. Why was that girl reading a magazine when she was in the next setup? Who was the grip who chewed gum so noisily? Why couldn't that assistant lighting man wait to take a leak later? People who couldn't stand a kvetch didn't work for him twice, but many workers in the film community so admired his perfectionism that they willingly put up with Vito, nicknamed "That Italian Mother." When he wasn't actually on the set of any one of his films, he was always expected momentarily, was temporarily in conference, couldn't be disturbed for five minutes, would be with you as soon as he finished, or had had to leave the set but would return shortly. And invariably, like royalty, he was where he was reported to be and always met people on time. Many people suspected there were two Vito Orsinis.

A passionate producer spends his evening sitting through dailies of the picture currently shooting and screening rough sequences that have been put together from prior dailies. When he isn't on the set during the day, he's out raising money for future projects, seeing his last film through postproduction trauma, attending editing sessions, finding the right music, omnipresent at the looping, dubbing, and sound mixing, and then, staying right on top of the film until the advertising campaign is running smoothly, watching carefully as the film rentals come in, auditing, if necessary, the distributor's books to make sure he is getting his proper percentage. And, of course, making deals to sell films in Kuwait and Argentina and Sweden. Before he goes to bed he may make a half-dozen phone calls to theaters that are playing his most recent film to ask the theater manager about the daily box office. A crowded life with many manic moments, many depressive ones—a life only a passionately obsessed man would choose.

In the fall of 1974 when Maggie was first assigned to interview Vito Orsini, he was on location in Rome, with two more weeks of shooting left on a film starring Belmondo and Jeanne Moreau. The excitement of going to Europe for the first time more than made up for Maggie's disappointment that it was Orsini she was going to be talking to, not Belmondo, for whom she had always had a major yen. The magazine had made reservations for her in the modest Hotel Savoia, a mere half block away from that famous moviemakers' headquarters the Excelsior, on the Via Veneto, but only one quarter of the price. The

Hearst Magazine Corporation is nothing if not conservative in its attitude toward expense accounts.

Before going off to interview movie stars, Maggie had always consulted the recent periodical file at the New York Public Library to get the background from which she could devise her fiendishly unexpected, acute questions. But to interview a producer, that inconvenient, time-consuming trip to the library, the searching through the files, the most important one of which was invariably missing, just seemed like too much trouble. She'd been to Orsini's last two pictures—both of them critics' delights—and that should give her enough to start on.

Orsini's suite at the Excelsior was exactly what she had expected: ornate, impressive, phones ringing, two secretaries typing, a number of people waiting around in varying attitudes of despair and anxiety while they ordered from room service, Telex messages being delivered. Maggie knew it was a bummer. How do you do an interview with somebody who, to begin with, doesn't particularly interest you and, second of all, is the center of a whirlwind? Maggie's touch depended on intimate conversation in intimate circumstances. Yet, at the promised minute, one of the secretaries ushered her into Orsini's inner sanctum, the smallest of the three sitting rooms of the suite.

Maggie's first intimation that common wisdom about movie producers might sometimes be faulty came when she laid eyes on Vito Orsini. In some ways he looked the part. The custom-tailored Brioni suit, the obviously Italian haircut, the Bulgari watch, the highly polished thin leather shoes. But where was the little fat man with the cigar? Where was the little balding man with the funny accent? She'd expected Vito Orsini to look Italian but not like a noble Caesar. She brightened considerably.

"Welcome to Rome, Miss MacGregor." What's more, he spoke English without an accent and did a neat hand kiss.

"My goodness," said Maggie, who made a specialty out of deliberately gauche remarks, "I thought you'd be a lot older."

"Thirty-eight," said Vito, favoring her with a smile that indicated clearly that even if she was deliciously young, he was not yet old. His smile came *through* his eyes, not just from them, his nose had a proconsular boldness, and his coloring was bronze all over. His presence radiated a kind of flash. He had the physical authority of a great orchestra conductor.

"Tell me," said Maggie, still in her most naïve manner, "what is it exactly that a movie producer does?" She had decided that ignorance was not just sensible in this case but downright appropriate—it might provoke him into making some comment for which he would be everlastingly sorry. Those were always the best interviews.

"Thank God you asked," Vito said. "You've no idea how many people have interviewed me without knowing precisely—or even vaguely—what I do. They're too lazy to bother to find out. I'm going to tell you all. But not now—I have to be at the studio in fifteen minutes. Could you possibly have dinner with me tonight? We could talk then."

Like taking candy from a baby, thought Maggie, nodding agreement.

"I'll pick you up at eight and take you to one of my favorite places. Meanwhile, remember that the Gucci shop here is just as expensive as the one in New York, so don't go crazy."

Movie producers who survive inevitably develop a high degree of ESP.

That evening, at the Hostaria dell' Orso, Maggie didn't need her bag of interviewer's tricks: the ability to go for the jugular, to ask just the wrong question to get the right answer, to give just enough of her own self to disarm suspicion, to be neither too deferential nor too cozy. All she needed to do was listen. Vito hadn't stopped talking for three hours and he had, so he insisted, only scratched the surface.

"Please, Vito, I can't take any more. I'm out of tape, I have writer's cramp, I know more than any reasonable human being would want to read."

"I keep doing that to people. Well, you should never have asked. Nobody warned you about me, eh?"

"Nobody told me anything. Just said, get on a plane and talk to you."

"Why don't we go back to my hotel and talk about you."

"I thought you'd never ask."

From Vito, Maggie learned what had been bothering her about star fucking. It wasn't making love. Vito Orsini was a great romantic. When she went to bed with him, Maggie suddenly understood that she was the star of this particular production. She learned, for the first time, that her large breasts and voluptuous bottom were a stupendous plus when they weren't being regarded in comparison to the American ideal. She learned that there existed a famous man who did not think that he was doing her a favor by letting her get acquainted with his cock. There was in the first night, and all the following nights she spent with Vito, none of that feeling she used to unconsciously ignore in her star-fucking episodes, an intimation of being an inferior who was allowed a short peek into the way the better people live. Vito cured her, once and for all, of what he called her "upstairs maid" complex in which she shone only in borrowed fame.

Maggie stayed two weeks in Rome in that warm early fall of 1974, sending cables to the office every three days that she was having trouble with the Orsini interview because he was too busy to see her. Everyone back at *Cosmo* understood perfectly. They all knew about Italian movie producers. Impossible people. Maggie and Vito became loving friends, fellow conspirators in an unnamed sense against an unnamed force, sincere appreciators of each other's body and mind. Maggie wondered, from time to time, whether this encounter, like the others she had had, would come to nothing once the article was researched, but gradually she learned to trust Vito. They would not always be lovers, but they would always be friends.

Vito let Maggie sit in on all his conferences, listen to all his phone calls, follow him around on the set, watch dailies with him. By the end of two weeks she knew more about the mechanics and business aspects of movie production than almost anyone writing on film in the United States, knowledge that stood her in good stead when she got her television show. But that was almost six months in the future, six months during which Maggie wrote five more movie-star profiles and found out that she didn't need to fuck a star to write about him. In fact, the ability to keep her distance became one of her most powerful weapons. Only when she stopped needing to be loved, even if only for a night, was she able to see movie personalities clearly, put them in absolute focus. Her interviews lost the faint flavor, so common in such writing, of revealing more about how the reporter feels about the star than about the star himself. Rereading her first profiles, she felt sick at the opportunities lost for devastatingly truthful reporting because of the memory of just another pretty face bending over her.

In the spring of 1975, six months after Maggie had said good-bye to Vito in Rome, she learned that he was producing a new picture, *Slow Boat,* on location in Mexico. The star, Ben Lowell, was one of the five leading male box-office attractions in the United States, a specialist in strong, stalwart roles, admired as much by men as by women. The female lead was being played by a brilliant, notorious English actress, Mary Hanes, who had a reputation as a devil in bed and the possessor of the foulest, funniest mouth in what was left of the British Empire.

Maggie persuaded her bosses at *Cosmo* that the time was right to interview Ben Lowell, that most all-American of performers in an age in which all-American boys were getting scarce on the scene. Her real reason for going to the Mexican location, infamous for its heat, discomfort, and bad food, was, of course, to see Vito again.

Maggie was the only member of the press to brave the location. Joe Hyams, Jane Howard, Laura Cunningham, and a dozen less important writers had all politely declined the invitation to suffer through a long trip in a chartered plane to a decayed fishing village on the coast, attractive only for its dependably calm sea and its authentic tropical sordidness. There were other, more agreeable invitations. Always.

Vito embraced Maggie as she stumbled out of the small plane on the badly kept landing strip.

"How's the picture?" murmured Maggie even before she said hello.

"A dog."

"How can you be sure?"

"I smell blood in the water."

"What does that mean?"

"I can't tell you exactly—many reasons, but so far I only know some of them," answered Vito. "But I smell it, Maggie, I'm positive."

After a day on the set, just watching and taking mental notes, as she usually did when beginning an interview, Maggie was more baffled than she had ever been since she started writing. She was accustomed to the deliberate pace of movie making, but on the set of *Slow Boat* there was an air of tension that she had never felt before. She found herself getting an anxiety attack just from hanging around, and Maggie had learned to dissociate herself from the normal temper flare-ups of a set since, in a way, they were all grist to her mill, just as a reporter doesn't feel personally involved in a traffic accident he is covering.

She was staying in the room next to Vito's in the motel, the best of the three mangy motels in the town, all of which had been rented to house the actors and crew. They were built to accommodate the California deep-sea-fishing buffs and private plane pilots who were the only non-Mexicans who usually came to this remote spot.

Vito and Maggie had had dinner together at the commissary set up for the entire company. The local food was a one-way ticket to gastroenteritis and all the film company's needs were taken care of by California cooks cooking California style. The supplies were flown in from San Diego, the nearest large city, even though it was six hundred air miles away. The company doctor had also been imported, from Mexico City, since there were none in this flyspeck of a village.

Back at the motel, Maggie changed into a robe, went to Vito's room, and snuggled into bed with him.

"Vito, if I didn't love you, I'd go home tomorrow, Ben Lowell or no Ben Lowell. But I do love you—very dearly —so tell me, what the fuck is going on here and why is the light and life of the Via Veneto in this place. Can you even call it a place?"

"Maggie, did you ever hear the old saying that when a fish begins to stink, it starts at the head? This project started to go wrong from day one. I allowed myself to be persuaded to set a start date even though I knew the screenplay wasn't right. One of the majors is putting up the money—a bunch of fucking banditti—and they insist on having the picture for a Christmas release. So we had to find sun and sea—otherwise no picture. It's raining everywhere in the world but here and Saudi Arabia, excuse the expression. Also it's the only time Ben Lowell and Mary Hanes are free—if I don't use them now I don't get another crack at them together for two years. So it was now or never—I let myself be stampeded. It's not the first time I've ever had this happen, but the other times we squeaked through. But, this time it's unreal, incredible—my screenwriter is so sick he can't do anything but throw up and shit; I think he must have gone out for tacos. My favorite gaffer broke his leg and we had to fly him back to L.A., the generator has already gone out ten times during night shooting, the script girl is deaf, blind, or both—I had to hire her at the last minute when my regular girl got married on me—I could go on but why bother?" It was the first time that Maggie had ever seen Vito drained of the optimistic air he always maintained in the midst of crisis.

"But, Vito, you're talking about details. How are the dailies?" He made a marvelously Latin gesture that indicated hope and despair in equal parts.

"So maybe it's gonna all be worth it?" Maggie felt a great need to cheer him up. She didn't want to mention the peculiar tension on the set, since he hadn't brought it up; perhaps, she thought, it's a result of all the accidents.

"It had better be." Vito said this in such a pale voice that Maggie was startled.

"So if it's not? It won't be the end of the world. Canby, even John Simon, liked the one with Moreau and Belmondo. Your last two pictures got fantastic reviews—"

"They did *niènte* at the box office. *Bubkes*. Nothing. If I ever see profits, the Pope will get married. Like everyone else, you still think good reviews automatically mean money. Only in New York maybe—"

"Oh." Maggie was conscious of a great feeling of shocked surprise. The openhanded, on-top-of-the-world way Vito lived, the way he shaped his life, had led her to believe that he had endless resources. She had never stopped to consider that a producer's fee is the only thing he is sure of when he undertakes a film, and that he is dependent on profits for his real reward. "I simply can't understand it," she said finally.

"Maggie, how many pictures make a profit?"

"Well, my God, lots and lots—otherwise why would they keep making them?"

"One in four. Don't you remember what I tried to teach you in Rome? Only twenty-five percent of all the pictures made show a profit, but that twenty-five percent make so much money that they keep the studios going."

"But your producer's fees—you get them up front, even if the picture doesn't make a profit."

"It depends," he said as wryly as if he were tasting foul medicine. "As it happens, on my last film and on this one too, it was so difficult to get financing that I deferred my fees until we show profits. The Belmondo film went down the toilet, I'm in hock, Maggie."

In hock. She looked at him, magnificent in his silk pajamas and monogrammed silk robe.

"I never knew."

"No one ever does. It's a secret of the producers union. We're all gamblers—worse than playing the horses. That's why we don't really have a union—we're afraid someone might tell."

"Oh, Vito! My darling. It's going to be all right. With Ben Lowell and Mary Hanes—you can't lose. All that animal sex up there on the screen—between them they're the six sexiest people in the world. Everyone's dying to see a really good love story. Vito, I know this is going to be a smash." Maggie wrapped her arms around him as tightly as she could.

"From your mouth to God's ear," Vito answered, using the favorite expression of Maggie's mother.

Within a half hour Maggie was too sick with tourista to do anything but flee to her room. She hadn't touched anything but commissary food. Still, Mexico. There was another casualty within the twenty-four hours she spent in misery, one that couldn't be cured by Lomotil. That night a handsome, young actor, Harry Brown, Ben Lowell's stand-in, tripped over a garbage can in the dark alley behind the motel and fell. He hit his head on a piece of broken concrete in such a way that he was knocked unconscious and bled to death before he was discovered. While the company doctor was making out the death certificate, Ben Lowell talked to Vito.

"Christ—I've known the kid for years. I still can't believe it. It's a terrible thing! He's been my stand-in for my last three pictures. He has nobody in the world—a drifter until he came to Hollywood. I gave him the job two years ago—the kid used to hang around wanting to be an actor, but he had no talent. Poor kid. Poor Harry, Jesus. He was brought up on some God-forsaken farm somewhere, but he'd never tell me where. We've got to have a funeral, Vito, and fast. This is a hot country."

"Was he a Catholic? Do you have any proof?"

"Shit, no—who the hell knows those things?"

"We can't bury him here then. They don't like us anyway in this town, and they won't let us bury a non-Catholic in their graveyard."

The two men looked at each other. It meant chartering a plane to fly down from Los Angeles and take the body back. It meant making funeral arrangements at long distance and considerable expense.

"Vito, the kid loved the sea, really had a thing for it. Is it against the law to bury him at sea?"

"I think we had better send his body back to L.A., Ben. The studio will just add it to our overages."

"Vito, I'm telling you, the kid would have wanted to be buried at sea. I feel strongly about this. Harry had terrible fears of—of being cremated, of being buried under the earth—*I have to insist* about this, Vito." The actor was shaking with some emotion Vito didn't understand. It wasn't grief and it wasn't anger at being opposed. He repeated again, in a voice that was suddenly shrill and violent, *"I have to insist,"* and Vito recognized his emotion. Fear. "Vito, I won't be able to finish the picture unless he's buried at sea. I'll be too sick thinking about him being buried in the earth when he hated that idea—too sick to work." Fear *and* blackmail.

"OK," said Vito, "I'll work it all out."

Harry Brown was quietly buried at sea before the day was over.

Vito had too much riding on the completion of *Slow Boat* not to give in to Ben Lowell's blackmail. He had not told Maggie the ultimate fact, the fact that because of the poor box-office performance of his last two pictures he had also had to put up a completion guarantee on this picture, selling his house outside Rome and his collection of lithographs to raise it. He had done it with his eyes open. A producer must believe in his judgment even if it means risking everything he owns to make sure he has money on hand to finish his picture.

But Vito Orsini knew that he had to find out why he had been blackmailed. The picture was slipping out of his hands. The day after Harry Brown had been lowered into the sea the director had worked all day shooting and re-shooting a key scene between Ben Lowell and Mary Hanes, but, without waiting for the dailies, Vito knew that the elements of good film weren't there. Vito had spent all of that day on the set, disregarding the director's pique, watching, watching, watching. He saw many little things, none of them exceptional in themselves, but with his highly developed extrasensory perception, his high-rolling gambler's instinct, Vito saw enough—of what he couldn't have explained—to make him wander over to Mary Hanes's room after dinner. Vito found her wearing the bottom of a black bikini and a transparent halter that she had made out of one of her large, red chiffon scarves. In spite of her thinness, she exuded a dark carnal quality that made Vito feel as if he were entering the wildcat cage at a zoo every time he was alone with her. There was something truly evil and dangerous about this seraphically pretty girl, a combination that was the reason for her stardom.

"So, so—our bloody producer himself. Or should I say our bloody undertaker?" She was lying sprawled on the unmade bed in a room reeking of marijuana.

"Mary, in Mexico it is dangerous to smoke pot. And even outside of Mexico it is dangerous to mix it with whiskey. But, primarily, I thank God you aren't drinking it on the rocks—the water might be even more dangerous."

"Vito, you're not a bad old cunt. I think I like you." She passed him the joint and he took a drag, careful to keep the smoke in his mouth. "I'm almost glad you dropped in, you sodding Wop—I was getting just a bit blue."

"I had a feeling something was wrong today."

"Mary doesn't like to have her pretty boy taken away from her and thrown into the deep blue sea—like a rat, just like a stepped-on rat. Christ, Vito, I can *see* him, fishes eating him." She began to quiver, her eyes skittering away from the horror she saw.

Vito had made a successful picture with Mary Hanes only three years ago. In spite of the scandals she had been involved in, in the past, he had never seen her out of control before. Even her most outrageous remarks were carefully calculated to attract attention, her shocking witticisms were rehearsed and honed until she made copy every time she opened her wide, oddly ugly, utterly alluring mouth, the mouth that gave her the touch of strangeness that beauty must have. Tonight she was merely paranoid from grass.

"Mary, how long have you been smoking this stuff?" He passed her the joint with a smile that had nothing in it to indicate that she and her agent had assured him before he signed her that she hadn't used drugs since she had been busted over a year ago on her return to Britain from South America, an affair that had been hushed up with difficulty.

"Since I was eleven—hasn't everybody?" she said, giggling, in a sudden change of mood.

"No," Vito said patiently, "I mean today."

"What day is today? Wait—no—don't tell me—it's Friday. Right? Yesterday was Thursday, tomorrow—Saturday. Right?"

"Right, Mary, one hundred percent. So, how long have you been smoking?"

"Oh, that—since yesterday I think. I didn't bring any with me. My bloody agent made sure of that—packed me up himself, he did—anyway, those turd-eating Mexican border guards'll put you away, Vito—didja know that? So, afterward, I got some from that quack you brought from Mexico City—one hundred bucks and the bastard only gave me twenty joints—but it's good stuff. Want another drag? Come on—"

Vito took another small drag, clamping the end of the joint lightly between his teeth to prevent the smoke from reaching his throat. He realized that Mary Hanes was far gone, but, like so many grass smokers, she had become too restless to stop talking.

"So you started after Harry had the accident?" Vito asked her calmly. "I understand. It was very sad. Such a young, good-looking kid. A sad, silly way to die. You found him simpatico?"

"Simpatico? What's with these bloody Italian words, Vito? That pretty piece of rough trade? Ben's cock-sucker—Ben won't make a picture without the kid around—stand-in! He had more talent in his mouth than anywhere else—a tongue that could drive you crazy—he'd do anything for a buck. Simpatico!" She seemed to muse bitterly on what she had said. "More whiskey, Vito." She held out her glass. In her skimpy bikini bottom and almost nude halter, stoned out of her mind, Mary Hanes looked as innocent as a cherub on the ceiling of a small Roman church.

"Rough trade?" Vito knew what the words meant. But did she—in her condition? She looked at him scornfully.

"Sweetums, momma's baby boy, come to mama." She grasped Vito's hands and pulled him to her, guiding his hands over her hard, flexible body, pushing them between her legs. "Even that nasty bit of work, even that little whore, that gorgeous slab off the meat rack, wanted Mary. They all want Mary. And I wanted him. Ben knew it too—bloody queen—wouldn't let Harry out of his sight—fucking faggot, wanted pretty Harry all to himself—and now he's got bloody fuck-all. Serves him right, shit-licking murderer—who'll suck his cock now?"

"Harry fell, Mary—"

"Harry FELL? You believe that too? Fell! How could the kid fall while he was fucking me?" Suddenly she laughed. A nasty wet sound. "You should have seen Ben's face when he opened the door—I'd won, Vito, and he knew it—I'd won."

"So—?" Vito said without expression.

"So he bashed him, you asshole, with the butt of that gun he carries—didn't know that—did you—and dragged him outside—that's all."

"And left him to bleed to death?"

"Too true—too too too true. Dead and buried like a squashed roach—a rat—deep, deep under the sea. Oh! Help me Vito! I keep seeing it!" Vito got a bottle of mineral water and carefully fed the crazed girl three Valiums from the bottle on her bureau—the only way he knew to help bring her down safely. Hours later, when she was snoring, finally unconscious, he left her room after rousing her dresser and exacting her promise to stay with the actress until morning.

It was Maggie who figured out what to do. When Vito staggered back to his room at dawn, he found her up, recovered from her bout of stomach trouble and anxious about his absence. Vito Orsini was a man who had learned that in the film business you trust no one, and quite possibly he would never have told Maggie what he had just learned except that he realized that even if Mary Hanes managed to finish the picture without revealing the truth about Ben Lowell and his murdered stand-in, she would return to London and, given her lack of control, within days, rumors or perhaps the entire story, would be in the world press. When he had finished, Maggie sat speechless for a minute and finally said, *"Actors."*

"A comment in the great Hollywood tradition." Vito, with nothing left to lose, found he could still be amused.

"Shut up, darling, and let me think." Craving a respite, Vito slumped on his bed and fell into a light sleep, while Maggie took out her pad and pencil and started making notes, scratching them out, making others. An hour later she woke him.

"Listen to what happened yesterday. Ben Lowell saved Mary Hanes from rape. He's a hero, she's an innocent victim. Like it?"

"Swell. Perfect. You're insane, did you know that?"

"Even my mother knows me better than that. Vito, you're not thinking creatively. It plays perfectly when you shift the details around just a bit. Now, pay attention:

366

Harry Brown, a very bad guy, started to bother Mary from the day she got here. She was terrified of him and told Ben. So, last night when Ben was walking by Mary's door, he heard her screaming for help. Brown was on top of her, raping her; she was fighting back, desperately. Ben grabbed the guy, he put up a fight naturally, Ben had to hit him. He fell, hit his head on the corner of the dresser. Now comes the important part. They revived him and he was OK. Still very drunk—but subdued. He left *alive*. Ben stayed to reassure Mary, then left. It wasn't until the next morning that Brown was found. Obviously, he had been dazed, stumbled on the garbage can in the dark, fell again, passed out, and bled to death. The doctor didn't question it. Burial at sea was for the reasons Ben gave you. Where's the hole?"

"Who's going to believe it?"

"Everybody. Ben will tell that story more convincingly than he's ever played any part. Mary too if you put the right kind of pressure on her—everyone knows how much scandal she's been involved in and this would finish her too. No one else knows anything about what really happened."

"Maggie, sweet, God knows I appreciate what you're trying to do, but *Cosmo* couldn't get that story into print for months and by that time this will just be old, bad news and all the damage will have been done."

"Not if I can get it on television. You have to get a plane here as soon as possible. I'll fly up to Los Angeles, talk to one of the network-news boys and we'll have a TV camera crew here by tomorrow night, latest. It will be on the air before you've even finished shooting. Fantastic publicity for the picture and nobody can prove it *didn't* happen that way. Hitting a man who's raping a woman isn't a crime—it's a mitzvah. Vito, Vito, it's your only chance!"

While Maggie was in Los Angeles, Vito did his work well. He found Mary Hanes shaken and sober when she finally woke up. He locked the door of her room behind him and hit her heavily on both sides of her face. Then he put his hands around her neck and squeezed, stopping just before she lost consciousness. He deposited her gently on her bed and waited, girmly, till she gasped, "What—what!"

"There is a moment in the life of a woman like you when she finally goes too far. You've reached it. I've cabled your husband."

"You cunt, you bastard cunt! You know he's determined to leave me if there's any more mess—and my *babies*—he'll get them—oh, Christ, how could anyone do this—it's all over—over." She was racked by loss.

"Don't be absurd. Harry Brown was raping you and Ben Lowell saved you, possibly saved your life. Look at the way Brown beat you up, hit you, choked you. Your husband is terribly upset. You know how much he loves you. He'll be here tomorrow."

"Vito—?"

"The television-news camera crew will be here tomorrow, too. They will want to interview you, of course—perhaps we should go over the story you told me yesterday. Mary, look alive! I know you've been through a nightmare but you're not usually a slow study."

She smiled as she washed the blood off her battered face. "You're a smart little swine, Vito. Right! Read me my part."

The incredible ratings of the show "Who Was Harry Brown and Did Ben Lowell Murder Him?" which preempted two half-hour situation comedies, told the network news chief that he had stumbled on a gold mine. There was a huge audience out there, addicted to television and hooked on celebrities. They could wallow in the pop-cultural peepshow of Maggie's program, feeling virtuously well informed about the doings of the world, without having to actually tune in to *Washington Week in Review*. The news chief had as little trouble talking Maggie into signing a contract for a weekly show as Maggie had had in getting him to send the camera crew to Mexico. They both knew a ripe thing when they smelled it. The only surprise was how good a thing it was. More than good. It was majestic. A new genre of television had been born: the movie magazine dressed in the superior style of the news documentary. A new media star had been born:

Maggie MacGregor. There were only two losers along the way, Harry Brown, still bitterly, secretly mourned by Ben Lowell, and Vito's picture, *Slow Boat*. Even with the enormous publicity it received it didn't do well. By the time it was released, the Mexican episode had long since dimmed in the public consciousness. Nobody cared, really. And besides, Vito had been right about it. It was a dog.

Billy Ikehorn was restless. It had been five months since Scruples had reopened and in this April of 1977 she had become accustomed to its raging, tearing success. Nice for Spider and Valentine, she thought, gratefully and fondly. However, in the small hours of the morning, for lately she had again been waking up before dawn, the thought of the triumph of Scruples was not enough. She had retained too much of her basic honesty to avoid the realization that now that Scruples was no longer a festering disgrace, now that no one would ever snicker about it, the daily details of running a store were not enough to fill her life. She even took for granted the bimonthly dancing parties, which had first captured her imagination as a form of victory over her hideous memories of dancing school, now that they had turned into California's most anticipated social events. As for the shifting sands of the supposed "A" list and "B" list, it was too silly to take seriously, reminding her of the politics of the sandbox. Her life at the moment felt as confining as the house she had visited with Ellis in Antigua where all the windows were hermetically sealed so that the salt air of the marvelous night breeze didn't spoil the millions of dollars' worth of French Impressionist paintings on the walls.

Billy was almost six months away from her thirty-fifth birthday. She had just barely attained the prime of a beauty that would last for many years; she was rich beyond even her ability to comprehend the extent of her wealth—and she was bored. Disgusting, she thought to herself, imagining what her late Aunt Cornelia would think if she knew. She, Billy, found it more than disgusting; she found it immoral and humiliating. Immoral because anyone with all that she had should, *must,* be happy, and humiliating because obviously she was not, so the fault must lie in her nature. Probably a lack of inner resources, she thought wryly, remembering the Boston code. Undoubtedly, a life devoted to good works, large dogs, and weekly attendance at the symphony would have left her enriched and fulfilled.

The entire world was available to her she observed, as she flipped over the pages of *Architectural Digest*. For three hundred thousand dollars she could own an air-conditioned pavilion in Bali, built in a coconut grove next to the ocean, with a swimming pool of course. In Eleuthera there was a house for sale that had twelve hundred feet of pink sand beach and a private overseas telephone system—all for less than three million dollars, furnished. (Did the list of private phone numbers come with the furniture?) Or, if she preferred something less tropical, she could live in England at Number 7, Royal Crescent, Bath, for no more than seventy-five thousand pounds, owning a house that had been built in 1770 as part of the most splendid example of Georgian architecture in the world, and which now possessed a sauna and a five-car garage. If she chose, she could adopt the life-style of someone like Bunny Mellon with four fabulous homes, two full-time interior decorators, everything from her tennis hats to her ball gowns to her servants' uniforms designed especially for her by Givenchy. They said she kept apples boiling at all times on the stoves of her one hundred thousand-acre Virginia estate to perfume the air with an authentic farm aroma. Such precious attention to detail made Billy's teeth hurt. Too much!

She could have anything in the world she wanted. Just name it. She couldn't—that was the problem. She didn't want another house. She still maintained a plane, a new Learjet now, but only Valentine and the other buyers used it for their trips. The St. Helena vineyard made a substantial profit and there was no reason to sell it. Perhaps a horse? Adopt a baby? A pet mouse? Obviously there was something wrong with her. Billy decided to accept Susan Arvey's invitation to go to the Cannes Film Festival. She couldn't think of a good reason not to.

Susan Arvey was the wife of Curt Arvey, head of the Arvey Film Studio. She was not a particularly interesting woman, but Billy felt comfortable with her, primarily because she never showed any of the sycophantic delight in

Billy's every word that so many other women did. She had gone beyond the nervously enlightened largesse of the new rich to the taking-for-granted of good things, which made her company fairly relaxing. As the wife of a studio head, she was a divinity in a community where Billy Ikehorn, rich as she was, was merely a curiosity. She was an accomplished hostess, clever enough to hide her pretentiousness. Most important of all, Billy, like everyone else, had always been fascinated with the world of the movies. As a miserable teen-ager she lived for Saturday matinees. During the years of Ellis's sickness, the projection room of the Bel Air mansion had become a refuge from reality. But Billy knew few movie people, although she lived in the midst of them. She would never admit it, but they did have a certain—intriguing quality.

The Arveys always spent the two weeks of the Festival at the Hôtel du Cap, at Cap d'Antibes, which is a good three-quarters-of-an-hour drive along twisting roads from Cannes itself. No one who stayed there did so for the sake of convenience. The symbolism of staying at the Hôtel du Cap was profound. It meant that you expected people to come to you rather than your going to them, an enormously important point to score in the business. It meant that you could afford to set yourself apart, out of the hurly-burly, holding court in your own artfully remote and tranquil space, rather than fighting like a member of the common herd to secure a table at the bar of the Carlton or the Majestic. It also meant that you could afford to pay two to four hundred dollars a day for a suite, with taxes and tips and breakfast and all sorts of unexpected, cunning additions on top of the basic rate. The Arveys always took two suites, one for Curt to do business in, one to sleep in.

"Billy, do come with us," Susan had said a month ago. "Curt is busy shaking and baking all day long—I have nothing to do but wander around by myself. I always rent a car and driver and go all over the Côte—it's heaven in May—and then, at night, we'll all go for a big late dinner somewhere, with a mixed bag of amusing people. It's great fun if you manage to stay out of Cannes—it would be so much more fun if you'd come and keep me company. Anyway, you've been in southern California too long. It's time you got away. Scruples can struggle along without you for a few weeks—we could stop in Paris on the way back—do come!"

"Don't you have to go to see films every night?" Billy asked curiously.

"Heavens, no! Well—I suppose some people *do,* of course—but Curt can see anything he's interested in at a private screening. He just asks for a print." Susan was always amazed at the people who thought that one went to the Cannes Film Festival to see movies. If you had a film in competition you had to show up, but otherwise— goodness, what a bizarre idea.

No one at all in the film business has a good word to say about the Cannes Film Festival. Yet nobody stays away. It is an indispensable trade fair, the commercial aspects of which drown out almost entirely the artistic window dressing. More deals are made at the Festival than anyone can count. Perhaps one in ten, or one in twenty, comes to fruition. It is not a place for the purely creative people of the film world. Directors and writers and actors are scarce, seen there only if they are involved in films that are being shown in competition before the jury and, even then, only if they have been strong-armed by their producers. Any actor or actress who is at Cannes without a good reason is a frank publicity seeker.

But all the agents and producers and distributors and public-relations people and advertising people and business-affairs people are there, from Egypt to Japan, from Canada to India, from France to Israel, muttering to each other the ritualistic words that attempt to indicate they are above this unutterably vulgar rat race, even as they compose the rat race itself. The hookers of the world are there, male and female. The world press is there. And so are the movie critics, who even go to the films, along with the townspeople of Cannes and people so unpreoccupied with buying and selling films that they have time to actually watch them.

Vito Orsini was also there, squeezing out some sales of the foreign rights to his Mexican dog and trying to drum up some financing for a new book he had discovered. Vito now had behind him three pictures in a row that had not shown a profit. Yet, in a world in which public reputations live on endlessly, he was still a very important producer. Only a few men knew exactly how empty Vito's bank account was, even fewer knew how much he owed. They were the very men from whom he hoped to find new financing. In the eyes of everyone else at the Festival, Vito's reputation was that of a brilliant producer with an impressive record of success.

Even those who knew the precise truth about Vito did not count him out. Many a producer before him had had a streak of bad luck and then come up with a winner, a box-office success that had enriched everyone who had a part of the profits. Movie making, more than most businesses, survives on taking enormous chances, on eternal optimism. Even the hard-eyed business-affairs men, armed with pages and pages of figures, couldn't last long in the industry if they didn't occasionally say yes to a new idea, instead of no. Studios and their distribution companies, as well as independent distributors, survive only if they have a product to sell. But that product, by its very nature, is unknown, an unproven element, until it has been made. And then, for good or for bad, the money has been spent. No one can guarantee, in advance, which picture will make money, which will not.

Vito was still very much in the ball game—not to the extent that he could stay at the Hôtel du Cap but surely to the degree that a small suite at the Majestic was a necessity. A sitting room was imperative. He could hardly do business sitting on beds. And the Majestic had a certain dignity, a certain class that the Carlton, the center of the frenzy, lacked. It was fractionally more expensive, but, on the other hand, every inch of the impressive lobby had not been rented to film companies, as it was at the Carlton, where you couldn't push from the door to the bar without winding your way through a crowded maze of decorated booths from which publicity pamphlets for dozens of pictures were thrust at you. Was the crowd in the lobby of the Carlton more like a convention of camel drivers or rug merchants, Vito wondered, or more like a gathering of international crooks or international cops? It was impossible to tell from the faces, impossible to tell from the polyglot babble. He understood perfectly why everyone in that lobby seemed to be looking past everyone else: They were looking either for people who owed money to them or for people to whom they owed money in order to avoid them.

Vito's suite looked out on a crescent of beach beyond the Croisette. At twilight, with the sun setting behind the spars and sails of the boats anchored at the far end, where the old port still thrived, it was one of the most indisputably romantic spots on earth. He stood on his balcony and thought about money.

To be at Cannes, at Festival time, with a winner behind you is one of the most intoxicatingly delightful experiences known to man. He had known many such seasons, years when a dozen different distributors lined up patiently next to his table at the bar, like men waiting to cut in on a debutante, for their chance to propose their deals to him. His time would come again, he reflected, but not this particular year.

He left the balcony and started to change for dinner. Curt Arvey had asked him to join his party at Pavillon Eden Roc, the restaurant of the Hôtel du Cap, reached from the hotel by a splendid, long, wide path through a vast fragrant gardenlike park in which many birds sang.

Eden Roc is most noted for the hotel's swimming pool, a nasty misshapen bit of 1920s concrete buried in a great rock formation on the edge of the water, which, for some reason, had once been a symbol of the gilded life. No self-respecting citizen of any country would entrust his body to the strangely dubious-looking water of that miserable pool, although many sunbathe there. However, the Pavillon, a highly rated, elaborate restaurant next to the pool, still attracted crowds.

Vito was sure that Arvey must have asked him to dinner in order to function as an extra man. There was no love lost between the two of them. Arvey had made money with Vito in the past, but his studio had partly financed two of Vito's last three pictures, and although they had perhaps recovered their investments, they had not made any profits according to their bookkeeping departments. Vito suspected that, although the studio claimed they had barely broken even, they were hiding profits somewhere, but he could prove nothing. Much as he disliked Arvey, he had accepted the invitation. At Festival time any casual meeting can lead to something.

Or, as Doris Day would sing, *que sera, sera*. Vito felt very Italian tonight.

Susan Arvey, had she been a man of mildly criminal disposition, would have made a fine pimp. But her marked predilections toward bringing a man and a woman together for sexual purposes with financial advantages did not include introducing Vito Orsini to Billy Ikehorn. She had indeed found a number of wives for men who didn't clearly understand that they needed them as well as she did, but in her conventional mind the girl must be in search of the protection, the wealth, and the security of the male.

She had given a lot of thought to Billy Ikehorn. It would be her crowning achievement to marry her off—but to whom? What could a man offer Billy? Her future husband must be a man who was so clearly above marrying for any consideration other than true love that it baffled even Susan's inventiveness. On the political side, she would consider nothing less than a senator or a governor from a large state. She had hopes of Jerry Brown, but he and Billy had not hit it off. In the film business there was absolutely no one. All the major studio heads were taken or had sworn never to marry again. And, unless they happened to own a great deal of stock in their company, like her own husband, they weren't financially secure enough to suit her. President Carter was married. And Billy was taller than he was anyway. Royalty? Not in Cannes. The invitation to come to Cannes had been extended because Billy was nice. Susan was very proud of the fact that she thought Billy was nice. So many women didn't, quite obviously, in her opinion, because they found Billy overwhelming. They were envious of her. It was delicious not to have to be envious of Billy Ikehorn—it proved to Susan exactly how high she stood in the world. She felt very pleased with her warm heart. Susan's heart was warm only for a tiny group of people she thought good enough to deserve it. Lesser folk she treated like friends she had dropped years ago but still felt faint pity for, mingled with vague suspicion.

Like most practiced hostesses, Susan Arvey liked her guests to feel honored by each other's presence. This demanded that they be familiar with each other's outstanding achievements. If one of her guests owned a giant savings and loan company and was as unknown to the general public as a shoe-repair man, Susan simply worked his savings and loan company into the introduction. She was so adept at this that hardly anyone was aware of what she was doing, but the subliminal impression was made. Not just a superior pimp but a great P.R. person existed in Susan Arvey. Many guests, of course, didn't need explanation. They were the most satisfactory. She certainly didn't have to tag a phrase of identification onto either Billy Ikehorn or Vito Orsini.

Tonight Susan had invited fourteen guests, all meeting first to have a drink in one of the Arvey's suites before going on to the Pavillon. It was not at all one of her more illustrious gatherings, in fact, frankly, rather a mediocre crew, but at Festival time you took what was available. In other circumstances, Susan wouldn't have invited Vito until he had a new hit picture, but she needed an extra man, and Curt had suggested him.

For the first half of the cocktail hour, Susan was so busy putting a little high gloss on everyone's reputation that it was a while before she realized that Vito Orsini seemed determined to monopolize Billy Ikehorn. They weren't circulating. It wouldn't do, not at all. As she herded her guests down the walk from the hotel to the restaurant, Susan found time to whisper to Billy that it was too bad that Vito Orsini's last three pictures hadn't made money.

"So he told me," said Billy. "Amazing, isn't it? The taste level of the world is lower than low. I loved every one of them. I think he's a genius—almost a Bergman. You have put me next to him at dinner, haven't you?"

"I don't think so."

"Please do, Susan dear." There was an edge to Billy's voice that only a very few people would have caught immediately: Valentine, Spider, Hank Sanders, Jake Cassidy, and Josh Hillman.

"Well, of course," Susan agreed unwillingly. Perhaps Billy just felt like a little flutter of flirtation. Heavens, it must be years since—naturally, that explained it.

'You haven't been into Cannes at all?" Vito asked with curiosity, as he and Billy ate dinner.

"Susan says it's simply too grotesque. Tomorrow we're going to the Maeght museum to see the Giacomettis and, if we have time, there is a wonderful old house in Grasse, restored in the period—sixteenth century, I think."

"Tomorrow you are going to the Cannes Film Festival."

"I am?"

"Of course you are. You're dying to go. It's not just grotesque, it's Dante's *Inferno,* painted by Bosch, with a touch of Dali, a little George Grosz, and if you look out at the sea, it's pure Dufy. Susan amuses me. You come six thousand miles to the world's most famous circus and she is too damn dainty to set foot inside the tent. But I don't think you are."

" 'Dainty' is not a word anyone has ever used to describe me."

"What words do they use?"

"You know, I haven't any idea. I'm not being coy—I just don't know."

"Let's use the process of elimination. Not dainty and not coy, to start with. Not ugly and not insignificant. Not stupid but not very self-aware. Not immature, yet not quite grown up. Not terribly happy but not melancholy. Perhaps—yes, I believe, a little shy."

"Stop it!"

"You don't like to talk about yourself?"

"It's not that. You embarrass me."

"Why?"

"All this instant character analysis. You just met me an hour ago."

"But have I said anything you don't agree with?"

"No—that's what I don't like. I had hoped to be a little more mysterious." Now she did sound coy, she thought, annoyed at herself.

"But you're very mysterious to me. I'm only talking about some of the obvious things I see—it's in my profession to see these things, as if you were a character in a script. In the treatment for the script—the outline—we write something like 'Billy Ikehorn is a beautiful, rich young widow who does not have a fixed center to her life, so she goes to the Cannes Film Festival with a friend, hoping for some distraction' and then we have established the character and we can go on from there. But that doesn't mean we know the really important things about her, the motivations, the nuances. Some will come out in the script and some in the actress we pick to play Billy Ikehorn—she must bring her own quality to the part. And the audience supplies the rest—each one of them brings something different to the idea of 'rich young widow.' So you remain mysterious still."

"Just three lines in a treatment?"

"Something more. After all, you're playing Billy Ikehorn."

"I *am* Billy Ikehorn!"

"Perhaps it is the same thing."

"Oh, that old bit about everybody playing a role," she said scornfully.

"No." He didn't explain further but adroitly changed the subject. Nothing could have piqued Billy's interest more, Vito was well aware. He was just letting his extra-sensory perceptions take him where they willed. He didn't have plans for Billy other than amusement. It gave him a mischievous pleasure to think of rescuing her from Susan Arvey's overly rarefied atmosphere, if only for a day. The workingman in him was offended by the idea of someone who was too grand to dip at least a toe into the bazaar of the Festival. And she was so very beautiful.

Billy took refuge behind an expression of ancestral Winthrop hauteur, with her eyelids lowered so that Vito couldn't penetrate her feelings about spending the next day with him. She had known, from the minute they met, that he was a virtuoso—would have known even if she had never seen one of his films. He had the unmistakable air of a man who has crossed a number of border lines, a man who didn't waste time questioning the importance of what he was doing but just went ahead and did it—an impulsive, fearless man. At first she had thought that he looked classically Latin with his large, aquiline, aristocratic nose and his firm, full lips, his thickly planted hair as tightly curled as that on a Donatello statue. But he burned an energy that was purely twentieth century in its lack of formality, its direct, intent concentration on its object.

Charm, she thought abruptly, is just one of the symptoms of energy.

Vito picked Billy up the next morning. She had been into Cannes before, of course, when she and Ellis owned a villa at Cap-Ferrat, the millionaires' compound near Beaulieu, but she had only dashed into town once or twice to pick up something in one of the branches of the great Paris shops or to buy some of the marrons glacé that Ellis had liked so much. They had used their villa for only a month or so in early spring and late fall, before and after the tourist season, and her strongest memory of Cannes was of a row of huge, rather empty hotels, bordering the wide Corniche, across from a stony beach.

Vito secured a tiny table on the terrace of the Carlton, by the arcane magic of having heavily overtipped the same headwaiter for fifteen years in a row, and let Billy look around. Within a space of a few hundred yards in each direction she saw thousands of people, swarming about in no perceptible pattern, yet each one looking purposeful and hurried. No one glanced at the sea beyond the beach, which was dipping and flirting with the sun. No one looked at the brave display of flags of all nations, which flapped on tall, white flagpoles all along the Croisette. Everywhere there were knots of men, jostled by the impatient crowd, who had stopped, sometimes in the middle of a driveway or on the steps leading to an outdoor terrace, to carry on what looked like deeply complicated conversations. The broad Corniche had become a seemingly permanent wall of unmoving cars, all honking furiously. There was something of the feeling of Grand Central Station at rush hour, something of the feeling of a stadium crowd looking for their seats for the big game of the season, something of the feeling of the floor of the Stock Exchange on a day of heavy trading. All under the bright, calm Mediterranean sky, ignored by the preoccupied throng.

"It's exciting, isn't it?" Vito finally asked.

"Terribly," Billy smiled in agreement. "I had no idea. Tell me, who are all these people—do you know any of them?"

"Some. In fact, too many perhaps. That man over there with the hat on, he's made fifty million dollars making

381

dirty movies in Japan. He's here to find some big-breasted Swedish girls who will agree to have their eyes made Japanese by plastic surgery. Then he will use body makeup and make even better dirty movies with them because he thinks that Japanese girls are too small breasted. The man with him has fifty Swedish girls to sell—they are dickering over the price. The tall, blond woman at that table over there is a man. He is waiting for his lover who is a woman casting director who only likes men in women's clothing. She spends forty thousand dollars a year at Dior to keep him well dressed. The three Arabs behind us are from Kuwait. They have nine hundred million dollars and the dream of establishing a film industry in their country. But nobody wants to go and live there at any price. If they go home without a film industry, they may be killed, so they are getting nervous. They are seriously planning to kidnap Francis Ford Coppola and possibly Stanley Kubrick, but they're not sure they can afford them. The Russians, who are waiting for a table, are trying to induce George Roy Hill to remake *War and Peace* so they can rent him their entire army as extras. But they want it to be set in the future so they can use their air force and their new nuclear subs—"

"Vito!"

"If I told you the truth it would be boring."

"Tell me anyhow." Billy's dark eyes were as flirtatious as the sea.

"Percentages. Pieces of the gross. Pieces of the net. Pieces up front. Pieces deferred. Points and fractions of a point. Film rentals in Turin. Film rentals in Cairo. Film rentals in Detroit, in—"

"I liked it better the other way."

"And yet you strike me as a woman to whom the truth is more seductive than the fake."

"I like to be left with some illusions."

"You'd be a failure in the movie business."

She turned to him, suddenly serious. "Do you know that Susan thinks you're on the verge of becoming a failure? It isn't true, is it?"

"No, I don't think so. I've made twenty-three films and only six have been failures at the box office. Seven that made money weren't critical successes. The other ten were successful both ways. It's a very good record. Right now I owe three hundred thousand dollars and I've had three pictures, one after the other, that didn't show a profit but didn't actually lose money, so I think my luck is due to turn."

"How can you be so cool about it?"

"You can be a silly girl, can't you? If I were worried, I'd get out of this business. It's simple. I'd rather make movies than do anything else in the world. I do it very well. I don't always know what the public wants, so sometimes I lose money. But I can't concern myself only with the public or I'd end up imitating others. For me, the thrill is in creating something that pleases me. That's worth all the struggle. I believe in myself, in my ideas, in my way of working. That's all there is to it."

"Doesn't it bother you to be up one day and down the next? Don't you feel afraid that people might be laughing at you behind your back?"

He looked at her, astonished. "Where do you get these fears? Certainly no one likes to be laughed at, but I don't worry about it. This is a fickle industry. If I weren't willing to take a risk, I'd go back to my father's business and manufacture silverware."

The simplicity of Vito's self-affirmation irritated Billy. She was envious of it.

"You've got a hell of a nerve for a man who's in debt!"

"Said in the true Festival spirit," he laughed. "You're catching the mood. Come on, let's take a walk. There is a prominent member of the New Hollywood waiting for our table so he can buy some cocaine." She looked around, trying to spot another of his jokes.

"But, that's—! Does he, really?"

"Yes. You'll find out—I generally tell the truth."

After lunch in a bistro on a side street, they spent the afternoon wandering around Cannes, poking through the antique shops and the old port, away from the Festival crowds. Later, after Vito had taken Billy back to the Hôtel du Cap to change into an evening gown, they went to the huge Salle des Spectacles to see an English film. The Cannes audience is the most purely vicious since Christians were thrown to the lions. The Leftist press whistles and screams insults. The Free World press screams insults and boos. The Third World press boos, whistles, and screams insults. Every year, by some strange combination of coincidence, a few films appear that do not offend the press of any country. However, they often offend members of the jury, a mini-U.N. with less in common than the real one. The choice of the winning film is rarely popular.

"Did you ever have a film in competition?" Billy asked Vito.

"Yes, in fact twice. Ten years ago I had *Street Lamps*. And three years ago, *Shadows*."

"Oh, I remember them both well, I loved them—*Street Lamps* the most."

"I wish you'd been in that audience. I could hear the tumbrels coming for me."

"As bad as that?"

"Worse. But *Street Lamps* made a lot of money for me later on."

"What happened to your money, Vito?"

"Whenever I had it, I spent it, living well and having a marvelous time. For my sins, I have often invested in my own pictures—unfortunately, they were often the ones that didn't make money. I don't regret a penny—I'll just make more." There was no way to doubt him, Billy thought, no way at all.

After the film, Vito took Billy to a late supper at the Moulin de Mougins, which is given three stars in the *Guide Michelin*.

"The food will be simply awful, so don't expect much," he warned her cheerfully. "During Festival time the chefs lose all their ability, the waiters become more surly than ever, the headwaiters look as if they would like to refuse your tips, though they never go that far, and even good wine turns to vinegar."

"Why on earth?"

"I don't think they approve of movie people."

As Vito drove her back to the hotel, Billy found herself wanting badly to know when she would see him again. Since he didn't say anything, she finally ventured a question.

"Would you like to come out here for lunch tomorrow?"

"Sorry, but I'm going to be busy all day. Two men are arriving here tomorrow and I have to see both of them."

"Oh." Billy couldn't remember a time in her adult life when anyone had refused one of her lunch or dinner invitations. Not since she had married Ellis Ikehorn, and that was fourteen years ago.

"Well, what about the day after?"

"That depends. If I see both of those men tomorrow, I think I can make it. But I won't come here. Susan might join us. She reminds me of the headwaiter at the Moulin de Mougins. I'll take you to the Colombe d'Or. I'll call tomorrow night to let you know if it's on or off." He took it entirely for granted that she wouldn't make any other plans in the meanwhile, she thought wrathfully. Nor would she. Fucking conquistador! That knowledge made her even more angry.

"I may not be here," she lied.

"*Que sera, sera,* as they say in the old country."

"Balls. That song was written for *The Man Who Knew Too Much.*"

"My God! A Doris Day fan!"

"As it happens, yes," she said, caught out.

"Ha! One more thing we have in common. Goodnight, Billy."

"Curt?"

"Oh, shit, Sue, I was almost asleep."

"I'm worried about Billy."

"What now, for Christ's sake?"

"She's spending almost all of her time with Vito Orsini. I haven't laid eyes on her for the last week except when she flies in to change for dinner."

"So what?"

"How can you be so dense? He's after her money, of course."

"So what?"

"Curt!"

"Sue, you're acting like a nervous mother. Billy's old enough to watch out for herself. She needs a good fuck. That's probably all there is to it. And who wouldn't be after her money?"

"You're revoltingly crass. I should have known better than to marry anyone from Bayonne, New Jersey. Mother warned me."

"I think you're the one who needs a good fuck. Good luck. Goodnight, Sue."

"Vito?"

"Yes, darling?" They were lying naked, in tousled splendor, in Vito's bed at the Majestic. Billy could feel her heart expanding. It was as if a small, dry, pale paper flower had been dropped in a bowl of red wine and allowed to soak up as much of the intoxicating liquid as it could hold, until it turned into a great, round, red poppy, moist with morning dew. She was feline and slumberous with direct, most excellent sex.

"Vito, will you please marry me?"

"No, darling, unfortunately no."

"But why not!"

"You have too much money."

"I just knew you'd say that. It's absolutely, totally ridiculous!"

"Not to an Italian."

"You're an American, damn you."

"But I've got Italian ideas, Italian pride. I'd have to be master in my own house. How would that be possible? Even if we signed twenty prenuptial agreements that I would never touch your money, we'd still be living in the style to which you're accustomed, on your money."

"Vito—I can't *stand* not having you!"

" 'Having me'—darling Billy, you even think in the wrong terms. I do love you, which is my problem, not yours, but I don't think of myself as someone you can *acquire.*"

"Why do you put me in the wrong?"

"Because you are. Turn over and kiss me. What are you waiting for? That's better. Much better. You don't have to stop."

Billy wouldn't have stopped even if she could have. She had never been in love like this before. Vito was a blinding encounter. It was utterly different from her youthful dreams of glamour with her French count, an infatuation that was based almost entirely on her own self-discovery. And Ellis, whom she had loved so dearly, had been so protective, so gentle, so much older than she that there had been no bite, no well-matched struggle in that love. It had been like falling into a feather bed. Vito—Vito drove her crazy, as in some witless teen-age song. He wouldn't bend to her will, he wouldn't give an inch on any of his convictions, he saw through her, even worse, he understood her. He was only seven years older than she, but he condescended to treat her like a girl! She bit him. Gently. She knew already that if she bit him too hard he'd bite back.

Vito, staring out to sea while he felt the lovely little nips and nibbles of her inflammatory mouth, was seriously worried. So far he'd managed to conceal his romantic nature from Billy. He'd realized, as soon as he met her, that she was extraordinarily spoiled and would surely take any advantage she could in any game she played. He certainly didn't intend to fall in love with her, but he hadn't been able to prevent it. Her insistent beauty was like a trumpet note, the line of her long throat, the curl of her ear, the heaviness of her hair, the striped irises of her eyes—no woman had ever pleased him so. Still, he might have saved himself if he had not quickly seen through her airs and graces to the lonely woman they concealed. Understanding her had been his greatest mistake because understanding made her vulnerable and, therefore, lovable. She was becoming more and more real every day, less and less the "rich, young widow" of his scenario. His heart felt bruised with tenderness and pity and the reluctant dawning of an imminent recognition. She had the most perfect sensuality he had ever known—no holding back, no modesty, no self-consciousness. They were truly well mated. But she was too rich.

"Vito, what if we just lived together? I wouldn't 'have' you that way—couldn't we—?"

"No, Billy. Anyway, the man is supposed to ask the woman."

"That was fifteen years ago. Now women can ask for what they want and get it."

"Not from me, my darling, not unless I want to give it."

"You're holding back progress." Billy felt suddenly shrill, false. She'd never given a thought to the liberation of women, and now she sounded as if she'd been a dues-paying feminist for years. But better to sound absurd than rejected, better to make a bad joke than to admit how she yearned for him to love her, to marry her, like one of those silly besotted nineteenth-century literary heroines she had always sworn she would never be like, long, long ago.

Curt Arvey, a first-rate son of a bitch, was a man who would go a long way to score a point. He was seriously annoyed with his wife, Susan, with whom he lived in a state of constantly fluctuating weights and balances even when they were getting along without an overt struggle. She had taken the tone that this business of Billy and Orsini was all his fault since he was the one who had thought of inviting Vito to dinner. She was acting as if Orsini were a fortune-hunting gigolo, a not too subtle way of reminding Curt that it had been Susan's money that first got him started. True enough, but it hadn't been her money that got him to the top, not her money that permitted her now to lead the life she led in Beverly Hills, and he'd be damned if he was going to let her tell him whom he should invite to his own dinner parties and whom he shouldn't. Arvey telephoned Vito and asked him to come out to the hotel for a late breakfast.

"The grapevine says you have a new project, Vito. Tell me about it."

"A first novel by a young French girl, another Françoise Sagan, only much better. I optioned it for peanuts. It's a love story about—"

"Another love story? Didn't Mexico cure you of that?"

"Would catching the flu cure you of breathing, Curt? The day people won't go to see a love story—a good one, Curt—is the day the world ends. I have a strong feeling about this book. It's selling fantastically well in France and it's being published in the United States and England —be out this spring."

"Does it need names?"

"It could survive without them—the lovers are very young—it could be brought in for two million two, maybe two million even, depending on where I shoot it. It doesn't have to be set in France; it's a universal story."

"Romeo and Juliet?"

"Yeah. But with a twist—a happy ending."

"Sounds good. Go ahead and talk to our business-affairs people and get the deal worked out."

"Absolutely not, Curt!" Vito went white.

"Why the fuck not!" Curt dropped his napkin in astonishment.

"Billy put you up to this. I'm not about to let a woman finance my pictures—"

"Christ, Vito, you're paranoid! The day *I* let some rich dame give me a couple of million dollars to have *my* studio make a movie that *we* distribute, that I *personally* have given the go-ahead on, that I have to account to my stockholders and board of directors for—that'll be the day! I don't deal that way and you know it—no studio does."

Vito took a deep breath. "According to you, you didn't make money with me on those last two pictures we did together."

"So? We broke even; it helped pay the studio overhead. And we did make money on a lot of dreck I didn't even enjoy making. At least your pictures were the kind I could run in my screening room and feel good about, class product. And where is it written that every picture has to make money? Breaking even isn't as bad as we did with some others. Do you realize how fucking stiff-necked you are, Vito? You should have come to me with this project instead of waiting till I called you."

Arvey was right and Vito knew it. His one major failing as a producer was his deeply ingrained pride. Ideally, a producer of any kind should be eager to do business with Lucifer himself if the Prince of Darkness has money to finance his production, and if he finds Lucifer reluctant, he should return the next week and try again. And again, if necessary. Whether he should also sell his soul is strictly a matter of individual choice. True, he didn't like or trust Arvey, but that should have had nothing to do with his holding back from seeking Arvey's financing. His soul was still his own.

"I'll be in touch with your people as soon as I fly to the coast." Vito's matter-of-fact manner was apology enough.

"Staying till the end of the Festival?"

"Yes—unfinished business."

"I'm glad. But bring it in at one penny over two million two, and I'll have your balls—oh, and Vito, come out here for dinner tonight if you're free. Sue will want to congratulate you. She's going to be tickled pink when she hears the news. She loves a good love story."

As Curt Arvey watched the door close behind Vito, he allowed himself a mighty, malicious, vindictive chuckle. It was easily worth two million two to show that Philadelphia snob he'd married just who was in charge.

As he drove back to Cannes, Vito found himself plunged into an unprecedented bout of introspection. Normally, at a time like this, with the go-ahead finally given for his next picture, one that he had more hopes for than any he had yet produced, he should have been totally engrossed in making mental lists of potential writers and directors. He felt an expansive elation, but the elation seemed to be somehow mixed up with Billy. Yet what had she to do with it?

He was stuck in the prenoon traffic jam outside of Cannes when it finally came to him that the same impulse in him that took a book or an idea and immediately envisioned what it could be as a film also made him want to mold, shape, and change Billy's life. He saw the unhappy girl and wanted to make her into a happy woman. The fact that no one saw the unhappy girl under Billy's facade except himself made the prospect all the more tempting. He was enchanted by her big feet, her long bones. The lusciousness of her body when she took off her ridiculously beautiful clothes astounded him. So much was hidden in her. He wanted to listen forever to the faint Boston accent he thought no one else noticed. He would like to make her pregnant.

If only she were a poor young starlet and he the all-powerful producer who could say "There, that's the girl, that's the one I'll make a star" and change her life—if only, Vito thought to himself, laughing at his potentate fancies, she had been the young Sophia Loren and he Carlo Ponti. Those fantasies had been all right for the young man he used to be, but today he had to deal with facts. With an effort, he turned his mind to the question of the ideal director for his next production.

Billy wandered around the park of the Hôtel du Cap, losing herself in the overgrown paths, avoiding the clearings where she might come upon another guest sunning himself on a bench, prowling through the kitchen garden where flowers for the hotel and vegetables for the restaurant grew in well-tended rows. Everyone was either sleeping late or having breakfast in their rooms. Except for a stray gardener, she had the acres of park to herself. Finally she sat under a tree in the sun-splotched, buzzing green shade, which smelled far different from any American earth, the smell of centuries of civilization she supposed, and tried to think.

She was acting like a love-sick child. Perhaps it was merely sexual. Vito had a knowledge of how to please a woman she had never known in another man. There was such a—she could only think of the word "generosity"— in his lovemaking. In recent years she had become a taker, a commander who told a man exactly what she wanted him to do to her, where and in precisely what manner she wanted him to stimulate her, and for how long, and if he wouldn't or couldn't, she left him flat and found another. She made her demands unconditionally and took her satisfaction as quickly as possible. That was what they were there for, those young male nurses who eventually went their way with such generous bonuses. Whatever happened to them afterward, whatever their private worlds were, Billy never knew or cared to know. To her, although she had never used the words, even to herself, they were male whores. She understood that now, and understood that she had had contempt for them. Did she have contempt for herself, with them? It was something she didn't want to think about.

Oh, but with Vito she didn't even remember her predatory, peremptory ways. She felt as if he were browsing in her, a man enjoying a long, lazy stroll over his beloved property, treasuring everything about her as if the very happiness he gave her made her more precious than she had been before. When she came, he was like a man who had received a priceless gift, yet it was he who had given it. He was so perfectly unhurried. Lying with him, it was always as if they had all the time in the world, no urgency, no pressure, no goal except the moment. He had washed the cynicism out of her and the hardness and left her as soft and helpless and open as—as she had never been since Paris.

Billy stood up, left the shade of her tree, and walked back to the hotel, a golden-white château with tall shutters painted in the palest gray-blue. It wasn't purely sexual and she knew it. Whatever happened, she felt in her bones that Vito was the love of her life. It terrified her.

The last few days of the Cannes Film Festival are like the last few days of college after exams. Everyone whose picture has already been seen leaves town as quickly as possible. Those who remain are aware of a change of mood. The carnival atmosphere melts away as if it had never existed; the press, nursing hangovers and bloat, drifts off; the facades of the hotels regain their dignity as the elaborate advertising signs are removed from them; it becomes possible to find a waiter from whom to order a drink; and the food improves.

Susan Arvey was in a snit. She and Billy should have already left for Paris as they had originally planned before coming to the Festival, but Billy seemed glued to Cap d'Antibes. It was all Vito Orsini's fault. He was still milking his Mexican dog. In an excess of wild energy he had sold it to a dozen foreign countries. With the certainty of seeing his next movie through production, he seemed unable *not* to make a sale, even if he didn't know where the country was located on the map. How he found time to do business while he saw so much of Billy, Susan couldn't imagine, but she was a woman of little imagination to begin with. She did have enough, however, to stop herself from telling Curt what she thought of him for financing Vito's next picture. Anyway, this delay could last only one more day, two at the most.

On the day before the end of the Festival, Vito invited Billy to have lunch with him at La Réserve, in Beaulieu. The restaurant of this small, gem of a hotel is a long, open, shaded marble gallery, decked in pink, facing the ocean, certainly the most elegant outdoor dining room in the world.

As Billy listened to Vito ordering lunch in his fluent Italian, a lunch she didn't want to eat, she realized that, through the screen of her sunglasses, she was observing the scene as if to memorize it for the future. She was trying to photograph Vito, just as he was now, glowing bronze, as Mediterranean as the sea at his back, explaining to the headwaiter with words and gestures that the crayfish should be served with three different kinds of sauces. She was behaving as if the die had been cast and the game had been lost long ago, as if there was nothing for her to do but save her pride by treating the whole episode as just another impulse of a frivolous woman flirting wildly but not seriously, a sensation seeker, a maker of empty, affectionate phrases and promises. She was reducing her emotions to the size they had been stuck at for years, shrinking, diminishing with every minute that passed.

Slowly she took off her sunglasses and put them down on the pink linen tablecloth. She was not going to permit herself this failure of character. She had to risk another rejection, no matter what humiliations it would cost her in the middle of the night for as many years as it took for it to become a memory. She felt obstinate, urgent, awkward —even brutal—and she didn't care.

"Vito." There was a resonance in her voice that made him look up abruptly. "Vito, I don't have the essential argument."

"What are you talking about?"

"I wanted to captivate you with my flexibility, be whatever you wanted in a woman, convince you that you could never let me go, but I was wrong."

"I don't understand, Billy."

"I was wrong, because my money will not go away—I couldn't get rid of it if I wanted to, and I don't."

"I don't blame you."

"No, you can't turn it into a joke with a twist of your voice. I'm rich and I'm going to always be rich. It is very important to me. But it's not fair, is it? If I were a man and you were a woman, and I were rich and you were not, there wouldn't be any problem, would there? We could try, couldn't we, without anyone thinking anything except that it was natural—normal—to be expected?"

He looked at her brave, unbeaten, lyrical eyes and said nothing.

"Vito, I'm sure that there are other men in the world

besides you who can't be bought—but they're not in love with me. You are. You're throwing it away to prove how far you are above temptation. But the whole thing becomes an exercise in useless pride because you won't stop loving me after you've made your gesture. So we're both going to lose, aren't we, for the rest of our lives?"

"Billy—"

"But I told you I didn't have the essential argument, didn't I? It's just such a waste—I hate waste."

"So do I." It went beyond love, Vito thought. It simply *was,* like destiny, like nationality, like inevitability. He put his hands over hers. "I'll give you the essential argument. You must promise never, under any circumstances, to buy me a Rolls-Royce." Billy stood up abruptly. "And," he added, "never to give me a surprise party." Tiny crayfish and wineglasses crashed to the marble floor, skittering in every direction. His words hadn't quite made sense to Billy yet, but her stomach or her heart or whichever part of her it was that knew things before her head was filled with an intimation of happiness. Everyone in the urbane restaurant looked at them, wondering what insult this man could have offered this woman to cause her to advance on him in such an uncivilized manner.

"If you're teasing me, *I'll kill you!*"

"I never joke about family matters." The diners turned back to their plates. Just another pair of lovers it seemed. Surrounded by waiters whisking away the debris, Billy sank back in her chair. She flamed with joy and felt as bashful as a child.

"Just don't say, 'I told you so.' " He traced the outline of her lips with his finger and caught a tear on her cheek before it had time to fall into the herb mayonnaise, the only dish left on the table.

The headwaiter, a hardy Communist from Milan, was thinking that the *poulet à l'estragon* and the lemon soufflé were going to be wasted on these two. On the other hand, he felt assured of a monstrous tip. If only all the lousy capitalists in the world were as much in love, it would be a better world for the working classes.

The cablegram was addressed to Valentine. She tore it open and, after one incredulous look, rushed into the office she shared with Spider and thrust the piece of paper at him. GETTING MARRIED IN A WEEK TO VITO ORSINI. HE'S THE MOST MARVELOUS MAN IN THE WORLD. PLEASE MAKE ME SOMETHING BRIDAL TO WEAR. I'M SO HAPPY I CAN'T BELIEVE IT. LOVE AND KISSES, BILLY.

"Holy shit! I can't believe it either—this doesn't sound like our employer—Valentine, why the hell are you crying?"

"Elliott, you don't know a fucking thing about women!"

Maggie heard the news during a meeting with her head writer.

"Hey, how about that! Maggie, isn't Orsini your buddy, for God's sake. Don't you think you could get an exclusive to cover the wedding? It's the biggest thing of its kind since Cary Grant married Barbara Hutton."

"Oh, shove it up your ass!"

ScruplesS
12

The period of almost eight weeks between the final days of the Cannes Film Festival and the Fourth of July weekend of 1977 was one of settling accounts, in various and different ways, for both Spider and Valentine. For Vito it was a period of renewal, of calling in old markers, of revving up. For Billy it should have been a honeymoon, but, in retrospect, the only honeymoon she and Vito ever had took place during the eleven hours it took their plane to make the polar flight from Orly to Los Angeles International Airport, and at that point they still weren't married.

Valentine had searched for a place to live as soon as she was assured of the future of Scruples. Her one absolute requirement was privacy. She couldn't consider a small house where there might be observant neighbors or an ordinary apartment building where people could come and go at will. She needed a place in which she and Josh Hillman could meet and love in security. It had to be reasonably near Scruples, reasonably near his home, reasonably near his offices in Century City, since the time they spent together was carved out of his busy, public life. Finally, a few blocks east of the border of Beverly Hills, in West Hollywood, she found a penthouse in a splendid, new apartment building in Alta Loma Road. It had the advantages she had been looking for. There was a guard at the desk in the lobby who questioned every visitor. No one could go up in the elevator without being first announced over the house phone, and permission given.

Of course, Valentine reflected, there were bound to be disadvantages. Inescapable walls of glass partly surrounded the living room and the bedroom. If she approached them without mental preparation, she found herself confronted with too vast, too wide, and too high a view of all of West Los Angeles, right out to the horizon of the Pacific Ocean. For a dedicated city rat like Valentine, so much air, so much light, so much space, made her feel like a visitor from another planet. But she was an illusionist, a conjurer of the first water, and when her furniture arrived from New York, the same furniture she had sent ahead of her from Paris more than five years before, Valentine devoted her wistful necromancy to re-creating another atmosphere, another time. This was particularly true at night when she closed her new white wooden shutters, drew her new rose-and-white curtains made from a romantic toile de Jouy, almost a duplicate of the old ones that were now too shabby, and lit her red-shaded lamps. She re-covered her old velvet sofa and deep armchairs in an old-fashioned Boussac print, sprigged in a rustic green-and-white print, which reminded her of Normandy, and covered the floor with her one great extravagance, a beautifully faded, very old, flowered needlepoint rug. The new kitchen was a great improvement on her improvised cooking arrangements in New York. She raided Williams Sonoma in Beverly Hills and made it perfectly French, filled with shining casseroles and earthenware crocks, wire whisks, copper-bottomed pans, and heavy, white pottery dishes banded in blue. Josh, who was frustrated by her independence, showered her with the only kinds of gifts she would accept, plants and lithographs, too many for her limited wall space, so that she had to hang them right up to the ceiling, even in the kitchen.

In spite of the abnormal expanses of glass Valentine was well content with her new home because it served its purpose, and she was certain that no one guessed why she lived where she did. Certainly Billy was too wrapped up in her new marriage to be curious about anyone else's affairs. According to Josh, his wife saw nothing suspicious in the three nights a week he spent with Valentine; the habit of working late during a lifetime had paid off. And as for Elliott—well, that had been a close call, but he had been fooled. On the very night she finally moved in, while she and Josh were tumbled together in her new bed, Elliott had been announced by the man on duty in the lobby. In a panic, Valentine told the guard to say she was already in bed, exhausted, almost asleep, but the next day, at the office, Elliott had looked at her curiously.

"In bed, Valentine, at seven-thirty? And anyway, why couldn't I come on up even if you were in bed? It wouldn't be the first time."

"That's precisely it." Her eyes shot bits of green stone at him. "You treat me without respect. Good old Valentine, let's go and see what she's dishing up for dinner. I am not your seventh sister, Elliott!"

"Aw, Val, you're not fair! That stinks! I never treated you without respect—you're my best friend."

"Don't be absurd." She tossed her small bonfire of curls so that she didn't have to look at Spider's hurt eyes. "Nobody believes that a man and a woman can be just best friends. Do you imagine for a minute that people won't assume I'm just another of your many girls, just another in the famous parade? I refuse to be taken for that, Elliott, especially now when we are practically in each other's pockets as it is—we share an office, even a desk, for heaven's sake."

"An office that I'm almost never in, and you have your studio all to yourself, Valentine. But if you like, I'll find another place for my desk." Spider looked as stunned as if she'd lunged at him with her sketching pencil. "Don't worry—I won't come to see you without an invitation. All I wanted to do was bring you a housewarming present and show you a funny letter I got—my first fan mail."

"Oh, don't be silly, Elliott—just call before you come over, that's all." Valentine retreated hastily from her studied indignation. She had carried it too far. What a baby he was under all that masculine strut. She touched his hand. "I'm sorry—will you still give me my present?"

"Ask your fancy doorman for it—a fucking heavy case of champagne—he helped me lug it all the way to the elevator. Let's hope he doesn't get a thirsty hernia and drink it all up before you get home."

400

"Oh, Elliott, thank you! Come and drink some with me tonight—please?" She tilted her bright head and peered demurely up at him from behind the twin fringes of her eyelashes and her hair. Somewhere, he thought, she's finally learned how to flirt. Bad-tempered bitch.

"If I have time."

"Please try—I want you to see my place. And what was your funny letter about?"

"Oh, it's just from the sexy broad I took free pictures for in New York when I didn't have any other work, remember? She called herself Cotton Candy? She saw a picture of us in *People* last week, that story they did on Scruples, and she recognized me. She wrote that my pictures changed her luck and now she has her own business, thanks to them. She took the best one of all and made it into a sort of calling card—take a look at this! Phone number and all. I should have asked for a percentage of her action."

Valentine took the photograph he handed her and gazed at it, wide-eyed. "Compared to her, I look like a boy. I like your fan mail better than mine. I got a letter from Prince, that bastard, saying how glad he was that I had become such a success. What nerve—Elliott, you *will* come tonight, won't you?"

"Of course I will."

He did, and stayed on for dinner, as he used to, just as she had expected him to, but Valentine knew that the warp and woof of their friendship had changed to make room for the secret of Josh in her life. It was the first thing, except for the facts about Alan Wilton, that she had had to hide from Elliott, and it altered their relationship in subtle ways, making her guarded, tentative, and withdrawn in small matters that she didn't think he'd notice, but which he saw as clearly as he saw the new double bed in her bedroom.

When the evening was over, Valentine felt queerly hollow, unexpectedly depressed. She had to expect it, after all, she told herself with firm logic. One cannot have it all. And what she did have, ah, that was worth giving up a great deal to guard. Valentine gloated over her thoughts of Josh, wrapping her knowledge of his love around her like a snug blanket that she could pull right up over her head if she wanted to. He worried furiously that she might resent the fact that he couldn't dare take her to a really good restaurant because of the risk of being seen together. If they didn't eat at the 94th Aero Squadron or some obscure place in the Valley, Valentine cooked for him in her kitchen. Once a month or so they even managed a weekend together without ever leaving her apartment. He was afraid that she might grow restless, but the very lack of any open arrangement between them suited Valentine perfectly. For the first time in her life, and she was now twenty-five, she was settled with a man, and she felt no need to pin this joy up for public inspection, to make this romance official by telling even one other person. Her love for Josh was all the sweeter for being unknown, like a secret garden blooming away in the middle of a city.

Their only quarrel had been over his offer, his expectation, actually, that he would pay her rent. *"Ah, ça jamais!"* she had shouted in unexpected fury, so surprised by rage that she lapsed into French. "What the hell do you think I am—a kept woman? You do not keep me, like men used to keep their mistresses. I have my independence, my own life. Never mention that again!"

The skin tightened over his high Slavic cheekbones, and he bent his serious head in consternation.

"Valentine, sweet love, I'm so sorry—I've never done anything like this before—I thought—It was unforgivably stupid—" She took his bowed head in her arms and pulled it close, ruffling his short, dark, graying hair with her breath, finally kissing his sad mouth.

"You thought it was the correct thing to do in such circumstances. Do you get these ideas from your law-books? Do they teach the proper conduct of a love affair at Harvard? Where is your sense of romance? They must have left it out of the curriculum, eh? We must make up for that—and quickly."

Several days later, right after she obtained her California driver's license, Valentine, moved by a curiosity she thought she hadn't felt, drove her new, little Renault past Josh Hillman's house on North Roxbury Drive. It was on a corner lot, with high walls, behind which she could see the mesh of a tennis-court fence and the tops of many large trees. The whitewashed brick facade of the huge

402

house spoke of absolutely rock-solid wealth, the hundreds of blooming rosebushes bordering the low wall around the property and the path to the front door spoke of loving maintenance and at least two gardeners. Valentine couldn't connect it with Josh; still less could she connect it with herself. The house had a permanence, a right to be where it was, that was so unquestioned that she couldn't envision the man who was the master of that house living anywhere else.

She roused herself from the memory of the house she had never returned to look at again to thoughts of the weekend to come. It was the Fourth of July and she had been invited to Jacob Lace's great annual party. Billy and Spider had been invited too, but they weren't going. Valentine hadn't been able to resist, even though it meant flying three thousand miles for just a few days. All the world of fashion would be there, and now that she too was an indisputable member of that world, Valentine of Scruples, she wanted to go back to New York and see how it looked to her from the vantage point of a peer.

Since Miss Stella of I. Magnin had retired in November 1976, Valentine was the only designer running a custom-couture operation in any large store in the United States. True, Scruples wasn't a department store (and Bergdorf's in New York was reproducing some custom copies from the Paris collection), but her workrooms, swelled by the addition of many of Miss Stella's former seamstresses, patternmakers, and cutters, bustled with the orders of the many West Coast women to whom ready-to-wear still was three dirty words. Billy had been entirely right about the prestige that expensive custom design would bring to Scruples. And they did much better than break even, thought Valentine gleefully. Thank God she'd held out for a piece of the profits.

Josh was coming with her to Lace's party. Precisely how he was managing it, she didn't ask, what excuses he had made to his wife, she didn't want to know, but he was determined to take her to the party, arguing that in such a large crowd they wouldn't appear to be necessarily together as they would in a restaurant, and there was never any press coverage of Lace's yearly festival.

The only cloud on Valentine's horizon was the prospect

of packing. For a woman whose profession consisted, in part, of totally organizing other women's wardrobes, she found herself in the grip of a doom-laden, nervous constriction when it came to filling a suitcase for herself. Only yesterday she had sent a customer off completely outfitted for a summer that was to span a tour of the Greek Islands, a conference in Oslo, and a semiroyal wedding in London; and Valentine had designed clothes to carry her through it all in splendid style without requiring more than two suitcases. She looked at the dress she had made for herself for Lace's party: a pleated blouse of apple-green chiffon, with an off-the-shoulder neckline and full sleeves, tucked into a vast, poufed skirt of eight separate layers of pale lilac-lawn with a wide, stiff sash of a green velvet the color of her eyes. Very *fête champêtre,* thought Valentine, appalled, but how do you pack it? In its own suitcase, of course, she could imagine Elliott informing her in his new role of fashion dictator.

While Valentine packed, Spider Elliott was feeling sorry for himself for no reason he could imagine, a state of affairs as foreign to him as an outbreak of boils on his ass. He stretched out by his pool with a large Friday-night drink in his hand and decided to change his mood by counting his blessings.

There was his newly rented house, for example. Just around the corner from Doheny Drive, north of Sunset, tucked into an easily missed cul-de-sac, it was an inspiring example of just how superbly a man can arrange to live when he has neither wife nor child to cater to. It had been remodeled by Spider's landlord, a famous director, father of nine, who had taken a vow of non-chaste, non-celibate, bachelorhood immediately after his fifth divorce. This vow, written in his business manager's blood, was symbolized by the large, plant-bordered Jacuzzi in one corner of the two-story living room. Something must have gone wrong, or else exceptionally right, in that Jacuzzi, Spider suspected, because the director was now married again, and his sixth wife refused to live in a house in which she sensed the aura of too much forbidden fun and games.

Fun and games, thought Spider morosely. Did anyone really have fun and games or were they just kidding themselves? He grimly resumed the list of his blessings. Scruples was the hit of the world of retailing and it was largely due to him. Hooray for Billy Ikehorn Orsini, since the store belonged to her. The women of Beverly Hills and places north, south, and east of Beverly Hills were invading Scruples and clamoring for Spider to tell them how to look at themselves with another pair of eyes. He was more important to them than their hairdressers, their house-plant doctors, even their tennis pros. Hooray for the good women of Beverly Hills. Perhaps one day he would become as indispensable as a good analyst or even a plastic surgeon. No, strike the plastic surgeon. His friend Valentine was riding high, coming into her own as a top designer, the talk of *WWD* and *Vogue* and *Bazaar*. Hooray for Valentine O'Neill and her mysterious little secret, whatever it was, and not that he gave a fuck, not even a fart did he give, if she chose to shut herself up in style with as many guards to keep people out as a rock star. Rotten, irritable, chit of a girl, a secretive, cunning French broad. Thank God he hadn't gotten mixed up with her. Another blessing to count.

His phone rang. Spider hurried to answer it. Probably Valentine checking to make sure he was there to mind the store tomorrow while she was in flight, off to show off at Lace's party. But it was his telephone answering service with two messages, which had come in during the day. One was from Melanie Adams saying that she just wanted to say hello, and the second was from Melanie Adams, cancelling the first message. The service was not sure if he wanted the messages or not, so they thought they'd better give him both of them, just in case. Spider hung up. Hooray for them too. Was there no end to his blessings? He was the only man in Hollywood with an efficient answering service.

Melanie Adams. The thought of her didn't lash him anymore. He'd even gone to see her first film, just to make sure. He supposed he should be glad for her—although it seemed as if that were asking a bit much of himself—but she had been born for the camera to make love to. Exquisite though she had been in fashion photos, the genius of cinematographer John Alonzo had doubled her beauty as it captured her grace of movement.

Now, in the last two weeks or so, she had taken to

phoning when he was sure not to be at home, leaving noncommittal little messages with his service and invariably cancelling the messages within an hour. He didn't know what sick, childish game she imagined she was playing, but whatever it was, he was not about to be involved. He had never returned a single call. Was it really only a year since that last Fourth of July, the night they had gone together to Lace's party? It felt like ten years. Spider had been invited to five parties this Fourth of July weekend and he had decided to go to every one of them. If he spent any more time counting his blessings he might decide to drown himself in his blessing of a swimming pool.

The phone rang again. This time he let it ring six times before he finally answered.

"Spider?" There was no mistaking that voice, smoking ice, haunted by the inviting ghost of a lascivious, wickedly prim southern belle. He couldn't answer. "Spider?" she repeated. "Spider, I know it's you and not the service because they always talk to me."

"Hello, Melanie. Good-bye, Melanie."

"Don't hang up! *Please*. Just let me talk to you for a minute. I've been thinking about you for so long, Spider, but I didn't have the nerve to call when you'd be home."

"Why d'ya bother?"

"Oh God, I understand why you sound so unfriendly and you're right. I've never forgiven myself for writing to you that way—"

"Grand."

"No please, let me explain—it was some sort of fear. I didn't really mean what I said—it wasn't true, not at all—but I was so afraid of being tied to you—oh, Spider, I just couldn't handle things, I had to be terrible because I was so scared—"

"Melanie, I really don't care. No harm done. Goodbye."

"*Wait!* Please wait! I need to see you, Spider. You're the only person out here who loved me once and I need to talk to you—I really need to see you."

"What about that Svengali of yours—Wells Cope—doesn't he love you?" Spider damned himself to eternal hellfire for continuing this conversation, but he had never heard that openly begging tone in her voice before; she had always been so unbreakably, eternally distant, beckoning with one hand and pushing him away with the other.

"Wells? Not the way you mean when you use the word love. I'm so lonely, Spider—please, let me see you."

"No, Melanie. It's a lousy idea, an exercise in futility; we have nothing to say to each other."

"Spider, Spider—" She was sobbing openly now. Spider had weaknesses for almost any female characteristic, but none was so strong as his response to an unhappy girl. He had loved Melanie too much once to turn away from her now when she was in some sort of trouble, he told himself, knowing perfectly well that the real reason was not humanitarian but simply that he couldn't resist her.

"I'll be here for the next hour, Melanie. If you want to come over for a few minutes, OK, but that's it. I have to be out at the beach by dinnertime."

"Just tell me how to get there. I'll be right over. Oh, thank you, Spider—" Tears still ran down her face as she finished scribbling down the directions to his house, but as she put down the receiver there was the beginning of a tiny curve of satisfaction on her invaluable mouth.

"Tomorrow," said Vito, with deep satisfaction, "back to work." Billy laughed at his joke. They had arrived at her twelve-acre estate in Holmby Hills the day before and spent most of the time since then sleeping off jet lag. They weren't unpacked yet, at least she wasn't, and, now that she came to think of it, they weren't married either.

"I should have started this morning," he continued, pacing restlessly around the great four-poster, hung with billowing loops of geranium silk, which stood in the center of her thirty-five-foot-square bedroom. "Fucking writers, you can never reach them on Sunday. I know that they all go out in their damn boats just so they can't answer the phone—actually they hate the water, those pricks."

Billy got out of bed and walked, naked, to where he was brooding out of one of the many windows of her magical room, not even seeing the English walled garden below or the shady wilderness beyond with its acres of woodland paths, thick with wild flowers, which led to the greenhouses patterned after the Victorian glasshouses at Kew. She put her hands on his shoulders and stood nipple to nipple, looking into his deepset eyes to where yellow lights were swimming behind his irises. Barefoot, he was only two inches taller than she was and she pretended that they were twins. She rubbed her nose with his nose. How did men with small noses breathe? She inspected him gravely, trying unsuccessfully to disarrange his tight, thick curls.

"You're serious." It wasn't a question.

"I'm behind schedule already, for Christ's sake. It's almost the end of May. I have to start shooting no later than July. So I have only June to get a script, find a director, cast the picture, get the right cameraman—"

"What if you didn't start shooting until September or October. What difference would it make?"

"What difference?" Vito was stunned until he remembered that some people didn't understand everything about making pictures.

"Darling, beautiful Billy, this is a love story I'm making. It has to be out, finished, in time for a Christmas release, not a single day later." She still looked bewildered. "Christmas, Billy, that's when the *kids* are out of high school, home from college, vacation time, everybody goes to the movies. Who goes to see love stories? Kids my sweetheart—young people, the biggest movie audience."

Billy looked wise. "Of course, it makes perfect sense. I should have realized. Well, naturally, Christmas. Vito— what about our wedding? I've planned it for Friday, but if you're going to be so busy—"

"Just tell me where and when. Don't worry—I'll arrange my appointments so that I'll be there in plenty of time, but try to make it after six-thirty, all right, darling?"

In the weeks and months to come, Billy, who now had her first piece of knowledge about the film industry, was to learn a great deal more about it, more, she often thought, than she cared to know.

The French novel, *Les Miroirs de Printemps,* that Vito had optioned he now called *Mirrors*. With the budget of two million two hundred thousand dollars, *Mirrors* would be what is known in the industry as a "small" picture. Such pictures fall in the gray area between the "big" pictures, which cost upwards of eight million dollars and use stars as insurance against failure, insurance that doesn't necessarily work but is deemed necessary nonetheless, and the "exploitation" or "low budget" pictures, which cost well under a million dollars to make and are destined to appeal to some section of the audience that can be counted on to go to a drive-in or a neighborhood house and pay to see movies about car chases, cheerleaders, or vampires.

Characteristically, Vito had become enchanted with a project that went against the grain of the tried, if not true, folkways of the industry. With a budget of just over two million dollars, he couldn't afford stars. Yet the superb quality of the novel and his own dedication to making a fine film out of it demanded that he work with a fine script, a fine director, and a fine cameraman. When Vito Orsini used the word fine, he did so in the same sense that Harry Winston would in describing a diamond. He meant *flawless*.

During the flight back from Paris he had made a short list of the men he wanted: Fifi Hill as director, Sid Amos to write the script, Per Svenberg as cinematographer. Currently Hill was getting four hundred thousand a picture. Amos wouldn't expect to take less than two hundred fifty thousand dollars; Svenberg made five thousand dollars a week and Vito would need him for seven weeks. All together, six hundred and eighty-five thousand dollars of talent. Vito intended to get them for no more than three hundred thousand plus percentages out of his own piece of the eventual profits of the picture. It was time to collect on certain favors, time for fancy footwork, time for Vito Orsini's luck to change if it ever intended to.

Sid Amos, the scriptwriter, phenomenally fast and the ideal writer to adapt a love story, was the first of the three Vito tackled.

"Well, Vito, sure I'd like to help you out. You've done me favors when I needed them most. But, I mean I'm busy, man. My shit-eating agent thinks I'm a two-headed electric typewriter. He's got me working steady for the next three years."

"Sid, I've got the book of the year. I've got Fifi and I've got Svenberg. I'm asking you to tell your agent that you're taking this job because you owe it to yourself. You'll never forgive yourself if somebody else's name is on

Mirrors. The book is a beautiful piece of material, you said so yourself. Naturally, it goes without saying that you'll be paid in cash, right into that Panamanian Company of yours. Seventy-five thousand dollars and you can tell your agent and the IRS that you did it for scale, for an old friend."

"Seventy-five thousand dollars! You're joking. Not nice, Vito."

"And five percent of my share."

"Seven and a half—and I'm only doing it to screw the IRS—and to see the look on my agent's face."

One down—two to go.

Eight years before, unknown and untried, Fifi Hill had been given his first job as a director by Vito. It had been Fifi's first success, and from there he had gone on to many others. But Vito didn't presume merely on gratitude, a condition even more unfashionable in Hollywood than virginity. He knew that Hill had always dreamed of making a picture with Per Svenberg. Vito hadn't even talked to the great cameraman, but he promised Fifi to obtain his services.

"If I can't deliver him, Fifi, we don't have a deal."

"You said a hundred and twenty-five thousand, and what percent was that again, Vito?"

"Ten."

"Twelve and a half—and Svenberg."

Cameramen have a long-standing and well-founded grudge against the movie industry. Svenberg in particular. He was famous only inside the business; although critics vied with each other in comparing his work to Vermeer, to Leonardo, to Rembrandt, no moviegoer, except for the sophisticated film buff, would recognize his name. Vito knew that Svenberg would do almost anything to see his name become famous. He promised the enormously tall Swede that "Director of Photography—Per Svenberg" would appear prominently in every piece of paid newspaper and magazine advertising, every piece of studio promotion and publicity devoted to *Mirrors*—if he worked for two thousand dollars a week. The studio would fight Vito to the last inch on this assurance, which he had no right to give. But nothing comes easy.

At the end of a month of negotiation, Vito felt that the

410

chief elements of his production were finally buttoned down. His own producer's fee had been worked out with the studio. Although he normally would have received, by virtue of his reputation, two hundred and fifty thousand dollars, he was taking only one hundred and fifty thousand because the budget was so small. On one of the memo pads, which were now scattered over Billy's house like too many clues in an insane paper chase, Vito jotted down the approximate figures for the rest of the picture: cast and crew salaries; secretarial services, which would include every last phone call and Xerox copy; rentals; transportation to the location; living expenses there for everybody; sets; wardrobe; makeup; and the most gruesome item of all, studio overhead of 25 percent of the entire budget. In addition there was interest on all money outstanding and, of course, the standard 10 percent of the budget as a contingency in case anything went wrong. Although less than four hundred thousand dollars was devoted to such major items as script, director, producer, and cameraman, he now had a budget swollen to two million dollars, give or take two hundred thousand. In the film business it is almost always give, never take.

It was a budget, Vito decided, he could live with, provided that nothing—absolutely nothing—went wrong.

The question of deciding what to wear to see Spider made Melanie feel more alive than she had since she last stood in front of the camera. She was filled with a surge of erotic excitement at the problem of how to present herself for this confrontation, toward which she had been inching for weeks. She went through her closets in Wells Cope's guest house in a delighted panic, considering and discarding a dozen possibilities, from the obvious nonchalance of jeans to a simple but powerfully seductive short Jean Muir in the most delicate shade of pink. In minutes she found the dress that expressed the way she wanted to look. It was the most innocent of pale blues, batiste, with a deep, round neck and tiny puffed sleeves, tied at the waist with a blue sash. It needed only a sunbonnet to make the illusion complete, but Melanie settled for a blue ribbon in her cinnamon-nutmeg hair. Almost no makeup, bare brown legs and feet in thin, low-heeled sandals and she had completed the effect she had set out to project: unspoiled, childish, almost countrified, and, above all, vulnerable.

As she drove to Spider's house her hands shook on the wheel. At last, something was about to happen.

Melanie Adams's discontent had started again soon after her first picture was completed. All during the making of the picture she had existed in a state of grace. Just to wake up in the morning and know that she would spend the day acting seemed like a benediction. She attributed this newfound ease with herself to the idea that she had been born to be an actress, that she had finally found her métier, that the strange, inexplicable anguish she had felt for so much of her life had simply been her search for her proper work. When the picture was finished, during the traditional wrap party, Melanie stayed in character, still talking with the innocent hesitation and unworldliness of the girl she had played, while all around her, cast and crew members were relaxing into their everyday selves, getting ready to put the picture behind them.

The next morning she woke up to desolation. There was no studio to go to, no makeup people and wardrobe people waiting for her to appear, no director to confer with, no camera to establish her existence. Wells Cope told her it was a perfectly natural reaction, the letdown that comes after any sustained creative effort has been completed. All actors and actresses go through this, he assured her, but it passes quickly; normal life can be resumed until the next picture comes along.

"When will it start—my next picture?"

"Melanie, Melanie, be reasonable. I've still got months of post-production work on this picture before it's finished. And even when it's all done, I don't plan to release it until exactly the right time, until the right theaters are available. I'm not running a Melanie Adams film factory, you know. The whole point is to use you in such a way that you become a great star—and you're not there yet by a long shot. It'll take a careful, controlled buildup. I don't intend to flood the market with you. No, your next picture can't start until I've found the perfect property. I'm looking, I'm reading galleys and scripts every day, but there is nothing even faintly right available at the moment. Why are you so impatient? You should use this time between pictures to enjoy yourself—eat lunch with friends, play tennis, maybe take a dance class, buy some clothes. You're studying with David Walker—that should be enough to keep you busy, darling." He turned back to the pile of scripts by the side of his chair.

Although Wells Cope entertained frequently and any of the women in his carefully culled circle of friends would have been delighted to lunch with Melanie, she never telephoned them. Woman-talk had never interested her, even in high school. She had no talent for intimacy, even superficial intimacy. Her life was reduced to studying with her drama coach, who no longer could spare her more than two hours a day, taking a modern-dance class, and waiting. Everything would change, everything would begin to happen for her, she promised herself, when her picture was released, not really sure what she meant by "everything," except that she had come so far, so rapidly, that some wonderful change must be in store for her.

When Melanie's picture came out in the early spring of 1977, not a single critic failed to fall in love with her. There had not been such a personal triumph for an unknown in many years. Five of the most important critics in the United States were not amused to find that four of their detested colleagues also thought that Melanie Adams was "The New Garbo." She read the reviews in a burst of glory. Wells Cope gave a thrilling dinner party. Nothing changed. There were dozens of messages of congratulations from people she had known in the past. She reread the reviews from all over the country. But nothing changed.

"But what did you expect?" Wells asked in mild exasperation, the strongest emotion he permitted himself outside of the cutting room. "It wasn't a coronation, just the first step in your career. It's business as usual out here for someone like you who makes her first mark. If you want to feel that your life has changed, go back to New York and visit the girls at Eileen Ford's or, better yet, go home and visit your parents—they'll treat you like a celebrity in Louisville, but here? All you'll get are requests for interviews—and maybe somebody will recognize you in the street or in a store, but otherwise—you're just the new girl in town, Melanie. What did you imagine actresses do between pictures? The best of them? They wait and they take classes. If they're married they can fix up the house or be with the kids, and wait. If they're on television they can do game shows and wait."

"I can always take up needlepoint," Melanie muttered, tears of chagrin and deception in her eyes.

"Good thinking, you're on the right track," said Wells absent-mindedly, turning back to his open script.

Melanie ran her film dozens of times in Wells's projection room. Now that she wasn't before a camera, the woman she saw on screen could have been another actress. She couldn't merge again into that figure on the screen. She found herself still sitting in the projection room, just Melanie being—what? She began searching her eyes in the mirror again. More and more often she fell into daydreams of being another. She wished she had been born looking like Glenda Jackson. Melanie was sure that she would have become totally *there*, a complete person, strong and arrogant and absolute, if only she had had to build herself up from scratch, had to overcome bad skin and an ugly body. If she looked like Glenda Jackson, she would know who she was.

The failure of her first film to fill the inchoate, questing need she had harbored all her life made Melanie more greedy than ever to see what she could get from other people. Trying to manipulate Wells was hopeless. No matter what she did or said, he was endlessly patient with her. It was his form of love, but their sex life, as elegant as a saraband, which had first been so soothing, and his lack of curiosity about her began to make her feel that she existed less and less.

It was then that she started to make tentative phone calls to Spider. His remembered passion, so insistent, so probing, so demanding, began to seem like an answer to her questions. Spider had never let up on her, never stopped trying to find out who she was. Perhaps, this time he could tell her.

Her timid knock sounded twice on Spider's door before he brought himself to open it. Melanie stood there, innocently proffering her towering beauty, waiting, eyes downcast, for him to invite her in.

"Oh, cut out the nonsense, Melanie," Spider said

414

roughly. "Don't act as if I intended to bar the door in your face. Come on in—we have time for a quick drink."

"Spider, Spider, you sound so different," she said. He had forgotten the sweetly painful impact of her voice. Possession of a voice like that, he thought savagely, should be limited by law to ugly women. He gave her a vodka and tonic, automatically remembering what she drank, and motioned to the far end of the long couch in his spare, white living room. Surrounded by a landslide of objects all day, Spider chose to live in as empty a space as possible. He pulled up a canvas folding chair just far enough away from Melanie to esablish an uncomfortable distance between them. She moved considerably closer on the couch. Short of moving his chair again, Spider was locked into position. He waited in silence.

"Thank you for letting me come over—" her voice trailed off. "I had to see you, Spider—maybe you can explain things to me."

"Explain!"

"I'm so confused about things—and you used to ask me all kinds of questions about myself—maybe you could figure out what's going on."

"Lady, you've come to the wrong place. Go to couch canyon over on Bedford Drive and you'll find dozens of good men who have trained for years for the chance to help you find out what the fuck is wrong with you, but I'm not an analyst, and I'm not about to start practice now. If you need advice on your wardrobe I'll be glad to help, but otherwise, you're on your own."

"Spider, you were never cruel."

"And you?"

"I know." She was silent, looking gravely at him with no hint of plea in her eyes, an absence of coaxing, which in itself was consummate artistry. The silence lengthened. She refused, mutely, to play on his emotions with words. She knew she didn't have to.

"Ah, shit! What's the problem? Wells Cope? Your career?"

"No—no—not really. He's as good to me as he could be to anyone and he's looking for another property for me as hard as he can—I can't complain about that. It's just that nothing seems to have turned out the way I thought it would. Spider, I'm not happy." She said the last three words in genuine astonishment, as if she were just discovering the fact for herself, putting words to her feelings for the first time.

"And you expect me to tell you why you're not happy," Spider said flatly, finishing her thought.

"Yes."

"Why me?"

"We were happy once—I thought you'd remember why." She was simple, sad, wondering, denuded of her mystery, a state that she conveyed as if it were a last surrender.

"I know why I was happy then, Melanie, but I was never sure about you." Spider's voice was harsh. He didn't want a victory now.

"Oh, yes—I *was*. And then I was happy again when I came out here and happy while I was working and then—I wasn't happy anymore."

"And now you think you can come back to me and feel happy again, is that it, Melanie?" She nodded her head shyly. "It doesn't work that way—don't you even know that?"

"But, it could! I'm sure it could. Oh, I'm not a simpleton; I've heard all that stuff about you can't go home again, but I don't believe that it is true for everybody—we might be different. I've changed, Spider, I've grown up, I think; I'm not the same person—you're the only one I've ever felt—*connected* with. Please, please!"

"I'm going to be late for my dinner party, Melanie." She rose from the couch and walked toward him. He remained seated in his chair. She knelt down on the bare floor and clasped his legs in her arms, resting her chin on his knees like a weary child.

"Just let me stay like this for a minute—then I'll go," she whispered in a diminished voice. "Oh, it feels so good to be close to you again, just touching you, just being close—it's almost enough." She lifted her head from his knees and looked into his eyes. "Please?"

"Christ!" Spider picked her up and carried her into the bedroom. As he undressed her, she covered him with hasty kisses on any part of him she could reach, as if she were

416

afraid he might change his mind. As she felt his hands on her naked body, his lips searching all the places he had loved, she moaned aloud with pleasure; as she felt his mouth warm between her thighs she said "Good—good—good" between clenched teeth, and when he entered her, she sighed with fulfillment, her body following his every step of the way. When it was over, they lay together for an exhausted moment before Spider abruptly pushed himself away and sat on the edge of the bed, contemplating Melanie who was sprawled in abandonment. Lazily, she turned and focused on him with a satisfied smile.

"Ah, that was *so* good—God, I feel marvelous all over." She wriggled her toes and stretched her arms over her head and gave a deep groan of relief. Spider was certain that this time she wasn't acting. He was too familiar with the after-aura of a sexually pleased woman to make a mistake. Her smile deepened into triumph as she put out her hand to caress his bare chest. "I knew it—I was sure—see, wasn't I right? We *can* love each other again."

"Feel happy now?"

"Terribly happy, darling. Darling Spider."

"I don't."

"What!"

"I feel about as happy as if I'd had a good massage. My cock is saying thank you, but *happy*—happy in my heart—no. It was the words without the music, Melanie." He tightened his hand over hers when he saw the look of fear cancel her smile. "I'm sorry, sweet girl, but I just feel empty, empty and sad."

"But how can you when you've made *me* feel so happy?" Her plaintive voice was the most genuine note he'd ever heard come from her lips since he'd met her.

"That isn't good enough for me anymore. Melanie, you don't love me, you just want me to love you."

"No, Spider, I swear it—I do love you—honestly!"

"If you did, I wouldn't feel this sadness, this emptiness. When my gut talks, I listen. You love the way I make you feel good, you love the way you walked in here and seduced me, you love the attention, the stroking, the listening, the questions, the talking about Melanie and what isn't working in her life. But love me? Why, you never even asked how I was. You love what you can take, not what you can give. Look, maybe you really wish you could love me, but it won't work."

"How can I convince you—what can I say—how can I make you believe—"

"You can't. Don't be sad, darling, but you just can't."

She looked at him and she saw that he knew more about her than she did. She needed that knowledge, wanted it for herself.

"*Spider*—"

"Give it up, Melanie. It's not going to be." His voice was implacable, disengaged. Worst of all, it was frankly relieved. Even Melanie could recognize defeat when she saw it, for the first time in her life. The light in her eyes faded as abruptly as a television set being turned off.

"But, but—oh, Spider, what am I going to do now?" she wailed.

He touched the curve from her ear to her chin with a finger so impersonal that it was more final than a blow.

"Go on home, Melanie. Something's sure to turn up for the most beautiful girl in the world."

"A hell of a lot of good that does me!"

"Don't knock it, baby, don't knock it."

Jacob Lace's party was in full swing by the time Josh and Valentine arrived. She had deliberately planned for them to get there rather late in the evening so they wouldn't be conspicuous. Lost in the crowd, they walked across the rolling green lawns, reveling in the unaccustomed sensation of being out together in public.

But they hardly went unremarked. Valentine, with her air of a young sorceress surveying her rightful domain, her light, dancing step, and her shamelessly romantic dress, looked as if all she needed to be declared Titania, Queen of the Fairies, was a little wand with a star sparkling on its tip. Josh, who was accustomed to a Valentine contained within four walls, cooking dinner, drinking wine, and making love, could hardly believe she was the same person who now passed in the midst of hundreds of celebrated and distinguished people with as much aplomb as if she had been born on center stage.

A short man detached himself from a crowd and ran up to them, throwing his arms around Valentine without a glance at Josh.

"Jimbo!" She laughed in delight.

"I should spank you, that's what I should do, you sexy, crafty slut." She just laughed harder, running her fingers through the stranger's hair, while Josh watched, not believing that anyone in the world could talk to her like that. "We've all missed you like crazy, Prince most of all, no, *me* most of all—how dare you run off just to become rich and famous? I may never forgive you. Where's your gratitude, you wench? Did I ever get even a Christmas card?"

"Jimbo, I never forgot you—but things were busy—oh, as if you don't know! This is Josh Hillman. Josh, Jimbo Lombardi is one of my former playmates, a very naughty one I'm afraid." The two men shook hands awkwardly. Valentine still clung to Jimbo's arm. "Tell me what you've been up to, you evil creature. Who have you corrupted lately?"

"As a matter of fact—"

"Tell!"

"Well—they say all the big trends start out on the Coast, but this time I think New York's first and I'm numero uno in New York."

"Stop being so mysterious," she teased.

"Beautiful young married things." Jimbo cocked his head at her in pride. "Almost newlyweds."

"Jimbo—that *is* wicked," Valentine said mockingly. "What do you do, lurk outside the church steps and lure them away?"

"Certainly not, Valentine, how gross of you. I wait till the first anniversary, my dear, it's the least one can do, and then—well, all I can tell you is you'd be surprised at how easy it is."

"Oh, no I wouldn't. And what happens to the poor brides?"

"Oddly enough, they're mostly so thrilled to be included in Prince's parties that they couldn't care less. Oh, they find ways to amuse themselves, I dare say. It's great fun and you're missing it all."

"How does Prince feel about your branching out?"

"Heavens, sweetie, Prince and I are as good as married! You know that—he's got me for life—the details don't bother him. Prince doesn't believe in a tight rein."

"He certainly kept me on one," Valentine said lightly but still resentfully.

"But darling Valentine, that was business! Listen, he's somewhere around and he'll be devastated if he doesn't see you. I'm going to find him and tell him you're here and we'll track you down later." He darted off with another kiss for Valentine and a wave at Josh.

"What was *that?*" Josh asked, nonplussed.

"Just an old buddy. Really a marvelous friend. You just have to get to know him, darling."

"I hardly think that's in the cards."

"Now, don't be stuffy, everyone can't be a lawyer." Valentine was flushed with the pleasure of seeing Jimbo again; she'd always enjoyed his banter and his seductive ways and his immediate championship of her in Prince's circle. "Actually, Jimbo was a very brave soldier, tons of medals from Korea. And straight too, at the time, I mean. He tells the drollest story I've ever heard about how he was seduced on his hospital bed when he was in traction, absolutely helpless to defend himself, an orderly I believe it was, or maybe a doctor. That's what started him on his merry way."

"I'll bet," Josh said, trying to keep the grumpiness out of his voice.

Half an hour later, as they were waiting for the bartender to make their drinks at one of the pavilions scattered over the grounds of Lace's estate, Josh stiffened in anticipation as an impressively handsome man caught sight of Valentine and obviously recognized her. He had half turned away, as if he wanted to avoid her, when she called out to him imperiously, "And how are you, Alan?" He turned back and advanced with a tentative smile. "Josh, this is Alan Wilton, who was my first employer on Seventh Avenue. Alan, Josh is a friend of mine from California."

"Yes," Wilton said nervously, "I've been reading all about you, Valentine. It's the most marvelous success. I'm absolutely delighted for you and not a bit surprised. You were always going to be a great designer; it was just a matter of time."

"Tell me, Alan," Valentine purred, "how is your little friend, Sergio? Is he still with you, still doing just exactly what you want him to do, still taking orders—or is he still *giving* them, Alan? Didn't you bring him tonight? No? Not invited? A shame, such a very beautiful, such a very alluring boy, Sergio—in fact, quite irresistible, don't you think so, Alan?"

Josh watched, uncomprehendingly, as the stranger turned a dark red under his smooth olive skin. "Valentine—" Alan said pleadingly.

"Well, Alan, is Sergio still with you or not?" Josh had never heard such frozen wire in her voice.

"He still works for me, yes."

"How wonderful a thing faithful service can be, can it not? And loyalty, and honesty—my, Alan, you are a lucky man. As a matter of fact, I already knew the answer to my question—I've seen your new line and Sergio is still using my old designs. Isn't it time for a change, Alan, or has he become too—indispensable? Perhaps you find you can't do without him, is that it? What a thin line separates the master from the servant—or should I say the slave? I've often reflected on that. Have you, Alan?" Valentine turned away from him, took Josh's arm and walked away quickly, shaking with some emotion Josh couldn't understand.

"What was that all about, for God's sake?"

"That lousy faggot!"

"I don't get it—you love Jimbo, you hate that guy—it's crazy."

"Don't ask me to explain, Josh. It's too complicated." Valentine took a deep breath and shook her tumble of paprika curls as if she were putting the whole incident behind her. "Come on, I see some people I want you to meet—there's Prince and his gang—observe the Vivid People, darling; we don't have anything quite like them out in Beverly Hills, some pallid imitations but nothing really close." She drew radiance around her like a veil of light and advanced on a group of excruciatingly fashionable people, all of whom, Josh saw, as he hung back slightly, were greeting her with the kind of acclamation usually reserved for presidential candidates and Oscar winners. As Josh reluctantly approached, at Valentine's urgent signal, he heard a man who looked signorial and tweedy, even in his dinner jacket, saying to her as he held both her hands in his, "—so you see, Valentine my dear, you owe it all to me—if I hadn't fired you, like a blithering idiot, you'd still be working for me instead of being the biggest new star in fashion."

"Oh, no Prince, don't fool yourself," Valentine told him with absolute sureness, "I would have found a way to get there, even without your lack of manners." And she kissed him forgivingly.

Prince looked with interest at Josh when Valentine introduced them. "So this is your California beau, my pet?"

"Oh, Prince, you are too silly. Mr. Hillman is my lawyer. I brought him along for protection against all my old friends."

"Hillman, of course—Josh Hillman. How foolish of me." He turned to Josh with speculation alive in his eyes. "Your wife, Joanne, is one of my most adored customers— Joanne and I go way back, Mr. Hillman, as you would know if you remember paying my bills. A lovely, gracious lady. Please kiss her for me when you get back to Los Angeles."

"I won't forget, Mr. ah, Prince," Josh said.

"Just Prince, Mr. Hillman, just Prince," he said with a chuckle worthy of Henry VIII.

Smoothly, Valentine extricated them from Prince's circle and turned a white, concerned face to Josh, her eyes filled with alarm.

"Good God, I never thought—and Prince will tell her every detail, you can count on that—I know him too well to think he'd pass up that opportunity. Maybe if I talk to him—"

"Absolutely not," Josh answered. "It would only make everything obvious. He's not sure of anything now, but if you talked to him, he'd know. After all, a lawyer can be seen in public with a client. Don't give it another thought, darling, it's not important."

Shaking, she tugged his arm and led him into the cover of some trees. "Oh, Josh, it was a mistake for you to come. I'm terribly worried."

"Don't be. I promise you. You're much too beautiful

to worry. You'll spoil the party—tonight you're an Irish witch and you're wasting that marvelous dress here in the shadows. Let's dance. No? Well, if you won't dance, we'll just stay under the trees and neck." He grabbed her and kissed her until he could feel her relaxing and beginning to respond in spite of the shock Prince had given her. "That's better, my darling. *Now,* we'll dance." And Josh whirled her off onto the dance floor, crowded with beautiful women, not one of whom could outshine Valentine on this night of triumph.

Near dawn, when they returned at last to their hotel suite, Valentine fell asleep immediately. Josh Hillman sat by the window and watched the sun come up, something he hadn't done since his law-school days after a night of study. He was thinking about the new Valentine who had been revealed to him that night, a Valentine who could be caustic, gracious, vicious, teasing, and loving, all in the passage of a half hour, a Valentine who could take care of herself in any encounter, who could match wits and spirit with kinds of people Josh had known existed but had never dealt with himself, a Valentine who was perfectly at home in the most smotheringly grand gathering he had ever seen in one place, a Valentine whom these same people treated as a heroine. He realized that of all the emotions he had felt last night, alarm and resentment had played a large part, as he saw Valentine slipping away from him into a world, a role, a position she had never prepared him for. It was like a magician's trick and, proud as he was of her, he didn't like it one bit.

Over the course of time since Valentine had returned from her first trip to England, Josh Hillman had occasionally, in his dispassionate legal way, considered that he had arrived at a perfect balance in his life. He had it all: the position of sage and brilliant man of law in his firm; a rock-solid place in the power structure of his community; a wife who ran half the charities in Los Angeles and managed to be a good mother and superb hostess; and to cap it all off, Valentine, who provided the romance he had never had before and who was so fiercely independent that she wanted nothing from him.

Now, looking out over the towers of New York, Josh

Hillman cast a long view over his ideal life and asked himself a most uncharacteristic question: Why had he rocked the boat?

He had known, from the day Valentine told him that she was going to Lace's party, that it was impossible for him to go without meeting at least one person he knew. At a certain level of achievement people tend to know each other anywhere in the world. He had set himself up to be discovered. Therefore, it followed that he had wanted to be discovered. Yet he was not a self-destructive man. On the contrary, he had led a constructive life for forty years, a life carefully, cautiously, *seriously* planned to get him all the goods and benefits a sensible man could possibly want for himself. He was the most sensible man he knew.

Wearily, Josh Hillman concluded that no man could live an entirely sensible life and have any self-respect left. He felt a lot of tumblers falling into place in his mind. Having arrived at some conclusion, whatever it meant, he felt an overwhelming need for sleep, a need not to carry his train of thought any further. It was quite enough novelty for one night for a man to see clearly that he is no longer the man he had always thought he was.

Again, Valentine and Josh had planned to take separate flights back to Los Angeles so as not to be caught arriving together. The morning after the party, Josh changed his ticket so that he would be on Valentine's flight, explaining that no one was meeting him at the airport because he had just telephoned his family to warn them that he didn't know when, precisely, he'd get back.

There is no other intimacy so heady as that special quality that two people feel sitting together and drinking champagne in a first-class lounge thirty thousand feet above the ground. There is a particular quality about being literally out of touch with the earth and the people on it that creates a timelessness and a euphoria that adds an extra dimension even to the closeness of people who feel close under normal circumstances. Valentine was sitting next to the window, going over in her mind some of the more delectable moments of Lace's party, when Josh broke into her reverie.

"Stop dreaming, darling, and listen to me." Valentine

turned to pay attention to him, but her mind was still on the party. "I have something to say to you," Josh said, taking her hand in his. "I want us to be married."

"Oh, no!" Valentine, no less than Josh, was stunned by the violence and immediacy of her response. Unexpected as his words had been, her answer had come instantaneously. "You can't be serious; it's *impossible!*"

"It's not at all impossible. I've been thinking about it for months; I just didn't know I was. I only realized it last night."

"No, Josh, no, it's absolutely crazy. You're just in a good mood because there aren't any telephones in this plane. What a folly!"

"It has nothing to do with that, darling. I'm not the kind of man who goes in for follies, now am I?" She looked at him with anger now added to her earlier surprise.

"Even the most reasonable man has his insane moments," she snapped. "Josh, you know it's impossible. I don't even want to discuss it. I'm perfectly content with the way things are. We have each other—why should you ruin your life, your wife's life, your children's lives?"

"Christ, you're more conventional than I am. 'Ruin my life'—do you think a divorce would ruin my life? It's a common, everyday occurrence, happens to the best people. The only thing that would ruin my life would be to spend the rest of it without you."

"How can you be so selfish? What about your wife? You've been married nineteen years! She loves you, she must!"

"I think that if she had to choose between me and the Music Center, oh, with maybe Cedars-Sinai thrown in, she'd take them and let me go. It's been years since we've had a good life together, you know that. If I'd loved my wife, I could never have fallen in love with you the minute you walked into my office. I would just have thought, what a peppery, cute little thing you were and forgotten you." Valentine was entirely unpersuaded.

"And your children? *Three* children. You can really think of—even consider—getting a divorce with three children?"

"That's the worst part of it, I admit. But look, Valentine, they grew up in a very secure home, they're good kids, they're formed already, they've passed the most vulnerable stages of their lives; I can't live the rest of my life without you just because of teenagers. In six years they'll all be finished with college and going their own ways—why, in only two years they'll all be in college and only home for vacations anyway. And Joanne is still young enough and attractive enough to remarry." Valentine considered his reasoning for a moment, her anger fading but her unwillingness as strong as ever.

"No, it's impossible. I would be in such a false position, they would hate me; people—people would say—oh, I can't bear to think about it."

"That wouldn't last more than eight days, my darling, and you know it. We live in Beverly Hills, not in some English village in the Victorian Era. You're being upset about things that don't have any real meaning when you compare them to our being able to live together for the rest of our lives."

"But what about me? What if I wanted to have children? You already have a family, all grown up. Don't you see?" she cried querulously.

"I'd like to knock you up tomorrow. You can have all the children you want as far as I'm concerned. I happen to love babies—I just never told you that about me." He grinned. "It's my secret vice."

"And my career, it's just getting started, Josh. I have to work all day, even Saturdays. I couldn't run a house the way your wife—"

"Dopey, darling Valentine. You're talking nonsense. Look, you can have as many kids as you can manage *and* your career *and* all the servants you need to run a house *and* I don't want a big establishment anyway. Valentine, don't you love me enough? Is that what this is all about?" She shook her head in negation and turned her eyes away from his probing gaze.

"You're too much the lawyer, Josh; I can't explain it logically. It's too big an idea. We were having such a wonderful love—now everything has to go Boom! and all the lives get rearranged and everybody changes places, all because you want to get married. It's just not—*comme il faut.*"

Josh smiled with relief and indulgence. He'd been carrying this idea in his subconscious for so long that he hadn't realized how surprised, how actually shocked, Valentine would be. She was, after all, the product of a culture that didn't take marriage or divorce lightly. Nor did he for that matter.

"Listen, darling, if you won't say yes and you won't say no, can you give me a definite maybe?"

Unwillingly, but unable to maintain her position entirely, Valentine said, "Only an *indefinite maybe,* and that is absolutely *all*. Please, Josh, I warn you, don't think it's more because it isn't. And don't make any plans that involve me and don't speak to anyone, *anyone*—or I will say no, I promise you. I won't be rushed into anything, I won't be pressured, I won't make any decisions until I'm ready."

"It's harder to negotiate a deal with you than with Louis B. Mayer. And he's dead. OK, we'll start with an indefinite maybe and I'll see if I can improve my position."

His legal mind was already busy with plans to get a divorce from Joanne with the minimum of recrimination, the maximum of dignity, and the least loss of community property. Josh Hillman was reasonably sure that any kind of "maybe" from Valentine would eventually become a "yes."

Vito and Fifi Hill set about casting *Mirrors* with the special gusto and sense of playing God that comes from a budget that doesn't allow for star salaries. Denied the crutch of a star, they could browse majestically through the hundreds of working actors—not to speak of the many thousands of nonworking actors—picking, considering, rejecting, reconsidering, putting together combinations of players, taking the combinations apart, all with a kind of innocently arrogant delight that would totally disappear once they had made their choices and had to live with them.

Well before the Fourth of July the three most important parts in *Mirrors* were cast, those of the two lovers and a third part, that of a girl who is a friend to both the lovers. This last part, essentially a strong supporting role, was filled by a girl name Dolly Moon. Two years before she had been a regular member of the cast of one of those summer replacement television shows that lean heavily on the brand of humor known as "zany," consisting largely of sight gags and the sight of appealing people making cheerful fools of themselves. Dolly Moon had caught the nation's fancy for a few weeks with her distinctive laugh, a cross between a gurgle, a yodel, and a whinny; which invariably greeted her good-natured acceptance of the witless humiliations the show's scriptwriters visited on her each week. She possessed the rare and particular beauty of a born comic actress and no one who saw her ever forgot what she looked like: gawky, stubbornly silly, brave, and unsinkable; her too big eyes always amazed by events; her too big mouth always ready to smile; her too big bottom and her too big breasts seeming to make her more vulnerable to the thinly veiled sneers of the writers.

That particular show had never been renewed, but following it, she had made one unimportant movie, playing a pea-brained secretary, and stolen the picture. However, before she could capitalize on this early success she had fallen in love with a rodeo rider and disappeared, to her agent's disgust, to follow the rodeo circuit. Vito had seen her in that one film, and with his memory for an interesting face, he had tracked her down and found her back in Los Angeles, finished with rodeos forever and out of work.

The two lovers were going to be played by Sandra Simon and Hugh Kennedy. Sandra Simon was a nineteen-year-old actress of fluid grace and a waiflike, poignant charm. She was currently starring in an enormously popular soap opera, and her agent had had the utmost difficulty in getting her written out of the script for seven weeks so she could work for Vito, but she was intent on moving from television to motion pictures and she finally had her way.

Hugh Kennedy had graduated from the Yale Drama School and done a lot of little-theater work before he landed his first movie role in a minor costume epic. Vito, who made it his business to see as many films as he could, sometimes as many as three a day, had noticed that, in spite of his turban and false moustache, Kennedy had romantic good looks of a contemporary masculine type, which seems to have all but vanished from the screen, to the dismay of female filmgoers.

Before June came to an end, these three principal players and almost all the smaller parts had been cast. Sid

Amos, working at his top speed, had delivered three quarters of a script, which was even better than Vito had hoped for, and the rest of it was promised for the following week. The frenetic pace of the past weeks had left Vito rejoicing and expectant. The last thing he wanted was a free Saturday, but after trying, unsuccessfully, to make a dozen phone calls, he bowed to the inevitable and spent a few hours relaxing with Billy.

"Know what I'm going to do?" he asked her.

"Call Tokyo?"

"Take you to dinner. You deserve it, a great, big, gorgeous, cunty girl like you. A romantic dinner—pasta!"

"Wow," said Billy. Her sarcasm was wasted on Vito, who had eaten dinner at home with a phone by his side ever since they'd been married. When they came home from Cannes he had had three separate telephone lines installed in the bedroom, his bathroom, his dressing room, the library, the dining room, the living room, and the pool house. These twenty-one phones, each of which had its own extra-long cord, were for Vito's use only, since he had a distrust of hold buttons and liked to keep his separate conversations going on separate lines entirely. Otherwise, he hadn't made any changes in Billy's weathered, timbered English manor house, which had been built and lived in continuously by one family since the early 1920s on twelve acres that were the last of the original Spanish land grant of the Rancho San José de Buenos Aires. She had paid two and a half million dollars for it in 1975 and put almost another million into remodeling and redecorating the thirty-six-room house, which now had only twenty rooms, twenty perfectly voluptuous rooms, full of treasure and comfort, rooms which, having made his decision to marry Billy in spite of her money, Vito thoroughly enjoyed between phone calls and business meetings.

"Let's go to the Boutique," he said. "We can probably get a reservation if we try now. Why don't you call Adolph and get a table for eight-thirty?"

"If you want a romantic evening," said Billy tartly, "why don't you start by calling Adolph yourself?"

The Boutique of La Scala Restaurant is owned by Jean Leon, who also owns the more costly and elaborate La Scala, which shares the same kitchen, but the Boutique attracts the prettiest girls and the most interesting-looking men in Beverly Hills. La Scala is just another good, expensive Italian restaurant; the Boutique is a way of life. It is the only restaurant in Beverly Hills that would feel totally right in New York City. It opens at twenty minutes before noon for lunch, for which it does not accept reservations, and five minutes later every one of its seven booths and fifteen tables is filled, with a line of people waiting at the bar, cursing themselves for having once again imagined that the place couldn't possibly be that crowded so early. At three in the afternoon on a Saturday there are still people waiting to eat lunch. The Boutique's windows, which look out on busy Beverly Drive, are filled with boxes of rare brands of pasta and bottles of imported olive oil, packages of breadsticks, jars of olives, anchovies, pimientos, and artichoke hearts. There are flasks of Chianti hanging from the ceiling, wine racks rising to meet them, and, in one corner, an open delicatessen counter at which Adolph, who is the headwaiter at night, chops a special salad at lunchtime, so that the hubbub of conversation, surprisingly urbane and electric for southern California, is constantly punctuated by the sound of his knife. It is crowded, inconvenient and noisy, and nobody cares. At night the Boutique accepts reservations and becomes relatively peaceful and intimate in a hole-in-the-corner way that most California restaurants, with their vast open spaces, never achieve. But if people don't arrive on time, Adolph may still give away their table.

Vito and Billy were being led to the very best booth when Vito spotted Maggie MacGregor and a young man seated at one of the small tables in the center of the room. He waved at Maggie, and as soon as Billy was seated, he went to greet her with an enormous hug. They talked quickly for a few minutes and Billy saw Maggie and the man with her both rise and approach the booth.

"What luck! They haven't even ordered yet, so we're all going to sit together," said Vito, beaming. "Just push over a bit, Billy, there's plenty of room. Darling, you know Maggie, of course? And this is Herb Henry, who produces her show. They've just finished taping and Maggie's having a pasta fit. God, I'm starving too." Satisfied that everybody was squeezed into the booth, Vito turned his attention to the menu.

"I didn't want to intrude on your dinner," Maggie said apologetically to Billy, "but Vito absolutely insisted, and you know how irresistible he can be when he wants something."

"Oh, it's no intrusion. I couldn't be more delighted," said Billy, feeling a gracious smile, worthy of Aunt Cornelia, mask her annoyance.

The two women did know each other, since Scruples considered Maggie among its very best customers, but they had never done more than exchange greetings. Maggie, in Billy's opinion, was like an aggressive toy poodle, snappish and dangerous unless treated carefully, with a kind of open and unabashed need for power and influence of which she didn't seem ashamed. Billy, who possessed in herself such a strong need for domination, could sense it in others more quickly than any other quality they might possess, just as one dedicated social climber can spot another social climber in a crowd of hundreds. To cap matters, Maggie made Billy feel like a gawk. Maggie had become so entranced by the way she dressed on her show that she had bought an entire wardrobe from Scruples for her private life, so understated, so artful that she had transformed herself, with Spider's advice, into an ambiguously virginal courtesan, like a tiny, immaculate bawd, a rosy Fragonard or Boucher in modern dress.

Maggie, clever as she was, had a blind spot when it came to Billy. She saw her only in one dimension, The Woman Who Has Everything, not just the obvious advantages but also the unbeatable Winthrop-ness, which Maggie never forgot, as well as that marvelous, enviable height and leanness, and even, goddamn it, Vito Orsini. She was awed by Billy and disgusted with herself for feeling that way. She knew that Maggie MacGregor should not have been awed, but Shirley Silverstein turned to custard in the presence of Wilhelmina Winthrop. Frozen custard. Maggie turned her attention to Vito, who had finally finished ordering.

"Pussycat," she cooed, "what's all the talk I hear about your next picture? Fifi told me you're going on location. I want to come visit with a crew—we might pick up another good story."

Vito made a sign of warding off the Devil. "Jesus, Maggie, I'm not a superstitious man, but do you really think that's such a good idea?" They both gave a laugh that bewildered Billy and Herb Henry by its undertone of complicity.

"Listen, baby, the way I figure it, I owe you, know what I mean?" Maggie asked. Vito nodded his head in agreement. He was entirely aware that Maggie's quick thinking in Mexico had not been untainted by self-promotion. Given the opportunity, he would have grabbed the same brass ring.

"When you've got your location picked," Maggie continued, "just let me know and we'll set things up. I'm so sick of doing pieces on actors I could spit. I want to do a show on producers, a day in the life of a producer, something about a mensch for once. Yeah, I like the idea more and more—a change of pace. And you're the most mensch-ish producer in the business." She looked at Vito with an appreciative, nostalgic eye and then, remembering her manners rather late, turned to Billy. "Don't you think it's a good idea?" Before Billy could answer, Vito interrupted.

"We're shooting in Mendocino, Maggie. Start date July 5th, all seven weeks up there." Billy felt her charming waxwork smile being replaced by blank, outraged surprise. She'd known that Vito was considering various locations in the north of California, but this was the first time she had heard that it was all decided. She'd learned to listen to his side of phone conversations to pick up these details of what he was doing, which he didn't remember to mention to her, but this was a major chunk of new information. "So," Vito continued, "if you're serious about coming, get the network to pull some strings and make your reservations now, because the tourists will be all over the place."

"Anything would be better than that Mexican motel we were in the last time," Maggie said, with a laugh that again excluded everyone but Vito.

As the four of them attacked their cannelloni and shrimps marinara, the conversation took an even more bewildering course. Vito launched on a discussion of some-

432

thing he called "creative accounting." This was his hobby-horse, the exposure of the ways in which the major studios of Hollywood have pioneered ingenious methods of reducing actual profits on their financial reports so that the people with participating shares in the profits of a picture, the producers, the directors, and often the actors, are left with a fraction of what they really deserve, if anything at all. Here and there Billy caught a phrase in the animated discussion, and then she was lost again as Vito, Maggie, and Herb Henry explored the devilishly complicated twists and turns invented by the business-affairs departments of the studios.

Billy felt utterly shut out. Incredibly, sitting there in the Boutique with the husband she loved, she was reminded of meals at boarding school, when she would find herself trapped at a table with some of the popular girls, forced to listen to them chatter on about mutual friends and parties to come, while she, invisible and negligible, was drowning in the thick soup of her own mortification, her own hatred of her own alienation.

Before that dinner came to an end, Billy had learned an emotion that she had been spared during her life: jealousy, the most filthy, the most thoroughly vile emotion of all.

All the forms of pain she had experienced while growing up had been forms of envy, feelings that others had something she wanted terribly to have but could not obtain. But there had never been a triangular relationship in her life in which someone threatened the love she wanted all for herself. The love she had known as a child, that of her father for what little it was worth, that of Hannah, the cook-housekeeper who took care of her, that of her Aunt Cornelia, all of those loves had been given with a steadiness. They had not been enough to make up for the disdain of her peers, but they had been hers alone. Then Ellis had loved her to the exclusion of the world. Never, in their life together, had she been less than everything to him. But here was Vito, her husband of little more than a month, totally caught up in a conversation with a woman who was part of his working world, with whom he obviously had secrets, forgetting that she, Billy, was there, enjoying himself with gusto, eating with relish, as if she didn't exist for him. She felt her stomach turn bilious with jealousy, and her sense of self was equally sick with the understanding that she could feel this foul and demeaning emotion.

On the drive home, Billy asked carelessly, carefully, "Vito, you've known Maggie for ages, haven't you?"

"No, darling, only for a couple of years. She came to Rome to interview me once, you know, the picture with Belmondo and Moreau."

"Is that when you had an affair with her?" Brightly, still casually. Another man might have been fooled.

"Now listen, Billy, we're not children. We didn't wait to meet each other before we lost our virginity; we agreed not to discuss the past before we got married. Don't you remember the talk we had in the plane." He shook his head gravely at her. "I don't want to know, ever, *not one word*, about the men you have had in your life. I'm a terribly jealous man. I know that particular fact about myself and I wish it weren't true. But I can refuse to think or hear about your past. And I expect the same consideration from you, about my life before I knew you." He took one hand off the wheel and put it over hers. "Maggie was rubbing your nose in it tonight and I don't blame you. Yes, we did have a little affair in Rome, not terribly important, but it left us good friends."

"Aren't you forgetting Mexico?" Billy felt her mouth making an ugly grimace of distaste at herself as she spoke, but she couldn't keep back the words.

Vito roared with laughter. "Mexico! Silly, silly, darling *idiot!* That terrible motel was where—don't you remember the Ben Lowell story, the stand-in he hit who died later? My God, where were you? The whole world was talking about it."

"I remember it vaguely. I was busy with Scruples. But did you—in Mexico—with Maggie?"

"Look, love, you're going too far. This is exactly the kind of sordid conversation we promised each other not to have. 'Did you do this, did you do that, how many times, where, was it good, did you feel this or that?' all those other ridiculous, hurtful questions. In Mexico, Maggie had the trots the first night, since you want the sexy details, and from then on, it was sheer nightmare, a dead man on our hands and hell breaking loose all over. Now, the subject is closed, permanently and forever. You have no reason to be jealous of any woman in the world and I'll never give you reason. There is no one else I love. No one else compares to you. You are my *wife*."

Billy felt the nausea of jealousy grow less in her belly, but it was not banished by his words. She hadn't been really jealous of Maggie, as another woman, but of Maggie as someone who had a part in Vito's obsession with the world of films. A new place in her mind had opened up, a putrid place in which there was poison. So long as Vito loved his work as much as he did—as much as he loved her, Billy thought—that new place could only be scabbed over, never healed. It would be scraped raw again and again as long as he could forget she was by his side while he talked business. She felt tattered and diminished by her newly born understanding.

As they walked upstairs together, arms around each other's waist, on their way to their bedroom, Billy angrily reminded herself that the only kind of man she could respect was a dedicated man, a passionate man, a man who cared desperately about his work, who did it with total commitment. When Vito had told her, that first time she asked him to marry her, that he wasn't the kind of man she could "acquire," she had thought he meant that he couldn't be bought. Now she realized that he meant he couldn't be owned. She had rushed headfirst into the heart of the paradox; she who insisted on ownership had sought, as she had never sought anything else, a man she could never own. Using all her strengths and wiles, she had contrived to build her own prison.

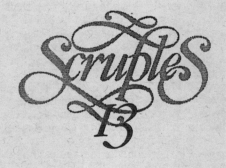

*I*n early July, on the Monday following their dinner at the Boutique, Vito, accompanied by Fifi Hill and the art director of *Mirrors,* left for five days of preproduction hunting in Mendocino. When he left, loneliness fell over Billy like a dusty curtain. Billy had neglected Scruples since her marriage six weeks earlier. She fled to her own office, the only part of the store that had not been redecorated. She had loved the richly tranquil room, but now she found it curiously melancholy. The blue-gray velvet walls hung with a collection of watercolors by Cecil Beaton, the delicate, elaborately inlaid and gilded Louis XV furniture, the *bureau à cylindre* at which she worked, although it should have been in a museum, even the Fabergé document case, made for Czar Nicholas II, in which she kept her most important papers, all seemed as lifeless as if they were missing one crucial dimension. The room gave her no comfort. She left her office impatiently and made a tour of Scruples from top to bottom, finding nothing to criticize. The store had flourished indecently in her absence.

After lunch she had an appointment with Valentine to talk over her fall wardrobe. It seemed to her, as they worked together, that Valentine had changed in subtle ways, which Billy found most intriguing. Somehow, in the past year, the girl had slowly acquired the delectable patina of the celebrated person. It was as if she had been lightly, almost imperceptibly brushed with coat after coat of, not gloss, not sophistication, not fame—perhaps assurance. She had always been decisive, but there had been something just a little overly defiant in that spunky manner of hers, as if she'd go off like a firecracker at the least opposition. Now she had softened and matured into a calm certainty of touch. She no longer double-dared Billy to contradict her by her attitude; she had a quiet, seasoned conviction about her work, which made an amusing, yet oddly impressive contrast to her spirited girlish figure, which had now been photographed a number of times. Aside from the profits generated by her department, the magazine and newspaper publicity it attracted was priceless.

All together, a most successful idea of hers, bringing Valentine to Scruples, Billy congratulated herself, but what did the girl do for fun? She wasn't having a bit on the side with Spider Elliott, that was certain.

No, it could hardly be Spider, unless he had a twin brother. From what Billy picked up here and there and all around, Spider was so involved with several women that she was amazed that he still had the strength to come to work. Yet he was the first person at Scruples in the morning and the last to leave at night. They walked through the entire store together, and Billy observed how he could change the mood of a room by entering it, banish tension, create excitement, and give tired saleswomen energy, charm dull women into feeling witty, let pretty women know they were intelligent, convince certain intelligent women, who, Billy thought, should have known better, that they were beautiful. He was a splendiferous one-man band, she decided, kind and funny and smart. He made every woman want to present him with her best qualities. Yet he, too, had changed. The pagan smile, so ready for joy, seemed to have dimmed. Now it was just a smile, not an expectation.

Valentine O'Neill and Spider Elliott, both invaluable to the great caravan, the baroque bazaar, the fantasyland that was Scruples. Billy realized that although they were her partners, her employees, she didn't know either of them very well. It never occurred to Billy that these thoughts would never have concerned her a few months ago. She might have been indignant, certainly puzzled, if someone had pointed out that her sensitivity to the changes in Spider and Valentine were signs of an even greater change in her.

Mendocino, the seacoast town Vito had settled on for the setting of *Mirrors,* is California's true Brigadoon. Some two hundred long, winding miles up the coast, north of San Francisco, it seems, to even the most unimaginative traveler, to have just risen out of the mists of a hundred years ago, intact and untouched by the twentieth century. It is set on a steep, rounded bluff jutting high out over the Pacific. The entire town is an official historic landmark, and once inside the village limits the traveler will look in vain for a McDonald's or a Burger King or even any minor indication that modern day has arrived to lay a disfiguring hand on this enchanted settlement, an old mill town, which was first built in the early 1850s in a simple Victorian style known as Carpenter's Gothic. Unlike anyone's idea of California, the houses are all wooden, timbered and shingled, once painted pinks, yellows, and blues, now faded into weathered and romanic pastels, surrounded with vacant lots overrun with old rosebushes, briars, and wild flowers. Any new construction in Mendocino—and almost none is allowed under any circumstances—must exactly duplicate this Cape Cod-style of architecture; even the signs for the one hotel, the bank, the general store, and the post office are of the period. On all three sides facing the Pacific, Mendocino is protected by wide stretches of fields, like Scottish moors in their windswept bareness, fields that are all state-park land and will remain forever in their natural condition.

However, the population of Mendocino is far from frozen in the past. The town attracts many young artists and craftsmen, sturdy individualists who find a way to live there by selling their work to the annual invasions of tourists or by running shops and art galleries and little restaurants tucked away in the few rows of old houses in the center of town. In general, the people of Mendocino County are a proud, pugnacious breed, who have, in the last few years, officially "seceded" from the state of California several times.

Vito had decided to shoot *Mirrors* in Mendocino for several reasons. *Les Miroirs de Printemps,* the French novel he had bought, had to be translated to an American setting. The original story took place in Honfleur, that much-painted

Normandy fishing village that also is a haunt of artists and tourists, and the weather in both places is similar, often chilly and foggy even in midsummer. Honfleur, a favorite target for invasion since long before Henry V, is less warlike in character than the northern California town but equally undisturbed by time.

Before the shoot started the locations in Mendocino had all been chosen, the necessary rents agreed upon, the legal contracts signed, the licenses obtained, and a number of Mendocino residents, picturesque as a band of young gypsies, had been recruited as extras. Vito had rented a small house for himself and another for Fifi Hill, the director. The cinematographer, Svenberg, was staying in the Mendocino Hotel, along with the principal actors; other actors with smaller parts would arrive when they were needed by small plane from San Francisco, landing at the tiny Mendocino airport. The crew members were installed in motels in Fort Bragg, an exceedingly ordinary city a few miles up the coast.

Billy had never been to Mendocino. Although it is only some hundred miles or so northwest from the inland Napa Valley, it is impossible to go from the valley to the coast except by two narrow little country roads with many hairpin turns. She had heard about the picturesque village for years, and she was in a state of high excitement as she prepared to spend the midsummer weeks there while the filming of *Mirrors* took place.

Billy now assumed that she knew a fair amount about movie making, having spent almost all of the last two months listening to Vito's end of the details of the preproduction activity, details she supposed were the necessarily dull and irritating prologue to the actual creative excitement that would take place once the cameras started rolling. She packed the simplest wardrobe possible. She didn't want to look ostentatious, she thought, as she picked her plainest linen pants, her oldest silk and cotton shirts, her most classic sweaters. For evening, she assumed, she and Vito would dine together at any one of the several excellent restaurants in the country inns around Mendocino; she added a few long skirts and several understated, yet elegant tops, and a few heavy jackets against the cool evening temperatures. Shoes —God, how many shoes a woman needed! Billy's passion for clothes had never overcome her annoyance at the necessity of having the right shoe for each outfit. Damnation, her largest shoe bag, which she had hoped not to have to take, was already full. She could manage with four handbags, she calculated, and only the simplest gold earrings and chains. Nothing really. She filled another bag with lingerie and dressing gowns. At least she'd be able to look glamorous when she and Vito were at home together. True, he'd warned her that their house, one of the few available at the height of the tourist season, was simple, on the verge of falling apart. But Billy was sure that it couldn't be all that bad, and anyway, what did it matter? The important thing was that she and Vito would be together in this adventure —a summer on location in Mendocino—just those words themselves had a thrilling ring.

Vito had been concerned that she might not find enough to do during the week. He'd even suggested that she fly up just for weekends, but Billy had been outraged by the idea. Did he think that she had so little interest in his work? Quite the contrary, she could barely wait to become a part of the film-making process.

Mirrors had started shooting on Tuesday, the 5th of July. By lunchtime on Thursday they were still working on an outcropping meadow across a bridge from Mendocino from which they could view the entire town. The camera crew and lighting technicians were setting up on the edge of a perfectly round lily pond, surrounded by tall, wild grasses, which lay in the rough, scrubby field like a hidden miracle. If someone didn't know exactly where it was, he could blunder right into it.

Billy already had. Exploring the terrain on the first day of shooting, when the lily pond had not yet been used, she had slid down its steep, muddy sides and landed in mucky water up to her armpits. Her white linen slacks and her favorite Hermès bag, white canvas and leather, had been a total loss, but the major damage had been to her pride. She screamed and two grips had had to be sent to pull her out of the deceptively deep pool, and one of them had been detailed to drive her, dripping, in humiliation, like a miscast Ophelia, back to the rented house where she changed into dry clothes.

And yet, looking back, that note of low burlesque had, at least momentarily, made her a member of the group. Her few minutes in the spotlight had been the first and last time that Billy had felt the cast and crew had been aware of her as more than an unnecessary bystander. Because that was exactly what she was, a useless onlooker. Everyone in Mendocino who was connected with the production of *Mirrors* had a job to do, except Billy. She was the most unproductive of all items, The Producer's Wife. She had never felt so invisible and, paradoxically, so visible, in the wrong way. The tailored pants and plain shirts she had brought with her looked as out of place as an Edwardian Ascot dress. Billy couldn't help the fact that her oldest sports clothes were no older than last year, fit perfectly, were made to order from the finest fabrics, in the most melting of summer colors. She couldn't help the fact that she was incapable of wearing them without her stupendous built-in chic, which was only emphasized by their simplicity. She couldn't help the fact that her personal style, her height, her very bone structure, all made it impossible for her to fade into the working group, dressed in the scruffy, well-seasoned, obviously *right* uniform of denim jackets and jeans, which were worn by everyone from Vito to the lowliest grip. She realized that she looked as eccentric as an Englishman having dinner in a black tie and a boiled shirt in the middle of Darkest Africa. But even that odd formality had been accepted years ago. Billy merely felt obsolete.

However, she reflected, as she searched the shops of Mendocino and Frot Bragg, in vain, for jeans that would be long enough and slim enough to fit her, the problem was not really how she looked. That was minor compared to the old enemy she was battling, that betrayed misery of an outsider, the sunless climate of her youth, when whatever group she was in never included her in their busy activities and complicated arrangements. Even when surrounded by blood relatives she had felt as if she were staring while she pressed her nose against the restaurant window and watched the people inside happily and obliviously eating their dinners. Whoever the fuck it was who said "Time heals all wounds" didn't know what the fuck he was talking about, she thought savagely. *Nothing* heals old wounds. They were waiting there, inside, ready to incapacitate her, each and every time a situation came up that thrust her back into the emotional atmosphere of the past. Then everything—all the glamour, all the money, all the power—that had come after those first eighteen years suddenly seemed to be no more than window dressing. Was she stuck with her old wounds for life? Somehow she had to climb out of that dark corner, she decided, with an expression on her face so determined that she looked even taller and more self-confident than ever.

On location, Billy put up a good front. Someone had found a spare folding canvas chair for her and put it next to Vito's. In theory she had her appointed place to sit and be near him. In practice, Vito almost never used his chair except as a drop for his jacket, his sweater, and, as the day grew hotter, his shirt. As he came by to shed each garment, he ruffled her hair absently, asked if she was all right, if the book she was reading was good, and dashed off before she could answer any of his questions. She felt, flushed with fury, like a dog without an owner.

During the shooting he was here, there, and everywhere, an Italian-American Scarlet Pimpernel, checking and double-checking to make sure that everyone was performing his job at 100 percent efficiency. While the cameras were rolling, he made notes so that Fifi could have the additional observations of a pair of fresh eyes.

Once a picture is being shot, the set or location is under the director's supervision, but if Fifi Hill had now become a general, Vito had been transformed into an entire army of top sergeants, as well as always remaining, in the final analysis, commander in chief. During the lunch break, Vito and Fifi were invariably huddled out of earshot, busily conferring, often sending for Svenberg or some other member of the production staff to discuss new ways of approaching the material.

Hill's greatest strength was in his flexibility, his willingness to use the script as a jumping-off place rather than as a bible. Like Vito, he never forgot that what they were all doing there was essentially playing; he never forgot that playing meant having fun. He wasn't a self-indulgent director of the sacred agony variety, the oh-sweet-Jesus-what-happened-to-my-dream school. He made the dream come true, and it was that quality Vito had seen in him when he gave him his first directing job. Fifi was able to create an atmosphere in which the actors and actresses all felt that they were a little in love with him and he was a little in love with them. Meanwhile, it suited him perfectly if everybody who needed it had somebody to hate. With Vito protecting his flanks, ready to kick ass if anybody was fucking up Fifi's picture, as he now thought of it, he was in the best of all possible worlds.

After her misadventure in the lily pond, Billy felt all but nailed to her canvas chair. Electric cables, of an unknown but unquestionably sinister nature, were lying in wait almost everywhere. If she walked around she knew she risked getting in the way of one set of technicians or another, and she had sworn to herself not to cause one more second's worth of trouble. But even from her fixed viewpoint, Billy was able, after several days of shooting, to come to the accurate perception that making a movie was 98 percent waiting and 2 percent action. No events in her life, certainly nothing she had ever read about films, had led her to expect the unrelenting tedium of the experience. At first she thought that things were going slowly because the shooting was just starting, but soon she perceived that the tedium was the natural rhythm of the process. It would have been more interesting to watch a doddering old man build a boat out of balsa inside a bottle, she decided balefully.

Could she be the only person in the world who found that spending half a day waiting for a setup, only to find it had to be relit, was not inspired living theater? There was no one she dared ask. She'd rather rot on her chair than say anything to Vito, and, in any case, the only time they had alone together was late at night, after the dailies. Sitting there in her director's chair, Billy smiled to herself and sucked down hard on her lower lip. No matter how thin Vito spread himself all day long, busy with other people, she could hardly fault him at night. He kept her so blazingly and so thoroughly fucked that she generally made her observations of the tiresomeness of movie making through a haze of sensual anticipation. She caught sight of him a hundred feet away, naked to the waist, gesticulating with his dazzling energy like the leader of a great troupe of followers, and thought that she wanted him again, *now*, damn it, not ten hours from now. She felt an almost irresistible, quite unbearable tug throughout her whole body as she imagined walking off the field with him and into the

Winnebago, which was parked there for his use, locking the door and peeling off her clothes. She would just stand there, her legs wide apart, absolutely still, while she watched his prick rise and stiffen, his face assume that blunted, half-blind expression that came over it when he saw her naked body, like a sacred bull, like a forest god in a Jean Cocteau drawing. Thinking about it, imagining how he would smell, already sweating in the sun, Billy closed her smoky eyes and rubbed her thighs together imperceptibly.

"Lunch, Mrs. Ikehorn!" someone boomed in her ear. She started up, almost overturning the chair, but whoever had spoken to her was gone.

Lunch, she thought, blushing and furious. How did they dare to call that revolting meal lunch? It was supplied on the set every day by a company that specialized in catering to movie locations. By tradition the food was abundant: huge trays of fried pork chops, platters of fried chicken, casseroles of spaghetti and meatballs, vats of potato salad, mounds of barbecued beef ribs gleaming with fat, and crocks of hot dogs and baked beans encrusted with brown sugar, each dish as heavy and indigestible as the next.

Confronted with this spread, fit for teamsters, Billy had finally unearthed some Jell-O and, miraculously, a plate of cottage cheese decorated with grated carrots, a dish she had hated since her school days. But at least it wasn't fried. Since Vito spent his lunch hours in conference, she ate alone, self-consciously, for two days, before she decided to take her tray into the Winnebago.

Billy sat in the trailer, her world reduced to a mound of cottage cheese, and knew she was too angry to eat. She felt her anger like a hard rubber ball that filled all of her belly and realized that only a minor part of it came from her rage at her own hard-core shyness and her own sharp vision of how alien she must appear to the company of *Mirrors*. Alien or not, she knew that most people don't really pay that much attention to others, not nearly as much as every individual tends to think, and that she could probably appear in a trailing, flowered garden-party dress and a parasol and no one would give a damn.

The biggest part of her rage came from another source. She was angry at Vito who was neglecting her, as he had to in order to do his work. She was angry at his work, which, necessarily, made her an outsider. She was angry at her own wanting to be with him that had stuck her up here in Mendocino, useless and self-pitying. She was angry because if she went back to Los Angeles now, she would have failed the challenge she had imposed on herself. If she left she would be proving that she couldn't take it when life wasn't going the way she wanted it to go. She was angry because she couldn't have what she wanted when she wanted it and how she wanted it. She was about to detonate with rage because she'd made her bed and now she fucking well had to lie in it.

She grabbed her plate of salad and Jell-O and left the trailer. Who to approach? That clump of gaffers roaring with laughter? Perhaps not, for her first try. Svenberg? He was sitting alone, his Norse eyes visionary, seeing his name in lights. He wouldn't welcome any interruption. The cast? Only Sandra Simon and Hugh Kennedy were on call today and they had disappeared into another Winnebago. She found herself stalking over to the makeup trailer. The two gay hairdressers were gossiping there in the shade.

"Mrs. Ikehorn!" They jumped to their feet, flattered and flustered.

"It's Mrs. Orsini really, but don't bother with all that—call me Billy."

They glanced at each other in hidden astonishment. So she wasn't the stuck-up richissimo bitch everybody figured she must be.

"Why don't you sit here, Billy? My, I love that watch."
"Your hair's heaven—who does it?"
"Love your pants—"
"Love your belt—"

Well, it was better than nothing.

The film that was shot each day was flown to a local laboratory in San Francisco to be developed and flown back to Mendocino. The production manager had discovered an unused movie house in Fort Bragg where they could view the dailies under fairly good conditions. So much, Billy thought, for dinners in little country inns. Vito had just time enough to return to their house, take a quick shower, and put on another pair of jeans before they joined Fifi, Svenberg, Sandra Simon, and Hugh Kennedy for a quick bite at the International House of Pancakes before the screening.

Billy had been looking forward to seeing the dailies. Her imagination, fed by Hollywood, saw a large private screening room, deep leather chairs, a wisp of smoke from expensive cigars, an aura of privilege and position, possibly the ghost of Irving Thalberg. Reality was an ancient movie house smelling of piss, with lumpy seats, which must be giving everybody some unmentionable disease if any of the germs in them were still alive, and a screen full of an incomprehensible multitude of images. After Billy had seen the same scene repeated four or five times, each version only slightly different from another, and listened to Vito and Fifi and Svenberg heatedly discussing them as if there were major and important differences among them, she began to rage inside at their endless nit-picking. Why couldn't they ever reach any decision without such agony; didn't any one of them have a clear vision of how it should be? She suspected that they were prolonging the problems because each one of them wanted to exercise his power to the full and exaggerating the difficulties of choice so that their individual creative viewpoints could be indulged. Creative? Balls! They were making tiny little mud pies. Piddle. Piddle. Piddle!

On a Saturday, when Vito had finished discussing some script changes with Fifi Hill, he finally had time to turn his attention to his wife. The picture was on schedule, the dailies promised great things, Sandra Simon and Hugh Kennedy had started a real-life love affair, which gave their scenes together a rocketing sensuality that soared off the screen and which, Fifi admitted, even he couldn't have extracted from them. Svenberg's camera work was the most inspired he'd ever done and, reassuringly, the generator had already broken down. Since this was to be expected at least once during the course of any shoot, Vito was glad it had happened sooner rather than later. Things were as they should be: The texture of a shoot, compounded of accidents and misunderstandings, mistakes and corrections, tension and belly laughs, clashes and reconciliations, and fuck-ups and ingenious solutions, was all happening, just as it should.

"Vito," Billy ventured, as he reached out his arms to pull

her into his lap, "don't you ever get—impatient?" She had almost said "bored," but then "impatient" seemed a better choice. Less judgmental.

"Impatient, darling? Like when?"

"Well, remember when the generator broke down and you all just had to sit around for almost two hours until they fixed it? Like then." Like always, like every single stupid day, she thought.

"Yeah. That always bugs the hell out of me. But basically it doesn't matter—after all, the whole business is so boring that one hour more or less doesn't make any difference in the long run."

"*Boring!*"

"Of course, sweet. Darling, sweet Billy. Put your head here, in my lap. Ah. Nice. Shooting a film is the most boring thing about the movie business."

"But you don't act bored! You don't look bored! I mean —you're totally engrossed in the whole thing—I don't understand at all—" Billy raised her head from its warm nest between his legs and looked at him in amazement.

"Look, it's simple. *It's* boring—but I'm not *bored*."

"You don't make sense."

"I'll give you an example. It's like being pregnant. No woman is going to tell you that for a large part of the nine months she isn't bored numb—who can think about the 'miracle of birth' day and night? But every once in a while the baby gives a kick and that's fascinating, that's exciting, that's something real. And the whole time she's growing bigger and bigger and that's damn interesting, too, and at the end there's a baby. So it's boring, but she isn't *bored*. Anyway, the most fun comes later, after production, in the editing and mixing." He looked pleased with himself for his explanation.

"I understand perfectly," said Billy and she did. It meant that Vito was the mother *and* the father of the film, and she was not even a relative, except by marriage.

Shit. Oh, shit. The man she loved was having the time of his life doing the thing he did best, and she was choking with resentment. All that crap about babies—what the hell did Vito know about being pregnant? Making movies was a job for children and madmen, all joined together in the common delusion that they were giving birth to a work of art. Maybe Vito wasn't bored but she was—bored, bored, BORED right out of her fucking skull.

Josh Hillman and his wife were eating cold poached salmon and cucumber salad in their dining room on Roxbury Drive, a splendid room in which they could accommodate forty-eight people for a seated dinner or hold a buffet for three hundred, as they often did. They were alone tonight, their children off improving their French in France for the summer.

"How was your day?" Josh asked Joanne, having run out of legal gossip to tell her but not willing to let a silence fall.

"Mine?" She looked mildly surprised. "Lunch with Susan Arvey. I think she's a bit of a prune. Maybe she always was, but she seems to have gotten worse. And Prince was in town with his collection, so I went to Amelia Grey's and ordered some fall things."

"How is Prince?"

"How is—Josh, you've never even *met* the man."

"Well, it's—you've been talking about him for so many years that I think of him as practically a member of the family."

"Hardly," she said, laughing. "I doubt that he'd fit in. We're not nearly grand enough for him. But he was fine, just the same, always adorable to me. And he had some great-looking clothes, better than last year."

So Prince hadn't mentioned him, Josh thought. Why did he feel such a sense of disappointment? His clever brain, too long and too well trained in seeking the right answer quickly, supplied him with the answer he didn't want. He had been counting on Prince to do his dirty work for him. He had been so sure, so convinced, that the man wouldn't be able to resist telling Joanne about seeing him with Valentine at Lace's party. That would have precipitated everything. Now he had to make the first move. Certainly Joanne, sitting placidly in her chair, ringing for the maid to clear the table, seemed well contented with her lot in life. Damn it all to hell, he thought, and damn himself for being a coward.

"Iced tea, dear?"

"Please."

Dolly Moon didn't arrive in Mendocino until the first two weeks of shooting were over. Vito had carefully planned to shoot the scenes in which she wasn't involved during those weeks, saving, by this means, at least a thousand dollars on her room and board, as well as paying her three thousand dollars less because of the shorter shooting schedule. Four thousand dollars might not seem like much of an economy in a budget of two million two, but he knew that in *Mirrors* every penny was going to count.

Billy first noticed the new addition to the cast as Dolly and Sandra Simon were being filmed walking along a Mendocino street together. The contrast between the two girls was delicious, Billy thought. Sandra so poetically beautiful, so lyrical, and this girl so—so funnily bouncy and kind of awkwardly bountiful.

At the lunch break she lined up at the caterer's long table, dreading in advance yet another chapter of the lives, times, and tribulations of her two hairdressers. As she passed the fried pork chops, she heard a voice just behind her.

"I think I'm going to be sick."

Billy turned, alarmed, and saw Dolly Moon looking appalled.

"What's wrong?"

"What's wrong! Do you realize that there isn't anything on this table that isn't *swimming* in fat?"

"There's a carrot and cottage cheese salad when you get to the end of the line."

"Oh, never! That would be an insult to my stomach. Say, listen, unless you like this junk, why don't we split and eat together—I saw a spot that has do-it-yourself sandwiches, avocado, prosciutto, roasted peppers, cold sliced turkey, things a human being could put into herself and not turn into a whale. How about it?"

"Point the way."

Since so many of the tourists were engaged in watching the movie people eat their lunches, Billy and Dolly were able to squeeze into a free table at a nearby lunch bar that served health food, delicatessen, and homemade lasagna. Wordlessly, Dolly demolished half a huge sandwich while Billy, picking at a tuna salad, observed her with intense curiosity. Some strands of Dolly's haze of hair were exactly the color of orange marmalade, others a nondescript light brown, her blue-gray gaze was seraphic, and her waist and nose were tiny—everything else about her, however, was just a little bigger than too big.

"They're something, aren't they?" Dolly said conversationally.

"Huh?"

"Oh, come on—the bosom and the bottom—you don't think I don't realize? Listen, I went to a Mormon junior high and I couldn't even try out for cheerleader when I was twelve—they said I'd project the wrong image. That's when I left the church. Still, maybe without them I wouldn't be able to earn a living."

"But that's just not true! I've seen your work—I saw the movie you made and you're a truly talented actress, a tremendously talented actress!" Billy cried, in a tone that contained no taint of flattery.

Dolly smiled with uncomplicated, candid joy. "Gee, you know, you're almost the only person who's ever said that to me? Usually they get stuck looking at the boobs and ass and don't pay attention to what I'm saying. I bet even if I were playing Lady Macbeth or Hamlet's mother or Medea—"

"Or Juliet or Camille or Ophelia or listen, I can almost see you as Peter Pan." Billy and Dolly joined in laughter at the range of roles Dolly would never play.

"Gosh, I'm glad I met you," Dolly said finally, subduing her last extraordinarily individual giggle. "I just got here last night and I don't know a soul in the company. I've got the room next to Sandra Simon and she and Hugh Kennedy were making the most embarrassing noises half the night and that means I won't get friendly with her, and gee, a location shoot is tough without a friend."

"I've noticed," said Billy tightly. "What do you mean, 'embarrassing' noises?"

"Well, they were having such a ball that I was turned on, but, on the other hand, I didn't think I should be listening to something private like that—so I was embarrased. Today I'll buy earplugs."

"So that's why they never show up for lunch."

"You can do a lot in an hour. They probably eat a big breakfast. Ain't love grand?"

"Oh, yes, yes it is," Billy said wistfully.

"A girl who looks like you—say, what's your name?—Billy?—cute—a girl who looks like you must have a million guys."

"I used to," said Billy, "but now I'm a one-man woman."

"I've just given up being one. It lasted a year, but my guy, that bastard, Sunrise, loved his broncos more than he did me. Gosh, I'd like to find someone steady, but it's hard when you look like a bimbo. Once I tried putting on a plain brown wig and glasses and a dumb dress two sizes too big for me, and the first time I crossed the street a truck driver yelled, 'Hey, four eyes, how about a slice of my sausage?' and then the moving man said that with knockers like mine I didn't need to see where I was going, so why did I bother with the glasses?—it's sort of hopeless," Dolly sighed, like a mournful Druid. "Yeah, I really need a steady guy, but not dull, sort of like a dentist maybe or an accountant or, what other kind of man is supposed to be steady?"

Steady. Here was one subject on which Billy felt superbly qualified to guide Dolly. She was awash with the desire to do something good for Dolly Moon, and she blessed the fate that had put her in a position to pass on some of the best advice she'd ever been given.

"Oh, just listen, you just listen to me, Dolly Moon. When I was a few years younger than you, I went to live in New York City. I had a roommate—"

Dolly listened in intent silence as Billy told her of the days with Jessica, the days at Katie Gibbs, the days of the glorious Jews. Billy hadn't had a truly intimate, unguarded talk like this with any woman except Jessica since those long past days, but Dolly didn't know that. She just thought her new friend was kind and smart and had sort of pretty clothes and was beautiful in all the ways Dolly admired. By the time they walked back to the roped-off part of the street, they had decided to meet for lunch every day.

As they approached the makeup trailer, Dolly said reluctantly, "I have to check in here first, Billy. Say, what do you do, anyway, wardrobe, hair, script girl?"

"They also serve who only sit and wait."

"I don't get it."

"I sit around and wait for my husband, Vito Orsini."

"Oh my God! You're The Producer's Wife!"

"Dolly, if you ever say that again, I won't tell you one

more word about how to find Jews. I'll hide all the best ones from you and never even give them your phone number. I'm Billy and you're Dolly and that's that."

"But gee, aren't you proud to be the—the you know what?"

"I'm terrifically proud of *him*, but *not* of being the you know what. Nobody here knows why I'm hanging around, but we've only been married just over two months and—and—"

Dolly put her arms around Billy comfortingly. "Listen. I followed a rodeo rider for a year and I'm petrified by horses, so I know exactly how you feel. At least I bet Mr. Orsini doesn't reek of horseshit when he gets home at night. Listen, Mr. Hill told me he wants me to watch the dailies every night. Will you sit next to me and explain them? I never understand what the hell they're all about. I've only made one other movie and I get kind of totally confused. Hey, what's so funny about that? After all, you're the produc—Billy, you're getting hysterical—hey, come on! Oh, my goodness, where's my Kleenex?"

On a Wednesday, with everything in full swing, Maggie MacGregor and her camera crew arrived to spend five or six days gathering material for her television show on Vito, tentatively titled "A Day in the Life of a Producer."

Billy watched, her dark gray thoughts sunk down behind her eyes, as Maggie bustled merrily about, full of the justified conviction of television journalists that the business of the entire world is their personal playpen. Maggie herself was the first real star to appear as far as the crowds of Mendocino natives were concerned. By now they had become so accustomed to watching the progress of the *Mirrors* company that they treated it as casually as they might observe the antics of their own dogs and cats and babies. Although they had a friendly interest in all the *Mirrors* people, they didn't recognize any of them except for Sandra Simon, and she was only familiar to those housewives who followed her particular soap opera. But Maggie MacGregor! Now there was a somebody. At least a third of the households in the town tuned in to her program every week. Isolated as they were, it gave them the feeling of knowing what was going on in the complicated cities they had fled in disgust.

454

Maggie bounded around, skipping heedlessly over cables, intruding without a second thought into every group of workers, as if she owned the entire *Mirrors* company from Vito right down to the last stick of eye liner in the makeup trailer. She stood surefootedly at home in the center of that forbidden working territory, that world of film making, from which Billy was barred by invisible but absolute barriers. Her eyes like chips of granite, Billy thought bitterly that Maggie had all the goddamned CREDENTIALS. Christ, who the hell did she have to fuck to get *off* this picture?

She decided to take a long ramble through some of the wild fields around Mendocino. She'd get away from the shoot, find a comfortable place in the grass and just stretch out and get herself in a better, more reasonable mood. Dolly, her friend Dolly, was on call, so she'd just wander off alone and come back refreshed, renewed, relaxed.

Three hours later she returned, feeling like another woman. The sun and the wind and the breeze off the Pacific had all had their way with her. And so had the poison oak, which grew as freely as the field flowers and brambles but less conspicuously. A day later Billy was on her way back to Los Angeles and the best dermatologist on the West Coast. Trying not to scratch, she looked out of the plane window and wondered if it was worth getting poison oak to avoid enduring the rest of the time in Mendocino? It was hardly an ideal alternative, but Christ, anything had to be better.

She soon changed her mind. Poison oak, Billy discovered, made poison ivy look like diaper rash. And there's not much any doctor can do about it except relieve a small percentage of the itching and prescribe tranquilizers and sleeping pills. She spent the next five days in a wretched daze of unending discomfort, her misery lessened only slightly by the fact that it didn't spread to her face. Vito telephoned every night, but their communication was inescapably unsatisfactory. Discussion and commiseration over an itch can last only so long as a subject of conversation, and while Vito tried to cheer her up over long distance, Billy could hear Sven's or Fifi's voice shouting in the background and imagine Vito's mind concerned with them even as he spoke to her. She asked how the picture was coming along but didn't really pay attention to Vito's brief answers, and eventually the words "Everything's going to be fine, darling, just fine" became the joint theme of their nightly, frustrating, half-lying phone calls.

After the first ten days Billy felt that she'd turned a corner: The huge blisters on her hands, between her fingers, and all over her legs were slowly drying up, and she no longer woke up twenty times a night, horrified to find herself scratching in her sleep. She still looked like the dog's dinner, she told herself, but suddenly she was desperate for company. Oh, how she missed Aunt Cornelia and her bracing frontal attack on life. Perhaps Lilianne would come to visit if she sent the plane for her? No, she remembered sadly, every summer the Comtesse visited Solange and Danielle who were both now married and living in England. There, she reveled in being called "Granny" by proper little English tots and in being asked to demonstrate the art of toasting a slice of bread in the fireplace. On impulse, Billy picked up the phone and dialed Jessica Thorpe Strauss in Easthampton.

"Jessie? Thank God you're home."

"Billy darling, where are you? In New York?"

"Back home in California, recovering from poison oak and about to slit my wrists if I can find them."

"Good grief, and I've been thinking of your having such a glamorous honeymoon with a divine man."

"Not precisely. How are your five beautiful children and my sweet David?"

"Dearie, just don't ask."

"What's wrong?"

"The son of a bitch has them all out learning how to sail, all day, every day, and you know how I get seasick in a rowboat. All they want from me are endless supplies of dry tennis shoes—top winders or top spinners or whatever they're called—I refuse to learn—and dozens of clean socks. What a dreary summer."

"Jessie, if I sent a plane for you, would you consider coming out for a few days to see me? We'd have to stay at the house because I can't go out yet, but it would be such fun," Billy pleaded.

"How soon can that plane of yours be here?"

"I'll notify the pilot and call you right back. You're sure that it isn't too much trouble, leaving your family right in the middle of the summer like this? Seriously?"

"Too much trouble? Ha! I won't even leave a note. Serve the bastards right. Let them go crazy tying to figure out what happened to me, if they even notice. Remember that old drinking song, Billy, about never trusting a sailor an inch above your knee? It's the story of my life."

Jessica arrived the next day, still divinely droopy, although now, because of the fifteen pounds she'd put on her frail frame, her droop was temptingly voluptuous rather than poetically pathetic. She was close to thirty-eight, but men still sighed when she blinked her myopic lavender eyes at them through the careless tangles of her cloudy haze of bangs, which she absentmindedly trimmed herself with her cuticle scissors whenever they flopped too far into her vision. Jessica's husband, David Strauss, was now one of the country's most important investment bankers, and Billy had long envied her friend her happy, fruitful marriage and her wide circle of friends, her wonderfully organized and complete life, so unlike Billy's own.

The two women resumed their conversation right where they had left off on their last visit together some four years before. By the end of two days they had almost filled each other in on the major events of the intervening years, during which they had only talked by phone. Billy now felt well enough to sit outside by the pool in the shade of the lanai, while Jessica sat in the sun nearby and dabbled her toes in the water with delight.

"Oh, the bliss," she sighed, after a short silence, "the absolute undiluted bliss of having no children and no husband. You can't imagine what heaven I'm in. Whatever nirvana is like, it can't be half as good. Who would want pure nothingness when there's California?"

"But Jessie," Billy said, suddenly vaguely alarmed, "you adore them all, don't you? It's not just show-and-tell, your wonderful life, is it?"

"Oh, Lord no, dearie, I adore that scruffy rabble but sometimes—well—often—oh, I don't know, perhaps half of the problem is just planning the menus."

"Jess, that's ridiculous. You have the best cook on the East Coast."

"Had, dearie. Had the best cook. Mrs. Gibbons left three months ago. It all started about a year before when the girls became strict vegetarians. Well, who can argue with that? It's so holy and pure and *such* a ghastly bore. Then the twins refused to eat anything but pizza for six months. Don't ever have twins, lovey, their willpower is staggering. To keep them from malnutrition, we had to chop up vitamin capsules and sprinkle them artfully around the pepperoni. Mrs. Gibbons demanded a real pizza oven, so I got her one, but the thing that really prevented her from leaving was cooking for David. You know he won't touch anything that isn't fine French cuisine, so that kept her pride intact. No, the breaking point came when David Jr. had his religious experience."

"Religious what?"

"He keeps kosher." Billy stared at her blankly. "He decided he wanted to have a Bar Mitzvah. He started studying Hebrew and reading the Old Testament and the next thing I knew he demanded strictly kosher food. We turned one of the pantries into a little kitchen for him, and he cooks in there on his hot plate, eats off paper plates with plastic knives and forks. But it wasn't so much that he wouldn't eat her food—one day he told Mrs. Gibbons not to go near his kitchen because she was *trayf*. She started thinking about how she had made his baby food for him, never using the canned stuff, and her feelings were so hurt that she just packed up and left. I don't really blame her, but since then I've had a dozen cooks. They all say they didn't know they were supposed to run a restaurant and flee in the night."

"Oh, poor Jessie." Billy rocked with laughter at her doleful friend. "Sorry, but it's the idea of David Jr. brewing up his own chicken soup. Does he light the candles on Friday night too?"

"Of course."

"Have you ever thought of getting in touch with your local branch of Jews for Jesus?" Billy choked.

"Bite your tongue. It's bad enough as it is, but at least I know what it's about."

"So you did bring them up as Jews after all," Billy said.

"Oh, no, only the boys, dearie. The girls are Episcopalians, baptized in the church I was baptized in. It's rather like the Rothschilds, you see—the boys have to carry on the tradition of the father's family, but the girls can pretty much please themselves." Jessie paused and looked at Billy sideways. Satisfied that what she had been observing in her friend's face for the last few days was no illusion, she turned away from the pool and changed the subject. "When are you going to stop playing at good soldier and tell me about it?"

"Tell you what? I've nothing to hide. I've been complaining about my poison oak since you first arrived and felt better with every little whine and whimper. Some good soldier."

"Come on."

"Whatever are you getting at, Jessie?"

"Vito."

"Vito?"

"Your husband."

"Ah."

"Indeed, the very one," Jessie persisted, implacable. "Vito the bridegroom."

"He's wonderful, Jessie. I never knew a man could be so incredibly dynamic, so creative, so energetic."

"Bullshit."

"I never could fool you."

"Is he a ten?"

"Oh that, definitely. Trust me on that."

"All right, then, what's the horrible drawback, the intolerable dilemma, the unforeseen and absolutely permanent catch?"

"Who said anything about a catch?"

"Every wife I know, including myself, sometimes at night when I'm getting ready for bed and David is fast asleep. Every woman's husband is hopelessly irredeemable in one way or another."

"Ellis wasn't," Billy said in a muffled voice.

"Ah, Billy, that's not fair. You were Ellis's child bride for seven whole years. You never really became an ordinary wife because when he was well he simply did everything to please and protect you and make you happy. His own life's work became second to you. And then, after all, once he was incapacitated, you could hardly be an ordinary wife either. I'm not criticizing you, love, but you never had to learn to play by the rules of the game."

"Game? Rules? You sound like one of those books about

dressing up in black leather tights and waiting for your husband with six ounces of gin on the rocks in one hand and a humble request for a raise in your household allowance in the other. Not that from you, Jessie, I just don't believe it."

Jessica shook her head at Billy in amusement mingled with pity. Why wouldn't Billy deal in realities? Leather was beside the point, and, anyway, David was freaky about Fernando Sanchez's satin teddies. "The game," she said slowly, "is called being successfully married. The rules are all the compromises you need to make to get there."

"Compromises," cried Billy, stung. "Compromises are all I've been doing since we got married. One fucking compromise after another. Little Billy, meek and mild. Believe me, you wouldn't recognize your old friend if you'd seen me up in Mendocino being The Producer's Perfect Wife."

"And hating every single second of it."

"Just about, all except the times when we were alone together at night. The only time I think Vito knew I was really there was when we were making love. I wonder if he'd even recognize me if he couldn't see my pussy—the rotten son of a bitch."

"Well then, get a divorce if it's that bad."

"Are you out of your mind, Jessie? I'm absolutely mad about him. It was hard enough to get him—I'm not about to let him get away. I couldn't live without that fucker."

"Then start compromising. Gracefully, willingly, graciously, and with a whole heart."

"Oh, God, that's just asking too much! No, come off it, you sound like those neurotic put-upon Brontë sisters all rolled into one. Haven't you heard of Women's Lib? Why the hell shouldn't he do some of the compromising?"

"He already has. He married you against his better judgment and is willing to live your way knowing that ten tenths of all the people he meets probably think of him as some sort of kept man, and he hasn't let that bother him or forced you to make changes in your life-style."

"Oh, that."

"It's a lot, Billy, especially for someone like Vito with all that Italian male pride you talk about so much."

"I suppose you're right. All right, you are right. But still—" Even Jessica couldn't really understand, Billy thought bitterly. What compromises was she really thinking about? The usual New York-Easthampton-Southampton banking crowd's discreet infidelity, the times one or another had too much to drink at a party, the real but hardly earthshaking irritation over an annoying habit David didn't even know he had? After all, for all her bitching, what was David doing now? Mucking about in boats, with his children as any normal man would do during a summer's vacation instead of concentrating his whole mind, soul, and will on making a piece of film come out right. And anyway, what else could Jessie expect, since she got seasick?

Jessica looked at Billy with an almost maternal glance, compounded with tenderness, foreknowledge, and a reluctance to hurt. Poor Billy, she thought, dissatisfied already, and yet how can anyone tell you the truth about what goes on in the heart of any marriage that endures? Who can teach you about the times when the well of love seems to run almost dry and you just have to keep going on faith, the moments when both of you wonder what wonderful *other* thing might have happened if you hadn't met each other? Who can really explain about learning to communicate your true feelings to each other in spite of the traps of words and gestures—the days, even months, when communication somehow fails? And that wasn't even taking into consideration the unescapable problems of a grande dame mother-in-law and the strange difference that becoming the father of five children makes in a man who was a passionate ten. No, she really couldn't help Billy. Even the best of friends can't help each other on the earthquake-quicksand landscape of marriage, except in superficial ways—by letting the other know she wasn't alone.

Jessica walked over to kiss Billy on the top of her head. "It's just post-honeymoon depression. Everybody has it," she said. "You wait, in a few months you won't even remember this. Listen, let's have something incredibly fattening for dinner and fast tomorrow, or at least till lunchtime. We both need it."

"How can you use the word 'need' about something fattening?" Billy asked incredulously.

"Simple. Haven't you heard that European theory about dieting? If your metabolic system is used to never getting fattening foods, and you suddenly give them to it, your

461

body goes into shock and immediately loses weight. Of course you can't make a habit of it."

"You're positive you're right about that?" asked Billy, eyeing the small but unmistakable potbelly her friend had sprouted.

"Absolutely. I'd weigh a ton if I didn't do it from time to time."

Both women laughed and dropped the subject of marriage for the rest of Jessica's visit. At the end of the week she returned to Easthampton, reluctant to leave Billy to go back to menu planning but rather shamefacedly lonely for her sunburned mob. She had, in spite of her earlier threats, telephoned them every night and her husband had spent enough time on dry land during her absence to find an Oriental couple who treated David Jr.'s kosher kitchen with respect and even brought their own woks in which to cook for the vegetarian members of the family.

"Billy, darling," Jessica said, as they both stood outside the Learjet saying good-bye, "I'm afraid I wasn't much help, but what I told you was the best advice I know. Remember, 'All government—indeed, every human benefit and enjoyment, every virtue and every prudent act—is founded on compromise and barter.' "

"Now where on earth did you find that little homily—stitched on a pillow?"

"Edmund Burke, if I'm not mistaken." Jessica smirked wickedly. She had always been proud of her summa cum laude memory for quotations, which permanently kept her one step ahead of her terrifying mother-in-law.

"Vassar girl, get out of here," laughed Billy, hugging her tiny friend one last time. "Go and sin no more, or some such thing. Remember, I'm the only person in the world who knew you when you weren't so beastly virtuous and bloody tolerant."

Back in Mendocino the dailies were over and Vito and Fifi Hill had driven back to Vito's house in heavy silence, not speaking until they poured themselves drinks and settled into the sagging, slip-covered chairs in the damp living room.

"It's gone, Fifi," Vito finally said.

"Even a blind man would know that," Fifi answered, "just from their voices—"

"It's been two days. Yesterday I thought maybe she wasn't feeling well, but today on the set, I've been watching—"

"So when don't you watch?" said Fifi mildly, too sunk in gloom to attempt sarcasm.

"—and hoping they'd come out of it. But we can't kid ourselves another minute; there's not one foot of film we can use. So. We're two days behind schedule now and those fucking kids are giving us turds for performances."

"I've used every trick I've ever learned. Nothing, nothing, Vito. Sandra won't talk, Hugh won't talk, they say they're doing their best, she cries, he cries—a firing squad is what we need!"

"A picture, Fifi, we need a picture. I didn't have time to tell you before we ran the dailies, but right after dinner they both grabbed me, separately, and announced that they weren't going to do the scenes we've set up for the next two days."

"Weren't going to do—!!" Fifi rose from his chair like a madman.

"Yeah, the nude scene, the big, fat love scene we *have* to have to make the whole picture add up, the most important scene in the whole fucking thing. They will not, repeat *not,* appear together in a nude scene."

"Vito! What did you say? What did you do? *They can't do this!* For Christ's sake—do something!"

"Fifi, cancel the shoot for tomorrow morning. There's no point. You and I will go and talk to each of those two moronic kids together. We'll get to the bottom of it. We will *fix* it. Worse things happen on pictures and they still get made, you know that."

"Sure, sure, but when you have a love story and your boy and girl come across like the other is a piece of rotten meat, it's not like having a shark that doesn't work or rain when you want sun. Come on, Vito, you know that everything, *everything* in this picture depends on believing that those two love each other more than Romeo and Juliet. And till two days ago they even had me convinced that they did."

"Fifi, let's get some sleep. Meet you for breakfast at the hotel. Then we'll get down to it."

After Fifi took his gloomy departure, Vito sat down to think some more. If Fifi was deeply worried about the quality of the acting he was getting from those two brats, Vito was confronted with a far graver problem. When Maggie had been in Mendocino two weeks before, she had told him news he had hardly been able to believe.

"Vito," she had insisted, "I can't tell you who told me, but believe me, it's no mere rumor. Arvey has said that he intends to exercise the Take-over Provision on *Mirrors* if he gets the slightest opportunity."

"Why, Maggie, why?" As they both knew, the Take-over Provision, which is standard in most contracts, provides that the minute a producer goes over budget he can be replaced by the studio. This provision is almost never exercised, and many hundreds of producers less highly regarded than Vito Orsini go over-budget and over-schedule without more than a few rumbles from the studio.

"From what I could make out, he's been doing a slow burn about putting up the money for *Mirrors* ever since Cannes. He gave you the go-ahead on it to shove a broomstick up the ass of that bitch of a wife of his, to let her know who ran the studio. He was just showing off, as far as I can understand it, and then when you and Billy got married, he felt he'd been conned. He makes a grandiose gesture to spite his wife and a week later you walk off with one of the richest women in the world and he's left with that Philly snob who never let him have a dime without reminding him of it a hundred times."

"Billy's money—it has nothing to do with me!"

"Yeah, try telling Arvey that. He thinks you should be financing your own pictures with her dough instead of his studio's money. I know, I know, you don't operate that way, but he's in a rage. He's a mean, envious man and he's out to get your balls, Vito, if he can."

Yes, thought Vito, remembering what Maggie had told him; he should have been much more suspicious when Arvey gave him the green light so quickly. He believed everything Maggie had told him. It fit entirely too well. Unfortunately, it made perfect sense.

The next day, shortly before noon, Fifi Hill and Vito sought out a secluded corner of the Mendocino Hotel and sat amid the Victorian clutter, lace antimacassars, and potted palms, like two defeated samurai, trying to decide on the proper place for ritual self-slaughter.

"It's insane," Vito grunted. "Fifi, if Sandra had been stone cold dead, she would have come back to life with what I said to her. I used it all, the truth, but even the truth didn't work! I told her this was the chance of a lifetime; I told her it would make a star out of her; I told her she couldn't do this to me and to you; I told her she'd never work again; I told her, her mother would die from the disappointment; I told her she'd be blacklisted with every casting director and producer in the world; I begged, I screamed, I did everything but fuck her. I would have done that, too, but she was like ice."

"Vito, I was *there*, please spare me."

Vito paid no attention to the weary director. "And that little cock-sucker Hugh Kennedy, he should have his prick rot off, he was just as bad. 'Call my agent!' I'll call his agent, all right. Doesn't he know he's committing professional suicide?"

"He's not smart enough to figure it out—not one of your brighter people, Vito. And there's another thing. Even if we could get them to play the nude scene, what good would it do us, in the mood they're in?"

"Maybe it's only a lovers' quarrel. I'm going back alone to talk to Sandra—"

He was interrupted by a timid voice at his elbow. "Mr. Orsini?"

"Dolly, Dolly darling, the only sane person left on earth. Go away, sweetheart, we're talking."

"I thought I should tell you. It's not like I'm a snitch, but I'd tell Billy so she could tell you, only she's not here, so I thought—"

"What?"

"See, it's not what you said. I heard you say 'lovers' quarrel,' but it's worse. I heard it all through the wall—never got around to buying earplugs—it started when Sandra accused Hugh of upstaging her, stealing scenes. And—"

Fifi interrupted. "He was. I caught him at it and warned him, but he kept trying."

"And then Hugh turned nasty and said she couldn't act, a lousy soap queen, and he's a real stage actor, you know, and then she said he had a cock as big as a baby's thumb but, unfortunately, not as hard, and then he said you wouldn't even know where her tits were unless you could

465

find her nipples, and she said he had pimples on his ass with pus in them, and he said she was the worst fuck he'd ever had—and her cunt smelled like a fish market—and it got a lot worse. I can't even repeat most of the things they said—I'd be embarrassed."

"I get the general drift," said Fifi.

"So," finished Dolly, "it's not a lovers' quarrel because they aren't lovers anymore. They really hate each other. I mean, they went too far. The thing is, he really does have a tiny cock; she'd mentioned it a lot before, but not like that, more like, she'd say, 'it's small but it's in the right place,' that sort of thing."

"Yeah, they definitely went too far, Dolly. Thanks. It's a help to know what's going on. Now, beat it, honey, we need to talk."

"We've had it, Vito," said Fifi. "A man can't forget that sort of thing even if he wants to, and this kid doesn't want to."

There was a long silence. The ornate Victorian hotel lobby filled up slowly with thirsty tourists, who were served by pretty female bartenders.

"We'll use photo-doubles," announced Vito. "It's doable Fifi."

"In a nude scene? You're mad!"

"I didn't say it was sane. I just said we'd do it. There are enough kids in this town so we can find one who can be made up to look like Sandra from the back and the same for Hugh. Wigs, Fifi, wigs. We'll find them this afternoon. Then we'll shoot the scenes twice, once with a photo-double of Sandra with Hugh and then the other way around. We'll never see the photo-doubles' faces, just the backs of their head and their bodies. And we'll intercut."

"You can't get away with that!"

"Do we have a choice?"

Svenberg was enchanted with the idea. To him flesh was flesh, light was light, and the challenge was the real game. While Sandra played her scenes with Hugh's photo-double, Vito read her the lines Hugh would have been saying, and she responded to them. While Hugh played his scene with Sandra's photo-double, Dolly read Sandra's lines. Later, this would all be incorporated into a single scene with corrected sound. Vito insisted that Hugh be present on the set while Sandra worked and that Sandra be there while Hugh worked. The two former lovers engaged, as he had hoped, in an Olympics of acting, competing with each other to see which one could put more fervor and pathos and sensuality into the scene, abandoning their totally naked bodies to equally naked strangers with flaunting erotic wildness he had never seen on any set. They were on fire, dangerous in their desire to act each other into the ground. He and Fifi didn't need the dailies to know they had made film history, if only in that one scene.

When the two draining days were over, Fifi reminded Vito that they still had those two days of film, shot before the nude scene, which had to be redone. All the rest of the script involved scenes in which Sandra and Hugh were not alone together, so he didn't anticipate trouble there, but what about those two missing days?

"I've been rewriting the script at night," said Vito. "Here —it's a new way around but we come out at the same place. I've just given Dolly more to do—it'll work with the changes I've made."

Quickly Fifi read the new pages. "It works, it works. But where do we get the time?" Vito handed him another batch of pages.

"These scenes we don't shoot, we don't absolutely need them. I've provided for the gaps, the transitions. It all makes sense. So now we're only one day behind schedule, Fifi, and if you can't make that up, they'll kick you out of the Directors Guild."

"Feeling good, you old bastard?"

"Just the normal joys of being in show business."

ScrupleS
14

*H*aving been a victim of poison oak, Billy discovered, when she finally returned to Mendocino for the last week of the shoot, was the magic leveler. Many of the grips, lighting crew, set dressers, and camera crew had had nasty touches of the vile disease themselves. From being The Producer's Wife, she was transformed into the wounded comrade who had returned from the field hospital to the front to carry on the war side by side with the troops. Everyone from Svenberg, wrapped in his dreamy isolation, to the drivers of the honey wagons, as the indispensable portable toilets are called, hailed her and wanted to know how she felt. Many of them could hardly wait to compare symptoms, and often Billy found herself the center of a brotherly knot of assorted crew members discussing the virtues of cortisone shots verus plain calamine lotion.

Dolly and Billy managed to have lunch together every day. Billy, who still counted, and always would, every calorie she put into her mouth, couldn't help but notice that Dolly, whose Rabelaisian bosom and bottom were flourishing superbly, was eating a sandwich that combined slices of avocado with Russian dressing, piled on a layer of brie, a layer of pastrami, and a layer of chopped liver, between two thick halves of a buttered, seeded roll, and on the side, potato salad with an order of extra mayonnaise.

"Damn," said Dolly, scraping up the last of the bowl of potato salad, "we don't have time for another sandwich, do we?"

"Are you still hungry?" Billy asked in awe mingled with reproof.

"Starving. See, after I throw up breakfast, it's a long wait 'till lunch."

"Throw up—?"

"Sure. But it won't last. I'm just in the very beginning of the third month and everyone says that's the worst time for morning sickness."

"Oh, Dolly! Oh, good heavens—how did it happen?"

Dolly rolled her huge eyes heavenward. The sounds of her heavenly chortling mingled with Billy's half-repressed yelps. Eventually, Billy quieted down enough to ask, "What are you going to do?"

"Gee, I guess I should do something, but somehow I just want to have the baby. It's kinda crazy but it *feels* right, you know. I've been pregnant before and I didn't even consider going through with it, but this time—"

It seemed to Billy that her friend was confused in a way she wasn't trying to clarify. It was as if Dolly was as willing as she was slightly slaphappy.

"What about the father?" Billy aked, trying to get Dolly to focus.

"Sunrise? He'd marry me tomorrow, but I don't see spending the rest of my life around rodeos. Why'd they have to play L.A. on the Fourth of July anyway? I'll tell him afterward. Who would think that forgetting to take the pill for just two days could do the trick?"

"Any gynecologist. Dolly, what about money? It takes money to have a baby and pay for a nurse and buy maternity clothes—" Billy's voice trailed off. She knew there were other expenses connected with having a baby, but she couldn't itemize them offhand. Maternity had never been one of her interests.

"I can live for a year, year and a half, on what I'm making on *Mirrors,* and then I'll worry about it. If I can't get work, there's always Sunrise. Gosh Billy, that'll all sort of take care of itself, like things always do if you want them enough." She seemed marvelously casual, almost disoriented, in a fuzzy, purring kind of way.

Billy eyed her friend, whose pleasure in her pregnancy could scarcely be contained. If ever she'd seen a cockeyed optimist, Dolly was it. "Could I be—do you think—the baby will need a godmother—?"

"*Oh, yes!* Yes!" Dolly hugged Billy so enthusiastically that she engulfed her. "I wouldn't want anybody but you."

At least, Billy thought, this would give her a chance to make sure that things would be taken care of properly. Her godchild would not be born without certain amenities. Visions of Bostonian christenings popped into her head. Silver cups and old sherry, bishops and biscuits and tiny sets of sterling spoons and forks; perhaps a subscription to a diaper service would be more welcome. A crib, a layette, a baby carriage? All of them, to begin with. And then she'd see.

Work on *Mirrors* finished on schedule, on Tuesday, August 23rd, and the wrap party was scheduled for the next night. Vito and Fifi, both totally worn out and yet dancing with nervous exultation, explained to Billy that the close of any film production traditionally calls for a wrap party, which serves a dual function; it celebrates the completion of the weeks of work and gives everyone a chance to get drunk and bury the many hatchets that have been waving around during the course of any shoot, even the rare harmonious one.

The *Mirrors* production had taken over the private rooms of the Mendocino Hotel for the party and by ten o'clock it was in full swing. The elaborate buffet had been demolished, replenished, and demolished again. The bar would stay open until the last man or woman decided to go to sleep. With the picture finished, there was no need for anyone to turn in that night, but two people nevertheless, seemed to be leaving rather early, with an unmistakable intention in their attitudes.

"Vito," said Fifi, almost stuttering with outrage "do you see what I see?"

"If what you see is Sandra Simon and Hugh Kennedy together making for bed, yes."

"TONIGHT they made up?"

"Naturally—it's too late to do us any good. Sometimes, if I didn't control myself, I could get to really dislike members of the acting profession, but thank God I'm a tolerant man."

"He should drop dead with a hard-on," Fifi hissed.

472

"Nah, all his ejaculations should be premature," Vito corrected.

"He should never be able to get it up at all."

"No, Fifi, no, that's not subtle—he should get it up—and no one notices," rejoined Vito.

"Excuse me, Mr. Orsini," said the manager of the hotel, "but there's a man outside in the lobby who insists on seeing you. He said he was from the Arvey Film Studio."

In the lobby Vito found a stranger, dressed in a suit and tie. He quickly introduced himself as being from the studio's Legal Department and handed Vito a letter, which he opened with an instantaneous apprehension of trouble. No communications from the studio should be arriving in this fashion. He skimmed it rapidly. "Pursuant to paragraph . . . contract . . . relating to production of motion picture entitled *Mirrors* . . . you are hereby notified that . . . Studio has exercised its right to take over production by virtue of producer's failure to maintain the agreed-to budget. . . ."

Vito looked at the lawyer, the calm of his manner effectively hiding his desire to batter, maim, murder. There was no point in arguing with this man. Vito was, according to his calculations, within the budget. However, it would be months before the business-affairs people and their creative Accounting Department would or could prove whether he was actually over budget. And by that time, it would be too late.

"So," said Vito, "would you like a drink?"

"No thanks. I've come to collect all the processed film you have on hand, every foot. Sorry about that, but those are my instructions. And the negative, too, of course. I have a van and a couple of men outside to carry everything. We got lost driving here from San Francisco, that's why I had to break in on your party like this."

"Hey, that's rough. I'm afraid your trip was wasted. But maybe they can get you a room here for the night."

"Wasted?"

"I don't have a foot of film. No negative. Nothing. They must be back at the studio."

"You know they're not." The lawyer was getting angry.

Vito turned to Fifi Hill and Svenberg, who had followed him out to the lobby. "Fifi, did you do anything with the

473

work print? Do you know where the negative is? Arvey's taking over the production and this gentleman wants it."

Fifi looked amazed. "What the hell would I do a thing like that for? Maybe Svenberg knows. Per?"

The gaunt Swede shook his head. "I just run the camera, I don't keep film under my bed."

"Sorry," said Vito, "but it's probably in transit somewhere—or other. It'll turn up—films don't just get lost, you know."

The lawyer looked at the three men confronting him so blandly. Monday they'd get a writ and force Orsini to deliver the film, but until then there was nothing more he could do. Life in the studio Legal Department had taught him much basic wisdom.

"I'll take that drink. And I missed dinner. Is there any food left?"

Billy was standing in the corner of a group of openly admiring men when Vito appeared at her elbow and whispered to her that they were leaving. First she thought it was too early to go, then she realized that, now that the picture was finished, Vito must be dying to make love to celebrate.

She bid her newfound pals a sentimental good-bye and hurried off. Vito found a side door so that they could slip away unnoticed from the crowd, and grasping her by the elbow, broke into a run, racing to the car. Billy's jubilation was short-lived: Fifi was waiting there for them. They drove back to the house in a silence Billy had the good sense not to break.

As soon as they got inside the front door, Vito explained to her, as he had to Fifi and Svenberg weeks before, what Arvey's intentions were. It took Billy a minute to fully understand that the Take-over Provision could be exercised whether Vito was over budget or not.

"I don't have the time to show that they're wrong," said Vito grimly.

"But what can they *do* to it?" Billy asked in baffled, innocent anguish and ignorance. "It's all on film, the work print's finished, the whole movie is *made*—why do they want it now?"

"If they get their hands on it they'll give the work print to any one of their regular editors to cut, any way it suits him, butchering it most likely, doing a hack rush job, never letting us see what sort of hash they make out of it. There'll be nothing to stop them from using the cheapest possible background music. Then, knowing Arvey, and knowing his mood, I'd say that he'll slap it together as quickly as possible, throw in a few sound effects, and release it, bleeding from every pore. They can take this film and turn it into a movie nobody would believe Fifi had directed or Svenberg had photographed. Post-production is where pictures can be made—or destroyed."

"Oh, Vito," Billy groaned, "I can't stand it!"

"I couldn't either, darling. That's why I have every foot of film tucked away under lock and key in Fort Bragg. The negative has been removed from the lab in San Francisco and stored under my name. The minute Maggie warned me, I decided to take these precautions."

"What about Arvey?" asked Fifi, who had known what Vito was doing all along. "He's not going to lie down for this."

"That stinking turd isn't going to have any choice," Vito answered, grim and concentrated. "I'm not turning it over to the studio until the film's complete, not until it's edited, scored, and mixed."

"Toronto? Is that what you've been planning?" Fifi asked.

"No, we'll work in Hollywood. You know our technicians are the best in the business. Even if we have to rent hotel rooms it can be done. It's been done before."

Billy interrupted him excitedly, with a rush of joy that at last she had something to contribute.

"Hotel rooms! When we have the house? Vito, it's perfect, don't you see? Private property, all the rooms in the world, and the guards won't let any strangers through. Oh, Vito, you can't say no! Please let me," she pleaded, seeing his uncertain expression.

"Guards? What guards?" asked Vito.

Billy blushed slighlty. She didn't realize that he hadn't known.

"I've always had armed guards twenty-four hours a day since Ellis died. I was sort of afraid of someone trying— oh, I don't know—to get into the house or steal my jewelry or, well, kidnap me or something. They're inconspicuous unless you know where to look. And then there's the gate-house."

Both men were silent with surprise. Mafia *capos*, rock stars, Sammy Davis, Jr.—they had guards, but Billy? Anyone as rich as Billy would not have thought twice about it. Billy took the guards so much for granted that she never remembered them from one month to the next. They weren't a major expense. It was like panty hose. Once a year she bought a dozen pairs in every color so that she'd never find herself without the right ones—a simple precaution.

"The house will never look the same again," Vito warned her.

"Accept it, Vito, or I will," said Fifi. "I imagine you have a spare guest room, Billy love? I'll be moving in. If I'm going to work eighteen-hour days, it's going to be in style."

"Twenty-four-hour days, Fifi," Vito answered, "and this one begins now. We'll take the Winnebago and go to Fort Bragg to pick up the film. I'm not leaving a scrap behind. Billy, pack for us both while Fifi and I load up. We have about twenty big cartons to move—we'll be back in two hours. If we drive all night we should be home before the lawyer even wakes up."

"Yes, darling," said Billy with well-hidden resignation. It didn't seem the best of times to suggest making love—one for the road as it were.

During the weeks that followed, Billy found a few spare seconds to wonder if she had ever really thought it might be something of a lark to edit a film in her house. Nothing in her history could have prepared her for the almost-never-ending days and nights of single-minded, feverish, obsessed, and beleaguered activity that entirely dominated her life and the lives of everyone connected with the editing. Billy's vast, mellow Tudor mansion took on, simultaneously, all the aspects of a sweatshop, a boiler room, a very odd sort of house party, a submarine under battle conditions, a high-class cafeteria, and a rather lavish mental institution.

Besides Fifi, two other permanent house guests were immediately installed in the house: the editor, Brandy White, a brilliant woman with whom Vito had worked often in the past, and her lover and assistant, Mary Webster. They had told all their friends that they were going off on vacation together, which surprised no one in their talented Lesbian circle, and then they moved into Billy's biggest guest room.

"We'll need another of the guest rooms for the script clerk," Vito had told Billy during the long night's drive back to Los Angeles from Mendocino.

"What does a script clerk do?" Billy asked.

"Takes notes on everything the editor and Fifi and I say while we're looking at the film and types them up so that we have a record for the next day's work—plus take messages, answer phones, attend to all sorts of things."

"I'm going to do that," said Billy.

"Look, sweet, I know you want to help, but you have no idea how tedious and detailed that job is—you'd go crazy in a week."

"Vito, I'm the script clerk. If you don't like my work you can replace me and I won't be hurt. But I don't want to be standing around sucking my thumb while the rest of you finish the picture. I have a vested interest in the success of this film, too, remember? I'm The Producer's Wife. *And* the script clerk! This is one area in which I have a skill you can use."

"What about the house—you're letting us have that?"

"Vito, I'm not talking about offering you something I happen to own because of money I happened to inherit. I'm talking about making a contribution of my skills and my time and energy—don't you understand?"

Reluctantly, Vito had agreed, convinced that Billy couldn't endure for long in the heated gloom and tension of the editing room, but within a day her reliable Katie Gibbs' skills came back and all her frustrated desire to *produce* kept her on the job, alert and totally willing. As the days went by, Billy began to learn the language of film as she had once learned to speak French. Little by little, she came to understand more and more of what was being done to the film as it was delicately carved out of the "rough assembly" they had carted down from Mendocino. She started to recognize why the control of an artist was vital in the editing process of even the most perfectly photographed, beautifully acted scenes; to appreciate how the choice of a close-up instead of a medium shot could totally change the mood of a scene; to sense why it was sometimes necessary to discard even the most exquisite piece of film in order to maintain pace or mood.

Billy's library, filled with rented equipment, became the editing room. The larger of the two living rooms was turned into a projection room. Mick Silverstein, the composer for *Mirrors*, sat at the Steinway grand in the former game room and began working on the various themes for the picture. Within a week two sound-effects editors arrived and spent every day working at their craft as each reel was completed. They made such a distracting noise, even tucked away in a corner of the big house, that they had to be moved to the garage. The dining room was in permanent use, since it was impossible to know in advance when anyone would have the time to eat. Breakfast was at seven for Fifi, Vito, Billy, Brandy, and Mary. From eleven in the morning until midnight there had to be food, instantly available.

Billy's knowledge of housekeeping was limited to two items, how to get out bloodstains with cold water and how to keep help. Aunt Cornelia had given her that first piece of information when she reached puberty; Ellis the second. "Hire only the best professionals," he had said, "treat them with every consideration, pay them at least twenty percent over the going rate—and hope for the best." Both Billy's butler and chef had worked for her for years, but ten days of the erratic, permanent, hot-and-cold running buffet caused the cosseted chef to decamp, muttering about strange goings-on and inconsiderate employers. The butler, however, was made of more adaptable stuff. He hired two extra kitchen maids and brought in two mates who had served with him in the Quartermaster Corps during World War II to do the cooking. The three regular maids kept the house as clean as possible, although they were scandalized at the amount of debris that was mysteriously produced; the overtoppling heaps of cigarette butts; the marks on the walls; the rented equipment making holes in ancient Persian rugs; the dining room carpet that looked, in spite of their work, as if an army had walked over it, spilling creamed chipped beef, as they went.

Josh Hillman was also a member of the team, riding shotgun from his office to reply to the legal demands that the studio made steadily on Vito with a barrage of answering documents. One day when he arrived to see Billy, he noticed, as he was admitted by the stern gatehouse guards, three men waiting stolidly outside the gates to serve subpoenas on Vito if he stepped outside the grounds.

"Arvey's an unimaginative man," he told Billy. "If he really wanted to, he could hire a helicopter, land on the lawn with his troops, and force his way into the house and serve Vito that way."

Billy laughed wearily. "It may come to that. He's so enraged that who knows what he might try next?"

Hillman hardly recognized Billy in her working clothes: the terry jogging suit, now baggy in the seat, the tennis shoes, the careless ponytail. If it hadn't been for the great diamonds she still wore in her ears, he might have taken her for—he wasn't sure, but Billy Ikehorn seemed to have disappeared into this rather worn, efficient, carelessly thrown-together woman. She had become a full-time, diamond-decorated ditchdigger, he thought. The insane working rhythm of the professionals was normal to her now, an eight-hour day would have been laughable; quiet, contained crisis was the constant, relaxation an aberration.

"I'm holding them off, just barely," he told Billy. "How's it coming along here? How much longer do you need?"

"The end's in sight," she sighed. "We've been sending the film back and forth to the lab every day for reprints, optical effects, titles—other things I don't really understand."

"How do you manage to get it past those thugs outside the gate?" he asked curiously. Josh dealt only with words and papers, not with the actual film, the subject of all the struggle.

"We use panel trucks. Sometimes they say 'Pioneer Hardware' on the side, sometimes 'Jurgensen's'; we change around—tomorrow they'll say 'Roto-Rooter.'" Billy was proud of this dodge, which had been her idea.

"How many more weeks before you're finished?"

"Probably two weeks of editing left. Fifi's agent called him last night and told him that Arvey was blacklisting him from the studio and proceeding against him with the Directors Guild, telling them that he was in breach of his contract, party to theft. His agent's afraid Fifi might lose his director's card."

"What did Fifi do?" Josh asked, alarmed.

"Told his agent to tell Arvey to do something unmentionable to himself and that he could survive without the studio, that the members of the guild were his friends and he wouldn't get anywhere with them."

"I hope he's right," said Josh gloomily.

The next day Fifi's agent telephoned again, more agitated than before.

"Listen, Robin Hood," he rasped, "you'd better get your ass out of Sherwood Forest. I had calls from Metro and Paramount today—they *were* going to be your two next jobs, in case you've forgotten. Arvey's been bad-mouthing you to them and they want to pull out from their deals, and we've got nothing on paper yet. Those studio heads stick together, you know. Do you want to commit suicide? I'm serious, Fifi, your whole future is on the line and the DGA can't fight the studios for you. Stay with *Mirrors* and you'll be back making commercials. That film is legally not yours, no matter how you try to justify it to yourself."

The following morning Fifi's place at breakfast was unfilled and under the door of Vito and Billy's room there was a letter from him, a combination of deep regret and matter-of-fact necessity.

"I can't blame him," Vito said gravely. "He did more than I had any right to expect. But Christ, if only we could have had him for the next two weeks—"

"I have about thirty pages of notes on the last reels," said Billy.

"How many?"

"Thirty, maybe more. He spent a lot of time looking at the whole picture, over and over and over, and every time he said something, I took it down. I figured he might forget—some of it is repetitious, some places he changed his mind two or three times, but it's all here. I'll transcribe it right away."

"First," cried a transformed Vito, "you'll eat a good breakfast—a working girl needs all her strength. I'll finish cutting the picture myself—Brandy and Mary and I—and Fifi's notes. Jesus! I love you, Billy!"

"Now," asked Billy, "now can I say I told you so?"

"Absolutely!"

At breakfast, Vito told Brandy and Mary what had

happened and warned them that the same thing might happen to them.

"I'm just cocky enough," answered Brandy slowly, "to think that Curt Arvey or no Curt Arvey I can get away with it. Anyway, Vito, you don't know how to run an editing machine, and I'll be damned if I'll let you try to mess around with one. It took me six years to get my editor's card and I'm not about to let you in on any of my secrets. Don't worry about us jumping ship. We're in this to the end. Right, Mary?"

"Right, Brandy," said Mary, repeating the same two words she had murmured hundreds of times a day since the work began.

The final stage in the completion of *Mirrors* was the "mix," which took place during five all-night sessions in an independent mixing studio, where no questions were asked, not even of the hardest of hard-core porno producers as long as he paid his bills on time. Nevertheless, as an extra precaution, even the mixing engineers were told that they were working on a picture called *The Mendocino Story*. In the course of the mix the music track, the voice track, and the sound-effects track were all fit together, and the resulting sound track combined with the images made a single piece of film called the "answer print."

"Show me an answer print," said Vito, pointing with thanksgiving and weary glory to the six double reels of film that filled two metal carrying cases, "and I'll show you a motion picture."

Limply, Billy thought that, if nothing else, marriage had added to her vocabulary.

The two cases held the net results of months of virtually nonstop work, the cooperation of hundreds of people, the total commitment of one small group, the expenditure of more than two million dollars, and an incalculable number of small miracles. Bad weather, illness on the part of the actors, accidents in labs, or any one of the hundreds of other things that can go wrong during the shooting of a picture *hadn't* happened. The inevitable series of minor and major crises had somehow been surmounted by Vito's absolute determination to make this movie and make it fast. Luck and Billy had been on his side.

It was mid-November when Vito had his answer print at last. Curt Arvey was in New York. His difficulties with Vito were merely infuriating compared to the huge disaster the studio was facing with its major production, a star-studded musical based on Dickens' *Pickwick Papers*, a fifteen-million-dollar film, which the studio had been counting on for Christmas release and the family trade. *Pickwick!*, which should have been finished months ago, was still a month behind schedule and bogging down day by day. It was now almost three million dollars over budget and Arvey's board of directors had summoned him to New York to explain. *Pickwick!* had been booked into two hundred and fifty carefully chosen, topnotch, first-run houses, and it was obvious that no combination of events would enable them to meet those dates.

Vito telephoned Oliver Sloan, the head of sales at Arvey Film Studio.

"You fellows can see the answer print of *Mirrors* now, Oliver," he announced casually.

"Jeezus! That's—" The head of sales checked his unseemly astonishment at the incredible speed with which the picture had come through postproduction. "I'll have to call you back on that, Vito."

"Anytime," Vito responded, knowing that Sloan would have to report to Arvey before he said anything more.

With difficulty, Oliver Sloan reached his employer in his hotel suite in Manhattan. After a brief conversation he hung up and sighed to his assistant, "Arvey said to burn the fucking print when Orsini walks in the door and to throw his ass in jail."

"What are you going to do?"

"We'll see it first, I think, before we burn it. Mr. Arvey wasn't in one of his better moods." Sloan then called Vito and set up a screening for the next day with the gloom of a medical examiner about to perform his ten-thousandth autopsy.

The next afternoon at two the big screening room was half filled with the upper echelon of the studio's Sales, Advertising, and Promotion departments, some sixteen men in all. Four of them brought their secretaries, who, by virtue of seniority and tradition, often deigned to come to screenings of new pictures. Since there were no big stars in *Mirrors,* they had scant interest in the film itself, but each of them wanted to be among the first in the studio secretary population to know what Billy Ikehorn's husband had come up with.

The sixteen men, as was their wont, made no audible reactions to the picture except for a few coughs and the sound of cigarettes being lit. As the film ended, the four secretaries scrambled out a side door as inconspicuously as possible and the men sat a minute in the traditional noncommittal silence, but this time it was deeper and longer than usual. Everyone waited for the reaction of Oliver Sloan. Eventually he said, "Thanks, Vito. See you around," and walked out. He was followed by the other men, discussing business matters in low tones, either ignoring Vito or else greeting him with tiny, meaningless nods. Vito waited until the last man had left and quickly slipped out of the screening room. He walked down the hall to the executive men's room. There he slid quietly into a stall and waited. Oliver Sloan's voice was the first he heard.

"Jeezus! This is the first time I've been able to go in four days. This job is getting more binding every year."

"You should complain! I get the runs—had 'em a week."

"Jeezus, Jim, Arvey'll have a heart attack, but this picture is going to save his ass. We can use it to fill all those dates for *Pickwick!* Fucking Orsini—what a fantastic picture. Beautiful! Fucking beautiful!"

"Yeah, it's gonna work, Oli, gonna make it. How many prints do we order?"

"Say two hundred seventy-five, be on the safe side. Fucking Orsini!"

"Why'd the girls leave like that? In such a hurry?"

"Embarrassed, I guess. They'd run out of Kleenexes. Dripping tears all over the place."

"Secretaries—emotional types."

"Yeah, Jeezus, a happy ending'll do it every time. Females, they've got no emotional control. I thought Gracie was about to start sobbing right out loud—had to pinch her hard. Who knows from women? Gracie eats nails for lunch and then goes all sentimental."

Vito had heard enough. Smiling like a conquering Caesar, he left the stall and stood at the door to the men's room, addressing the four well-polished shoes planted on the floor under the stalls.

"I'm delighted that you like the picture, gentlemen. Enjoy a good crap. My treat."

Valentine lay full length on her puffy couch, reveling in the luxury of putting up her feet after a mad day at Scruples. A November breeze blew through the open doors to her terrace, and if she waited there she knew that in a few hours she would see the moon rise. What a day it had been! Tonight was one time she wouldn't give Josh anything more exotic to eat than a pizza, but she was too weary to even phone in an order. There had been the final fittings on the Portland, Oregon, wedding party; everyone from the bride and bridesmaids to the mothers of the bride and groom, plus the bride's entire trousseau. Valentine wondered where the girl would wear those outfits in Portland. She had a vague idea that Portland was a strictly industrial city somewhere up north, but, on the other hand, a forty-thousand-dollar trousseau indicated some anticipation of galas.

She'd finally finished the sketches for Mrs. Byron's winter cruise as well. If Mrs. Byron, at eighty-two, still saw herself as a shipboard femme fatale, Valentine had, at least, made sure that her wrinkled arms and shoulders would be appropriately covered. And, of course, all of her least favorite clients had chosen today to come in to order their Christmas Eve and New Year's Eve dresses. Her favorite clients had ordered them last August, as any sensible woman would. Valentine twitched her ravishing nostrils at the idea of anyone who had so little knowledge of couture that she allowed only six weeks for a made-to-order dress, but she knew she'd manage to deliver them. She took enormous pride in the scope of her designing and the efficiency of her workrooms. She could switch in seconds, from concocting artfully, alluring black lace for a withered grande dame to creating a bridesmaid's dress so pure of line that a girl could still proudly wear it five years frow now. She loved the many challenges of her job. Designing one ready-to-wear line had been so limited, compared to what she was now doing at Scruples. And, heaven knows, she had no one to tell her what to do or what not to do. Billy had totally vanished except for a phone call now and then, just to say hello. Valentine knew that something mysterious was going on at the Orsinis, since Josh had told her a little about it, but it was strange that Billy hadn't ordered any new clothes in months, not since her wedding. Now that she thought about it, Billy had never planned her fall wardrobe, bought nothing except for those jeans. Jeans—Billy. They didn't go together she thought as she slipped into a light doze.

The sound of the house telephone woke her an hour later. She had refused to arrange with the desk downstairs to let Josh up without being announced. The idea that he be allowed to come up without a warning call displeased her. He had his key to her apartment—that was enough. Josh had been irked, even hurt, but she was still her own mistress.

Tonight, she thought, still groggy, he looked a little different than he usually did. He seemed to be suppressing some excitement, some inner agitation. His hair was as perfectly groomed as ever, his conservative four-hundred-and-fifty-dollar suit hung precisely as it should on his well-designed body, but his eyes, those serious gray eyes were filled with some emotion she felt but couldn't analyze. She inspected him more closely. Even his tie was perfectly knotted, yet he looked as if a hurricane had just blown him in the door.

"Josh, I'm too tired to phone. Will you call out for a pizza? Do you think the big one is enough or should we order one big and one small?"

He disregarded her words and came to kneel at the side of the couch where she still lay, stretching and yawning. A nap like that left her as vague as if she'd flown the Atlantic.

Josh kissed her round, white neck and the tender translucent insides of her elbows and her eyes and mouth until he was quite sure she was wide awake.

"No pizza tonight, my dearest. Put on your favorite pretty dress. We're going out for dinner. I've reserved a table at The Bistro for nine o'clock."

"Josh!" Of all places in Los Angeles, The Bistro was the most likely to be filled with friends of Josh and Joanne Hillman. They, along with many of their intimate group, had been among the people who had first financed the fashionable retaurant. To dine at The Bistro with anyone but his wife was possibly the most unwise thing a man could do.

"That's my surprise," Josh said, stumbling over his words. He held her head tightly between his two hands and looked intently into her eyes. "Oh, not The Bistro—I didn't mean that—but from now on we can go anywhere we like in public. I've arranged my divorce." His voice rang with youth and happiness and something like bravado.

"*Divorce?*" Valentine sat up suddenly, almost knocking him down from his kneeling perch on the carpet by her couch.

"Yes—it won't be final for six months, so we can't get married till then, but all the legal business has been taken care of—" He had no intention of telling Valentine, but it had not been easy at all. However, he had prevailed, as he had known from the beginning, since there is no longer any way, at least in California, in which a woman can prevent a man from getting a divorce when he really wants one and is willing to pay the price, nor the other way around for that matter.

Valentine jumped up from the couch and hurled words in a tone he'd never known could come from her.

"You decided to do this without telling me?" she accused him, her pointed face white and distorted with fury.

"Oh, but darling, you *knew*. When we talked on the plane I told you what I wanted. Did you think I was just playing with words?"

"Did you think *I* was?"

"I don't know what you mean—"

"I gave you a very precise answer, an *indefinite* maybe. You can't have forgotten that! And with an indefinite maybe you went ahead and got a divorce?" She was sputtering with burning scorn, twisting her curls as if she'd like to pull them out.

"Sweetheart, when a woman gives a man that much of a go-ahead, he naturally knows she really means yes—I mean, it's implicit, it's understood, it's just not spelled out."

486

"Goddamn it, how *dare* you tell me what I meant? How dare you make me feel that because I didn't say positively, absolutely NO, I said yes? What do you take me for? A coy flirt who hides behind ambiguous words? Who won't commit herself but will smile like some little doll when a man presents her with a fait accompli? You live in another century, my friend." She stood blazing at him, insulted to the core.

Josh was aghast. He was so used to having things his way that he underestimated Valentine. Christ, he'd started out underestimating her from the first day he met her. Abruptly, he turned away from the sight of her and stood blindly fingering the rim of a table lamp. Eventually, he spoke in a voice of such defeat and self-punishment that she listened in spite of herself.

"I can't endure it when you get angry at me—I just don't seem to have the understanding—the intuition—to make the right moves where you're concerned. The only reason I didn't tell you sooner was that I didn't want you to feel responsible for my getting divorced. It was never, never for a minute because I took you for granted." He turned back to her and she saw that his eyes were filled with tears.

"I love you so terribly much, Valentine. It makes me foolish. You love me, too—don't you?"

With a heavy heart, Valentine nodded assent. She supposed she must love him or else why had they been together so long? And what was done was done. But if she had only said a plain no when he asked her to marry him, this wouldn't have happened. It was partly her fault, letting herself be trapped by his clever persistence. She felt as guilty as a child who has accidentally set fire to a house while playing with matches—a house filled with people who couldn't get out. She felt three emotions struggling with each other: love, guilt, and—a more significant emotion—the beginning of a deep, important anger.

"Go away, Josh. I have to think this over. And I wouldn't dream of going to The Bistro with you—what a hideous notion—all those people there knowing that you are getting a divorce and then seeing you with me."

"Oh, shit! That's got to be the worst idea I've ever had!

Valentine, I'm going crazy. Please, please, just let me order the pizzas? I won't ask you for one more decision. I swear it."

Reluctantly, uncertainly, Valentine agreed. She was suddenly terribly hungry. Whether it was filled with love, guilt, or anger, her stomach still functioned with French precision.

"Two pizzas with *everything* on them." She agreed. "Tell them if they forget the pepperoni again you won't pay."

During the first week of December, *Mirrors* opened in the two hundred and fifty excellent first-run movie houses previously chosen for *Pickwick!* now still incomplete and almost four million dollars over budget. Arvey didn't put *Mirrors* in those houses because he wanted to, that was certain. But, faced with an empty stocking for Christmas, he had no choice. While other studios were each releasing their holiday blockbusters, he was stuck with a small-budget love story without stars, which had received virtually no advance publicity buildup. He called his faithful radiologist to make a date for yet another series of upper-GI X rays—he'd just avoided an ulcer for years, but this time the burning pain every time he swallowed a mouthful of food was too sharp for Maalox to soothe.

The newspaper reviews, as they started to come in, did nothing for his digestion. Everyone knew that critics don't mean much of a damn any more as far as movie attendance was concerned. People had a way of going to pictures the critics hated and avoiding those they doted on. Arvey, like most of Hollywood, considered the critics out of touch with the average American, too intellectual, too artsy-craftsy. So what if *The New York Times* said it was "a wonder, the peak of a genre, an act of beauty, a masterpiece." Who the fuck knew from genre out in the Midwest? And the Los Angeles *Times* said that Fiorio Hill and Per Svenberg "had writen another new chapter in film history." Big deal. Film history was full of chapters. *Newsweek* said, "The cinema has never before given such amazing and disquieting visual emotion." Do people stand in lines to see "disquieting emotion," whatever that meant? The only reviews that mattered to Arvey were the trade reviews in *Variety, Daily Variety,* and the *Hollywood Reporter.* "Not since *Love Story* has there been . . ."—that just might be a money review. "Not since *Rocky* . . ."—knock wood, the guy should be right. "Not since *A Man and A Woman* . . ."—a foreign film, but still, it had done business.

But the first week was slow. The heads of his Advertising and Sales departments persuaded Arvey to put more money into advertising, particularly television advertising. They knew that both of their secretaries had gone to see it again, away from the masculine tyranny of the screening room, where they could sob to their hearts' content. No matter what clichés they uttered about emotional women, they knew those girls were tough old tomatoes; you couldn't make them cry with bamboo shoots under their fingernails—and if they were willing to pay to see a film, that was as good as the Oracle at Delphi.

The average motion picture does its best business in its first week of release. *Mirrors* doubled its box-office gross in its second week and almost tripled it in the third week, as the college kids, home for the holidays, began to hit the theaters. If a picture maintains its first week's business for a period of time, it is considered to have "legs." *Mirrors* was showing signs of being a centipede. What was doing it? Word of mouth? The critics after all? The holiday season? No one knew why—they never do—but *Mirrors* had become an indisputable "sleeper." The studio allocated more money for advertising and the public relations began to take care of themselves.

Newspaper and magazine writers like nothing more than a movie they can discover for themselves, a movie that hasn't been shoved down their throats three months in advance by public-relations men. Each reporter who went to interview Sandra Simon or Hugh Kennedy had the feeling of opening up fresh territory. They interviewed Fifi Hill; they even interviewed Per Svenberg, who was a cult figure in any case, the kind of cult figure that fewer than a thousand people know about. Now, millions had heard of him, and he basked in the recognition for which he had waited so long. No one bothered to interview Vito Orsini; he was only the producer.

By Christmas, *Mirrors* was number one on *Variety*'s

box-office weekly chart, and Vito judged the time ripe to break the silence that still stretched between Arvey and himself. Every night he and Billy had driven into Westwood to feast their eyes on the long, patient, good-natured lines waiting to get into the theater in which *Mirrors* was playing. Both of them had had time to get back to knowing each other, Billy's mansion was almost restored to its former tranquillity, and Vito wanted to put his particular house in order.

In Arvey's office the atmosphere was chill. Arvey, having been outwitted in the matter of taking over the picture in postproduction, now clutched it even more possessively than he would have normally. *Mirrors* was "his" picture now, just as it had been Fifi Hill's while it was being shot. Hadn't he given Orsini the opportunity to make it? Hadn't he released it in time for Christmas? Vision, that was what a studio president had to have, vision and daring.

"Vito, I'm putting *Mirrors* into over fifteen hundred houses all over the country next week," Curt Arvey announced imperiously.

"What!"

"Face it, Vito, it's a fluke. It's the kids who're making the box office. When they go back to school in ten days, the picture'll die." Arvey smirked with pleasure at Vito's face. "I want to milk it bone dry before then. Take the money and run—don't tell me you've never heard of that."

"Curt, you just can't do it." Vito jumped up, keeping his voice logical. "This picture is just starting. When Christmas is over the parents of these kids will be coming to see it, young married couples will be coming to see it, everybody in the whole damn country will be coming to see it! If you ruin the distribution pattern now, if you book it into second-rate houses, you'll dissipate the whole word-of-mouth buildup." Arvey's expression hardened. "In one week you'll end up with half the cash—maybe less—than you would have if you keep it where it is, letting it grow, build, naturally. I've been talking to the kids on those lines; some of them are waiting to see it for the third or fourth time. Curt, those *lines* are just as important a lure as the picture itself. Book it in fifteen hundred houses and in a week you won't have any lines left. Don't you see that, for Christ's sake?" Vito was leaning forward, both hands on Arvey's large desk. He couldn't believe the other man could fail to agree with such basic business logic.

Arvey looked at Vito vindictively. *Mirrors* was his, damn it, and he could do anything he liked with it. No gigolo of a Vito Orsini was going to tell him how to run his business. It was a nice switch to have Orsini by the balls for a change.

"You are entitled to your point of view," he drawled, "but I happen to have another. And I'm in charge now. Cash, quick cash is what interests me, not pie in the sky. You're a romantic, Vito, and a thief as well."

Vito moved swiftly. Tall and lethal, he leaned over Arvey's desk and switched the desk intercom to "Sales."

"Oliver? Vito Orsini here. I'm with Curt. He plans to string *Mirrors* out in the dates we presently have instead of going into a wide break. What do you think?"

Arvey, gaping in his swivel chair, was about to bellow into the intercom when Oliver answered.

"He's a hundred percent right, Vito. Anything else would be totally ridiculous, cost us millions in the long run."

Vito released the switch and aimed a look like a rifle barrel at Arvey's congested face.

"What would your board of directors think about that, Curt? Are you in a position to blow millions in box-office grosses just to prove you're boss? How's *Pickwick!* coming along? I hear you took full credit for that idea before it started to go sour."

"Get the fuck out of here, you shit-ass, you—you—" Arvey, too angry for more invective, pushed the button for his secretary and screamed, "Get Security! Right away!"

"Careful, Curt. Remember your ulcer."

Vito strolled out of the office like a big tawny panther. As he passed Arvey's secretary, he blew a kiss at her frightened face.

"Don't celebrate yet, darling, unfortunately he'll survive."

In spite of the sprinkling of smugly overorganized women who delight in declaring by the first of November that they have finished their Christmas shopping, most retailers find that December 10th, not a day earlier, is the magic moment for the Christmas rush to begin. Scruples was no exception to that rule. Although few customers were buying clothes, they jammed the Country Store, and the entire first floor, being systematically stripped of its treasures, swarmed like an anthill under attack. Spider had spent the day exerting his benign influence, trying on dozens of sweaters for women unsure of their husbands' exact size—"He's about a head shorter than you, Spider, and weighs twenty pounds more, would you be a darling and just slip it over your head?"—and giving advice to the perplexed: "What would *you* send to your mother-in-law if you positively *detested* her but had to spend at least three hundred dollars? A Waterford jar of sour balls and a gold-plated nutcracker?—Spider, you're a genius."

By closing time on December 23rd, both he and Valentine felt that the worst was over. Christmas Eve was on Saturday this year and all of Valentine's special holiday party dresses had already been picked up or delivered; tomorrow's gift buying would be light, an in-and-out last-minute sort of business except for the few wise people who knew that the best day to shop after December 10th is December 24th. These were usually businessmen with imposing lists who made up their minds in seconds, the saleswomen's delight.

Spider and Valentine sat facing each other on either side of the old partners' desk. There should have been a comfortable, relaxed silence between them, as there so often had been at the beginning or the end of a Scruples day, but the air in the room was filled with watchfulness. Spider thought that Valentine looked troubled. Her impertinently tilted nose was held as delicately high as ever, but some of the aggressive, coruscating shimmer seemed to have been chipped away from her great green eyes. He knew his Valentine. She wasn't happy.

From her side of the desk, Valentine was considering Spider Elliott. He looked tired, she thought. Older in a way that couldn't be explained by the mere passage of time. It seemed difficult to connect this polished, sophisticated, elegantly dressed man of the world with the carefree blond boy in a UCLA sweat shirt who'd carried her wine bottles home from the market, made her countless melted-cheese sandwiches when she was miserable, and listened to her old Piaf records by the hour in her little loft room.

"Are you just exhausted, Val, my darling, or is there something wrong?" he asked gently.

Valentine felt an ignominious, totally unexpected prickle of tears begin at the sound of his voice. She was longing for someone to confide in about her situation with Josh Hillman, but, of all the people in the world, Elliott was the last one she would discuss it with. Some mysterious but imperative reason lay behind her obstinate determination not to let Spider guess how far matters had progressed or how confused she still was.

"Oh, it's just these women, Elliott—so demanding, so difficult to please. They gain ten pounds between one fitting and another and they think it's my fault."

"Come on, darling, you know they dote on you. And you never hesitate to lower the boom on any of your ladies when she's changed her measurements—why, you're the reason behind half the diets in this town. What is it, really? Is the mystery man giving you any trouble?"

She sat bolt upright, alarmed and defensive. Her desire to weep disappeared.

"What are you talking about?"

"The mystery man, the one who keeps you so busy that I never get to see you alone anymore. If he's not treating you right, I'll kill the son of a bitch!" To his amazement, he found that his fists were clenched, every muscle in his arms and shoulders was tense with rage. Killing the son of a bitch seemed like a very good idea. Never mind a reason.

"You assume too much, Elliott. Your imagination is running away with you." Valentine pressed her attack, suddenly as infuriated as he. "Do I ask you why you make all those women crazy over you? No wonder you look so tired—how do you tell them all apart anyway, all your little friends? Is there a magic in numbers, Elliott?" She was overcome by the injustice of the situation. "Am I not to have even *one* lover?" she blurted. "I'm not accountable to you, Elliott."

"*You damn well are!*" he shouted. The air between quivered, with amazement. Neither of them could quite believe that they had become embattled so suddenly. They glared at each other in a momentary, baffled hush. Finally Spider spoke.

"There must be something wrong with me, Valentine. Of course you're not accountable to me. I don't know why I said that—just because we've known each other so long I guess."

"It still doesn't give you the right—"

"No. Forget it, OK?" He looked at his watch. "I'm late, see you tomorrow."

As he retreated hastily, closing the door behind him, Valentine sat motionless in her chair, stunned, puzzled, shaken by the intensity of the gust of emotion that had been released into the air. Elliott had spoken without any right, without any reason. She should be furious. She'd been furious for less cause. Yet she felt—pleased. Pleased? Yes, unquestionably pleased. What a terrible bitch she must be. So he thought she was accountable to him, did he? An involuntary smile crossed her face without her knowledge.

As several weeks passed without *Mirrors* being shifted from the theaters in which it was currently playing, Vito became increasingly confident that Oliver Sloan's understanding of the best way to make a buck, combined with the unwilling corroboration of Arvey's sensitive digestive system, had triumphed over Arvey's attack of bad judgment.

However, Arvey's personal animosity to Vito was more virulent than ever, and he showed his spite and thwarted wrath by placing only a bare minimum of trade ads in the *Hollywood Reporter* and *Daily Variety*. Under normal circumstances with a top-grossing picture, the studio would have thrown the success of *Mirrors* in their competitors' teeth. No, thought Vito, he could expect nothing from the studio, but the beauty of it was that he didn't need them now. Two things told the only story he cared about: *Variety*'s weekly box-office chart, on which *Mirrors* remained number one, and the yearly lists of the "Ten Best" pictures, as judged by critics all over the country. All of them, to date, included *Mirrors*. Vito decided to proceed with the plan he had been forming since he first saw the answer print.

Several days before Christmas Billy drove out to Venice, that raunchy, Coney Island-like seaside colony of Los Angeles where a number of slapdash Bohemian houses still have not been replaced by the rapidly growing mass of new condominiums. She was going to visit Dolly for lunch and see for herself how she was feeling halfway into her sixth month of pregnancy. Loaded with Christmas presents, Billy climbed to Dolly's two-room apartment on the third floor of an old stucco house, painted pale pink with magenta trim, on a street where everyone seemed to know everyone else, where neighbors chatted as they basked in the winter sun in their front yards or watered their potted plants or avoided skateboarding kids. So far none of these houses had been sold to developers, and Dolly's landlord, a captain in the Los Angeles Fire Department, managed to pay the escalating taxes on his modest but increasingly valuable house by renting his top floor, now that his children had left home.

One look at Dolly convinced Billy that the pregnancy was going well. She stood in affectionate contemplation of the blooming milkmaid of a girl, euphoric, rosy, blessed with positively Restoration amplitude, although totally lacking the Restoration waist, or any waist at all.

"You're a toothsome dish," she told Dolly, surveying her from all sides.

"What does that mean?" Dolly asked, laughing, demurely delighted with her majestic belly.

"Tasty, I think. Anyway it sounds good."

"Wait till you try what I made for lunch, Milton Berle's Gefilte Chicken à la Fish," Dolly pronounced impressively.

"What on earth—?"

"I almost did the Senator Jacob Javits Cheese Blintzes or the Irving Wallace Matzo Brei, but then I remembered how careful you are about gaining weight so I compromised."

"*Where* did you get those—those recipes?" Billy asked, torn between laughter and skepticism. Dolly produced an oblong pink-and-red book.

"It's the *Celebrity Kosher Cookbook*—it's marvelous. Yesterday I practiced the Barbara Walters Stuffed Cabbage."

"But why?"

"I figured that as long as I wasn't working, I should do something useful. Remember what you told me about finding some wonderful Jew? Wouldn't it help if I were a terrific kosher cook?"

"Unquestionably," said Billy dryly. "But is this the time to catch one?"

"Some men are attracted to pregnant women," Dolly answered impishly. "Especially when they can make a fabulous Neil Diamond Pot Roast. Actually, I guess I'll have to wait until after the baby is born, but you just never know, do you? The other day I went to see *Mirrors* again —it's my eleventh time—and about fifty people asked me for an autograph, and three guys asked me out for dinner."

"Did you go?" breathed Billy.

"Of course not—weirdos, all of them. But still, they asked."

"What's it like," asked Billy curiously, "seeing *Mirrors* with an audience, all the way through?"

"Don't *you* know? Billy, you've seen it over and over!"

"Only in an editing room or in a mixing studio, never with strangers, not where they have to pay to see it."

"That's simply terrible." Dolly was shocked. "Why, the audience is the best part of all. You know the scene after I've told Sandra how Hugh really feels about her and she finds him on the cliff—"

"Know it?" Billy groaned. "I know it so well I think I wrote it."

"But, Billy, that's when they start to cry—all over the theater you absolutely feel the emotion growing, swelling, people responding—I even get tears in my eyes."

"But, my God, Dolly, you were standing right there when Fifi made them do it over for the sixth time and Sandra kept complaining about the burrs in her shoes and Svenberg was screaming that the light was going—"

"I forget," Dolly said stubbornly. "I just don't remember all of that—it's all fresh to me, each time. Look, let's go together, after lunch, OK?"

"Your twelfth time and you still want to see it?"

"Maybe I'll get to be like one of those *Sound of Music* addicts, remember? Some of them saw it seventy-five times or more. And they weren't even *in* it—don't ever tell Vito, but mostly I go to watch my own performance. You know all those interviews when actors say they never see their own films? I don't understand that—I just adore seeing myself up there!" She whispered the last words, hugging herself gleefully, half guiltily, half pridefully. "I guess I'm just a ham."

"You're unreal," said Billy. "You're a most beautiful and touching actress—I've told you before but you'll never trust me."

Dolly turned aside bashfully. She could never quite believe or accept praise for doing what came so naturally.

"Here, I almost forgot," she said, "your Christmas present." She handed Billy a filled, covered earthenware crock. "It's George Jessel's Chicken Liver Pâté. You won't believe it!"

"I don't already," Billy answered.

Vito wanted to get a Best Picture nomination for *Mirrors*. He hadn't dared to do more than dream of it until he saw the answer print, but from that day on the thought was never out of his head. *Mirrors* was the finest production of his working career. In it he had achieved a film that became far more than the sum of its parts, expertly chosen though they were. It *lived* with a beating pulse of its own; it *worked* on every level from comedy through poetry. It would be a landmark picture, he felt in his bones, but first he had had to wait for the confirmation of the rest of the world to justify his belief. Until the reviews came in, until the box-office responded, and, finally, until the picture appeared on the "Ten Best" lists, it would have been an exercise in wistfulness to do more than dream. But now he had the necessary prerequisites to act.

Mirrors had all the credentials it needed, but it lacked the one thing commonly considered necessary for a shot at one of the five Academy nominations: studio support. Lavish advertising campaigns, unabashed promotion, specially hired publicists, all these could have been provided by the Arvey Film Studio, but Vito had no illusions. Curt Arvey wouldn't spend one extra penny to push *Mirrors*. Perhaps, in fact certainly, if Arvey had been convinced that this small picture had an excellent chance to actually win the Oscar, he would have brought himself around to seeking a nomination, since an Oscar means an average addition of ten million dollars to the box-office gross. But Arvey could see, as could Vito, that the past year had produced a number of superstar, super-expensive films, which had powerful studios behind each one of them. Any one of them could legitimately merit the Oscar. A nomination for *Mirrors* would only mean some glory for Vito, and Arvey would travel far to prevent this, even if some of the glory could be expected to rub off on him.

So, quite simply, Vito would do it alone.

He pondered the membership of that group of some three thousand three hundred working people so elaborately called the Academy of Motion Picture Arts and Sciences. Only this carefully limited number of people was entitled to even *decide* for which films and performers and craftsmen votes could be cast, something comparable to permitting only the population of Westport, Connecticut, to vote for President of the United States.

The Best Picture nominations are the only ones voted on by the entire membership of the Academy. Nominations in all other categories are voted on by the branches involved, so that only actors nominate actors, only art directors nominate art directors, and so on. However, the final voting in all categories is by all members. This meant that Vito had to influence every one of the Academy members in order to get a Best Picture nomination.

When a studio is actively promoting a film for a nomination, it gives any number of special, luxurious screenings at the studio's expense. Vito couldn't afford that. But he had never forgotten the response of the four secretaries at the first screening of *Mirrors*. He narrowed his entire campaign to capturing the attention of the wives and the mothers and the sisters and the daughters and the cousins and the aunts of the male members, who are a preponderance in every branch of the Academy.

Get the women, he told himself, and they'll take care of the men.

Vito sent invitations to afternoon screenings to the women who lived in the residential communities all over Los Angeles in which sound men and cameramen and editors and short-subject men make their homes. Every single day, from Christmas until the day during the first week in February when the ballots for the nominations are

498

filled out, there were at least three, and sometimes as many as seven, screenings of *Mirrors,* playing from Culver City to Burbank, from Santa Monica to the far stretches of the San Fernando Valley. Vito didn't care if the female relatives of the Academy members brought every woman friend they had; he simply wanted them to see *Mirrors.* "Operation Matinee," as Billy dubbed it, was a complicated affair logistically. Vito had to find local movie houses that were empty in the afternoon, make deals with managers, borrow prints, arrange for their delivery and return, and see to rounding up projectionists.

"How's it going, darling?" Billy asked, looking at Vito with worry. During the tension of the shoot he had never seemed so preoccupied. Stubbornly, in her opinion, stupidly, he wouldn't use her money for this project.

"I'm perfectly swell, except for a nasty heart murmur, those mysterious shooting pains in my head, a spastic colon, and fallen arches. But I can't complain, I think my hearing is coming back in one ear, and I barely fainted at all yesterday."

"Are you even sure it's worth it?" she wondered, refusing to be put off by his diversionary tactics.

"No. Of course not. Sometimes there are only a dozen women at the matinees, and for all I know, they are just somebody's curious neighbors. Sometimes there are almost a hundred. But if I don't do it, nobody will. And if I don't make the attempt, I'll never forgive myself."

"I think *Mirrors* will be nominated simply on merit!" she flashed.

"I wish you were a member of the Academy."

Vito never knew how or why *Mirrors* was one of the five pictures nominated in the second week of February 1978. The element that finally swung the vote might have been actors voting for a picture in which three almost unknown performers were given a chance to do their stuff; it might just have been Fifi's year for a nomination; it might have been the more than three hundred Academy writers voting to salute a film that depended so much on a sensitive script; it might have been because people had wanted to see a love story or a film of exceptional visual beauty, or liked to cry at a happy ending—or even because of his matinees. Afterward, it was as impossible to single out one single reason, although it was as irresistible a subject of conversation as trying to decide which ethnic or socioeconomic group was responsible for the election of a President of the United States.

But it was not a fluke. *Mirrors* also received nominations in three other categories: Dolly Moon for Best Supporting Actress, Fiorio Hill for Best Director, and Per Svenberg for Best Cinematography.

"Thank God!" exalted Billy. "Now you can relax."

"Are you mad, girl? Now we have a crack at the Oscar! I could only relax if we hadn't gotten a nomination."

Dolly Moon, thought Curt Arvey, he'd have to do something about her. Now that *Mirrors* had the nominations, his feelings toward Dolly, Fifi, and Svenberg had become paternal to a degree. Just as *Mirrors* was *his* picture, Dolly and the others were *his* people. He successfully blocked out any memory of Vito's role in any of the glory. Fifi and Svenberg were established, respected, famous professionals, and he could do litle to add to their reputations at this point. But Curt Arvey fancied himself as a star maker. And he was a devout tits and ass man. Cute, sexy, little Dolly Moon deserved her own full-time publicist, he told the vice-president in charge of Promotion and Public Relations.

All of the top people in the Promotion Department, presently deployed in the salvage of *Pickwick!* which was now rescheduled for an Easter release, were beset on all sides by the piranha fish of the press who flock joyously to munch and suck on the bleeding carcass of a big picture known to be in deep shit, an event far more productive of copy than anything else Hollywood provides except the suicide of a top star. Surveying his depleted troops, the head of Promotion picked out his youngest employee, one Lester Weinstock.

He had to do something special for young Weinstock, who was the son of the president of the company that supplies all the honey wagons used on locations. Like an army, a film unit travels on its stomach, but unlike an army, its members demand decent toilet facilities. Although young Weinstock was a brilliant graduate of the Film Department of the University of Southern California, he could, at best, have aspired to a job in the mailroom if his father had not been "Honey Fitz" Weinstock, an influential man indeed.

Young Lester Weinstock was a throwback to another time, another civilization. Just to look at his round, cheerful, bespectacled face, his shaggy head of hair, his warm, delighted, delightful, delighting smile, was to feel that he had tumbled out of a more innocent past, one of the Three Musketeers perhaps, although too plump to be much good at duels, or a youthful Falstaff, before he gained all that weight. He was tall as well as bulky, with hair the color of a Teddy bear's and nearsighted eyes the color of anybody's favorite dog, sort of brownish, and indeterminate but pleasant features, which no one really could describe because his smile was what they focused on. Women invariably had one of two reactions to Lester: They wanted to adopt him or they wanted him to adopt them, as sisters. Since Lester possessed a deeply romantic soul, this familial state of affairs was not really what he had in mind, but, at twenty-five, he was not discouraged. Life was too good.

When Lester got his assignment to become Dolly Moon's personal public-relations representative until the Academy Awards, he was overjoyed. His ultimate ambition, as is almost universal with film students, was to become a director, but, meanwhile, realistically, he knew how lucky he was to have this happen after less than two years as lowest man on the Promotion Department's totem pole.

He had already seen *Mirrors* and been utterly enchanted with the austere, fatefully beautiful Sandra Simon. Now he screened it again, concentrating on Dolly. Physically she wasn't the type of girl he generally went for. Lester lusted after moody, fascinatingly neurotic, miserable, will-'o-the-wisp beauties with haunted eyes. There was nothing haunted about Dolly Moon, but she was one hell of a splendid actress, Lester realized, and saw the picture through again. Much, much too big fore and aft for his taste, but he was supposed to nursemaid her, not date her.

He telephoned Dolly right after lunch to announce his mission and to make an appointment to meet her.

"What did you say your name was, again?" asked Dolly, somewhat befuddled from the block party that had begun in the morning as soon as the nominations were announced.

"Lester Weinstock."

"Could you say that again—slowly? Spell it?"

"Hey, are you OK? You sound a little, sort of, dizzy."

"Oh, no! I'm perfect. Come on out here, Lester Weinstock. We've got eggnog and rum punch and sangría and Tequila Moonlight and hot toddies, and I'm baking strudel. If you get here in less than an hour it'll still be hot. Goodbye till then, Lester Weinstock."

Jesus, thought Lester, his first movie star and she turns out to be a bit bananas. His next phone call confused him even further.

"Mr. Weinstock, we haven't met, but I'm Billy Orsini, Vito Orsini's wife. Now this is very, very important, so listen carefully. Dolly Moon is my best friend and her only fault is she doesn't know how to dress. Not a clue. Understand? So you're in charge of getting her to Scruples no later than this afternoon so that Valentine O'Neill—got that?—can design a dress for her to wear to the Awards. Don't let her ask anything about who's going to pay for it or what it costs—it's on the house but I don't want her to know. Tell her the studio is picking up the bill. Is that all perfectly clear? Good. We'll be meeting soon. What? Yes, of *course* I'm thrilled for my husband. Yes, I'll tell him. But, Mr. Weinstock, Lester, there are only *six weeks* till the Awards and Dolly's got to see Valentine *today*. You do understand? Never mind, you will!"

Lester climbed the stairs to Dolly's apartment with his heart, reacting to the excitement, almost not beating at all. Billy's breathless phone call coming on top of his conversation with Dolly had plunged him farther into a world in which anything could happen. His mother and his oldest sister sometimes shopped at Scruples for extra special occasions, but he'd never ventured inside. Now he was going to be taking a gorgeous, well, an adorable potential Oscar winner there for an evening gown under mysteriously urgent circumstances, and the strudel smelled wonderful. Just for today, he decided, he'd forget about his diet.

The wife of Dolly's landlord opened the door, revealing a room filled with celebrating bodies. Lester stood uncer-

502

tainly in the center of the room, wondering where Dolly Moon was and how he was going to spirit her away from all of this. After a moment an unmistakable voice from behind him said, "I've saved you a piece of strudel, Lester Weinstock, and believe me it wasn't easy." He whirled around and met the full force of Dolly's huge eyes, profligate in their blueness, smiling welcomingly at him. Automatically, he reached out for the plate she held just above waist level. WAIST LEVEL!

"I know," giggled Dolly deliciously, "I can't believe it myself. Every morning I wake up and see myself in the mirror and I just don't think it's possible to get any bigger, but I do. Eat your strudel while it's still hot."

Without knowing what he was doing, Lester put a piece of pastry in his mouth and chewed.

"Don't you like it?" Dolly asked apprenhensively.

"It's—great, just great. Would it be rude if I asked—"

"For the recipe?"

"How many—months?" She looked like an explosion in a pillow factory, he thought. No, a mattress factory.

"Seven months and one week, give or take a day or two," Dolly answered, pleased with her accuracy. "It happened over the weekend of the Fourth. People should always get knocked-up on holidays, don't you think? It makes keeping track so much easier."

"Wait a minute, wait a minute." Lester looked wildly for a place to sit down and finally lowered his bulk to the floor. Dolly maneuvered herself down to sit beside him. He definitely needed a haircut. Why was he counting on his fingers? He looked smarter than that. He looked very sweet, steady, reliable but fun. Just as she had known he would. And Lester went so well with *Weinstock*. But why did he seem so concerned?

"There's nothing to worry about," she said softly.

"Eight months and three weeks," he sighed, "on the night of the Awards."

"I don't have to go, if you don't think it's a good idea."

"Oh, yes you do. My boss made that very clear. Everyone connected with *Mirrors* is going to be there. He says it's the worst kind of public relations when the nominees don't show up, unless, of course, they're working on location somewhere on the other side of the world. And even then. You'll be there with your husband—no? OK, your guy—no?—your father? No? Shit. Look—a date, somebody who's just some old buddy, a high-school sweetheart?"

Dolly smiled at this absurd man. She might not know much, but she knew whose job it was to escort her to the Academy Awards if she didn't have another date. And she didn't.

"Have some more strudel, Lester."

Valentine had never imagined that a day that started out in such a normal way could end with such frenzy. As she had predicted to Spider, the comedy had begun, but it was only a comedy to nonparticipants. Because the Awards ceremony is telecast by satellite throughout the world, the estimated audience is something more than one hundred and fifty million people. Fortunately, it is quite impossible to visualize that many people. Nevertheless, each of Valentine's customers knew that they would be seen by more people at one time than they ever had been before, and that thought did nothing good for their anxiety levels or their senses of inner security.

Maggie MacGregor, ordering the first custom-made dress of her life, was the most atwitter of them all. Since she was going to be on camera, interviewing various stars as they arrived and then backstage with her minicam crew, she would be visible for much of the broadcast.

"Valentine, I should never have gotten into the business," Maggie moaned.

"Nonsense," retorted Valentine, who was fed up with a day of feeling more like an English nanny with a houseful of bad children than a designer. "You'd poison anyone who tried to take the job away from you, wouldn't you? So shut up and let me think." There was no question that Maggie had a difficult figure. In the half-slip and bra she was standing in, her miniature but lushly ripe body did not inspire thoughts of chic. Spider had done wonders in getting her into quiet, elegantly forgettable dresses, but what was suitable for her weekly show just would not do for the awards. Maggie had to be as glamorous as the occasion, in all fairness to herself and the network. Valentine peered closely from behind her stockade of black lashes.

"Maggie, push your breasts up with one hand your bra down with the other. Farther down. And farther up. Hmm. That's it, that's it all right, the tops of your breasts, seductive but not indecent. Thank God for the Empress Josephine."

"Valentine," Maggie protested "you know Spider won't approve. He'd never let me get away with showing so much of my boobs on camera, you know how strict he is about that."

"Do you want *me* to design a dress for you, or do you want to buy ready-to-wear from Spider?" said Valentine, joking very little.

"Oh, my God, you know I want you to make me the dress, but are you *sure,* I mean, won't I look—vulgar, just a little?"

"You will look utterly, totally elegant, and the only ornament on the most simple, most slender, most refined, and most restrained dress I've ever designed will be your breasts, right down to the top of the nipples. And when the show is over, hundreds of millions of people will know two things: who won the Oscars and that Maggie Mac-Gregor has fantastic tits. Now, off you go. My assistant will take your measurements and we'll set up a first fitting for two weeks from today."

"What's this restrained dress going to be made of?" Maggie ventured, as Valentine turned impatiently to her sketching table.

"Black chiffon, of course—how else would we get the maximum contrast? And Maggie, no jewelry except earrings, not even a string of pearls. Tits and chiffon, it can't fail. It never has, not in thousands of years."

As Valentine quickly sketched a low-cut Empire dress, with bare arms too, of course, for Maggie had beautifully rounded arms and pretty hands, she realized with another part of her mind that she wasn't feeling the elation she should be experiencing. From midmorning on she had had a flood of world-famous customers, women so beautiful and talented that it was a pleasure to dress them, a prideful thing to be called upon to create the gowns that would set off their particular points to their best advantage when they were called on to present awards or, possibly, to receive them.

Yet now, at a moment of triumph, with all her creative juices flowing, Valentine was aware of an uneasy place somewhere in her mind that somehow made her bones feel bad inside her skin. She had done as little self-searching as possible lately, living each day on the surface, postponing, putting off, filing away, and turning her back on any resolution of her future. She hoped that, like unanswered letters put out of sight, this method would eventually make the decision for her by itself. Somehow, thought Valentine wryly, it doesn't seem to be working. Whenever she managed to pull herself together and resolved to think things out, her brain performed a neat backward flip, away in the opposite direction. Fantasy failed as limply as logic. She couldn't project herself, even in fantasy, as Mrs. Josh Hillman. She kept seeing that big house on North Roxbury, but she could never imagine herself living in a similar one. It just didn't fall in place. Some essential gear wouldn't mesh.

Although Josh said nothing more to her, as he had promised, Valentine finally told him that she couldn't tell him if she was going to marry him until after the Academy Awards.

"What on earth does that have to do with us?" he had asked, baffled and disconcerted.

"I'm too busy to think about myself, Josh, and, anyway, until I know who wins, my mind is all wound up with Billy and Vito and hoping for them." Behind the diversionary protection of her bangs and her eyelashes, Valentine wondered if that sounded as ridiculously lame—even false—to him as it did to her. In any case, it was the best answer she was prepared to give him and it would have to do. He knew better now than to push her. It was not, Valentine realized, that she was too busy to think about herself, but rather that she had no inclination to think about herself. Obviously her fatalistic Irish genes were dominating her French ones—so much the worse, or so much the better, as the case might be.

Valentine shrugged her unreconstructed Gallic shrug at her shamelessly ethnic excuse and waited, impatient now, for her next client, Dolly Moon. Billy had been so insistent this morning, so unusually nervous when she told Valentine to design for her friend the most marvelous dress she'd ever made.

Valentine had seen *Mirrors* twice, and she had a good idea of the problems involved in dressing Dolly, but she suspected that Miss Moon could wear almost anything and get away with it. She had the kind of personality that would inevitably triumph over whatever she put on. Billy had no need to worry. One did not look at her clothes, one looked at her funny-beautiful face, her wide, beguiling smile, her entire person, so adorably awkward and sexy.

Valentine stretched her arms to the ceiling, bent to the floor, and stretched up again. She felt tight from all the drawing she'd done. Time for Dolly Moon. Billy hadn't made this much of a production about her own wedding dress.

A little more than an hour later, Billy had swept Dolly and Lester off to have dinner at home with her, as relieved as a mother who has watched her child perform in a school play for the first time.

"Well," said Spider, handing a glass of Château Silverado to Valentine, "you can't say that Billy has lost her capacity to astonish and confound us. How on earth are you ever going to upholster Miss Moon?"

"Oh, there is a way," Valentine answered airily. "It's merely a question of using one's imagination. Obviously, it's a little more difficult than the sort of thing you do all day, Elliott, but it can be done." She put down her glass, took off her smock, and put on her coat, ready to leave.

"Wait a minute, Val. This dress for Dolly is something I could help you with, and, God knows, you've got enough on your plate already. Sit down for a few minutes and we can talk it over."

"No thank you, Elliott. I can handle it and I'm late for a dinner engagement already. I can't spend any more time here today."

Spider stopped dead at her dismissive tone. "Can't? My, my, this guy really makes you toe the line, it seems. Got you just right where he wants you, hasn't he? Somehow, I never thought I'd live to see the day—Valentine tamed at last." There was the slightest sneer in his tone, but Valentine picked it up instantly.

"What do you mean, Elliott? My private life is private. I thought we'd agreed about that weeks ago, but obviously you can't leave well enough alone."

"Oh, your little hole-in-the-corner arrangements don't bother me, Valentine. I'm just rather amused by it all," he said loftily.

Circles of wrath appeared around Valentine's eyes. "You are hardly one to speak of holes-in-the-corner—you spend your whole life in one, Elliott. I didn't know, when I managed to get you this job, that I was providing Beverly Hills with its stud of the year. If I had, perhaps I might have persuaded Billy to give you a slightly higher salary."

"Ah ha! I was waiting for that. I knew the day would come when you'd take credit for keeping me off Welfare. Listen, my pet," he snarled at her, "you would have been out of here on your ass in two weeks if I hadn't come up with the ideas of how to change Scruples."

"That was a year and a half ago. What have you done since then except act like some bloody floorwalker? A self-appointed arbiter of elegance. Ha! The thing that gives Scruples its cachet is my department; you're just too mean-minded to admit it." Her voice ripped the air.

"Your department! On the profits of your department we could barely pay the telephone bill." He was caught in a rapture of rage. "You and that white smock, as if you were another Givenchy, giving yourself grand airs and graces because you've suckered a bunch of spoiled rich women into letting you design for them—it's all supported by the rest of the store and I'm responsible for that—a store doesn't run itself, or are you too much above it all in the fucking rarefied air you breathe to realize that?"

"You lousy, rotten—"

"Oh, ho, our Valentine's about to embark on one of her famous temper fits; if she can't get what she wants she gets all French and kicks her heels and foams at the mouth and frightens horses. Temper, temper." He wagged a finger at her. He might just as well have shot an arrow into her face. Her hands and feet went numb with fury.

"You cheap prick. No wonder even Melanie Adams rejected you. And how typical of you, how typical of your standards, to have picked a hollow little creature like that to love, just another pretty face with nothing inside, all

508

surface, no substance, a doll-child, as immature as you are —and *that* was the love of your life! I find that 'amusing,' Elliott. At least my lover is someone of substance—I wonder if you even understand what substance is?"

In a rusted, painful voice he said, "I hope he's not another Alan Wilton, Valentine. I really couldn't take it if I had to nurse you over a tragic love affair with a fag again."

"WHAT!"

"You thought I wouldn't hear about it? Half of Seventh Avenue knew—eventually the word got around to me."

Valentine felt as if a weight like a great slab of stone had knocked her in the chest. She couldn't speak. She crumpled in her chair, reaching blindly for her handbag. Suddenly Spider felt the greatest shame he'd ever known fall over him like a net. Never, never in his life had he been cruel to a woman. Good Christ, what had come over him? He couldn't even remember how this had all started.

"Valentine—"

"I don't want to talk to you again," she interrupted, in a small, steady voice. "We can't work together anymore."

"Please, Val, I went crazy—I didn't mean—it was a lie, nobody knew. Nobody. I met the guy once and figured it out for myself—Val, please—"

"One of us has to leave Scruples." She said this in a way that allowed no room for apology or reason or discussion.

"That's ridiculous. We can't do that to Billy."

"I'll go."

"No, you can't. Nobody else can do your work. She can replace me."

"Fine." She was unmoved, frozen.

"I can't tell her till after the Oscars. She's get enongh to worry about with Vito."

"As you wish." Valentine picked up her coat and left. Spider heard her taking the fire stairs, not waiting for the elevator. For an hour he sat there, rubbing his hands on the oxblood leather of the partner's desk, as if the slight friction might make him warm again.

The documentary Maggie had done on Vito, *A Day in the Life of a Producer,* had never been shown on the network. Other, more controversial topics had superseded it for a few months and then it had languished in inventory waiting for an appropriate time slot. Maggie had almost forgotten it, particularly now, as she was bombarded by various studios competing for her attention as Academy Award time drew near.

A week after the nominations were announced, screenings of the five nominated pictures were begun in the Academy's own marvelously comfortable Samuel Goldwyn Theatre on Wilshire Boulevard just east of Beverly Hills. With only three weeks left before the ballots were marked, Vito knew that whatever his last effort was, it had better be made soon. If Maggie's show was ever to be helpful, it would be now. Vito telephoned her at her office.

"Maggie," he asked, "who is your very favorite person in the whole world?"

"I am."

"Who's next?"

"Vito, have you no shame?"

"Certainly not," he laughed.

"You want something," she said suspiciously.

"Damn right, I do. I want you to schedule that piece you did on me before the voting for Best Picture takes place."

"Jesus! Vito, do you realize how that would look? I mean, my God, that would be the most barefaced piece of propaganda—how could I do a thing like that even if I wanted to?"

"Which you do, don't you, Maggie?" He was relentless.

"Well obviously, Vito, I mean I'd like to do whatever I could for you but—"

"Maggie, remember the night we all had dinner at the Boutique and you said you figured that you owed me?"

"Vaguely."

"You've never been vague in your life. My Mexican dog made your career."

"Yeah, but my quick thinking saved Ben Lowell's ass."

"So Ben Lowell owes you. Only you can never tell him. But now you have a chance to pay *me* back."

"You'd really put the squeeze on me?" She could hardly believe this was Vito.

"Of course. What are friends for?"

There was a silence. Vito gave Maggie time to think, as he knew she would, that if she did this for a friend, she would have demonstrated her power so effectively that the demand for her friendship would be even greater, among the people who count in Hollywood, than it ever had been.

"Well," she said finally, "I could talk to the vice-president in charge of Programming, I suppose, and maybe I might be able to con him into it, but I can't promise anything."

"It couldn't be more topical," said Vito helpfully.

"You Wop bastard! Topical! Political is what it is."

"Oh, Maggie, just one of the things I love about you is that I don't have to beat around the bush."

"If this does get on, you'll owe me. Win or lose."

"Fair enough. You've got a deal. We'll go through life doing each other favors and paying them back."

"Yeah," said Maggie, suddenly wistful. "Well, I'd better get started. It's going to mean a lot of reshuffling if I can make it happen. Shit. Listen, Vito, give my love to Billy, will you? Know something funny, I truly like her, and I never thought I would."

"She's not envious of you anymore, Maggie, maybe that's why."

"Was she? Was she honestly?" Maggie sounded like someone who had just opened a fabulous and unexpected present.

"Didn't you know that? I thought you were my smart Maggie."

"That smart, Vito, no one is."

Lester Weinstock found himself in a state of considerable confusion. Was he, floundering, a victim of a cultural time lag, out of touch with the Now Generation, a regressed fuddy-duddy from the 1950s, when he had not yet been born, or was Dolly Moon out of sync with reality? Did having an illegitimate—no, wrong word—a one-parent baby only happen in the wilder reaches of Bohemia or was it being done every day all over the United States, with the same happy, wacky abandon Dolly displayed? He pondered these questions while finishing his second helping of Henny Youngman's Sweet and Sour Ragout. No, he decided, wiping up the last of the prune-and-apricot-laden gravy with a piece of Dolly's homemade challeh, he still didn't think it was fair to the baby, no matter how good a mother Dolly would be.

Lester had now been Dolly's public-relations man for two weeks. He'd gained six pounds from her cooking and his first gray hair from worrying over her plight. The only fixed bright spot in his suddenly troubled world was the thought of Dolly's dear old Jewish grandmother, the one who had taught her how to cook so miraculously.

"Lester, you've simply got to let me give you a haircut."

"I'll go to the barber tomorrow."

"You've been saying that for ten days. You never have time, you're so busy making up excuses about why I can't meet the press and arranging those hilarious telephone interviews."

"Dolly, you know what the studio thinks. If there is the slightest chance that you might win an Oscar, you'd blow it if people knew you were pregnant. And if you told them about Sunrise—the rodeo—and don't think they wouldn't get it out of you—forget it. There's still a lot of ol'-time morality around, you know."

"Maybe I'd get the sympathy vote," Dolly dimpled. "Sit down and I'll put a towel over you. Now—where did I put my cuticle scissors?"

As if in a dream, Lester let her lead him to a chair. There was something so, so—immediate—about Dolly's face. She simply refused to inhabit the safe distance between people. It was disgraceful, really, the way she just dove into him, feet first. He'd already told her about his boyhood bed-wetting problem; the catastrophe of his first love affair; the time he cheated on an algebra final at Beverly Hills High School and got caught; his innermost feelings about owing his good fortune to portable toilet trailers, a subject he had learned to joke about many years ago, but which he had never really felt was all that funny to live with; the catastrophe of his second love affair; the near-miss of his third love affair; the potential he felt he had to make wonderful movies someday. Christ, he'd just about told her his life story. About the only thing he'd left out were the circle jerks at summer camp. And only because he'd forgotten, not because she'd be shocked.

"I think you're getting it too short," he complained.

"Not for all the world. It's just taking me longer because it's kind of hard to get close enough to you. There, it's finished." She sat down heavily on the chair. "Go look at yourself in the mirror and then tell me that's not an improvement."

Obediently, he took a nearsighted look and liked what he saw. Turning to compliment her, he caught sight of an unexpected expression of pain on her face.

"Hey, something wrong?"

"Just my back. You know, people shouldn't have to be pregnant standing up; it puts too much strain on the back muscles. All pregnant women should go around on their hands and knees. Maybe someday they will."

"Is there something I could do?"

"Well—"

"Really. In return for the haircut."

"It's kind of a drag, but I've run out of oil—for rubbing my stretch marks—oh, Lester, don't you even know about stretch marks?"

"I'm an obstetrical innocent," he said humbly.

"Could you go down to the all-night market and get some oil for me? That would really be a blessing."

Ten minutes later Lester was back with a bottle of imported Italian olive oil, a bottle of domestic olive oil, a bottle of safflower oil, a bottle of peanut oil, and a bottle of Johnson & Johnson's baby oil. A clinking Santa Claus, he deposited his brown paper bag on the table. Dolly had vanished.

"Where are you?"

"In the bedroom. Bring it on in." Dolly, pink and burnished from her quick shower, was lying on her bed in a pair of lace and satin pajamas, one of Billy's Chirstmas presents. Shyly, Lester emptied the heavy bag on her night table.

"I wasn't sure which kind—"

Dolly contemplated the oils, biting her lip to keep from bursting into laughter. Gravely, her eyes brimming with tears of merriment, she pointed to the baby oil. He handed it to her. She opened it, poured some into her still outstretched hand and raised the top of her pajamas and lowered the bottoms. Her belly, magnificent, monumental, and velvety white, seemed to Lester to be the most extraordinary sight he'd ever seen. He averted his eyes, shocked and fascinated. Unable to resist, he looked at it again. Had there ever been so wondrous a work of nature? An alp dwindled by comparison. Art was a pastime for the dilettante. My goodness!

"Kind of a knockout, isn't it?" Dolly asked, patting it lovingly.

"Splendid," he choked.

"Don't just stand there, Lester, the oil will drip. Sit down and rub."

"Rub?"

"Lester, don't you know *where* stretch marks are?"

"I haven't made a study of it, no."

She took his hand and guided it to her side and slowly nudged it over the mound of her abdomen. "All around here, from one side to another. Oh, my, that feels so good. Just keep rubbing, Lester—and I'll dribble the oil. You can use both hands if you like." She sighed voluptuously. "It feels so much better when you do it for me. This is what I call luxury—sheer luxury. Take off your jacket, Lester, you look awfully hot. Mmmmmm. There—that's better, isn't it?"

Three hours later Lester woke up. Someone was pushing him slowly but relentlessly, like a large, soft fist in the stomach. Who was in his bed, pushing him, he wondered in sleepy alarm. He groped around with his hand and encountered Dolly's belly, or rather Dolly's baby, turning a lazy somersault inside of Dolly. Then he realized that Dolly's hair was tickling his nose, Dolly's head was on his chest, and Dolly's feet were mixed up with his legs. Pinned down, immobile and incredulous, he opened his eyes in the dim light of the bedroom. Without his glasses, everything was a blur, but his mind was clear. He, Lester Weinstock, had made love to a woman who was eight months' pregnant! Furthermore, he, Lester Weinstock, had never *ever* had such a sublimely erotic, altogether delectable experience in his entire life, and he, Lester Weinstock, would like to repeat it immediately. He was a monster of depravity, no doubt about that, but he felt like a member of the Now Generation at last. Why had he been so nervous about everything, he wondered? Dolly stirred in her sleep. He jiggled her a little. He supposed he really shouldn't wake her up, but he wasn't so far gone that he would make love to a *sleeping* pregnant woman! He jiggled her some more and played with her bountiful breasts with his free hand. Talk about good!

After the fight with Valentine, Spider Elliott started counting the days until the Oscars. They couldn't pass fast enough to suit him. Since he was going to leave Scruples, he wanted to get it over with, but until Billy knew, he couldn't start looking for another job. He had no doubt that he could almost write his own ticket in any number of large stores: His success with Scruples had been widely noted throughout retailing. Or, if he didn't want to stay on in retailing, he could go back to photography, perhaps here on the West Coast. Or maybe the Harriet Toppingham vendetta was forgotten and he could go back to New York. In any case, he had saved his money. Why not go around the world on a slow boat? To China? And stay there? Oh, he had a number of options.

As far as Valentine was concerned, he had put the matter behind him. She was totally unreachable. He had tried to apologize half a dozen times and each time she'd left the room without even looking at him or letting him speak his piece. He was willing to take all the blame, in spite of her cheap shots, but she didn't want to know about it. Whoever said that a man and a woman could never be real friends was right. It was a chapter in his life and it was over, finished, forgotten. On to something else. Naturally he felt bad about it, but that was a temporary state of affairs.

The weeks passed and still Spider couldn't shake off the grayness of his inner landscape. This was nothing like the state of rage, grief, and loss that he had felt in New York when Melanie left him to come to Hollywood and Harriet Toppingham bitched up his career. Those emotions had had clear outlines; he had known why he felt the way he felt. But lately he had taken to waking in the middle of the night and lying sleepless for hours, thinking thoughts that made no sense at all the following day, thoughts in a key Spider had never known before, thoughts that he judged as self-pitying even as he had them, absurd thoughts about who really cared about him, who gave a damn, why was he doing what he was doing, what difference did it make, what was there to look forward to, why, in short, was he alive?

In all his healthy, carefree, rambunctious, self-confident thirty-two years, Spider had never for one minute indulged in wondering about the meaning of life. As he saw it, he had had the great good fortune to have been the product of one lucky ripe egg and one aggressive sperm that met on just the right night at just the right time of the month in just the right woman. Chance, pure chance, dumb luck it could be called, had caused him to be born instead of that other child his mother and father would have had if they had not made love on that auspicious night. Having had the good fortune to be born, he took the world as he found it, riding it like a splendid horse. The meaning of life? To *live it!*

But now, in early March of 1978, he woke up every morning feeling bad after a lifetime of waking up feeling good. Taking a shower, getting dressed, making breakfast, and driving to Scruples became the most stable part of his day, as hasty routine tasks absorbed his attention. Once at work, he found that the well of energy on which he had always drawn unthinkingly seemed to have a bottom.

At least that was the cause he gave to what he called the "bubble," a feeling that he was not connected, in the way he used to be, to the outside world. The bubble became in his mind an actual physical sphere, like those transparent balloons that have grains of something inside of them that bob around at random. It made voices seem muted, food taste bland, physical contacts less real, less actual. It took the edge off everything. Spider was able to get through his day at Scruples by consciously forcing himself to behave as he had behaved naturally in the past, but his heart wasn't in it; so that although the customers didn't see any difference in him, the fun was gone. Passing a mirror once he noted without surprise that his eyes were about as lively as the Dead Sea.

Rosel Korman, the first saleswoman to be hired at Scruples, was one of the few people who noticed the change in Spider. She thought—to herself since she was infinitely discreet—that where once he had looked like Butch Cassidy *and* the Sundance Kid put together, he now looked like a pallid remake of the same movie.

Billy, one of the other people who was aware of Spider's sudden lack of zest, thought it must be the need for a vacation. Since he had come to California in July of 1976, he hadn't been away for more than a long weekend. There was fresh powder in Aspen that March and the ladies would just have to do without him for a while, she informed him.

"You know, you're a pushy dame," he observed. "How do you even know I can ski?"

"People who look like you always can. Now get out of here and don't let me see that face for three weeks."

From a skier's point of view, Aspen was a success. But the bubble was waiting for him when he arrived. One day he found himself alone on a mountainside and he came to a stop, leaning thoughtfully on his poles. He checked out the pure air and the undiluted sunlight and the crisp, creamy quiet; it was all there and accounted for. No one could possibly ask for more. On other days of skiing, before he had gone to New York, a moment to himself such as this would have been an affirmation of the goodness of life, a time to gather in the realizations of his luck. He had always looked for those rare opportunities to ski alone so that no other human being came between him and the full joy of being part of the mountain. Why now did he feel so *abandoned?* He dug his poles into the snow and pushed off, recklessly skiing the fall line as if he were running for his life.

Back in Beverly Hills, he decided that he probably needed a change in his love life. He eased himself out of his current involvements, which he had never allowed to become so serious that they couldn't be untangled without any loss of pride or self-esteem on the part of the women in question. They would miss Spider, but they would never doubt that he had deeply liked and enjoyed them—because he had. Spider had perfected a way of dropping a woman so that she felt more cherished than if he had continued the relationship.

Within a week, he found a new girl; soon yet a different one. No question, thought Spider in despair, he was fucking more and enjoying it less. Suddenly it seemed so auto-mated, so predestined, so ultimately unimportant. He could go through the motions, exactly the same motions that had given him such gorgeously simple pleasure in the past, and afterward—finally he knew what the fellow was talking about who had sagely said that after coitus all men felt sad. He didn't know who the philosopher was, but all his life Spider had thought the guy must have been screw-ing the wrong girls. He had more respect for him now.

Maybe it was his age. He had never paid attention to birthdays, but, after all, he was over thirty and it could be some physical thing. Spider had a complete checkup with Billy's doctor, who told him to come back in twenty years and stop wasting his time.

There was something else too, but he didn't see what he could do about it. He was getting sentimental, or at least that was what he called it. If he picked up a newspaper or a magazine and read about some couple celebrating their fiftieth wedding anniversary, surrounded by their children and grandchildren and great-grandchildren, he felt tears come into his eyes. He felt the same way for the guys who won the Super Bowl, television beauty-contest winners, teen-age kids who saved small children from burning houses, blind people who managed to graduate from col-lege with honors, and people who sailed around the world by themselves in small boats. News of death, disaster, and other routine horrors affected him not at all, but good news turned him to mush.

He was too young for male menopause, Spider thought, in deepening worry, and too old for adolescence, so what the fuck was this all about? He dragged himself into the kitchen of his wonderful bachelor house and opened a can of Campbell's Cream of Tomato Soup. If that didn't help, nothing would.

It didn't.

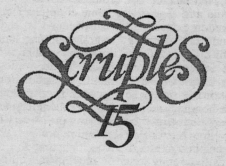

As Dolly entered her last weeks of pregnancy, she found herself less enthusiastic than she had been about trying out new dishes from the *Celebrity Kosher Cookbook* or the precious, tattered copy of the *Molly Goldberg Jewish Cookbook* she had found in a secondhand bookstore. It wasn't that she had lost her appetite, she told Mrs. Higgens, her loving landlady, the fire chief's wife, but that it was kind of hard to get near enough to the stove. And she couldn't go out to eat because the case of measles that Lester had fabricated for her to keep the press at bay had been followed by an announcement of a case of mumps, which wouldn't be cured until tomorrow, the night of the Awards. Not that hordes of people were calling for interviews anyway, but three weeks ago Lester had decided that the duties of a public-relations man included moving into her apartment in case she needed him for anything in the middle of the night, like driving her to the hospital or something.

"Lester Weinstock, that baby isn't going to be born until a week after the Awards, and that's eight whole days away. You're just taking advantage of a poor knocked-up female who hasn't the heart to say no."

"I am a devil with women," he admitted, beaming. "Hey, you know how to play footsie?"

"You can teach me, as long as that's all you have in mind," she said judiciously.

"Dolly, I am pure of heart and besides, anything else wouldn't be good for the baby." Lester felt a strong bond with the force that gently pummeled and prodded him every night, as if trying to make friends in a necessarily difficult situation, like the Prisoner of Zenda tapping through the walls of his prison.

"Let's play footsie later," Dolly said.

Lester sighed and returned to his copy of the *Herald-Examiner*, Los Angeles's afternoon newspaper. "Jesus! I just don't believe it."

"What happened?"

"There was a fire at Price Waterhouse this morning. They put it out, thank God, and all the final Oscar results have been removed elsewhere for safekeeping—that's what it says here. Can you imagine the freak-out there would have been if everything had gone up in smoke?"

Dolly was unimpressed. Her mind was on food. "Come on, Lester, Mrs. Higgens invited us for dinner tonight. She's worried that I'm not eating right."

"I brought in Chinese food every day this week, just the way you wanted," Lester said, aggrieved.

"That's the point. She's afraid it might not have the right things in it for the baby—all that MSG and stuff. So she's made corned beef and cabbage."

Lester brightened. He hated Chinese food, although he'd never told Dolly. It might have upset her. "Wonderful—absolutely wonderful!"

"If I'd known you were a corned-beef addict I would have made it while I still could," Dolly pouted angelically.

"It's not just that."

"Then what's so wonderful?"

"Everything." He gave a great contented sigh and came to kneel by the side of Dolly's chair, his nose pressing her nose, peering at her through his glasses as if he were trying to merge their eyes. Giving up, he compromised and kissed her at length on the lips. Kissing was still allowed, as much as he liked.

Dolly hummed pleasurably. Lester Weinstock was coming along very nicely indeed. And he was one terrific kisser.

Dinner was delayed because Mr. Higgens, known as Chief, was late. Finally, they started without him. He arrived just as second helpings were being served.

"Sorry folks, but we had a hell of a day, and I had to hang around until everything was settled."

"I know you put out fires, Chief," Mrs. Higgens said with some exasperation, "but I didn't think you had to 'settle' them."

"Some fires are more unusual than others," he retorted, looking mysterious.

"What was it, Chief? A fire in a house of ill repute, the house of a city councilman's girl friend, Hugh Hefner's mansion—sounds like monkey business to me." Mrs. Higgens spoke with the air of worldly wisdom she put on to hide her pride at her husband's position. "We'll read about it in the paper anyway."

"Not more about this one, you won't. It's being played down."

"Ah ha—funny money," said Lester knowingly.

"Oh no," said Dolly, looking stricken. "I bet it was in an orphan asylum or a maternity hospital."

"Aw, hell," the Chief grinned, "I shouldn't have brought it up at all, but there's no harm—just between us. Anyway, Dolly, you do something in pictures, don't you? This should give you a kick. The fire was at a place called Price Waterhouse, an office downtown—you know, these fellers who give out the Oscars every year—"

"My God," Dolly interrupted, "did somebody get hurt? They didn't put that in the papers."

"Nothing like that. Nobody injured. But it was damn funny. Some crazy stunt man set it—they found him there fanning the flames and laughing like mad. He said it was his revenge, he'd been waiting years for them to give an Oscar for stunt men and this was to call attention to the injustice of it. Had to take him away, crazy geezer. Burned out half the office, smoke damage something terrible, some of the floors are unsafe to walk on."

"But what happened to the ballots?" Lester asked impatiently.

"Oh them, I think they keep them in a computer or something. No sweat. But all the final scores or whatever, they were kept in a special safe in the office that had the most damage, so we had to move them to another place."

"Say, that's really interesting, Chief," said Lester, eyes gleaming. "Maybe I could get you in the papers, 'Noble Fire Chief Saves Oscar Envelopes,' stuff like that."

"Les, the Inspector says we treat this very carefully,

don't want to give people ideas about arson, you understand."

"Yeah. OK. But it's a shame. Tell me more about what you did—it's really a great story."

The Chief was delighted to oblige. It was seldom that anyone showed a genuine interest in the details of his work. They tended, he felt, to take fire fighters all too much for granted until they needed them.

An hour after dinner, Dolly and Lester were back upstairs in her apartment finishing a half bottle of framboise. Dolly had a theory that any drink made from fruit couldn't possibly hurt the baby because it contained vitamins. Lester bought her peach brandy, plum brandy, Cherry Heering, triple sec, blackberry wine, but something about the bottle of framboise—raspberry liqueur—had caught his fancy. The price, perhaps, because it was very expensive and he yearned to give Dolly expensive things. He didn't know that it was very old, very rare, and very lethal, and even a Frenchman wouldn't dare to take more than two or three tiny glasses of the precious stuff. Raspberries sounded very healthy to both Dolly and Lester, and the drink, crystal clear with almost no taste but a delightful fragrance, went down easily and in quantity, almost evaporating on their tongues as they lapped it up.

"I think we should do it," he anounced after a long, pensive silence.

"What?" Dolly was mildly curious.

"Take the strain off you. It's not good for the baby for you to be under all this strain."

"Lester, what strain?"

"Of not knowing about the Awards. I'm aware—don't think I'm not aware—that you're under considerable, abnormal, not at all unsinister, strain."

"You're so adorable when you're drunk. Take your glasses off and kiss me a whole lot."

"Excessive, unrelieved, unrelenting, untidy, unnatural, unprovoked, incessant, constant, permanent, unendurable, *intolerable* strain!"

"Silly boy—come here."

"Well, if you're not, I am under considerable strain, and it's not good for the baby either. He is under strain, so he wakes me up and then I start to worry. He wouldn't want that to happen, but he can't help it. Let's do it."

"Sleep in different beds?"

"Never! What a terrible thing to suggest. Dolly, apologize!"

"I'm sorry, Lester. What were you talking about? Why did I apologize? I think I'm drunk, too. How could raspberries make you drunk?"

"Let's—let's just take a lil' drive down 606 South Olive Street where the Chief said the envelopes were kept and take a lil' peek at 'em. Put you out of your strain, get a good night's sleep for a change—be fresh for tomorrow night. If you know you didn't win, you'll be relaxed tomorrow, not fair for a poor pregnant lil' person to have to go through the strain of not knowin'—cruel and inhuman, I say."

"That would be cheating, I think, or something else bad."

"I don't care. Goin' to do it anyway. Now, just sit there and I'll come and help you up, poor, helpless girl."

"I'm perfectly able to get up myself," Dolly said, heaving herself out of her chair and swaying slightly.

"Problem is, getting downstairs holding you up," Lester muttered. Dolly was already halfway down the stairs and came back when she heard him talking to an empty room.

"Lester! Over here, the door, see it, now just walk in this direction, that's right. Are you sure this is a good idea, Lester?"

"Stroke of genius. Simply brilliant. Shoulda thought of it myself."

"You did."

"Oh? Good show, good show. Wait a minute, Dolly, I'll help you with your seat belt—buggers didn't consider poor pregnant people when they designed it."

By the time Dolly and Lester reached South Olive Street, they were considerably less drunk yet far, very far, from sober. They had reached that particular plateau of drink in which an idea conceived earlier now seems to have been chiseled on stone tablets by Moses himself. It was a self-evident duty to put Dolly out of her strain, something no right-minded citizen would question. They were gifted with raspberry-inspired cunning and determination.

There was a guard sitting at a table in the lobby of the office building. Half-asleep and totally bored, he was mesmerized by Dolly's stately progress toward him. Lester waved a case full of plastic cards under his nose and said authoritatively, "I'm from Price Waterhouse. Come to check on things."

"Identification, please," the guard said. Lester presented him with his Visa and Diners Club cards.

"No, Price Waterhouse identification."

"Damn, got so many of these things kicking around, where did it go to? Wait a minute, it's probably in my wallet—"

Dolly clutched her belly and gave a sudden grunting howl. The guard and Lester stopped dead and looked at her helplessly. "My God, sweetheart, I've simply got to pee—at least I hope that's what it is."

"Jesus! This is an emergency, fella," said Lester. "I've got to get her up to my office—there's a ladies' room there. Damn fucking office dragging me out with her in this condition! But I couldn't leave her at home alone, could I?"

"No sir!" said the guard, pointing to an open elevator. "Need some help?"

"Nah, I can handle her. Dolly, talk to me, Dolly. Can you just hold it in, hon?"

"Oh, Lester, *hurry*."

As the elevator doors closed behind them, Lester turned anxiously to Dolly. "Are you all right?"

"Had you convinced, didn't I?" she smiled with mischief. "Was that method acting?"

"I'm not sure, but I doubt it—you're not allowed props."

On the third floor the offices were just as the Chief had described them. Lester bypassed the charred double wooden doors with the name of the company emblazoned on them and went directly to the fourth door on the left, the one the Chief had told him about. He took out his Swiss Army knife and worked intently on the lock for a minute.

"Are you sure you can do this?" asked Dolly.

"Please, a lil' respect, you're talking to the champ. Lock picking is my middle name."

"You rich kids have all the advantages."

"Jus' how many hours a day can you play tennis in tennis camp?" Lester continued to work the lock. Three long minutes passed. "Damn jerk, that Benny Fishman, he must have left something out when he taught me. Don't worry, Dolly, I'll get it open if I have to kick the door in."

"Lester, we don't have to—"

Abruptly Dolly shut up and Lester put away his knife as a cleaning woman appeared from around the corner. "Good evening," Lester said, sounding businesslike.

"Evening. Some mess, huh? And nobody even told me till just now. Nice thing to find when you get to work, soot all over, cinders, everything soaking. Wattsa matter. Key won't work? Big deal—leave the place in a mess and don't even tell you which key." She opened the door with one of the many keys she carried. "Don't try and go into the other rooms—they're not safe."

Lester thanked her and he and Dolly went into the room and closed the door behind them. Lester switched on the light by the door for the benefit of the cleaning woman and then, after a few seconds, switched it off as he heard her continue down the corridor. Raspberry cloud or no, he had brought his glove-compartment flashlight with him and with its aid, he went directly to the filing cabinet in one corner.

"This I can do—I think. Dolly, hold the flashlight." He fumbled a minute and finally opened the tall filing cabinet. They looked at each other in consternation. It had five drawers, all jammed with papers.

"Now what?" whispered Dolly. "How can we ever go through all that?"

"It's obvious. They'll be under 'A' for Awards. Just hold the light and don't make a sound." Lester didn't find anything under Awards, so he tried "M" for Motion Picture Arts and Sciences. Nothing. Back to "A," smiting his head as he realized that it was the *Academy* of Motion Picture Arts and Sciences. Academy proved fruitless. "Shit! I'm stupid. Naturally they'll be under 'O' for Oscars." But they weren't.

"I'd say," Dolly hissed, "if I were going to file them, I'd have put them under 'E' for envelopes."

And there they were. All twenty-one stiff white envelopes containing everything but the Honorary Awards and the Thalberg Award. Lester fumbled among them, blaspheming under his breath. "Fuck—Best Screenplay Based on Material from Another Medium—cock-suckers, Best Foreign-Language Film—damn it to hell, Best Original Song Score and Its Adaptation—who the hell gives a flying shit—"

"Lester, I think I hear somebody coming." Dolly quavered in a terrified semigiggle. She put out his flashlight and laid it on the floor, while Lester grabbed all the envelopes in both hands, and they both stood absolutely still as two men passed by the door of the office. When they didn't return, Dolly peeked out. "Nobody—keep looking, Lester."

"You've lost my flashlight. It rolled away. We can't turn on the light. Come on, we're getting out of here."

The fire stairs, required by law to be unlocked, were only a few feet away. For a woman one week away from giving birth, Dolly found herself amazingly quick on her feet. Within minutes they were safely inside the car.

"Oh, Dolly, where is your lap when I need it?" Lester groaned.

Dolly looked at him for the first time since they had scampered out of the Price Waterhouse office. He bulged strangely above the waist and had his arms tightly crossed below the bulge.

"Lester! You took them! Oh, how could you? We just wanted a peek. Oh dear, oh my—" she bellowed with laughter, finally able to unleash her mirth.

"I'm sweating blood and you're laughing," hiccuped Lester. He looked at his chest in wonderment, afraid to unclasp his arms. "Dolly—do something! I can't just sit here." Still unable to speak, she fished a paper shopping bag from the floor of the car and took the envelopes from Lester's jacket and tossed them into the bag. Released, he started the car and within five minutes they were far from the scene of the crime.

"Can't we stop somewhere and have our peek," Dolly suggested when they had both resumed normal breathing.

"Dolly—you're missing a sense of occasion," Lester said grandiosely. "We will do this in style. This is no ordinary night. Tonight we have made history."

"What about all that strain I'm supposed to be under?"

"Patience, my angel, patience. Let us not put selfish considerations before historical imperatives." Lester was still drunk, but now he had entered the phase in which the broad view obscures petty details. Horizons opened, vistas beckoned. And after a long drive, the Beverly Hills Hotel came into sight. Lester had never had occasion to take anyone to be interviewed to the Polo Lounge of the Beverly Hills Hotel, that tacky, overrated sanctuary that has, for some inexplicable reason, retained a reputation for glamour that hasn't existed there for more than twenty years, but he had been brought up on its name.

"What we both need, Dolly, is some more framboise—it restores the mystery and gives wings to the imagination." He turned off Sunset into the driveway of the hotel, left the car with a carhop, and escorted Dolly and her shopping bag into the Polo Lounge. It was partly empty at that late hour and they were able to get a tiny table under a window surrounded by green plastic leaves that hadn't been dusted in ten years. "Two triple framboises and a telephone," Lester told the waiter; he knew the form if not the substance. The phone was brought immediately. The waiter went into conference with the barman and returned with two pousse-cafés.

"Bartender says he's out of that stuff—this OK?"

"Marvelous," said Dolly, clutching the shopping bag under her chin and trying to read the writing on the top envelope in the dim light.

Lester toasted Dolly. "To the best actress in the world, whoever the hell wins!" They drained their pousse-cafés and Lester signaled to the waiter for two more.

"Oh, Lester," Dolly whimpered, "I really don't want to see my envelope after all. This is such a wonderful night— I don't want to spoil it."

"But the strain, the *unendurable* strain!"

"Lester, you can stand it for one more night if I can."

"Then let me have the shopping bag."

"Lester, Lester! What are you doing?"

"I'm not looking for supporting actress, take it easy, ah ha—right at the bottom naturally."

"Which is it?"

"Best Picture, that's all."

"Oh, Lester, should we?"

"How can you ask?"

"We'll get into trouble, I know we will," Dolly wailed.

"We already are. So let's enjoy it." With ceremony, Lester carefully inched open the lightly sealed envelope without breaking the flap, and then, with almost as much ceremony as the professionals who usually do it, he peered through his glasses at the name written inside. "Hmm, they need a new typewriter rib—*Mirrors*—*MIRRORS!* Dolly, *Mirrors*—we did it. WE DID IT!" Dolly clapped her hand over his mouth. People were looking at them from all sides of the room.

"Shhh—Wow! Wow! Wow! Wow!—I'm so happy— what do you mean, *we* did it? Vito did it."

"It's the studio's picture—we did it!"

"Let's not fight—everybody did it—oh, Lester, we have to tell Vito right away. Give me the phone," she said, tears of joy pouring down her face. But as she reached for the phone, the shopping bag fell open and spilled the other twenty envelopes on the carpet. Lester took off his glasses so he could see at a distance. He noticed that their little table, with Dolly sobbing unrestrainedly, envelopes scattered on the floor, and the two new pousse-cafés threatened by the phone cord, was attracting more and more attention.

"Dolly, freeze! Don't make a move. Let me get these back in the shopping bag, understand? Put down the phone. No, waiter, we don't want to check the bag, just a little spill, all under control. No, it would *not* be more convenient. Just bring some pretzels. Dolly, do you think you could stop crying? They'll think you're in labor. Good, Dolly, that's fine. Drink your nice pousse-café. That's my baby. All right now. We're all organized again, smooth as silk." He stroked Dolly's hand abstractedly. He suddenly felt sober. Not entirely sober perhaps, but opening that one envelope, actually doing it, had shocked him badly. Christ, this wasn't a crazy caper, this was reality. Dolly's voice interrupted his thoughts.

"Oh, Lester, please let me call Billy and Vito. And then we'll sit here and open all the other envelopes and call all the other winners and put them out of their misery and then you could call the wire services, the papers, the radio stations, the television stations—Lester, you'll be the most famous publicity man in the world."

"Famous! I'd *never* work again! Dolly, try to understand what I'm saying. We're in trouble. It's all my fault. This could ruin the whole big Oscar night—don't you see, it's *got* to be a surprise. Oh, shit on a stick, why did I take those envelopes? I must have been temporarily insane."

"We could burn them," Dolly said helpfully.

"Yeah, or throw them in the garbage or flush them down the toilet—but they'd still be gone tomorrow morning and that guard and the cleaning woman can describe both of us. They might not recognize me, but they'll never miss you."

"Maybe we could take them—back?" she quavered.

"One break-in, yes, twice, no, we'd be caught. Anyway that office door locked behind us, I heard it."

"Oh, Lester, I'm sorry!" Dolly's face was so woebegone that Lester had to kiss her several times before he restored her to some tenuous equilibrium. He'd never seen her really upset before.

"Don't worry. I've just had an idea." Lester took out the little book he always carried that was filled with the precious unlisted VIP numbers that the studio's Promotion Department had on hand, numbers he had noted down just in case someday he'd be asked to call a very important person.

Maggie answered her phone with irritation. She wanted to get a good night's sleep before tomorrow's big show, and someone was calling on her private number at nearly midnight.

"Lester Weinstock! You what? You WHAT? You're where? You're not kidding because if you are—no, I believe you. I'll be right over. DO NOT MAKE ANOTHER PHONE CALL UNTIL I COME! Promise? Ten minutes. No, five."

Six minutes later, Maggie, without makeup, her hair covered by a scarf, wearing a mink coat over her nightgown and slacks, confronted the two of them.

"I still don't believe it," she said slowly. Lester bent down, lifted the battered shopping bag and held it open while she looked inside. She shook her head, looked again, picked up one of the envelopes, scrutinized it, put it back, and shook her head again. "I believe it."

"Maggie," Dolly said eagerly, "Lester wouldn't even let me make a single phone call until you came—he says you'll know what to do."

Maggie was dazzled by the magnitude of the folly of this innocent who, daintily licking up the last of her third pousse-café, looked as divinely springlike as an apple tree in full bloom. Did she have any idea of the business implications of the Oscars? Didn't she understand that the Awards presentation represented millions of dollars in advertising revenue to the network, incalculable millions of dollars' worth of renewed public interest in the entire movie industry, that the sheer *suspense* of the Oscars was like having a national election every year?

"Better give me the bag, Lester," she said, "unless you want to go into your family business."

"Can you keep it quiet?" he asked her desperately.

"Lester, no matter how dumb you were to do this, you made up for it in being smart enough to call me. Not only will Price Waterhouse get their envelopes back, but, as a member of the press, I don't have to answer any questions. Think of yourself as Deep Throat."

"Maggie, I'll be forever in your debt. There's just one thing—could we just take a peek at the Best Supporting Actress envelope, just to put Dolly out of her strain."

"I don't wanna," Dolly wailed, as Maggie spoke.

"No, absolutely not. That would make three of us who'd know the winner and when three people know a secret everybody knows it. It isn't safe. Dolly can wait just like the rest of us. You didn't open any of the envelopes, did you?"

"Of course not," said Lester righteously, clasping Dolly's foot between both his big feet and pressing hard. "I called only you."

"You'll go far, Lester, you heard it here first. OK, you two, this hasn't happened."

"Not a word to anyone," Lester assured her.

"I've forgotten it already," said Dolly.

"I always wanted to hear people talk like that in real life," said Maggie, and before anyone could say another word, she swept out of the Polo Lounge, the bag firmly tucked under her arm.

"But you didn't even tell her about *Mirrors,*" Dolly gasped.

"She won't let us peek, we won't let her know—she can wait just like everybody else. Fair is fair."

"Oh, Lester, you're so wise."

A few minutes later Maggie was home in her kitchen. Driving back to her house she had calculated quickly the various difficulties she was going to encounter in returning the envelopes without giving Lester and Dolly away. All her prestige would have to be deployed and very cleverly too, but, after all, Price Waterhouse had at least as much interest as she did in keeping the public from knowing that this deepest of secrets had leaked before the big night. Oh, it was a sticky business, but it could be done.

She gazed at the stiff envelopes neatly laid out on her kitchen table. The kettle on the stove was beginning to send up satisfactory quantities of steam. One by one she steamed open the envelopes, wrote down the names on a pad, and sealed them closed again. A girl had to look after her own ass in this life, thought Maggie. Oh, what fun she was going to have tomorrow. She'd probably put together a dozen deals by noon—*everybody* in town would *owe* her. And the show tomorrow night—incredible. She'd open it with her own list of projected winners—which should she get wrong? Best Achievement in Sound and Best Documentary Short Subject? Sure, nobody cared about them except for the hundreds of craftsmen involved. Maybe one other—Best Costume Design? Those were always up for grabs. But otherwise—could this little girl pick 'em! And she'd brief her camera crews so they would be exactly in the right place at the right time and she'd know just how long to interview each nominee—heaven protects the working girl, no question about it. She felt a rising sense of excitement as she got to the last five envelopes. She'd been opening them in the same order that holds during the program. Maggie always felt that professionalism was all important when engaged in white-collar crime. She opened the envelope for Best Picture last. *"Oy, gevalt!"* Her shout was so heartfelt, so fervent, so stunned, that her guard dog barked wildly outside the house.

Professionalism can go only so far, thought Maggie, as she picked up the phone.

16

*M*aggie's phone call had come an hour before, and Billy and Vito finally began to accept her news as real, as a part of their lives, not just as a transcendent victory after a long race. They began to assimilate the win, to incorporate it into themselves by dint of repeating certain phrases.

"You're sure she was sure?" Billy asked for the fifth time, more for the pleasure of hearing the answer than because she doubted it.

"No question."

"But why wouldn't she say how she knew. Isn't that odd?"

"That's how Maggie operates. Believe me, she has unique methods."

"Oh, Vito, I still can't believe it."

"I can."

"*Mirrors is* the Best Picture," Billy said. It was an affirmation, a declaration, yet somehow it managed to sound like a question.

"Maybe," Vito said thoughtfully. "Actually, it's not possible to make an absolute judgment about a film. You can take five brands of cake flour, test them, and decide which one of them really works better than all the others —but a film? All it basically proves is which picture in a field of five got the most votes—like a primary. And the only reason I'm able to be so lofty and detached and philosophical is because we won. If we'd lost, I'd say *Mirrors* was the best, without any question, and that they

534

gave it to another picture for all kinds of complicated, wrong reasons."

"But how do you feel? I mean, do you feel as if you've gotten an Olympic gold medal or something?" Billy asked curiously.

"I feel like Jack Nicholson when he won for *Cuckoo's Nest*—he said that winning the Oscar is like making love for the first time—if you've done it once, you never have to worry about it again. You have to believe you *are* good just to have the nerve to be a producer, but when all those people tell you *they* think you're good—well, I don't care if you do know it inside yourself, it's nice to get some feedback from the outside world. Better than nice, it's beyond fucking words."

Billy looked at Vito as he prowled around their bedroom in his pajamas and a bathrobe. He was like a blowtorch. Even she, accustomed to his pulverizing energy, his nervy assurance, had never seen him so phosphorescent. He looked ready, she found herself thinking, to start work on a dozen new projects. Suddenly, in the middle of her tumult of thanksgiving, she felt her heart give a strange, nasty little dip of apprehension.

"Does an Oscar really change your life—or is it just a big bang, like king for a day?" she asked casually.

Vito stopped to consider for a minute before he answered. Slowly he said, almost as if speaking to himself, "For anyone in the business it *has* to change your life—inside and out. Permanently. I know that in a week—hell, in three days—half the people who'll be watching tomorrow night will have forgotten who won what. But, from now on, I'll always have that Oscar under my belt. It'll always be there, somewhere, in the minds of the people I do business with. It won't affect the raw problems of my work; every picture will still contain as much crisis and agony, in its own particular way, as any other, but this is a company town, and for a little while—I'll own it! That crap Arvey pulled on *Mirrors*—that sort of thing isn't ever going to happen to me again. Right now, just for a while, I'm untouchable."

"Deals! You'll be able to make them the way you want?"

"Not with ten Oscars," he laughed. "Still, they'll be a

lot easier than the last few. I really don't know yet—I'll have to find out. But I promise you, my darling, no more editing a picture in the library. That sort of thing won't happen again."

In disbelief, Billy felt herself beginning to dissolve into tears. She tried to hold them back, but it was impossible. A convulsion of loss was contracting her chest. It was several seconds before Vito noticed, and then he was holding her tightly, kissing her dark hair, rocking her in his arms until she was able to speak.

"I'm sorry—so sorry—what a terrible time to cry—but it's so silly, it's just that—oh, I *loved* having the editing here—I was so much a part of it, and now that's gone—we'll never have that closeness again—you won't need me to work with you—you'll have all the real script people you want—so dumb of me, darling. I don't mean to spoil your fun." Her face was desolate as she tried to smile.

Vito didn't know what to say. She was absolutely right. The situation with *Mirrors* had been a once-in-a-lifetime happening, like a shipwreck. He hoped he'd never be forced to work in that kind of frenetic, insane haste again. It had worked out, miraculously, but it could far more easily have been a total disaster. And he didn't see Billy having a future as a script clerk. It simply didn't fit her at all, and he was sure she knew it.

"Is that the only reason you're crying, my darling?" he asked tenderly, holding her tightly and licking up some of the tears on her face. "How can you say we'll never have that closeness again—you're my wife, my best, my dearest friend, the most important, beloved person in the world to me—no one can ever possibly be as close."

Billy was lured by the immense sweetness she felt flowing toward her to dare to express the thoughts she had hidden for months.

"Vito, you're always going to be a producer, isn't that right?" He nodded gravely. "And that means that you'll always be busy, and when you've finished one film you'll be right on to another because that's the way you've always worked, at least two balls in the air—three is better—at the same time or you're not happy?" He nodded again, with a glint of amusement in his eyes at her solemn tone of voice. "You can't have me always trailing after you like a lost child at a fairground, wailing for her father, now can you? All right, I've finally learned how to make friends on a set without half-drowning myself in a pool, but helping you with *Mirrors* didn't make me a professional—I know that. So what are we left with, realistically? The more successful you are, the less I have of you. Tomorrow night you enter a whole new level as far as your work goes. But, Vito, *what about me? What do I do now?*"

He looked at her helplessly. He had no answer. It was not a question to which any man has an answer if he loves his work and puts his best energies into it.

"Billy, darling, you knew I was a producer when we got married."

"But I didn't have the faintest idea what being a producer really means. Who the hell could? It seems perfectly natural to you—that's your rhythm, you've had years to get accustomed to it, Christ, by now you wouldn't know how to lead a normal life. When did you last take a vacation? And don't tell me Cannes, that's not a vacation, that's business." Billy was working herself into anger as she saw the expression of concern on his face being replaced by the obstinate firmness of someone who is saying to himself, this is the way I am, what are you going to do about it?

"Have you ever thought what it's like for me when you're shooting a picture?" She pulled away from him and tightened the belt of her robe. "If I go with you or stay home it doesn't matter. Either way I'm lonely. And the shooting is only half of it anyway—what about the nights you have script meetings or disappear into an editing session? Ten to one the president of General Motors or U.S. Steel works a shorter day than you do—and when you're not working, you're thinking about working." She was breathless with rage.

Vito didn't jump to respond. What could he promise her? That he would work an eight-hour day, do only one film every two years? Unless he was working on a picture he was only half-alive. His face, with its strong lines, took on a solid, immovable expression, which made him look more like a Donatello sculpture than ever. This was what he had been afraid of before he agreed to marry Billy, this itch to possess all of everything, to have him on her terms, the way she wanted it.

"Billy, I can't reshape myself into your idea of a convenient husband. That's the way it is and that's the way it's going to be. Whatever I don't give my work I give you. There is nobody else and never will be, but I can't give you my work too."

Billy was suddenly terrified by the note of finality in his voice. He had never sounded so far away from her. Vito remote was like Vito without energy, a frightening dart in her own heart. She heard the shrill, complaining echo of her own words and realized that she'd gone too far. She had forgotten how entirely his own man Vito was. She walked over to him and took his hand, magically reassuming her familiar huntress quality. The furious little girl was gone, the strong predatory, invulnerable millionairess armor was buckled back in place in the blink of an eye.

"Darling, I'm being foolish. Of course you can't change. It's some sort of crazy reaction to your Oscar I guess— I'm probably just jealous. Please stop looking like that— I'm fine—pay no attention—please?"

He looked back at her unsmilingly, searching her face. She looked straight back at him, offering her lovely eyes to his inspection, chastened but not furtive. "Darling, I can't wait till tomorrow! There's so much to look forward to. More than anything I can't wait till I see Curt Arvey's face. He just won't be able to stand it, will he?" She had changed the subject effectively.

"No," answered Vito, brightening. "He won't believe it when he hears it. And then he'll probably demand a recount until he realizes it's his picture. I think—I think I'll have lunch with him tomorrow."

"Vito—why on earth? With that scum?"

"The Orsini family motto, 'Don't Get Mad. Get Even.'"

"You just made that up." She bit his ear playfully. "But I like it. I think I'll adopt it. Can I use it, sweetheart?"

"Of course—you're an Orsini." He kissed her questioningly. She kissed him back in a way designed to block out all questions, particularly ones she didn't want to answer.

The next morning Billy got to Scruples as soon as it opened. She knew that toward the end of that late March afternoon it was going to be a scene of confusion. A number of women had decided to leave their new dresses hanging up at Scruples so that they wouldn't be crushed, planning to come there to dress before leaving for the Awards. There had been no way to prevent them from arranging to have their hairdressers there for a last-minute comb-out, and by midafternoon every dressing room would be filled with fussy ladies and coveys of coiffeurs. Billy only hoped that the fuses wouldn't blow when they all plugged in their hot rollers at the same time as they inevitably would. She'd remind Spider to have an electrician standing by just in case.

Driving along Sunset she mused on the conversation of the night before. Of course, nothing had been settled—how could it have been—but she hoped she had convinced Vito that what she had said was a temporary spot of crazy-lady vapors on her part. She hoped, but she doubted. Vito was too damn smart not to know the truth when he heard it. He was off and running now; he had it made, but the only difference in her life was that she would have to find the right place in the house to put the Oscar, not too conspicuously displayed yet not pretentiously used as a door-jamb. Who the fuck had said, "All human wisdom is summed up in two words—wait and hope." She'd like to get her hands around the fucker's neck.

She greeted Valentine with a hug whose warmth surprised both women.

"I bet you'll be glad when today is over," Billy said.

"Actually, tired as I am, I'm looking forward to it. Tonight I'll get to see everybody finally wearing my clothes outside of these fitting rooms."

"Well, not all of them," Billy noted. "More than half of those clothes were bought to wear at private parties, after all."

"No matter."

"Where's Spider?"

"Oh—who knows? I'm too busy to keep track of him," Valentine said coldly.

"Is that any way for a partner to talk?" Billy teased.

"That partner business—it's not legal you know,"

Valentine said hastily. "Just an expression. It all started when I talked you into giving him a job. He's not my partner, Billy."

"Whatever you say, my pet, as long as he works for me." They seemed to be talking in mysteries, Billy thought, only she didn't know why. She dismissed the subject. She had her own problems.

"Look, I'll just grab my dress and leave you to it."

"Billy, try it on again."

"Why? It was finished ages ago and it fit perfectly. I don't know why I didn't take it home then—I must have been too jittery about *Mirrors* to think straight."

"I'd really like to see you in it once more. Just to be sure. Humor me?"

Valentine beckoned to an assistant and told her to bring Mrs. Orsini's dress.

"Did you ever stop to tote up how much business we did just for the Awards and all the other parties given tonight?" Billy asked as they waited. "I tried to figure it out the other day and I stopped when I got to a hundred and fifty thousand dollars. And we're only one store. If you look at it in a certain way, the Oscars are given for the retailers of Beverly Hills."

"Which is as it should be," Valentine replied smugly. "Ah, here it is." The assistant had brought in a shimmering strapless length of finely pleated, hammered satin in a subtle, luscious shade of crimson. Billy took off her shoes to step into the skintight taffeta slip, which kept the satin sheath from clinging to her body at any point.

"What jewels are you wearing with it?" Valentine asked while she bent to zip up the slip.

"Not my emeralds, too much like Christmas. Not my rubies, one red is enough. And not the sapphires either, I'd look like the American flag. I think just dia— Valentine! The slip doesn't fit!"

"Just hold still a minute. I must have done something peculiar to the zipper." Valentine unzipped it all the way and tried again. Again the zipper stopped moving at Billy's waist. Valentine's hand started to sweat.

"Was it dry-cleaned by accident? This is impossible. That slip had nothing wrong with it before." Billy was dismayed.

540

"Billy, what have you been eating?" Valentine asked accusingly.

"Eating? Nothing, thank you very much. I've been too nervous to eat. Just the thought of it makes me sick. No, there's something wrong with the slip. If anything, I've lost weight."

Valentine whipped out her tape measure.

"For heaven's sake, Val, you know my measurements by heart. Put that away. This is getting ridiculous."

Paying no attention to Billy, Valentine measured her waist and then, after a second of reflection, her bust. She muttered something to herself in French.

"What are you saying, damn it? Stop that crooning and articulate. I hate it when you speak French as if I couldn't understand it!"

"All I said, *Madame,* is that the waistline is the first thing to go."

"To go? Go where, for God's sake. Are you trying to tell me I'm losing my figure?"

"Not exactly. An inch and a half in the waist, an inch across the bust. That's how much you've changed. Most people would still consider that an acceptable figure, but you can't wear this dress without this slip."

"Damn," Billy said, aggrieved. "I've only missed exercise class for five months. I've been working like a dog for this body since I was eighteen and when I neglect it for a few months, look what it does—it's not fair!"

"You can't fool Mother Nature," smiled Valentine.

"Stop smirking. This is serious. Oh, what the hell, it's not the end of the world. I'll wear something else tonight, and start exercising at Ron's every day, get Richie to really push me hard, and in a month I'll be back to normal."

"In a month you'll begin to show."

"Show?"

"*Show.*" Valentine made a gesture with her hands, puffing out an imaginary belly.

"Nuts! Valentine, you have gone completely nuts! Do you think Dolly is infectious? Christ almighty, give you one maternity dress to design and you develop a raving case of babies on the brain."

Valentine said nothing, quirked her eyebrows knowingly, obviously holding her ground.

"You're a designer, not a gynecologist; you don't know what on earth you're talking about," Billy was shouting.

"At Balmain we always knew first, before the doctor, even before the *woman*. The waistline is the first to go, it's well known," Valentine said, softly fervent. Her small, amused face was thrilled with certainty.

Billy was throwing on her street clothes, screaming all the while. "You fucking French! Always so fucking sure of yourselves. Know-it-alls. It couldn't be that the slip doesn't fit, it has to be that I'm pregnant. How far can you carry that sort of crap? One of the damn models wore the dress out dancing and had it dry-cleaned. Check and you'll find out! I'll never leave another dress here, that's for sure." She turned to leave.

"Billy—"

"Please, Valentine, no excuses. I can't even get a decent dress to wear out of my own store. Damn, damn, *damn*." She slammed out the door.

Valentine stood gazing at the crimson pools of satin and taffeta on the floor and the tape measure in her hand. She knew she should be angry. Where was her famous temper? But a tear rolled off the tip of her little pointed nose. A tear for Billy.

Curt Arvey had been pleased with Vito's phone call. The bastard wants to make up, he thought grimly, as he accepted Vito's invitation to lunch. "Bury the hatchet." What a marvelously original way to put it. Obviously, Orsini had seen he had gone as far as he could go and was trying to mend his fences before it was too late. It was so overt, but still it satisfied Arvey's sense of importance to be wooed and courted by someone with whom he'd been in bitter conflict only a few weeks ago. Sure, *Mirrors* was making him a fortune, but Orsini was crazy if he thought that made every cheap trick he'd pulled smell like roses. The man was a tricky son of a bitch. But why not let Vito pay for his lunch? They'd have to greet each other at the Oscars tonight anyway.

They met at Ma Maison, another sharp bit of business on Vito's part, Arvey considered. At the table next to them Sue Mengers was drinking a banana daiquiri. After lunch everyone in town would know they'd eaten together and suppose that they were friends again. Well, let that cock-sucker hang on to the studio's coattails for another few hours, for all the good it would do him. After tonight Vito Orsini would be just another producer whose picture didn't make it. Back to square one. Could anybody remember who had produced the four pictures that didn't win last year's Oscar? Or even the one that had? But a studio went on forever and so did a smart studio head.

Arvey enjoyed the conversation over lunch. He had a fresh audience for the topics closest to his heart; the record of disasters at other studios, the names of leaders in the industry who would find themselves looking for a job any day now; the number of pictures that were behind schedule at other studios and their nonexistent chance of recouping their cost; the inside gossip of what Wall Street firms were unhappy with the earnings of which studios and what they were going to do about it.

Vito nodded with interest, encouraging this gloating recital.

"But you, Curt? You're in good shape I take it?"

"You'd better believe it, Vito. Experience talks in this business, and if I say so myself, I guess right more than I guess wrong. We'll show another twenty-five-cent profit per share this year—the stockholders should be satisfied for once, those leeches."

"I wonder how much of the profit comes from *Mirrors?*"

"Some of it, no question—credit where credit is due. If I hadn't given you the go-ahead, without even a script, the dividend would be a few pennies less. A nice little money-maker."

"I heard you had luck selling those television stations that the company owned and that the rest of the profit, the bulk of it, comes from *Mirrors.*"

"Where do you get your financial information from, a gypsy tearoom?" Arvey became faintly mottled.

"Or maybe you expected to make it from that big picture of yours—*David Copperfield?*" Vito inquired politely.

"*Pickwick!*" Arvey put down his fork with a bang.

"*Pickwick!*—*David Copperfield*, it's the same picture,

just retitled it, who'll know? It won't show up in the earnings till next year anyway—and it might show up as a loss. I hear they haven't even started to edit the thing. Yeah, better retitle it." Vito smiled encouragingly.

"*Pickwick!* happens to be opening at the Music Hall for the Easter Show," Arvey said scathingly.

"The Music Hall? Didn't *Lost Horizon* open there? Good place for that kind of kiddie picture. Nice thinking, Curt, if anything can help it, the Music Hall should."

"Vito—" Arvey began, choking with indignation, but Vito interrupted him briskly, reassuringly.

"Listen, you've got nothing to worry about. With that rise in earnings, the stockholders'll come in their pants. I'm sure, almost positive, that they'll renew your contract, Curt, you're in a great position this year. And if *Mirrors* wins tonight—"

Arvey broke in viciously. "Give a producer a decent break and he thinks he knows it all. Better enjoy it while it lasts, Vito; *Mirrors* is going to be yesterday's news—and today is half over."

Vito answered as if he hadn't heard Arvey's last words. "Yeah, if *Mirrors* wins, I think I'll do a big picture next. A creative man needs variety—and I've always wanted to see Redford and Nicholson together—there's a property they're both dying to do—question of getting together on price—but I think I can buy it."

"Come off it, Vito. I can tell a snow job when I hear one. Redford and Nicholson. *If* you win! You know as well as I do that there isn't a chance. I want you to win as much as you do—after all, we're in this together—but against those four blockbusters, *no way! Mirrors* is a small picture; remember, I told you that right from the very beginning. Small pictures almost never win. *Rocky* was a once-in-a-lifetime fluke. It certainly can't happen twice in a row. Don't build up false hopes, you'll just feel worse tonight," Arvey said, regaining his patronizing tone.

"Maybe I'll get the anti-blockbuster vote," Vito answered dreamily. "People in the industry know that every blockbuster that fails means six or eight or even ten other pictures that don't get a chance to get made—thousands of jobs lost. Disappointing big pictures—and we've had more than our share this year—turn off the public—the industry knows that."

"Dream on, Vito, dream on. Look, listen to the voice of experience. Have you any idea how long I've been head of the studio—since before you knew a lens from a viewfinder. And I know all about how you got your nomination—those housewife matinees—did you think I wasn't aware of the stunts you were pulling? But from a nomination to winning—it's a whole other ball park, my boy."

Vito addressed himself to his individual chocolate soufflé served with chilled whipped cream in a separate dish. He ate judiciously. Arvey studied him curiously.

"So you're thinking of buying something?" he asked at last. The bastard wanted something from him. It would be a pleasure to turn him down.

"Uh huh. A book. *The WASP*. Heard of it?"

"What do you think I am, illiterate? My readers loved it. Susan loved it. I don't have time to read, but I get outlines. Eleven months on the best-seller lists—if you can trust them, which I don't. But one million five for the movie rights—they're crazy. Nobody will pay that."

"Billy's wild about it—wants to buy it for me. If you don't want your soufflé—?"

"Take it, I shouldn't eat chocolate anyhow. So Billy wants to buy it, huh? I take it you have a birthday coming up? Nice, very nice."

"It *is* nice, Curt, when your wife has faith in you. She's got almost as good a nose as mine. You think *Mirrors* won't win—my Italian nose says it will. Call it a hunch if you don't want to be ethnic."

"When you run a multimillion-dollar company you don't play hunches as easily as when you have a rich wife—no offense, just the facts. Nicholson and Redford—do they really want to do it?"

"Yeah."

"I just can't believe that. And their salaries alone—Jesus—you'd be up to five, six million before you even bought the book. You're talking a twenty-million-dollar budget. No, Vito, those deals are a little rich for your blood."

"Tell you what, Curt, I'll buy the book myself, or

545

rather Billy will, and I'll give you a free option of thirty days if you're right about *Mirrors* not winning."

"What's the other half?"

"If I'm right, you buy the rights for me. Simple."

"One million five?"

"The odds are against me and you don't think I have a chance. But don't sweat it. If you're unwilling to risk your judgment, I'll buy the book and find another studio. Shit, it'd take too long to order another soufflé, wouldn't it? They're so damn small."

"You eat too much. Vito, I still think you're a schmuck, but if you want to make this deal, OK. If you don't mind, why don't we make a memo of agreement while we're here?" He signaled the waiter and asked for a menu.

"Curt, Curt—you can trust me," Vito sounded hurt.

"After you stole my picture?" Arvey asked, busily writing.

"You got it back."

"Nevertheless—I prefer something in writing." Arvey and Vito both signed the memo and the waiter and Patrick Terail, the restaurant owner, witnessed it. Vito reached for the menu and started to fold it to put in his pocket when Arvey grabbed it from him.

"We'll let Patrick hold it for us, eh Vito? Remember, this is the only copy. And I'll pay for lunch. Otherwise it would cost you one million five, *plus*. I'm feeling generous today."

Billy drove home from Scruples with all her senses focused on getting there safely. The short distance between Scruples and Sunset Boulevard is full of opportunities to hit jaywalkers and she knew she was so angry that she was afraid not to concentrate. Her self-control held as she ran through the enormous house, not speaking to any of the servants. She crossed her sitting room, her bedroom, and her bathroom, at last locking herself into her final refuge, her main dressing room. This room, thirty feet square, thickly carpeted in ivory, with pale lavender silk on the walls, held rack upon rack of clothes. In the center of the room a Lucite island was divided into hundreds of drawers, each one

546

holding a different accessory. Beyond it, in another locked room, cooled to a permanent 45 degrees, hung Billy's furs. Neither of the rooms was ever entered by anyone but Billy and her personal maid.

There was a deep bay window in the center of one of the walls, with a wide window seat covered in ivory velvet and piled high with silk cushions in the colors of anemones and Iceland poppies. She sank down, panting from her race through the house, and pulled up an old afghan she had never been parted from since Aunt Cornelia had knitted it for her. She tucked her cold feet under her thighs, wrapped one arm around the other, and made herself as small and as warm as possible. This hidden window seat was her ultimate private place where she came to think things out. It contained a phone, which only she ever used, and a buzzer to summon her maid. As long as she stayed in the bay window no member of her household dared to disturb her, and in her present mood Billy felt she might well spend the rest of her life there. The bastard had trapped her!

Oh how convenient, how very well timed, how marvelously well planned! Trapped, by Christ, in the oldest trap known to man. The minute Valentine had spoken, she'd felt the trap close. No doubt Vito expected to turn her into an old country Italian wife, contentedly producing bambino after bambino—perhaps learning to cook with lots of olive oil and garlic—certainly getting *fat*—while he gallivanted around the world making movie-producer magic, occasionally returning to his family just long enough to knock her up again. Oh, what a Machiavellian son of a bitch he had turned out to be! Mama Orsini—who would have thought that she, Billy Ikehorn, would turn into La Mama Orsini? How had he done it, the sneaky rat fink? How had he timed it for today, just when she had finally told him some of the things she had been so miserable about; *how* had he planned this to happen to her just at the right moment so that he would be able to pat her on the head and say that she had other things to do than worry about being lonely *now*? What an infernally clever manipulator he was!

Billy squinted her eyes as she calculated. She'd always had irregular periods, and while waiting for the nominations, she'd been under such tension that she hadn't given her missing periods a second thought. When, exactly was the last time? She consulted the week-at-a-glance diary she kept on a table next to the window seat. Then she jumped up and unlocked the door to her bathroom and peeked out. No silent-footed upstairs maid was in there putting out fresh towels or watering any of the flowering plants. She tiptoed quickly over to her supply closet and found the pile of round, plastic, birth-control pill containers she kept there. She counted them twice and returned to her dressing room, locking the door. She rechecked her journal. She had seen her gynecologist the morning of her Christmas visit to Dolly, and she had just finished a period then. Her doctor had a roguish way of making sure that all his "girls" over thirty saw him twice a year by only prescribing pills every six months. Then why did she still have six full pill containers?

If she didn't know that it was impossible, she'd have to say that she hadn't taken a pill since Christmas. If she didn't know it was impossible. If she didn't know.

In the empty room Billy suddenly threw back her head and roared out loud with laughter. Oh, but she had screwed herself up good and proper this time. Really done a very thorough job—almost three months gone, my dear, how's that for a slip?

Billy didn't have to be psychoanalytically oriented to see and accept immediately that she'd done this on purpose. But then why, if she wanted to have a baby, had she been so angry at Vito just a few seconds ago, why had she been so absolutely hateful to poor Valentine?

Billy rocked back and forth, still snorting with laughter, her arms clasping her knees, while she pondered the workings of—was it her mind or her subconscious or her unconscious? She didn't really know, didn't have the vocabulary or the insights—it was the only resolutely unfashionable thing about her. She'd operated on impulse for so long, flinging herself into situations, floundering around in them, making them work out in one way or another, more or less successfully, but never with the benefit of foresight.

Foresight? In hindsight, she thought, there was something rather strikingly determined about a woman who forgets to take her birth-control pills for almost three months. Billy patted her flat stomach tentatively. This baby would be another product of her inveterate impulsiveness—like—like all the rest of her life. Her fingers wandered to her right breast, then to her left. She weighed them experimentally in her hands. Bigger, and somehow warmer, than they had been since she was eighteen. How could any woman, especially one as conscious of her body as she was, overlook such elementary clues? What kind of woman carefully traps herself into having a baby but doesn't want to face the fact that she is pregnant? And why?

Good question.

Billy pulled over a pad and pen from where they lay on the seat and started making notes, grinding her teeth in determination to get to the first layer of this. The bottom layer, she knew, was lost in murk.

First of all, she just didn't feel ready to be a mother. Once she was a mother she would never again be a carefree woman without any absolutely irrevocable responsibility.

Second, she wanted to be Vito's honeymoon bride for a long, lovely while. But, in that case, she'd lost the battle to *Mirrors* even before they had been married. A wife yes, she was that, but a bride?—hardly. They'd skipped that part.

Third, she wanted to make all the decisions in her life by herself, in her own good time, at her election or pleasure, with the authority she had enjoyed for so many years. None of this being crept up on and shaken by the scruff of the neck by nature. Billy did not accept being bossed around by life. But, in that case, why hadn't she married one of the tame, decorative, amusing, caponish men available to women with money? It wasn't by mistake that she had chosen Vito, would choose him again today, knowing everything she now knew, not only because he was the particular man she loved but also because he was the *kind* of man she loved. *His* authority, *his* ability to make decisions, *his* autonomy—all the things that would permit him to work apart from her much of the time—were the very things she admired most. She couldn't cut off his air supply by suffocating him with her needs—for one thing, he wouldn't let her. Life gets a little paradoxical, Billy told herself ruefully, when you start to grow up.

Fourth. She wanted to come first with Vito, before any other person, to be the be-all and the end-all in his life, never to have to share him. And that was the most absurd reason of all. She had shared him from the very beginning, from the first moment she saw him, shared him with his preoccupations, his scripts in development, his endless meetings, with the whole circus caravan that had to be pulled together to make any movie, with Fifi, with Svenberg, with the Moviola. Collaboration is the soul of movie making. But for emotion, for absolute trust, for simple human warmth, he would always come back to her. A baby wouldn't be someone who took Vito away from her—on the contrary, a baby was someone she could share with Vito.

She looked at the three or four key words she had scratched on her note pad. The only one that still made some sense was that at thirty-four she still didn't feel ready to become a mother. Thirty-four? She chortled out loud at her own absurdity, for she'd also managed to forget her thirty-fifth birthday in November when they were in the full spate of editing. She had certainly been up to some monumental forgetfulness lately. Did she plan to wait till she was sixty?

And yet, and yet—how difficult, how really wrenching it felt to relinquish freedom. Obviously, her subconscious, or was it unconscious, mind had made that decision for her. The un or sub probably knew best, worked on a lunar clock or some such thing. Billy contemplated her list with gloom. No question that she was a slippery bitch indeed. In fact, a damn silly cunt. She wanted it *all,* the possible and the self-evidently impossible, and she gave up only with reluctance, dragging her feet and screaming foul play until the last possible moment. A fine example to set for a poor innocent baby. She looked at the piece of paper with the few words she had written on it. Slowly, carefully, and decisively she crossed them all out. Then with strong strokes of her pen she wrote: CORNELIA ORSINI? WINTHROP ORSINI?—and studied the two names with a mixture of acquiescence, slow, tender captivation, and the fast-fading remnants of sheer surprise. It was a half hour later before she came out of her reverie to realize that she still hadn't decided what to wear tonight.

She put out the piece of paper carefully on the table, slithered out of her clothes, and went directly to the section of her dressing room in which her evening gowns were hung. She flipped through dozens of garments, each encased in its own plastic covering, and quickly found the white silk Mary McFadden two-piece dress she'd bought a month ago. Over her head she flung the fragile pleated tunic, painted in a multicolored abstract shell design, quite beautiful enough in itself to frame and hang on a wall. Then she stepped carefully into the long skirt, finding that it still closed at the waist, just barely. She hesitated between seven pairs of silver slippers, chose a pair, and put them on. As Billy walked toward the triple mirror with the special lighting that reproduced evening illumination, she tightened the corded belt of the tunic.

Not bad. In fact, good, really very good. Billy inspected herself in each of the three panels of the mirror; front, both sides, and finally a full back view. Not as smashing as Valentine's red number but quite acceptable. She wandered over to her daybed and picked up a small silk pillow; then she loosened and lowered the corded belt and stuffed the pillow under the tunic. She sauntered back to the mirror, approaching it sideways, as if to take her reflection by surprise. Hmmmmmm. Not without a certain style—rather Botticelli, all those soft billows. What if she added just one more little pillow? No. Not really. The tunic wasn't that ample. But what if she substituted a long, loose Geoffrey Beene top woven of gold and silver thread? Surely there was enough room in it for three babies. She tied the Mary McFadden belt over the Beene top at crotch level and added a third pillow. A strange effect indeed. Something like a Memling Madonna—but it missed. Still, it *did* have a look, though not one either Beene or McFadden would acknowledge.

Now Valentine could design maternity clothes to her heart's content. Oh God! Valentine. How could she possibly apologize? The truth was entirely too complicated. She was only beginning to understand it herself. Never mind—she'd figure out something, she thought, and picked up the phone.

Maggie had arrived at Scruples shortly after a lunch date with an actor whom she had gently persuaded not to sign for his next picture until after the Awards, no matter how much pressure his nervous agent was putting on him. She earned that actor's lifelong gratitude when, Oscar in hand, he was able to get an additional three quarters of a million dollars for the part he had almost accepted twenty-four hours earlier. It had been that kind of morning. For every award there were five potential winners. Some of Maggie's dozens of phone calls conveyed the unmistakable message, "Take the money and run." Others counseled, "Wait and see." Not everyone Maggie talked to took her advice, but they all remembered it later. Her legend grew, during that one morning's work, from mythical to almost mystical proportions. Maggie MacGregor knew how the movie business *worked* all right, which made her one of the very few—perhaps the only one in the world—who did.

Valentine had Maggie's dress ready to be taken to the dressing room Maggie would be using at the Dorothy Chandler Pavilion where the Awards would take place. They had had a final fitting on it several days ago, but Maggie insisted on trying it on for Spider.

"Let him see it on television, that's what I designed it for," objected Valentine.

"I want to see the look on his face when he sees what you've done," Maggie insisted, with a swagger, her round, brown eyes screwed up with her sense of fun and clever power. "He'll freak."

But Spider, when he had been found and summoned to Valentine's studio, looked at Maggie through his bubble, reverently and absentmindedly brushing his fingers across the top of each superb breast. He nodded approval as if he were feeling the cool smoothness of a statue.

"Ravishing." He gave her an approximation of his old smile. Looking at Maggie and touching her, the bubble thinned out until he almost didn't feel it. His smile deepened. "I can only allow this once a year, Mags. Otherwise your public will stop taking you seriously and just spend their time waiting for one—or the other —to fall out entirely. Good luck tonight—and *don't bend down.*" He kissed her automatically and left the room, weariness apparent in his graceful lope.

"He must be coming down with something," Maggie said anxiously.

"Probably the clap," Valentine snapped. "Listen, gorgeous, Colette here will help you out of that invitation to riot and put it back on the hanger. Remember, no jewelry. I'll be watching, so don't try to cheat. I must go now and return a phone call before this place turns into bedlam. You'll be the best-looking one on that screen tonight. *Bonne chance!*"

Valentine retreated into the little room where she did her sketching and reached for the phone. She simply had to call Josh. He had phoned her twice yesterday and she'd been too busy to talk to him. Last night she'd been so tired that she had shut off her phone and let the switchboard downstairs take her messages. He'd called her once and been told that she wasn't accepting calls, and today he'd already phoned again while she was busy with Maggie. Slowly she dialed the number of his office, hoping that he'd still be out to lunch. His secretary put her through immediately.

"Valentine! Are you all right? You must be exhausted, poor sweet." His voice was deep with concern.

"Yes. It is quite crazy, Josh, but I'm having fun, too, you know. If only each woman that I help make beautiful didn't seem to be taking a few drops of my blood along with her dress."

"I hate it when you work so hard. Billy shouldn't let you."

"She has nothing to do with it, you know that. It's

just me—I could have refused any of the women who asked—don't worry." Valentine was aware that they were making conversation, like two semi-strangers. She sighed, waiting for the words that were sure to come.

"Darling, will you be too tired tonight to have dinner with me?" He was as casual as she had ever heard him, as if they had nothing in particular to talk about. Suddenly Valentine felt an overpowering desire to push away the moment of the final decision, for just one more day at least.

"Forgive me, Josh, but I'm practically falling down on my knees and it's only early afternoon. I won't get my last woman out of here for hours and by that time I simply won't make sense. Not tonight, dear—tomorrow. I'll sleep late tomorrow. Maybe I won't even come in to work at all. You do understand?—Josh?"

"Of course." He had the feeling that he was sitting at a table conducting a very delicate piece of negotiation, but one in which he was in perfect control. "I'll let you go back to your work." Christ, he thought, talk about the reluctant bridegroom. Valentine was a woman who had to be lured just to make a commitment to make a commitment to make a commitment. Still, wasn't that very elusiveness a very large part of the delight he took in her? The phone still in his hand, Josh sat for longer than he was aware of, meditating on a future in which coming home to Valentine would be a daily affair, one which would eventually become routine, marvelous, of course, but still routine. He knew enough to anticipate that inevitability. Would he miss the thrill of leading a double life, the pleasures of a love affair kept successfully secret from all his businesslike working world? Would Joanne's friends and the wives of his associates ever forgive Valentine or would he simply have to make an entirely new group of friends? And what would it be like to have a diaper can in the house again, after so many years? Funny how you could always smell them, no matter how big the house. But he had to face the possibility. He'd seen too many middle-aged men with second families to think he'd manage to avoid that. Still, they did have disposable diapers now, so perhaps diaper cans had gone the way of the spittoon. Well, in any case, after he and Valentine were married, he'd be settled down for the rest of his days; one division of community property in a lifetime was enough. Settled down. Strange how those words had a musty ring to them. At this point Josh took his hand abruptly off the phone, told himself not to be adolescent, and rang for his secretary. Second thoughts at the last minute were for other people. Josh Hillman was a serious man, and when he made a serious decision, he stuck to it seriously.

At the very end of the frantic afternoon, with all the ladies dressed and combed out and whisked away from Scruples by a fleet of hired limousines, Dolly pottered in, half dumpling, half moonbeam, with Lester's shaggy, anxious bulk hovering never more than a few feet from her side.

"Valentine," Dolly crowed, "I feel just like a girl again."

"Indeed?" Valentine inspected Dolly's childishly chaste face with a tired smile. "To what miracle do you attribute that?"

"The baby dropped! Oh, don't you know? A couple of weeks before you give birth the baby drops down into position. It's just a few inches, but gee, what a relief. I honestly feel as if I've got my waistline back."

"I can honestly tell you that you have not. But Lester has. He's lost ten pounds."

"It's prenatal tension," moaned Lester. "She gave it to me. Also a hangover. Don't ask."

Valentine called down to the kitchen for an extra spicy Bloody Mary for Lester, to make his liver turn over and start ticking again, while she took Dolly away to dress her and let Helen Saginaw, that pro of pros, work on her hair and makeup. After forty minutes and two Bloody Marys for Lester, Dolly emerged, bringing Lester and Spider, who had joined him, to their feet in astonishment. Dolly's little round head on its long neck was set like one bright star on top of a swirling, whirling cloud of a dress, misty gray-blue, in the twelve different sea shades of her eyes. Beginning safely above her bosom it was sprinkled with thousands of twinkling, hand-sewn brilliants. Her neck was long enough so that Valentine had been able to give her a ruff, a sparkling, pointed, stiff ruff, rather Elizabethan. Her hair was done up on top of her head and dusted with more brilliants and in her ears were Billy's great diamonds. She seemed to be bathed in baby spotlights, although there was no special lighting in the room. Dolly looked like the sugarplum fairy nine months after a minor indiscretion. Only her giggle, that welcome assurance of the existence of an endless well of laughter, seemed familiar. Both men gaped in admiration and a kind of reverence. Valentine watched her with intense satisfaction. A designer who knew her business—and wasn't afraid to borrow tricks hundreds of years old—could show even nature a thing or two. Lester, gulping, broke the spell of silence.

"We're going to be late. Dolly, you haven't got a minute. Hey, where'd you get those earrings?"

"Billy. She lent them to me for luck. Would you believe they're nine karats each?"

"Lord have mercy on us poor sinners," gloomed Lester. "I just hope they're insured."

"Gee, I never thought to ask—maybe I shouldn't wear them if it's important." Dolly looked like an eleven-year-old offering to give up her favorite doll.

"Nonsense," Valentine said briskly, herding them toward the door. "Billy's feelings would be hurt. Go—your pumpkin is waiting."

"Valentine," whispered Dolly, turning back for a final kiss, "if you take the dress in a little, I could still wear it afterward, couldn't I?"

"We'll make at least two out of this one. I promise."

Standing at separate windows in their office, Valentine and Spider watched Dolly and Lester drive off in the long black Cadillac the studio had rented for the occasion. Now, except for them, Scruples was empty, from basement to roof. They both waved even though they knew the couple at ground level couldn't see them, and then turned to each other, their faces still lit with the almost parental frolic of being part of a Cinderella story. It was the first kind look they'd exchanged in many weeks.

"Dolly is going to win," said Spider softly.

"How can you be sure?" Valentine was puzzled by the quiet conviction in his voice.

"Maggie told me, just before she left this afternoon. But nobody else, not even Dolly, knows yet. It's a dead secret."

"Oh, but that is glorious! What glorious news, Elliott!" Valentine hesitated a minute and then announced, not to be outdone, "As it happens, Vito's going to win, too."

"What! Who told you?"

"Billy. But it's another dead secret. Maggie told them last night. I'm not supposed to tell anyone; Billy only let me know to apologize for something," Valentine said vaguely.

"Maggie and her dead secrets," Spider said in wonder. "Holy shit, Val, this is *marvelous*. I'm beginning to—Vito—Dolly, *Best Picture*—Valentine? Valentine? Valentine—what's wrong? Why are you looking like that? Why the hell should you be crying?"

"I'm just so happy for them all," she said in a disconsolate, tiny, devious voice.

"Those aren't tears of joy," said Spider in a peremptory tone. In her refusal to be honest with him, he felt something very bad hovering in the air, which surrounded his bubble. He saw her take a deep breath, like someone about to step off a high diving board, and then let it out in a shuddering sigh. She half turned to him and said something so softly that it seemed to him that he hadn't quite heard it. Impatiently, instantly, irrationally terrified, he shook her shoulder.

"What did you say?"

"I said, I am going to marry Josh Hillman."

"Oh no, you are fucking not," roared Spider without a millisecond of reflection. The bubble burst with an explosion only he heard, the rupture of an invisible membrane of depression he had constructed to shield himself from the blow he had been expecting for months. He fell with a crash into reality; in a blaze of belated insight, barriers crumbled, tumbled, crashed down in his mind, he saw the light flaming at the end of the tunnel. All his senses were as refreshed, as renewed as if he were awakening from an enchantment. He reeled at the joy of his captive heart. He had never seen Valentine so clearly, even in this half-light. He knew that she didn't understand yet even before she spoke.

"Are you telling me again what I can do?"

"You're not in love with him. You can't possibly marry him."

"You know nothing about it," she said, sniffing delicate disdain.

Ah, but she was still as stupid as he had been. The thing he now knew in his blood and in his cells and in his marrow he would have to explain to her until even her sublime stubbornness was overcome. He mastered his impatience, his flame of anticipation, and dragged his eyes away from her mouth to her defensive, bewildered eyes.

"I know so much about you that I need only to look at you to see that you're not in love with Josh. Jesus, have I ever been a total, incredible moron!"

"Perhaps you have been, Elliott, but what has it to do with me? Or Josh?"

"Right down to the wire, that's my Valentine—struggling all the way home." He put his hands over hers and held them firmly, speaking in the tone he might have used to tame a wild pony. "Now—come here, over here and sit down on the couch. Now, Valentine, you are going to listen to me and without interrupting because I have a story to tell you." His look was so complex, so filled with an unflinching, golden blue tenderness, so limpid in its candor, so triumphant, so unpuzzled, that he swept all her objections out of her mind for once in her life. Silently, she allowed herself to be led across the room. They sat down, her hands still in his.

"It's a story about two people, a young, smart-ass stud who thought all girls were interchangeable and a feisty little broad who thought that the guy was hopelessly frivolous. Five or six years ago they met and became friends, even though she disapproved of him. In fact they became best friends. They fell in and out of love—they thought—with some wrong people, but they stayed friends. They even saved each other's lives from time to time." He stopped and looked at her. Her eyes were downcast and she wouldn't look up at him. But she wasn't interrupting. She was so still that even Spider couldn't tell that within Valentine there was a storm of wild speculation, a wonder booming in her blood. She concentrated on his hands. If she moved, she was afraid she would stagger.

"Valentine, these two people didn't know the first thing about the long way around into the heart of love; they were impatient, they kept getting sidetracked, they missed obvious opportunities, they were so busy that they didn't give each other a chance; when one zigged the other zagged, but all along, without knowing it, ridiculous timing and all, they were becoming completely necessary to each other, permanent, as permanent as—as the Louvre."

"Permanent?" The word seemed to rouse her from the spell she was in. "Permanent? How can you talk of permanence with all of your girls, ever since I've known you?" She spoke shakily and there was a reservoir of suspicion in her eyes.

"First, it was because I was young and dumb. Then, later, there were so many because no one was the right one. No one was the one I really wanted—and, God knows, you never encouraged me—so I kept looking. Oh, you, *you*. Valentine, you are all I have ever wanted, all I ever will want. Christ, why didn't I see it? I just don't understand. Damn, I should have kissed you the first chance I had, back in New York, and saved us five years of walking around in circles. That fight we had—I was just jealous—pig jealous. Didn't you guess?"

"Why did you never kiss me—back in New York?"

"I think I was a little scared of you. I thought it would frighten you off and I didn't want that."

"And are you still scared?" Her question was exquisitely mocking. Taken off guard by a forest fire of happiness, Valentine could still laugh at the man she had loved and refused to admit she loved, too proud and too stubborn to compete for him, from the first moment she saw him.

"Oh—you—" He enfolded her in his arms, clumsy, almost shy, until at last he kissed for the first time the tilted lips he knew so well. At last, he thought, the land of lost content.

After a minute she pulled slightly away. "You're right, Elliott, it would most assuredly have been a shortcut." Irresistibly, impetuously, she ran her hands over all the planes of his face, touching, touching, touching at last the flesh she had ached to touch for so long. She messed up his hair, scratched herself against the grain of his whiskers, kneading and pushing and smoothing his skin with the questing abandon of a passion too long held back. Her eyes were closed in joy as she possessed herself of his face, of his texture, of his smell. She buried her little nose in his neck, ferociously sniffing, biting, tasting, sucking, feeding like a fastidious French vampire off this masculine treat.

"Ah, you big dumb creature, waiting so long. I'd like to shake you until your teeth rattle, only you're too big for me."

"It's not entirely my fault," he protested. "You've been untouchable for months—I couldn't have gotten to you even if I'd tried."

"But we'll never know that, for sure, will we? You could have tried to kiss me before, idiot. In any case, don't bother to make out a case—I plan to hold it over you for a long, long time." He had never heard words as triumphant as her threats.

"As long as we both shall live?"

"At least that long."

It was growing darker outside and only one lamp was lit on their partners' desk. Spider started to unbutton her white smock, his usually nimble fingers fumbling with the big buttons until she came to his aid. For all their experience, both of them were curiously clumsy, as if each separate movement was happening for the first time. And yet each gesture, as they undressed each other, felt as if there was no possible way to do otherwise. When they were naked at last, lying on the wide suede couch, Spider thought that he had never seen such wholeness, such perfect unity. Her small, up-pointed breasts were as delicately alive, as impertinently arrogant as her expression. Her tousle of pubic hair curled more tightly than the hair on her head, but it was the same spicy red. He felt, even as he touched it gently for the first time, that he knew its springiness, its soft tangle, from many dreams. Valentine, who had been so voracious when she bit his neck, now lay motionless as he looked at her naked body, offering herself proudly to his gaze, like a hostage princess, the prize of a great victory.

She was so luminously white, next to the tan of his chest, that Spider thought she would be fragile, but, as

560

he began to stroke her breasts, she grasped him in her fine, young arms and pulled him close, flinging one smooth thigh over his hip so that he was trapped. "Stay, just stay like this for a while—I want to feel the whole length of you next to me—to learn your skin," she whispered, and he stayed still, a fiercely tender prey. They lay on their sides, pressed together, breathing together, pulses touching, listening with their bodies as their passion gathered like warm mist on a lake and covered them in a swirling cocoon. Soon they were both panting, still motionless but ravenous with curiosity and need. When he knew that she wanted that simple, irrevocable act, more than anything in the world, he entered her, directly, simply. She was small. She gasped, once, in pleasure, and then she was small no longer. He was clasped, utterly clasped, and he felt no overpowering desire to thrust, so hot, so tight was the dream. But Valentine rocked her pelvis languidly until she pushed them over the edge into urgency, wild, flash-flood urgency, as much an urgency of the soul as of the body, to finally know each other, be joined, made one. They invented lovemaking for each other as that March twilight faded into night, and afterward, they were as humble as nonbelievers who have suddenly become pilgrims, so great was their astonishment at their ability to create together a new thing neither had ever known before.

Valentine slept for a long while, enclosed in Spider's arms like an exotic bouquet of pink and red and white blossoms, damp and aromatic and tumbled every which way, abandoned to him in sleep as trustingly as she was now pledged to him awake. Spider could have slept too, but he wanted to watch over her, astonished and at the same time absolutely sure. She was Valentine, yet not Valentine. For all that he had thought he knew about her, he had never suspected the existence of a Valentine who concealed such a treasure of deep, pure sweetness under her fiery surface. The whole world was full of splendid surprise. Their office was transformed into a bridal chamber. Could he ever sit across from her at the desk and talk business without remembering the room as it was now? Could he ever see her in her white smock without wanting to take it off? If not, Spider smiled to himself, they'd probably have to redecorate and she'd have to find something else to wear when she worked.

Waking in Spider's arms, Valentine knew quite simply that this was the happiest minute of her life. Nothing would ever be the same again. The past was another planet. The search for a native place was over—she and Elliott were their own principality.

"Have I been asleep long?"

"I don't know."

"But what time is it?"

"I don't know that either."

"But—the television—the Awards—we've probably missed them."

"Probably. Does it matter?"

"Of course not, my Elliott. Between us, we only had about two hundred customers in the audience or on the stage—we shall just tell each one she looked sensational."

"Are you going to call me Elliott for the rest of my life?"

Valentine considered the matter. "You don't insist on Spider, do you? Why not Peter? It is your name, after all."

"No. God, no."

"I could call you darling or I could call you sailor—I rather like that—sailor. What do you think?"

"Whatever you like—just call me."

"Oh, my darling—" They were profligate with kisses, no longer awkward, growing together like a strong tree. Finally Spider asked the question he knew had to be asked.

"What are you going to do about Hillman?"

"I shall just have to tell him tomorrow. He'll know anyway, the minute he sees me. Poor Josh—but still, I never did give him more than an indefinite maybe—"

"But—the way you told me—I thought you'd made up your mind."

"I hadn't decided yet, not really—I couldn't."

"So you told me before you told him?"

"It does seem that way, doesn't it?"

"I wonder why?"

"*I* don't know." She looked as innocent as a celestial puppy. Spider decided to keep his leaping intuitions to himself. Some questions are not meant to be asked as long as the answers are right.

"Just think," he said, pulling back her curls so that he

could see all of her small, splendid face, "how surprised everybody is going to be."

"All but seven women," said Valentine with pure mischief now spilling out of her great, green eyes.

"Hey, hold on!" said Spider, his suspicions newly aroused. "Who have you told?"

"How could I tell what I didn't know? I'm talking about your mother and your six sisters—they knew—everything, I think, the day they met me."

"Oh, lovely, silly Val, that's pure imagination—they just think I'm irresistible to all women."

"Ah, but you are, sailor, you are."

Billy had stayed in her dressing room all afternoon, dreamily roaming around, while all sorts of ideas passed through her mind, restlessly inspecting various garments with an all-seeing but vague eye, even going through sixty empty handbags in her peregrinations and reaping a harvest of twenty-three dollars and twenty cents in change. She felt too tender all over, almost as if she had grown a new skin, to leave her retreat, but suddenly she realized with a start that Vito must already be home, dressing for the evening, while she was still incommunicado. She had long ago taken off the Mary McFadden so as not to wrinkle it, and she was wrapped in a favorite old at-home robe from the great days of Balenciaga, deep saffron silk velvet lined in shocking-pink taffeta with shocking-pink cuffs. Finally, as she realized the time, she unlocked the door and crossed her bathroom. It was like entering a spring garden, filled with the fresh perfumes and earth smells of the pots of daffodils, narcissus, hyacinths, and violets that banked both sides of her sunken tub and stood massed, in the large room, under the dozen rose trees that had been brought in from the greenhouses by the head gardener. They were covered with buds. In two weeks, she thought absently, they'll be in full bloom. She rang for her maid and crossed the bedroom looking for signs of Vito. He wasn't in his dressing room or in his huge, green-and-white marble bath or his sauna. She finally found him in the sitting room, which formed part of their suite, an intimate room hung entirely in shirred Paisley in rich browns and yellows, with glimmers of black and gold from an antique Korean screen and a group of seventeenth-century Japanese cachepots holding eight dozen half-opened tangerine tulips. He had been to the butler's pantry off the sitting room to fetch a bottle of Château Silverado from the refrigerator there, which was used to hold white wine, champagne, caviar, and pâté de foie gras, and it looked as if he was about to drink a toast to himself. Billy took a second wineglass from the heavy silver tray on the lacquered black Portuguese table and held it out to him, her face serene, her eyes withholding some strong emotion.

"Oh, sweet, I'm so glad you're home—I'm late but I'll hurry. How was lunch with the chicken-shit pussy?" she asked.

"Gosh darn," said Vito, "the language you rich girls use. You shouldn't be so tough on that poor mound of buffalo droppings. My accountants just got the final figures on *Mirrors* and, it turns out, we were almost fifty thousand dollars over budget when he tried to take over. Would you believe?"

"I'd believe, and he's still a chicken-shit pussy. Who paid for lunch?"

"He insisted. I had him by the balls, so his heart followed." And, thought Vito, it only cost him a little over forty dollars plus one million five. Coming home, he had decided not to tell Billy about his bet with Arvey until tomorrow, until after the Oscars. She'd have enough of his success to swallow tonight without knowing that his next production was all set except for the screaming poor Arvey would do. And who knew, maybe Redford and Nicholson really would be interested—it was the book of the year, maybe of the decade.

"Well, that was the least he could do," Billy said. Her mind was evidently on something Vito didn't know about, but her spirits had never seemed so high.

"What, may I ask, lit you up like some fucking wonderful Christmas tree?" Vito inquired.

"My God, Vito, this is the big night. When am I supposed to get excited—Boxing Day, Bastille Day, Fidel Castro's birthday, Amy Carter's graduation from eighth grade?" She whirled around, her robe flying, drinking the wine, draining the priceless old crystal and throwing it at the fireplace where it shattered in a hundred pieces. "I must have had some Cossack blood," she said, very pleased with herself.

"You'd better have some racehorse blood. You have exactly fifteen minutes to be dressed and in the car." He gave her a smart smack on her bottom and watched, puzzled, as she blew him a kiss and strode away. There was something different about Billy tonight and it wasn't just that she wasn't wearing her earrings. Some—potency, some secret victory. She looked the way he felt.

The Academy of Motion Picture Arts and Sciences had finally become aware that except for a few long-awaited minutes, the Award ceremonies could use a little jazzing up for the television audience. More than any pomp or lavish sets, those hundreds of millions of watchers really wanted to see famous faces in moments during which the average person could empathize with them, moments of tense waiting, of hope, of crisis, of concealed disappointment, of nerves and bluff and explosive joy.

The Academy officials had allowed Maggie's crew, all properly dressed in dinner jackets, to take up positions right down on the floor of the Dorothy Chandler Pavilion, with their hand mikes and their minicams. This way, instead of those brief flashes of the stars sitting somewhere in a row of people, sometimes accompanied by a zoom close-up of the blink of a celebrated eye, which more often than not vanished from the screen before the public managed to get a decent look, this year's audience was treated to an orgy of lingering close-ups and was able to listen in on snatches of conversations in various moments during the presentations when the audience wasn't silent in expectancy. Maggie's men were so unobtrusive and blended so well into the audience that after a while they didn't seem to be there at all and the nominees for the various Oscars, all seated in convenient locations near the stage, almost forgot they were on live television.

Billy and Vito didn't reach their seats until long after Maggie had finished her interviews with the arriving stars, but they managed to slip in before the ceremonies began. By now Maggie was backstage. She had finished talking to the presenters in their dressing rooms, most of whom were so hyped-up with stage fright that they welcomed her with a spate of words, and now she had retired to the control booth with her director to cover the Awards themselves. Maggie had worked out a game plan based on one simple directive, which she had issued to her troops.

"If Sly Stallone is scratching his ass while the guy who gets the Best Sound Effects Oscar is trudging up the aisle, *STAY ON SLY* until they actually hand the son of a bitch his statue and then, only then, cut to him."

"What about his acceptance speech, Maggie?" an assistant director asked.

"He gets twenty-five seconds—no, make that twenty—and then cut back to the action on the floor."

It made for an interesting show. Unfortunately, the Academy never granted this permission again.

The Oscar audience is truly captive. Not even heaven can help the person who feels like going to the bathroom during the duration of the telecast. There are no commercial breaks for them, no seventh-inning stretch. Billy found herself sinking into a reverie during the first, endless production number of one of the five nominees for Best Song.

Her brain, she realized, had never worked so logically as it was doing now. Something about figuring out and facing the facts of how she had managed to get herself pregnant had liberated powers of reasoning that she dimly sensed were beginning to vanquish her old habit of impulsiveness. There had always been a lot to say for making a list. Even as she had taken up her pen, earlier in the day, she had heard Aunt Cornelia's voice saying sternly but lovingly, "Wilhelmina Winthrop, pull up your socks."

She knew now that she was about to arrive at the center of her life and she didn't want to do it in a scramble of grabbing and clutching and flailing about, trying to keep her world tied down and under her control as if it were a runaway balloon. It was time to let the balloon loose and allow it to take her with it, soaring tranquilly over a new, broad, sunny landscape, with a light hand at the controls. Did a balloon have controls, a tiller, ropes, what? Never mind, she told herself, at least she wouldn't be alone in the balloon. There would be the baby and, of course, another baby to follow. She had been an only child and she wouldn't let that happen to her own child. Perhaps three children in all? There was time, if she hurried. No, she told herself, here's exactly where you start grasping, snatching, and arranging it all just so, and get into trouble. First this baby and then she'd see. In fact, next time, she and Vito would see. What if she did, after all, spend some years in the role of La Mama Orsini? If she just let it happen, she might find out that she loved it, she reflected warily, feeling an unpremeditated and rambunctious quiver of anticipation.

There was applause for the song and two new presenters, one ravishing boy and one ravishing girl, gibbering with nerves, were trying to announce an award for, as far as Billy could tell, the Best Animated Film. As the titles of the films and the names of the animators, many of them Czech or Japanese rolled, with many mispronunciations, trembling off their lips—didn't they rehearse? —Billy resumed her thoughts.

It would be easy, in fact inevitable, to slip, under the providential cover of fruitfulness, into the joys of motherhood, but she was beginning to know herself too well now—and not a minute too soon—to imagine that she would be satisfied with late-blooming maternity into the indefinite future. What if she tried to compensate for her inability to control Vito with an attempt to control her children—child—children? It would certainly present a temptation and she wasn't awfully good at resisting temptation, but it must not be allowed to happen. Vito would always belong to himself and, therefore, it followed that her children would ultimately belong to themselves too. She didn't have to like this piece of basic knowledge so recently arrived at, but she had to learn to live with it. Finally. No, the only person with whom she would always come first, who would always belong to her, was herself.

Finished, long, long ago, were the days when Ellis had put her first above everything. Finished not so long ago, the days when she could separate the life of her body from the rest of her life and decide how to lead it, as much in cold blood as a bitch in heat could be. All those cocks of all the various male nurses, Jake included, had been exactly what one of the words for them was: tools. Pieces of machinery. Vito's penis was like those other words, the evasive Victorian ones: a member, an organ, just as an arm is a member of the body, just as a heart is an organ. When it was in her it was not an "it," it was Vito, the love of her life, come what may.

Billy turned her attention back to the stage where four identically black-bearded gentlemen were all receiving Oscars. Animators? Raskolnikov, Rumpelstiltskin, Rashomon, and von Rundstedt? Surely not? Yet they were from Toronto, so they must be animators. All quite as usual.

The next nominees were for Best Costume Design. Billy watched, distracted from the flow of her thoughts, by the images flashed on the giant screen. As the winner was announced—would it be Edith Head again winning her ninth Oscar? No, not Edith this time but another designer. What misguided impulse had made her try to bring back sequin-paved body armour tonight of all nights?—Billy picked up her drifting interior monologue.

There was a major dilemma at the bull's-eye center of her life. In fact she could put it into one sentence. If she wanted to stay married to Vito, *and she did,* without too much resentment, without too much jealousy and without more than the normal strain and pain of any marriage, she had to establish an abiding interest in life that did not depend on him in any way. Could this by any chance be the compromise Jessica had been so unenlightening about?

She didn't need to make an Aunt Cornelia list to know where, amid all the interests the world offered, that choice lay. Everything pointed to Scruples. She had had the original idea. She had managed to see it through until it became workable. True, she had almost loused it up. When she made a mistake it was not just a beaut, it was a goddamned work of art, a bloody masterpiece. But she had known that it was wrong and she had picked Valentine to fix it. The fact that Valentine had turned up with Spider, who had had the imagination to turn Scruples around, would have meant nothing if she hadn't coöperated fully as soon as he showed her the way. In other words, if she said so herself, she had what was usually called executive ability.

Billy interrupted her self-congratulations as the award for Best Achievement in Cinematography came up. Svenberg had been nominated and she found she was holding her breath. Damn. John Alonzo. Poor Per, but he was so happy with the ads for *Mirrors,* and he did have two Oscars already.

As another song was given a production worthy of Radio City Music Hall in the 1950s—where did they dig up these songs?—Billy's head filled with ideas the way a Fourth of July sparkler gives off flashes of light. There were still rich women in the world who lived much too far away from Scruples. She could open branches of Scruples in cities flung across continents. Rio was ripe for it—Zurich—Milan—São Paulo—Monte Carlo—all full of very rich, very bored, very elegant women. Munich—Chicago—either Dallas or Houston.

And New York. Ah, New York. Once, at lunch, about six years ago, Gerry Stutz had told her why she had never opened a branch of Bendel's. She'd said that there weren't enough women in any city in the United States except New York who could understand and support the Bendel approach to retailing. She'd enjoy giving Gerry a run for her money. The Scruples approach was not as confined to avant-garde chic as Bendel's. It could be modified, tilted, angled to suit any metropolis so long as the country in which the city was located held a large leisure class.

Billy felt her fingertips tingling with the excitement of her visions. All those cities to visit, locations to scout, offers to be made on land, deals to be consummated, architects to be found and commissioned, interior decorators to hire, to consult with, the habits of the local wealthy community to explore. Each Scruples would be different from any other store in the world except for its basic kinship to the Scruples in Beverly Hills. There were salespeople to be trained, new buyers to be discovered, store managers to be hired, an infinitude of new refinements on the one basic theme of Scruples. Enough to last a lifetime. Billy shivered in delight. She felt, she realized, the way Vito must feel when a new picture went into preproduction. No less love for her, just more passion for something that had nothing to do with her, didn't threaten her place in any way. Oh, lovely! But one thing at a time, or her balloon would grow too heavy and fall to earth.

Vito nudged her gently. She seemed lost in some sort of dream and the nominees for Best Director were about to be announced. Billy came alert immediately and was surprised by the surge of tension she felt. She did so love Fifi. The two presenters—Christ, who chose them?—seemed more engrossed in their jokes, bad jokes too and poorly memorized, than in getting down to the envelopes. It was sadistic. The reading of the five names seemed to take five minutes. The ritualistic fumbling with the envelope went on for an eon. How was it humanly possible for two normal people to be unable to open one envelope? Fiorio Hill. Poor Fifi. Why was Vito jumping up and—it was Fifi. As she watched his familiar figure, clad almost unrecognizably in an elegant brown-velvet dinner jacket, run up to the stage, Billy wondered if she'd ever known Fifi's whole name or was she just too full of her own ideas to make the connection?

Thank God, another song. Time-out. She wished she'd brought a pad and pencil. No, no, *no*. That was wrong. That was exactly what she must not do. She knew that if, in a mood of gut-thrilling covetousness, she so much as wrote down the names of the cities in which she was dreaming of establishing a branch of Scruples, she'd be on the phone within hours, avariciously and imperiously giving orders to real-estate brokers, pouncing on choice corners, ravening to get started, impatient to the point of frenzy to see her ideas come to life. She had changed enough, she told herself solemnly, to see the ease with which she'd make such a mistake. She had even changed enough to avoid it. Fleetingly, but implacably, Billy reminded herself of some of the things she had gobbled down in her life; once, long ago, it had been food; then, in New York, all those young men; then, after she met Ellis, the rich years of travel, too many houses, all the jewels, coming when she was so young that she was surfeited before the end of her twenties; then the clothes, the mountains of clothes, more than nine tenths unworn; and finally again, the men, Jake in the pool house, the others in her studio. She'd had too much, so very much too much, and so much of it unsavored, swallowed without chewing. Now she knew where she wanted to go. The days of unfulfilling cupidity were over, the days of a sensible, discriminating choice of priorities lay ahead.

How very Bostonian of her. So she hadn't left Boston totally behind after all.

Billy resolved not to make the mistake of trying to plan the future of Scruples alone, in secret, self-indulging acquisitiveness. She just wasn't smart enough. It took executive ability to admit that. Valentine, and in particular, Spider, would be in on everything. They'd both be vice-presidents of the new branches, of the new company that would be formed, with more money and bigger profit shares for them both. Who knows—it might even cheer up Spider, cure whatever ailed him?

Vito pinched her sharply, bringing her back to the vast, crowded auditorium. He hissed in her ear, "What the hell is Dolly doing?" and pointed to Dolly who had, until now, been seated a few rows in front of them.

The two presenters for the Best Supporting Actress Award had just arrived at the podium. They stood still, without speaking, gorgeous faces fixed in expressions of paralyzed confusion, watching the floor of the theater where Dolly Moon was on her feet, saying something into the hush. A big man was lumbering up from the seat next to hers. It was unimaginable. Perhaps it was some sort of protest, a Marlon Brando number only with bad timing? All over the auditorium people were looking at Dolly, aware that something had gone wrong with the smooth functioning of the Awards. This was the moment of sacred suspense. Tradition dictated that, like all nominees, she was supposed to be sitting quietly, with a serene, unfocused look on her face, every feature in disciplined repose, ready to smile falsely when the winner was announced, or crumble slowly into disbelieving joy. Instead, she was standing and speaking at length in a tone of some mild agitation. Maggie's producer got both the minicam and the mike on her in seconds. The audience in the Dorothy Chandler Pavilion couldn't all hear what the television audience heard, so many of them half rose to their feet to crane in Dolly's direction.

"Now Lester, Lester, darling, don't be so upset—it's only the waters breaking—there's still plenty of time—oh, my goodness, poor Valentine, I've ruined the dress—" She was walking up the aisle now, the minicam right behind her, the mike man next to her. As Billy said later, it would have looked neater and unquestionably more glamorous if the camera had been in front, but the cameraman knew a classic shot when he saw one and Dolly's rear view, the huge wet patch on her sea-foam dress, the copious rivulet of amniotic fluid that she left behind her on the carpet as she made her unhurried progress to the exit, were worth a thousand glimpses of her face. Anyway, she wasn't rushing anywhere, she was turning her head from side to side, talking to the amazed audience.

"Would you all look and see if there's an earring on the floor? I seem to be missing one—it's probably rolling around under your feet—now, stop it Lester, there's nothing to worry about—just everybody look for an earring—it's a nine-karat diamond and I'm not sure it's insured—what Lester?—no, don't be silly, why should I say it's a rhinestone, Billy wouldn't wear rhinestones. No, Lester, I can't walk any faster, it's uphill, don't you see, no, please don't try to carry me, I weigh more than you do—oh my, this wasn't supposed to happen for a week— *honestly*—but it just went 'pop'—I didn't mean to do it *here*—", and she giggled. And giggled and giggled. In millions of living rooms, all over the world, people were laughing. More people were laughing together at that one time than at any time since history began as Dolly Moon made her historic exit from the Oscars.

Billy sat through it all in a state of shock. Dolly's face as she walked past her! She'd never forget that look of expectant rapture as she passed by, intent on one important task, even as she dealt with the embarrassment of the moment in her own artless fashion, which always seemed to work in the end. Dolly, her own Dolly, knew the secret. She waited patiently and eventually it all happened—even if her timing was just a little off. What did it matter? No one, Billy realized, not even she, could make her life "come out even." Perhaps it was all for the best? Not that she had a choice. How interesting to realize, finally, that even with all her vast options there were areas in which she had no choice. Just like everyone else. It was such a relief. She felt rigid bands loosening somewhere in the area she had always thought of as her stomach but which she would now have to treat with a little more respect.

While the great earring scramble died down, the presenters announced Dolly's Oscar, and Fifi, tears of laughter streaming down his face, hastily accepted it for her. Next the presenters had come to the awards for the Best Actor, Best Actress, and Best Picture. Vito squeezed Billy's hand tightly. As they waited for the Best Actor Award to be presented, Vito was also casting the male leads in *The WASP,* in the event that Redford or Nicholson wasn't available, while Billy was blown here and there in her balloon, the wind deciding the direction. Was there a history of twins in Vito's family? And while the Best Actress made her acceptance speech, in one tiny corner of her balloon Billy had started to wonder if the word Scruples should be translated into Spanish for the Rio store or should it remain in English, and Vito was thinking about many points of profit he was going to be able to negotiate on his new film.

In the momentary wait, during which Oscar fever reaches its height, while the presenters walked out of the wings and downstage to read the list of nominations for Best Picture, Vito began to sweat. What if Maggie had been wrong? Jesus—he'd have to buy the rights to the book out of his own profits on *Mirrors,* which were beginning finally to mount up. But what the hell. He shrugged his shoulders and smiled. Right or wrong, and when had Maggie ever been wrong, he had to have that book. It had been written for him to produce. He knew it.

Billy had no such last-minute panic. Dolly had called her first thing that morning, unable to hold back the good news, and told her the whole mad yarn. But Billy hadn't wanted to tell Vito because she suspected that he might feel that in some way it diminished his Oscar to have had the envelope opened by two sets of people before the actual presentation. Just as she wouldn't tell him about the baby until tomorrow, when the glory of this night was less fresh. The news, for bambino-loving Vito, would upstage whatever industry recognition he could ever be given. And, as she felt Vito's hand tense more firmly than ever over her own, she told herself to be honest. Wilhelmina Hunnenwell Winthrop Ikehorn Orsini did not have the faintest intention of sharing that particular spotlight with any little gold-plated statuette that the Academy, in its infinite wisdom, might ever bestow.

"Will anyone ever find your earring," Vito suddenly whispered in her ear as the presenters started to read the list of five pictures and their producers.

"Forget my earring," said Billy, kissing him full on the lips. "We've got better things to think about."

Best Of Bestsellers from WARNER BOOKS

__**THE CARDINAL SINS**
by Andrew Greeley   *(A90-913, $3.95)*
From the humblest parish to the inner councils of the Vatican, Father Greeley reveals the hierarchy of the Catholic Church as it really is, and its priests as the men they really are.

THE CARDINAL SINS follows the lives of two Irish boys who grow up on the West Side of Chicago and enter the priesthood. We share their triumphs as well as their tragedies and temptations.

__**THY BROTHER'S WIFE**   *(A30-556, $3.95)*
by Andrew Greeley   *(In Canada A30-650, $4.95)*
A gripping novel of political intrigue does with politics what THE CARDINAL SINS has done with the church.

This is the story of a complex, clever Irish politician whose occasional affairs cause him much guilt and worry. The story weaves together the strands of power and ambition in an informed and clear-eyed insider's novel of contemporary politics.

__**THE OFFICERS' WIVES**
by Thomas Fleming   *(A90-920, $3.95)*
This is a book you will never forget. It is about the U.S Army, the huge unwieldy organism on which much of the nation's survival depends. It is about Americans trying to live personal lives, to cling to touchstones of faith and hope in the grip of the blind, blunderous history of the last 25 years. It is about marriage, the illusions and hopes that people bring to it, the struggle to maintain and renew commitment.

THE BEST OF JACKIE COLLINS